# The Programme

**Other novels written by Andrew Arden**

The Motive Not The Deed
No Certain Roof
The Object Man

**(writing as Bernard Bannerman)**

The Last Wednesday
Controlling Interest
The Judge's Song
Orbach's Judgment

# The Programme

*by*

**Andrew Arden**

ARAMIS
**AB**
BOOKS

Aramis Books
13 Stockleigh Road
St Leonards on Sea
East Sussex TN38 0JP

NOTE: ARAMIS BOOKS LTD DOES NOT ACCEPT
UNSOLICITED MANUSCRIPTS OR OTHER MATERIALS

First published in 2001

ISBN 0-9540215-0-9

A CIP catalogue record of this book is available from the British
Library

Typeset by
David Chaproni̇ère, Streatham, London

Printed and bound in Great Britain by
Bath Press Ltd, Bath

For Jo and Emma

# *Acknowledgements*

The quotations from Aleister Crowley were taken from his *Magick in Theory and Practice*, Castle Books, New York. Other useful works include *A Dictionary of Angels*, Gustav Davidson, Macmillan, 1967; *The Encyclopaedia of Witchcraft and Demonology*, Rossell Hope Robbins, Crown Publishers, New York, 1969; *Black's Bible Dictionary*, 8th ed., Harper & Row, 1973; and *Ancient Christian Magic, Coptic Texts of Ritual Power*, ed. Meyer & Smith, Harper, San Francisco, 1994. Quotations from the Bible are from the King James Version.

It was Arnotts' largest partnership meeting ever: only Carey Arnott would be absent.

There was just one item on the agenda – The Programme – and just one question: whether or not the firm would continue to act for the cult, regardless of Carey's involvement in it: to refuse to do so would mean the final break with Carey herself. There were two sides: on one of them was her father Charles; on the other, her brother Colin.

They met in the largest of the conference rooms. Charles Arnott sat at one end of the long table, frequently and pointedly looking at his watch. The other end of the table was still vacant: his son Colin was uncharacteristically late.

At Charles' side, Alistair Mathison was grim-faced. It was the confrontation he had urged his friend to avoid: he had to let Carey go, they all did. He too glanced at his watch in annoyance: what was delaying Colin?

Charles said:

"Graham – go and see what's holding my son up, will you?"

"I'll go," Jessica Harvey offered, rising before Graham could do so.

It was the first time since the merger with Andrew Chettle, Jessica Harvey and their associates that Charles had used his right to call a special meeting. He could not help himself. It was the only way he could reach out to his daughter, to reassure her that they would do anything to provide her with support, even if it meant also continuing to support The Programme.

He lay in bed at night, his heart pounding with anguish, tossing and turning and crying out to her. He awoke sweating and incapable of further sleep, tried to read, sometimes to work, most often drinking and watching the continuous news channels, muttering along with recurring sound-bites, wanting something about The Programme to crop up and afraid of what it would be. The Programme was on everyone's mind: that cult, people said – the one that killed the Rockworth boy.

His mind was wandering. He found it harder and harder to keep moving along a single track. He told himself it must be the want of sleep: losing his mind was the greatest fear of all, greater than death itself.

1

Where was that damned boy?

As if in answer, the double doors flew back and Colin entered, followed by Jessica, now carrying a sheaf of papers. There was something going on between them, Charles was certain of it. He watched them part, Jessica to return to her seat, Colin to head for his.

Colin did not sit.

He was ashen-faced as he stared down the table at Charles.

He was holding a letter.

He cleared his throat, on the verge of tears.

"I don't think we need this meeting. This is a letter from Carey, from my sister – uh, Carey Arnott," he added formally, as if it might help him to feel less emotional. "Jessica has copies for you all. I'll read it anyway. It is very short. It says: 'I, Carey Arnott, hereby resign my partnership. I would like arrangements to be made as swiftly as possible for my partnership share to be valued and released to me so that I can use it for The Programme.' That's all it says."

A hammer struck Charles across the chest; not a hammer but a wrecking-ball. He gasped for breath. Alistair reached out but Charles brushed his hand away, thrusting himself awkwardly upright, leaning forward to use the table top for support.

He glowered at Colin. The partners were stunned both by the announcement and by the intensity of Charles' fury. Many of them were wondering how they would react if their own father were to face them down with such studied hatred.

Alistair muttered a plea:

"Charles."

The single word shattered the concrete silence that was the final barrier between father and son.

"You bloody fool, Colin, you bloody, bloody fool. I told you that you didn't understand her – now will you believe me? Look at what you've done. You've destroyed your sister, you've destroyed me – and all for what? For this firm? Look around you, Colin: how much respect do you see, how much admiration, how much support? You're arrogant, vain and pompous; you're a coward; you've destroyed this firm too. I shall never forgive you. Never."

Charles pushed himself fully erect and strode from the room, leaving the partners – and the partnership – behind; Arnotts too.

\* \* \*

Outside a small town in upstate New York – Hedgerow – a couple of weeks later, Carey was thinking about Colin. She was in a low-ceilinged punishment cell in the basement at the Hammer Reach farmhouse. She was clothed in a thin cotton shift that barely reached her thighs. She was cold. She was scared. She had been in the cell for days, she could not remember how many. For the first couple of days, she had been given water and pitta bread, with a slice of vegetable pâté just enough to be able to digest it and a solitary orange for the vitamins. Latterly, only water.

All she had for solace was an offprint of Matthew's latest visit to The Programme's Website, which she had been clutching when she was brought to the cell. It was a response to Arthur Rockworth's repeated public accusations that Matthew had brainwashed and murdered his son.

> *The evidence of evil is too great to ignore, however hard you try. Why even try? Why not admit it: there are bad people and there are good people and what we want is to be whole. But it's not enough to say it; we have to do it; we have to become whole. One thing that means is that there has to be a part of us capable of doing evil; something else it means, because everything has to exist in contrast, is recognising that some are not and never will become whole. Whole, not whole. We call ourselves The Programme; it is a way of life – a way of being; also, it is a way of dying. Sometimes, only death can make us whole; for some, death is the ultimate achievement – a beginning not an end. It is not brainwashing to share with another what we have learned and experienced about our capacity to make a whole of our lives. It is a gift.*

He had come to see her in the cell. Stooping, he had stroked her cheek like a parent. For a moment, she thought he was going to take her there, on the dirty blanket on the dirty floor where she lay while time had come to a halt. Part of her wished he would. Physical power over her was not his objective: he wanted her mind; her crime had been to let slip that it was still her own. He had caught her using the phone: Colin was out there, she had seen it on the news; surely they would let her talk to him.

In the cell, Matthew played the martyr.

"You were my favourite, Esther." He called her by her inside name. "You were always my favourite".

She remembered a time when Matthew had been contemptuous of survivalists – "fundamentalists by not much of another name" he mocked them – but now he was suffering from the same siege mentality, the belief that they were going to destroy him and that if he was not careful, they would do it before he could destroy himself. The thought of destruction terrified her but it was also attractive. It was an easier route out of this mess than a return to London, to the contempt of her friends and former colleagues, and to their pity too, which would be far worse, a world far more lonely than when she had left it – no Emily to share the despair.

She wished she could pray: if she could pray, she would pray to Marion, her mother. Marion had God's ear; she would help. Instead:

"Emily," she cried: "I'm sorry. Please, Emily. Please."

There was no answer from the cell across the hall.

\* \* \*

Richard Fielding was on the phone to his lawyer. It was nearly midnight but he did not apologise. They owed him. The first time he had brought up the subject of The Programme, it had been to accuse Carey Arnott of dragging his emotionally frail wife into the cult with her. He had wanted his lawyer to use the accusation as leverage to get Carey to withdraw the proceedings that had led him to a suspended prison sentence for assaulting his wife. Emily would never have sought a court order against him on her own. Therefore, tortured logic dictated, it was Carey's order and Carey should be the object of attack.

His lawyer had been reluctant, insisting that Arnotts were merely doing their job as they were instructed. Eventually they had compromised on a private call between partners and the threat had fizzled out. Life had been on hold until the news stories had begun.

Suddenly Richard was the victim. His own momentary lapses were forgotten. If he had struck her once too often, he had been provoked. It made no chronological sense – his violence had preceded her approach to Arnotts and, therefore, her friendship with Carey and introduction into The Programme. Emotional turmoil kept its own time.

He had become the deserted husband rather than the partner who had driven her away. She had been seduced by Carey, seduced by The Programme, as surely as if it had been an affair. The time leading up to their separation had all but evaporated. The Programme was exclusively responsible for it. It was a common enough tale, a couple torn asunder by a cult; it gave him rights over Emily he had not expected to recover.

"'The Morning Show' rang, wanted me to go in and talk on the air. I said I'd do it."

The lawyer said wearily:

"Do it."

4

"I'm going to," Richard sneered, as if to say he was doing more for himself than his lawyer was doing for him.

* * *

In her own low cell, Emily heard Carey crying out. She wished she could forgive her. Too much had happened: too much love in too little time; too much hatred; no food for days, longer than Carey had gone without.

There were no windows in the cells. She tried to imagine the clear, New England winter sky, strained to light it with a star.

She had only spoken to Carey the once. She had been in the cell by then for a week, three or four days longer than Carey. Carey had put her there – Esther. She had been locked up before. Then Berlinger's man had helped her to escape. She told the authorities she had to go back for Carey. They tried to prevent her. She threatened them: unless they agreed to take her with them she would not swear out the affidavit they needed to secure their warrants. They had to give her a chance to talk to Carey, to try to get her out of it before the trouble began.

They had cajoled, threatened back, made promises they had no intention of keeping, but in the end she was – for that brief window of time – more important to them than they were to her and, they privately admitted, if she succeeded in persuading her friend to leave, it would significantly increase their information about The Programme and what they would have to confront at Hammer Reach. They were nervous: Waco was never far from their thoughts, nor Ruby Ridge.

They had not asked Sergeant Romero, the local State Policeman, for his opinion until it was too late. Emily was already inside the house, he was asking what the hell was going on. When they told him, he had laughed at them, assured them that Carey would not come out, predicted Emily would not do so either.

The escape had been pointless. The hike across the hills inadequately clothed and starving hungry; the kindness of the people at the Inn; the frantic calls home – in desperation, she had even called Richard; on a hunch, she had rung Charles Arnott in Antibes. Finally, she had passed into the hands of the authorities whence she had – in effect – jumped right back into her cell, exactly where she had begun.

Carey had been brought to the cell opposite a day after Emily had been forced to give up the name of Berlinger's inside man. That was when they had their only conversation. Carey had cried:

"Emily, Emily, I'm sorry."

"What happened, Carey?" For the first time, she spoke to her friend.

"He killed him," Carey had sobbed.

Emily had frozen. She had been halfway between relenting and continued contempt. She said – her last words to the friend she had loved more than she had ever loved anyone:

"Then you're responsible for that too."

\* \* \*

Matthew conducted the Midnight Meditation. Some members had never meditated under him until they had retreated to Hammer Reach from the Chapters in America and England, fleeing the onslaught of media attention, fraud charges, deprogrammers, Rockworth's civil litigation and that of other former members who had donated money and property to the group, and – most threatening of all – a police investigation into the disappearance of three of their members.

He said, his voice rich and rolling like the hair that flowed down his shoulders, slowing hypnotically with every word:

"I want you to think about the person nearest to you, not about yourself. It doesn't matter who it is, or how well you get along together. Think of him or her as the most loved person in your life, until he or she matters more to you than your life itself. Fix that idea in your head as you begin to meditate, as you begin to float, stop thinking about it, let the idea take you over, let it become you, let it be your very breath, let it be your very last breath – love that person as he or she is loving you, become one another, do this for each other, until between us we are whole being called love. You will never know this love again; you will know it forever. We are one, we are many, together we are whole, whole love. This is what they cannot destroy or take away: it is the fire beyond that is too hot for them to handle."

He watched them and was the idea himself. He loved them all. What happened to them mattered more than life itself, more than his own life. They were his children, his lovers, his companions and comrades: they had become his world, his breath. If it was to be complete, a whole, he had also to be theirs. There was no room for questions. Damn Esther.

\* \* \*

The day her resignation letter arrived had been bad; the next few were worse. Charles departed immediately for the apartment in

Antibes. Colin only found out from his secretary that he had gone.

Colin spent the days – and long into the evening – ringing around. He had rung Hammer Reach of course, but she would not take his calls. He had established that they had a fax machine, e-mail: neither had procured a response. There was no reply from any of the Chapters. The London number had been disconnected. On his first calls, Boston and New York had rung and rung – later they too were out of service. The Programme had holed up at the farm.

He even called Berlinger – the deprogrammer who had button-holed him at his sports club and who had warned him, prophetically:

"It's a sorry feature of my business, Mr Arnott, how often people don't decide they need me until it's too late."

Berlinger was in Boston but not in the office; then he was out of town, expected back; then gone again. Rockworth, too, had refused to take his calls. Colin was certain that things were happening, but he was outside the loop. He even rang a firm of lawyers in New York with whom Arnotts had contacts and they had promised to make enquiries: again, no news.

The disconnection of the Chapters made him think of Jonestown, of Waco, of the Order of the Solar Temple, cults which had turned away from the world until all they had left was their own vision of nirvana and apocalypse, unchecked by any outside reality, spinning out of control, group pressure preventing anyone standing up to the leader or simply no one left who wanted to do so, until there was no test left of faith, loyalty and themselves but death.

No one ever thought it could happen to them, to people they knew, to family, to a sister his wife always said he loved more than anyone else, more than her, perhaps even more than his children.

It was the sheer absence of hard information he could not cope with. He barely worked; he was obsessed; several times, he decided he would go over and find her himself. The trouble was that Charles was right – of course Charles was right, he was always right. Colin had done precisely the wrong thing and provoked the wrong result. There was no point going over to see Carey: by her actions and her silence, she had told him she would not forgive him either.

A week after the partnership meeting, he sat in his study drinking whisky, the third or fourth too many of the night. Though it was past eleven, it would not be the last. In what he referred to as normal times, he might have a drink when he got home, a glass of wine with dinner to keep Jan company, and – if he did not have to work any more – a final Scotch to see out the evening.

Across the room, he had installed a television on which to watch the cable channels: CNN, Sky News, at half past the later hours they ran CBS, ABC.

"Come to bed," Jan said from the doorway: "Nothing's going to happen tonight."

She crossed the room, stood behind him: he was almost thirty-six, balding and what was left of his hair was turning to grey.

"Later," he muttered. "I want to see one more news."

For a moment she thought of trying to dissuade him but then she shrugged, gave up. He had plenty of time for Carey's problems, never for hers.

The story broke just as Colin was about to give up for the night. The cameras cut to a picture of a farmhouse, open fields with a light covering of snow, woods on a rise, police cars, TV vans, a solitary fire-truck marked Hedgerow, ambulance, other unidentified vehicles, dozens of people, uniformed and not, caped and capped, armed. Colin knew it was Hammer Reach before the reporter told him.

"This breaking story in upstate New York. A special force of FBI and ATF officers, accompanied by local police and New York State troopers, have surrounded a farm known as Hammer Reach near to the Pennsylvania border occupied by The Programme, a religious-based community – or cult, some would say – which has increasingly featured in news stories both here and in England in the course of an angry confrontation with wealthy tycoon Arthur Rockworth. Rockworth has accused them of causing the death of his son and has been trying to evict them from premises he owns in London.

"Now The Programme has also been at the centre of a court hearing brought by the sister of a member – Amanda Kroger – who owns Hammer Reach and who gave cult-leader Matthew Crane a life tenancy of it. The family claim Kroger was under Crane's influence when she deeded the farm to him and was not responsible for her actions. They want the farm – and other money Kroger gave the cult – back."

"Bob, can you tell us what's happening in this breaking news at the farm now?" The anchor asked from Atlanta.

The screen cut back to Hammer Reach, and the square-jawed, reporter in weather-beaten close-up, wind blowing in his hair.

"Suzanne, what we've got here is the beginnings of a stand-off Waco style. Now it seems, a small force arrived here quite early this morning to execute a search warrant: sources are talking about both a cache of weapons and possibly the bodies of former members buried in the grounds. At first, they met with passive resistance. Apparently, the Bureau of Alcohol, Tobacco and Firearms had executed another warrant just a few days ago and today some of Crane's supporters refused to allow officers to approach the house, claiming harassment. Initially, there were about a dozen officers involved and when they tried to push their way inside, armed Programme members appeared at the windows and, in a flash, battle was joined. They seemed to be ready and waiting for the visit, though it's not clear yet whether they'd been given any explicit warning. During the day, reinforcements have been arriving hourly. There must be fifty or sixty law enforcement agents from one jurisdiction or another at the farm now."

"Bob, do we know if anyone has been hurt? Have shots actually been fired?"

"We understand that a few shots were fired either in the air or in the general direction of the police, enough anyhow to force them to pull back. Now there's a number of buildings involved: they're all occupied and we're told that they've all got armed members in them. One of them – I don't know if the camera's giving you this clearly – is a strange building, more like a silo than anything else, but round, in the shape of the cult's symbol, and it's a pretty solid construction with slits in the walls through which, if you look hard, you can see the barrels of weapons."

"And Bob, has anyone been hurt?"

"Suzanne, not so far as we know. There's one bizarre twist here. Apparently, the source for the warrants is a former member who only left a few days ago. Now she apparently managed to persuade officers to let her go inside and talk to some of her, well, brothers and sisters I guess you'd have to say. What we're told is that it's when she didn't come out, when officers asked to see her, that's when they tried to go in and the fuse was lit."

"Do we know anything about that member?"

"We don't have a name, no, Suzanne. She's an English woman – there's quite a few English members. Now from what we've pieced together, The Programme has just recently – possibly only in the last few days – closed up what it called its Chapters – it had Chapters in London, New York and Boston – and all of its members converged on Hammer Reach."

"Do we know how many people that is?

"Suzanne, we have no idea. Hold on, now, something's happening."

The screen shifted from a close up of the reporter to an awkward long shot of the front doorway of the farmhouse where Matthew Crane stood, cradling a rifle in one elbow, his hand grasping the neck of a woman, turning her head away from the camera. Beside him stood Carey, in a brilliant white cloak, holding a pistol straight-armed to the woman's head, screaming something that the microphone could not pick up directly.

The reporter was having the words fed to him by a technician nearer to the door, repeating them back in his own voice a few seconds later like badly-synched acting, handling each word as if it came from outer space.

"'Get away from here'. 'Get away from us'. 'We've done nothing wrong'. 'Get away – she'll die'. That's what I'm told she's saying."

Before there was any reaction, they had retreated into the house dragging their hostage with them, slamming the door behind them.

Colin did not hear another word of the commentary: all he could see was his sister, waving a gun, in confrontation with a troop of armed police any one of whom could end her life with a twitch of his finger.

His too.

*Part One*

# Chapter One

"Mr, uh," Colin fumbled for the slip on which his secretary had written names and other details about his new appointments for the day. "Mr Crane." He offered his hand. "Sit down, please."

For a split second longer than necessary – long enough to have an effect – Matthew clung onto Colin's hand while he lowered himself elegantly onto an upright chair across the desk, allowing his leather satchel to drop lightly to the floor.

Matthew was probably older than Colin and certainly much taller – five or six inches – and he had a much more substantial presence. Colin was both impressed and disturbed: there was something haunting about the man, other worldly, mesmeric was the word that popped uninvited into his head. He was almost physically drawn to him.

Colin's secretary brought in a tray: coffee for Colin, tea for Matthew. Mid-morning biscuits neither of them would touch. While she set the cups out, the two men sized each other up.

They were a study in opposites. Matthew was wearing an off-white suit: silk, Colin thought. His jacket hung loose, as if he had almost forgotten to put it on. He wore a silk shirt, too, also white, open at the collar. His shoes were a smart version of a basic deck-shoe. He could be anything from Colin's age – recently turned thirty five – to his fifties, it was impossible to say. He wore his hair long, almost to his shoulders, framing his face; he was lightly bearded. It was a faintly familiar image, though Colin could not quite place it.

Colin flipped open the thin cardboard folder with Crane's name on it and studied the almost empty pro-forma stapled to the inside cover. Only two columns had anything in them: Crane's name, and the sum of £500 – plus Value Added Tax (£87.50) – as a payment on account.

"How can I help you?"

Colin pushed his high-backed leather chair back on its rollers and crossed his legs beneath his desk, twisting the gold Dupont between each of his thumbs and forefingers.

Matthew said:

"I don't know if you have heard of The Programme." The way he said it made clear he was talking about an organisation.

Colin logged the soft American accent. Taken aback by it, and by the question, Colin shook his head, repeating:

"The Programme?"

"It's a group – an organisation – a way of life. A belief system, I call it." It was a gentle accent, dulled by Matthew's years in England; it was not only accent that he had acquired, but style and mannerism. He spoke slowly, deliberately, pausing for an echo to follow each phrase.

"Like – uh," Colin fumbled for the name of a sect, without wanting to use the word. "Scientology? Children of God? A religion?"

He was already thinking: whatever it is, this is not for us. He did not like religions; he did not like sects or cults or recognise any distinction between them. His mother had been religious; she had used it to assert her moral superiority against both of the children and against Charles; it had led to their separation.

Matthew noted the expression on Colin's face and smiled.

"A cult?" He was not frightened of the more pejorative expression. "Some people would say so; some people do. Everything's a cult when it begins. I founded The Programme nearly ten years ago; now there are several hundred members. There are bigger cults but smaller religions."

There was nothing defensive in his tone.

"Are you, uh, a registered charity?" Colin grasped at the first legality to come to mind.

"We're not incorporated," Matthew replied. "It's built on trust; the people in The Programme trust each other; they trust me."

"Forgive me, Mr Crane..."

"I'm known as The Teacher inside the group; Matthew otherwise."

"Matthew." He was the client. It was his money.

"What were you going to say?" Matthew prodded him along.

"I was going to ask," Colin corrected, "what it was you wanted from me, from a solicitor?"

"One of our members – former members, I suppose you'd say, though we prefer to think of it as a temporary separation – deeded some property over to the group; now, er..."

"They want it back," Colin supplied.

"Right."

Colin was tempted to say: so give it back. Instead, he asked:

"How much property?"

Matthew shrugged carelessly.

"It's a farm, upstate New York – Hammer Reach; I don't know what it's worth. It was – it is – going to be the base for an American

14

Chapter. There was some money, too. A quarter of a million."

"Dollars or pounds?" Colin pulled a notepad towards him, rolled the Dupont one last time between his forefingers and thumbs and removed its cap. Despite himself, he felt his interest stir. He had no idea of New York agricultural land values, but nowhere could be worth less than six figures. They were into a half-million dispute – dollars or pounds.

"Pounds," Matthew said. "I don't remember exactly how much it was originally."

"Who was he?"

"She. Amanda Kroger. American," he added.

"Was it her own money? How did she come by it?"

"Inheritance. Her father made some kind of patented dairy product. There was – is – a trust fund; that's untouched; this was additional capital. Entirely hers."

"And the land?"

"It had been left to her outright. There were several children; she was a bit wild; I think the idea was to try and get her away from the city. Does it matter, as long as it was hers?"

"What was your relationship with her?" Colin asked bluntly. If this was about domestic property, someone else would have to handle it. He knew nothing and cared less. Carey maybe.

Matthew snorted.

"The usual preconceptions? She was a member of The Programme; she gave it to me as a member of The Programme. Members of The Programme trust me with their worldly assets as they trust me with their lives. They would not be members otherwise."

Colin noted that he had avoided answering.

"Has she issued a writ? Here? Or there?"

"It's not her. One of her sisters, acting as administrator. There's a court order, appointing her to manage Amanda's affairs. She's, uh, undergone some sort of breakdown."

"Deprogramming? Forgive the pun," Colin failed to hide his discomfort. Maybe a half-million wasn't worth losing sleep over. Or the firm's image.

"Perhaps. It's the vogue. I've got a letter."

Matthew picked up his satchel and extracted a sheet of paper which he slid casually across the desk. Colin finished scribbling a note, skimmed the letter quickly, pressed a button on his phone. Before he could say anything, his secretary appeared and, wordlessly, took the letter from him. Colin explained:

"She'll take a copy. I take it, from the fact that you're here, you're not willing to give it back?"

"I would give it back to Amanda in a moment if she asked for it herself. But I'm not giving it back to anyone else. Amanda gave it to me, to The Programme; I think she'll be back one day; I think when she does, she'll expect us to have used it for the group, the way she intended. Who is to say what is in her interests? Her sister, or me?"

"According to the letter, the court says the sister," Colin replied dryly.

"That's just one side. What if I appealed against the order, or had it set aside, however you do it?"

"I wouldn't know; not in New York State. But if the court there approaches it the same way as here, I'd tell you not to waste your money. The best you could get, if you managed to persuade a court the sister isn't acting in, uh, Amanda's best interests, would be to get someone else appointed. It wouldn't be you; and they wouldn't let you keep the money."

"Not without Amanda, right?"

Colin nodded, seeing at once where Matthew was leading.

"And a court case takes a while, right?"

Colin thought before saying:

"It's an American case."

"The money's here."

"True. They haven't issued proceedings here, though."

"Not yet."

Still prevaricating, Colin asked:

"Chesterfield Gardens?" The address on the letter. "Is that your home?"

"It's our home, our base."

"Expensive." In the heart of Mayfair, in the shadow of the London Hilton, around the corner from the historical Shepherds' Market. There was real money in the background all right; real as in big.

Matthew shrugged.

"If we went into court, you realise it would mean, uh, declaring everything about the organisation – financially and otherwise." "Exposing" was the word in his mind.

"I have nothing to hide," Matthew would still not be drawn.

Colin said:

"I don't think, to be honest, I'm not sure we're the right firm for you. I'm not even sure why you came here." He hated to turn work away; he hated to turn away a case with money in it; but – however Matthew dressed it up – it was closer to a domestic dispute than to anything that might be called a business enterprise; and, it would be controversial.

16

"I looked around a bit. Read up on the Net."

Arnotts had been one of the first firms to post their own board. If one knew the sitename, it could be accessed directly; otherwise, it was accessed through half a dozen different directories, from community advice through corporate finance. It hadn't been intended to attract clients like this.

"You seemed to be the best for civil rights."

"Civil rights?" Colin didn't disguise his surprise. "What does this have to do with civil rights?"

"Isn't it? If this was property deeded to the Catholic Church, you think they'd be trying to get it back?"

"Questions of consideration," Colin answered lamely, admitting that Crane was right and no one would – as did the letter – be alleging undue influence or unfair advantage. "All the same, it's not what you might call a conventional civil rights issue; people, uh, tend to see these things from the individual's perspective, not the organisation's."

"That's your job, isn't it? To get them to see it the other way around. Individual rights aren't worth much if you can't exercise them. And that's what we're talking about here."

"Which is what? What is The Programme?"

"That's a question. I'll tell you what, Colin, I'll leave you a couple of booklets; you have a look at them and make up your own mind. If you're willing to act for us, fine; if not, well, it won't have cost you anything."

Matthew's tone was light, carefree, as if none of it was his problem, none of it touched him. Colin found it unnerving. This sort of first interview was supposed to be his forte, yet it was as if it – and he – had been completely controlled by Matthew; he often felt a similar helplessness when he confronted his father.

They rose simultaneously. Matthew took the booklets – and the most recent edition of their magazine – from his satchel and placed them face up on the desk. The cover of the magazine was a portrait of Matthew in a pose suggestive of Christ. That was what had been familiar. The covers of the magazine and the booklets were all glossy, richly coloured, expensively produced. Colin casually flicked open one of the booklets: well printed, too. Each of the volumes bore the group's symbol, a circle, in four segments, not joined up, the sides of each segment ever so slightly curved inwards – concave: it was evocative of, yet clearly was not, an Iron Cross.

Colin walked Matthew to the front door.

"I still don't think we're the right people for you, but I'll read your, uh, books and I'll talk to one or two of the partners and, uh, I'll give you a ring."

They shook hands. Matthew held onto his, smiling gently.

"It's not worth it if it's going to make you unhappy."

"If I only took the work that made me happy, I wouldn't have much to do," Colin barely managed to reply.

He watched Matthew walk down the road towards Smithfield. Their offices were on St John's Street: halfway between the City and the Angel, Islington, a spit away from Clerkenwell Green. That was about right. Historically, Clerkenwell Green had been a centre for radicalism, and the Angel once an immigrant and working-class melting-pot – Charles' constituency. The City was money – Colin's.

Just as he was about to go back in to work, his father's car pulled up. From one God to another, Colin thought as he leaned down and spoke through the window:

"I didn't expect you in today."

"Sorry," Charles answered cheerfully, not meaning it. "I'm having lunch with your sister. Care to join us?" he added as Carey came out of the office behind Colin.

* * *

Arnotts was listed in Community Advice, Legal; Community Advice was a sub-directory of Advice and Assistance; so also was Self-Help, which led to Self-Improvement, which led to The Programme. Or enter http://www.the-programme.org.uk (turn on sound card if available).

> *Why do some find self-fulfilment and others do not? We know we have an infinite capacity to expand and to advance ourselves, so why don't we do it? What holds us back? We say fear: fear to let go of the same codes of belief and behaviour that everyone around you adheres to even though you know that it confines you; fear to invest your imagination and hopes – you might as well say – except in the same stocks everyone else invests in, even though it's the stock with the lowest return! The only thing The Programme can offer you is courage; after that, you're on your own. How do we do it? Example, support, love: that's our programme. Come and meet us; we have a home in Chesterfield Gardens in Mayfair; you're welcome to drop in just to say hello, or for a meditation, or come and eat in our Coffee Lounge. There are no conditions, no catches, just people.*

* * *

Carey was a forceful lawyer, strong enough to dominate her own clients, and when she needed to be she was also an aggressive litigator. In her private relations, however, she was just the opposite: almost timid at first meeting, tentative – fragile was a word that came to people's lips, brittle was a less flattering alternative.

She had been an unhappy child and she was an unhappy woman, darting between relationships and experiences, unable to commit herself to a particular person, desperate for love and direction, terrified in case she made the wrong choice, most frightened of all that if she let anyone get close enough to love her, they would learn just how unlovable she really was, anyone but Charles and Colin who must – surely – by now already have found out and forgiven her.

Colin was the older by five years. When their parents separated, he was in his teens, she was just shy of them. They had been supposed to go to live with their mother. They had prevaricated and postponed the moment until, in less than a year, she had died of a violent, unannounced colonic cancer and it was too late. After that, it was just the three of them and their guilt.

Carey was tall for a girl, the same height as Colin. Colin was stocky, she was slight. Colin was beginning to bald; her hair was as fine and as full of lights as when she had been a child; she looked not much older than when she finished university. She had her mother's high cheek-bones, which enhanced the sense of fragility – china doll; his were flat, giving the impression of a straight, flat surface from jaw to forehead. Sometimes they joked that they must have had different fathers. It was only a joke because the idea of their mother being unfaithful to Charles was absurd; almost as absurd as the idea that he might ever have stayed faithful to her.

Their parents had met on an Aldermaston – Ban-the-Bomb – march in the 1950s: Charles propelled by politics, Marion by religion. In hindsight, it seemed as if it was the last time they had anything in common: he looked as if he had slept in a hedge, tufts of hair protruding from his head and most of its orifices, while she was always impeccably prepared and presented; the children were spoils of war to be fought over; Charles always won. When she died, and they were released from the obligation to go and live with her, it seemed like even God – even her God – was on his side.

Their mother had taken them to school or to the doctor, shopping for clothes and to children's parties. Charles took them skiing – water and snow – and into town to adult restaurants, gave them too much pocket money, asked what they thought, then argued with them when their opinions differed from his. His cases were in the newspapers and sometimes he appeared on television commenting on this or protesting about that. When he disappeared for a weekend with the latest young female articled clerk he had taken into his firm, it was for a conference. They were none of them fooled but, given the choice between their mother's dour sufferance – her tiny voice haunting them with scriptures full of doom and wrath – and his childlike exuberance, they took his side.

Charles was the *force majeure* in their lives. He was a magnet. Colin and he were identical poles and therefore they conflicted. Carey was the opposite and could adhere to both of them. She was all that prevented them going their separate ways. It was a battle and a pursuit and a role which she alternately relished and resented. Though often she thought that she would like to walk away from it and from them, each passing year meant she would be leaving more of herself behind. Besides, she had nowhere to go.

She filled herself up with work, occasional male companions – too often, because she had so little life outside, from within the firm – and irregular recourse to women friends from college with whom she had less and less in common with each passing encounter. She drank wine – too much – and nibbled cheese alone in her tiny, cottage-like terraced house with the front window that looked right out onto the street, watching the people pass beneath the street light directly outside, smoking in solitude. She wanted something to fill the void, but she didn't know what: it could be almost anything, but nothing that she could imagine. Sometimes, she heard secret beats inside her head – sometimes a jig, sometimes a dirge, sometimes a throbbing that was discernibly sexual. It came upon her at the strangest times – sometimes in front of her window, sometimes in a law library, sometimes in court.

"A guinea for 'em," Charles prompted as they drove to the restaurant, an old joke, meaning her thoughts were worth far more than the conventional penny.

"Nothing," she shook her head. "Who was that with Colin?" The striking man she had seen from behind as he left the hallway, and could still see in the distance when she emerged from the building.

"I don't know. Ha." He spied a parking space and aimed the car at it like a javelin. "That's a piece of luck."

She wished he would let her drive. At the best of times, he had not been a good driver, but neither his eyesight nor his hearing were what they once had been and it told. He was growing fiercer with age, not more mellow, and that too showed when he drove. She was relieved when he cut the engine, leaving the car at a modest ten degree angle into the traffic.

They ate at Oscars, a little known restaurant tucked into the basement of a massive, anonymous, fifties brownstone building full of small businesses in clusters of tiny offices sharing facilities on Temple Avenue, backing onto the Inns of Court.

Over pre-prandial drinks and, for her, a cigarette, Charles announced: "I'm going down to Antibes soon. When are you coming?"

They owned an apartment overlooking the bay, on a small, well-maintained estate, bought with the money their mother had left. Because they had not been divorced, the money went to Charles; because they were separated, it had not been right for him to take it. He had resolved the ethical difficulty with customary aptitude: first, he had settled the money in trust for the children; then – as trustee – he had spent it on a property that would become his own.

Charles went down for six or eight weeks before the season and another couple of months afterwards. He despised people who had apartments on the Côte d'Azur, and loved to be near enough to let them know it. She usually went down for a visit – as Colin, Jan and their children did – but it had to be planned in advance. There were always visitors, some of them from the covey of widows and divorcees with whom Charles managed still to surround himself, others would be friends of his own age who had retired or, like him, who worked less than a full year. His sojourn in the South of France had to be organised so that he was never left alone for too long at a time.

"How's the book?" she asked non-sequentially as they were brought their food. She watched as her father tasted the wine. Tried not to appear too eager for her own. She had a meeting to attend and clients to see that afternoon, but nothing too serious for a couple of lunch-time drinks.

Charles had been promising – or threatening – to write his autobiography since, shortly before his sixtieth birthday, he had decided that the active part of his life was over and that it was time to arrange it into a permanent record as if it had all been a coherent whole.

He grunted. He was no further forward than the last time she had asked. Or the time before. It was an idea, and though years ago he had shown her an outline, she doubted there was much more than jottings and notes.

He pushed his food around on his plate, asked:

"How are you getting along?" She and Colin.

"Fine," she said. "We always get on fine."

He found it difficult to understand how she could be so close to him and yet so close to Colin.

"And Jan?"

"Ah, Jan." Jan – Colin's wife – Colin's pretty wife – wife and mother. They were both jealous of her.

"She's the reason," Charles said darkly.

Carey knew what was coming. Colin wanted to take the firm in a new, more commercial – more profitable – direction. It was Jan's fault: Jan who wanted their children in expensive private schools, delivered in expensive cars by smartly turned out nannies; Jan who urged Charles to spend more money on his appearance – especially, when he was planning to be around his grandchildren.

"It's the times," Carey said. "No one survives on legal aid anymore; all the others are doing the same."

\* \* \*

Http://www.the-programme.org.uk (turn on sound card if available).

*What people fear most is being controlled; what they want most is to be taken care of. The only people who can be controlled are those who are not in control of themselves. Ask yourself why you are not in control of yourself. Ask yourself if you want to be. Then comes the difficult question. How? We don't have the answer; we don't think there is one answer; there are as many different answers as people asking the same question. We think everyone has to work it out for him- or herself, but we don't think you have to do it alone. We don't think anyone can do it alone. The crucial, hidden – difficult – difference is between control and care; none of us needs to be in anyone else's control, yet all of us need someone to care for us. How can you be cared for – safely – unless you are also in that person's control, which defeats the very purpose? That's what we offer: a way to be cared for, and to care, without being controlled or controlling. Example, support, love: that's our programme.*

\* \* \*

Matthew strolled confidently from the Arnotts office all the way back to the Chapter, enjoying the solitude. He was always at work and on show. He was the public face and spokesman of The Programme. He was The Teacher. He was the father and the leader, the guide and the shepherd, the vessel through whom the message was interpreted. He had dependants at every level.

He did not waste too much time thinking about the meeting with the lawyer. He knew that Amanda Kroger – or, rather, her sister – was a threat, but she was not the first and he had not yet been defeated. It was a challenge; in the final tally, it would not count. He would find a way to reach out to her. He had enjoyed crossing swords with Colin Arnott: they would never be friends; there was no empathy; they might yet prove fruitful allies.

It was a fine, spring day. The journey did not take him as long as he would have enjoyed. Through Smithfield to Fleet Street and along the Strand, then through back streets until he reached Green Park. On Piccadilly, he stood and watched from a distance as a small group of Initiates and Acolytes in linen suits cut much like his own sold their magazine to strollers. Donating, they called it: donating, not collecting; they were offering more than they asked for.

Tourists, for the most part, were generous with spare change, perhaps adventurous and open to a new experience. Some would be students, others unemployed; occasionally, a shop- or office-worker killing a lonely lunch hour. Often, the Coffee Lounge in the basement of the building would be full from midday to midnight; most of those who visited once would return. He had something people wanted; they surrounded him, looked up to him and loved him; that was what fed him.

Donating in the street did not produce an income on which they could thrive; nor did takings from the coffee shop; possibly fifty per cent of their outgoings could be met from this sort of income, including meditation, lecture and course fees. Some of the members, some of them residents, worked in outside jobs: one was an accountant; yet another was a personnel officer in the civil service. The balance came from the private incomes of members, legally or in practice made over to The Programme, from capital gifts, from the donations which members made when they committed their lives to The Programme and no longer needed an independent safety net. Donations like Amanda Kroger's: if it had to be given back, then none of the group's money was his; it was all no more than a loan.

He supposed he had enriched the truth for Arnott. Several hundred implied more than the two to three to whom The Programme could at any one time lay claim, and this included not only the full-time, residential members and active outside followers but those who flitted in and out of the group as the mood took them and a number who had never made a formal commitment to it but who had hung around long enough for Matthew to consider them a part of the group's life. Even so, for a boy from the nowhere state of North Carolina, it was a sort of success; no one else he knew had achieved anything like it.

This was why he had come to Europe: to find success. He had been born in Asheville, the home-town of North Carolina's greatest writer, Thomas Wolfe. Another one larger than life. You can't go home again, he had written; but, look homeward angel. Move on, but do not forget where you come from.

He did not have Wolfe's talent; he did not have any other obvious talent, yet he had always believed – to a certainty – that he was destined to accomplish something special in life, that would make people say, yes, Asheville, Wolfe – and Matthew Crane, of course.

He had charm and wit and because he was a big man people wanted his protection. For a while, he had been a soldier, in Vietnam; he had commanded men and killed enemy; he had no regrets – it was the most fulfilling time of his life. He had studied the Bible, read it cover to cover several times over, pondered its secrets and the hold it had over so many people for so long. He had wondered about it as he gazed on fire-wars: gun flares, flame-throwers, napalm, ritual bombings, shattered limbs and broken bodies – these too were the story that the Bible was trying to tell yet somehow fell short. He had discovered a natural ability to lead. That was what he wanted to do: to lead and to protect. Though he could have stayed in the army, it was not a real choice; he was meant to fight his own battle, not someone else's war.

He had used GI Bill money to fund his travels; he had enlisted at the University of London. He had put his birth-family to one side and begun to create one of his own. He lived a dual life. For one part of it, he was merely the American philosophy student, older than most, with dark secrets that mystified and attracted but no discernible direction; for the other, he was plotting a way to create something that people would stand up and take notice of – in the end, that they would applaud. He had set to work with a clear sense of where he needed to be, even if he was not yet sure how to get there.

He had been amused when the lawyer mentioned Scientology. He had been approached outside Tottenham Court Road Underground Station, lured into their shop-front fly-trap, answered their questions, attended meetings, paid for e-meter readings, made love to their women and thought: I could do this too.

He had learned that once people were dependent, they would do almost anything he wanted: that was what he offered them; the capacity to do things they would not have the courage to do on their own. Peer group pressure was a particularly potent drug: take an act that a person might be able to imagine but would not have the confidence to perform; show that person one other who was willing to do it and it was within grasp; show that person two others – or five or ten – willing to do it, and the only questions that remained were how soon, how often, how much. He had tested the theory and proved it incrementally: spiritual exploration and abasement alike, mental, moral, even physical.

It was astonishing how many people – mostly young, many well-educated, all of them superficially self-possessed – were desperate for something more than friends and families could offer. He was the Big American, a big brother; he was charismatic; he combined novelty with security; he offered them something that was new, gift-wrapped and with a guarantee for life; gradually, the flotsam came together to form a floating island.

He had learned one thing early. Not quantity, but quality. He rejected as many would-be followers as he accepted. Every rejection bound each of those he accepted ever more tightly. People cost money; monied people cost nothing. Nothing would be achieved if he did not build a net strong enough for the wider trawl. The lonely, the emotionally dispossessed, the frantic, the hungry with something financial to contribute were every bit as worthy of his attentions as those whose neediness was their solitary asset.

Many of those who joined him were American exiles: there was a post-Vietnam generation addicted to cynicism and despair, living like Matthew against the backdrop of fire, who could not switch off and settle into the family business; some had fallen foul of the law – one or two had been to prison; although there were exceptions – like Amanda Kroger – they tended to bring less capital wealth into the group than their British and European counterparts, but they were much quicker to find ways to make money and most of them had at least a small income-stream from home, intended to keep them as far away from it as possible.

Matthew had attended meditations organised by Asian gurus and discovered there was nothing so potent as the mantra he had chanted when bombs fell about him at Xuan Loc: give me until tomorrow, and then I shall start again, carried forward on an ocean of fire. He had found that a few, select words on a photocopied sheet – latterly, on the Internet – could be as effective as any novel or prayer. He had learned that if you hold out enough hope, some people will be motivated to try and find it, whatever it cost them materially, financially, socially or emotionally. If those with least to leave behind were the quickest to sign up for the journey, that was only natural. The self-styled anti-cult specialists and deprogrammers focused on where membership led; Matthew preferred to think about where members had come from.

\* \* \*

Http://www.the-programme.org.uk (turn on sound card if available).

*People talk about brain-washing, mind-cults. We do not ask for your mind. We ask only for your body and your heart. The mind will follow of its own accord – or it won't. We cannot ask for your mind; it is not possible for you to give it to us, to give it up. If you try to do so, then by definition you are not doing so, because some part of it is being kept back, that part of it which is making the decision to do so. All we can offer is example, support, love: that's our programme.*

*This is what The Programme is like. It is like the secret place you hid in as a child: maybe you were a little scared, because you were hiding, but also you felt safe, safe as only a child can be, in the sanctuary of his or her parents' keep. You are scared and at the same time you are drawn to it. What does it mean? It is an admission that we need something more than we can create for ourselves; it is an admission that we need someone to take care of us; we cannot go back and find our parents – we have to go forward and find something to take their place. It is something we need others to build with us; that means we have to trust them, and earn their trust; that means we have to know that no one of us is more committed – and no one of us has held more in reserve – than the others. In the end, it is like any other relationship – the sum must be greater than its parts.*

\* \* \*

Matthew arrived back at Chesterfield Gardens shortly after lunch. Outside, a new follower – a non-resident member – was polishing the discreet brass plate that announced the way into the basement Coffee Lounge: there was no additional sign on the portals or at the front door. The house itself was busy. He could hear noise from the

kitchen; chattering in the Coffee Lounge. In reception, Sister Rebecca
– ungainly, overweight, awkward in motion but quick with her mind
– was detailing last night's Coffee Lounge receipts in an account book
overlooked by a vast portrait of himself, the same picture that was
on the magazine cover.

She glanced up as he entered, rose urgently, half-bowed and half-
stumbled, finally remembered to smile.

"I am one," she said.

"We are many," he murmured as – without breaking his stride –
he mounted the sweeping stairs that led first to the huge, high
Meditation Hall and meeting room and, beyond, to the private
quarters where the junior ranks of resident members lived in virtual
dormitories and – beyond them – where he and Cassandra each
occupied separate quarters of their own. He was home; he was God.

\* \* \*

Http://www.the-programme.org.uk (turn on sound card if
available).

*Do not ask me who or what God is. Ask me what godliness is.*
*Godliness is what we put up there on a pedestal, to represent that*
*special quality we see in ourselves and in humankind generally*
*and that makes us better than we appear to behave. Godliness can*
*be kindly, it can be harsh, it can be profoundly challenging.*
*Godliness is good just because it is godliness, not because it is*
*nice or kind or forgiving. Godliness is our sense that we are more*
*than flesh and bones and the limits of our daily lives; godliness is*
*soul come to mind. Psychoanalysts might call it superego,*
*individual or collective; moralists, the conscience – again of a*
*person or of a people; religionists believe that it is a quality that*
*belongs to – and is given to us by – God. We believe that it is the*
*other way round. God is the manifestation of godliness; God is the*
*representative on earth of what we hold up on high; God, to repeat*
*an earlier lesson, is the sum total that is more than our parts.*

\* \* \*

In his bedroom, Matthew changed into black slacks and a black high-
necked, roll-top sweater. At one time, they had all worn black – black
capes in the street, a black uniform like the one he had just put on.
Around their necks they had worn The Programme symbol in

different metals to distinguish their ranks, worn outside sweaters or T-shirts. He and Cassandra – The Seer – wore platinum; the Superiors wore gold; Senior Messengers wore silver; there were Junior Messengers and Initiates with brass symbols, and the outside Acolytes stainless steel. The segments represented the four elements, fire always supreme.

That was in the dark days when their message was of gloom and despair, when God was Satan and The Teacher their only hope for salvation. Members of The Programme would be saved from the final holocaust, but only at a price of punishment and penitence. Although he had played his part, and commanded unquestioning obedience to the rituals of humiliation and shame that Cassandra had devised, he preferred tunnels with shafts of unexpected light to caves of unrelenting night. When their personal relationship changed, he seized the opportunity to separate their spiritual paths. The Teacher and The Seer no longer spoke with a single voice; instead, he costumed the members in white while Cassandra and her clique hid in the shadows, waiting for prey.

Cassandra was his lawful wife. She was therefore the source of his legal right to reside in the United Kingdom. She was a small, sharp-featured, heavy-breasted, black-haired Welsh woman, with an anomalous high-pitched giggle. A decade his junior, she was the sister of one of his earliest followers – Huw – who was also one of the first to leave the group: they had been uncomfortably close; it had been a relief when he left.

Matthew and Cassandra made an odd couple. They had turned the complex dimensions of their relationship as it used to be into a fount of tension through which the tenets of The Programme had emerged like a howling, new-born child, violent and innocent, knowledgeable and unlearned, instinctual and physical.

Then they had used their disunion to reshape the group. The Teacher was now both darkness and light; he could be a wrathful, disciplinarian God one moment and a forgiving Christ and joyful Cherub the next. He could choose at will. Cassandra remained The Seer, but she was always and forever harshness incarnate. It created two centres within the group and thus enhanced its range: the innermost core of senior members – Superiors – were immediately below The Teacher within the hierarchy; but a cross-section of members at every level were additionally the private property of The Seer, Satan's troops.

The most secret ritual of the resident members – still called the Midnight Mass – brought these two internal factions into direct conflict – light versus dark. From within this energy, The Teacher rose magisterially to decide which element was to emerge victorious for the next round. Exhausted, they curled up on the floor of the Meditation Hall to sleep, limbs entwined, comforting one another, all of them touching, some of them clinging on to one another, welded to one another, a molten whole.

In the Chesterfield Gardens Chapter, Matthew wore black or white as the mood took him, but – like the other residents – only white when out and about in the world. The Seer alone wore no uniform when it suited her mood not to do so; she was a triumphal star on the crest of the hill. Symbols around necks had gone altogether, replaced by belt buckles; the passage through spiritualism was ostensibly in the past, even if they returned to it in private; now it was about minds – giving up an impotent individual freedom in favour of a collective freedom of inifinite power. The disciplines this change imposed on the resident members – and, before their initiation, on outside Acolytes on track to full-time – were acts of liberation.

Matthew stood before the mirror on the inside door of his wardrobe and looked at himself as if for the first time he saw that he had dressed in black, as if the image in the mirror was telling him his mood. He smiled thinly, momentarily short of breath, excited.

There was a knock at the door to his living-room. Except in an emergency, no one disturbed him in his private quarters uninvited except Sister Helen.

"Come in, Helen," he called.

If anyone threatened Cassandra, it was Helen. Helen was Matthew's future. Helen was the closest thing to a second wife. Helen was an ethereal, West Coast Canadian and younger than Cassandra by more than another decade. Unlike Cassandra, she was slender – small-breasted, small-waisted – and taller, like a model. Her face was gentle, devoid of cutting angles and bruising knots. Helen was his child, his hand-maiden, his mistress. Helen was everything Cassandra was not. Helen was quiet; Helen was graceful. Helen would glide into a room which Cassandra would take by force. Helen could stand still for an hour but Cassandra not for a moment. Helen did not demand, she waited patiently until she was given.

"I am one," she said automatically.

Matthew smiled, passed a hand over her fine red-blonde hair.

"We are many," he replied.

"Together we shall be whole," she concluded.

She saw he was wearing black. Her face revealed no emotion. When he was in a dark phase, life was turmoil: for all of them; for her too. That was what he wanted: to shake them up, to displace their complacency, to turn them on each other and even on himself; he wanted to throw everything up into the air and see where it came down; it meant that he was unsettled or perhaps even frightened; at its lowest, he was bored.

As she stood passively before him, he fixed himself in her eyes, passed the back of his hand over her cheek, first one side then the other, he ran a finger the length of her torso, between her breasts, from the hollow in her throat to the silver symbol-buckle of the white belt of her white skirt, only recently exchanged for brass. He leaned forward and kissed her gently on the forehead.

"Later," he murmured.

"I came to see if you'd eaten," she said. It was her destiny to ensure that he was fed, for whatever he was hungry. "There's soup. Fresh bread. Some rice." They baked their own bread, made their own soups; they were vegetarian, making a virtue of necessity: it was cheaper than meat.

"I have work."

"May I stay here?"

She did not want to be in the open hold if Matthew was determined to create a storm. She knew where he would go first to feed the anger – Cassandra; she did not want to watch where he went on afterwards. If she stayed there, he would return to her when he had worn himself out.

"I was working on an article for The Programme," he said, meaning the magazine they sold in the streets and at reception. "It's on screen." Finish it for me, Sister Helen, he was telling her.

As she had anticipated, he sought out Cassandra. He passed Rebecca on the stairs, relieved from reception duty, on her way to her dormitory to meditate and rest, asked her where he might find her. Rebecca told him Cassandra was teaching, in The Temple.

The Temple was the sound-proofed, back room on the first floor, to which outsiders never had access, its high ceiling painted to resemble the hanging sheets of an eastern pagoda. It was the room in which the Midnight Masses were held once every two or three months. One wall held a giant painting of The Programme symbol: unlike its normal representation, when the areas between the segments were blank, in this painting they were rich in detail – storm and fire.

At a push, The Temple could hold thirty. Now, though, Cassandra was seated cross-legged on a huge, square floor cushion – four feet by four feet – so tightly packed she hardly dented it, surrounded by a mere half dozen of her Initiates and Acolytes, kneeling around the cushion. Matthew let himself in silently; if she heard him enter, she did not acknowledge it.

She wore a thin red robe big enough to cover her from head to toe; her body was shapeless within it. The members' eyes were shut, their arms outstretched towards her. She took one of their wrists in her hand, someone with his back to Matthew, and drew it down herself, much as Matthew had stroked Helen, but across her breast, lingering, sensual.

"What do you feel?" she murmured.

There was a long silence. Then, dry-voiced, the youngster replied: "Love."

Matthew said:

"Agony."

As the youngster turned, Cassandra let go of his wrist. Matthew recognised Brother Lucius, a slim, fair-haired, attractive boy in his early twenties, Lucius of Cyrene.

"I am one," Brother Lucius acknowledged The Teacher.

The others of the group intoned the greeting.

"We are many," Matthew replied.

"Together we shall be whole," they spoke in harmony.

Cassandra giggled but said nothing.

"Why agony, Teacher?" Lucius asked.

"Do you think that when you reach out to someone with love, it is necessarily what they receive? It can be painful, agonising. Especially if it is not what they want."

"I love Cassandra," Lucius answered. In this group, that was what they called her: not Seer.

"Yes, but does she love you?"

"I love Lucius," Cassandra said. "He knows that I love him."

She took his hand again and led it to her breast.

"What do you feel?" She repeated her question.

After another silence, Lucius answered, lowering his head in shame:

"Agony."

\* \* \*

Http://www.the-programme.org.uk (turn on sound card if available).

*I am one, but we are many. It doesn't matter whether you know it or not, or merely sense that you belong: none of us is wholly alone*

*– even if your contact with others is minimal, and fraught, if you rarely speak with anyone else, or only to give or receive spiritless commands, we are surrounded by other people and if we were not, we would quickly begin to doubt that we even existed.*

*It is not sufficient merely to acknowledge that we are but one amongst many. It has to mean something to us, do something for us, bring something into our lives, something special. In turn, that raises for each of us the question – what do we want, what do we want out of others? Contact to reassure us of our existence; communication, meaning someone to talk to at least as much as someone to hear; love, to banish the demons of self-doubt or self-loathing and to stimulate the desire to give love back; and, something with which to warm and to protect ourselves.*

*We say "I am one", and someone answers "We are many". What we mean is that together we have created that special something we each want; it is not an incantation but a positive reminder that there is a purpose to our coming together in a group, in The Programme. We want to make sure that – day on day – we do not take each other for granted; instead, we are here to work together – every single member of The Programme is here to work with each and every other member towards that purpose, every time one of us passes another on the stairs, or sits down to enjoy a cup of tea, or to share a mundane, housekeeping chore. What we are doing is taking the slightest, smallest – in an everyday sense the most meaningless – task and focusing on how, doing it together, we can get something positive from it.*

*People spend an enormous amount of time rushing through irritating, boring functions so as to get onto something else which is supposed to have more meaning. How often does that something else prove to have that meaning, how often does it bring you anything that might be described as "satisfaction"? Mostly, we are still struggling to get some satisfaction from it by the time we have to get back to one of those other functions we've only just put behind us. What we're talking about is altering the balance between looking and finding, between doing things because we have to do them and doing them because it takes us forward. It's not the function that is different; cleaning house is cleaning house. It's doing it together with someone else, who is doing it together with you; it's doing it for the purpose of doing it with someone else, not merely to have it done.*

\* \* \*

The Management Committee was composed of Colin, Carey, and four others – with Charles in attendance, when he wanted to be, *ex officio*.

"It's a straightforward decision," Colin insisted. "Either we tender or not." Historically, Artnotts acted always for employees, not the bosses. Now they had, for the first time, been invited to bid for the employee relations work of an employer, and not just any employer, but a major, formerly nationalised and still national industry. If they won, it would be followed by others.

"Nothing's that straightforward," Alison Hansen fought on. "If we tender and don't get it, we get the worst of both possible worlds: we lose unions because we wanted employer work; and we don't get the contract to compensate."

Alison Hansen knew more about employment law than any of them had forgotten. A lean, spare, hard-looking woman in her mid-forties, recently and suddenly deserted by her husband of twenty years, there were General Secretaries – tough and working-class to a man – who would not call a strike without consulting her, nor would consider settling a dispute if she raised an eyebrow in disagreement. She had a love-hate relationship with Arnotts: she loved where it had come from, but hated where it was going.

"Where is this leading, Colin? Where do you want it to go?"

"I'm asking you. At the moment, income is thirty per cent crime, against expenditure of nearly half; family, domestic, small claims, petty problems, say ten per cent income, fifteen percent cost; your union work – fifteen per cent income, about the same expenditure. About eighty per cent of our expenditure generates fifty-five per cent of the income. The remaining twenty per cent of our expenditure generates forty-five per cent of our income. The margin is profit. I, uh, rest my case."

"Which is what?" Alison pressed, ever the negotiator.

"That if the balance doesn't change, dramatically and soon, we'll have to choose between continued investment in the firm and what we can personally take out of it. That's a conflict that will ultimately tear us apart."

"Then we might as well do it," Graham said. "If the firm'll tear apart anyway, we've nothing to lose."

Alison raised her eyebrows in despair. Before she could speak, though, Alistair chipped in, ever graphic, vulgar only by design, when a few blunt words would save him the trouble of a speech.

"Sometimes, it's better to die for principle than to spread your legs for the enemy, son."

If Charles had a *consigliore* within the firm it was Alistair Mathison, former and first articled clerk of Charles Arnott, much married and as many times divorced, a compact man of nearly sixty and carrying it well, the leading criminal light of his generation.

Alistair's position within the firm put him above factions. He was personally and professionally loyal to both Charles the father and Colin the son. His reputation and practice had been based at and on Arnotts but now stood alone.

The sixth member of the Committee was Patrick Preston. He, like Colin and Graham, was a civil lawyer; he, like Alistair, had been articled to Charles, but only nominally: he had worked instead with Alistair for half a year, with Colin for another, and had finished up with Wendy Brett, their then family practitioner, whom Charles had ushered out of the firm to make space for Carey. Now, he was Head of Litigation.

Patrick was in his early thirties, of a generation with Colin. He ran each year in the London Marathon. He could name every film that had been made in black and white. He sang in a choir. The tapes in the Walkman he wore as he walked to work contained Law Society updates. He drank New Zealand Chardonnay. He had worked out the cost to the firm of the time he spent flossing. His father was a preacher; his mother bought antiques. He came from a family that could trace its origins back for more than two centuries, and had lost its fortune long before the depression. He lived alone in a flat in the Barbican. He was an archetypal English eccentric. He was in love with Carey.

"Can we get back to the budget," he asked, preferring statistics to personalities.

Alistair boomed:

"Budgets be buggered. I've a pair of long-term fraudsters to see in the Scrubs at four o'clock."

Carey asked:

"What do you think, Alistair?"

She wanted to know whose side he would come out on before she declared her own position.

"I do my crime; I'll take any case that comes along. Well, maybe I won't touch paedophilia, but that's about the only limit I set; give me a man who's cut up his innocent wife of twenty years, and I'll turn it into six figures of legal aid money without breaking a sweat. I'm no one to tell others what they ought to do." He loved Carey but at times like this her reluctance to commit herself irritated him. "What do you want? Clients who never do anyone any harm?"

34

"This doesn't need to be personal," protested Patrick.

"Sonny," Alistair affected a Scots accent that wasn't his by more than a generation, "it's all personal. You may have lineage; me, I want a cheque in the bank big enough to hear the interest adding up."

"Then you agree with me," Colin insisted.

Alison shook her head.

"It's not that simple."

"Here we go again," Carey sang. "Around and around."

She was right, thought Colin: it was deadlock. He and Graham formed one faction. Patrick supported them intellectually but usually sought to straddle the fence rather than risk antagonising Carey, who all too often would not say. Charles and Alison were the other faction. Alistair, like Patrick and Carey but for different reasons, wouldn't take sides.

Colin sighed.

"We'll have to call a partnership meeting, then."

"Soon," said Carey, thinking that their father was going abroad shortly.

As the others bustled from the room, Carey hung back.

"Nice lunch?" Colin leaned back, eyes teasing.

"Who was the Man in White?" she answered, sliding up to sit on his desk, facing him with her legs crossed.

"Funny you should ask," he pulled out the file – fattened by the booklets and magazine Matthew had left with him – from a pile of a half dozen others.

Over the course of the Management Committee discussion, Colin had reached his decision. He was not going to turn away paying work without good cause; they would take on The Programme; it would infuriate Charles.

"I was wondering if you might let me know what you thought about this. Odd sort of business – cult type action – people wanting their property back – sort of thing." He shoved the file along towards her, conscious of her proximity and her position. "Good thing you're my sister." He covered up his embarrassment. "I'd be up on some sort of employer charges."

"Good thing you're my brother," she answered tartly, picking up the file, "not my employer. This is him?" Matthew.

"The Teacher," Colin announced sarcastically.

"You want me to take him on?" She wasn't fooled by his request for her views; if he hadn't already decided, he wouldn't have asked.

"As a client," Colin laughed. "Only as a client."

* * *

At the Midnight Mass, the Teacher raged:

"None of you, none of you is committed – not wholly committed, not truly committed, not committed until you can feel the rough edges of your soul as it rubs against the raw need of The Programme, the hunger that causes it to scrape and scratch for more until the last drop of blood dribbles from the broken skin.

"What do you think I am doing with my life?" he screamed at the assembled Superiors. "My life is your life; my needs are yours; my hunger is your failure. Purpose and counter-purpose: if you have not learned to throw yourself entirely into your purpose, how can you expect the Messengers and Initiates to do so? Every inch of your being that does not achieve perfection is an act of hostility against me, an act of theft from me, an act of war.

"I am your Teacher, your father, you owe nothing to yourselves, nothing but what you can give to me; you cannot love yourselves except as you love me; you do not live unless and until it is my life that you are living. We may take many forms and even more directions – there is but one direction: mine, The Programme – you are many; I alone am whole."

# Chapter Two

Carey had put off looking at The Programme file until the last moment. It was a busy time, with several trials coming on within a few days of each other.

She usually got to the office at about nine, savouring the fifteen minute walk from her house in Islington when she was no longer alone in her house but not yet lost to herself at work. She had been looking for a flat when she had spotted the tiny house and, defiantly, decided she would live there alone. She liked the silence: it helped her to keep calm; she lived with troubled instincts that needed space; if they escaped, she might never get them back under control.

There were times when she felt her mother must have been like this, straining to contain it all until it had become impossible: at least, Marion had religion to comfort her – and God to hold her hand in those final, swift, dying months. Carey could admit to a similar inner yearning yet deplored religion, like Colin blaming it for the break-up of her parents' marriage and – somehow – even for her mother's subsequent death.

The morning of her meeting with Matthew she arrived at the office early. She had to be at the High Court at ten, to make one last attempt to persuade a client to agree to a settlement before she left counsel to conduct the hearing. Though there ought to be enough time to get back to the office to prepare for the midday appointment with Matthew Crane, Carey knew from experience how rarely conferences outside court kept to schedule.

Accordingly, she arrived that morning at eight, tired, regretting a couple of glasses of wine too many the night before as she had boredly channel-surfed, unable to settle herself for sleep, chain-smoking. After three coffees, however, she was as alert as ever. She skimmed Colin's brief notes, and a facetious post-it that she threw away: "Remind you of anyone? Perhaps we should start the day with a meditation or a chant?" She smiled at his image of Charles as cult-leader; at least the tensions between her father and her brother had not destroyed the private humour she and Colin had shared since childhood.

She studied the cover symbol and read The Programme materials with a bit more care, after a while feeling something akin to prurience, as if she was spying on a shameful, personal activity, something that, though she would never admit to it herself, none the less struck a reluctant, closet chord – like a secret eating binge, or masturbation, or the sudden, inexplicable impulse to pocket something belonging to someone else.

Q: *Teacher, what do you hope to achieve?*
A: *I don't think we can save the world; it's past saving or not worth saving and not our business. I do think, though, that one can create a place – or a space – for people who want to save themselves; I think at its simplest, that's all I'm trying to do.*
Q: *What do you mean by "save"?*
A: *Safe enough to want to stay, safe enough to satisfy one's faith in oneself without a residual urge to go out and find new challenges at which to fail.*
Q: *Surely you mean at which to succeed?*
A: *No. I mean at which to fail. Most people spend their lives throwing themselves at this or that challenge, knowing they will fail, because if they succeed they'll have to move on to something yet more difficult. I don't believe that it's natural to be always ambitious, forward-moving, upwardly mobile I suppose we'd say today. I think what we want most is to get back the feeling of belonging into which we were born; a sort of peace, an "at one-ness", being – and being accepted as – a part of something larger without needing to prod and probe to find a place and prove oneself within it; a time when we felt a part of something whole, because it made sense – without question – and that was complete in itself. The further forward we move, the further away from where we each began.*
Q: *No man is an island?*
A: *An island is static. No man is a river might be better.*
Q: *And God?*
A: *Say God, if it pleases you; call it collective unconscious, if you want to talk in a different language. My simple assertion is that we come from something more than mere flesh and blood and bone, grown from mere seed; that's my faith; most people believe it. To allow yourself to get back in touch with it is the challenge, and – for us – what we call The Programme. You don't have to agree with me; I'm not trying to force it on anyone. But if you do agree and if you still haven't found your own way to get back in touch with it, then maybe my way will work for you. That's all. There's no mystery, nothing to be afraid of.*
Q: *Teacher, thank you.*

* * *

From the window of his own office on the first floor, Alistair watched Carey hail a taxi to take her to court. He had known her as a child, as a teenager, as a college student, as a trainee solicitor, now he saw her daily not just as a woman, but as the end product of that long history. He still could not say what made her tick or what she wanted out of life.

His door opened without a knock. His secretary, his trainee or Charles. It was the latter. He was not surprised.

"I thought you'd be in today."

Charles lowered himself into the comfortable, leather armchair beside the window.

They all had offices to suit their personalities. Colin's was uncluttered, lined with *Halsbury's Laws* and *Halsbury's Statutes*; his clients sat on high-backed chairs across from his desk; the photograph of Jan and the children was at one side, at right angles, so that clients could see at once that he was a family man. Carey's had piles of folders and files on every available top, pictures lining the walls reflecting tastes during different periods of her life – a Mexican bark painting, a framed poster of a William Morris exhibition, a Picasso bird of peace, a watercolour that belonged to Patrick Preston's collection but to which she had taken a sudden liking and that – failing to persuade her to accept it as a gift – he had put up for her on permanent loan instead.

Like Carey's room, Alistair's was littered with mementoes. Some of them were of his wives; sometimes, they were things brought into the office while he moved out of one home or another, until he found somewhere new to live, and which he had never taken out again – *objets*, small sculptures, photographs of himself with friends and mentors, trophies from sailing when he was young and from the solitary competition he had won since he took up bridge. Others were gifts from clients, reflecting victories.

He displayed most proudly of all the rock-climber's pick with which his client was said to have murdered his boss and which, in the confusion of an unexpected acquittal, his client had pocketed from the evidence table.

It was mounted on a board into which had been etched the alleged angle of entry into the victim's frontal lobe, and on a bronze plaque Alistair had caused to be inscribed the memorable words with which his client had presented it to him in the pub after the verdict:

"Perhaps you'll use it on yours some day."

"What do you think, Alistair?"

"I think you're working your way round the firm, finding out what everyone thinks before the partnership meeting so you can decide how to get your own way," Alistair was amused at Charles' transparency. "Let's see, the way I calculate it, we're about evenly split – which means it could go either way. Which is a risk you won't take. So if you can't talk them round with a main course of reason I imagine we're in for a dessert of fire and brimstone. 'It's not Arnott & Co but Arnotts'; 'this is my firm, I built it and if I have to I'll bring it down'. That sort of thing?"

Charles laughed.

"I'm getting too old for this game. Perhaps I should give it up."

"No one's stopping you," Alistair replied tartly.

"That's what I like about you, old friend; you don't pull your punches."

"That's something you taught me. But you also taught me that it's sometimes important to let people do things, even when they're wrong, just to find out for themselves."

"So?"

"So, you've fought Colin every inch of the way for too long, Charles. He's a good Managing Partner; he won't harm the firm."

"No, but he might sign it up for the Tory Party."

"Balls, Charles. He's still your son. His instincts are still good. You've locked onto the idea that he's your enemy. Don't be so stubborn; give him a chance to do it his way."

Charles raised an eyebrow.

"Stubborn, Alistair? Me?"

\* \* \*

"I want to talk to you," Cassandra slid onto the bench of one of the Coffee Lounge booths opposite Matthew. Matthew was eating his breakfast: tea, fruit, bread baked by the members. The Coffee Lounge was not yet open to the public.

She was followed onto the bench by Father Caleb, her archangel of destruction, a self-educated student of the black and paganic arts, of whom "Do what thou wilt shall be the whole of the Law" was the Aleister Crowley saying – of the many that he liked to quote – that contained the whole of his philosophy.

Matthew did not acknowledge them immediately. He finished his melon and sipped his tea. Then he looked up calmly at Caleb and waited. Caleb met his gaze with something close to defiance but was unable to hold it without muttering:

"I am one."

"And we are many," Matthew replied heartily.

He thought of Nabal: "The man was churlish and evil in his doings; and he was of the house of Caleb."

Caleb used to think that the sun rose and set on Matthew; like others too quick to follow, he had also found it easy to abandon The Teacher when he saw that Cassandra was the lone star of evil within The Programme.

"Good morning," Matthew added, addressing Cassandra.

"I want to talk to you," she repeated.

One of the Coffee House Initiates approached the booth, head bowed, with a fresh pot of tea. Matthew gestured towards The Seer and her lieutenant. Caleb shook his head, but Cassandra, keen to keep the younger members on her side, said:

"Thank you, Brother Martin."

After he had retreated from ear-shot, Matthew said:

"This is about Anthony."

"I told you we couldn't handle him," she said.

\* \* \*

Anthony, son of Arthur: the bad blood of the Rockworths. At the age of eight, Anthony had been expelled from his boarding school for peeing on a sleeping child in his dormitory. At ten, though small for his age, he had managed to punch a maid to the ground and kick her unconscious. At eleven, he was arrested for kidnapping and torturing the five-year-old son of a neighbour in the wealthy hamlet in which the Rockworths lived outside Marlow. The police, welfare agencies and child psychologists had all been involved: the case had been blanketed by a financial snow-storm that included a million pound investment in the neighbour's business and a peremptory move across the border into Oxfordshire.

Arthur Rockworth was the wealthiest man Matthew had ever met. He was rarely at home, rarely in England: his corporate interests straddled both the Atlantic and the Pacific; he was written about in the language of Maxwell, Murdoch, Hansen, Goldsmith. He was also said to be personally shy, though he used the media as part of his business weaponry like an accomplished general.

Rockworth and his wife had been married for twenty-three years: in addition to Anthony, there was an older son, who had also been difficult, but not in Anthony's league of psychosis. He had finally fallen onto the right side of the line. After dropping out of university, he worked now for his father and – unexpectedly – had recently become engaged to a girl Arthur believed was strong enough to keep him under control.

Anthony, though, had gone from bad to worse. They had managed to keep him in schools – with lashings of money conferred on individuals and institutions – until he was sixteen. Subsequently, he was taken care of by what was euphemistically termed a private tutor, but whose duties more closely resembled those of a warden.

Much of this Matthew had learned during a strange talk in the back of a stretch-limousine parked alongside a village bonfire party for which Rockworth like a squire had paid. One of the properties in the village was a house which belonged to the parents of a member who were now living abroad and which they allowed The Programme to use as a retreat.

That weekend Matthew was present with Helen and a small party of Programme children. The older children lived in a sprawling, mansion-block apartment in South Kensington that had been rented for so long it was hard to remember whose lease it had originally been, which at one time had been Matthew's home, and which still provided a useful annexe to the Mayfair Chapter.

The house was in walking distance of the village green. He tried to spend some time with the children every few months, talking with them individually and in groups, telling them stories, teaching them games and educating them in the rituals of The Programme. He found the presence of children in the group the most exciting part of The Programme. These children were growing up – the oldest had just begun her teens – believing in his teachings and in himself from such an early age that they had never known anything else; when they came to adulthood and – in the fullness of time – succeeded to The Programme, he would finally be complete.

Until a couple of years before, they had sufficient qualifications within the group to be allowed to provide education at home. As Tamar – the daughter of Brother Micah and Sister Hannah – turned eleven, however, it had become necessary for her to attend secondary school and, now, so also did her brother. Meanwhile, Micah and Hannah had separated; for a time, Hannah had been with Father Simon – Matthew's closest ally and friend – while Brother Micah had embraced celibacy and, to date, had yet to depart from it. They were sometimes called the union of opposites, an incarnation of the principles of The Programme: Micah was tall, rangy, with flaming red hair; Hannah was tiny, dark and hawk-like.

The attendance of the children at state schools posed the challenge of preserving the dominance of Programme teachings. Matthew intensified his personal attention; Cassandra, too, sought competitively after their minds and their vitality. Between them, just as they had forged The Programme out of tension, they had convinced the children of the singular reality of their lives within it. They taught them to hide their disdain for the childish attitudes and antics of their school-mates; they were Junior Messengers – a rank to which they had been elevated over members many years older – who knew the importance of keeping their own counsel; their teachers believed that they were angels – Matthew and those closest to them alone understood the truth.

The visit to the bonfire party was a treat for the children. They normally saw fire only in spiritual terms: the fire beyond was the key goal of The Programme.

Matthew was standing at the edge of the crowd watching the children, preferring their pleasure to his, when a voice spoke softly behind him:

"That's a smart pack of children. They can't all be yours."

Matthew did not turn around.

"No. I don't have any children of my own."

"I have two," Rockworth added.

"I know," Matthew replied.

They stood in silence for a while. Rockworth observed:

"You're watching the children, not the fireworks."

"Men made fireworks," Matthew answered, keeping his tone light, meaning but not saying "God made children".

"Are you visiting the village?" Rockworth commented on Matthew's accent.

"We have a cottage."

Another long silence. Then:

"That's my younger son," Rockworth pointed to a spot near to the fire. "I have to be here." He apologised without any need to do so.

Helen left the younger children in the care of the older. She waited to make sure she was not interrupting before she said demurely:

"Matthew. The youngest children are tired. I think I should take them home."

Matthew looked at her and nodded. She read the activity in his eyes.

"You stay a while."

"Yes."

Rockworth – surprising himself – held out a hand.

"I'm Arthur Rockworth."

"Helen," she said, taking his hand. "Will you excuse me?"

They watched as she went back for the children. Rockworth said:

"Lovely girl." When Matthew didn't comment, he asked: "I don't know your name?"

"Matthew. And, yes, she is lovely." He turned to share a smile.

"What do you do, Matthew?"

"I work with people."

"People in trouble?" Rockworth understood.

"Some of them; some of the time."

Rockworth wanted to talk. It was the need Matthew often brought out in people, sometimes on sight alone. It had to be Rockworth's decision.

"Do you drink, Matthew?" Rockworth made up his mind. "I don't mean wine." He gestured towards the trellis from where hot mulled wine was being dispensed to adults, hot chocolate for the children.

"I'd like that," Matthew said.

Rockworth led him to his car. It was a Packard, perhaps twenty or more years old, parked across the road from the green. As they approached it, a uniformed chauffeur scurried back from watching the fireworks. Rockworth waved him off.

"We'll be a while yet, Kevin. Enjoy the show." The man nodded, translating the invitation as an order to keep an eye on Rockworth's son.

Rockworth ushered Matthew into the spacious rear of the vehicle, pointing him towards the back seat.

"I'll sit here," in the jump seat facing Matthew. "It's easier to reach the bar."

It was neither more nor less easy than from where Matthew was sitting but less comfortable: Rockworth was a well-mannered host. He opened up a wood-panelled bar between the jump seats.

"Scotch okay? Ice?"

"Fine, both."

Matthew was not a drinker; he might go months without a touch of alcohol. He had no taste for it. He had never made abstinence a part of his teaching, however, using it instead and selectively for individual programmes.

He watched Rockworth busy himself. He was older than Matthew, approaching sixty; he was shorter – but then, most people were; he was trim but not thin; his eyes were as fierce as a warrior's, but his voice as controlled as a priest's. This was not a man to cross; on the other hand, he was someone from whom Matthew could gain a great deal – mostly materially, but also in terms of acceptance, acceptability; the safest course would be to keep his distance – for Matthew, that amounted to an obligation to get involved.

"Tell me more about your work, Matthew."

Rockworth listened in silence as Matthew talked about how difficult some people found it to make a way in life that brought them any kind of personal satisfaction. He thought there were too many people on the scrap-heap in one way or another – economically, emotionally, spiritually. Work was a solution – he emphasised to the man who had made several fortunes by dint of hard work – but it was not the whole solution. Nor did everyone have the same capacity to make sense of their lives on their own. What he did, he said, was to work with people to find out what it was that would make them feel whole; for some, they were simply looking for a partner, for love or companionship; others persecuted themselves with their inability to believe; for many, work was the key. He did not claim to have any universal panacea, or even a solution for large numbers.

"Some, though, need to be part of something bigger than themselves; they can't be whole in themselves, so they need to be with others who are likewise incomplete – imbalanced in one sense, though I don't mean clinically. Or," he laughed formally, "perhaps I do. I'm talking about people who might turn to drugs, or drink, or violence or psychotic depression: but I'm also talking about those who do have something positive – creative – to offer, potential is probably the word I'm looking for; not the no-hopers but the simply lost. It's a small task," he concluded modestly. "It's just something I do, with some others, to provide a framework that allows people who can't make it on their own to belong to something different."

Rockworth asked suspiciously:

"Where does the money come from?"

"Some of our members work; we run lectures and courses; we write our own magazines and booklets and sell them. A few of our members had money or property of their own. We had a Coffee Lounge in Earl's Court, but we've just had to leave it. We'll find somewhere else. We don't need that much; you know the saying, two can live as cheaply as one; it works when you multiply it."

Then it was Rockworth's turn to talk. And what he talked about was Anthony.

* * *

Two years later, Matthew was still hearing about Anthony.

Cassandra frowned to conceal a scowl, came up with one of her unnerving, high giggles instead. This was why she loved Matthew; and it was why they were still – in their way – together in The Programme; he already knew it was about Anthony; he always knew – everything.

"What has he done now?" Matthew asked.

"Thomas," she announced melodramatically.

"Ah," Matthew understood.

For the last two years, Anthony had been kept away from the children. This was his weakness. Rockworth had admitted it that first night, frankly and without equivocation: his son had always been violent, his son was sexually disturbed, his son was destined to do harm and he feared that his most likely victims would be children.

The way Rockworth told it, nothing could be done until he committed some terrible act and the law could take its course towards incarceration, one way or the other – prison or secure mental institution. Death, he confessed, would be a better fate, though he did not spell out whether he meant for the boy or for himself. The Programme – as it emerged as the evening wore on – was an attractive alternative.

Until she heard about the financial side of the deal, the most important part of which was the tenancy of the vast building in Chesterfield Gardens at a peppercorn rent, Cassandra had been opposed. It was outside their remit and outside Matthew's abilities. She did not want a specific obligation to one particular member. Nor did she see as quickly as Matthew that the address alone was worth something they could never otherwise afford – prestige, instant establishment.

He took her to see the house: it had once been the headquarters of a company which Rockworth had taken over. Because of the depression in the London property market, it had not yet been sold. Rockworth was willing to rent it to The Programme, at a nominal rent, for a period that they had eventually agreed as seven years. Thereafter, they had an option to buy it, or to lease it for a further five years but at a market rent. Rockworth said bluntly: if Matthew could turn Anthony around, if he could control him, if he was no longer a threat to himself, to others or to Rockworth's peace of mind, neither purchase price nor rent would prove a problem.

Cassandra was, however, excited once he took her to see the house itself. It was unfurnished but carpeted and in good decorative order. Within minutes, she was muttering that this was it, this was their home, there was nothing they could not do with it. They sat cross-legged on the top floor, staring into each other's eyes, knowing that a new world was opening up for The Programme.

The heat was intense; quickly, it became sexual. It was the first time they had made love for months, perhaps a year. However separately they lived, together they were still The Programme. Afterwards, she straddled his naked back, massaging him, humming, maybe thinking of Huw, at one point she repeatedly thrust her pelvis hard against his backside.

"God, there were times I wish I was a man," she sighed and giggled.

"I thank God daily that you're not," he murmured in reply.

She had stood up, stood on his back, perfectly balanced and poised.

"We can do anything, Matthew; we can do anything, with anyone."

That was then; this was now. She hissed:

"I told you we couldn't handle him."

Early this morning, as Father Caleb related the story, Anthony had offered to go to the flat in South Kensington flat to collect a stash of booklets for members to take out on the street donating. He had taken the spare key to let himself in, in case no one was at home. Thomas, meanwhile, had apparently been sent back from school, because a boiler had broken down and there was neither heating nor hot water. Sister Gloria – who was in charge of the flat – had gone out shopping for food. Thomas was accordingly alone when Anthony let himself in with the spare key. When Gloria returned, they were in one of the bedrooms. Thomas was naked; Anthony had his trousers undone.

There had been no time for anything to happen. Gloria had rung for help. Cassandra had caught the call and expropriated the problem, though the reception member had also mentioned the call to Helen, which was how Matthew knew something was going on around Anthony. For the moment, Thomas was confined to his room and Anthony was under guard by a couple of Caleb's Initiates. No one had yet told Micah – who was at work – or Hannah, who was upstairs conducting an early meditation for non-residents.

"Perhaps I should turn him over to you," Matthew said to Caleb.

Caleb was a sadist. With the exception of Cassandra herself, he was the most naturally, comfortably evil member of The Programme. His contribution was entirely hostile. That was its attraction – few could offer such naked, unrelenting, unrepentant malice. His face was lop-sided, and he cultivated the unsettling effect with a bushy, untamed, beard – black but tinged with copper – that fell in thick waves almost to his chest, although the hair on his head was close-cropped, curly and greying. His eyes and mouth were in a permanent sneer.

An American, he had served time as part of a hot-car ring; he could be as brutal with his body as with his tongue. He preferred boys but used the women too – what he liked was the power, in every shape and form he could take it. In some respects, he was the perfect choice to deal with Anthony.

Matthew came to a quick decision.

"He can go with me to America."

\* \* \*

Http://www.the-programme.org.uk (turn on sound card if available).

*God is basic, elementary. God is the elements. Fire, earth, water and air. The four elements in constant interaction and constant revolution: fire scorches the earth; air feeds fire; water puts it out, feeds the earth, lets us breathe the air. The different faces of God – wrathful, benevolent, lightness and dark – are the elements, likewise in constant revolution. They are in personal relationships, too: think about your own relationships with people you love; you feed each other, then douse your emotions when they start to frighten you; it's a cycle – repetitive and ultimately unrewarding because it takes you nowhere.*

*Some talk of fire as purifying. It is a difficult exercise, to purify without destroying. Fire melts things down and welds them together. Water stops fire. The skill is to pour on the water at the right moment between the end of purification and the start of destruction. The right moment is just at the moment when it is re-formed into the shape – the combination, the unification – that makes something new. These are images, metaphors, and they need to be undertaken in practice, not merely theory. That is something we can only do with others; otherwise, there is no one – nothing – to which to be joined.*

*Perhaps it is dangerous; but that which is dangerous is exciting. Without danger we can only do that which is an already trodden path. A path – what is more – that was trodden not by ourselves but by others. That does not make it wrong or bad or worthless. It is a path that others first trod in quest of the same sort of peace and satisfaction that you are looking for. That made it seem right for them, at that time: but if it did not work – and if it does not work for you – then it is stupid to ignore its deficiencies; nor does it make it right for you, now. The Programme is not a fixed path, but a method of finding the right path for each person individually.*

\* \* \*

"You were given the money here?"

"Yes, I'd say so."

"What does that mean, Matthew?" They had already been around the block with Mr Crane, call me Matthew.

He held out an open hand, palm downwards, rocking it directly over the crease in the trousers of his white suit, as if to say "maybe".

"I'm probably being obtuse, Matthew," Carey sighed, "but in the end, she had to give it to you somewhere."

"A lot of it was meeting bills; some cash. She was in England when she told me she wanted me to have the money, but some of it was in the States."

"And came here?"

"Right. She was living here with us by then; so, yes, the idea was that we would use it here."

"How did it come here?"

"Mostly, it was brought here by people."

"I want you to think carefully about this next question. If the people who brought it here were working for you, as your agents, then you would have received the money from her there, where they picked it up on your behalf. On the other hand, if the people who brought it here were doing so for her, then you would not have received it from her until they arrived here with it, on her behalf."

He watched her as she spoke, shaking his head in mock-admiration.

"I thought I was the one who was supposed to talk nonsense."

She blushed.

"I didn't say that. All I said was, I don't have much patience with religion – I thought you should know that at once if I was going to act for you. I was just trying to be clear about my position."

"They were her friends."

"Excuse me? Oh, right; the money was brought here by her friends?"

"Yes."

"Not your people."

"Well, they were my people too, members of The Programme. But, if I had to decide one way or the other, I'd say they were bringing it here for her, to give me once it was here; I wasn't sending them to pick it up. Have I understood the question right?"

"Perfectly, Matthew." Carey kept the sarcasm out of her voice.

"Okay, so where does that take us?"

"Nowhere. It brings them here. At the time the money was given to you, put into your hands, it was in this country, received by you in this country, for use in this country, and therefore the proper location for any action for its return is in this country."

"And?" He enjoyed watching her work. She was a performer, a magician. Not since Helen had he experienced quite such an immediate desire to possess a woman. He could sense that she, too, was aware of – and affected by – his physical presence.

"And we file a defence saying that the money was given for a specific purpose – the purposes of The Programme – and it has been spent, one way or another, on those purposes, and therefore there's nothing left to return; put another way, you've changed your position on the strength of the money, and it would be inequitable to make you pay it back. Would that be a problem?"

"To show it? I don't think so. I'll have to talk to George about it."

"George?"

"Brother George Cohen. He's our accountant; he's one of our members."

"You have Jewish members?"

"Sure. Everyone. It's not a religion," he said, not for the first time.

"Mr Cohen is a practising accountant?" She could not bring herself to call him "Brother".

"He has a small, one man practice in Hammersmith; we went to him when we were living in South Kensington."

"Is he, er, a resident member?" She fumbled with the terminology.

"Sure. Why not?" He lived with Gloria at the flat in South Kensington.

"He might not be the best witness," Carey commented.

"He can give me the answers, prepare the accounts."

"It's enough for now. We'll have to retain New York counsel, of course."

"Why? I thought you wanted to get the case over here?"

"I do. But unless they carried Hammer Reach back with them in their pockets, I don't think we can claim jurisdiction over the farm."

"I'm going over soon anyway." For some time, four members – two Superiors, two Junior Messengers – had been in New England, travelling around, a mission not a Chapter, exploring the prospects for a fully-fledged stateside operation. The idea of visiting them had not come into his mind until he had talked with Cassandra and Caleb about Anthony and then it had been a spontaneous suggestion. Now, the idea was becoming whole.

Carey looked up from her notepad sharply, displeased. She might or might not like what The Programme stood for – whatever that was – and she had no more time for cults, organisations, sects, movements, cells, factions or revivals than she did for more traditional religious institutions; but she found something appealing about Matthew; she had been struck by him – even at a distance – the first time she had set eyes on him.

"I don't think that's a good idea at the moment."

He raised his eyebrows in surprise.

"We ought to consider whether it will hurt or help the jurisdiction claim for you to be there; I'd like New York counsel's view first."

He was as used to people being attracted to him as he was to them wanting to talk to him: they were variations on a theme.

They talked money. She did not like asking for money on account. Charles never found it a problem; it fit his style to make people pursue him to obtain his services. Colin had no trouble with it either: some of his clients could write out cheques for thousands on demand. Her clients were usually on legal aid and needed only to complete the forms; cash did not come into it. Matthew was unworried.

"I'll write you a cheque now."

She relaxed, smiled, she was at her most appealing. He added:

"On one condition."

"What?"

"That you let me take you out to lunch first."

"Now?" The smile fell from her face. She rarely went out to lunch during the working day: her father, an occasional friend, an even more occasional client she liked or perhaps a professional, referral client she wanted to treat for venal reasons.

"All right," she said suddenly, "if you let me take you." She slid the event into an established package. He was a private client, a paying client.

"Fine."

He could receive as well as give.

* * *

"Is Matthew your real name?"

They were at Fredericks in Camden Passage. It was within a brisk eight minute stroll of the office; they used it for office parties, private

51

conferences between faction partners, taking commercial clients to lunch.

They were seated in the Garden Room, for smokers. It was a vast conservatory, with a fifteen or twenty foot high smoked-glass ceiling forming a sloping roof, two trees growing inside, and one wall also in glass which opened onto the garden and patio where, in the warm weather, an extra half-dozen tables would be installed beneath parasols.

"Yes," Matthew said. He raised his glass of wine to her: "Matthew was a publican," in the Bible.

"It meant tax-collector," she corrected him. Memories of her mother were never far from her mind, and with them fragments of religious memorabilia.

He inclined his head to one side: *touché*.

"Which are you, Matthew?"

"Publican or tax-collector?" *Bon viveur* or someone who extracted money from others? "Neither, I hope. I love life but I don't need to drink to enjoy it; nor do I ask for money from anyone – though they often give it to me."

"I'm sure they do." She was combative: the side of her that liked him fighting the side of her that despised and feared what he did. "It's why they do it that matters."

"I give them something they need," he answered unperturbed.

"That makes you a salesman." Between *hors d'oeuvres* and main course, she lit another cigarette.

"No more than you: people need peace as much as they need law."

She shrugged: she was no defender of the legal faith.

"It's a lot more powerful," she replied.

"Which? Law?"

"No. Law is government; government is powerful; but it doesn't own you – at least in a democracy."

"Correct. Which leaves the whole area of your private life and your private feelings to work out all on your own."

"Which gives you terrific power over your members, doesn't it?"

"They award me that power – much like a democracy."

The waiter brought their food. He covered his glass after the waiter had refilled hers, nodded when he was offered more mineral water instead.

She flushed. "I don't normally drink during the day. We've got a meeting this afternoon – a full partners' meeting. This is anaesthetic."

"Will your father be there?"

"Why do you ask?"

"Just curious," he grinned.

"You're too direct for me. Too perceptive, too."

"It's not a difficult conclusion. Brother and sister in famous father's firm. Full meeting; drinking to protect yourself."

She looked up and held his eyes. Briefly, she shivered; suddenly she felt the warmth of him physically well up inside her, almost sexually; not almost. She reminded herself he was a client. Skipped around for something with which to bridge the discussion back to work. Asked:

"The Seer – Cassandra?"

He nodded, leaving her to make the pace.

"Is she your wife?" Damn; wrong question.

"Legally. We don't live together. It's about The Programme now."

"I don't understand the, er, structure of, er, The Programme," she was still not sure whether to refer to it as a group, a church or an organisation.

He was studying her as she spoke. Like Helen, Carey could not have resembled Cassandra less. There were other similarities, including age – and, Matthew suspected, the extent of repression – though there was something more substantial about Carey. Helen was spiritual, serving him as an act of grace; she was intuitive, while Carey was analytical, mental.

"You should come and visit us," he said. "Come and see how we live and work. Come down to the Coffee Lounge one evening."

"I'm too old for that sort of thing," she laughed nervously, wondering how he had known she had time to burn of an evening.

"What sort of thing?" he asked with affected naivety.

"Going to a coffee bar; it's the sort of thing students do. Especially when they've got nothing else to do." And when they had no one to do it with.

"Oh, yes. Young people have got a monopoly on wanting to meet new people or find new ideas?"

The waiter arrived to offer dessert. Both refused. She shook her head when he sought to pour the rest of the wine into her glass, asked for coffee; Matthew ordered tea, lemon tea. She said:

"I know what you're saying; but it is true, isn't it? As you get older you're not looking so hard, you don't want constant change."

"Yes. It's like a blank canvas. You start off with nothing on it, and fill it in a bit at a time, giving the blank space a colour or a shape of your choice, with less of it left as time goes on; the choices keep getting harder, because you've still to find what will make the canvas into a complete picture that works and there's less and less room left to do it in. What do you do if you can't find the right way to finish it?"

She shook her head; it was his image, not hers.

"How old are you?" he asked.

"Twenty-nine. Why?"

"It's not so old."

"How old are you?"

"Fifty-one," he laughed. "More than twenty years older."

"You don't look it." She would have put him in his early forties. "You've kept well," she laughed to cover her embarrassment.

"You too," he said quietly, affirming the undercurrent between them. "You're far too young to be afraid of new ideas, or new people."

"You never answered the question," she reminded him.

"What you do if you've filled the canvas up and it still doesn't work?"

She nodded.

"Oh," he laughed, "that's easy. You paint it all over and start again."

* * *

Http://www.the-programme.org.uk (turn on sound card if available).

*We all want to belong somewhere. The difficult choice is deciding what it is we want to belong to soon enough to make a commitment to it, yet late enough to make the choice an informed choice, and still not too late to get out and start over if we make the wrong choice. For some, the choice is easy: their birth or social circumstances may lead them in a clear direction: perhaps they follow their father into his line of work, politics or religion or law; there might even be a family business to take over; or they might imitate their mothers, get married, give birth – passing onto their children the burden of finding a new path. Or, they might do everything in reaction, opposition. For some, there are no such footsteps to walk in; they have to make a choice at large.*

*You can only make a choice by committing to it wholly, holding nothing back; otherwise, it is half a choice which is worse than none, creating the impression of having made a choice, yet guaranteed to fail – simply because you have not tried it out wholeheartedly. Catch-22: without committing wholly, you cannot find out for sure; if you commit wholly, and find out you have made the wrong choice, you think you will be lost. That is the fear that holds us all back. It is wrong. Even if you commit every inch of your being to something, you are still you and you will be stronger for having done so; you cannot lose from the choice you make; you gain at least the ability to make it.*

*You only have one life. How are you going to spend it? Afraid – like everyone else? Surfing the Net – like now, like everyone else? Failing to make a choice – like everyone else? Or using your freedom to make the choices that suit you and stop worrying about what suits anyone else?*

\* \* \*

Charles was trying to control himself. Alistair had been right: they were fairly evenly split. Carey had yet to speak up, had sat to one side in a reverie of her own. Charles hoped she was distracted by a case or some other kind of problem and that she hadn't been drinking too much – again.

Graham Engel waved his banner from the moral high ground.

"Life changes. Today, helping the poor means creating jobs, not defending their right to unemployment benefit or social security. Back in Alistair's good old sixties, youngsters mugged and robbed because they were socially deprived, psychologically abused, undernourished saints or geniuses *manqué*; nowadays, they're nasty little villains we'd hang or shoot if we could be sure we were getting more than half the convictions right. It's not unprincipled to change but stubborn to stay the same."

It was the second time that day Charles had been called stubborn, and he would not take it from young Engel the way he would from Alistair.

"Oppression is timeless, and it is a practice that is exclusive to the powerful. Those little villains weren't born that way, they were made," he thundered.

Colin – at the opposite end of the long conference table from his father – held his hands up in a low gesture of surrender.

"You can't help it, Dad, can you? It's always got to be about the big picture."

"This firm wasn't built by small ambitions," Charles rasped. "Every time you take a step, you're choosing a direction: and the next step forward starts where the last one ended. I'm the first to agree we need to do more private work and the first to say we need to survive.

You don't hear me object to your finance packages or offshore investment work. That's realism. Taking sides with employers is just that –
taking sides; and we'd be taking sides against the people who made
this firm what it is."

"I've had a quiet word with one or two of my clients," Alison
chipped in. "Put it abstractly, but enough for them to know what I
meant. They made quite clear what sort of reaction to expect."

"It's always in the way you ask the question," Colin brushed aside.

"I'd like to hear from some of the others," Charles suggested,
meaning those who were not on the firm's Management Committee.

They went around the table, some responding in a few words,
others with a wave of a hand to say that had nothing to contribute, a
small number speaking at length, with feeling, almost all of these –
as Charles had found out earlier – in favour of staying away from
the new opportunity, hanging for a while longer onto the firm's
reputation and their own idealism.

Charles stared triumphantly down the table at his son.

"Well?" He asked whether Colin wanted it put to a vote.

Colin glanced around, checking the figures, and nodded to
concede that – close though it still was – he would not win. His eyes
narrowed as he stared back at Charles.

\* \* \*

At about seven thirty, Patrick came into Carey's room.

"So?"

She smiled, beckoned him in, flirtatious.

"Watcha doin', Mister P?"

He lowered himself into one of the two comfortable armchairs
across the desk from her.

"What are you up to, Carey?" he asked in reply.

"I'm not sure, really," she admitted. "Some cult-type thing..." She
paused to see if Patrick knew anything about it. He shook his head.
"I'm not sure if it's Colin's revenge on the rest of us, a bad joke, or a
real case."

Patrick reached across and took the magazine with Matthew's
picture on it. He glowered at it, held it by a corner as if it might smell
bad.

"And you all think I'm mad?"

She smiled again.

"I think you're rather sweet, really, Patrick. Far more sweet than
mad."

He laughed: she could say things like that to him; she could say anything to him.

"All the same, I've seen this sort of thing before. Mind-nazis. What are we doing acting for people like this? Jesus, to think people object to acting for employers; this is what I call objectionable."

She came around her desk without any shoes on and, as she had done in Colin's room, slid up onto the desk: she supposed it was how she had sat in Charles' study at home, when she was a child, when she wanted to attract his attention. She watched Patrick's eyes divert from the portrait of Matthew to her legs, his tongue flash across his lips. She said artlessly:

"I have got nice legs, haven't I."

He reached out and ran a hand up beneath the skirt of her suit, to the point where the flesh met; he waited for a second to see if she parted her legs and, when she did not, withdrew without trying to force her.

"What do you want, Carey?"

"I want dinner. How about you?"

They had been on-again and off-again, serious and casual, lovers and mere companions, for almost two years. In the beginning, he had set the pace and – unsure of his feelings for her – might fairly have been described as blowing hot and cold. By the time he realised he was in love with her, she had slipped back into her shell, willing only to continue it for company. It did not stop her continuing to see him, and sometimes to sleep with him, but it left her feeling guilty because she knew how much more he wanted of the relationship than she would ever give it.

They ate and talked, and Carey drank and smoked too much, and then they went back to his flat as they always did when she had decided to sleep with him. She put up a good show of enthusiasm. As he stood in his kitchen opening a bottle of wine, she threw her jacket onto a sofa, unbuttoned her blouse and reached behind to unclasp her bra. Then she came up behind him and pressed her breasts against his back, refusing to let go as he wriggled to turn around, sliding one hand inside his own shirt while with the other she unzipped him and scratched lightly at the erect penis beneath his briefs before she pulled it out and, finally, let him turn around.

He was mashed against the kitchen counter. They kissed feverishly. He hiked up her skirt and slid his hand onto her backside to reach her from behind. Over his shoulder, she picked up the ice-cold bottle and swigged from it: first one for herself, then – holding it in her mouth – one for him. She pulled away from his grasp, slid to her knees and – careful to let none of the wine escape – sucked him into her mouth. He moaned as she drove him into the wine; the cold made the skin contract but also made him twice as hard. It was not until later, however, in bed and pounding her violently and anonymously from behind, that he finally burst.

At about two o'clock, she slid out of his bed, careful not to wake him. This was why she always slept with him at his flat, not her house: maybe once or twice she had made herself stay until morning; usually, though, she dozed off lightly, thrashed around for a while, then failed to sink into a real sleep. She would get dressed and either walk home – it took about twenty minutes at that time of night – or cab it, struggling with the troubled memories, profoundest fears and private, unfilled ambitions that had disturbed her post-coital slumber.

It had always been that way. Just after sex, sometimes during, not in exclusive control, her mind would be stabbed by tiny darts of despair, grouping until they took on an identifiable face, something secret, something buried, a pathetic cry of loneliness, a prayer to be rescued.

She did not worry about walking home alone through the deserted City streets around the Barbican, or the ugly and abandoned roads that led through the Angel: if she got lucky, an act of violence might release her from it all – terrifying, overwhelming, terminal – as her mother had been released. It never happened: her black turmoil frightened others off, not the other way around.

It didn't frighten Matthew, though; the face that had kept her from sleeping in Patrick's bed.

## Chapter Three

"I am one," The Teacher said. He was sitting cross-legged on his throne-cushion in The Temple, his back to the wall, looking up at his assembled Superiors and Senior Messengers – fifteen of them in all; with two more Superiors on the mission in America, they represented about a fifth of the resident membership.

He was clothed and cloaked in white: that was a sign. Also, significantly, he wore the platinum version of the symbol around his neck, instead of as a belt-buckle.

"We are many," they responded in unison. They were standing, holding hands with one another, likewise clothed and cloaked in white.

After he told them to sit, the door opened and The Seer entered.

She picked her way between the members, pausing occasionally to smile at or touch one of her own, and settled down, legs beneath her, to Matthew's left. She wore a dark green dress, a black cloak. Like Matthew, however, she was wearing the platinum symbol around her neck. The question rippled silently through the congregation: "What does it mean?"

"Let us meditate," Matthew said, as each of the members retook the hands of those nearest to them.

He looked around the room, smiling, encouraging them to not take themselves too seriously: it was easier to absorb the ridicule of the outside world if one could share the joke. It was something that, as a man so much bigger than others, he did not find difficult to do.

"Close your eyes, breathe deeply, take your time," he said. "I want you to think about your first meditation within The Programme. I want you to remember what it felt like to take that first step to come together with The Programme. I want you to capture an image from that moment – the image that is most real to you – the moment of your change. Breathe deeply, take your time, slowly, it's easy now, let it flow, go with the flow." His voice rolled over them in waves; they were empty vessels waiting to be filled.

Matthew, too, closed his eyes, though he did not meditate in the same way as he was telling them to do. He was still receiving what he was going to say. This was the monthly meeting of the hierarchy, not so much a religious occasion as a council; none the less, it was preceded by rituals to remind them that their discussions were not to be material; it was an opportunity to be a channel for the ulterior forces by which The Programme was ultimately guided.

"Come in now, come in now, slowly, open your eyes, come in," he said when long enough had passed.

He looked around: the members opened their eyes at their own paces, some taking more time than others, some because they wanted to give the appearance of greater profundity, others because they had genuinely distanced themselves from the moment. Mother Naamah, Sisters Rebecca and Helen fit the latter class; Father Christopher – Caleb's closest friend – was an example of the former.

Matthew nodded once: permission to proceed.

The Seer rose and started to point – you and you and you and you – two men, two women – by choice not convention. She began to chant:

"I am one."

The chosen ones sang back:

"We are many."

She began to sway, waving her arms above her head and to her sides; they followed, mirroring her movements. Gradually, she picked up the pace.

"I am fire."

"We are fire."

"I am earth."

"We are earth."

I am fire; we are fire; I am earth; we are earth; I am fire; we are fire; I am earth; we are earth.

Air; water.

Faster and faster, arms akimbo, frenzied.

She tossed her cloak in the air, catching it, twirling it around; they followed suit.

"I am good, I am evil."

"I am good, I am evil," they responded.

She threw her cloak to one side; they threw theirs away from them; some of them landed outside the circle of members, a few landed within; they were quickly seized, rolled up by cross-legged members, swaying along with the designated dancers, clapping their hands to the rhythm.

The Seer had left them behind. She ran her hands up and down her body, frenetic, sexual, drops of sweat flying off her forehead.

"Touch me, burn me," she screamed: "Touch me, burn me."

"Touch me, burn me, touch me, burn me," her chosen ones echoed.

Some of the unselected members of the congregation got up to join in; others remained seated, stomping their heels on the ground, clapping harder and faster, a rising crescendo of noise and energy, everyone was touching, everyone had joined in, everyone was participating – except Matthew.

Matthew watched approvingly: it was a game – they did not know what fire could mean; it was insane; they were insane; he could make them do anything.

If this had been a Midnight Mass, he would have let them go until they dropped but this was a meeting. He clapped his hands together once, loud enough to be heard and to distinguish the sound from those clapping along.

"Come in now, come in."

It took The Seer minutes to slow down, for the others to follow her down. Matthew knew she was taking longer than she needed. Her eyes met his, almost smiled, insolent, his frown was her reward and enough.

He said, slow and sonorous:

"I want to go back to basics. I want to go back to what we're about. I want to talk first about the very idea of The Programme itself. I don't mean historically, although what we are is what we came from, but you all know the history; I want to go back to what our past lives and times were about – what they meant, and why. I want to remind you that we were once small. 'I am one; we are many' is how we have long greeted each other, but everything is relative," he smiled to allow them to share his joke.

They loved him but they were frightened of him, even Cassandra and Caleb and others of their ilk: they might feign contempt, but in their hearts they quaked – he had designed their lives and like any other child rebelling against a parent, it was the most awesome rebellion of all. His eyes could see into a soul, could pierce the deepest hidden deceit, could puncture the longest-held precept; yet they could bathe with warmth and sparkle with love. His hands could heal; but they could hurt. A hug could become a crush; a touch could be reassurance or invasion. They never knew what to expect; they were constantly off-balance; they knew only that whatever they were prepared to withstand, he could set aside.

"Once, The Programme was The Seer and myself, a handful of followers, a half dozen, then ten. Look at us today. Why did we grow? Not how: it is easy to answer how; we had found something that all of you wanted to be a part of; there's no surprise – it was never a novel idea that people – many people – were discontented, looking for something new, wanted to be with others of their own kind, it was the oldest idea of all, it was Moses' charter as much as Christ's; it is the premise of gods, emperors, dictators and presidents.

"The question I am asking is 'why'; 'why did we want to grow?' I am asking you to stop for a moment and challenge the assumption that it was natural to grow, natural to share what we had with others, natural to allow you all in. It's not natural to share: animals don't share – to the contrary, they fight to protect their own space and their hoardings; people don't share – go and ask a rich man for a dollar or a pound."

He paused for a change in direction. When he began talking again, it was in a different tone, less rational, evangelical, almost a hum.

"What is it that we believe life itself is about? It is the core of our teachings: our teaching of life is simple, elementary almost: that is its attraction. We only take one premise: life is energy. That is all: life is energy.

"Energy needs expression, expression is its very nature. If all that exists is energy, then energy – a single, whole energy – is all that it can express." His voice was rhythmic, hypnotic.

"Energy cannot express itself to itself: that is a nonsense. It is like trying to see a room that you are in: you cannot do it; you are in it, yet you are looking at it; you are inside looking out, not outside looking in. Looking at a mirrored ceiling or wall is the best that you can do and it is still not real, merely an image.

"Energy – being – isn't there to be looked at; we have to become it, not watch it. We have to perform its different parts, between us to make up the whole: conflict and peace, love and cruelty, confusion and clarity – it all needs to be expressed. We have to go on trying to create the whole, because unless we do so, we have no purpose; and to be whole is the purpose.

"It is walking on the very edge, dangerous, untrodden ground, looking for the fire beyond. It beckons from over the horizon – promising relief, release, we reach out to it, something bigger than each of us and all of us, more powerful, all consuming, consuming us – conflicted, separated, battered by life, beleaguered by isolation, exhausted. Water and fire, the eternal symbols. God. The fire beyond."

His voice shifting gear, he switched back to reason:

"The reason we needed to grow was because we could not complete our purpose – our Programme – without more energy, more people; we did not have or could not perform enough parts to complete the whole. If we were incomplete, then we needed something else – and that meant something else which we did not already have. Surely, it might have meant something deeper from within the existing group but we had gone as deep as any of us could at the time, far deeper than some of you can imagine."

He paused to allow flashes to enter, then clear, his head.

Flash: finding he could make people do anything he wanted them to was a journey too full of promise not to explore, and a temptation too great to resist. He had pushed and touched and used – and turned them to push and touch and use each other while he watched – in ways that most could only imagine as fantasy. In the end, there was nothing they could not do with – or to – their own bodies and each other's.

Flash: a drug-besotted night on a hillside high in the Andes, five of them naked and holding hands, building image on image into a vision of the new life, the new God. Flash: their passages through black magic, white magic, mysticism, spiritualism and religion, celibacy and profligacy, each phase contributing something new to their philosophy.

Flash: the first time a stranger approached him and told him that he had heard he was the way and the truth and on his knees begged to be allowed to serve.

"We needed more of you, to contribute your energies, to contribute your experiences and the particular, peculiar aspects of your being, because we had yet to make it whole: we were building a house and had insufficient bricks; we were telling a story without enough words; we were creating children without enough parents. We had taken on a tremendous task. We had looked around and around and what had we seen? We had seen people in hunger and in misery – throughout the world, and on our own doorsteps; not just physical hunger, nor just spiritual, but in profound, human need of comfort. The world was a mess and we were a mess. It wasn't news; what was new was our refusal to tolerate it for and of ourselves.

"What we saw was waste. We saw the battle between good and evil and we could see that it was a waste – a waste of time, a waste of energy, a pointless battle designed to secure the triumph of good over evil – one over another – which meant expending energy fighting ourselves, within ourselves, one part of purpose against another, so that – in the end – there could be little left to use in any other way. In familiar imagery, God and Satan were at war and it was a war that, in the end, neither could win; it achieved nothing but to kill the soldiers.

"This was the seed from which The Programme grew. What we learned was that the only hope lay in reconciliation of the opposing forces within each of us. This is what The Programme is about: the reconciliation and unification of opposites; the reconciliation of good and evil, of God and Satan; they are each halves of the same whole being; they need to be treated as such, brought together not set against one another.

"We need to remind ourselves of this every day. When we recognise different facets of each other – when we say of this member or that, he or she is good or evil, Godly or Satanic – we are not saying this person is purely one or the other, or that this person exists in isolation from us. The purpose is to acknowledge the different parts of the whole as an act of reconciliation and unification.

"What we say is that good – true good – and reality – true reality – can only emerge from that reconciliation; only by unifying opposing elements can we make something that is whole, and only by making something that is whole can we bring the whole of our energy, the whole of our being, to bear on the task of creating a way of thinking, living, learning, loving, sharing, teaching, achieving.

"It's a constant exercise, a constant challenge. The desire to feel a sense of arrival, of completion, is so great that we can easily slide into a false sense of achievement. We can look around – go on, look around – touch the person next to you, turn to him, look into his eyes – ask yourself, is this the end, or merely another step on the path, is he or she the last person in The Programme or a partner with whom to look for another? If God is dynamic, if life is dynamic, if energy is dynamic, then we have to keep moving, we have to keep changing shape, we have to keep growing, to feed the exercise – the moment we stop, we cease to have any purpose and the time will have come to break it all down and begin again. We are many; but we need to be more."

He gripped the platinum symbol around his neck.

"It is time for change. 'Be clean and change your garments and let us arise and go,' it says in the Bible. It is time now for us to change and to arise and to go: at least," he added with a twinkle returning to his eyes, "some of us."

* * *

Http://www.the-programme.org.uk (turn on sound card if available).

*I was in Bolivia, Sucre, the political capital, not La Paz which is the economic capital. Sucre is high in the Andes, so high you can feel the shortness of your breath. Above the town is a monastery,* on a square. One side of the square is an arched terrace, overlooking a part of the town, then out into the country. It was late; dusk. Earlier, students had sat and studied, or read aloud as they strolled up and down the terrace; a little later, the monks had emerged from the monastery and paraded silently around the square, like prisoners allowed out of their cells for exercise. I must have been sitting there for close to five hours: I had nothing to eat and nothing to drink yet I was neither hungry nor thirsty; I hardly noticed the time go by.

After dark, alone, unafraid, I heard a noise on the hillside beyond the town. The night was cloudy, and I could barely see by the light of the moon. I knew that what I had heard was an animal: a sheep or a goat or some kind of a llama. Gradually, as my eyes adjusted, I watched as the animals – still too indistinct to make out exactly what they were – gathered in a herd of their own; there was no shepherd, no farmer; they were gathering for the sake of it. I thought: that is what I would do, I and others, if we were on the hillside, at night; we would gather together for comfort and protection – perhaps merely for company.

It was such a natural thing to do; it was what tribes and other rural peoples had done throughout all time; I could not fathom why we had stopped doing it – just because we had relocated to the towns and the cities. It made no sense to me at all. I began to feel that it must have been a design to separate us into little boxes or compartments, to make us need the accoutrements of urban life in place of the comfort and protection – the company – of each other. They are things, not people; they can be bought and sold and stolen and withheld; they take sense of self and turn it into materials which we own and which, being owned, can tell us nothing new about ourselves.

That was when I saw my way. I saw that if I followed the conventional course, the course I was supposed to take, the course that others had already followed, I would end up being owned by the things I was supposed to own, and I would be dependent on being able to replace them with new things, as an addiction. I saw that what I needed was to be on a hillside, finding in the company of others whatever comfort and protection that we could afford to make for ourselves. What I had seen was the idea – the framework – the way for us to do that together. It sounds simple, doesn't it? Elementary, even? Believe me, it is.

\* \* \*

Another day, another injunction, another client – another battered woman.

This one was different. For a change, there were no children; they were middle-class; it was too soon, they didn't want to give up their freedom, the enjoyment of money to spare, holidays to be taken, cars to driven across the continent, restaurants they couldn't afford when they were at college, lying in bed at the weekends, making love if they weren't too hungover, reading the newspapers, drinking coffee.

"Life is this: work, money, sex," the woman said bitterly.

Emily Fielding, late twenties, sharp-featured but attractive, close-cropped, curly dark-brown hair, fit, management consultant, liked to ski, jogged, played tennis, looked as if she could give as good as she got, trying to explain to Carey why she let it happen, why she had let it happen again and again until, finally, she couldn't take it anymore. He was still living with her when she came to see Carey; he was given no warning before they sought the injunction *ex parte*; her affidavit candidly admitted she was scared what he would do when it was served. Now it had been granted, was about to be drawn up, and she was still terrified to do anything with it.

Outside the High Court, she asked Carey:

"Will you have lunch with me?"

Automatically, Carey shook her head.

"I'm sorry, I have to get back."

"Just a drink, then?" Emily was desperate not to be left alone. "Please."

"All right," Carey heard herself say.

They found a table at the back of The George, opposite the court: they were early for lunch, the crowds had not yet arrived. This was where barristers' clerks gathered to drink; if she wanted, Carey could walk from one end of the bar to the other and be offered a drink every step of the way.

They bought sandwiches, g-and-ts, Carey lit a cigarette, Emily said:

"You always read about women who think they deserve it; I never thought that. I thought… I'm not sure what I thought. I suppose I thought a lot of different things. Richard's under pressure at work." He was an accountant: they worked for different arms of one of the top six firms, all of which now offered management consultancy alongside accountancy. "It's because he loves me too much, he doesn't know how to cope with it: that was another, that was a favourite, it lasted for months. Then, sometimes," she looked down at her drink, glanced up shyly, "I think there were times I almost enjoyed it. That's a terrible thing to admit; I mean, I'm not a masochist, we weren't into anything, well, you know, kinky. I'm not even sure I mean that I physically enjoyed it – no, I don't mean that at all – more like, I enjoyed the feeling of superiority."

Carey shuddered: she could imagine it happening to her.

As if she had read her mind, Emily asked:

"Have you ever… I mean," she tailed off lamely. She knew Carey was unmarried, without a partner, it had cropped up casually when they were waiting outside the court. "You didn't say."

"I've never even lived with anyone. Isn't that awful? You've been married for eight years, and I've never spent a week with one man except on holiday."

"It doesn't sound awful to me," Emily murmured enviously.

"The grass is always greener. No, I don't really regret it. But I feel," she struggled to explain herself, much as Emily had with difficulty admitted the different reactions she had to her husband's violence. She wanted to honour the confidence; she liked the woman; she identified with her; she wanted to give – and get something – back. "I suppose I'm beginning to feel it may be too late now for any of those conventional relationships, those dreams. And it worries me where it leaves me."

"Being alone?"

"Maybe. Or slipping into a relationship that isn't right, just to have one."

"It's what kept me with Richard," Emily admitted. "You get into a pattern of life until that's all life is. Life is this: work, money, play, sex. You feel, if you let go of it, there won't be anything else. When will it be served, the injunction?" she asked suddenly.

Carey glanced at her watch: a male para-legal from the firm – Gordon, a former policeman – would serve the order at his work. He would do it politely, asking to see him privately, but if Richard Fielding responded true to the norm in these cases, there would be at the least a verbally violent reaction, sometimes physical.

"Before he goes to lunch, I hope. Are you going to go back to the office this afternoon?"

"No way. What do you think? Should I go home? Should I be there when he comes for his things? Should I pack them first?" They had an order excluding him from their flat; he was allowed to collect clothes, personal belongings; Gordon would tell him, would insist on being there, had been given a key. Emily wasn't needed; it would become a flash point. "Gordon won't know what's mine. How will he stop him taking my things?"

"He's got a lot of experience," Carey reassured her. "Let me get you another drink."

They were talking like old friends. Carey almost forgot Emily was a client. She could not remember when last she had slipped into such an easy familiarity – almost intimacy – with a stranger. She was needier than she had been prepared to acknowledge; as needy as Matthew appeared to have recognised. Emily bummed a cigarette off her, protesting that she did not smoke. They giggled over men tales, then frowned; Emily would start to recount an adventure with Richard and be overtaken by despair; Carey talked about her father and her brother. She found herself talking about Matthew.

"I don't know. I tell myself, people like that are charlatans, cults and sects are cons. There's something appealing about it though: getting away from all this; doing something different."

"Escaping?"

"Sure, yes. I mean, I don't think I know that many people who are really happy doing whatever it is they do. Or in their private lives. How many people do you know who are really happy? Well," she remembered who she was talking to, "that's not the right thing to say to you at the moment."

"It's just the right thing to say. And you're right. We're always struggling half the time with what's wrong in our lives, or doing things we don't want to be doing. I don't know how some people survive. I suppose that's what kept me married so long: watching the news, you know – seeing some mother whose child has been murdered, or film footage from Africa and Bosnia, the terrible things people do to each other – and that they do to themselves – you end up thinking well, if she can survive this or that, I can put up with Richard. There's a sort of perverse logic in it somewhere."

"Perverse is right," Carey muttered. "It gets harder to know what's perverse. The Programme – this group I mentioned – I think everyone would say it's perverse – closed-in groups, believing they've got the only solution, fanatics I suppose: but Matthew doesn't say that – he just says, well, it's one way of living, if you don't like it, fine, and if you do, you're welcome. What's wrong with that?"

"I'm not the right person to ask. I've made a hash of my own life, but I don't think I can solve it by, well, giving up, giving up control of it to anyone or anything else. Maybe that's what's wrong with it: it's too much control to give to someone else. Like a marriage."

"I know," Carey sighed. "It's just so attractive, sometimes, though: the idea of letting someone else decide."

"I thought that was half your problem?"

"What?"

"Too much decided for you by your father and your brother."

"You're astute," Carey acknowledged with respect. Immediately, though, it provoked a question of its own. "I mean, if you can see things that clearly," she let the sentence tail away of its own accord.

"Oh," Emily answered gaily, two gins to the wind. "I'm trained to see problems – organisational problems aren't that different from personal, they're usually about relationships between people at the end of the day; but I'm only trained in business solutions. You can't put a marriage on the open market, or reorganise it into different departments. I mean, there aren't enough parts, are there – people. Not without children," she added.

"Do you think it would have been different if you had a child?"

"It would have made it worse, more of us under his thumb, to wreak his revenge on."

"Revenge?"

"Yes," Emily said, as if she was as surprised at her choice of word as Carey. "Revenge – because it isn't all as nice and as happy and as easy as he was always led to expect. That's most of it, isn't it?"

"Don't go back home," Carey said firmly. "Let him do it alone. If he wants to take anything of yours – let it go. Gordon'll stop him doing any serious damage. Please."

"Why? Why should he get away with it?"

"Because you're doing the same as him: getting your revenge. This morning, the order, that's self-preservation, self-protection; watching him eat it is revenge. And," she added after a moment, "even with Gordon there, you don't know what's going to happen. I don't want you to get hurt. Either way." Physically or mentally.

They left the pub together, knocked back by the fresh air. Impulsively, Carey gave her client a hug and a quick kiss on the cheek.

"Call me. You've got my numbers." She always gave her domestic violence cases her home number: domestic violence most frequently came out to play at night. "If you need to get away, I've got a spare room; really, it'd be fine. I'm going to my brother's for dinner, but I never stay late – I'll be home before eleven. Or if you just want to talk."

"I will," Emily said, "I'll call you later."

* * *

The meeting continued through lunch. Junior Messengers brought salad sandwiches and cold drinks to The Temple on trays. The talking would stop as the door opened. As the Junior Messengers entered, they would mumble shyly:

"I am one."

The nearest couple of members would turn and reply comfortingly:

"We are many."

The Junior Messengers would leave the room as quickly as they could, overawed by the power that hung in the atmosphere.

When the door shut behind them, the debate resumed.

The Teacher did not forbid discussion, even argument; The Seer positively encouraged it.

Father Christopher – Caleb's friend – led the attack.

"If we're going to be across the Atlantic, we've got to have autonomy; we can't be expected to create a Programme that is dependent on England; it would be two halves. Who is going to lead us?" He was tall and angular, lean and predatory in his movements, and wore wire-rimmed spectacles like a revolutionary.

"Are you going, Christopher?" Matthew asked, mildly reprimanding him for the presumption.

"We are going – whether I am one of them or not."

"Right. That's exactly what I'm saying: it's still us, we're still one group."

"I can't go," said Sister Hannah, ever practical: the children.

"Ah, yes, now," Caleb's eyes lit up, "that raises another question, doesn't it?" Who would take care of Anthony?

"Give us your poor, your oppressed, your psychotics?" Brother Micah offered sombrely. He had taken the news of the assault on his son with his customary fatalism; it was Hannah who had waxed hysterical. When Micah had next seen Anthony, he had gripped his arms, stared into his eyes, finally said: "I forgive you," and turned away before he could see the sneer in Anthony's eyes replace the fear of physical retaliation.

Matthew had meditated with Anthony, for hour after hour until Anthony could take it no longer, had sobbed that he was sorry, that he had meant no harm. Matthew had kissed him, full on the lips, gripping the boy's shoulders so that he could not break free. Anthony did not know if it was punishment or pleasure. The Seer had rocked Tom in her arms, telling him that he was nearly a man, it wouldn't be the last time, it meant as little as this – she kissed him – and that – she took his hand and placed it on her breast.

"Hammer Reach is...out of reach," said Father Simon, one of the earliest members of the group and one of Matthew's closest allies within it. A thickset man with shoulder-length hair tied back in a pony tail, Simon was patient, stoical. English upper middle-class, public school, a Cambridge rugby blue, he had studied as an architect before he committed to The Programme. A number of the early members had been in or around architecture – architects were drawn to form, tried to recreate inner forms as buildings. Simon had decided to pursue the real thing.

"What can we do at Hammer Reach?" Father Christopher brought the discussion back to the subject. He was a practical man; there were times when his friend, Caleb, verged on the mystical; for Father Christopher, the hard line was the way to get things done.

Christopher had been a computer consultant. He had set up The Programme's Website. He had helped Brother George Cohen computerise their financial records. He made himself useful, and useful he made Caleb powerful. They were the left hand and right hand of The Seer. Cassandra bestowed on them the right to be near to her; she bestowed on them her confidences; she bestowed on them her visions; sometimes she bestowed on them her body; always, she bestowed on them her authority.

Through Brother George, Christopher still undertook some free-lance consultancy work. According to the rules of The Programme, everything he earned – as a resident member – belonged to the group; The Seer gave him dispensation to slice something off the top for the two of them, a private fund. His mastery of The Programme records also allowed him to funnel the occasional donation or Coffee Lounge profit to that fund. Over the years, it had grown. The move to the States was a unique opportunity to put it to use.

"Boston," Matthew announced. "It's only a few hours from Boston. We'll keep Hammer Reach as a base, a retreat; Boston is where we should be." It was one of a half dozen cities the small group of missionary members currently exploring the States had suggested would be ripe for a Chapter. The student population of Cambridge, the numerous colleges elsewhere in Massachusetts, the port and the drug-trade, new age New Englanders, relative proximity to the ever-fruitful recruiting grounds of Canada, relative wealth.

"It doesn't answer Christopher's question," The Seer reminded him.

Matthew knew she wanted to lead the mission. She wanted to take her band and make of The Programme in America something that was different and separate from The Programme they had established in England: something made over in her image, not his.

"Is there an answer?" Matthew asked. "The Programme is The Programme; the whole is the whole; there are no two wholes; if we have two identical images of one whole, what do we have – two Programmes or one?"

Sister Rebecca replied, as if the alternative was too awesome to contemplate:

"There can only be one Programme." The Programme was The Teacher. She did not understand what he was doing; it was as if he was dividing himself in half.

Father Caleb rasped:

"Simpleton."

Sister Rebecca flushed an unattractive deep purple, tried to attack back, bit on her tongue. Mother Naamah – Job's sister – tall, thin, austere, white-haired and ghost-like, a former New York publisher who was now in charge of all The Programme's publications – who could spend weeks at a time without ever leaving the Chapter House – came to her defence.

"Simple and complex; unification of opposites; I am one, we are many; together we are whole."

"Why did you say that, Father Caleb?" Matthew asked, curious not critical: "What did you mean?"

"The notion that everyone has to be different to make up a whole; that's not the way of it, it's not what you said either. Some are different – Naamah's unification of opposites – but some are the same. 'Every individual is essentially sufficient to himself. But he is unsatisfactory to himself until he has established himself in his right relation with the Universe'," he quoted Crowley. "'For these, there is strength in numbers, in uniformity, an army'."

"With all our symbols clanking in time," Simon – least afraid of Caleb – ridiculed.

Caleb glowered at Rebecca as if Simon's attack was her fault.

Matthew ruled: "Caleb's right." Caleb nodded at Rebecca: to the victor the spoils. "One can make a fetish of being different; the purpose of the mission to America is to expand; I said, 'we are many; but we need to be more'."

Brother Enoch held up a hand to speak. Enoch who had lived for a year of years – three hundred and sixty five years – and had risen to Heaven without death; the man-mountain Brother Enoch who spoke so quietly sometimes it seemed as if he had not spoken at all, just as he had not died. Enoch whose stammer had ceased the day he met Matthew in the street in Exeter, when The Programme spent some time in Devon, which was the day that he had joined The Programme, which was the day he had stopped injecting heroin – cold turkey. Brother Enoch said now:

"I never had a home before. I have a home here. I am comfortable. Therefore, it is time to go." Enoch in the Bible had walked. He ran a hand through his long, scraggly hair and shrugged, as if apologising for interrupting Matthew, his saviour, his father.

Sister Meredith – Merry – a dark, attractive New Englander in her late twenties who like Matthew had come to England for her studies – leaned forward from behind Enoch, stroked his hair and kissed his hand until he settled down.

Caleb snarled:

"We're all in agreement, Teacher." Get on with it, he meant.

"Then it's decided," Matthew said.

They waited. He looked around at them all, until he had looked each one individually in the eye.

"The Seer is to lead this mission. Father Caleb, Father Christopher, you will go with her. Father Simon and Mother Naamah will stay here. So will Brother George and Sisters Hannah and Rebecca. Brother Enoch, Sister Meredith, Brother Micah and Sister Helen – you too will all go. With Father Nahum and Mother Jemima, there will be eight Superiors and Senior Messengers." Father Nahum and Sister Jemima were the two Superiors already in the States – the advance mission. In all, Matthew was sending almost half of the hierarchy. "I will decide on the others later." There would need to be Junior Messengers – as well as the two already in the States – to service the hierarchy. No Initiates, the most junior resident rank of all; the missionaries would be expected to find new Acolytes and bring them into the fold as Initiates over there; if they could not do that much for themselves, the mission would fail.

No one needed to say anything as he crossed his legs, held his hands outwards palms open and facing up, closed his eyes and began to intone:

"We look to the energy that is the source of all life and of which we are but a tiny part to guide us and to feed us in this next step on the journey of re-unification; I am one but we are many: together we shall be whole. We seek to be channels of conflict and vessels of the elements; I am one but we are many: together we shall be whole. We seek to be free of the petty aims and ambitions of our past lives – our vanities, our insecurities, the will to hurt in order to protect ourselves; I am one but we are many: together we shall be whole. We seek to stride confidently towards the fire, hands outstretched; I am one but we are many: together we shall be whole."

As he prayed, The Seer rose from her place beside him and came and knelt down in front of him; if he was aware of her, he gave no sign. She reached out and touched his fingertips: while doing so, she looked up at The Programme symbol above his head, and said:

"I am one; we are many."

She picked her away through the membership and left the room, shutting the door behind her.

Matthew, oblivious, continued:

"In conflict, we shall be free and we shall find harmony; in war, we shall be free and we shall find peace; in fire, we shall be free and we shall find our release; I am one but we are many: together we shall be whole."

Father Simon was the next most senior member present and he, accordingly, came first to kneel before The Teacher, touch his fingertips, look up at The Programme symbol and mutter:

"I am one; we are many."

He too shut the door behind him as he left.

One by one they took their turn, first kneeling before Matthew, then proffering their allegiance to the group, finally leaving and shutting the door until the person next to perform the ritual decided he or she was ready.

Finally, only Sister Helen was left.

He waited; she waited.

"I know you are not ready," he said.

"Why?" Helen asked, barely concealing the emotional hurt.

"I need you to be there, Helen, to be there for me. Surely you of all people can see that?" Helen with her ability to identify the politics of The Programme. "You must be my eyes and my ears – and my voice, too, when I need to be heard."

"You know what she will try to do?" Cassandra worked through others; her pleasure was not to voice her own malice directly, but to encourage others to give voice to their own.

"That's why," he said, beckoning her to come and kneel before him.

"What can I do?" Helen was crying now, quietly but distinctly, tears running down her cheeks.

He stroked them away with the backs of his fingers. Then her hair, the way she liked.

"I'm frightened," she admitted.

"Of what will happen over there?"

"Yes, and."

"And? Of our separation?"

She nodded silently: petty aims and ambitions – vanities and insecurities.

She wanted reassurance. It would have been easy. He, too, stayed silent. No one owned him; the hardest path led up the highest mountain to the furthest view.

She gazed mutely into his eyes: help me be strong.

He smiled, held out a hand.

"Come. Come with me."

* * *

The Temple was not the only sound-proofed room in the building: in the rear part of the basement – which also housed the Coffee Lounge and the kitchen – was a private studio, where Matthew recorded his Internet messages.

It was also sometimes used for punishment; it was where Caleb's men had confined Anthony while his future was decided.

Sister Rebecca stood before Father Caleb. She was naked. Her fat breasts and her fat thighs hung disproportionately from her painfully thin frame and narrow back; two of her toes were joined by a web. Her nudity humiliated her and her humiliation thrilled him. He too was naked: his chest was thickly matted with grey hairs. His erect penis was thick and stubby, like the rest of him.

He reached out, placed his palm flat on the top of her head, and thrust her down towards the floor. At first, she thought he was going to put it in her mouth but he changed his mind and continued to push down until she fell backwards onto the hard, cork-tiled floor. With his foot he prodded until she rolled herself over and lay prone, her hands stretched out along the floor above her head, her breasts squashed against the ground, jutting out either side of her in globs of flesh.

He stepped down and straddled her like a horse. He reached around and placed one hand against her mouth for her to lick it wet. He used her spit to moisten his penis, his thumbs to pull her cheeks apart. Once, after a private meditation for a half-dozen intimates, he had watched through an open door as Cassandra mounted Matthew like this; he was doing what Cassandra could not.

Positioned to begin, he put one hand around her face to grip her mouth shut, the other on her back to hold her in place, and thrust himself directly into her backside, riding her as she bucked and writhed in agony, savouring the conquest, ramming her in stone silence: giddyap, giddyap – slap; giddyap, giddyap – slap.

As he came, he had both of his hands around her neck, squeezing lightly. He controlled himself: not yet; not this one.

* * *

Colin played squash and worked out in a gym: this was something else his father despised.

While he worked out, he watched women and fantasised.

Then he went home to the wife to whom he had never been unfaithful and the children he loved more than life itself, the way he wished his father had loved them.

Unless he went to his gym, Colin usually arrived home at about seven thirty. There were a half-dozen parking spaces at the back of the office, of which two were for clients and the remaining four allocated to the Management Committee: perks of office. Though it would have been quicker by tube, he always drove. They were the two parts of the day he had to himself, his private time.

Tonight, Carey was coming to dinner. She had arranged it with Jan. No one had consulted him. Irritated, he kept to his squash date; but, loving her, he did not ask her to rearrange her visit.

"What's up?" Jan asked at the door to the study to which he invariably first retreated to put out his files for later, or to scribble down a thought he had en route before it was swept out to sea by family noise and news.

"Nothing."

They touched lips lightly; she took his raincoat to hang it in the hall cupboard; he smiled as he was reminded that this was the life he had wanted and that he had not begun yet to regret. She was a good-looking woman and bright, though she had dropped out of university shortly before the end of her first year and surfed undemanding jobs until they had met at a lunch party and, over a six month period, decided that neither of them would be likely to find anyone more suitable. She had set herself the task of establishing a family frame-work from which the children would be able to waltz into any stratum of society they chose; she worked at it as hard as he worked at his job. What his father failed to appreciate was that it was neither snobbism or vanity that motivated her, but a fundamental insecurity with which she was terrified she might otherwise infect her children.

She accepted his answer at face value, not because she believed him but because Carey was due at any moment and there would be no time to finish a discussion. As if on cue, the doorbell rang and she went to let in her sister-in-law, the other woman in Colin's life and the only one by whom she felt threatened. They kissed the air and let go in time for the girls to grab at Carey's skirt demanding attention and presents.

"Sophie, Alice, I've told you," Jan reprimanded exasperatedly.

"It's all right," Carey laughed. "I like it really."

She had come straight from work. From her briefcase, she extracted Matel boxes: a Barbie for each of them. As they snatched them away from their aunt, Jan was torn between further, futile scolding of her children and resentment towards Carey: they were her children with Colin, not Carey's. She opted for polite admonition.

"You spoil them, Carey; you shouldn't."

"I don't see them often enough to spoil them. Besides, children should be spoiled. Where's Tim?"

"Here I am," he said from the doorway to the kitchen.

He was a strapping lad, far bigger than his years, with a face that was so obviously Charles it constantly reminded her of nature's mystery: a generation skipped – but, she hoped, not lost.

"I didn't think you'd want Ken," Carey laughed, bending to be kissed. She didn't remark that he had grown again: he was sensitive about his size. "Have you got one of these?"

She had bought him a child's version of a pocket electronic organiser, with quizzes and games as well as address book and diary. His face lit up with unfeigned joy: it was an exciting gift, a real present not just a token.

"Help me, Mummy," Alice said, unable to open her box.

"There're so many of them," Carey apologised. "I can't keep up with what they've got."

"Last count," Jan said grimly, "nearly thirty between them. I don't think they've got either one, though: you were lucky. We give them names: Barbells Barbie, Biking Barbie, Bedtime Barbie, Alice has got one that talks – we call her Babbling Barbie."

"What about Bonking Barbie?" Colin joined them, still clustered in the hallway. "She's my favourite."

"Colin," Jan hushed him.

"What's a bonking?" Alice asked.

"Here comes the boss, all fit and trim." Carey put her arms around her brother and kissed him: they saw each other every day but these visits were different.

In a group, all but Jan who had food to prepare, they made their way into the living room. The girls would have to go to bed shortly: it was after eight and a school night. The nanny was off: it would be all hustle.

"Five minutes, now, girls." Colin opened the negotiation.

"Ten, Daddy, please, please."

They clambered onto the sofa for protection, one either side of

Carey, clutching their dolls. Sophie's was a teacher Barbie with a blackboard and two tiny doll pupils at their own desks.

"Bossy Barbie?" Colin proffered.

"Barber Barbie?" Carey held up the one she had purchased for Alice, a doll with detachable hair, plastic scissors. "I don't remember there being so many of them. I wish I was a child now; the toys are incredible." Tim was sombrely punching the keys of his organiser, already mastering its features.

"You are, Carey, you are," Colin teased. "Drink?"

"When did I ever say no?"

She was still slightly pissed from lunchtime.

They bantered until Jan called through that dinner was nearly ready. Tim was to be allowed to eat with them, though on a promise to go straight to bed afterwards.

"Come on, girls. If you're good, perhaps Carey'll read you a story."

They shared a room; the age difference was slight; they could squabble and fight and cry bitter complaints about cruelty to one another but in truth they were as close as twins and if one of them was hurt in the playground or about the house, the other felt it as deeply.

"Come on, I said," Colin upped the irritation quotient a notch. "I mean it." He hovered over them, parentally threatening.

"All right, all right, don't be such a lawyer," Sophie whined in reply.

Colin and Carey exchanged a glance of surprise, then both of them burst into laughter.

"The other day," Colin crowed over his children's wit. "I told Alice to get down from the swivel chair in my study. She said: 'No, no, no, I repeat, no'."

"Don't be a lawyer," Alice imitated her sister. "Don't be a lawyer."

From cute to irritating in ten seconds flat.

They had wine at dinner. Jan raised an eyebrow at Colin as Carey helped herself to a second glass. Carey spotted the gesture.

"It's all right. I'm not driving."

"I didn't mean," Jan blushed but didn't bother to finish the sentence: she did mean it and they both knew it.

Tim sat next to Carey and showed her how his organiser worked. He had figured most of it out already. Carey shook her head.

"That's amazing, Tim. The man in the shop tried to explain it to me and I still couldn't understand it."

With an offer that he could keep the lights on for ten more minutes to play with his new toy, they got Tim up to bed without any greater persuasion. Carey offered to help clear up; Jan refused; Colin suggested they take their coffees through to the living-room. The format of these visits never varied, there were no surprises.

"Are you all right, Carey?" Colin asked.

She read the question the way he intended it.

"I'm all right," she answered, sliding in the equivocation. "You know me. I get on with it."

"How are things with Patrick?" He had known from the beginning.

"Oh, Patrick. You know. Much the same. Going nowhere."

"Pity," Colin murmured. He liked Patrick. They were on the same side. Though eccentric, he could not imagine anyone more ordinary making a match with his sister; and, at heart, he was a kind man who treated her well. If there had to be someone, it was all Colin asked.

"What did you make of Matthew Crane?" Carey tried to sound casual.

"I sort of found myself quite drawn to him, sort of in spite of myself. You know? I didn't like it; like he was making me."

"Yes, that's more or less how I felt to begin with. There is something quite special about him, though. How much of that stuff did you read?"

"I skimmed it. Enough. Crap on toast?"

She laughed despite herself.

"Yes, I'm sure that's right."

"Only?"

She hesitated, then admitted:

"Only not quite certain. I mean, when you look at it closely, there's very little in it to take exception to."

"Pulls in as many punters as he can," Colin scoffed.

"Maybe." She stirred her coffee.

"Do you want a brandy?"

"No. I'm fine. Even I know my limits."

"So what are you saying?" he asked cautiously. They were close; they loved each other; there was nothing they could not tell each other. Yet the relationship remained brittle, touchy even: the wrong question at the wrong time could spark an answer that neither of them knew was lying in wait.

"Oh," she was exasperated, with herself not Colin, "I don't know. I've seen him a couple of times, had lunch with him once, read a few of their books, looked at their site on the Web." It was her job to monitor the firm's Website: to see it was kept up to date, to log on changes, to note the hits, to compare their site with others. It was a job she often undertook from home, late in the evening when call charges were cheapest, when she had nothing else to do. Sometimes, a drink too many and lonely, she'd add an hour surfing at random. "I've corresponded with New York too. There's more to the Amanda Kroger case than appears; I couldn't put my hand on my heart and say who was the bigger charlatan – Matthew or the sister; it's not her first time out, either."

"Whose?" This he could relate to: a case.

"The sister. The good Missus Gruenfeld has a track record: first she tried to argue the division of the fatherly spoils; then she successfully argued mummy into a rest home with a consensual guardianship appointment. The legal information network they've got up on the Web makes us look like we're still developing precedent over dinner in the Inns."

"Good work," he complimented. "How's the jurisdiction argument?"

"Not so good; they get to have a trial over there on who gave what to whom and where the brown envelope was delivered."

Not for the first time, not for the first thousand times, he was struck by how agile she was when she was talking law. He wished it was enough for her; he managed to contain his own yearnings for something more.

"Are you going over for it? Is he?"

"I didn't want to let him originally; I suppose I didn't trust how he'd come over on the stand. But now, I'm not sure he couldn't pull it off. Either way." On jurisdiction, or on the substantive, capacity issue.

"I take it, uh, you're not trusting him too far in other ways," he asked delicately.

"No," she laughed. "Don't worry; he's paid up front."

Jan joined them.

"Talking shop. Who'd've guessed."

\* \* \*

After he saw Carey to the door, Colin went directly to his study. A few moments later, Jan brought him a last cup of coffee: it was no surprise that he was returning to work. Tonight, though, instead of leaving him to it, she asked:

"What was that all about?"

"What?" He acted as if he didn't understand.

"I don't know. Just before I came in, there seemed to be something going on, something in the air. Something's worrying you."

"I'm not sure. I gave her a case; I think she might be getting in a bit over her head."

"Carey?" She had never heard him say that his sister was not capable of doing her job.

"It's the client, really. It's unusual: I shouldn't have given her the case."

"Why? What?" She leaned against the sideboard. He deliberately kept no extra chairs in his study; on the few occasions when he needed to talk to a visitor in the study at home, one was brought in; it served to discourage the children from disturbing him, and Jan.

"Ever hear of something called The Programme? Cult-type thing?"

She started to shake her head, then – to his surprise – nodded.

"I've seen them on the King's Road, selling their magazines. White suits, capes?"

"That's them. His is silk though."

"Who?"

"Their leader; The Teacher, he's called."

"A lot of mumbo-jumbo, I always thought; well," she laughed, "I assumed. I've never bought any of their books."

"Nor did I. But I had a look at them."

"And?"

"And you're right, it's a lot of mumbo-jumbo."

"So, what's the problem?"

"Oh, you know Carey; she's always brooding, always discontented; always looking for something new, or someone."

"What about Patrick?"

"He's probably too nice to her. She says it's not going anywhere."

"So? What are you saying? You think she's getting involved with this, um, this Programme thing?"

He smiled sheepishly.

"No, of course not. It just seems to be a bit more under her skin than I would have expected; or else he is." Matthew.

Jan laughed and turned to go.

"Phooey, Colin. You're carrying worrying about her far too far, my dear. Carey's got her head screwed on as tightly as the rest of us."

*    *    *

Http://www.the-programme.org.uk (turn on sound card if available).

*What do we believe? We believe that as we came from mere energy, we shall return to mere energy: ashes to ashes, dust to dust, the spirit returns to the spirit and the flowing river rejoins the sea. We are like drops of water off rivulets off streams off rivers off the ocean. We do not float; we do not sink; we are the sea. We believe that no one can feel complete on his or her own and that so long as we are on the earth, there is a natural longing to be at one with others. We believe that this is how we recreate the sense of belonging that is our nature. No ghosts and Gods, no belief in the super-natural or the superstitious, no pagan rituals or mystical ceremonies, just a journey taken together by people who began together and who it is inevitable will return together.*

*It's not so unusual or so dangerous, is it? Then why do people always descry private groups and gatherings such as ours? Can it be that they feel threatened? Can it be that they want their way of living to be the only way to live? Can it be that they shun and condemn what is new for fear of finding out that they have been wrong all along? We do not say they are wrong; we do not even believe it. It is their business and we look after only our own; that's what we ask of them in return – to be allowed to follow our own path.*

*There is an end to the path, a fire in the hearth. We may never be aware of reaching it, not with our heads and our minds and our bodies, but we can stretch out towards it, and in reaching for it we can experience something of what it must mean to arrive – a destination is a product of its journey and if the journey is all that we are to enjoy then it is its own arrival. A fire in the hearth – the fire beyond.*

\* \* \*

Carey had rung for a cab to take her home. She had identified Islington as her destination. She let the driver head towards town before she told him otherwise. She had known all along that this was what she was going to do but was putting off admitting it.

"I've changed my mind," she said. "I want to go to Mayfair: Chesterfield Gardens, do you know it?"

She saw the driver's eyebrows rise and guessed what he was thinking: at this time of night, a good-looking woman on her own.

The driver did not answer; she did not explain.

He let her off at the end of the *cul de sac* that was Chesterfield Gardens. It was a short road with huge double-fronted Georgian houses in three terraces – one each side and a short one at the end – tall and wide and proud of their heritage. Each house had double porticoes, steps down to a basement. Some of them had brass plates suggesting businesses or diplomatic uses. The Programme occupied a building about half-way down on the right. She could see the lights from the basement and the main entrance hall from the end of the street. No other houses were still so alive. She glanced at her watch: nearly eleven o'clock; she had read that the Coffee Lounge remained open until midnight, two o'clock at the weekend. That was fine; she would not be staying long.

She dithered between going down into the basement and ringing at the upstairs front door buzzer. She wanted to get a feel for The Programme as it was yet at the same time she did not want to seem to be a mere visitor. Between elitism and discretion, the latter won and she trod carefully down the stairs to the Coffee Lounge entrance self-conscious about her work clothing and her briefcase. The door was painted black, as was the porch by which it was protected from the rain, but there was a port-hole in it through which the light shone and through which she could sense movement.

The door opened to her touch. Inside was an open foyer to the left-hand side of which were stairs which would lead up to the main entrance-hall while to the right a door led into the Coffee Lounge itself, the famous Coffee Lounge, she protected herself with gratuitous sarcasm, of which she had read on the Internet. There was a table between the internal door and the door to the outside on which were displayed issues of the magazine, two of which she had read. Above it, the now familiar round symbol of The Programme, the segmented circle. The door to the Coffee Lounge was shrouded by a curtain, but she could hear music and laughter from within. She felt like a party-crasher, wanting to be a part of it and acutely conscious that she did not belong.

She was at the point of telling herself not to be silly, to make up her mind whether or not to go in, when a young woman emerged from the Coffee Lounge, smiling and humming. She was one of the members: she was wearing a white sweater, white slacks; around her waist was a belt, held together with a brass buckle in the shape of the symbol. The woman – an American – said:

"Hello. My name's Lilith. What's your name?" She was not asked what she was doing there or what she wanted, the questions she was preparing to answer.

"Carey," she answered nervously. "Carey Arnott."

"Hello Carey," Sister Lilith held out a hand. She was also wearing a ring in the shape of the symbol: it was rapidly moving from familiarity to ubiquity. So far as she had noticed, Matthew did not wear one. Though it now struck her as odd, he was still the only member she had met. "Would you like to come into the Coffee Lounge?"

The woman was warm, welcoming, almost physically comforting, yet there was something distant about her too that spoke of an inner world she was either trying to keep hidden or, perhaps, to contain.

"Yes, all right," Carey replied, feeling as lame as she sounded.

Sister Lilith led her into a vast, light room – more of a chamber or a hall – which had been divided into two levels. There was a spiral staircase to the left of the door, leading up to a second-tier platform. It was all built in blond wood: despite the polished perfection of it, she guessed that it would all have been of their construction and handiwork. It was impossible not to be impressed.

At both levels, tables were in individual booths. Above each table, there were drawings or paintings in a common style which most immediately brought Richard Dadd to Carey's mind: writhing figures, faces distorted by madness, entangled with one another and divided by fire. Few of those seated were members of The Programme; most of them were young, though here and there was an older face looking to her as out of place as she felt. There was a distinctly American atmosphere – accents, clothing, music. Matthew had told her that – as well as himself – many of the members were American and it seemed so also were many of their followers and customers. Several people turned to stare at her, openly and unashamed.

"Would you like to sit upstairs?" Lilith asked, sensing her discomfort. "It's easier to just watch."

It was taken for granted that this was not an ordinary coffee lounge or restaurant: people did not come here for a bite to eat or a drink; they came to meet, to talk, to join in – ultimately, Carey supposed, some of them came to join.

She nodded and followed her hostess up the narrow steps to the less crowded upper level, allowed herself to be ushered into a booth at the other end, overlooking the whole room. She slid into the booth, grateful for the consideration, glad to recover her anonymity.

There was a menu on the table, emblazoned with the symbol, with a small selection of snacks and more filling foods on one side, drinks on the other. The food was mainly vegetarian: she glanced down the list at an "exotic melanesia – rice, nuts, vegetables, raisins," and vegetable stew concoctions with "our own, home-baked bread". The drinks ranged from conventional coffees, teas and soft drinks – Coke, of course, another ubiquity – through mixtures of their own making.

Still waiting, Sister Lilith suggested:

"Have the 'Job's Reward'. It's my favourite."

Carey raised her eyebrows but it sounded good – frozen yoghurt, crushed nuts, chunks of grape, slivers of melon, she wondered whether it was a meal or a drink.

"Okay. Thank you."

"Is there anything else you want?"

Carey almost let it go. Suddenly, she said firmly:

"Yes. There is. Could you find out if The Teacher might be free."

Lilith started to protest: no one walked in and saw The Teacher on demand; The Teacher was the reward at the end of the game.

Carey raised a hand to forestall her.

"Actually, he invited me here." She almost said that she was his solicitor but realised that the general membership might be unaware of any need for legal counsel.

Lilith looked at Carey as if to make sure she wasn't insane then nodded.

"Carey Arnott, you said?"

"Right. Thank you, Lilith."

Her first reaction as Lilith left was to regret asking for Matthew. What if he did not want to see her? Or see her here? It would be humiliating to be told he was too busy; it would be better if he was away from the building.

Her second reaction was one of surprise. She did not usually issue instructions in a social setting. It had been easy. She had enjoyed it.

She did not have long to wait. In a few minutes first his handsome head then the rest of his long body rose out of the spiral staircase like a god from the fire. She smiled, raised a hand to tell him where she was sitting, then let it fall to the table as she saw he already knew, was walking around the balcony directly towards her. In contrast to the way people had stared openly at her when she entered the Coffee Lounge, they lowered their eyes modestly as he passed, as if it tempted fate to look upon a god.

She started to get up to greet him but before she could do so he had sat down opposite her. He smiled and took her hand across the table in both of his, holding onto it.

"Carey," was all he said.

"Hello, Matthew. I hope you didn't mind my dropping in like this. I just thought, well, I wanted to see the place, get a feel for it. Besides, you said."

He could have told her to stop apologising; but that would have been as redundant as the apology itself.

"And?"

"And? And what do I think of it?" He nodded. She laughed. "I only just arrived. But people seem, well, very nice, very friendly. Welcoming."

"You are, you know: welcome."

"Yes. I think I do know that. I mean, I feel welcome."

\* \* \*

At her house, the phone rang. When the answering machine picked up, the caller disconnected without leaving a message. Ten minutes later, it happened again. And again. The caller did not stop trying until after one o'clock. It was Emily, calling from the hospital.

# Chapter Four

Guiltily, she took Emily with her to the South of France.

It was a first, to befriend a client and bring her into the family.

Emily was not too badly hurt, blamed herself, claimed that something she had said when Richard rang about his belongings during the afternoon might have led him to believe that he would be welcome to return that evening despite the court order, might even actively have caused him to return. She was one sentence shy of claiming it was her responsibility that he had lost all control, had gone further than ever before, had beaten her until her screams forced the neighbours to call the police.

When Carey visited her at the flat the next morning, one side of her face bruised black, one side of her body still bandaged, her legs either side of a pillow, Richard was under arrest: even if Emily did not want to pursue the complaint, the physical evidence was overwhelming; she could withhold evidence to support a charge of attempted rape but not the assault itself; besides, there was breach of the court order.

The flat was a cracked mess. Carey asked about other friends she might stay with. They were friends of the couple and did not want to take sides, or run the risk, or get involved. She could not let her stay at her home alone.

"I've got the room. Stay a while."

"I can't," Emily was sincere in her protestations. "You've done enough. Look, it was my fault. I shouldn't have rung you."

"It's not your fault; none of it. Stop blaming yourself. I said to ring, then I went out and forgot. Leave me my mistakes, please."

They were fighting for responsibility. Emily burst out laughing, then clutched her cheek.

"Ouch, that hurts. I'm sorry." Which made them laugh again.

\* \* \*

Carey had stayed late at the Coffee Lounge, long past closing time but, she noticed, so did many others, people she had thought were visitors.

"Acolytes," Matthew explained his world. "They are also part of The Programme. Everything needs an opposite: residents need non-residents."

"We all need to feel superior to someone?"

"Different, let's say."

"I don't know how people do it," she said, admitting ignorance and interest in equal measure.

"Do what?"

"Join something like this: give up everything else. I mean, I can see the attraction: complete change; the freedom to redesign yourself. I just don't know how people have the courage."

"Is it that much different from joining anything else? It's just a question of degree."

"It's the size that makes the difference; the perimeters, perhaps."

"Which is a question of how you measure them. We're used to measuring space by reference to external criteria, houses, jobs, friends, money: success. Here, we build on a sense of our own identity: the stronger it is, the less we need things to which to attach it. It's enormously liberating, owning nothing, needing nothing: you don't need to worry about what to wear, where your next meal's coming from, what you're going to be doing tomorrow or at the weekend. You give everything you can to, and get everything you need from, the group."

"You make it sound like socialism."

"We're not interested in a new world order; only our own."

"This world order or that of the next?" She tensed as they passed over to the religious side.

"I don't know the difference. The next can only be something that follows something else."

"Like God and Satan?" Of which she had read.

"Right. Two sides of the same coin."

"I don't know, Matthew," she said, stirring the watery remains of her drink with the long-handled spoon with which she had picked out its fruit.

As if on cue, Sister Lilith approached the table deferentially.

"I am one," she said.

"We are many," he replied without self-consciousness.

"Would you like anything, Teacher?"

"Some tea would be nice. Carey?"

"All right; thank you."

Sister Lilith smiled at her.

"Did you enjoy the Job's Reward?"

"I did. It was delicious. Thank you."

After Sister Lilith had left them, she said:

"She's a nice woman. How long has she been a member?"

"I'm not sure," Matthew admitted. "A couple of years, I think."

"What did she do before?"

"You're looking for types. Everyone did something different. Everyone did something alone. Everyone had something missing. After that, it's mostly window-dressing."

"You've got it all so worked out, Matthew. I envy you."

"All I have worked out is the need to keep on working it out. I don't know where I'm going, or where The Programme is going; I don't know how this case will work out. I don't know how you'll work out either."

She shivered: she didn't either.

"All I know is, you have to take the next step just right; if each step is right, then the journey is right, then the destination will be right." His voice was soothing, mesmeric, mellifluous.

Carey looked up to see that someone new had brought their tea.

The woman was carrying a tray, bearing three glasses, not two, each in a plastic holder. She sat down next to Matthew without being invited. She was small, dark, heavy-breasted. Carey knew she looked familiar, was about to place her when she introduced herself.

"Hello Carey; I'm Cassandra."

"The Seer," Carey murmured despite herself, trying not to think how ridiculous the name sounded.

"That's right. I thought if I didn't come up and introduce myself, Matthew wouldn't introduce me to our own solicitor."

Carey couldn't remember the last time she had heard anyone bury so many barbs in so few words.

"I'm pleased to meet you," Carey said. "I'm sure we would have met soon."

Cassandra giggled.

"Excellent, excellent."

Matthew was amused: no matter how much they fought, no matter that there were locked into combat for the soul of The Programme, no matter the different paths they took within it, they were still its twin poles.

"Will you come to America?"

It could have meant many things. Carey took her at face value.

"It's too early to say. I don't know if the case will need it."

"But we might need you. Or, perhaps, we might just want you."

Carey's eyes flashed.

"I wouldn't know about that. It's too far away. I thought we were only supposed to look one step at a time."

Cassandra reached across, took her hand, held onto it.

"That's why I'm called The Seer," she warned her.

As suddenly as she had arrived, she was gone.

Carey stared at the table for time to recompose herself. She asked Matthew:

"Is she always like that?"

"I've known her for twelve years; I don't think she's ever the same twice."

"How do you keep up with it? With her, I mean?"

Matthew took the same hand that Cassandra had let fall on the table with one of his hands, stroking the back of it with the fingers of the other.

"I don't. She rushes ahead, then darts into a corner to hide and watch, and I think, all I can do is take the next step, my own next step, just right."

"I am one?"

"Right. I am one; we are many; The Programme moves forward on many feet."

"And if they don't all move in the same direction?"

"Then that's the direction we'll move in."

Carey sensed that Matthew's answer meant something but didn't understand what.

"We arrive at the destination that is the product of those differences."

"How is it different from compromise?"

"Compromise is the decision reached by people who disagree; it involves setting aside their disagreements in favour of some sort of middle ground agreement. If you and I walk a hundred yards in opposite directions, we'll be two hundred yards apart: and that marks out our perimeter."

"I'm just a lawyer; it's too abstract for me. I need to know what the destination is so I can plan the tactics for getting there."

He sipped his tea.

"It's where you think you're going, but when you get there it won't be what you think."

"Because?" She couldn't help herself; she could listen to him for hours.

"Because what you see at a distance is not the same as what you see from close up: at the least, it has proportions which are different."

"Different to?"

"To you."

"And?"

"And, secondly, because once you enter it you become a part of it; then you cannot see it the same way."

"This is the room you are a part of?" She had read it in a magazine, or heard it on the Internet: you cannot describe a room that you are in.

"Right."

He leaned across to touch her cheek. She blushed and took his wrist in her hand, but – immediately – she was not sure what to do with it and quickly sensed that it was the wrong thing to do in this place: she had touched The Teacher.

"I'm sorry," she said, letting go, glancing around to see if anyone had noticed.

Again, he did not brush the apology aside or tell her it was unnecessary.

"So you concentrate on the next step, just the next step. Taking it right," she repeated what he had said earlier. "That's all you can do, right?"

"You're a quick study, Carey."

She backed off.

"I'm just curious."

"Fine. If that's the next step. Do curiosity."

"What if you don't like where it leads you?"

"Then stop."

She struggled to voice her concern.

"If you've taken a step, but then you don't like where it's led you, it may be too late."

"Sometimes you have to let go, let yourself go."

"That's what scares me. That's what stops me taking the first step."

"Think about a bottle of rancid water. How do you make it whole?"

"Excuse me?" She didn't see the connection.

"It's an old Zen saying. You cannot make it whole by pouring it away a bit at a time, and filling it up again. You have to pour it all out until the bottle is empty; then you fill it up anew."

This time, she did not make the mistake of taking his hand, but she reached across the table and laid her own in front of him, open and facing up, for him to take if he wanted.

"'You just paint it all over and start again'?"

He took her hand.

* * *

"I've got an idea," she said to Emily.

She had persuaded Emily to pack some things, come to Islington with her.

"After the hearing, let's take a break."

"A holiday?" Emily sounded doubtful. Her eyes were all on the hearing, the committal application to deal with Richard's breach of the original order not to molest her. Carey had warned her it was possible that he would be jailed. It had been one thing to consult a lawyer, another to get the order, yet another to serve him with it; but to cause arrest crossed a line. Before they were finishing, now they were finished. "Why?"

"Why not?" They were stretched out on Carey's two, right-angled sofas, talking, drinking wine, nibbling cheese, listening to music, smoking – both of them: Carey had never shared her living-room with anyone like this; there had been visitors, but the fact that Emily was staying at the house made a difference. She could not switch her off when it suited, get her to leave. If the mood became tense, Carey had to delve inside herself, find a way to cope. It was surprisingly easy, surprisingly pleasant.

"I'm on sick-leave," Emily protested weakly. She had not gone back to work since the assault. There had been a meeting at Carey's office – two of them, a man and a woman – and Emily and Carey. The man was Emily's boss; the woman, from personnel.

The man admitted:

"We've got some difficulties here. Richard's partner level."

"Emily's not asking for him to be sacked; their offices aren't even in the same block. She just wants reassurance about her own position; she wants to know that he'll be kept away, no one's going to put them into contact; and, of course, that there'll be no indirect, er, consequences."

The woman rushed in.

"Absolutely. There's no question of it. When Malcolm said there were difficulties, he meant that all of us, well, naturally, we want to give Emily all the support we can, we're all on her side here. He's just saying, Richard can't be, well, you know, sacked."

Carey was at work; she did not need a bullshit dictionary. She said:

"And, er, if he wasn't at partner level, you'd sack him, right?"

"No, I'm not saying that either," the woman blushed. "But we'd have more room for manoeuvre; he could be relocated, for example, further afield. Another town, perhaps."

"But because he's at partner level, you can't? Please." Carey pulled a face. Partners had little more power than any other employee; maybe their payoff wasn't called redundancy but buy-out, but they could be, and were, sacked as often and as easily as everyone else.

"What do you want, Ms Arnott?" the man asked.

"I've said what Emily is after," Carey repeated. "And of course she's going to need some time off."

"Absolutely," the woman said. "As much as she needs."

"The longer the better, you mean?" Carey said.

"I don't know why you think that. I don't know what you think we want." The woman shifted uncomfortably in her seat.

The man was harder by a head.

"If Emily feels it's going to be too difficult, then we'll just have to work something out."

"Yes, I thought so," Carey grinned. They wanted her to write the overture for an opera called gone.

"Will you all stop talking about me as if I wasn't here?" Emily pleaded. "I want my job; I need it; I just don't want to have to worry that he's going to come around the next corner; and I don't want any of his friends taking it out on me. Is that so much to ask? Look at me, damnit." She pointed to her face, still swollen.

The man nodded at Carey.

"Right, then. Why don't we all step back and consider our positions for a while? Time's no problem; Emily is obviously entitled to some sick-leave; that gives us an opportunity to review the situation clear-headedly."

"If you're prepared to put that in writing, that it's what you want, then I'll advise my client to agree. Without prejudice to all her rights."

They shook hands and started to leave. At the last moment, Emily's boss turned around, took her hand again, and leaned in to kiss her good cheek.

"I know you think we're all bastards, Em; but I'm sorry, I'm truly sorry."

Emily said nothing until he left, then snorted:

"The only thing he's sorry about is having my time off on his budget."

Carey laughed brittlely.

"We did all right. They can't come at you for the next couple of months. And if they do," they could sue for unfair dismissal.

"So?" Carey said at the house. "We'll go to the South of France; people go there for their health; you can recuperate in the sun."

"I can't afford it."

"All it'll cost you is the flight. We have a flat. There's room. I have to go down anyway. My father's there."

* * *

The Programme was all about the move. Not just for the residents but also for the Acolytes. No secret had been made of the plan: to the contrary, a moment such as this was seminal for those who were hesitating about joining. There was an opportunity for some to move into the group in London. Though The Programme would not take Acolytes, there was nothing to stop them going with their own accord; a few were thinking about combining the opportunity with a visit home for its own sake. The Junior Messengers nominated for the States after the monthly meeting were particularly keen on camp-followers: with no Initiates, they were on the bottom rung; a few outside friends could help both with the mundane tasks of establishing themselves in Boston, and to make contacts in the community from which they wanted to recruit.

Father Nahum flew back to brief them and to consult with The Teacher: Mother Jemima stayed behind. She was British; her immigration status was unsatisfactory; it was one thing to tempt fate or the gods, quite another the INS.

Father Nahum was a round, happy man in large, red-framed spectacles that would have suited a circus clown, who would have been a monk in the middle ages, a vicar in the nineteenth century, and who had been an architectural school drop-out turned shoe salesman named Bob Eccles in the second half of the twentieth. He discovered The Programme when it was still little more than a group of friends, travelling around Matthew during a long summer, post-university vacation, the tour that had taken them – and Eccles – to Bolivia. At that time, he had been separated from his wife and was about to separate from his job. He was already halfway to the right attitude: Matthew helped him make it complete.

Matthew took Father Nahum out to dinner with Helen. They went to a Dutch Pancake House: they ate vegetarian pancakes and luxurious ice cream pancakes and drank alcohol-free cider.

Matthew was spending as much time as he could with Helen. Their time was coming to an end. He was offering her to Nahum. Nahum was an ally: Matthew wanted to forge them into a partnership to represent him. Alone, neither of them could succeed in standing up to The Seer, least of all to The Seer supported by Fathers Caleb and Christopher.

Helen's eyes told Matthew she would not accept the party line. She had not accused him of other motives for wanting her out of the way, but when she had finished her work the night Carey visited with Matthew, she had sat in a dark booth and watched him talking to the woman solicitor, the way he had talked to her in the beginning.

Matthew asked Nahum:

"Have you heard from Amanda?" Kroger.

"Not directly. Jemima had lunch with Rosalyn – Amanda's old room-mate?" Matthew shook his head to say he didn't remember. "She'd been out to see her." At the clinic where she was held. "Claims Amanda's planning on checking herself out; wanted Rosalyn to bring her some clothes, money, says there's a credit card in another name, a car in a parking lot. Rosalyn says she won't do it, but there might be someone else. It doesn't look good."

"I don't understand," Helen said. "If she's well enough to get out, won't that help the case?"

"Not if she's nowhere to be found. They'll think we've kidnapped her or hidden her away. What are you thinking?" Matthew asked Nahum.

The jolly man shrugged, his chin wobbling.

"Give her up? Stop the break out."

Helen shook her head.

"No. Help her."

Nahum started to protest. Matthew liked Helen's suggestion.

"Produce her at trial. Can you do it?"

Nahum caught up. He wasn't stupid though he could be slow.

"With some help." He turned to look at Helen with admiration. "No one knows you over there, do they?"

"What do you want us to do, Matthew?" Helen asked, changing tack. "We're no match for them." Cassandra and her crew.

"Do you think they want to split?" Nahum picked up the thread.

"Split? No. I think they have fantasies of taking it all over."

"You are The Programme, Matthew," Nahum protested. "It's impossible. They'd destroy it."

"It won't happen; like I said, it's just a fantasy."

Helen looked at him sombrely. It was not that The Programme without Matthew was unthinkable; Matthew would never let that happen. It was what he would do to stop it that frightened her. Meltdown; final unification; the fire beyond; the demons unleashed. She asked:

"Why let her even try?"

"Let her?" Matthew raised an eyebrow in reprimand. "It has to run its course. If they need to try, if they need to take it to the extreme, then we have no choice except to go along with it. That's The Programme; that's the only route; you know that."

* * *

Charles met them at the airport: he had delivered his last guest just as – in a week's time – he would bring them back and fetch someone new. Before them, an editor from a publishing house which had long ago expressed interest in his book. Carey had heard about her, never met her: Charles liked to keep his people in boxes.

Immediately after them, an American lawyer and his wife were due to visit, someone with whom Charles had once joined in an international civil rights campaign and stayed in contact since. Later, Colin, Jan and the kids would come down, crowd the apartment. It was their apartment, Colin reminded Carey, theirs as much as Charles', perhaps more; their mother's money.

Though the season had not begun, the Côte d'Azur was already alive: the sun bounced off old mountain villages – Saint Paul de Vence and Haut de Cagnes amongst them – onto the shiny new buildings of the coast. Carey – sitting in the back – leaned forward to point out the famous Marina *Baie des Anges* at Villeneuve-Loubet Plage before the long stretch of sandy beach was lost to sight as the Autoroute curved in towards the hills.

"It's glorious, isn't it?" Charles crowed. "Sometimes I wish I could stay the whole year round; but I'd probably end up as stultified and as lame as the other old codgers."

He glanced at Emily, in the front passenger seat, and smiled for sympathy. She returned the smile uncertainly. When he returned his vision to the road, she looked quickly back over her shoulder at Carey who responded with an amused grimace.

No sooner were they on the motorway than they were leaving it. Their estate was on the East side of Antibes, between Nice and Antibes rather than between Antibes and Cannes, the exit after Villeneuve-Loubet and Cagnes-sur-Mer. Emily pointed to a road sign, exclaiming with surprise:

"Skiing?"

"Sure. The Alpes Maritimes; it's just a couple of hours' drive," Charles replied. "Why? Are you a skier?"

Emily nodded.

"I used to ski; haven't been for years, though. You must come down again, in the winter," Charles added.

He swerved without signalling off the main road which had led from the motorway to the sea and, within minutes, turned again into a short driveway, likewise without using his indicator, narrowly missing a car coming in the other direction. Carey said:

"The reason Charles likes France is because they drive as badly as he does."

Charles chuckled and used a swipe card to open the electric gates of the estate. The grounds were lush, rich green grass carpeting the terrain between roads and paths, palm trees rising here, thick bushes flourishing there, exotic and colourful plants flowered in well-tended beds, at brief intervals a sharp eye could spot sprinklers in the ground, at night – Emily would soon learn – they watered the grounds for hours at a time, creating mini-rainbows in the lights of the estate, from the balcony of the apartment it was a beautiful sight.

The estate itself was composed of a single, relatively high-rise block of flats, with two smaller blocks on one side of the walled enclave, and a line of mini-villas along the other. They were in the high-rise, on the sixth floor. Before she even showed her to her bedroom, Carey led Emily to the balcony, to look out onto the Bay. She sensed that it was almost too much for her: from the small flat in London where she had been abused by Richard to this luxury in a matter of weeks. She quickly led her to the third bedroom, the one that had been Colin's in his teens and student days. The apartment was stone-floored, with rugs not carpets, laid out like a "T" from one side of the building to the other, with the bedrooms – each with its own private bathroom – and the kitchen on a corridor of their own at the back, through the living-room onto the balcony at the front.

"You'll be all right," Carey reassured her.

"I know. Thanks, Carey." She held her new friend's eyes for a moment then, unexpectedly, stepped forward and hugged her. "No one's ever done so much for me."

Carey went in search of her father. She kept spare clothes in the flat and did not need to unpack, nor did she need time and space to feel at home. She loved the apartment: in her private fantasies, she liked to imagine herself living here permanently, not Charles.

She found him on the balcony, setting out the accoutrements for an alcoholic tea: thin biscuits, a bottle of gin, small bottles of tonic, ice in a bucket, a bowl of fruit. Carey laughed.

"I see you plan to get us straight into the holiday mood."

"Your friend looks as if she could do with some relaxing," he said gruffly, somewhere between considerate and a complaint.

Carey glanced around to make sure Emily was still in her room, led her father to the balcony railing and explained in hushed tones:

"She's had a rough time, Daddy. Husband thing. Go easy on her."

"She's a client?" Charles asked doubtfully.

"She's a client but she's a friend. She's been staying in the house, too. Oh, I don't know, it seemed right at the time. I was lonely," Carey shrugged. This was not the time to touch on any deeper discontent, probably it never would be: she was the apple of her father's eye and she had to be rosy and fresh and unblemished if she wanted to stay that way.

Charles studied her querulously. It was out of character. Not that Carey was mean or unkind to those in need, but because she was always careful to draw a line around herself, not to let them – or their pain – touch her. She was – as, he supposed, he was – a sympathiser by profession. Despite himself, he heard himself ask:

"You're not, er, I mean," he looked around for the right – politically correct – words, "you're not involved with her, are you?"

For a moment Carey did not know what he meant, then she burst out laughing:

"Oh, Daddy, everything isn't always about sex."

"What about sex?" Emily came onto the balcony. "I thought that was the one thing I'd left behind in London – thank goodness."

Carey almost told her what Charles had said but thought better of it. She did not know Emily well enough; she had been through a terrifying ordeal; it would not be surprising if she was – as they used to say at college – off men for a while.

While Charles prepared her drink, Emily crossed to the rail and leaned out over it for another delighted inspection of the eye-stopping view.

"Can we go for a swim after?" Emily waved her hand in the direction of the pool. It was surrounded by plastic recliners and chairs, a few tables, sun-shades, but otherwise empty of people. "It looks, oh, idyllic."

"That's the right word," Carey replied, suddenly bitter. "But we ought to go down now, before it gets any cooler. And before we have another drink." Her eyes met her father's accusingly: the South of France was a fantasy he had imposed; she ought to be able to choose her own.

While Emily went to change into her swimming costume, Charles – equally unexpectedly – asked quietly:

"You're unhappy, Carey?"

She shook her head, rose, as she passed behind his chair, she leaned down and kissed the top of his head, murmuring:

"It's just that time of my life."

He did not join them at the pool, staying behind to clear up the drinks. A local woman came in to clean for him each weekday morning, but in between he managed on his own. Later, he would take them down to the harbour at Antibes to eat; the restaurants had all re-opened, if they dressed for it, it would not be too cold to sit outside, but because the crowds had not yet arrived, there was no need to book. Later still, when they had gone to bed, he would sit on the balcony, in the dark so as not to attract the mosquitoes, with a last whisky or maybe two, brooding about his life, wondering how so much of it seemed to have slipped away and how he could hang on to what was left.

\* \* \*

Http://www.the-programme.org.uk (turn on sound card if available).

*Everything is about fear. "What doth the Lord thy God require of thee, but to fear him," says the Bible. Fear is double-sided: it puts us off, but it only has the capacity to do so because whatever it is we are afraid of attracts us. Otherwise, we would feel nothing but indifference. Fear is like when we were young, and we could afford to be afraid, knowing our parents would take care of us. Fear is like the Big Dipper at the fairground, or Indiana Jones at Disneyland: we can experience the fear just because we know we will soon enough be safe again. Fear can be pleasant, warming, enticing. We learned early that fear comes before knowledge; fear is of the unknown; without unknown, no fear; fear and unknown are synonymous; you cannot discover anything new – about yourself or about anything else – unless you fear it first; if you do not fear it, it is not unknown, but something already within your grasp; fear-unknown, it is a partnership.*

*That's what The Programme is. Most organisations or institutions or frameworks for growing and learning to live in peace and in fulfilment would say the same: they are ways of moving forward despite the fear of what you have to learn, of the unknown. The difference is this: most belief-systems cope with fear by comforting you about what it is that awaits you. This is the fallacy: it defines what you are to learn, brings it within reach, diminishes it in order to do so. What we do is to provide something that does not pre-define the unknown, or teach you what to learn. We offer each other, and you, a way to fly, but where you fly is something only you can decide for yourself.*

*This is what The Programme does; this is its purpose: it creates an environment in which others, daily, show you not where to fly but that flying brings its own rewards, that it is not dangerous, it is not to be feared. At its simplest, there is the you that you know, and the you that you do not; it is the first part that is afraid, and the second that is the unknown; there can be and there is no reason to be afraid of your own self, your own nature, the very elements of which you are composed; to the contrary, it is not until all parts of yourself are brought to bear on the flight itself that you can truly feel safe; then there is nothing left that is unknown and therefore nothing left to fear. What should you be afraid of? You are embracing a god – and it is a god that comes from within.*

\* \* \*

They filled the week with trips, mostly on their own. They went up to Haut de Cagnes and wandered around the Grimaldi Castle and Museum and ate on the square. In Saint Paul, they bought cards and jewellery in a shop behind the Picasso Museum and took photographs over the ramparts. In Vallauris, they saw rows of shops with rows of pots that they were glad were too big to take home, they would never have been able to choose. Mornings they swam graceful and lithe in the pool and lay out on recliners, talking little, sunbathing topless like the French women of the estate, trying to seem as casual, self-consciously ignoring each other's bodies.

One afternoon, they drove out to Cap Ferrat and walked around the zoo, sipping cokes and smoking at the open air café. Another day, they did a half tour of the Loup Valley, scrabbling over the rocks at the side of the road to paddle in the pool at the base of the waterfall at the Loup Gorges. In the early evening, they spent more money than they ought in the boutiques of Antibes. In Cannes, too, they roamed the rue d'Antibes, where Paris couturiers had southern outlets, struggling to keep their credit cards in their purses.

The pavements were filling up with tourists and entertainers. Arabs and Jews predominated, co-existing in harmony: all that was needed to bring peace to the Middle East was to give everyone enough money to live in the South of France. Elderly couples, deeply tanned and crinkled from years of sun, roller skaters in skin-tight lycra biking shorts, clowns and jugglers in masks, a pony ride around Nice, the days were theirs and the evenings belonged to Charles. They ate one evening at the Carlton in Cannes. As they ate, he would be greeted by acquaintances – French and English and American – and he was known to all the waiters.

"What does Colin want?" Charles complained, slightly tipsy, treating Emily like family. "He's effectively got his own firm. It's not as if anyone stops him doing the work he wants."

"His firm?" Carey asked, voice rising in automatic anger.

"Both of you; I meant, both of you." He looked at Emily and raised his eyebrows. "Damned lawyers; they pick on your every word." Sometimes, he even flirted with her.

"I'm sure she had a good training," Emily replied, her voice bubbling with laughter. In less than a few days, the sun and the swimming had begun to heal the brutalisation of years: it had been what she needed; a visit to a foreign land to be treated like a lady. The sudden squabbles which burst out between Charles and Carey no longer bothered her: she understood that it was part of the fabric of their relationship, neither of them could do without for long. It was as addictive as what she had slid into with Richard, only less harmful: as cannabis is to crack cocaine, she thought to herself, smiling at the metaphor but refusing to share it when they asked what was amusing her.

They sat in the dark on the balcony with Charles after dinner, sipping drinks, watching the sprinklers below, talking quietly. Without any prelude, she began to talk about him.

"The first time he touched me," she hesitated. "Hit me, I mean, I couldn't believe what was happening. I mean, suddenly I was confronted with the most terrible, unexpected, shocking dilemma: it was such a small thing – that first time, he twisted my wrist until it brought up a scorched red welt, he claimed he hadn't meant to hurt me and, I suppose, the pain itself had worn off within a few minutes, anyway within an hour or two. But suddenly I was being forced, immediately, without any warning, into this gigantic choice, between the whole of the life we had led – all the years we had been together, and all the dreams for the future, all the investment in it – and one, as I say, relatively small incident. I knew inside that it was serious; otherwise, it wouldn't have struck me that way, as such a big issue, but because it was actually such a short incident, such an, I don't know, apparently small thing, I couldn't rationally compare the two. Almost as if, obviously," she stressed, "it was to be taken for granted that it couldn't threaten everything we had."

Carey murmured:

"Tiny eruptions."

"Yes."

Charles shook his head gloomily.

"All my life, I've been bemused by this. The major changes in people's lives always seem to be about the smallest things. If I look back at Marion and I, Carey's mother," he threw in for Emily's sake, "I know there was a great deal that was wrong, that when she went she needed to go, it was right; and I know we had great differences of attitude; but if I try to remember what this or that difference was about, what were the things that mattered, I can't. Like you say, Carey: tiny eruptions."

"It wasn't an original saying." It had been Matthew's: if we do not dig beneath the surface, then we are always vulnerable to these tiny eruptions and, ultimately, we will be destroyed by the accumulated lava.

"There's not enough respect paid to love," Charles added. "We take it for granted, but it's a gift."

"It isn't what I most remember about childhood," Carey looked at him quizzically, conveying tacitly that it no more coloured Charles' relationships with his children today.

"That's what I meant. The little things take over."

There was a long silence while each of them thought about the different little things that had taken over their lives. Finally, Emily broke it.

"It's all we can deal with, isn't it? The little things. Or perhaps I mean, it's the only way we can deal with everything else. It becomes about the little things, and then they're not so little after all; they're all there is."

Charles studied her with something akin to affection.

"I'm sorry," he said. "Sorry for what you've gone through; sorry a man should do that to you." He held out a wizened hand and, after a moment, Emily took it.

Carey watched them, frowning and confused.

The last night, they ate at *Les Vieux Murs*, a restaurant in the old quarter of Antibes town itself, on the battlement walls overlooking the sea. It, too, was uncrowded.

"Once the season starts, you'll need to book a week ahead to be certain of a table. People book just to come here for dessert."

The main dining room was on the ground floor of the stone building, with vast, oak windows that opened out flat along the whole of the frontage. It was approached through a narrow terrace, with tables along one side and a gallery on the other. They sat at an outside table, punctiliously attended by waiters with blue-waistcoats and impeccable English. Below them, on the road, a uniformed coachman guarded the restaurant's parking spaces to the death. They ate exquisite pre-prandial tasters, carefully blended *hors d'oeuvres*, fish that had been landed that very evening; to finish they had *crème brûlée* flavoured with essence of violet. Monsieur Romano himself came out to ask if they had enjoyed their meal, shaking Charles by the hand and greeting him by name.

"It means a lot to you, doesn't it, Daddy?" Carey said after the restaurateur had gone back indoors with their requests for a final drink, with his compliments.

"But what does it mean to you?" Emily asked intensely. "I mean, it's so different from everything Carey's told me about you, about the firm, about your work. Things I'd heard, too," she added, to flatter her host.

"I suppose," he answered her, ignoring Carey's question, "it's a bit like those tiny eruptions. There's a part of me that has always enjoyed the good things in life. Professionally I foreswore them in favour of, well," he laughed, "the good fight, you might say. But I was lucky; I had the means to find a place, carve a little bit out of my life for it. I don't know what I would have done if I hadn't been able to find something like this. I might have burst, though probably I'd have become a dry old stick like a lot of my contemporaries, pompous about the glory days, arrogant and over-confident in the knowledge that everyone else is too far behind to catch up, hypocritical about our failures and our contradictions. If you can survive like that this long, then you come to believe you can survive like it forever."

As they strolled back to their car – not on the road outside the restaurant but down in the park next to the covered market – he put his arm around each of their shoulders.

"It's been a lovely week; the best I can remember."

At home, he left them alone on the balcony to talk: he had preparations to make for his next visitors, including a long telephone call to their hotel in London, from where they were flying, as if he could not wait to exchange news and views and gossip until they arrived in the early afternoon the next day.

"It has been a lovely week," Emily thanked her friend. "I'd never have believed I could feel so much better so quickly."

"I'm glad," Carey answered simply.

"It's been a strain for you, though," Emily continued, as if Carey hadn't spoken.

"What? Having you here?"

"No, I didn't mean that. Though," she blushed as she realised how presumptuous it might have sounded, "I know you've been taking care of me, I really am grateful, please don't think I'm taking it for granted. I mean, taking you for granted."

They touched hands lightly.

After a while, Emily said, looking around to check he was not within hearing distance:

"I meant with Charles. He's not easy, is he?"

"He never has been. I'm used to him."

It still wasn't what Emily had meant, but it was how Carey had wanted to hear it.

"I just thought, well, you wanted something out of this week too; I wasn't sure you'd had the chance."

"I didn't come with the same sort of needs as you. I just wanted time away for its own sake. To see how it felt when I came back, I suppose." It, Matthew, The Programme.

"I'm going to move back to the flat when we get home," Emily said.

"Why? You don't have to, you know. I've enjoyed you being in the house. I've enjoyed being with you here too," she added.

She turned to pour the last of the bottle of wine they had been sharing. As she did so, she saw a sudden movement within. Her father was at the back of the darkened living-room, turning towards his bedroom, as if he had been watching. She felt unsettled, though whether by a sense of his voyeurism or by Emily's sudden announcement she could not say.

"I've enjoyed being with you too," Emily reassured her. "Very much. Perhaps I mean too much. I have to find out about being on my own, not having you to depend on."

"I've sometimes thought it was the other way around," Carey laughed hollowly.

"It's just, well, almost too easy, isn't it? We both needed someone; and there we both were. I don't mean," she rushed on, "that I don't trust it, you. You've been wonderful to me, for me, like a sister, and it's made the whole thing easier. It's made it possible; without you, I still can't be certain I wouldn't have gone back to him."

"And now?" She suppressed a twinge of jealousy at the idea that she might yet lose her back to Richard.

"No. Not at all. I know that. That's why I want to be home. I know, you know, in the divorce, he'll get half of it, I'll have to sell it, but I want to be there for a bit first. I need to spend some time in my own home, on my own, in a way I've never done. I'm not explaining myself very well. You, well, you've been alone all your life – adult life. I haven't. I need to do that, for a bit. It's not equal otherwise."

They went to their beds soon after. Charles had already shut his door, though there was a light beneath: he would be reading; he read until the early hours; still learning, he would say; still looking, said Carey.

She took a shower, smiling as she heard the water on the other side of the wall that told her Emily was doing the same. She imagined them taking a shower together, in the way they had lain beside the pool together at perfect ease – sisters, Emily had said.

In her bed, lying awake in the dark, she stared at the ceiling and wondered about what Emily had said. Her answer – that she wanted the time away for its own sake – had been a half truth. She knew that when she got home, she wanted her life to be different; the only thing she did not know was how.

As she was drifting off to sleep, she heard a door click. It jerked her out of the twilight. She stiffened beneath the single sheet by which she was covered, holding her breath, listening for further sounds. None of them had any need to leave their bedrooms to use a bathroom, but either of them might have gone in search of something to drink. She focused on the kitchen, but heard nothing.

Bare feet on stone floor, a scampering sound like mice. Her immediate image was Charles, going to Emily. From early in the week, he had fixed her with his attention and more than once she thought she had seen hunger in his eyes. She was less clear about Emily's own reactions. Emily was emotionally raw; however much she claimed to be healing, she was still needy. There had been times when Emily seemed to be responding to Charles – one evening on the balcony, another in a restaurant. She had not shrugged him off when he had put his arms around their shoulders. An older man would be a different animal than her husband.

Then again, at other times Carey had felt that Emily's needs turned towards her, though she knew it might be no more than the reflection of her own. Though Carey had never touched a woman sexually – aside from the usual explorations as children – she did not have any abhorrence of homosexuality, male or female, and there had been more than one occasion when she had wondered if it might not be a simpler way of life. She was in a mood for something new – The Programme was one option; she wondered if Emily was another.

In the hall, the scampering had stopped. It was like a freeze-framed video. She could barely hear her own breath. She watched her door handle as it turned. Without a knock, it yawned ajar. She could see by the light of the moon, entering through the kitchen window, seeping through the kitchen's open door into the rear corridor, filling it with a faint light, the consistency and comfort of a child's night-light.

"What do you want, Daddy?" she whispered, feeling not relief but queasy disappointment.

He let himself in, pushing the door shut behind him, and shuffled to sit on the side of her bed, wrapping his bathrobe tightly around himself:

"I wasn't sure if you were still awake," he excused the failure to knock.

"I'm awake. What do you want?" she repeated.

She could feel him shrug in the dark.

"I just wanted to see you for a moment. I thought you'd be asleep."

She was puzzled.

"You wanted me to be asleep?"

Her eyes had adjusted. She could see him as he nodded, embarrassed.

"Yes, I suppose I did."

"Why?"

"I used to do that, you know, when you were little. Whenever I came home late, and you had already gone to bed, I'd creep into your room and kiss your forehead and just look at you for a while. You were so beautiful, so peaceful, so good," he chuckled, reminding her that she had also been a stubborn, impudent, naughty child at times. "And you were mine. I used to think – did I make her? There you are, even I used to wonder."

He smiled at the memory; she returned the smile.

"I knew. I always knew you were there."

"No, no you didn't. That's your memory playing tricks. Sometimes you'd wake up, and roll over, and I'd lean down and tell you that I loved you. You'd mumble back: 'Love you too, Daddy,' is what I remember you saying. But usually, you were so fast asleep you wouldn't have known if I'd held a trial at the foot of your bed."

"Yes, you'd've done that too," she said wryly. Then: "Was that why?" She meant, why he had wanted her to be asleep. Perhaps he had been checking on her, before he made another visit.

"No. Not really. I knew, if you were awake, we'd talk."

Her brow knitted, confused, she asked:

"So?"

"I want to be here for you, Carey; I know you're not happy, I know you're," he hesitated, then admitted what he believed, "I know you're frightened. But I'm not very good at these things, not really, am I?" He had come to her room in duty, but it was a duty he had not a clue how to discharge.

She reached out a hand to pat the back of his where it lay on the sheet.

"Not really, Daddy, but it's all right, I don't expect more."

He shuddered at the insult, struggled for an answer, then leaned down and kissed her forehead and left without another word.

She was fully awake now. She darted from one thought to another. He had been Charles – as a parent, all form and no substance: none the less, she regretted dismissing him so harshly. She also regretted her earlier suspicion about his movements in the corridor and yet, despite herself, listened for more, as if should she strain hard enough she would be able to tell the difference between his door and Emily's.

She thought she was fully awake but she was drifting off again, her conscious deliberations interwoven with an fanciful, unreal image that disappeared in wisps, like a trailer for the dream to come. Another click, another door; she did not know if it was for real or only in her mind. This time it was Emily, pushing the door shut behind her, coming to sit exactly where Charles had sat.

"It's like a train station in here tonight," Carey managed to joke, touching Emily's shoulder through her nightgown to tell her that she was not complaining.

"I was frightened," Emily said. "I thought." She did not finish her sentence. Carey knew what she had thought: that Charles had been going to come into her room.

"It's all right," Carey said.

Their eyes met, engaged. Carey's hand was still on Emily's shoulder. She squeezed it lightly.

"Thank you." For coming.

Neither of them moved for the longest time. Then, Emily bent over to touch Carey's lips with hers.

"You too," she said.

She rose gracefully and left in silence.

In his bedroom, Charles sighed and snapped closed the book of which he had been unable to read a page.

# Chapter Five

"I feel humble," Matthew beamed. "No, truly," he joined in the wave of friendly laughter as it ran around the packed Meditation Hall. "I look around and see so very many friends; my family, my very own family. And, like other families, there comes a time when some of the children grow up and want to leave home, to follow education, career, a relationship, or an inner drive to travel and to grow that has no greater identity."

This was the last, grand, public convocation. Almost everyone who had any connection with The Programme – whether formally admitted as an Acolyte or not, all the way to The Teacher and The Seer – was present, excepting only those in the States and the handful who remained on Coffee Lounge and reception duty.

It was billed as a Midnight Meditation, the public version of their private Midnight Masses. Anyone could attend a Meditation; it was one of their income-generating activities – a charge of two pounds was made, and many people paid more voluntarily – and one of the events from which recruits could be culled. Normally, there would be from five to fifteen who could be identified as outsiders – casual visitors to the Coffee Lounge or friends of regulars – or who were still on the fringe, the Hall otherwise filled with resident Initiates and Junior Messengers.

The Hall occupied the massive front-room of the house. It was where parties would once have been held, or dinners: these had been the town-houses of the very rich; they could not replicate their country homes with separate dining rooms and living rooms each large enough to hold a weekend party of twenty guests and more, but they all had one grand room which could be turned to either use. Later, occupied by diplomatic missions or international corporations, they would be used for formal receptions.

This one was fifteen feet high, thirty-five feet across the whole frontage of the house, twenty feet deep; the walls were interspersed with alcoves which once had housed statues and which The Programme members had decorated with murals. The original chandeliers had been swathed in translucent, ballooning silk which cast two orbs of gentle, glowing red like moons in the sky against the dancing multi-colours of the ceiling. The floor was parquéd; the windows had been double-glazed and were hung with thick drapes to ensure that neither sound nor light filtered onto the street.

At a normal Midnight Meditation, there might be thirty or forty people seated cross-legged on the ground or on cushions, in a semi-circle that did not crowd the furthest wall of the room where the Superior conducting the meditation would be enthroned. Tonight, the Hall was jammed. For some weeks, the date had been announced: on posters in the Coffee Lounge, on display advertisements in the most recent magazine, and on flyers stuffed into the booklets they sold in the street, left on Coffee Lounge tables and ostentatiously piled alongside the reading material for sale in the basement foyer.

The flyers, advertisements and posters all bore both the symbol of The Programme and the familiar, Christ-like portrait of Matthew, together with a shadowy black-and-white photograph of Cassandra, deliberately out of focus, in profile, gazing into the distance, above the proud announcement that both The Teacher and The Seer would be in attendance and would conduct portions of the Midnight Meditation. This was to be the ultimate Meditation in Growth: The Programme was expanding, opening a Chapter in America; it was the last opportunity to share with all of its members the experience that had assembled into a movement.

The presence of The Teacher would have been enough to guarantee an audience larger than usual; with the added attraction of The Seer and the knowledge that this was some kind of last chance, the resident membership had rightly anticipated the largest gathering of all time. There were nearly a hundred and fifty people crammed into the Hall. By the time Matthew and Cassandra arrived in their flowing robes, heralded by Superiors, followed by Senior Messengers, there was barely room for a corridor through which they could reach their stage. The room was a sea of white: even the unadmitted had sought to wear white for the occasion; even The Seer.

Pressed against a wall, straining to contain her panic – near claustrophobia – at the crowd, even Carey, personally invited by Matthew to attend The Programme at its most complete, had unconsciously chosen clothing that was predominantly white.

As she just managed to watch Matthew make his way to the other end of the Hall, she struggled not to be overtaken by her confusion. She was not a member of The Programme. On the other hand, she had started to spend a lot of her evenings at Chesterfield Gardens, some of them in the Coffee Lounge, some of them in one of the private rooms talking with Matthew. She would no longer describe herself as a sceptic; whatever The Programme was, it brought comfort and peace to what seemed like – as this gathering proved – a large number of people, none of whom had yet struck her as reluctant members, oppressed or trapped into membership.

She had gone back to the Coffee Lounge after the first time on impulse. She did not ask for Matthew and if he was in the building, either no one told him she was around or else he did not want to see her. Despite this, she enjoyed herself, found it easy to strike up conversations with other visitors, junior members. There was little small talk; complete strangers slipped into inner feelings and fears, emotional experiences, tales of parental traumas. Occasionally, a member would draw the discussion into Programme-speak: this person was acting out an authoritarian impulse, believed he was a chieftain – in the Cabal, a guardian of nations; that one was in a phase they called cherubic, personification of goodness; Sister Rebecca was a nun and Sister Meredith – Merry – a social worker; Father Caleb was only ever mentioned in a whisper, Satan himself.

At times, she felt patronised: some people assumed an aura of seniority, even amongst those who were not members, offering explanations and acting with excessive familiarity. They were students or artists or straightforward drop-outs. She admitted her own occupation only reluctantly, with a nervous laugh: it felt totally out of place in the casual, formless atmosphere of the Coffee Lounge where people came to explore and to find themselves, not to boast of what they had already become.

When she told him, on one of her visits, Matthew told her:

"It's their embarrassment, not yours. They don't like the idea there are people around The Programme who have already achieved so much more than they have; it's straightforward competitiveness."

"I would have thought," she said lamely, meaning she would have thought they were beyond such petty resentment.

"It goes; in time, it goes. But don't make the mistake of thinking that what everyone does in The Programme is the same. We try to value it equally; but for most people it's a struggle."

"Isn't it a cause of, well, dissension, tension?"

"Sure, but it's what is. We work with it; use it; treat it creatively. Anyway, it's not for you."

"What do you mean?" she asked, flustered.

"I don't see you serving customers in the Coffee Lounge."

Nor did she.

She continued to visit in the evenings or at the weekend, and drink coffee or tea or one of their marvellous concoctions. Sometimes, instead of the legal journals she used to read in bed last thing at night, she would read one of The Programme publications, torn between cynicism and a gnawing sense that Matthew had it just about right, that his descriptions of how people functioned and what they represented fit too many she could recognise – herself included – to be brushed aside as coincidental.

\* \* \*

From *Programme and Progression*:

*All thought-systems – religious or rationalist – are trying to provide us with the complete understanding of life and of ourselves, not "a" complete understanding, but "the": yet all of them complete the comprehension by reliance on mystery, the inexplicable or that which simply has not yet been resolved. Indeed, some can be said to base comprehension itself on the inexplicability of life, called anything from soul to human spirit.*

*What we believe in The Programme is that you can look at life from any of these different points of view and what you will see is essentially the same: an infinite number of acts, impulses, intentions or thoughts, fit into categories in some sort of order, squeezed into a framework of thought in order to be able to say – "yes, see, our way is complete".*

*Nothing and no one exists in a precise or static fit to a pre-existing model – whether it is of a religious persona, a philosophical approach or a psychological type: no approach claims otherwise. None the less, each model purports to provide and to prescribe a method for comprehending life – on earth alone, or on earth and beyond. Ultimately, each is unsatisfactory because there will always be experiences which – or individuals who – do not and cannot be made to fit in anywhere. It is as if we are all seeking to complete a million-piece, plain white jigsaw: while there are different ways of piecing it together, none of them uses up all of the pieces, and none of them makes a complete whole.*

*This is the best way to imagine The Programme's view of life. Think of a globe, made up of billions of tiny strands, each a complete circle in itself, each constantly revolving so fast it is barely discernible to the eye. When a religious analysis is inappropriate, a strand of philosophy or psychology comes around. Types only exist in transience, as strands in common for a period of time. That which defines a person – or an experience – is the peculiar complex of strands of the moment. Beneath the surface, though, there are hidden strands, and hidden combinations, and – always – a new combination about to emerge.*

*The essence of The Programme as a thought-system is awareness of the constant change in ourselves and in one another, of the way we are comprised of numerous, contradictory, apparently irreconcilable aspects; not different parts performing different functions, but all with an equal claim to our names (even if, at different times, some are ascendant and others in abeyance). Where we believe we differ from others is in this: we do not seek to pin each other – and events – down for once and all in order to complete the jigsaw; our comprehension is based on movement, dynamism, change.*

*We do not believe that there is a single theory within which we can understand and analyse life and so we do not believe we should try. Comprehension comes from within; comprehension changes as we change; we set our minds to follow and flow with the changes; we accept that there is a comprehensive whole – but we reject that it is something that can be reduced to words or thoughts or ideas; they are themselves a part of the whole therefore they cannot (wholly) comprehend it. (The room from within). We can only be it.*

*The Programme as an organisation seeks to do just this: to be a cradle in which people can gather together, microcosmically, to be – to be in order to comprehend, macrocosmically. We believe that one day, perhaps for just one moment, all of the aspects of life will come into perfection, the perfect expression of the energy with which it all begins and ends; one moment it will be as far away as now; then a tiny – perhaps barely discernible – step, and it will be back in perfect order. When it happens, it will be done.*

*Hence: I am one; we are many; together we shall be whole.*

\* \* \*

Matthew said:

"I am one."

"We are many," the congregation replied, Carey amongst them.

Matthew said, beaming, almost laughing, rumbling from within: "I feel humble."

Carey joined in the amused reaction. Humble was not a word one applied to The Teacher: both humility and arrogance were superfluous, he had told her; just be what you are, and do what you do; don't explain, don't excuse; how others respond is their own choice, for which you are not responsible.

"Ten or so years ago, when what we call The Programme began, I don't think any of us who were privileged to be a part of it would have suspected that we could find ourselves in an assembly such as this; nor would we have expected to be on the verge of such a giant adventure as opening a new Chapter across the Atlantic, expanding our range a thousand times over, opening the way to undreamed of dimensions, unheard ideas.

"People sometimes ask me why I'm always a bit vague about when The Programme started. Perhaps they think I have something to hide. It's much easier than that. I do not say because I do not know. I am not even sure that it is correct to refer to The Programme as starting, because that implies there was something before it, something may come after it, that it is something that is separate. That is why I prefer to talk about what we call The Programme – meaning our group, our organisation, our space, our home, our way – as distinct from The Programme itself, which is all space, in every way, all that there is and that there can be, the ocean into which the river flows, and yet from which it sprang.

"But over a period of time – and over a long journey taking in a number of countries – we began to feel a sense of something, a way to live, and where it came from I cannot tell you, any more than I can tell you where it is going. It is about being together and going where that leads us, even if sometimes it seems as if it is leading us apart. The bigger we grow, the more directions we can take; the more directions we take, the more we have to offer, the more people will be able to find within The Programme, the greater the hearth and the heart. What we're about is warmth: that's what we have to offer each other; the warmth of certain support for whatever direction we feel we need to take.

"So when I look around and see so many people here tonight, I feel proud, and because I don't like feeling proud, I decide to feel humble. Actually, what I feel is an enormous warmth, a positive heat that comes from you, a fire that some may think threatens to devour but that I see as energy or fuel, the fire left behind by a space-ship taking off: watch the television shots, everyone is looking up in awe, everyone wants to be on board.

"Of course, few would be willing to mount the craft if invited. Most people would be scared. I doubt they would be scared of the launch, though doubtless they would be – and should be – in awe of anything so mightily powerful and it is well-known that it is the most dangerous part of a mission. But they would be much, much more scared because they did not know where they were going. Space is infinite, the largest concept we can think of; terrifying because we

113

cannot possess it or control it; it is the most frightening concept we can entertain because we cannot define it.

"I like to think that is what we are doing now. Of course, Boston is not the moon; it is not even Mars. For one thing, the food is a lot better." He chuckled, encouraging them to laugh: he did not want them to leave tonight without laughter to remember. "But we're not going to Boston. Oh, of course, many of our members are: The Seer is leading the mission and will lead the new Chapter when it opens and where The Seer goes, go we all. But Boston is just another point on the globe, it could be anywhere: The Programme is growing, touching down perhaps in Boston, but extending the parameters of its presence on earth to mirror a much larger portion of that whole, infinite being of which we are but a small part, and to become at one with which is the whole of our purpose.

"I see this mission as a launch-pad into inner space; we are stepping out from the defined limits of the space-ship in which we have been journeying hitherto, into an unknown, like diving into the ocean from a tiny fishing vessel or exploding like a fireworks display in the sky. Look up from Boston Common and you will be able to see us; you need only believe that back here we, too, will be looking up to the sky and watching you in return, and we will be. Those are the images of light that I want you to take with, while we will be the light left burning in the window. You are the fire beyond, and we will be holding out our hands to your warmth."

From laughter, he moved them to tears. He half-turned towards The Seer and held out a hand; she took it as they exchanged vows.

"I am one."

"We are many."

"Together we shall be whole," they ended in unison.

"I want you to close your eyes, now," said The Seer, still holding Matthew's hand. "We shall descend together, as one, towards the fire beyond of which The Teacher has spoken, by its flames we shall be devoured and in its ashes we shall be spread, from its sparks we shall grow anew. I want you to close your eyes now, breathe deeply now, breathe in, let it out slowly, let it go, let it flow, watch yourself approaching the fire, you are not afraid, it can only warm you, it can only release you, it can only bring us freedom."

\* \* \*

After the meditation, and after they had hummed and hugged together, Matthew conducted a novel but poignant ceremony of re-admission, during which he promised each and every individual member of The Programme – Superior, Senior and Junior Messenger, Initiate, Acolyte – the opportunity to join him in a spiritual adventure, a voyage into the unknown, to explore not the aspects of themselves with which they were already familiar, but the most unknown aspects of themselves, the hidden halves without which they could none of them be whole, without which The Programme itself could not be whole. In return, he procured their commitment to the journey: unquestioning, unqualified, unrestrained.

This, he reminded them, was the meaning of the exchange.

"I am one; we are many; together we shall be whole."

He started with The Seer; then the Superiors, one by one. Watching, Carey wondered at the way the exact same words could sound so different. The Seer's iteration of the exchange was a sensuous promise; Father Caleb's sneer converted the words into a threat; Mother Naamah poured them like a delicate sauce; Father Simon was distinct, with pride in each word; Father Christopher doled them out one by one. Matthew was teaching them: what it means is different to each of you.

As he moved from Superiors to Senior Messengers, they came forward in matched pairs: two here were pious, apparently resigned yet vibrant with virtue; another couple were defiant, they belonged but they were proud of their independence; some were simply serene. Then the Junior Messengers in ranks of four; the massed Initiates in packs of six; the Acolytes in groups of ten at a time. When they had all passed before The Teacher, he said:

"Are there those present who wish to come forward?"

This was the opportunity for those who had not yet made their commitment to join The Programme at the hands of The Teacher himself, the last chance to submerge themselves into The Programme gathered together in one place and at one time. Carey watched in surprise as many other members of the congregation stepped forward through the corridors left by existing members; she realised that it had been pre-arranged, that they had already indicated an intention to join this night, had been positioned in the Hall to be able to respond to Matthew's invitation.

Surprise gave way to another sensation. She was jealous, wistful, resented being an outsider; she was almost tempted to follow them to stand in front of Matthew and receive around her neck the chain on which hung The Programme symbol and exchange vows with him. She reassured herself – you're a lawyer; people like you don't join. It was small comfort.

\* \* \*

Colin waited in the bar at his gym for his squash partner to join him for a post-match drink, ignoring the dull background thump of beat music in the gym itself: the bar was plain and quiet, a place to wind down.

Unlike his sister, he was not a heavy drinker. He did not like the loss of control. His father had drunk too much. He did not want his own children to overhear violent arguments, blowing up out of nothing, casting a pall over the next day and sometimes weeks on end.

Andrew Chettle finally emerged from the locker-room, his hair still damp. Currently between wives, he had a date lined up for whom he had replaced the suit in which he had arrived with smart casual to complement his blow-dried blond locks and the boyish sheen on his cheeks. Colin joked:

"Teeny-bopping?"

Andrew stuck his tongue out, ordered a vodka-tonic at the bar, clinked glasses with Colin's.

"Good game."

"You always say that when you win," Colin complained. "And that's too often by half."

They had been at Cambridge together; shared a flat. Then at the College of Law for their professional examinations. They had gone on to their separate firms but stayed friends, had been each other's best man. Andrew had achieved great success, heading up a team in his firm that specialised in European work.

After Andrew's divorce, Jan had tried him out on a handful of her available friends. Andrew wanted his youth back, lusting after newly qualifieds and trainees, pretending it had nothing to do with his partnership status and the influence he could wield in their behalves, admitting to Colin he didn't give a damn why they found him attractive so long as the line was long enough that he couldn't see its end.

"What time are you meeting, uh, what'shername?"

"I'm not sure," Andrew twirled his glass in front of his face. "Annette, I think."

"And Annette does what?" He held up a hand to forestall the obvious. "For a job."

"BBC," Andrew said.

"That's a change."

"Not really; in-house lawyer, looking for a move."

They chit-chatted for a while until Andrew suggested a second drink.

"Just for once. Go on. Do something different."

"Why? I like being boring and predictable."

"It's not the only Colin I've known."

Andrew was leading somewhere. Curious, Colin accepted another beer without any intention of finishing it.

"Spit it out," he invited.

Sometimes, when he was with Andrew, he slipped back to another time, the other Colin to whom Andrew had referred: looser, easier on himself and on others, funnier. He started to laugh just ahead of Andrew's bawdy response.

"No, actually, she doesn't."

"Will you ever grow up, Andrew?"

"Like you? Have you?"

"I think so. I'm not sure, you know, that it was all quite as deliberate as it seemed, or maybe I mean that I didn't it to happen so fast, but, uh, well, here we are, wife and three monsters, what can you do?"

"It's not a lot of freedom," Andrew agreed. "Especially not on your sort of income."

"We get by," Colin acknowledged that his friend was right: it was hard to keep up with, let alone get ahead of, the game – schools, cars, house expenses, nannying, tax, holidays, if he added it up in round figures it exceeded his regular annual income by a significant margin. Hence his dependency on pay-out of profit.

Feeling the moment still wasn't quite right to broach his subject, Andrew asked after Carey: they'd gone out a couple of times; once for fun, the second time to check it was nothing more.

"It's all right for her," Colin joined together the two strands of conversation. "She doesn't have the outgoings."

"Presumably, when your father finally lets go, the firm is worth quite a bit in capital?"

"The building, sure. The library. It's difficult to estimate the goodwill value without Charles, though."

"Don't underestimate your own value, Colin."

Colin raised an eyebrow: mutual admiration was rarely spoken.

"They're both still too young for you, just," he joked his way out of his embarrassment. "If you're, uh, asking for a hand in marriage."

"Actually, Colin, it's a different kind of proposal I wanted to talk to you about." Andrew had finally, circuitously, arrived at his destination.

Colin waited in silence.

"Last time we met, you were talking about some work you wanted to tender for? What happened with it?"

"What do you think happened with it? Daddy didn't want to get his hands dirty on the money of the oppressor before he went off to the workers' paradise of Antibes for his pre-season holiday."

Andrew was too used to the bitterness to be shocked or disturbed.

"I've been wondering how long you'll hang on, doing the same thing, under the parental thumb and all that."

Colin's eyes narrowed, trying to identify the direction the conversation was taking:

"I'm beginning to feel head-hunted," he prodded.

"There's a small group of us, at the office. We're beginning to weary of 'big is beautiful'. Actually, we're sick to death of it." The guiding principle of the major law firms was size.

"You, Andrew? I thought you were set for life. You?" Colin studied him shrewdly: the other side of growth was downsizing; many of the firms who had aimed too high had been forced to let some of their number go.

"I'm fine. I'm niche. I'm even, dare I say it, safe, so far as anyone ever is. Most of it is work that'll follow me. I've got a few choices," he added.

"How many are there of you?"

"About half a dozen, give or take. You know how it is: people like to talk; somewhat fewer like taking chances; we're cautious, conservative people, lawyers. Half a dozen is my best end estimate."

"Are they all in your area?" Despite himself, Colin felt himself growing excited: Europe, where the future lay; expansion.

A burst of laughter from another table broke into their line of discussion. The lads were out in force tonight. Colin rose and went to the bar. He brought Andrew back another drink, and himself a tonic water to replace the beer he had barely touched.

"Are we all right for time?"

"She's meeting me here." He glanced at his watch. "She'll be late; she always is."

"There must be plenty of firms who'd snap you up."

"It wouldn't achieve anything; just more of the same."

"Is there a fit?" Colin asked. "We're still predominantly legal aid, crime, civil liberties. At any rate, that's the reputation."

"The reputation you don't want to be limited to," Andrew reminded him.

"Maybe. But what's in it for you?"

"Size; location; property; a friendly face I can trust long-term; very long-term. Besides, you've got some good people: Engel, Preston; I can work with them; there's overlap."

"And some people you'd want to eat for breakfast."

"So?"

Colin shook his head in admiration.

"You've been saving it all up, haven't you?"

"Every word of it," Andrew confessed. Every comment about every difficulty, and every difficult solicitor, that Colin had confided in his friend had been stored on disk until there was enough material to make into a programme.

"It's a lovely fantasy, Andrew, but it's off the map. Too damned many obstacles."

"Apart from Charles?"

"Charles and Alistair Mathison." He paused. "Alison Hansen. Carey, too, I would have thought: she wouldn't like the change."

"Ah, Carey," Andrew said wistfully. "No, it couldn't be done without her."

Before Colin could respond, a pretty girl of about twenty five approached, long athletic legs balanced on high heels, her blouse a button too open, eyes wide, lips glossy, smiling worshipfully at Andrew.

"I'm late. I'm sorry."

"Come and meet Colin. Annette, Colin. Colin's my oldest friend." He scowled at Colin. "And don't you dare say Annette's my youngest."

Colin rose to shake her hand but did not sit down again, trying to avert his eyes from her blouse.

"I was just leaving."

"Stay and have another drink," Andrew demanded, knowing Colin was already well beyond his self-imposed limits of alcohol and of time.

"Please do," Annette imitated with apparent sincerity.

"I have to get home; Andrew's worn me out."

"Hard match?"

"No. Not that," Colin offered a hand to his friend. "Let's lunch, shall we?"

\* \* \*

Then they were gone and everything was tranquil. The Coffee Lounge seemed emptier, though there were as many customers, but there were fewer Initiates and Junior Messengers waiting on them.

Sister Lilith had been left behind, which Carey welcomed: there was a relationship between them, as if Lilith's first night welcome meant more than the mere accident of passing through the foyer at a particular moment.

Sometimes, instead of spending time in the Coffee Lounge, she would sit with Lilith on reception: they talked for hours on end, rarely interrupted by calls or callers, much as Carey had talked with Emily, much as – she supposed – she had spent time at university or at the College of Law talking with friends, about this and that and nothing they could remember the next day, exploring the sound of her own thoughts more than the reply. Carey was no longer an outsider or a stranger; nor was she a member. She had a special status, as the group's solicitor or Matthew's; she cherished it and managed simultaneously to feel guilty about it.

Sister Lilith told her about her background. She was by qualification a State Registered Nurse, working in her hometown of Detroit, across the border from Windsor, in Canada. A couple of years before, she had been involved in an incident in the operating room: a patient had died in the course of a procedure that was designated routine. Accusations had flowed around the hospital like blood from a shotgun wound. Complaints had been filed against both Lilith – it was her own name, not a Biblical alias – and another nurse: anyone but a doctor who cost twice as much to train.

"They blamed you?" Carey guessed.

Lilith shook her head, square and determined.

"Uh huh. They blamed the doctor."

"So?"

"I couldn't figure, how come they spent more money finding out who was to blame than the cost of the operation: I mean, mistakes happen. You know?"

"So?" Carey repeated, despite herself ever the lawyer.

"So, I was just worn out by it. I mean, don't you ever feel just worn out by something – even if it's not your fault, even if you're not to blame? I mean, what's the big deal about blame – what's its street value? You know, sometimes don't you just look around and say, ugh, what kind of a game are we playing?"

"Every day. I'm a lawyer."

"Is it right, what they say, it's just a game? Law?"

"Sometimes. But a lot of the time, what happens is real, terrifyingly real, and you know that it's going to have an influence on the rest of the client's life. It's hard to think of that sort of thing as a game, whether it's a divorce settlement, a job settlement, a housing dispute, a claim for personal injuries or whatever. Very little of it is a game to the clients, you know?"

"Sure," Lilith said softly. "Or to a patient."

They sat in silence, each side of the reception desk, Lilith protected by it, Carey overshadowed by the portrait of Matthew.

"From there to here?" Carey asked.

"I sold my car, my stereo, my TV, most of my clothes, everything I owned really. I jumped my last month's rent, too, which doesn't make me proud, you know. I took the train to Montreal, flew into Paris, travelled around Europe on a train. I, well, I did some things I'm not sure I'm that proud of – guy things – and I managed to end up here, wondering whether to spend my last few bucks on a flight home or a score," of dope. "I met Merry in the street, selling the magazine, and I told her to fuck off, actually, I didn't want any religious shit to complicate it all."

Carey jerked back in her chair: she had been around enough to be appalled at the idea of telling a Messenger to fuck off.

"What happened?"

"Merry said right, who needs it? Let's go for a coffee. Just like that. I was a complete stranger and she just said, screw it, what she was doing was less important than whatever pain I was in. I guess that's about the whole story. A week later I was washing up in the Coffee Lounge kitchen; a month later, I was a member. I haven't thought about much since; I've been enjoying myself, you know; it's warm, there's so many people around."

"I can't see myself, well, you know, joining something – oh, like this, anything."

"So don't. No one expects you to join, anyway."

"What do you mean?" This was Carey's first feed-back on how Programme members saw her.

"Oh, you're a lawyer, and you're Matthew's lawyer, you're not like, well, someone off the street. Maybe you don't need the same things as the rest of us. You've got this, like thing with Matthew: The Programme's his thing; you're like, well, I don't know, what I'm thinking is like when we had a new med. student at Buffalo South – where I worked – you could see some of them were fast-tracking. That's you: on a fast-track to the top."

Carey was halfway between being flattered and appalled.

"It's still joining, though."

"No, it's not. One thing's joining The Programme; the other's about joining Matthew. Do you see?"

Carey nodded, confessing:

121

"I know what you're saying. It just seems so, well, er, amazing, really, that you can just come out and say it?"

"We don't have any secrets here. Conflicts, sometimes, maybe; secrets, no. That's what I like about it."

"About anything?"

"Not that I'm aware of," Lilith laughed at the contradiction. "Go on: ask away."

Carey took a deep breath.

"All right, then. Matthew. He and, er, Cassandra, they're not, well, together. Right?"

"Right," Lilith grinned cheekily. "You've got a thing for him?"

"Of course not; he's a client." Carey was blushing.

Lilith's laughter was infectious: despite herself, Carey joined in.

"You must be the only one, then," Lilith said.

"It frightens me. Only, I don't know what I mean: Matthew or The Programme. All this, er, Satanic-type stuff. You know, God and Satan, two halves of a whole. It does, it frightens me." Flashes of Marion, on her knees in a church as Carey had never witnessed but often imagined, praying to a wrathful God: flashes of herself, on her knees before God, asking for forgiveness; a flash of herself, naked, kneeling before Matthew, as she had erotically fantasised. "People like me, we don't join, er, well, cults, you know?" She repeated the thought she had at the Midnight Meditation.

"And people like me do?"

Carey barely heard her answer. She was thinking, as soon as the words had left her mouth, of the countless lawyers she had known who she had heard one way or another had given it all up, suddenly as it always seemed though doubtless it reflected months or years of inner debate, defeated by the aridity and the aggression and the arrogance of the job.

"The religion puts me off," Carey admitted.

"It's a metaphor, just a metaphor," Lilith reassured her. "What do you think? Can you see me, or, say, Rebecca or Merry engaged in some, I don't know, what do you think? A Satanic ritual, for Christ's sake? How about Mother Naamah?" The most ridiculous image of all.

"Of course not," Carey said quickly, suppressing the image of death stepping from a dark alley. She shuddered, hoped Lilith had not noticed, hurried along. "I suppose, what I'm saying, I suppose I agree with a lot of what The Programme teaches – about demons within, the impulses we all keep hidden; it frightens me – well, you know, to let them out."

"Like the man says – you have to let them out of the dark to see them."

"What about Matthew?" Carey asked hotly, suddenly bold. "What about his dark side?"

Lilith was less disturbed by the question than Carey had expected.

"It's not my business. Sure, he's got a dark side too. We all have. I've seen him be cold, dark, unforgiving. Perhaps cruel. We're not talking about him as a man; he's The Teacher."

"But without Cassandra, The Seer? What is he?"

"Tell me what you're asking about?" Lilith said patiently. "The Teacher or Matthew?"

"I don't know," Carey answered plaintively. "If I knew, I probably wouldn't ask."

Lilith rose and stretched. She came around the desk, stood behind Carey, lowered her arms around her and rocked her from behind, the back of Carey's head pressed against her breasts.

"I wish I had your answers for you. There are times, you know, you sound so like the questions I used to ask."

Carey held onto the other woman's forearms.

"I'm just trying to sort it all out, that's all."

Lilith returned to her seat, as if she had reached a decision.

"Did you meet a Messenger called Helen?"

"I think so; briefly. American, no Canadian. Tall? Blonde? Thin? Beautiful," she concluded reluctantly.

"You could have been describing yourself."

In her answer, she had communicated what Carey wanted to know. Carey asked:

"And now?"

"Helen has gone to the States," Lilith answered simply.

"Which means?"

"We pass in and out of each other's lives. We make what we make with each other until we're not making it anymore. Helen's gone with The Seer: The Teacher sent her. That's all I know."

* * *

She could not leave Patrick hanging in the wind. One morning, as she went out to court, she left a note for him saying simply – "Dinner?". When she returned, he had returned the note to her, with a tick through its one word, throwing the burden back onto her to decide when. She rang him from her room, instead of going through to his.

123

"Tonight?"

"Okay."

They both hung up, one dry with apprehension, the other with stale anger.

It was taken for granted that they would go out from the office once they were both finished working. She went to fetch him soon after seven. He was studiously turning the pages of a file, filling time.

"Hi."

He smiled, came around his desk: she hugged him quickly, kissed him on the cheek.

"Where are we going?" he asked: her date.

"How about The Island Queen?" She suggested a restaurant above a pub in Islington, in her direction home not his.

They walked up in strained silence. Waiting for a table, she told him about Antibes, taking Emily with her and how it had surprised Charles.

"I'm not surprised. He's conventional that way."

"What? Making friends with clients? It's how he built the firm up. He's enormously proud of his old political clients. Most of them came to the house one time or another." More after Marion's death than before.

"I didn't mean that. I meant as a father; he's protective; he doesn't want to see you involved in something, well, I suppose I mean stressful."

"He shouldn't have encouraged me to be a lawyer," she quipped, sipping her wine: she had been drinking less and less since she had started to go down to The Programme – this was her first drink for a week; she could already feel it going to her head.

"Arnott?" The barman called out.

"Did he?" Patrick asked when they were seated, studying the short menu.

"Did he what?"

"Encourage you to be a lawyer."

The question confused Carey: of course he had; everyone knew that.

"I'm not so sure. I've always thought it was something you assumed he wanted; then in turn, that he assumed that you did. I've never heard you talk about it."

She shook her head, flustered, shocked: Patrick was right; it was a truth so simple she had not seen it for the trees. She had indeed taken for granted that it was what Charles wanted; and Charles had acquiesced in what he believed she did. The most major decision in

124

her life had never been taken; it had happened of its own accord, almost by mistake.

Patrick's face was impassive, neither apologetic nor triumphant. Inside, though, he was pleased: first blood.

"Do you think that was it? He didn't like the idea of my making friends with a, er, well, a battered woman I suppose he'd say, you'd say?"

"I should think so. All parents want their children to be safe, kept away from trouble – and troubled people." Second blood: she was a troubled person. "Wouldn't you?"

They ordered: fresh carrot and coriander soup followed by filo pastry filled with leek and brie on a tomato sauce base for her; mussels followed by pan fried leg of lamb steak for him. She was also eating less meat since she had been spending time at The Programme.

"No, I'm going to move on to water," she answered when he asked if she wanted more wine.

The look on his face made her laugh.

"Disappointed?"

"No. I'm pleased for you." It was her point though.

"I never thought about children, I mean, how I'd be with them."

"Do you really not want them, Carey?"

"Like Dad? God, no."

"What about Colin? He's managed all right."

"Yes, but I'd have to be Jan. Or find one."

"You're so," Patrick fumbled for the words, "you're so principled; you never make a move without deciding on the principle first."

"I'm comfortable with what I know. I don't want to move on until I'm sure it's right."

"Sometimes, though," he forked a mussel into his mouth and chewed on it before continuing: "It isn't the way to do things; not everything is about principles; some things are just for doing."

He was talking about them; she was thinking about The Programme.

As if he could read her mind, he asked:

"Tell me about The Programme, then."

"What do you mean?" They had only talked about it as a case.

He flushed, embarrassed by the indiscretion: Colin had mentioned to him that Carey was spending time at The Programme, probing how much Patrick knew about his sister's involvement.

"I just gathered, well, that you'd been hanging about it a bit."

"I don't know what to say, really. It's not clear what it is – whether it's a religion, a psychological theory, a therapy group or a cult. There are times when it turns me right off. And it's not hard to see that there are people who don't have the strength to thrive on their own who could be taken in by it. On the other hand, there are times I find myself thinking, well, yes, it's got a lot of the answers."

"It? What is it?"

"Whatever you want it to be. There's a lot written or talked about what they believe, and there's very little to disagree with: Matthew says he positively wants the common ground; common ground in what people believe and in what disturbs them. It all turns on his purpose, I suppose."

"His purpose? God's purpose?"

"I forgot you had such a down on religion." As if she had not herself often spoken out angrily against it.

"I'm not down on it; I'm down on what people do in its name. I'm comfortable with the idea that there's something more out there, that I come from something and that I'll go back to it, and if you press me on it, I daresay I'll admit to calling it God, but I don't need a mysterious American with long hair trying to look like Jesus, asking me to give him all my money and spend my life in his service just to prove he exists. He doesn't give his followers anything; he needs them to prove he exists."

"You talk like you know him."

"Just the type."

"That's what I find disturbing," she admitted. "He's like someone – well, something – that we're all familiar with, and yet of course he's not."

\* \* \*

At the Mayfair house, Matthew wandered the dark corridors. He was disoriented. He had wanted and had organised the separation, but he felt the departure more keenly than he could show.

He thought of Cassandra and the early days, the early adventures, the times when they had discovered there was nothing they could do to each other that would destroy their love or the group, from physical or mental games, through role-playing their deepest fantasies and acting out their most powerful ambitions, to dark ceremonies and the worship of gods of their own manufacture.

Had they been aware that they were building a world in which he was God and she his right-hand angel? Yes. Had they thought they were creating an environment in which others would let go of their self-control, and in doing so would become dependent on them? Yes.

126

Had they enjoyed watching members strip down to their basest elements and lay them in separate piles at their feet like tributes? Yes. Had they knowingly indulged their drives with the bodies of near-children without guilt? Yes. Had they known it was dangerous, that it would accommodate a Caleb or an Anthony Rockworth as much as a benign Naamah, a wise Merry, or an innocent Rebecca, and lead to cross-infection between them? Yes. Had they known people would do things they would never be able to forget, that they would become addicted to, so that they would have to stay in The Programme, self-made exiles from the outside world? Yes and yes again.

He scourged himself with his crimes and comforted himself with the knowledge that it had been without malice. Above all, he comforted himself with the realisation that it had worked, so many of them were happy together, had found a way to be with each other's pain and, thence, with their own. Yet he could not bury the fear that their offences had outweighed the gains, that they had laden The Programme with more pain than it could bear. Nothing they had done while forming The Programme had separated him and Cassandra; he was not sure, though, that The Programme itself might not be the one thing that could. The fire beyond.

He let himself into The Temple, mumbling automatically:

"I am one."

He answered himself:

"We are many."

He thought, but did not say aloud: "Together we shall be whole".

From a spring-door cupboard so flush with the wall of an alcove that it could not be seen, he extracted candles, bowls, bottles of oil. He set them around the giant floor-cushion which was The Temple's only furniture, sometimes its throne. He poured oil into bowls, placed lit candles within them, lick-spittles of light arose from the flames, the air was heavy with scent. He settled himself cross-legged on the cushion in their midst.

He wanted someone. He could not say who. Cassandra; Helen; Carey. He got up from the cushion, stretched. He pulled his sweater over his head, unbuckled his trousers, quickly stripped. He was tumescent, not hard. He stepped across and pressed himself flat against the painting of The Programme symbol, his cheek cold against the paper, then flung himself around so that he was facing the room, his back to the wall, arms outstretched, a crucifixion pose, humming desire.

He was not surprised when the door opened; he would have been more surprised had no one come.

It was the boy, Lucius, whom he had made Cassandra leave behind, like a hostage. Matthew wondered how many times Lucius had come to this room in the middle of the night, to be played with by his wife. He could imagine Cassandra sprawled across the giant cushion from which she taught, and on which Matthew would himself sit bethroned during a Midnight Mass, being fucked by youth, pretending the years were still not taking their toll, savouring the abuse of their most hallowed place. He grew hard at the thought, made no attempt to conceal it, focused on Lucius as the boy's eyes adjusted to the dull light until they caught and were held like a magnet.

Lucius pushed the door shut behind him. Said nothing. Licked his lips. This was a rough trade game from the hidden alleys of Soho, tiny mews where men met boys and did them in desperation propped against a wall or bent over the hood of a car.

Lucius stood before The Teacher, waiting, remembering.

"What do you feel?"

Matthew said:

*"Agony."*

Matthew smiled thinly. In a corner of the room, he imagined Cassandra crouched, robed again in red and applauding. He nodded to Lucius: the boy approached.

# Chapter Six

Carey arrived at the office. Messages from Colin – he had to see her – from Patrick – if she felt like a drink, a chat, trying to tell her he was still her friend – from Alistair – wanting a few moments later in the day. There were also messages from clients, counsel, opposing solicitors: they took priority; as long as she kept working, she didn't have to face up to anything else.

It was mid-afternoon before she had time to slip in to see Alistair.

She had known him all her life or thereabouts. Intermittently, she had been going to marry him: when she was four years old and sitting on his knee, when she was a pre-teen, finally at fifteen or so, between a couple of his marriages, for a whole month she had convinced herself the crush was for real. After that, she had grown up, he had seemed to grow no older, the gap was closing and the fantasy evaporated with it.

In its place, real warmth: she had turned to him with the doubts – professional and personal – that she could not confide in her peers or her supervisors, least of all in her father or her brother. He asked:

"How long?"

"Maybe half an hour, if I keep her waiting."

He buzzed for tea, pulled an upright chair over to the window for her to sit in, lowered himself into his own seat.

"Age before beauty."

His secretary brought in a tray: tea, two small plates bearing slices of creamy cake. She explained:

"Lesley's birthday."

"Goodie," Alistair rubbed his hands together. "Cholesterol."

"You could both use it," remarked his secretary tartly. "I went without," she added, patting an ample hip.

"Without what? A second slice?" Alistair teased.

She stuck her tongue out at him and left.

"Everyone loves you, Alistair," Carey said wistfully.

"Not for too long, though. You're my longest-lived affair."

"I wish," Carey replied, smiling.

"You're unhappy," Alistair got down to business.

"Am I? Where did that come from?"

Alistair shrugged, code for Charles. He added:

"I've seen you in better sorts."

"What did he say?"

"You know Charles. Personal things like that, well, he never quite says what he means."

"Nor means what he says," Carey responded tartly.

"Sometimes I think I'm worth more to this firm as a family therapist than a lawyer."

"We could have done with one. But if we'd been able to admit it we wouldn't have needed it."

"That really was what Charles said, though. Or meant to say. He said you were unhappy but I think he meant you were unsettled, taking shots, banging them out, hard shots to see what they hit. You must have struck him a few blows."

"It happens. Parents, children; it's not a big deal." She was not going to tell him the details.

"No, I suppose not: never had any children, remember."

"That's why you've hung around all these years. The firm's your child, we're your children – Colin, and me, and Charles."

"I'm not that old," Alistair choked on his cake at the last name. "Nor's he."

"True enough. But it's suited us all well; he'd never have kept his idealism alive if he'd ever grown up."

"You did," she shot back.

"No, I was never as much an idealist as Charles; intellectually, perhaps, we shared the same goals, but not emotionally. I liked the game, most of all; still do."

"What does he like?"

"Different things at different times. One thing after another. The politics; the people's champion; well," he hesitated then shrugged, it was old news. "Women."

"Coming from you," Carey protested.

"No, I said women. I only wanted one woman, one at a time, and when that didn't work out, I tried again."

"Serial monogamy? You were a man before your times. So was he."

"That's a mistake the young keep making," Alistair said. "They always think they've discovered things that people have been doing for years. It's like original sin, I suppose: it wouldn't be so much fun if you knew it had been going on since time began."

"What else?" Carey steered the conversation back to her father.

Like all conversations with Alistair, one point leapt off from another in a series of forks: it was easy to forget the way back to the main road.

"I think he's beginning to realise, the only thing you can finally have – completely, truly have – is love; the people he loves are you and Colin."

"And he thinks he doesn't have us? Phooey: perhaps he's got a problem with Colin – I'm not surprised; he's spent more time pushing him away then showing him affection. But he and I, well, we may squabble but we've always been close."

"I know. But it's been an odd sort of closeness, hasn't it? Fragile. As if it could be snapped like a twig, accidentally stepped on."

"He knows I love him."

"You can love someone and still not be close; I loved my father, but I don't think we ever had a personal exchange in our lives. I think he's frightened you're changing and that you won't be there for him anymore."

"What else?"

"What else? What else should there be?"

"Don't play with me, Alistair. What else did he say?"

"He didn't say anything else. But, well, there might be something else I've heard about."

"The Programme? This is about The Programme?" Not Charles but Colin. "God, and I always thought you said what you meant."

"Sorry. Doing the best I can. Not my sort of subject really."

She glanced at her watch: their time had gone and ten minutes more. She got up.

"What I do with my own time is my own business."

"And what you do with your life is mine," he shot back.

"Is it?"

"I always thought so, Carey; I always hoped so; I always hoped you'd be happy here."

At the door, calming down, she asked:

"But did you expect me to be?"

He didn't answer.

"I'll always love you, Carey."

"I know." She opened the door to leave, then popped her head back into the room. "Me too." It sounded more like a farewell than she realised she had been ready for.

\* \* \*

"I've been trying to ring you." Emily. Nearly one o'clock. Carey was just through the door.

"I've been out," Carey smiled, peeling off her jacket with her other hand, getting comfortable, settling down to talk. "I'm sorry." She realised how much she had been missing her.

"Where have you been?" Emily demanded.

"At The Programme," Carey admitted.

"I didn't know, well, you were still into that." As if, when she had faded from Carey's life, everything else ought also to have done so, at least until they caught up again.

"Oh," Carey sighed, "I don't know that I am." A long silence while she thought about what she had said, realised it was no longer true: it was beginning to take over her thoughts entirely, at least when she was not at work, nor when she was thinking about Emily herself.

"Richard rang," Emily announced. "Tonight. I saw him again." At work: after all, she had gone back to her job. "He wants to come round."

"He can't," Carey snapped back into lawyer mode.

"I know," Emily said. "He knows, too. He was lucky last time." The judge had sentenced Richard to three months for breach of the injunction, but suspended it so long as there was no repetition.

Carey picked up the sympathy in her friend's tone. She asked:

"Do you want him to come around?"

"God, no," Emily cried. "It's hard enough when he's not here." She was still vulnerable to him. "The further it gets." As the pain faded, and memories of the good times together resurged, she was worried she would weaken. "I'd like to meet up, Carey. I mean, if that's all right?"

"Me too."

"In France. I don't think I've ever felt that close to someone else. I mean, apart from Richard. It was frightening. Do you understand?"

Another long silence.

"I didn't want to be alone; I still don't," Emily added.

"Are you all right now? Do you want to come over? Do you want me to come over?"

"No," Emily answered languidly, reassured: "I just wanted to talk. Tell me about The Programme."

"I don't know really. Part of the time, I find myself really resisting it: then I think, oh, it's just a place, just people, somewhere that's different and kind. The main thing is, it doesn't make any demands of me. I go there and drink coffee and talk with people and that's all I have to do. It feels a bit like starting over: no one's got any expectations of me."

"I'd like to come."

"Come tomorrow; come tomorrow evening, say about eight? We

can eat; have coffee." The idea of someone with whom to share The Programme thrilled her.

"Tell me the address."

* * *

It was happening too fast. Later, she would find it difficult to arrange events in any kind of order: snapshots, not a video.

"Well, the food's nice. And the coffee."

"I didn't have time to eat today," Carey said. "The client treadmill. Some days seem like a tour of the legal system. It's hard enough to keep my own head above water. Let alone clients'."

Emily had dressed for her visit to Carey's hideaway with an aptness that took Carey by surprise. She looked casual and smart: neither dressed down to fit, nor up to stand apart. She was wearing a simple white blouse, no jewellery, short, khaki skirt, bare legs, flat shoes, negligible make-up: she was showing off her natural good looks and, despite her complaints, she was glowing. Carey told her so.

"I go through a dozen moods a day. Sometimes, if I'm in the wrong mood, I go into work looking like a nun; oh, not that smart; like a bag lady." Carey pulled a face: she doubted Emily ever looked like a bag lady. "At other times, I look at myself in the mirror and," she glanced around to make sure no one was listening: "I do feel like that, glowing, and I want to go out like that, the best I can be." She gestured towards her body. "This is part of me; this is what I am; I like this part of myself, I hate the way I have become so frightened of it. I don't want to hide it all away; it's hiding me."

"No one's stopping you; don't let him beat you." Carey thought it was about the worse choice of all possible words. She glanced at her friend, embarrassed: "Sorry."

"No, you're right, I did let him beat me." She leaned back in their upstairs booth, the one at the end where Carey usually sat, and took one of Carey's cigarettes. "So, what are we now, beatniks, hippies, left bank artists?"

"Something like that. We didn't do so well as career women."

"You've kept it together. I worry, sometimes, you've let us get close, you've let the thing with Richard get to you, I worry that's it's my fault what's happening with you."

"What is happening with me?"

"I'm not sure. When we were away, it was, well, one of the best times of my life. Even though, you know, I knew you weren't happy."

"Why does everyone keep telling me I'm not happy? In France, Dad said it; Alistair, our next most senior partner said it; Colin hinted at it. I am happy. Alistair was closer when he said I was unsettled. I'll tell you what I feel like: I feel like someone coming to the end of a terribly long prison sentence, and I feel excited and anxious, and I'm not sure how to behave, but the one thing I don't feel is unhappy."

Emily watched her, eyes wide with pleasure: Carey strong was how she had first seen her and begun to love her.

"Well, that's telling me."

"I'm sorry. I didn't mean to attack."

"No, it's fine. None of us really knows what we mean when we try and talk to our friends about what we think's going on with them – even when we're asked. We just use the words that come closest to what we see and hope it, well, punches a button." Emily giggled. "And to think, I haven't even had a drink."

"That's the power of The Programme," Carey laughed.

"Well, it is about letting go, isn't it? I mean, letting go of the conventions, letting go of our assumptions, our inhibitions, too. The freedom to be anyone you want to be."

Carey raised her eyebrows in surprise. Emily shrugged.

"Hey, you think you're the only one can surf the Internet?"

Their eyes met: if Emily had spent time finding out about The Programme, she had been finding out about Carey. Boldly, Carey asked, pursuing something Emily had referred to obliquely during their telephone call the night before:

"Is that why you came into my room in Antibes?"

Emily reddened, shrugged again.

"Perhaps. I don't know. I'm not, well, I mean, I don't think I am, I mean, I haven't ever, oh, shit, you know what I'm saying. But I didn't want to be alone, and I wanted comfort and, yes, I suppose I mean I wanted comforting physically."

Carey frowned: for a moment, Emily thought she had offended or upset her, shot to the edge of panic. Instead, Carey asked:

"Then why didn't you stay?"

"It's difficult to explain. I can't honestly say it wasn't a little bit sexual; but it wasn't, just the same. I mean," she stubbed her cigarette out angry that she couldn't find the right words, "I mean, I didn't want to, you know, do anything, well, you know what I mean." She was flustered beyond words. Carey reached across the table for her hand, held it. "That's right," Emily nodded at Carey's hand. "Like that. I wanted that. I wanted someone – you – to hold me, and stroke my hair, and be with me, and I wanted to be with you the way I said, with my body as well, not hiding it away or drawing an artificial line down the middle between lovers and non-lovers. Am I making any sense to you?"

Carey nodded, affected by the emotion and by Emily's candour.

"A lot. There are similarities with what The Programme is about, why I like being here; it's about different ways, for different bits of ourselves; and, no," she pre-empted, "I don't mean sexually, either." She waited a moment, then looked up, grinning. "So, you never answered my question?"

Emily looked confused for a moment, then laughed.

"Why I didn't stay?"

"Sure. Why didn't you?"

"Was it up to me?"

"Don't get out of it like that – a question with a question; I'll answer for me; you answer for you."

"How come you get to ask all the questions?"

"It's my job," Carey was still holding Emily's hand.

"I wasn't sure. At the last moment, I wasn't sure." She knew she was still being evasive, so she went on before Carey could ask again: "I wasn't sure it was all I did want."

"And you thought I'd mind?"

"Something like that."

"Is this a private love affair, or can anyone butt in?" Matthew asked, hovering at their table.

Carey and Emily burst out laughing simultaneously.

Emily asked:

"Is this place bugged?"

"Sit down, Matthew. I'd like you to meet Emily. She's the friend I went…"

"Yes, to France with." Matthew slid into the booth next to Carey, until their legs were touching, put one hand on Carey's and held out the other for Emily to take.

Spontaneously, and again simultaneously, Carey and Emily took each other's free hand, completing the circle.

\* \* \*

Http://www.the-programme.org.uk (turn on sound card if available).

*There are references to fear in more than fifty books of the Bible. Sometimes it seems to be all about fear. "I will send my fear before* thee," Exodus 23:27. Or: "Thou shalt not curse the deaf, nor put a stumbling block before the blind, but shalt fear thy God," Leviticus 19:14. And: "Ye shall not therefore oppress one another; but though shall fear thy God for I am the Lord your God," Leviticus 25:17. "Only fear the Lord and serve him in truth with all your heart," Samuel 12:23. "Fear is on every side," Jeremiah 6:25. "And I will give them one heart, and one way, that they may fear me for ever," Jeremiah 32:39.

It is the notion of the need to stick to a single route – one way – enforced by this fear of straying – that is fundamental to the traditional religions and that ultimately defeats them. Either because the complexity of life as we now perceive and experience it is simply not containable along a single line, in which case it is the religion that is rejected or because single-mindedness revolts against that complexity and seeks to turn the clock back by eliminating it. In the west, religion fails; in the east, modern society is put to the sword by fundamentalism; gradually, western social values are moving eastwards and fundamentalism into the west and where they cross shall be Armageddon.

The final holocaust is inevitable; no sane person – spiritualist or rationalist – believes that the world can continue the same blind rush to destruction without finally arriving. We see it happening every day: global warming causing seasonal change and the Arctic to melt, pollution causing breathing sickness and destroying the plant-life, feeding habits creating new diseases – for none of them do we have the beginnings of a solution. Meanwhile, around us, we decimate our numbers in genocidal wars, bursting into flame like bush fires with no apparent warning until – when we can ignore them no more – we tell each other it was a disaster waiting to happen. There is always an historical explanation – we never do anything about it in time.

The Programme looks on new ways – new routes – with enthusiasm; far better to pursue a different way of understanding than to push the present models to their logical conclusion. Not because we believe that the end can be averted, or even postponed, but because we believe that this is the only way we can survive through it. We do not want to build camps beneath mountains or in the wilds, like the physical survivalists who are fundamentalists by not much of another name; nor do we believe we can procure a science that will prevail; least of all do we think we can construct a philosophy that will prevent the inevitable – it is far too late for that, and we are far too small.

*If you believe that there is a soul, an energy – something more than the physical and intellectual environment that we describe as reality or existence – then the one task we can set ourselves, and that makes awaiting the end worthwhile, is to ensure that it is protected from the destruction ahead, that love outlives hatred, that belief outlives fear, that there will still be a life – transmuted, transcendental, transformed as it must be – beyond an otherwise total death. This is The Programme: it is a way to recreate the whole, to anticipate its dissolution and to be ready to liberate life at the very moment that death descends, to save the doves. All of us have a little bit of dove within; together, we can make whole doves to fly beyond.*

\* \* \*

"How are you, Andrew?"

Lunch. Simpson's-in-the-Strand. Carnivore heaven.

"I'm well, Charles," he rose awkwardly in the narrow space between bench and table to shake hands with his friend's father: he had known him since college days. "And you?"

"This is Alistair Mathison."

"I've heard a lot about you; I'm glad to meet you. Can I introduce Jessica Harvey? She's one of my partners and, well, part of my team." Jessica was a small, dark, attractive woman of about Andrew's and Colin's age, doing her best to appear nonchalant but on edge, glancing around nervously, failing to meet the men's eyes.

"And Colin makes five," Colin arrived, separately but only slightly late, holding out his hand to Andrew's partner and slipping in beside his father.

They made small talk until they had ordered but Charles had no intention of putting off the main conversation until dessert.

"Colin tells me you're planning to set up your own firm."

"Is that what he told you?"

Alistair concealed a smile: he already liked the young man.

Charles scowled to hide his own amusement.

"Among other things."

"Ah, well, then, we're on the same wavelength."

"I thought that was what we were here to find out?"

"We could certainly benefit from any advice you could give us."

"We sell advice, don't we, Andrew?"

Jessica, for the first time, looked directly across the table, at Colin, and studied his expression with wonder: as in, is he always like this?

Colin winked: they were just warming up.

"I've never really made up my mind about Europe," Charles said. "What is it that fascinates you about it?"

"It's there," Andrew said. "We can't make it go away. It doesn't matter if we're in or out: we're going to be dealing with it."

Colin studied the wine list and ordered without consulting anyone else.

Jessica asked quietly for a bottle of mineral water. Colin would have liked to talk with her, get a handle on their work that was not pitched by Andrew, he felt a sense of affinity with her: around this table, they were the junior partners. Jessica smiled to acknowledge the moment, then turned her head to remind him they ought to be paying attention to their leaders.

Andrew continued:

"Part of what made me think about Arnotts was the volume of European work we're involved in which touches some of your own: competition law, equal social and employment rights, environmental issues. We're also increasingly involved in Convention work." The European Convention on Human Rights.

"Even if it touches some of our areas of work, it doesn't mean we want the same things out of it," Charles replied.

"I don't think the future is necessarily about conflict," Jessica asserted herself. "Anyway, not the traditional conflicts between, say, employer and employee for example. The conflicts are much bigger, between whole industries and between nations. The employer and the employee want the same thing: the laws that suit them, in their industry, to allow them to make the most out of it for themselves."

"And you think that's right, that's the way it should be, do you?" Charles engaged amusedly.

"I'm a woman, Mr Arnott. It's not for me to decide how things should be. I just get on with things the way they are."

For a split second, no one else around the table knew how to take her answer, then Charles bellowed with laughter.

"That's right. None of us can, right, that's what you're saying?" Not even the great Charles Arnott himself.

"Something like that."

"So tell me what we have in common, Jessica? Arnotts and you."

"I don't know that we do have anything in common," she answered thoughtfully. "But if you take any more than half a dozen lawyers, none of them has that much in common with all of the others and yet you can put them together in almost any combination you like."

She paused to gather her thoughts:

"You've built Arnotts up on certain common principles, and you've got a lot of good lawyers doing similar types of work, but I can't help wondering how many of them are committed to doing that work for the rest of their working lives, how many of them are committed to it because they don't know anything else and perhaps fear they wouldn't make the grade elsewhere, how many of them are committed because they've got no intention of staying in the law and don't want to bother changing track before they quit, and how many of them are, well, perhaps simply scared of admitting they'd like to do something different – scared of admitting it to you, that is."

Charles scowled: she had diplomatically and prettily accounted for just about every member of the firm.

Andrew chipped in:

"If you want to keep a firm together, you have to provide plenty of space for people, plenty of room for growth and choice. We're lawyers; that's what stimulates us most of all: once we've mastered one game, we want to master another. The big firms have fallen into a trap: they have to keep turning the money over, they can't afford to miss an hour's billing time, so they don't give people that room for growth and change."

"And us? What's the trap we've fallen into?"

Colin said flatly:

"We're old and stale and we've nowhere new to go; damnit, Dad, it's just plain boring."

"You, Alistair? Are you bored, Alistair?" Charles took a last stab at the past.

"Bored? No. But criminal work's different; every case is different – at least the cases I do. I don't think you can say that about most of our other work. And, I'm not looking for excitement any longer: any more than you." The ones who mattered were the youngsters – like these three, with the greater part of their careers still ahead of them.

The waiter brought back the menus – Bills of Fare – from which to choose pudding. Alistair was alone in ordering from the selection of old English stodge, gleefully rubbing his hands together, repeating what he had said to his secretary the day before:

"More cholesterol. Bread and butter pudding, please."

Andrew and Jessica had fruit salad; Charles, English cheese; Colin, nothing. Over coffee, they mumbled about numbers: turnover, personnel, equity shares. Alistair was the first to leave: his solitary client of the afternoon awaited. Andrew took the hint.

"We should be getting back too. Before we're missed," he added, only half-joking.

"I'll ring you," Colin said.

"I suppose we're paying for lunch," Charles grumbled, signalling to a waiter.

"Are you in a hurry? I wanted a word."

"I've got time," Charles was surprised that Colin, too, did not want to get back to a billable hour.

"More coffee, please," Colin told the waiter, before his father could ask for the bill.

He slipped around to sit on the other side of the booth.

"What's on your mind?"

"I wanted a word about Carey."

"What's wrong with her?" Charles demanded.

"I'm not sure. I had a phone call. A rather odd call. Do you know Jack Gatehouse?"

"Everley Ashurst?"

"Right. It seems, they're against us on a matter Carey's been dealing with: divorce case; Fielding. The girl Carey brought down to the apartment."

"I wouldn't have thought that was Gatehouse's type of work. Or are they wealthy?" It had not been his impression. "Nice girl," he added.

"No and no. He's the Senior Partner, rang me as Managing Partner – and as her brother, I daresay. It seems, well, I'm not really quite sure how to put this. You've heard of this Programme thing?"

"That, what do you call it? Cult? Sect? Religion?" It rang a bell, but Charles couldn't say why.

"That's the one. We're acting for them." Charles would have seen the name on the client list which was circulated to make sure no one took on a conflict of interest by accident.

"What are we doing acting for people like that?"

"It doesn't matter," Colin brushed the question aside. "There's a freedom of religion factor, if you like."

Charles snorted: freedom of religion meant Marion; he was no more sympathetic than before.

"What's the connection?"

"Well, uh, Carey's been taking a bit more of an interest in the case than, uh, might have been expected. It seems, well, according to Gatehouse, basically, he was hinting Carey was some sort of fully-paid up member and, uh, dragging this Fielding girl into it."

Charles sat bolt upright.

"Balls. Bloody balls. Where does he get off?"

"I think, uh, they were under a lot of pressure from the husband to make something out of it. And, uh, you have to admit, it's not exactly the sort of thing that looks good."

"What did you say to him?"

"Nothing. I told him The Programme was a client; it was Carey's case; Carey and his client had become friends – hardly surprising she needed a friend the way her husband had treated her – that sort of thing." He grinned. "I told him he'd gotten hold of the wrong end of the stick and hinted in a friendly way there was a place he might like to shove it."

"And?"

"I don't know. I thought you ought to know about it. I, uh, it worries me, I admit."

"She's not a child. She knows what she's doing. Besides, how can you stop her? You know Carey." The last thing Charles wanted was an escalation in the recent tension between them.

"I know. I've been trying to decide what to do. I could take the case away from her?"

"Might as well beg her to get more involved." He shuddered. "Religion," he muttered darkly.

They sat in silence, equally out of depth. Colin studied his father. Quietly, he asked:

"What is it?"

For a moment, Charles was tempted to tell him: he knew something was wrong with her; she had not been willing to talk about it to him. It was too much to admit.

"Keep an eye on her, Colin. Don't let her, well," he drew in a breath, "don't let her do anything stupid."

It was the most he was going to say; Colin did not push him. Nor did he feel that Charles was ready to leave.

"What did you think of Andrew?" He meant Andrew's proposal; he knew his father had always liked his friend.

"I can't work up any enthusiasm for it, Colin; it's not for me; I can't see it, I can't feel it, damnit I just can't touch it. It's too abstract for me: my people have been on one side, and there's been an identifiable other side, as long as I've been practising – longer as a matter of fact. But I'm not going to stop it either, directly or indirectly," he glowered at Colin. "I mean it, Colin; you've got Alistair interested; get the others on your side and I'll stay out of it. Of course, I'll come back in on the financial negotiations," he added.

The last remark came as no surprise: Colin expected no favours; nor did he expect Charles to fail to protect either his own position at the head of the firm or his financial investment in it.

"All of the others?"

"Never happen, you know that. All those lawyers. It's as that girl – Jessica – said. No, just get enough of them and I'll stay out of it."

"And?" Colin persisted. "Enough means?"

"Ah, Colin: she's your sister; I wouldn't expect you to want to do anything that made her unhappy." He stared into his coffee, thinking: more unhappy.

Colin couldn't help himself. He burst out laughing.

"You're an old fox, Dad; you're banking on her, aren't you?"

To his astonishment and to his chagrin, when Charles looked up from his coffee, there were tears in his eyes.

"I meant it. I want her to have what she wants. It's about time, isn't it?"

Though Colin loved Carey, he was not above jealousy of her relationship with their father or his willingness to put her happiness first, within the sense of which he included the way Charles banked on Colin always to do what was best by her. It was a form of emotional blackmail so devious no one other than Charles could have carried it off. This time, Colin was certain he knew what was best for her and for them all and he was going for it regardless of anyone else, even Carey.

* * *

She felt like she was being summoned to the headmistress' study, but it was only her brother's. She had avoided him for days, angry about the conversation with Alistair and distracted. The firm had lost its grip on her; she was doing days in order to get over to Chesterfield Gardens at night. None the less, she did not entirely ignore the rumour-mill as it ground out the gossip: merger; new partners; new work. She knew too that Colin and Charles had lunched with Andrew Chettle.

Finally, Colin broke the deadlock and asked his secretary to arrange a mutually convenient time with Carey's for them to spend an hour together. They met formally, across his desk, barely a peck on the cheek when she arrived.

"I haven't seen you for a while," he probed.

"I've been busy," she murmured.

"Never stopped you popping in before?"

"I was annoyed with you," she came right out with it.

He nodded expressionlessly.

"If you'd wanted to talk to me about The Programme, you should have asked; you didn't need to get Patrick and Alistair to spy for you."

"The Programme? I, uh, barely mentioned it."

"Isn't that what this little talk is for?"

He smiled disarmingly but did not quite deny it.

"Which are you talking about? The case or The Programme itself?"

"The latter, I assumed. There's nothing new on the case; the jurisdiction hearing's next month. The New York lawyers want Matthew to be there. I'm thinking of going with."

"That's new, isn't it?"

"Maybe. I won't be away for more than a few days."

"Can they afford it?" He meant her time: he was checking she was going professionally not personally.

"They're surprisingly well resourced: there's an accountant – George Cohen – one of their members; he looks after their financial affairs. He knows what he's doing. You could check," she nodded towards his computer screen. "We've put in some good bills: they're all paid by return. You should be pleased: we could do with more clients like them."

For a brief moment, he was tempted to let go of his own agenda, come around from behind his desk, make her tell him what it was all about, how deep was the water she was getting into. His lips were dry: he licked them. He brushed the impulse aside: there were larger issues at stake.

"Perhaps a break would be good for you," he closed the subject.

"If it wasn't about The Programme, then what? These rumours?"

"Uh, yes, it's time I brought you up to date," he admitted. "I've been trying to do so for a while, but you haven't been around."

She nodded at the computer again.

"They talk." He could have e-mailed her.

"And people listen," he replied, meaning that they weren't safe.

"So? I'm here now."

He cleared his throat.

"Well, uh, there is something else, though. About the Fielding case."

"Emily? That's nothing to do with you.

"I am the Managing Partner," he reminded her.

"And I'm your sister; don't be pompous."

"I had a call: do you know Jack Gatehouse?"

"I don't think so."

Colin told her who he was, twiddling his pen.

"Okay."

"He wanted to raise something off the record; claimed to be doing me a favour; mentioned our relationship straight off." He sighed. "Uh, their client is making a little bit of noise about you."

"Sounds about right: I'm his wife's lawyer, and her friend; he nearly spent a season in the slammer. As far as I am concerned, he should have. I'm sure he knows Emily came to the apartment with me. It's not unethical, Colin, making friends with a client."

"You've, uh, been taking her to The Programme with you?"

"She's a grown woman; she's met me there a couple of times. She's happy there. I'm happy there. So what?"

"Well, apparently Mr Fielding isn't happy, and he's threatening to make waves about it."

"About what? Who cares what Richard Fielding thinks. It's none of his business what Emily does, or me."

"You can hardly pretend that The Programme... Uh, well, it's not quite a church bake-in, is it?"

"It's not illegal; and they are clients."

"Yes. That was what I told him."

She studied him calmly: he expected her to be first worried, then grateful; he was using the phone call from Gatehouse for his own purposes. They were best friends, they loved each other more than anyone else; it wasn't that time anymore; her heart was heavy; heavy but determined.

"So this was about The Programme, then? After all."

"Look, Carey," he replied heatedly, "no one's saying there's anything illegal about it, or, uh, unethical; but it could be an embarrassment. Especially at the moment."

"Ah, the moment." She lit a cigarette before looking to see if the ashtray he kept for clients and for her was on his desk, forcing him to extract it from a drawer, momentarily throwing him off his course. She was trying to get ahead of him: Colin wanted to keep her out of whatever was going on.

"Well, look," he began awkwardly, "I would have told you about this sooner if I could. In fact, I have been trying."

She brushed her hand through her hair: it was a struggle to care.

"You know Andrew Chettle of course. Yes, of course you do."

She interrupted impatiently:

"I know you and Charles had lunch with him. The place has been abuzz. I can add up. Though," she added indifferently, "I don't think it does."

"Alistair, too. Alistair was there; and he thinks it does."

"What are we talking about?" She concealed her surprise.

"Andrew's group, they're well, obviously this is entirely confidential; but they want to make a move. And he's approached me, us. I know it's not an obvious marriage, but it makes a lot more sense the closer you look at it. We need to grow and change: but every time we try, it offends someone here – more than a few. The idea is, uh, instead of taking on different client-groups, to expand the areas of law we do, without keeping on coming into conflict with each other. Just think about Europe in terms of our union clients, or environmental groups."

"What sort of package are we talking about?"

"Two full partners; four associates. A couple of support staff. We've got the space," he added. "Let's put it to use."

She was curious despite her lack of interest.

"Tell me what Daddy says."

Colin paraphrased her father's intentions: a promise to stay out of the fight; and, almost by way of afterthought, that he wanted Carey to be happy.

"And will there be? A fight, I mean?" She was angry that Charles' concern for her happiness had not been enough to make him discuss it with her directly.

"Oh, sure; take two lawyers... But, uh, with Alistair on-side, and Alison beginning to think it might work without causing her any client problems, well, it's do-able."

"I see," Carey crushed her cigarette in the ashtray. If Charles was intending to stay out of the fray, and if both Alistair and Alison were on-side, she would be the most senior dissident. She had his game plan now: if she spoke out against, he would use the Fielding call to weaken her support – the hint of extraneous influence, unreliability, an embarrassment in the offing.

Colin was missing by a mile. He didn't realise that she didn't care. He didn't need to manipulate her – do a Charles. It was hurtful – if he had spent a little time talking with her, it would have been unnecessary.

She threw him a vengeful scare.

"It's only the first step, though."

"Meaning?"

"Oh, I'm sure that it can be made to seem very attractive; obviously, if you can convince Alistair and Alison, you'll be able to convince others; and in principle, the way you put it, there's no reason anyone should object, even if, as you say, a few are bound to. But it alters the balance of the firm, and that's the key issue, isn't it? Europe's only the first step; the ones that come next are the ones that count."

"They're not fools; people see that."

"There's a difference, though. Between seeing it and having it spelled out. People aren't all one way or another – I'd say, give or take, most people are close to the middle on a lot of issues, sort of forty per cent committed one way and sixty another. What you're proposing, it's sixty-forty the other way. People don't look much further than the ends of their noses; especially lawyers. The prospect of what might happen in the future isn't enough to push them back over the line, but once the prospect becomes a reality, around a real issue, it'll be a different head-count."

He smiled thinly: she had summed it up correctly. She had the strength of character, and enough respect within the firm, to be able to pull them around: just as he had known and feared.

"All right, then: say that's true. You know all the arguments: we can't just stand still. How do you think we ought to be developing?"

"I don't. I think you've realised how I'm feeling, Colin. Alistair has, Patrick has, even Charles has an idea – you're not that stupid. I can't say, you know, that I'm ready to give it all up for good – being a lawyer or the firm. But I know something's changed, I've changed. I know I need more than the firm can give me, and I know I can't go on, feeling as empty as I have been. And, I suppose, whatever comes out of it, comes out of this period, I'm not going to want to go back to exactly the way things were beforehand. So, no, you're right, I don't need to keep things the way they always have been. Especially if Charles is willing to let it happen."

Her brother exhaled visibly. He glanced at his watch and got up from his seat to signify the interview was over. He said:

"It is important to me; very. It's the sort of change we've been looking for, for a while."

"We?"

He flushed.

"Yes, I meant Jan too; it opens up possibilities for us; it can take us onto a different level." Financially. "It's not such a terrible ambition, is it? To want the best for your family; security."

"Money, Colin, money," she said, rising. "It's not the same thing."

He let the comment pass, took her hands, kissed her on the cheek.

"Thanks, Carey."

"What for? I didn't say I was going to support you, did I? All I said was, I didn't need to oppose you." She smiled at the confused expression on his face. "Just like you didn't need to threaten me over The Programme. Right?"

She did not give him the opportunity to argue, pulling her hands free and leaving the room without another word, seething at his handling of her, even angrier because she would despite it give them what they wanted – her menfolk – because she couldn't bring herself to care enough to oppose them. It was a sorry indictment.

\* \* \*

That evening, punishing herself for her indecision, she did not go to The Programme. She worked frantically and fiercely until late, the way she worked to clear her desk before a holiday. She stomped home, ignoring the people pouring out of bars and restaurants, not envious of them but uninterested. She did not look into their eyes; she did not wonder what they thought of her; she was not aware, and would not have cared, that she startled – even frightened – them. She wanted to be at home, alone. She had not called Emily from the office, nor did she return the call from her that was on the answering machine when she got in.

For the first time in a while, she opened a bottle of wine, took it to her study at the front of the house, lit a cigarette, staring out the window at the people caught in the street-lights as they walked by, trying to re-capture a past frame of mind, to remind herself how it had felt. Without thinking about it, she switched on her computer and clicked on the stored code for The Programme, following the familiar instruction to hear Matthew's voice.

Http://www.the-programme.org.uk (turn on sound card if available).

*Now is the time of our separation and therefore for our departure. No, we are not leaving London – but, yes, we are leaving the path we have been following for the past few years. It is inevitable: some of us have gone, some of those with whom The Programme began, and so we are of definition a different whole and we must take a different journey. It is an adventure: a glorious adventure; those who have gone have left room for new people and new ideas, just as – far away – they will find themselves liberated to develop new directions.*

*The Programme has no secrets, except the secret that is the moment that is the members in their most imminent state of being; all of our ideas have been exposed through this most public of media, the invitation has been cast world wide – indeed a world wide web. Many of you have responded, and now it is the time for us to take stock, to study what we have gathered together and to design the next step forward.*

*It is time for this series of messages to end; when next you come looking for us on the Internet, you will find information about where to find us, here and in the States, and how you can learn more about us, by writing to us or – as we would enjoy most of all – by coming to visit. No more lectures, no more exhortations, no more warnings, no more clues: it is time for you to do it for yourself. It is time for the theory and the words to end; time instead to act.*

*The only thing The Programme can offer you is courage; after that, you're on your own. How do we do it? Example, support, love: that's our programme. Come and meet us; we have our home in Chesterfield Gardens in Mayfair; you're welcome to drop in just to say hello, or for a meditation, or come and eat in our Coffee Lounge. There are no conditions, no catches, just people.*

She smiled. Matthew's voice was rhythmic and soothing and warm; she could feel his arm around her shoulders; she shivered with excitement. The contrast with Colin was striking. If he no longer wanted her, she knew someone who did.

\* \* \*

The Meditation Hall at the front of the building had never again seemed full to Carey after that grand, last Midnight Meditation when Matthew and Cassandra had parted. Yet she had enjoyed the meditations more since. It was the quiet place and the quiet time when she could absorb and catch up with all her changes and the relocation of the focus of her life from the firm to The Programme.

She was floating, in near trance. She was aware of Emily, seated next to her. She could hear Matthew, in the distance, inviting them to come in now, come in from their meditations. She could hear him ask:

"Are there those present who wish to come forward?"

Though she knew that there were others intending to join, she realised that they were waiting for her. She looked around at faces she knew: Father Simon and Sister Hannah; dear Brother George Cohen of whom she had grown so fond; Sister Lilith encouraging her with her eyes, recalling that what Lilith had said was that she was not expected to join, not that she would not do so – she did not have to, it was her own choice. She rose gracefully in her white dress, still floating, her eyes caught Emily's, she passed her hand lightly over her friend's hair, she knew Emily was not yet ready, but she knew what Emily was feeling, jealous, wistful, resentful of remaining an outsider. Yet it was not Emily's face she carried with her, but another from long ago: Marion, her cupped hands held out towards Carey bearing forgiveness.

She made her way between other cross-legged members and stood before Matthew. She could sense others joining her – two or three others at least – but did not want to turn around to check: this was between herself and Matthew. Matthew placed around her neck the chain on which hung the symbol of The Programme.

"I am one," he said.

"We are many," she replied

"Together we shall be whole," they spoke in harmony.

Afterwards, she joined the other new Acolytes in the Coffee Lounge. They gathered to share their excitement, reassure one another they had not gone mad – whatever the outside world might think – this was no lunatic cult, it could not be, it was made of them and it was what they made of it.

At one o'clock, the Coffee Lounge was closed to the general public: new times for a new time. Only admitted members could remain. Carey walked Emily to the door.

Emily hugged her.

"You're glowing, you're beautiful."

"I wish," Carey bit her tongue off before she could finish the thought, that she wished Emily had also joined. Regret for what had not happened was never a fruitful emotion. "I'll call you tomorrow," she said instead.

Carey watched Emily mount the stairs to the street slowly. At the top, her friend looked around.

"Enjoy," she said.

Carey went back inside to find that the Coffee Lounge tables had been pushed together in the middle of the lower area; members were sitting all over the place; Father Simon had settled himself at what, for that reason, had become the head of the table; he was holding a guitar; she had heard tell of these sessions. Simon was beginning to sing old Dylan songs, some of them rewritten with Programme words with which the longer-standing members joined in; she flashed on copyright, then banished the legalism; periodically from the kitchen would emerge snacks and jugs of mixed fruit juices; she found herself singing along where she knew the words, humming to the tunes, laughing, loving her new friends as much as they appeared to love her.

Shortly before two, she sensed his presence behind her. Simon acknowledged him with an exaggerated, but seated, bow and carried on playing. Matthew rested his hand on Carey's shoulder for the remainder of the song, then squeezed just the once to let her know it was time. There was no coy attempt at concealment: she got up, took his hand and followed him from the room.

They did not speak as he led her up the stairs to the Temple, nor were words necessary within. From a cupboard in an alcove, he extracted candles, bowls, bottles of oil and set them around a floor-cushion. He placed candles in bowls of the oil and settled himself cross-legged on the cushion.

She understood. This was not Matthew, her lover, with whom she was to lie, but The Teacher, to whom she was giving herself in tribute and in submission. She unbuttoned her dress without fumbling, let it fall open. She was not wearing a bra, just panties and low pumps, adopting Emily's understated style. She shrugged the dress back to drop to the floor behind her, stepped out of her shoes, quickly and easily peeled away her panties until they fell to the ground and she could kick them aside. She stood before him while he studied her. She did not fear disappointment: he would take her as she was.

He got up from the cushion, pulled off his sweater, let his trousers fall, stripped. He was not fully erect. He stepped back from her, turned and pressed himself flat against The Programme symbol, then, suddenly, swivelled around with his back to it, arms outstretched.

He had thick, grey, matted hairs on his chest, a scar on one side that reminded her he had been a soldier, fought in Vietnam, had been grazed by shrapnel. His skin was crinkled with age; he wore it like armour. She tried not to shiver, in case he thought it was fear. She could not help running her tongue over her lips, dry with anticipation; though it had only been a couple of months since that last time with Patrick, it seemed like it had been forever since she had been with a man; she was worried that her responses should be more spiritual but she was wet with excitement.

Then he was fully erect. She stepped forward so she could touch him. He remained completely still. She reached out a hand, cupped his testicles in it, then ran the back of a finger up the shaft of his penis. She leaned in to him, kissed a nipple, tangled her tongue in his chest-hair without letting go of his penis. She lowered herself to kneel in front of him, licked him slowly, all over his genitals, until they were slippery wet, gleaming in the dull glow of a background lamp. Finally, for the first time, she took him into her mouth; almost immediately, he emptied himself into her, thrusting so deeply she could not believe she did not choke, joyful to realise she could swallow him whole.

He did not lose his erection. He brought her to her feet, gently lifting her by the back of her head. He took her hand and led her to the cushion, lowered her onto it, limbs outstretched. Her back was arched to the point that he could enter her without needing to lie on top of her. With his thumbs, he pulled her open, did not check to see if she was ready, thrust into her in a single movement, once he was wholly inside he stopped, held himself there, impaling her.

She could not help herself. She moaned:

"Oh, God, Matthew, love me, love."

He withdrew slowly, held himself at the very entrance, thrust back within. It was a programme of individual stabbing movements, each one leaving her wanting more, time after time, clenching to try and hold onto him. She could not contain a tiny cry of pleasure, he was still far above her, not holding her but merely in her, one moment she was thinking, terrified, that if she was not careful he was going to slip out of her by accident, that she would lose him, the next moment she was coming, he leaned back to thrust singly into her again, his arms behind him gripping her legs apart, preventing them encircling and enclosing him, the minimalist contact created a focus she almost could not bear, it seemed to have no end, she had no control and no responsibility, it went on and on until, finally, he released himself inside her for the second time and they dissolved in the fire beyond.

*Part Two*

## Chapter Seven

"There are only two things that you do with one hundred per cent of your being: being born and dying. They're the only things you do with your body as a whole, your mind as a whole, and your soul. The rest of the time, what we are doing is what we most want to do, slowed down by the part of us that doesn't want to do it: we call what we do the purpose, and that which is left undone the counter-purpose. We have to beat being held back by our own counter-purpose," Matthew lectured.

They were in New York, SoHo, a brownstone town-house off Spring Street, about halfway between Washington Square and City Hall. This was the base for the New York mission, which Matthew was here to inaugurate into a Chapter, complete with ground floor Coffee Lounge, street selling, meditations and meetings. Within three months of her arrival at Hammer Reach, Cassandra had set up not just the one new, designated Chapter in Boston but one in New York as well.

Rapid expansion called for rapid recruitment to staff the Chapters, to raise money and for their connections. Matthew and Cassandra had approached Arthur Rockworth and convinced him that the move was as much in Anthony's interest as others' and Rockworth had let them use his name with people who did good works in New England, the sort of people who might be attracted to a new initiative. Through one of them they had lucked into Brookline, one of the smartest suburbs, on a deal not dissimilar to Chesterfield Gardens but without a lease or any other security.

The house in SoHo belonged to a middle-aged doctor who had thrown up family and a wealthy practice in pursuit of long-lost ideals: his wife had returned to her native Florida, the antiques were in storage, house and car were left in the charge of his children. One of them – Tanya – had joined The Programme in Boston; the other – Chad – lonely and abandoned, was studying at Columbia and, eager to appease his sister, had agreed to The Programme taking over all but one room of the house, in which he continued to live until he was absorbed into the group.

At the current rate, The Programme would have doubled its membership in less than a year. Matthew was not without worries:

rapid growth was bought at cost of dilution; the emphasis on self-development that The Programme placed in England dictated the sort of recruit they got. It was being replaced by pre-packaged gratification, with an accent on the mutuality of exploration, adventure, more than a hint of the esoteric and the exotic. Matthew recalled Micah's line: "Give us your poor, your oppressed, your psychotics." If visitors to the English Chapter were open to change, those in New York would be positively insistent – and they would want it at once.

Carey was over with him for the Kroger jurisdiction hearing, though it was still more than a week away and they were planning to take off for a few days first. Cassandra wanted the case to generate publicity for the new Chapter. If some might be put off by the avaricious, mind-bending cult that the lawyers for Amanda's sister – Petra Gruenfeld – would undoubtedly paint, there would be many more who would be curious, even interested, some would be attracted.

There were about thirty people at Matthew's inaugural talk, about a quarter of them existing members. The rest fell into two, distinct groups: those already familiar with the world of alternative religion or other kinds of cult – whether as operators or watchers; and the usual spattering of moody loners with their own peculiar insights into the psyche or soul, looking for others with whom to share it.

A member of the audience asked:

"What kind of 'you' is doing this? Spiritual? Physical?"

"We don't say that one part of what we are is more 'me' or 'you' than any other," Matthew answered cautiously, sensing hostility. As well as the Gruenfeld legal team and the press, other groups would be looking to cut the competition down to size. Every new member was a source – of income, energy, adulation, contacts – of power – and if it was not his soul they were all after, then his worldly attributes would do.

"A lot of people believe that the 'true' you is one thing or another: soul, of which body and mind are aspects; body, with a soul and a mind; minds which imagine a body and – optionally – a soul. What we say is that, right now, we are all of it and who are we to say that one is more important than the other: it's the way they relate that defines us."

From the back of what would be the Coffee Lounge when, after tonight, it opened to casual visitors, Carey listened intently. From the moment they had touched down on American soil, she had been troubled, oppressed by the idea that it was an error to have come over with Matthew, not professionally but personally. Yet it was not

The Programme doctrine that vexed her but her relationship with it: purpose, counter-purpose.

"What life is about, in the end, is a series of choices, from choices over what to wear, or eat, or what book to read, to choices about what job to do, or with whom to strike up a relationship. There are always choices, even if it is between action and inaction. And, whenever we have a choice, if we can envisage alternatives, there must be some part of us, however tiny, which is capable of each of them: otherwise, they could not come to mind. In practice, we normally have a range of choices, and as a matter of routine what we choose is the option which seems to us at that moment of choice to represent the strongest impulse; it's a sort of psychological fascism – the strongest impulse always wins out."

He paused.

"What I'm talking about is what happens to the choices we don't make, the ones we discard. We call this difference purpose and counter-purpose: we become what we do; but we are made up of all the things we could have done, or the choices we could have made. Purpose and counter-purpose," he repeated. "Purpose is what we do; counter-purpose is what is left behind."

"I could leave some of this behind," a heckler called from a corner of the room.

"You will, friend," Matthew retorted.

Another called out:

"Did the Jews choose to march into the gas ovens? Was that their purpose?" The last word was sneered.

"I don't recall they had much of a choice," Matthew shot back. It was not a new question; he had the answer ready, even if it was not what he believed. Yes, he would have liked to say, at the most abstract level, it was what they did, it must have been their purpose. "As I said before, being born and dying are the hundred per cent actions; choices arise the rest of the time."

When there were no more interruptions, he resumed his theme.

"This way of living is ultimately unfulfilling. It inevitably leads to frustration and repression; we're wildly variegated people, with minds that don't run along a single track and can't fit into a single seat, a single choice. No one can bring their full range of impulses into being alone; we'd be driving ourselves forward in too many different directions at once.

"We believe that people can only find fulfilment with others: if you have an impulse that you cannot fit into your own way of life, then it may fit into someone else's, through whom you can express it for yourself. This is not about surrogate activity, second-hand living or voyeurism; it's about finding a framework in which many people can between them make up a way of life together in which they can all be whole. What outside is called good and bad, moral and evil, is a set of judgements designed to make us all conform to the social order. It means that we are all – to a greater or lesser extent – unfulfilled. We all have to hide something away in a cupboard, which we only take it out at night when no one else is watching.

"We have to find a way to be whole. There is no halfway; halfway in is halfway out, just as half good is half evil. It's like loving someone: you either do or you don't."

"Couldn't you just love him?" a queen in the row in front of Carey stage-whispered to his friend. "Isn't he just the way you wished Daddy looked when he came calling in the night with that big hard thing of his?"

Carey suppressed a giggle. There had indeed been something sexual in Matthew's voice and in the way he was carrying himself and the atmosphere had acquired a nervous titillation, erotic and enticing. She exchanged a glance with Meredith. She had barely known her in England but they had become close in the week she had been in New York. Merry smiled, nodded and mouthed in confirmation that she had sensed the same:

"I am one."

Carey grinned back, mouthing in reply:

"We are many."

Despite her reservations, she was no longer embarrassed to participate in the exchange – on a busy day, it seemed like hundreds of times. She had learned how the words could bear a different meaning depending on the circumstances. Cassandra was currently at Hammer Reach – where she and Matthew were going next – but she had visited New York for a couple of days. When she said "I am one," what she meant was that she was *the* one and the reply was understood to mean that they were all in a cluster beneath her. Others could mean the exact opposite, that they were, humbly, but one amongst many. Merry meant that she was one who had understood and that Carey was another.

Briefly, Carey allowed herself to flash on home. She had yet to tell Colin how close she had become to Matthew and to The Programme. He hadn't wanted to know when it suited him, now he could wait until it suited her, when she was wholly clear about what she was doing. He was already concluding his negotiations with Andrew Chettle and Jessica Harvey: the one time she had seen them together, she had caught a frisson of attraction between Chettle's principal colleague and her brother, though she knew it would not happen nor, thinking guiltily of her nephew and nieces, would she want it to.

Emily was moving into Carey's house: Richard had offered her a price for her share of their flat which Carey had advised her to accept, hoping she was advising disinterestedly, knowing it was foregone that Emily would move in with her, not merely happy but anxious for her to do so, delightfully uncertain what developments it would bring to their relationship. She no more wanted to slip back to her former, lonely existence than Emily could afford to go back to hers.

She was brought back to the present as she realised that Matthew had wound up his talk and that some members of the audience were leaving. Others looked around, unsure where to put themselves, needing a lead. It was the job of The Programme members to help them feel at home. Carey spied a man on his own – half-way between staying and leaving – standing by the table-display of magazines and booklets in the hall, most of them imported from England, but a couple of them produced in America. She went to work, hovering beside him until she caught his attention:

"Hello. I'm Carey. What's your name?"

"Calvin," he answered nervously. "Calvin Wood."

"Hello Calvin," Carey held out a hand. "Would you like to come into the Coffee Lounge?"

* * *

When Father Caleb said: "I am one," Carey – despite herself – shivered.

It meant he was the one who could, at will, do anything he wanted to her, and to as many others as he wanted.

They were at Hammer Reach, the Kroger farm in the Catskills in upstate New York, the nearest town – Hedgerow – a ghost-town from which the youth had fled and which survived only to service the surrounding rural community, with turn-of-the century frontages, a fifties soda-shop, a hardware and farm machinery store with an archaic Sears catalogue sign in the window, a gas station and the Trading Post in which the proprietor fulminated evenly against excessive government intervention and people who exploited the freedom to carry weapons, and sold a range of goods from Indian pottery to fringed jackets in raw brown leather that he had stitched himself.

Until The Programme took it over, there had been no farming at Hammer Reach for more than a decade. They had put some of the land to a vegetable garden, there were chickens for eggs, a cow for milk and a couple of horses. The buildings showed signs of recent works: if there was one talent The Programme seemed to bring out in its members it was carpentry.

Cassandra – in black silk blouse and black shorts – came out of the house to greet them when they drove up in the former doctor's smoked-glass Lincoln, loaned them by his son in SoHo. It had not been a long trip from New York City: three hours up Route 17 exiting at Hedgerow. She was accompanied by a small, sharp-featured, black-haired man who could have been her twin.

"Matthew. Look who's here."

"Carey, this is Cassandra's brother Huw," Matthew introduced.

"Hi," Carey held out a hand, adding automatically, "I am one."

"Yes," Huw replied. "I know who you are."

Carey flushed: she knew enough of The Programme to have learned that being whole did not equate to perfect harmony, but this was the first time she had taken a strike against herself. She snapped:

"Together we shall be whole," as if Huw had given the standard reply.

Cassandra giggled the high-pitched giggle that was her unnatural trade-mark.

"Our first lawyer."

Their own sense of mystique had not diminished Carey's as a lawyer; they all wanted it – whether to own or, it seemed, to attack; either way, it rubbed off on them; even Matthew was not immune.

"Huw was one of our founder members," Matthew explained. "He left because there wasn't a title for him – anyway, not one of his own. Does this mean you're back in the fold, Huw?"

"Is there a vacancy, Matthew?"

They were standing in the driveway in front of the main house. The immediate area had been lawned; behind the house, on both sides, were outbuildings – two barns, one in breeze blocks, the other in wood; also, a storage hut. Between the house and the storage hut, some people were working on what appeared to be the foundations of a new building. The fields glistened golden in the sun, curving gently upwards and into the distance where they ended, so far as the eye could see, in a thick, silvery copse of mixed trees – sycamores, chestnuts, maples, fir-pines – with a wide, clear path cut between them.

Matthew looked around proprietorially.

"This is mine," he said. "I have a life-tenancy of it."

Carey watched the scowl flash across Huw's face. Cassandra took Matthew's arm.

"Ours, Matthew," she said ambiguously: ours, because they were married, or ours because it belonged to The Programme.

That was when Father Caleb emerged, sneering, but offering Carey his hand.

"I am one."

He led them straight through the house.

"We've repaired the deck," he explained to Matthew.

There were more than twenty members staying at the house, including a couple of children. Some of them were unknown to Matthew; they went about their business, self-conscious because The Teacher was present. Cassandra had not yet destroyed his standing or diminished its aura. She needed Matthew still: he was the US star of psyche and the supernatural who had made good in the UK; and, he was the respectable and reasonable social work wizard who could persuade the suits to hand over their cash. Others were Superiors and Senior Messengers who had come to Hammer Reach in order to confer with him: this afternoon, he would hold a Council Meeting.

"Where is Helen?"

"In Boston. I thought, perhaps," Cassandra glanced at Carey and let the sentence trail away.

"I wanted to see her," Matthew said, treating the excuse with disdain: people regularly, even routinely, changed partners in The Programme without embarrassment or jealousy.

Despite herself, Carey felt relief.

A youngster – head bowed – brought iced tea.

"Brother Anthony," Matthew said.

"I am one, Teacher," the young Rockworth mumbled.

"We are many. How are you, Anthony?"

The boy glanced at Caleb, as if he needed permission to answer.

"I'm fine, Teacher."

He started to go, but Matthew took his arm.

"You're nervous, Anthony. Why are you nervous of me, Anthony?"

Anthony shook his head, could not answer aloud.

Matthew let him go, waited until Anthony was out of earshot.

"The idea was to calm him down, Caleb; not to destroy his spirit."

Caleb sipped his tea before he answered.

"I know he's special to you, Teacher, but we've got a lot of new members. There were risks."

"He has a place in The Programme, too." He was more than rent on Chesterfield Gardens.

"He's all right, Matthew," Cassandra intervened. "I keep an eye on him."

A man in dirty shorts and sweaty T-shirt was walking towards them from the work-party, waving at them while wiping his forehead. It was Father Nahum. Matthew rose to greet his old friend, stepping down from the porch and striding towards him, they threw their arms around one another, Nahum's red-framed spectacles flashing in the sun. Matthew introduced him to Carey.

"The lawyer," Nahum chuckled. "Just what we've always needed." He poured himself a glass of the tea, gulping it greedily.

"We should talk about the case," Cassandra said. "Before this afternoon."

She tossed her head at Carey, reminding Matthew that she would not be attending the meeting: she was, after all, only an Acolyte.

"I thought it might be better to talk without her," Matthew answered realising at once that they were already talking as if she wasn't there. He apologised. "I thought there were things you might not want to know."

Carey digested this cryptic remark. She answered cautiously, slipping on her legal shoes.

"I wouldn't want to know about anything, er, illegal." It was difficult as never before to be his lawyer, sitting on the deck in the powerful American sun, bare-foot, bare-legged, her blouse open as low as hung The Programme medallion around her neck, witnessing – and being subjected to – the mind-wars that passed for casual conversation amongst the group's hierarchy. "Short of that," she did not care.

Matthew asked Nahum:

"Where is Amanda now?"

"Here," he answered flatly.

"Here?" Matthew did not try to conceal his surprise. "Where?"

Nahum looked at Cassandra but, after a moment, admitted:

"Downstairs. In the, well, in the basement."

When last Matthew saw the basement, it had been nothing more than a bare, damp cellar with an earth-packed floor. His anger was evident. Nahum reassured him.

"We've done a lot of work. She wanted it," he said. "Really," he added in an almost aside, quiet and for Matthew's ears. "She wants to see you, Matthew. She thought, well, if she was left to herself." That she might run away again.

"I'll see her, then," Matthew announced. "Now. Downstairs."

"I'd like to see her with you," Carey said, to her own as much as to everyone else's surprise.

Huw guffawed.

"Even your lawyer doesn't trust you, Matthew."

"Should you be part of this discussion, Huw? I don't remember your answer." To the question whether he had re-joined the group.

"Huw was re-initiated a couple of months ago," Cassandra said. "He's about to take the name Paimon." Paimon – fallen angel – king of Hell who answered to Lucifer, who commanded 200 legions of spirits, part angel and part potentate, and who commonly took the form of a crowned princess astride a dromedary. The androgynous and ambivalent image suited Huw.

"But you forgot to tell me?"

"I'm sure his name was somewhere on a list." They used the Internet to keep in touch: cursors flashing in a darkened room, dancing about unknown names, many more than expected; Brother George Cohen – who was monitoring USA income and expenditure through the same medium – had taken responsibility for drawing Matthew's attention to specially significant information. The name had meant nothing to him.

Unexpectedly, Matthew reached across to grip Huw's hand.

"We'll be friends again, then, Paimon. Remember?"

Equally unexpectedly, Paimon – the re-naming instantly effected by The Teacher – gripped his in return and smiled.

"Of course I remember, Matthew. I was there." At the beginning; on their tour of Latin America; in Bolivia. "We vowed, whatever we made of it, that was what we were supposed to make of it. Remember?" he repeated.

"Show me," Matthew commanded Nahum, gesturing Carey to accompany him.

The wooden stairs to the basement were rickety, the ceiling low, in the main area at the bottom there was only a tiny window, the light-bulb was dull and shade-less. Yet the floor was clean and hard, recently concreted over. The walls were likewise finished and white-washed. On one of them, a painted symbol was in progress.

Carey asked artlessly:

"Is this to be The Temple?"

Father Nahum shook his head.

"No; that's what I'm building. This is for," he hesitated, then finished, "punishment. And worship amongst them." Those being punished.

He studied Carey's expression with frank interest, to see how she reacted. Carey nodded but did not say anything. She had guessed as much from the look on Matthew's face when he had been told where Amanda Kroger was to be found. It felt odd, knowing the woman's name for so many months as a plaintiff and as a major player in the court case, to be about to meet her in person.

There were two doors on each side of the main area, three of them ajar, the fourth closed and with a key sticking out of the hole. There was a light-switch outside each. Carey logged the row of air-bricks between them, feeding each of the four rooms beyond. It was a cell-block for punishment inflicted not only by The Programme but also by members on themselves – as Amanda. With Cassandra's expansionist plans, four was not an excessive number to serve a continent.

Father Nahum twisted the key to Amanda's cell and stepped back.

"Do you want me to stay?"

"No." Matthew waited for Nahum to retreat up the stairs before he opened the door.

Inside, it was too dark to see. Matthew flipped the switch. The cell was tiny, its ceilings even lower than in the main basement area, barely high enough to stand up straight, especially not Matthew who had to bow his head to enter.

The cell was completely unfurnished. There were no chairs, no table or mattress, not even a bucket; just a single blanket scrunched up and lying disused against a wall. In a corner, on the floor, squatted Amanda Kroger. The smell of her hit them in a solid wave. She was dressed in a simple – once white – shift, and both it and she were filthy; around the crotch, the shift was soiled. She was a small woman, overweight and with brown curly hair grimily in need of a wash; her fingernails were bitten to the quick. As soon as she realised who it was, she flung herself at Matthew's feet, crying:

"I'm sorry, I'm sorry, forgive me, Teacher."

Matthew gestured Carey to help her up. For a split second, Carey was disgusted at the thought of touching her then instantly disgusted with herself for hesitating.

Amanda recoiled.

"What are you doing? Leave me alone."

Forced to crouch to her level by the ceiling, Matthew placed his hands on her shoulders, looked into her eyes as if he could read her mind, asked:

"Amanda, do you believe?"

The woman nodded fervently.

"I am one, Amanda. Remember?"

"I am one," the woman mumbled. "We are many. Together we

shall be whole. I told myself that, every day, in that place, a hundred times a day," she babbled. "Even when they did things to me – they gave me pills, they gave me, you know, shocks. They made me cut my hair. It was down to here," she held her hands to the middle of her rib-cage. "They were trying to make me change. They brought a man to see me. He tried to get me to tell stories about you; claimed he knew you; I knew he didn't. When I wouldn't tell them what they wanted to hear, they gave me more pills, more shocks. I didn't tell them anything, Teacher. I didn't," she babbled.

"I want you to come outside with me, Amanda," Matthew said. "I want you to come out with me and go with Carey. She's a friend; she's going to help you clean up; she going to help you be whole again."

Amanda shook her head violently.

"I have to stay here. I can't go out. If I go out, they'll come after me. Like before, when I left." The Programme. "I'm not safe. I'll run away, I will, I will," she threatened like a seven year old. "Punish me, Teacher; punish me for what I did."

"It was done to you," Carey spoke for the first time. "Don't blame yourself."

Amanda looked at her in confusion, then back at Matthew.

"It was what I wanted. If it happened, I must have wanted it to happen." Purpose and counter-purpose.

"It's all right, Amanda," Matthew said patiently: "Sometimes, we need to go one way to find out we wanted the other. You came back."

"Clean me, Teacher," Amanda begged. "You clean me."

"Come out now, Amanda, come with me."

The woman allowed him to take her hand and lead her out of the cell. None of them spoke as they mounted the stairs. They made a pitiable procession: Matthew in the lead, tall and Christ-like but sombre; the waif-like Amanda bearing demons on her shoulders like a cross; Carey in the role of warden. At the stairs, Matthew left them.

"If you need anything, ask," he told Carey. "I'm sure you'll get along fine." Getting along meant preparing her for the hearing.

"You get what you want, don't you, Matthew?" Carey said, mostly in admiration but not without fear.

"We all get what we want, Carey. Does it bother you?"

"No," she murmured. "It's just, er, unfamiliar." She squeezed his hand, to remind him – or perhaps herself – that he was what she wanted, and had got.

* * *

From *Programme and Progression*:

*If you ask someone what is the first quote they can think of from the Bible, most will say: "I am the Lord thy God" – it appears in just that form in Exodus, Leviticus, Numbers, Deuteronomy, Judges, Isaiah, Ezekiel, Hosea, Joel, and Zecheriah, and in mildly different forms in many other books. The image is of a being – God – speaking to someone, whomever it may be on the particular occasion but let us say now – you and me.*

*This is the issue: does the voice come from without or from within? We start with the notion of the voice from without. The notion of religion as authority is far from novel nor the notion of religion as a means of social control. In domestic politics, religion was once the law. Religious order is the most familiar tenet of history; religion was a major part of what we would today call politics – wars were fought in the name of religion just as in Vietnam we fought for capitalism, and elsewhere we fight along lines of ethnicity; we even continue to fight in the name of religion – look at South Asia, the Middle East, the Balkans, look yet closer to home in Ireland.*

*You can see the steps: mythical figures representing authority – the Lord thy God most prime of all; interpretation at the hands of the personnel of religion – priests, if one will; the state in the person of the Crown backed up by the priesthood; the emergence of the personnel of the state to service the government of an ever-more complex society – more people, more wealth, more machinery; the emergence of a separate identity of government; the struggle for control between the priesthood and government; finally, the struggle for control between these officials of government and the Crown itself.*

*Still these masters of society lay claim to the authority of religion. The solitary form of government which disclaimed it – communism – has fallen in the West and will fall soon in the East. In the West, the religion is Judaeo-Christian; in the East, Islamic; even Buddhism, which is closest to understanding that the source of religion lies within, needs its tales and images of Buddha.*

*To obtain control of the local God is to enjoy control of the local people. We do not need to dwell on this: it is plain; if to possess God is to possess the people, it needs a God-figure that is without – "I am the Lord thy God," God the glove-puppet. Look out for those who tell you who God is, what God thinks, what God wants you to do; they want you to believe in their God instead of the God within.*

166

*What The Programme is about is the God within; the God of The Programme is the God that is created by a shared vision, based on a shared experience, the experience of seeking out and realising the God within – in all contradictory aspects – and defining God as then can see. Is there a great difference between this God and the God we have been brought up to recognise and obey? No and yes. No, because we may yet call him "God," and worship God as that which gives meaning to the material of our lives; yes, because God belongs to us, and has been created by us, not the other way around.*

\* \* \*

"We must be disciplined; we must take control. With so many new members, they cannot be left to their own devices – we are one but they are too many," The Seer made a joke. "They must have time to learn how to relate to each other and to us. We must have the time to absorb them, organise them, to build enough space for them all. We must be able to use their energy now, to build the room for them, but they are not yet ready to draw on it themselves. We must explore them, find their hidden pockets, bring them to the surface."

"Discipline? Control?" Matthew enquired. "We're a community, not an army – salvation or otherwise."

"We need to take that direction for the moment, to carve out more territory, for yet more people."

"Where do we stop? When we've put the rest of the world onto a reservation? The impossible task that is never achieved? It's implosion, not ex-, every time."

Only a half-dozen of the members attending the Council could follow the argument. If you set a task that can never be achieved, commitment to it becomes a way of life in itself. The world becomes the enemy instead of a harmless flock. Build-up of paranoia follows – aggression, frustration, energy spent getting nowhere – which finally demands an attainable target. The only target within their reach is themselves. The energy turns inwards and upon each other, all that is left that is within their control; destruction by implosion, no fire beyond.

Mother Jemima, Nahum's fellow-Superior of the vanguard mission, spoke:

"Some of these new ideas – I mean, I understand the theory – but, Teacher, they're capable of considerable misrepresentation. Maybe dangerously so," she added. "The contact rules."

She was a striking woman with eyebrows either so faint or so plucked that they were barely discernible, and a prominent nose that could none the less not spoil the matriarchal beauty of her face: somehow haughty yet somehow warm. Like the majority of the full-time, long-serving members, who had lived frugally – and as vegetarians – for most of a decade, it had served her well physically: slender and fit, a state of body and health that professional women paid fortunes to procure.

She addressed Matthew, The Teacher. The Seer was not responsible for what she saw, she merely told it as it came to her. Matthew was not arguing with her, just probing and testing the words.

Contact was euphemism for sex. The Seer had told of a period of constancy to come. It would not be total abstinence: that would be as unattractive as it would be unenforceable; but sexual hierarchy, members available only to their seniors. She had not yet said whether the rules would be confined to opposite sex partners, or whether same-sex activity was likewise to be regulated.

Mother Jemima said:

"I can see that it could be useful in practice." The Programme might affect a fatalistic attitude towards sex, but all members were required to undergo an AIDS test before they were allowed to become residents. "But it could be turned on us."

"Meaning?" Matthew asked.

"Abuse, misuse of authority, maybe worse." Rape.

Nahum, loyal to both Matthew and Jemima, reminded them:

"We're already confronting more than one claim."

Amanda Kroger's case concerned the greatest amount of money, and Hammer Reach itself, but there were three other former members who were trying to recover lesser sums put into the group; two of them were already hinting that if they did not get it back, it would not only be psychological abuse that might be alleged against The Programme.

Cassandra observed:

"It is at the point just before a group becomes strong that the greatest number of enemies will gather to try – one last time – to destroy it: earlier, there will not have been enough people who will have been involved in or around the group who yet want to attack it; later, the group will be strong enough to resist."

Father Christopher proclaimed:

"Four out of every five people who come into The Programme want to be told what to do – want to be controlled, dominated even – sexually as much as spiritually; we don't need the others."

Father Nahum said:

"I'm sure some of us don't want them."

Because it was Nahum – because none of them was ready for a showdown – because none of them was yet out of touch with the essential humour of The Programme – everyone started to laugh, led by Caleb, the target of the remark. He rose and stepped across Christopher and a handful of other members between them, to kneel in front of Nahum.

"I am one," he said.

"We are many," Nahum replied.

"Together we shall be whole," the Council chanted.

\* \* \*

That night, Matthew took Carey out to dinner.

It was still light. He took her to the Moonlight Inn overlooking a calm, clear spring-water lake, surrounded by untouched forest and meadows, fern banks, moss-covered boulders, rolling hills, an abandoned railroad bed. The loudest sound was nature itself.

Moonlight Inn was a low-slung cluster of wooden houses, tennis courts, jetty, dockside sun-deck, Adirondack chairs and recliners. There were substantial, one-storey extensions built onto either side of the three-storey original house, one of them encased in glass. The upper storeys were painted green, the ground floor white. There were stone slabs for steps to the front entrance, which led directly into a cosy hall that fulfilled the dual functions of lounge and reception. It was furnished with deep armchairs and a sofa, a piano, and an antique desk behind which sat the matriarch who ran the Inn.

The atmosphere was – like Hedgerow – turn of the century; nothing much had changed since. Life was slow at Moonlight Inn. Before they went into dinner, they spent ten minutes visiting with the innkeeper, answering questions about their journeys, both immediate and to America. She nodded when they told her they were with The Programme, over at Hammer Reach, as if to say it was none of her business what people did so long as they did not disturb anyone else. Matthew charmed her; Carey was quiet but sweet. The woman told them that she had clients from all over the world, and of every imaginable occupation and opinion. Her repeat clients were her friends. In one corner of a photo-board, there was a black-and-white postcard of a tiny baby in a crib, eyes shut, one hand in view, fist tightly clenched ready to take on the world.

"She's from London," she said to make Carey feel at home. "Her name is Emma."

"She's beautiful," Carey meant it. She was reminded of her nieces.

"She must be four or five, now," the innkeeper replied almost wistfully. "We've never seen her."

"You will," Matthew said confidently.

They sat for a while at the stove-pipe bar before their table was ready in the restaurant itself. The menu was rich, varied, inviting: smoked trout, home-made linguine with whole-wheat pasta, jumbo shrimp to start; venison, pheasant, duck, pasta with seafood, fresh steamed fish to follow. The portions were plentiful: Carey could barely finish either course, refused dessert. Matthew had suggested wine: Carey had hesitated, then accepted.

"I thought you'd want to spend the time around the house," Carey quizzed him. "After all," it was an opportunity to see his disciples and to ensure that they saw him and remembered who The Programme was about.

"It's not really my style," he said. "I'm best one-on-one."

"I know," she blushed, thinking of their most intimate times alone.

It was not always the way it had been when he had taken her that first night. They could make tender love without a hint of power and position. Sometimes, she rubbed his body with massage oils, and he hers, until their bodies seemed like a single, joined, erogenous zone. At other times, urgently, they would fall on each other in a frenzy: one evening, when he came to collect her after a meeting in her office, they had screwed on her desk; another time in the kitchen at her house; in the shower, clinging precariously onto the shower-rod with her legs around his waist, he had soaped her backside, entered her in it by lifting her at right-angles to his body, there was nowhere she could not, would not, take him.

She had grown used to his body, ageing and blemished, still lean and fit but sturdy like a post planted in the ground long ago. He could not have been more different from the bodies of the younger men she was used to, perfected and polished in the gym – in contrast, poles still quivering. She liked to kiss his scar, lick her way up his spine, she could bring herself to orgasm that way clenching her thighs against him, straddling him, rubbing against him rolling him over afterwards and mounting him in a frenzy.

Once, during a Midnight Mass, she had watched Lucius watching Matthew and knew instantly they had been together. It disturbed her but – though she thought it ought to do so – it did not shock her. Later, in his private quarters, she had asked him. Matthew had said simply:

"I love them all."

She had said to Matthew:

"Can it really be this simple? Can we really change ourselves this easily?"

"What do you think? How does it feel to you?"

"I want it to be; it is. I just can't believe, well, that it can go along like this."

"The hardest part is to start. It'll keep happening as long as you want it to. Once you've begun, you've got choices that are at least equal, keep going or turn back. Mostly, once you've begun, you realise that there's very little to go back to, it isn't even an equal choice but far preferable to carry on."

"But I'm a lawyer," she cried, as if it was the greatest block of all.

"Lawyers think they're special; perhaps they are; perhaps that's what takes them into the law. But they're often unhappy at it, and that's what makes them look around for something different; there's more of them to be found in groups than people realise. There are many lawyers in Scientology, and the Moonies; three of the dead at Jonestown were lawyers; several of the members of the Order of the Solar Temple were lawyers. There was an English group in the papers recently, based in Portugal: the International Saturday Group; I've never heard of it, but the article said it recruited from the professional classes – including doctors and lawyers. What's the oldest sect of all?" She had shaken her head and he had said: "Freemasonry." She knew that it was positively riddled with lawyers, to the highest ranks of the profession.

"Is that what The Programme is? A sect? A cult?"

"It's The Programme. Beyond that, you have to make up your own mind."

Every inch of Matthew exuded wisdom, good-will, confidence; she had been looking for him – if she had but realised it – for all of her life.

At Moonlight, she said, for the first time:

"I've fallen in love with you."

"I know. Do you mind?"

She knew he could not respond in kind. As he had said in London, he loved them all. She shook her head shyly.

"It's comfortable. Appropriate is a word that I can't seem to get out of my head. I like being with you; I mean, all the time I'm with you, I like it." She had chosen him, as much as he had chosen her. It was not like it had been with, say, Patrick: then, she had reserved the major part of herself, chosen only to sleep with him. With Matthew, she had chosen a way of life.

After dinner, before they drove back to Hammer Reach, they walked along the side of the moonlit lake. On the grass verge, hidden by a decayed concrete bunker which once had served the railroad, they made love, quickly and easily, familiarly.

Later, they sat up at Hammer Reach until dawn, she listened as he swapped memories with others, brought one another up to date on members, traded gentle gossip. In their bedroom, undressing for bed, she said to him:

"Sometimes, they all seem so, well, normal. It's hard to associate say, I don't know, Nahum, Jemima, Meredith with, well, some things about The Programme."

She was most uncomfortable with its dark side. She was, Matthew had told her laughingly, a Seraph, one of the angels of love, light and fire, of whom, before his fall, Satan had been the prince. It was understood that Caleb's ascendancy within the authority of The Programme in America would lead to an upsurge in the power of the night.

He said, almost idly, distantly:

"The ingredients are there. It's a shorter step from acknowledging Satan to worshipping him than it is from agnosticism to God."

It frightened her: she was, at most, an agnostic.

\* \* \*

Leah, the former SoHo Tanya, came up in the morning from Boston, driving Helen at Matthew's request. Several other members had already left: Helen, too, would go straight back to Boston, although Leah was due for a stay at Hammer Reach. It was not a peripatetic life that they were living: instead, home and work were spread evenly over all of The Programme's properties of the time being.

Matthew went for a walk with Helen. He pointedly invited Carey along; Carey – equally pointedly – declined. Instead, she sat out on the deck smoking with Leah. Carey was in civilian clothes; Leah in white.

"How long have you, er, been involved with The Programme?" Carey probed.

"I met them the first day they were in Boston," Leah answered gleaming: she had already acquired that special intensity about her eyes that Carey termed "the look". "The first day," she repeated, as if any other day would not have been good enough.

"What were you doing there?"

"I don't know," she laughed. "Nothing, really. I was at Radcliffe for a while. Then, when my father did his thing, I dropped out but, um, I found I couldn't go back to New York either. I just stayed on." She shrugged. "I guess I was waiting for The Programme."

"Your brother said, both of you were thrown by it."

"I shouldn't think that was what he said."

"No," Carey laughed with her. "He said you were both fucking freaked by it."

"It was, I don't know, like everything we knew was just, well, chucked away. I don't mean we were especially close to our parents, that wasn't the sort of relationship we had. But it was solid, all the same. I thought, they knew what they were doing and we fitted in with that and that was how we knew what we were doing too. I was going to do medicine, go in with my father, you know?"

"I do know," Carey said. "My father's a lawyer: we were always expected to go into his firm, at least – that's what we believed. My brother and myself. And that's what we did."

"But you're here now?"

"Sort of," Carey admitted. "But I'm not a resident, just an Acolyte. I'm The Programme's English lawyer," she added.

"A bit more than that," Leah told her she knew about Matthew.

Carey nodded: it didn't call for a reply; something about the sly way Leah had said it had put her off. It was not so much prurience as sensuality, as if for a split second Leah had slid between their naked bodies. She noticed that, when not smoking, Leah laid her hands on her thighs, kneading them gently. There was something in the air between them that was sexual, not warming as it had been with Emily, but predatory.

"I don't think he thought about us. One night – well, I guess we knew something was up for a few days, my parents were hardly talking and when they did they just fought – he told us that he was giving it all up, it no longer meant anything to him, he wasn't sure it ever had. He said – this was his exact words – he had lost the will to heal, he had to find it again. Oh, sure, he kept saying how much he loved us, how he didn't want to lose us, but, bottom line, we weren't enough for him. In one sense, I thought it was quite admirable; he had enough money – plenty enough – and he wasn't going to live his life as a fraud anymore. But that made his life up to then a fraud – his life and his relationship with me – at least that was, you know, how it felt."

"And now?"

"Now I understand it a lot better. I was doing a lot of drugs – legal stuff, too – Valium, you know. I've stopped all that; my head's a lot clearer. The Seer's been helping me, personally. That's why I'm staying on here: to do some more work with her. I wish I knew where he was: I'd like to see him, or write to him, tell him what I'm doing, tell him I understand. It was his purpose. We all have our purpose," she repeated, sounding unsure, wistful, staring off towards the woods where they could just make out Matthew and Helen walking side by side, maybe hand in hand. She murmured: "Nothing's forever, right?"

"Sure."

"What's he like? Matthew, I mean."

"In what way?" Carey asked guardedly.

"I don't know. We've only got, you know, a vague sense of him; I mean, we know he's The Teacher, and we've seen his picture and read his writing; some of the people who came over just worship him, you know, but there's a feeling, maybe, I don't know, that maybe he's had his time and it's The Seer's time instead. Is that a terrible thing to say?" she asked artlessly.

Carey was appalled but all she said aloud was:

"We see what we want to see. The Seer's here; she's what you saw, who brought you in, who's been helping you. It's natural to relate most to her; but you should go back to the books once in a while; he's not The Teacher for nothing. Have you read *Programme and Progression*?" It was the book Carey could relate to most easily, in which Matthew wrote about religion, philosophy and psychology and progressed them towards his own idea of God. There was a number of other texts available to the general public and to junior members, and a number to which she had not yet enjoyed access which she guessed would be more overtly mystical.

"Oh, sure," Leah said, almost dismissively. "But The Seer's been giving her own Lessons and, well you know, maybe they mean more to me, you know, just now. I think, I guess, there's too much I've been keeping inside for too long, it needs to find its way into the open; that's what she's helping me with."

Carey did not say anything. She could not have said why, but there was something threatening in what was otherwise a straight-forward sentiment.

\* \* \*

From *The Seer's Lesson On Hierarchy*:

*The Programme hierarchy exists to serve the members. It can only do so if the members accept its absolute authority. The hierarchy of The Programme is the accumulation of the years of training and preparation in which we have been engaged, particularly the period in London during which we were few in number, drawing on our inner resources, achieving our inner vision, the shared experience of recognising the God and Satan that are within each of us, until they could take on an existence of their own that was strong enough and distinct enough to lead us forward as commanders of the army of their own unification.*

*We are growing as never before. The need for a new way of life, a new order, has never been so compelling. The grey forces who hold the reins of power in the world today demand uniformity from the greatest number. Uniformity of values. Uniformity of goals. Uniformity of approach. You must wear a mental uniform in order to be allowed to take part in the race for material success, howsoever it is defined. The greater the uniformity, the more who are alienated from it and yet who are left with no alternative.*

*We are the army of the alienated! We proudly wear the uniform of alienation! We will not accept singularity! We recognise only diversity – the diversity of God and Satan – the reconciliation between whom will bring diversity into reality! We line up in platoons behind these two great forces – some at one extreme, others at the other – so that we can all march together and in step! This is our way. It is the order you are looking for. The hierarchy of The Programme exists to allow you to find it. Its authority is derived from you. Doubt it, challenge it – you doubt and challenge yourself!*

\* \* \*

"I've been with Christopher," Helen told him as they walked in the woods holding hands.

Matthew had forgotten how pleasant on the ear was her gentle Canadian accent. He voiced neither surprise nor disappointment: he had wanted her to make a couple with Nahum.

"Nahum and I, well, it wasn't the thing."

"I miss you."

"And I you."

"Will we be together again, Matthew?" She bit on her lip.

Matthew stopped and turned her towards him, gripping her arms.

"When I was with you, you were the focus of my person; as much as anyone, as much as Carey is now. I could tell you it could be anyone, but that wouldn't be true. There are people, no matter what, you're never going to arrange yourself to be around – like you and

Nahum, I should think. Nothing's gone to have to come back again: it's still there, it's just not what we're doing right now."

She leaned against him, listened to the familiar beat of his heart.

"I know, Matthew, I know." She put her arms around him, stroked his back, looked up and accepted his brief kiss in exchange.

"Tell me about Christopher."

"Maybe there weren't that many choices."

"Caleb?" He only asked in order to find out if it had been mooted.

"I'd rather be with Enoch."

The giant Enoch bore the years of dissolution and despair in the lines of his face; he looked ravaged, exhausted, at the end of a long, hot march, without the energy to step into the shower or a bath before collapsing fully dressed on top of the bed. The idea of the elegant and fragile Helen lying down beside him was as alien as the image of her being clawed at by Caleb.

"I thought," she hesitated, then admitted, "I thought it would be useful. To you."

He thought briefly of reassuring her that she need not sleep with Christopher for his sake. He said nothing. It was no different in kind from his own hope that she should make a couple with Nahum. They lived in a small world. Whether the outside world was enemy, ally or indifferent, they coupled within. There were too few of them to spare at the upper reach; couplings were not bred exclusively of mutual attraction and desire.

"Tell me," he demanded as they began to walk back towards the farmhouse, holding hands again.

"I'm not sure; he's not, well, open with me." She glanced at Matthew shyly. "He's not stupid."

"No." Far from it.

"I know she went to New Orleans," Helen said. "I heard Christopher talking to her. I don't know why."

Matthew quickly guessed.

"Phillipe," he said. "Phillipe Lamarque."

They had first met Phillipe before The Programme was even a group, even the idea of a group. He was someone Huw knew; a big man, a black man. He had been around and about London's esoteric sub-culture at the time The Programme had begun to emerge. At one moment he was a Scientologist; the next Sunday afternoon he could be found taking tea with the Druids; if there had been a black Masonic Lodge, he would have put his left foot into it.

Phillipe Lamarque was part black, part Creole. He had been amused by Matthew, amused enough to cause Matthew himself to doubt what he was doing: in this, he was unique. Lamarque had said: do it; the only criterion that counts is if it works. He had gone away, come back, taken a little part like a sip of tea, then disappeared again without explanation.

He had returned shortly after Huw had left the group. During a phase of free contact – contact with outsiders – Cassandra, on the rebound, had picked him up and for a few, short weeks no one else had mattered. Matthew had not been troubled while it was going on; only after it was over.

Lamarque had finally ended up in New Orleans. If Cassandra had been to New Orleans, that was why.

"What do you think?" Helen asked, meaning developments generally, not Phillipe.

"I think… I think that if they had stayed in England, we would have lost them. I think they had begun to lose sight of the whole, were too focused on their own path. I think they needed to follow it down alone, to rediscover their part in the whole."

"And if they don't?"

"If they don't, they don't."

"Sometimes I'm scared, Matthew. What will happen to us?"

"When the time comes, follow your own path. The Programme remains whole."

"Let them go, Matthew; before it's too late. You don't need them; we don't."

He let go of her hand, turned and stared back at the path through the woods from which they had emerged.

"I can't let them down," he said eventually, simply. "They have a right; they are a part of it; until they don't want to be any more."

"And you think they have the same caring attitude towards you?" She sounded bitter; it was easier for Matthew to withstand them than for her.

"I think… I think we'll all find a way through. Together; together in the end. Maybe it will be hard; maybe some will fail or fall; maybe there will be pain. It can't always be easy."

"Me, Matthew," she insisted. "I'm scared for me."

"They won't hurt you," he assured her. "That would be to hurt me."

She wanted to tell him: that was what she was trying to say.

He was The Teacher; she could not imply that it could ever be otherwise.

* * *

Anthony – naked – in a punishment cell, not even The Programme symbol around his neck; Caleb cracks a stock-whip, points at the boy with its leather handle, licks his lips.

"Do you want it?"

Anthony, shivering, shakes his head violently. He has been beaten before.

"You like doing it to others," Caleb goads him.

"I've changed," Anthony whispers. "That was then. There."

Caleb snorts disbelievingly.

"I was just a child."

"You were never a child, Anthony," Caleb sneers. "You were just small; small and mean and growing."

"I didn't mean any harm. I wasn't going to do anything." He is still talking about Thomas. "It's been months; I've behaved."

"But it hasn't left you, has it, Anthony?" Caleb speaks almost gently. "It's always inside of you."

Suddenly, momentarily defiant, Anthony says:

"I thought that was what The Programme is about? It's in all of us. Always."

Caleb cracks the whip: do not answer back.

"What do you want of me, Caleb?" Anthony begs, crying. "This?" He touches his hands to his body. "That?" He points at the whip. "What would The Teacher think?" he adds, regretting the words before they are out of his mouth. The moment of defiance has passed.

"I know you. You and I, we're the same. I've been there, in a cell like this; but I handled it, and I learned to handle myself. That's what you have to do. And if you can't, there's no place for you to go – not in The Programme, not outside."

"I want to, Caleb," Anthony replies, his voice trembling. "I've always wanted to. You show me, Caleb," he pleads. "I'll do anything."

For a moment, Caleb is tempted. Then, without explanation, he pokes the tip of the whip through one of the top holes in the air-brick, leaving it dangling as he steps out and slams and locks the door behind him. Outside, he pulls the end of the whip through until there is enough to tuck back in through another hole in the brick, to make a knot with.

None of them understands him. He has traded being understood for fear. Cassandra thinks she controls him – with sex, with power – but it is because he lets her do so, not because of the buttons she pushes. Christopher comes closest: that dark mind – authoritarian, pleasureless. Even he does not see that within Caleb there had once been a wish to be loved, and to love others, to do the good for people that he daily saw The Teacher doing. It was a wish that has dried up for want of fulfilment, it was not his purpose. It was replaced by a gnawing jealousy, turning rapidly into a cocktail of resentment and hatred – resentment and hatred of Matthew.

Inside the cell, Anthony focuses on the handle of the whip, setting it in motion like a pendulum, struggling to understand what Caleb meant by it.

* * *

Impulsively, suddenly lonely, Carey called Emily.

"Carey? Are you all right?"

"I just felt like a chat. How are you?"

"I'm fine, Carey; really fine." There was something in her tone that was different; there had been changes.

"What's going on, Em?"

"I did it, Carey; last Saturday." Joined The Programme.

It was not something Carey had expected. She ought to have felt glad; instead, for some reason she shivered.

"Where are you ringing from?" Emily asked.

"Hammer Reach. The farm. How's work?" She changed the subject.

"Ah, well, they're re-organising. Merging two departments. And guess what?"

"They're going to make you redundant," Carey said. "I expected it; I just didn't expect it so soon. We can fight it, you know."

"No," Emily sounded sad but only just. "It's time to move on. As long as I'm there, well, you know." Richard around every turn in the corridor.

Carey asked after Chapter members. Shyly, Emily told her she had been seeing Simon. For a moment, Carey was jealous: she knew how good it felt at the beginning; Emily, too, was fast-tracking. Carey wanted to tell her that the waters got muddier the higher up she rose. It would not be fair to take this time away from her; it was her first venture with a man since Richard.

She knew these were not the real reasons for her jealousy.

As if reading her thoughts, Emily said:

"I want to come over."

"What, here?"

"I miss you."

"Don't you have to work any time out?"

"Yes, sure. But like you said, I could fight it. I haven't been in this week; they aren't complaining. I think they'll go for holiday time during my period of notice, don't you?"

Carey let her emotions get the better of her judgement: if Emily wanted to scare them into a more generous pay-off, she ought to turn up on time every day, make sure they saw her and then make plenty of ostentatious, loud and long calls to her lawyer – even if she was not there. She said:

"Do it, Em. Matthew and I are planning to take a trip, to the South, where he was born. Come over; join us."

"What about Matthew? Do you think he'll mind?"

Carey laughed.

"Matthew? When did he ever mind a following?"

## Chapter Eight

Father Micah, newly so promoted – tall, rangy, red-headed, smooth-talking Englishman in a white suit – leads The Introduction. There are between thirty and forty newcomers present, a little bewildered, a little scared, impressed by their own courage.

"This is who you are," Father Micah cries, clapping his hands.

"You are the army of God and Satan; you are the army of good and evil; you are soldiers whose battle is for a plot of earth to call your own – a plot of earth on which you are free of the demands and the rules which have left you drained, afraid, angry, isolated, hopeless, confused, unloved. Despairing you will ever find a way of life to be yourself. It doesn't matter if you might choose different language for yourself: here's two thoughts – if it was not true, you wouldn't be here; and, until we all start using the same language, we are all truly alone."

He looks around at them.

"Now; what we're going to do, we're going to have a short meditation; don't be scared; there's nothing mysterious about it – most of you have probably meditated some time or another; maybe a few of you are adept at it." He glances around, spots and memorises the faces of the members of the audience who glow and nod for recognition – these will be first targets as they gather to talk in the Coffee Lounge after; they have already been to the foothills for a solution and have been left wanting; they have come here for more.

"So, take a deep breath, let it out slowly; and again. That's good." The calm descending is almost visible. "One more time. Now, I want you to close your eyes; relax; let go. Stop thinking: stop thinking about me, about who I am. Stop thinking about what you're doing here. Just think about the here and now: you're in a room – we call it the Meditation Hall – there are people around you, they're here for the same reasons you are, whatever they may be; we're all here to learn, to change, to receive something and we all know that to receive something we have to give something; we've got to get ourselves ready for all of that – to give and to receive; we've got to learn to let go; relax, close your eyes, breathe deeply, think about the room, think about the meditation; let what comes come."

The voice fades away, people are breathing slowly, eyes shut and mouths ajar; a small number retain control of their consciousness, imitating others but squinting out from a half-opened eye; these too Micah notes and records – likewise, they will be priority targets. The most sceptical fall hardest and make the most fervent converts.

"I know you've read some things about us, and I've told you what we're about: we're here to help you to do things and to become some-one you've dreamed about but never thought possible; we're here to stop the war between God and Satan, to bring them into the same army, to march in harmony, towards peace. This is our fundamental message: reconciliation of God and Satan; reconciliation of good and evil.

"How do you go about it? The first thing to get out of your heads is that you know what you need to do; and, the first thing to get into your heads is that we do. We may not know specifically what this one of you or that one needs right this moment, anyhow not the colour and the shape of it; and the ultimate solution is going to have to come from within you anyway – it's your quest, your peace of mind, your destination. But we know how to help you get onto the road and find your way along it, far enough for your eyes to adjust to its darkness. And we know how to reconcile your personal God – and good – and your personal Satan – and evil; what you do with it, what it means, those are things you will work out for yourself later.

"For the moment, for the now, the very first lesson, you have to learn to let go, you have to learn to trust, trust us, trust me."

* * *

Cassandra had been disturbed by Matthew's presence at Hammer Reach.

There were times she almost managed to forget how much she had loved him – that long weathered body, the Christ-like head, the limitless compassion, the power with which he could draw people into his aura, the wisdom, the charm, the humour, the sex. Her life-long quest had been for men bigger and stronger than herself; they had to be bigger and stronger not merely than at any given moment was she, but than she could at that moment imagine she would ever become. As soon as she could see that she would outgrow them, she was gone; no point waiting for it to happen.

Matthew was different, not just in the degree of his strength but in its quality. It had been impossible for her to say: "This is me, this is what I am learning from him". The learning process had become her identity. As such, there had been no image of a time beyond – they were inseparable, she had become him, she could not see into the room that she was a part of.

Paimon had introduced them: Huw, then. They had been sharing a flat in Highgate. Huw was a year shy of a degree in architecture that he would never complete. At the time, she had already left a brief marriage to an actor behind her. Before that, she had been at the University of Aberystwyth, reading English Literature, with heavy emphasis on the Welsh poets with eyes and souls as dark as her own. From poetry to folk-lore, and from folklore to mysticism, were tiny steps, so small she could not now remember taking them. She lived, sequentially, with a student in college, a fellow-poet who was in charge of the local authority Environmental Health Department, and the Senior Fellow in her Department. Actor had visited the Department in her final year, to award prizes for dramatic writing, and had carried her back with him to London.

As it became apparent that minor success was too grand a term for what Actor would achieve, Cassandra began to drift. There was not even any property to divvy up: the flat was rented; their car was hired; his bank account was overdrawn. She brought Huw into the flat to pay the rent: he was still in receipt of an allowance from their parents.

Huw was three years younger, but they could not have been closer if they had been twins. They meant everything to each other, shared everything; if they had never quite crossed the final line, there were no modesties on either side, nor withholding of affections. The first time she had ever touched a woman sexually was when she crept into her brother's bed wearing only a T-shirt, not realising that the sleeping body within was not Huw but a woman he had brought back for the night. Shock on each side was followed by gales of laughter and laughter by adventure: neither of them thought twice about it; it was the early seventies; it was what people did.

Between Actor and Matthew, her only serious relationship had been with Donald, the famous senior partner of the architectural firm with which Huw had spent a part of his practical year. For a short while, he even left his wife for her, and she had moved into his London penthouse. Almost as soon as she had unpacked her clothes, she had known she would move beyond him; within a month, he knew it too. She went back to her flat and began desultorily to look around for a job, or a new man.

Huw was like her, yet completely different. She was small and dark and haunting; men wanted to protect her, and in exchange take possession of her ethereality. Huw was a man: likewise small and dark, he frightened women; they skipped within his reach without appreciating how complex were his designs, and were scared to withdraw, hanging about him nervously until he lost interest. Huw liked power far more than money or sex. That was why he had left The Programme: the power was Matthew's and – through Matthew – Cassandra's; the most he could ever be was number three.

Huw met Matthew first, at a New Age lecture. They were seated next to one another. Not long into the talk, they sensed that each was as unimpressed as the other. Huw mumbled a sly riposte to something the speaker had said, for Matthew's ears; Matthew did not visibly acknowledge it; a while later, he whispered a sarcastic commentary of his own; another few minutes, it was Huw's turn; by the end, they were soul-mates.

Huw brought Matthew back to the flat to show off his find to his sister. She had just emerged from the shower, wrapped in a towel. Unembarrassed, she made them tea before she went into her bedroom to put on a dressing-gown.

She listened as Huw and Matthew sparred for fun, then as Matthew began to talk about the group of people that was putting itself together around him. They were not losers, not drifters or nutters, but bright young people – like Huw and Cassandra – from decent backgrounds – like Huw and Cassandra – some of them with a bit of money – of which Huw and Cassandra had just enough to get by for the time being – who could not see a career or other kind of life that suited them, yet who were not ready to give up and settle for something less.

After a while, as Huw pressed Matthew on his plans, she went back to her bedroom to get dressed. When she re-emerged, she sat on the floor beside Matthew, forearm resting on his thigh, cheek resting on his knee, still silent, exuding confidence that she knew what she was doing until, after five minutes or so, he began to stroke her hair, casually but rhythmically, accepting her challenge.

Huw took it well: better than she had expected. Around two in the morning, he went for a leak; when he returned, he remained standing.

"Time for me to go to bed. I'll see you tomorrow?" He addressed the question at Matthew.

Matthew got up; they stood apart for a few seconds then, simultaneously, moved into the centre of the room to hug. They stood like that until Cassandra joined them, her arms around each of them, each of them with one arm around her, another around each other.

She had grown within The Programme, as Matthew finally named it during the trip to Bolivia, but Huw had grown apart. The night before he left – while they were in Devon – she slipped into his bed and they lay facing each other, lightly holding each other, whispering tenderly, the way they had done as children, and again when they had lived together at Highgate.

"You're leaving, aren't you?"

He nodded: he had given her no forewarning.

"Why, Huw? I need you with me."

"No. Not now. You've got everything you need."

"What are you going to do?"

"I'm not sure," he admitted. "Wait for a while; wait and see."

Their parents had died in a car crash. There was some money left, though much of it had already been poured into The Programme. He said:

"I'll take what's left."

"Sure."

They lay in silence for a while. He broke it.

"I'll miss you."

"I know. I love you."

"It isn't forever."

"Nothing's forever; everything's forever." One of The Programme aphorisms of the period: nothing is forever in the sense that it will continue; everything is forever in the sense that what has happened cannot be undone. They kissed and hugged a last time and she went back to bed with Matthew. In the morning, he was gone.

Shortly afterwards, Phillipe reappeared.

* * *

"Who said, 'if you can't fuck the one you want, fuck the one you can'?"

Phillipe Lamarque was forty pounds heavier than when Matthew had last seen him: New Orleans was fat city; the highest level of obesity in the USA; thirty-eight per cent overweight. It cooked good and ate better. He sat in an easy chair, legs stretched out and fat ankles crossed, smoking a joint in the back room of his house, a long-necked bottle of Miller Draught by his side.

"Was she here, Phillipe?"

"Sure; she was here then, you here now." He spoke with a lilt in his voice that had been absent the last time they had met; his English was wilfully and unnecessarily sloppy.

They had sat through part of a Voodoo ceremonial – a small part designed not to offend Voodoo's essential secrecy: Voudon, religion, way of life, banned by slave-owners, forced underground, admixture of conventional Catholicism and West African tradition, a pantheon of godheads – *loas* – a Supreme Being – *Gran Met* – to rival free-masonry's *Jabulon*: kind, cruel, violent and vindictive, wise and generous, all things to anyone willing to acknowledge his supremacy. Even the names were alike: *Danbhalah, Jabulon, Jahweh. Danbhalah* does not speak, but hisses: hence, snake fetish. *Langage* is Voudon's liturgy: *Danbhalah* governs water and sun, the sun on the water makes a rainbow, *Aida-Wedo*, his wife. *Aida-Wedo* is also *Erzulie*, goddess of beauty and love, dark and vain and angers easily: *Cassandra. Danbhalah* and *Aida-Wedo* make blood sacrifices; their communions are governed by *Papa Legba*, who is Christ, *Christopher*.

"God, I love sex," Phillipe eyed Carey, Emily, Matthew.

"It's not why we're here, Phillipe." Matthew contained the beast.

"It's not why you think you're here," Phillipe grinned wickedly, leaning towards Carey. "Take this," he offers her the joint. She reaches to accept it; he snatches her wrist, pulls her hand towards him, presses it against his cheek. "It is soft, no?"

"Soft, yes; gentle, no." Carey resented the familiarity; he scared her. She watched herself flee: no one stopped her – not Matthew, not Emily, not herself.

"You see," Phillipe says to Matthew, as if they are discussing philosophy, "it is universal." Not saying what it was.

"You always knew how to get what you wanted, Phillipe."

Before, Phillipe had greeted them as honoured guests: they were the only white people present at his service. Now, he treats them like servants. Carey inhales, passes the joint to Emily; they barely exchange a glance, just enough to remind the other she is not alone. Matthew takes it from Emily, studies her, it, passes it untouched to Phillipe. The older, bigger man laughs.

"You don't know what I want, Matthew; you never have done."

"Do you?"

"Yah; sure. I am Baron Samedi."

*Baron Samedi* is the undertaker who kills with his cock. He drinks and smokes and fucks what walks. He drifts easily from gentle *Rada* ritualists who wear white to sacrifice chickens, goats and bulls to the rhythm of oxhide-covered drums, and the *Pedro-ists* in red, who dance wild and menacing and demonic and who sacrifice pigs to the sound of two drums, covered in goatskin, struck only by hand.

"Stop playing, Phillipe."

"You came to see me."

"Yes," Matthew admitted. "Now I'm not sure why."

Phillipe asked:

"You want a drink?"

Matthew shook his head.

Carey said greedily:

"Yes."

"You," Phillipe pointed at Emily, "in the kitchen; bring us some beers."

Emily did not hesitate: the lessons were far and away above petty disputes over who fetched a beer from the refrigerator.

She gave Phillipe his beer first. He took it in one hand, her in another.

"Are you frightened, girl?"

"No," she said truthfully.

"Excited, then?"

"I think so."

"What are you doing here?"

"I'm here," Emily shrugged. "Make up your own reason why."

Phillipe roared with laughter.

"You always got the good ones, Matthew."

"Maybe."

"You want to know what it's all about, man?" Phillipe was suddenly a rationalist. "All we want, we just want the best chance to get laid. What do you think?"

"I think," Matthew hesitated, then grinned broadly, "I think it's not the worst part of it."

Carey took her beer from Emily, studied it like it was holy grail, hissed in anger and in pain:

"Is that what it's about, Matthew?" It was not what she had left family and firm behind for, so Matthew could fuck her.

Emily stood behind her; gripped her shoulder, leaned against Carey's back.

"What I said was, it's not the worst part of it. What do you say? Why do you sleep with me, then? Out of burden, duty?"

"Maybe I love you." She was sitting on her heels, hunkered down, rocking. "Do you ever think of that?"

Emily kneaded her shoulders from behind. This was about her too. They were lean, fit, aggressive together. Her eyes met Phillipe's while Carey and Matthew attacked one another. She thought: he's fucking me in his head; and, she thought, I like it. He grinned knowingly. She winked back. "Yah," he had said. She mouthed at him: "Yah."

Carey reached up to her shoulders, covered Emily's hands with hers.

"Sometimes, you don't seem to know what you want, Matthew – Teacher. How am I expected to follow if you don't know where you're going?"

"She's right," Phillipe jeered. "You don't know where you're going. If you're going to lead them off the path, be sure they can read a compass – and you can too."

"Tell me then, Phillipe," Matthew demanded. "I know what I think I'm doing; you tell me what you think."

"Communion," muttered Emily. "We're fucking taking communion together."

"I'll tell you some things, Matthew, things you know. I'll tell you and then you go away and you decide what you're doing, where you're going." He paused, sipped his beer, lit a cigarette, tossed the pack to Emily, nodded as if in afterthought. "Then maybe I'll come after you."

"Whose side are you on. Phillipe?" Matthew asked lightly.

"What are the choices? You know what I hear The Programme is now? The army of God and Satan. I love it – the army of God and Satan in a white uniform bought from a mail-order catalogue, like doctors and nurses? Matthew, my old friend, my dear old friend, there's a world out here, you know it, a twilight world, living by what they think are different codes and all of them, all of us, we are just the same. People like you and me, we're offering addictive soup in kitchens without a back door. We're building families and we think: yah, a family will do it.

"It doesn't work like that: build a family; become a threat. You know how it goes down: they can tolerate any kind of a different way of living if it's somewhere else, in some other country; here, make a life that lasts from the cradle to the grave – with its own family structures, its own educational system, its own rules of conduct, its own resources – and we become the threat from within, we're talking subversion, and we're talking about time to nip it in the bud. If nip means an assault at Waco, or at Ruby Ridge in the mountains of Montana, then so be it: they've got the gunfire.

"In the end, it's not enough to build a family: look at Charlie Manson; he built a family, if you like. David Koresh. Marshall Applewhite and his Heaven's Gate. Jim Jones: he had a family. I knew him, liked him too." He did not pause for reflection or remembrance but rushed on. "You've got to be going somewhere with it; you can't just plod along thinking the end is the means. If it ain't something worth fighting for, well, it ain't worth, you know, fucking either."

Carey snapped:

"Too much fucking this, fucking that. Who needs fucking

fighting?"

"You do, lady," Phillipe snarled. "You didn't come into The Programme as just a warm place to escape, did you? You've got drive – you've got balls between your legs, girl – it's got to be something you can make something out of, doesn't it? That's what I'm saying to you: something to fight for. Yah?"

"Is this what you told Cassandra?" Matthew asked.

"Maybe. Something like it. Can't say what she heard, though."

Carey – stoned – snorted:

"Bullshit. It's all bullshit."

Phillipe giggled.

"Maybe."

Suspiciously, Carey asked:

"What's your angle on The Programme?"

Phillipe replied promptly:

"Same as anything. It's there; so am I. Berlinger pays me."

"Berlinger?" Matthew asked. "You take money from Berlinger?"

"Sure. Doesn't everyone?"

Matthew, angry for the first time, crossed to him, fists clenched.

"Don't you believe in anything, Phillipe?"

Phillipe looked past his shoulders. Matthew glanced around. Through an open doorway, he saw red-robed black men, as if from nowhere. Matthew laughed.

"Am I supposed to be frightened, Phillipe? What is this? You fucked Cassandra – now you want to fuck me?"

Phillipe was placid, Buddha-like.

"If you're facing evil, Matthew, evil is what you'll have to do to defeat it. Remember that, Matthew – Teacher." He reached out a hand, took Matthew's in his, squeezed it gently. "Is that all right with you, Matthew? Teacher?"

It was not a question but a challenge, a warning, even a premonition.

\* \* \*

From *The Seer's Lesson On Pleasure and On Pain*:

*It's easy – if impossible – to forget about our bodies. Mind, body, soul. The three basic ingredients that make us what we are. We take our bodies for granted. Without them, we do not exist as people. We attribute their needs and their limitations to a state of mind. We treat the mind as standing between the body and the soul. We are one and we are whole. The relationship between body and soul is ignored. The body is a vessel. To stretch the vessel is to stretch its capacity. Do not think about it – be it.*

*The injunction to cease sexual activity on joining The Programme is not self-denial but discipline. It is not about liberation from sexual desire or dominance but redirection. To make your body capable of doing things it has not been able to do before is to show yourself you are capable of changing. To change is what you came into The Programme for. Do not tell me you did not come in to change your bodily activities. Do not tell me you are concerned only with the spiritual, or the mental. Do not tell me you – and you alone – can distinguish between them.*

*The Programme is about bringing all of ourselves into one being. Sometimes, we call it an army. Sometimes, we call it a religion. Sometimes, a way of life. Sometimes, even life itself. I am one, we are many, together we shall be whole. We each have to be able to take our parts in the whole. We have to be able to give and take with our bodies as we have learned to do in our hearts and in our minds and in our worship of God and Satan alike, with love and with hate. Our bodies are also weapons that belong to the army of unification. Our bodies are sacrifices to a demanding deity. Our bodies are what we bring to our way of life. Our bodies are life itself.*

*We associate sex with pleasure! We associate punishment with pain! We have to be able to control their exercise, redirect them, change them about! Sexual punishment! Pain as the ultimate – pleasurable – relief! Not sex as pain, nor least of all pain as sex! Sex is sex – hate sex, love sex! Pain is pain – love pain, hate pain! God as sexual hate! Satan as love that punishes! Learn to take it! More difficult, learn to give it!*

\* \* \*

They had driven down from New York in the Lincoln, through Maryland and Virginia to Asheville in the central mountains of the Western part of North Carolina; from Asheville, through Alabama and Mississippi to New Orleans. They drove, but it felt like they had stayed still as the South paraded before them like a line of whores waiting to be picked.

The Appalachians and the Blue Ridge mountains dominated the drive to Asheville, Matthew's home town: they came in on the Blue Ridge Parkway. Downtown Asheville was an architectural roller-coaster: neo-Georgian, neo-classical, Italian Renaissance, Spanish and even Art Deco. Matthew pulled up to point out a rambling old building – the Thomas Wolfe Memorial.

This was a defiant, luxury trip. They were like fugitives on the run, spending as if they were using stolen credit cards, staying in the best hotels, the financial parasites that Amanda's lawyers were going to try to make them look like. In Asheville, they had booked into the Richmond Hill Inn. The main hotel was an erstwhile Victorian mansion but they were lodged in a modern cottage in the grounds. The hotel housed one of the city's best restaurants, reservations and jackets required. The night they arrived, they ate there to soak up the atmosphere of the Southern city; Matthew made no secret of his wish to make a successful appearance.

Both his brother and a sister still lived in the city. His mother was in a retirement home on the outskirts. His father had died long since. He took Carey to meet his mother but she could barely appreciate who he was, let alone a stranger. Once, she called her Cassandra, a name lodged in her mind in association with her son, but she called him Jack, his father's name. She was wrinkled and frail and the smell of urine in her bedroom told them she was incontinent. Carey wondered if this was how her mother would have been had she lived, but Marion would still not be seventy while Matthew's mother was nearly ninety.

The second night, all three of them visited with Matthew's older brother – Eugene, Gene for short – and his younger sister Frances and her family. They were awkward together, wanting to ask Matthew about his life but frightened of what they might hear. Matthew had always been different; it was as if they had been two families – theirs and his – on two tracks. Frances eyed Carey and Emily alternately, not hiding what she suspected.

"We read about you in the papers," Gene said over dinner, meaning the Kroger pre-hearing publicity. "Hey, has God got any money to spare for Ma?" The cost of the retirement home.

"Gene," Frances warned.

Gene's latest wife – Carolyn – was younger even than Carey. There were three generations at the table: the brothers and sister; the brothers' three young women companions; and Frances' two, early-teen children. Carolyn spent more time supervising the servants than at the table, refusing the visiting women's offers of help.

"How's Gerard?" Matthew asked Gene, trying to change the subject.

"He's doing fine; pre-law, you know." Gene grinned knowingly at Carey. "That's where the big bucks are, right?"

"Depends what type of law you do, Eugene," Carey said in case she was the next person he hit up for money. "What's he interested in?"

"Sports, mostly; lot of money to make in sports-law."

"What is all that about in New York, Matthew?" Frances asked.

"Money," her husband growled.

It was the only thing they could talk about.

After they went back to the hotel with Emily, Matthew and Carey walked alone in the grounds.

"I can't connect up the dots," Carey said.

"Here to, well, here and now?"

"Yes. Them."

"Frances was a wild child; wild teenager. She was the one who was expected to lead the least conventional life. There were times, drugs, men, it wasn't certain she'd have any kind of a life. She burned herself up, out. Started over like it had never happened."

"And Gene?"

"Gene was Gene as long as I can remember. All Gene ever wanted was money; money and position, maybe, but money mostly. Carolyn's his third wife. I shouldn't think he noticed when the others left; went on working, making money, bought a new wife and car. They thought I'd do the best, be the big success."

"Are you?"

"What do you think?"

"I think you mean a lot to a lot of people's lives; you mean a lot to mine," she reassured him. "You've made a place for people who don't fit in anywhere else; you've given them a sense of themselves, a sense of direction. I'd say, that's a lot more than most people ever do."

"It's what happens now that makes me wonder."

"What did you learn from Helen?"

They had not yet talked about it. On the drive back to New York, they had carried Amanda Kroger, Nahum – to act as her minder – and a couple more junior members. Once they arrived, they had been caught up in further conferences with their lawyers: they had not told the lawyers about Amanda; as officers of the court, they would have a duty to disclose her whereabouts to the other side.

There were other members, too, with needs to which Matthew was bound and of which Carey was no part. For a whole day, while they awaited Emily, she had nothing to do except to hang around the New York Chapter. The pace of her life had changed: she was not at work, but she was not on holiday; she was with The Programme, but not as a client. There were no parameters, no comparators. She passed some of the time with her friend Meredith who told her that Calvin Wood had become an initiate, Carey's first convert. Carey said:

"You can understand your own reasons, never someone else's."

"Peace, most of us just want peace."

"Was that what you wanted?"

"I think so. There was, you know, nothing specific I was trying to get away from," Merry said. "I just felt worn down by the complexity of it all."

"The complexity?"

"Yes. Trying to balance everyone, everything. I liked my work." She had been a post-graduate in London, studying women servants in late Victorian urban England. Carey knew, from occasional remarks, that it was an area she still liked to read about in her spare moments, when she was not studying the latest *dictum* from The Programme hierarchy. "College was nothing but politics; home was politics – whether I was spending too much time with my mother, my father; relationships with men, too, were politics, maybe above all. It was like The Teacher says, too much energy spent getting to where I just wanted to be. I don't know; maybe in another life I was in a convent – maybe I would have been, anyway."

"There's politics here."

"I know," Merry admitted, though she tried to keep herself well apart from The Programme factions. "I'm not saying it's simple."

"Don't you ever wonder, er, well, if this is enough?"

"Sure. And one day, if I wonder long enough, if it gets too complex for me, maybe I'll go on to something else."

"Day at a time?"

"Absolutely; like all addiction-counselling. You should try it," she said.

* * *

"What do you want to know?" Matthew asked in the grounds of the Asheville hotel, in the middle of the night and, it seemed momentarily to Carey, the middle of nowhere.

"Everything that's going on. I want to be a part of it," she insisted. "Good or bad, whatever."

"Reconciliation of God and Satan? Army of God and Satan according to Cassandra. Are you ready for that, Carey?"

"You don't need to protect me from it," she protested. "I am a member, remember?"

"Sometimes," he answered lightly. "I'm not always sure if you're my lawyer who's dipping a toe into the water as a member; a member who's still my lawyer; or, just my lover."

"Ouch," she remarked sardonically on his choice of priorities. "You have so many people in love with you, I think you lose sight of what it means. I'm ready. For all of it. Whatever it is. I don't want you holding back on me; I don't want to hold myself back."

"I know you don't want to; but that's not the same."

"The same as what?" She was irritated. "Don't you trust me?"

"Trust? That's what we demand from new members."

"Meaning I get to trust you, but you don't need to trust me?" Trust; love. The words seemed interchangeable.

"Of course, I trust you as a lawyer."

She leaned back against a tree, glowered at him.

"Am I just another moment? Are we all?" The conversation wasn't going the way she expected, or the way she would have expected if she had thought about it beforehand: nor the trip.

"I don't think of it as moments."

"What, then?"

"What are the only two absolutes?"

"Being born; dying," she recounted by rote.

"Right. That gives me just one more; you too."

"What about being itself: can't that be an absolute?"

"Very good, Carey; very good indeed."

"Don't patronise me, Teacher," she taunted.

He placed his hands either side of her shoulders so she couldn't escape, leaned down to kiss her. For a moment she let him, then she ducked out from under, threw her arms around him from behind, squeezed hard, dug her nails into his ribs. He covered her hands with his own.

"Go on, then," he said tautly. "What do you want?"

"You're leaving me out of things; I want to know what; and why."

She had stopped squeezing in order to hurt him, rested her head instead against his back for warmth, stroked his chest. She wished he would understand how much she was with him; she wished she did. Being part of The Programme ought to be easier than this, easier than life; it was life's final departure tax.

"It's Cassandra's game for now, not mine to play – to leave you out of or let you in. I'm not even sure if I'm in or out of it."

"Cassandra's game? You wrote the rules. Or maybe what I mean is, you threw all the other rule books out."

"Are we back to Lucius again? Something like that."

She nodded, rubbing her chin against his back.

"Did it shock you so much?"

"No. I wasn't shocked. You want me to be, but I'm not."

"What, then?"

"I wonder sometimes, what did he think about it?"

"He? Lucius?"

"Yes, Lucius." She clutched her hands together behind her back, pulling away from him. The night was growing colder, or she was. She rarely wore a bra these days: she was aware of her nipples against her blouse; they were hard and itchy against the material; she wanted to scratch them. "I mean, I suppose what I'm asking – Lucius – other members you've slept with – one or other of you, you or Cassandra – I don't think I mean me, or Helen – but the casual adventures – the Amanda Krogers – what are they supposed to feel? Blessed? And what do they feel? Used?"

"You're beginning to sound like a lawyer again."

"I never stopped being one. That's one of the best things you've done for me. All my life, I've never really liked being a lawyer. There's so many times I decided I didn't want to be one any more. That's frightened me. What would I do if I wasn't a lawyer; and, if I didn't do it, what would I be? Now, I'm not so scared about losing it, so I don't mind it so much."

"Well, then, there's your answer."

She was about to ask him what he meant when she understood: they did not need to choose between being blessed and being used. Everything good and everything bad about human relations, in a pick-n-mix bag from the spiritual sweet-shop. She used his own words back on him.

"Very good, Matthew, very good indeed."

He chuckled, held his arms out: she stepped forward, let him put his arms around her, wriggled against him for fun and friction. He said into the top of her head:

"It's not my decision to leave you out; it's your decision how far you want to go."

"Maybe that's true," she sulked. She wanted to feel that the tough decisions had already been made; what he was saying meant that there were more to come. "It doesn't make it any easier."

"More difficult, really," he said cheerfully.

* * *

From *Programme and Progression*:

*There are no Gods who can do for you or to you what you cannot do for or to yourself; there is no faith that can make happen what you cannot make happen yourself; there is no power to invoke that does not come from within you. No one can enter your mind, let alone invade it; when so-called cults and like organisations – including The Programme – are referred to as "mind-bending," or "brain-washing," it would be amusing if it was not such a disturbing misrepresentation. The mind is not an entity with an independent existence which you can turn over to another. It is yours; it is you.*

*That is not to say that you do not learn from others, do not allow others to teach you, do not re-order your perceptions accordingly: that is precisely what The Programme invites you to do; but it remains your mind, and your decision whether or not to receive the information, what to do with it, how to let it affect you. The expression "mind-bending" imports the notion of something different from what everyone does each day – learn, absorb, use.*

*Mind-bending, mind-control, brain-washing are synonyms for new experiences, new perceptions, offered by those with something new to say; the energy that feeds it, that gives it life, can only come from within, from the listener who decides that he is going to do something with it, and what. The moment that is accepted, the accusation falls.*

\* \* \*

Andrew Chettle came in early to buttonhole Colin. He had been in Brussels the night before, channel-cruising in his hotel room when he flicked through CNN and saw a short report on his new firm's clients and the hearing which, he understood, was what had taken Carey to the States: it put what he knew of the Kroger case in a different and unwelcome light.

He had watched the report with a growing sense of irritation, perhaps even dismay, mostly professional, mildly personal: he had thrown in his lot with the Arnotts, but Colin was his friend and he had always enjoyed a soft spot for Carey. He was astute enough to appreciate that her relationship with The Programme was not exclusively professional: the idea of her being involved with them appalled him.

Andrew enjoyed life: he was not a careless or reckless man, but he was not overly-cautious: his team's move to Arnotts had been described in the legal press as unusual and imaginative. So far, the boldness seemed to be paying off; most of the clients they wanted to come with them were doing so; they had picked up some new work

– including two unions.

Still, he could do without a distraction like The Programme. Colin was in. A couple of others had also arrived, but it was too early for appointments with clients. Andrew dropped his overnight case in the room that since the beginning of the week had been temporarily assigned to him, poured himself a mug of coffee and brought a cup and saucer for Colin. Colin, hunched over the mail, looked up in surprise.

"I thought you were in Brussels?"

"I was. I came back early."

"No one to keep you warm in bed?"

"Now, now, dear boy; jealousy just makes it worse."

"Thanks," Colin pulled the coffee towards him. "What's up?" Like a new relationship, he was nervous; he was a worrier; it had been going too well for comfort.

"Should something be?"

"No," Colin said crossly: "It shouldn't. Now tell me what it is."

"I saw a clip of these Programme people on CNN."

"And?"

"How deeply involved with them are we, Colin?"

"As far as I'm concerned," Colin chose his words with care, "a lot less than with most of our clients."

"And as far as Carey is concerned?"

"I'm not sure. Too much," he admitted.

"I don't understand it," Andrew sighed. "She's always seemed so, oh, stable."

"We all have to break out once in a while," Colin took at stab at defending his sister.

"What?" Andrew mocked. "Even you?"

"Not me. I have to never break out. It's the only way I can handle it all."

"Yes," Andrew admired his friend's self-appraisal. "That's about right. So it's hands off Jessica, is it?"

"You really can be a shit, Andrew; I managed to forget that when we were bringing everything together. Yes, it's hands off Jessica; she's a nice girl, woman; that's all."

"That's where we differ, Colin: if I see a woman I'm attracted to, I need a reason not to do something about it; you need a reason to do so."

"I'm married and that's my absolute reason not to, that's the difference," Colin replied, mollified. "Anyway, I'm sure I'm not her type." Andrew raised his eyebrows: Colin had been thinking about her. "What are you trying to do, Andrew? Make me unhappy because you don't feel happy about The Programme?"

"Ouch. You're such a calm bugger, I forget how capable you are at defending yourself."

"Flattery won't cut it. What do you want from me?"

"Reassurance, I suppose; God knows, when we talked about European business, neither of us was thinking about the ashes of the Order of the Solar Temple."

"I think she's more involved than she intended but it's more this Matthew Crane character than anything else; once that wears off, the rest of it'll follow."

"I hope you're right."

"I'm sure I am," Colin replied cheerfully.

He did not to tell Andrew about the calls he had been receiving from Richard Fielding, Emily's husband. Following the previous threats through his solicitors, Fielding had called Colin at the office; when Colin's secretary wouldn't put his calls through, he had called Colin at home, late in the evening, drunk, demanding to know where Emily was, accusing Carey of leading her into The Programme, threatening Colin with dire consequences – professional and personal – if he did not bring her back. It was nonsense: nothing to bother about; nothing to bother anyone else about either.

\* \* \*

Matthew stayed back to talk.

"Tell me about Berlinger," he asked Phillipe after Carey and Emily had left.

"Tell me about the girl," Phillipe countered.

"Which girl? Carey?"

"Yah. That one."

"What's your interest in her?"

"Isn't what you think, Matthew. She'd drown inside of me; she don't like me."

"I know that. That's why I asked."

They were in the backyard, sitting on chairs still drinking beer, no more dope. They sat in plain view of his *hounfour*, his temple, a covered space in the walled backyard around an altar stone – the *pe* – on which were set candles and tiny brown jars, rattles, charms, flags, a model boat: there were also photographs in frames – Papa and Baby Doc, Mandela, Kaunda; black leaders of men, representatives on earth of the gods. Phillipe played with a rattle, bulbous, with

198

a long-handle, phallic – the *asson*.

"Are you happy, Phillipe?"

"You were the one with ambition, Matthew; all that time ago, still are I think. This suits me. I've got a congregation, maybe four, five hundred: that's a lot more than some of the regular churches about here. They tithe me two, three hundred dollars a year each. Works out good. They give me this house to live in: it isn't grand but they know where to find me. I get what I want – women, to eat and drink, a little bit of respect now and then too."

"Fear?"

"Yah; a lot of it is fear."

"And Berlinger – he pays you for what?"

"You ever think, Matthew, how many people I knew back then? I knew everyone in England; I came back home, knew everyone here too. I'm a gold-mine for that boy."

"He pays you for information?"

"Call it information if you like," Phillipe answered languidly. "It's more than that."

"What, then?"

"You think you're the only one comes calling? You wonder why you came to see me?"

"I came because Cassandra came, that's all." Matthew's eyes narrowed: Phillipe knew the way into his head.

That was the answer: what Berlinger was buying was how to get into their heads.

Phillipe watched him work it out, saw him bristle, too. He laughed, reached across, patted Matthew's knee.

"All these years, you've been doing it; me, I've been watching and learning."

Matthew sipped his beer slowly, thoughtfully. For a time, when the women were still there, they had all been a little stoned, him too. Now, he was clear. At the time, he had thought Phillipe was stoned with them; now, he was sure he had not been.

"What about her?" Cassandra. "What did she want?"

"Ask her. Maybe she wants be the one on top now, have all them people looking up to her, you too."

"Yes, I think that's what she wants."

"You going to let her?"

"If I let her, she wouldn't be doing it, would she? I would."

"Might not know it, though."

"You say you just like to watch but you're a player too."

"Have to play once in a while, remind yourself how it feels. But playing's just that for me, a game: I never took it seriously."

"You're asking if I did?"

"No," Phillipe said sadly. "I know you do."

"And you think that's my mistake?"

"That I know, brother. What you doing with that little girl?" Back to Carey.

"She's not so little; good lawyer, too. What's it to you?"

"This is where we came in: I told you about Berlinger." Tit for tat.

"He's coming after me, isn't he?"

"That's a safe bet; you or The Programme."

"Same thing," Matthew dismissed. "Whatever Cassandra may think."

"Same thing I told him too," Phillipe said cheerfully.

\* \* \*

Phillipe's red-robed *Guedes* had accompanied the women to their hotel, sullen though not rude. They drove riverside through the French Quarter, along the path of the Mississippi, past three-storey houses in weathered brick with huge, dormer windows and wooden galleries, pastel-painted. They had found a suite in a small hotel, two bedrooms adjoining with a common balcony overlooking a courtyard bar and plenty of space to sit within.

Emily and Carey talked, their first chance alone. Carey was still angry at Matthew's remark while they were at Lamarque's. Emily told her:

"That's not why you're angry."

"Why, then?"

"I don't know. What do you think?" Programme-speak.

"You're really getting into it, Em."

"It's bringing something out in me," she admitted shyly.

"What?" Carey was only half-attending: she was pissed in more ways than one and wanted the conversation to be about her.

"All the time I was with Richard, trying to care for him, trying to please him; I like that – caring for people, pleasing them. But now I'm doing it for me; it's dangerous to invest it in someone else."

"Simon?"

"Simon's nice; that's all. After Richard, well, you know."

"It's easy to, er, mix it all up," Carey warned her, warned herself.

"Men; The Programme?"

"Something like that. Warmth, love, wanting to belong."

"It's natural," Emily shrugged.

"Is it? I mean, The Programme – is it natural? Or just easy."

"I'm not sure it's that easy. I find it hard enough. Other members; people maybe I wouldn't have had five minutes for on the outside; trying to be completely open with them, share with them, accept them. I still find, oh, I don't know, I still get irritated, want to say – pull yourself together, you know," she concluded laughing. "Like someone at work. Don't you?"

"It's been easy for me," Carey reminded her that she had a special ticket. "Though I get scared sometimes."

"What of?"

"That's it's all a fantasy, a mistake. As London fades, I begin to wonder: was I that unhappy, that badly off?"

"I was," Emily said flatly.

"Yes. I suppose that's what I mean," Carey flashed back to the conversation with Meredith in New York. "You've got something specific to hang it on."

"I don't know how committed I am to it," Emily said. "It's something I have to find out about. That's all, really. Is that enough?"

Carey glanced over her shoulder, as if to say: "Who are you asking?"

Emily stretched, yawned, got up and strolled into her own room calling back:

"I'm not the one you should be asking either."

After she had showered, she came back in to find Carey still sitting where she had left her, in an armchair, smoking, a glass of mineral water at her side. She knelt down beside her, put her arms around her waist.

"Don't worry so, Carey; we're fine."

"I know," Carey stroked her friend's hair. "I'm just not sure I am."

She was stoned; she had drunk too many beers. Although the visit was intended to bring them back together, it seemed as if she and Emily were drifting in different directions, different stages. Nothing was the way it was supposed to be: not even Emily.

\* \* \*

When Matthew returned, he found her waiting up for him. She said without waiting:

"I feel like I'm on a roller-coaster."

He sat down opposite her.

"It's like that sometimes."

"Yes, I know. And I've gone with it, kept going with it, but it just doesn't seem to end."

"It is the end, Carey, not the means. That's all there is."

"Not the fire beyond?"

"The fire beyond is like this: you're on a roller-coaster; up and down, round and round, even upside down; one day, when you think you're going over the crest of another rise, you just keep going up and up and beyond."

"I thought this trip was supposed to make us feel closer. I don't understand why, but ever since Asheville, you've been somewhere else."

"No supposed to be, Carey, just what is."

"All right then," she said, annoyed by his pedantry. "Not what I wanted."

"Ah, well, that's different. This is Carey as was, isn't it?"

"What do you mean?"

"The one who doesn't like it when she doesn't get what she wants." Spoiled.

"What was all that about at Phillipe's?"

"I'm not sure myself. That's the thing about Phillipe. You can never tell if he's warning you about something – and if he is, whether it's for your good or someone else's – or if he's telling you something just to stir it up for the hell of it, to make it happen."

Matthew had walked back from Phillipe's, several miles through the old city and its more recent additions. It had been a long time since he had enjoyed the opportunity to be alone. Phillipe's focus on Carey had taken him by surprise, made him focus on her. He had wanted her since he set eyes on her, but only on his terms, which meant within The Programme. She had to come to want it at the same time as she came to want him. It was a difficult task, but he had to let her make it her own way without telling her how to do it. It was what Carey had meant when she accused him of keeping her out – holding back.

He said, as if he was answering a question she had asked:

"I belong to The Programme, Carey; the question is whether you do."

"I told you," she protested, "in Asheville."

"You told me what you wanted; I told you, it wasn't the same thing." As being there.

"What do I mean to you, Matthew?"

"I could ask you the same."

"You know what you mean to me. I love you; I respect you; I believe in you; I believe in The Programme."

"'I love you – I believe in The Programme'," he repeated, as if he had been listening to her conversation with Emily.

"Meaning?"

"Meaning you haven't separated it all out; meaning that until you do, you can't know how you feel about it's different parts."

"Do you want me to go home now, leave you here? Is that what it's about?"

"Doesn't matter what I want."

They stared at one another with something that was on her part akin to hatred, on his to anger. She said:

"I'm a fool, really."

"How so?"

"I really believed it was all about peace, love, being whole; I thought, well, er, there's some tensions getting there, a little bit of play-acting between members struggling for something they can't otherwise resolve, but at the end of the day – family."

"And? How is it not? Because I'm not immediately kissing it better?"

She blushed.

"Perhaps. You still haven't said."

"What?"

"What you want."

"What I want you to do?"

"Yes."

"See the case through; then decide what you want to do for yourself."

"How can I do that if I don't know what you want, what my choices are?"

"It's the only way you can be sure it's you who's deciding." She shook her head, tired, confused. He said: "The other way round, the question you're deciding is whether to do what I want."

She shook her head again.

"It's just as complicated as everything else, isn't it, Matthew?"

He smiled at last, rose, reached a hand out for her.

"Whoever told you it was any different?"

He led her to the bed and started to help her undress. She shrugged him off. While she was undressing, he went into the bathroom; when he came out, she passed him. By the time she was finished, he was already in bed, had turned out all but the night-lights on the wall. She slipped in on the other side from him, did not cuddle up for warmth or more. He rolled onto his side to look at her, staring at the ceiling. After a while, he stretched out and touched her breast, traced a finger down her stomach, slid it between her legs. She neither resisted nor helped him.

He pulled her legs apart, stroked the inside of her thigh, felt his way to the dry lips of her vagina. He brought his fingers to his mouth, licked them wet, dampened the opening enough to insert them without hurting her. Gradually, in spite of herself, she began to respond to the circular movements he made within, a second finger, then a third, he was forcing her to buck against him, bringing her manually to the edge before he pulled his hand out, clambered on top of her, pushed himself into her, moving slowly on top of her, to his own rhythm, he came gently, in his own time, emptying himself into her without waiting.

* * *

In the backyard, outside the *hounfour*, Phillipe raised the *asson*: it is the circle and the wand of magic, joined together. Within it were sacred stones and the dried vertebrae of serpents to represent the bones of African forefathers. He held it towards the sky, rattling it, whispering:

"Come, *Danbhalah*, come down."

It is three in the morning. He is alone. This is a private ceremonial.

He lays the asson down on the *pe*, picks up *ku-bha-sah*, the ritual sword, runs his thumb along the blade, cuts it until it bleeds, smiles, licks greedily, replaces the sword. He walks over and opens a door in the wall; it leads to a second yard, running along behind his own house and the one next door, which is also owned by the congregation, where the *commandant la place* – the master of ceremonies – lives. One side is taken up by coops; he reaches in and removes a chicken, holding it by the neck so it cannot bite him, but careful not to choke it to death. It is an easy, familiar activity, one he could do in his sleep and, sometimes, that he finds he has done.

He carries the bird back to the *pe*; the stone is already stained with the blood of a thousand earlier sacrifices; now there will be one more. These, too, are easy and familiar steps, he whispers the words, thrusts his body forward so that the bloody spray hits him full in the chest, looks again to the sky and smiles: fly away; fly away little bird. It is a spell he is casting, but even he does not know if it is a spell for good or ill.

* * *

For the first time since he had returned to The Programme, he slipped into her bed.

They were both naked.

They lay facing one another.

She reached down and touched him; he was erect.

He shuddered.

"Cassandra."

"Little brother."

"You like?"

She took his hand and placed it on her breast, put her own arm around his head.

Their lips met; they kissed fully.

He pressed against her, moved slowly against her, she did not pull away, but when he tried to roll her onto her back she resisted. One of his hands was trapped between their bodies. He let go of her breast, reached for her thigh, tried to lift her open. She seized his wrist, pulled his hand away, placed it back on her breast. He rolled the nipple around in his fingers, lowered his head to take it in his mouth, they kissed again, he asked:

"Why not?"

She put a finger to his lip; he licked it, sucked it into his mouth. He was still pressed against her. It would not wait much longer.

"It's still not the time, Huw my love. Not quite, not yet."

He groaned, tried to roll himself away, but she clung on to his spine so that he could not release the pressure and rocked herself against him until he came cold and sticky on both their stomachs, their mouths grappling fiercely. It was the closest yet, they have straddled the line, soon they will cross it.

## Chapter Nine

The New York State Supreme Court – the first level trial court – was at 60 Centre Street – in its original English spelling – in the City Hall neighbourhood, a few blocks north of Wall Street, not a long journey from the SoHo Chapter House to which Matthew and Carey and Emily had returned from New Orleans the night before the hearing.

The court was in a large, grey stone building, creaking with age, next door to the old Federal Courthouse and around the corner from the new one, a magnificent building of marble and brass with which its predecessor made a poor contrast. The Court was approached by a set of wide steps – as wide as the building itself – six inches deep, dominated by a set of four Corinthian pillars. They were in Part – Court – 37, a high-ceilinged, panelled room without a modern sound system: the voices of lawyers, judge and witnesses alike disappeared into the ceiling but, hopefully, were accurately caught by the stenographer.

They met their own lawyers in the corridor.

"Morning," Carey said. "We've got someone for you to meet."

Nahum drew out Amanda from behind Matthew. Carey said:

"This is the real plaintiff, Amanda Kroger."

"Pleased to meet you, Amanda." Danny Trask – their lead lawyer – held out a hand, grinning. Lawyers do love to win. They do not care how.

\* \* \*

Cassandra had not gone to New York. She had planned a Special Mass at Hammer Reach, in which only her closest confidants would participate: a trial of another kind.

\* \* \*

"I have never asked for money or other property from any member."

"You've never refused it?"

"There have been occasions when I've felt that money was being used to buy acceptance in place of earning it with commitment."

"Can you give me any examples?"

206

"By date, no. I have nothing to do with financial management. We have a member who is an accountant. My wife would deal with any questions. She might ask me if she should accept."

"Your wife would deal with it? What are we talking about here, the housekeeping?"

"I don't know what you're talking about. I'm talking about building a home that people haven't been able to find elsewhere. That's a full-time job, Mr Kennedy."

"You had sex with Amanda Kroger, didn't you?"

"I don't think that's your business, Mr Kennedy."

"Instruct to answer, Your Honour?"

Matthew answered without waiting:

"I was very close to Amanda; we were lovers at one time, yes."

"While your wife looked after The Programme?"

"We all looked after The Programme, Mr Kennedy. My relations with Amanda were not kept secret from my wife."

"So what have we got here? A group for free-sex? Or just for you to pick and choose?"

"A group with a lot of love in it, Mr Kennedy; something most of our members missed in their lives beforehand; sometimes, that would mean physical love, yes. If you sleep with a woman, Mr Kennedy, does she give you all her money?"

"It was more than sleeping with members, though, wasn't it, Mr Crane? We're talking about how they came to want to sleep with you."

"There's no accounting for taste."

Even the judge was amused; the audience laughed aloud.

"It doesn't answer the question, Mr Crane."

"For the life of me, Your Honour," Trask half-rose. "I can't see what the question is."

"I'll rephrase it, Your Honour, so even Mr Trask can understand it."

Carey thought: it was the same everywhere; aggression between lawyers who'd meet tonight for a drink; sarcastic repartee; skipping across the surface of the issues because lawyers did not know what lay beneath and had been trained never to ask a question to which they did not know the answer. None the less, the familiarity was reassuring. She was at the counsel table, where she had been permitted to sit, introduced to the court as The Programme's English lawyer; she glanced around to the public seats, sought out Emily, winked at her, won a comforting smile back.

"Would Ms Kroger have given you money but for The Programme?"

"I would have thought quite obviously not."

"Or the tenancy of Hammer Reach?"

"I assume the same is true."

"So what made her do it is The Programme, right?"

"She did it; she was – is – a member of The Programme. I don't think that means The Programme made her do it."

"You've accepted she wouldn't have done it if she hadn't been?"

"I don't put money in a charity box that isn't there, Mr Kennedy."

"The Programme wasn't there without you, was it, Mr Crane?"

"Nor Christianity without Christ."

"Are you Christ, Mr Crane? Is that what you're saying?"

"Mr Kennedy's twisting Mr Crane's words, Your Honour." Trask.

"Withdraw. Mr Crane, all I'm trying to get at, really, is this: it was The Programme that caused Ms Kroger to give you her money, right?"

"Ms Kroger gave the money to The Programme."

"Which you sent Mr Eccles to collect?"

"Ms Kroger asked Father Nahum to take it to me."

"Did you know about the money beforehand?"

"I knew she had money and that she was increasingly committed to The Programme. Did I ever think: Well, that means she will give us her money? No. Did I think, in general terms, that there was money amongst our members, which would help us develop? Of course I did; that is one of the ways we had managed to survive and grow."

"I'm curious, Mr Crane: how many members of The Programme have you slept with?"

Trask objected.

"This is none of Mr Kennedy's business, Your Honour."

"Goes to Mr Crane's domination of The Programme, Your Honour."

"I'll allow it."

"Mr Crane?"

"I couldn't tell you. If you're asking if I sleep with all the members, the answer is no. You already know I wasn't sleeping only with my wife."

"Where does it go, The Programme, Mr Crane?" Kennedy held up a hand to forestall the objection. "No, that wasn't my question. I just find myself wondering, if people abandon one set of values for another, don't they become kind of dependent on, well, whatever, whoever those new values come from?"

"It all depends on the person, Mr Kennedy."

"Calls for speculation, Your Honour," Trask interrupted.

The judge mumbled:

"That seems to be the area, doesn't it, Mr Trask?"

\* \* \*

Caleb is seated cross-legged on a bale of hay draped with a silk cloth on which the symbol of The Programme has been painted. He is naked. Beside him, on the floor, there is a bowl of oil in which stands a candle.

They are in the basement of the house at Hammer Reach, the large meditation area onto which the punishment cells open. Each of the cell-doors is closed, two of them with keys in their locks. There is silence from within them. The floor is covered with coconut matting.

Caleb is at one end of the basement; The Seer reclines at the other on a bed along the wall, also covered in silk but plain silk on which lie cushions for her to stretch out in comfort: against the middle of the bed is a much more substantial cushion, like the one in The Temple in London.

She is – unusually – wearing a white dress like The Programme's other female members usually wear, although – unlike their uniforms – hers is short, not reaching her knees. Instead of wearing it around her neck, however, she has extended the silver chain on which her Programme symbol hangs to use it as a loose belt, the symbol itself dangling suggestively between her legs. She is bare-legged, bare-foot. There is no member present – of any gender – who is not actively thinking of her sex.

The basement is lit only by candles, the rest in brass holders tied to long nails hammered into the walls. A gong hangs from the low ceiling, dangling like a disembodied head ready to look them in the eye. There are a dozen members present, not including the principal ceremonial protagonists. Between two of the cell doors, Christopher sits on a small cushion, his erect back to the wall, the master of ceremonies. He is wearing a loose, black robe. Opposite him, Paimon lounges between the other two cell doors, dressed wholly in red: red jeans, red sweater, red scarf around his neck, red socks, red sneakers. The reds do not match, but they are all bright, all promise blood.

The other members are – like The Seer – in traditional white. They sit upright on cushions or sprawl on the ground. Micah up from New York and Sister Gloria – recently arrived from England – lean casually against one another for support. There are others who were members in England, though several of those are American. Some are from Caleb's private unit of Initiates, now promoted Messengers, three slight youths, smaller than Caleb and not so stocky: Brother Reuben – Jacob's eldest son by his first wife, who had used Bilhah, his father's own mistress; Brother Lemuel – the mysterious king of whom nothing was known; Brother Ehud – who massacred ten thousand Moabites.

Sister Mary had been Mary when she joined, then Aholah the unfaithful; recently she had reverted to her given name, leaving unexplained whether it was a movement back or forwards onto the highest plane of all. Sister Pascale, likewise, was a given name. Sister Diana vied with Helen in Boston – as they had in London – for the title of Chapter belle; unlike Helen, though, she was openly vain about her looks and hoarded the interest she aroused in men as if frightened that it would one day disappear.

These three long-time friends sit in a group. What they are about to do is something that would have been unthinkable in London, in Matthew's Programme. They are scared. The Programme has kept them well for years. The Seer has asked them to join her, to experiment. She told them she wanted familiars, loyalists even. It was not a game that Matthew would play, she said with a giggle, but that did not mean it was wrong. It was part of the voyage that he had put her in command of – part of the purpose in coming to America; time to explore the extremes.

They are scared but they are excited; they make a pact to go down the road together; if any one pulls back, so would they all.

Those who had not been members in England are the elite of the new members. They have shown a natural gift, are the first to be made Messengers after the move, still only Junior Messengers but fast-tracking. They include the only black members of The Programme. Either side of thirty, they bore Biblical names from birth – Brothers Jeroboam and Jeremiah – given them by their father, the preacher of a Harlem fringe church with an undercurrent of Voudon, jailed for stealing from his congregation, dead from a heart attack on his third day inside.

The two Jays, as they quickly came to be called in The Programme, had an established taste for loud worship, black magic, sexual frenzy and mind control. They fit perfectly into Cassandra's image of how The Programme should develop.

Finally, a couple of Boston locals, one of them a woman friend of Leah's, the other a young man who wandered into the Coffee Lounge one afternoon shortly after it opened and sat in silence without food or drink until it was ready to close. When they came to ask him to leave, he said simply:

"No."

They had accepted him without more, not even the usual medical tests. His name was Lee. Leah's friend was Karen, recently released from an addiction unit, her place in college lost, shunned by her parents, broke, terrified she would fall back into drugs, her headlong dive into the life and language of The Programme was as logical as it felt natural.

\* \* \*

Caleb chanted his own version of an early magic spell:
"'Hail, lover of power, as he spits on the angels!
"'Hail, Adonai! Hail, Jehova! Hail, Satan!
"'Hail he who has beheld the mask of his father in pain!'"
The Seer intoned:
"This is the new beginning that we came to America for. This is the time when words alone are not enough, this is an exploration of energies of which others are too frightened to do more than pay lip service – even our brothers and sisters in The Programme. I shall make you into soldiers, into an army: I shall make you into the army of God and Satan."
She looks around, eyes brighter than any candle.
"Are you mine?"
This is new, being invited to address The Seer directly. The members of the ritual nod and reach out to touch one another and mumble:
"We are many."
She calls out:
"Anthony, can you hear me?"
From behind a cell door, a choked voice answers hesitantly:
"I am one, Seer."
"We are many," the members respond automatically.
"Leah, can you hear me?"
From within another cell, Leah replies, firmly and with evident joy:
"I am one, Seer."
"We are many," the members reply in harmony.
Paimon rises, steps into their middle, takes a small, brass gong-stick from his pocket, strikes the gong once and says:
"I am Paimon. I obey only Lucifer. Tonight we shall bring into our midst the goddess of love," he smiles at Diana. "We shall bring her into our midst to show that love can heal. Tonight we shall heal our brother Anthony, and we shall heal him with love. Can you hear me, Anthony?"
"I am one, Paimon," the voice trembles from behind the cell door.
"We are many," the members reply.
Paimon gestures and Diana rises and comes towards him. None of this has been rehearsed. They are making ritual on the run. It comes

easily. There have been years of Masses and Meditations within The Programme, and exhortations to share with one another their darkest impulses. For Matthew, there it stopped: he worshipped the capacity to realise oneself, leaving individuals to work out for themselves how far they wanted to take its enactment. For The Seer, that was the step short of ultimate control that had weakened Matthew and left him vulnerable.

Diana peels her dress over her head, stands naked before Paimon. She is unashamed: some of the men have seen her naked before, and – soon after arrival in Boston – she had accompanied Cassandra to New York, found herself sharing first a hotel room and then her bed. She is a full-bodied woman. She touches Paimon, fondles him through his trousers, strokes him until he reaches across her and strikes repeatedly on the gong, faster and more frenziedly until, suddenly, he stops and jerks away unspent.

Laughing, he steps aside and bows with arm outstretched towards Caleb. She crosses him to kneel before Caleb. Though the others cannot see it, he makes a twirling gesture for her to turn around to face them, her back to him. With a bare foot he pushes her down until she is on all fours. He slides off his throne of hay and silk, scoops oil from the bowl onto his erect penis and enters her from behind, just the once, gripping her hips to hold her still and firm, her cheeks flat against him, her breasts hanging down like honours, before he withdraws, waving his glossy wet erection triumphantly at the gathering as he hops back up to his pedestal.

"I am one," he says.

"We are many," she replies.

"Together we shall be whole," they chant in unison.

The Seer beckons. Diana strides through the gathering, kneels on the big cushion, The Seer strokes her hair, strokes her breasts, kisses her lightly on the forehead, whispers in her ear:

"Christopher."

Christopher is still seated against the wall. As she walks towards him, he lifts his robe. She lowers herself onto him. She is wet and he slides easily into her. She rises and falls lightly until she feels him come inside of her. As she pulls off him, she covers herself with her hand so that it does not drip away: blessed seed. She scoops to pick up her dress from where it had fallen, placing it beneath her to sit on as she lowers herself to the floor between her sisters.

The Seer says:

"Love is not sex. Sex is not love. Yet sex evokes love where love does not evoke sex. Sex is dominant. Sex is powerful. Sexual unison between two people can create love; love between two people does not create sex. Sexual unison between many people creates love for them all; love between many people does not create sex. We are using sex to create love, and with that love we shall heal all of us, we shall heal Anthony."

Christopher begins to hum. It is an almost tuneless humming, not recognisable music or a song. He is humming in sentences, some close to a groan, others full of light. Gradually, he begins to repeat some of his rhythms. Slowly, others join in as they pick up a repeated chord. They hold hands: Diana, still naked, holds hands with Pascale and Mary; all three of them have their eyes shut as they sway and hum, there are sensations in the air and within them that they did not imagine existed.

"Anthony," says Paimon, "before tonight is over you will be free of the devils which have beset you all these long years."

"I am one, Paimon," comes the voice from behind the closed door.

The Seer says:

"Come here, Lee."

He has difficulty standing. The older men might ebb to and from erection without difficulty; he is hard and it won't go away. The Seer pats the bed and tells him to sit. She whispers in his ear. He turns red. Now it is his turn to take off his clothes. Once he is done, he stretches out face down on the bed, next to the wall, unfurling himself behind her. She strokes his head, shifts to make space for him, reaches between his legs to fondle him. She bends down to kiss the back of his head, turns it to face the wall – things a child should not watch – and nods at Caleb to continue.

It is Christopher who – otherwise motionless – speaks next:

"Our Father who art in Heaven, hallow'ed be thy name, thy Kingdom come, thy will be done on earth as it is in Heaven, give us this day our daily bread and forgive us our trespasses as we forgive those who trespass against us."

Paimon is still standing beside the gong which he strikes once but hard to stop Christopher short of the plea not to be led into temptation.

Caleb commands: "Bring her out."

Leah is already naked. She emerges from her cell radiant, looking around for Caleb. Without any hesitation, she moves through them to kneel with her back to him, bending down to all fours without needing to be told. As he did with Diana, he splashes warm oil on himself and enters her the once, holds her still, withdraws and resumes his throne.

He whispers to Leah. The girl starts to advance across the basement, still on all fours, like a dog. As she pushes against the members, they push back at her, push her over onto her side, onto her back, grabbing and touching until she rolls full circle and rises again to her knees to continue her journey. Each time she falls, Paimon strikes the gong. When he, in his turn, kicks her off balance, he strikes it several times. It takes her forever, though the depth of the basement – and of the house – is only about forty feet.

Finally, she reaches the bed where The Seer is stretched out luxuriously. The Seer places her palm against the girl's forehead, grips it, twists hard until Leah understands that this is the final roll, she lies now with her back on the large cushion, head resting against the bed, looks around at the hungry gathering, opens her legs in readiness.

They take it in turns, the men pulling up their robes in order to enter her – just enough to establish ownership – before withdrawing, the women sliding fingers into her briefly. Finally, Paimon kneels between her legs, takes out his penis, enters her and brings himself to orgasm inside her, his eyes relentlessly locked into The Seer's. As he comes, he hisses:

"Cassandra."

\* \* \*

"Mr Crane, tell me exactly what 'the fire beyond' means."

"Exactly? Mr Kennedy, if I knew I wouldn't be here. I can tell you what I think it is, what we mean by it, though. The fire beyond is the fire beyond all our knowledge and experience. The fire beyond is the step beyond the end."

"And this? That God and Satan are two sides of the same coin?"

"Good and evil are opposites, hardly an original idea."

"Okay, and this: 'The fundamental union of God and Satan'?"

"I don't know what your question is, Mr Kennedy," Matthew replied calmly but quickly, before Trask entered the same objection: he was The Teacher, he did not want to be seen to need the protection of a lawyer. "It says in the Bible that Satan came down from Heaven – 'I beheld Satan as lightning fall from heaven' – Book of Luke, Chapter 10, Verse 18. 'And he showed me Joshua the high priest standing before the angel of the Lord and Satan standing at his right hand to resist him' – Book of Zechariah, Chapter 3, Verse 1."

"Let's get right down to it, this is black magic, isn't it? Pure Satanism, right? Union of God and Satan," Kennedy snorted.

"I think this is from our Website, isn't it?"

214

"Don't you know your own words, Mr Crane?" Kennedy was on a roll, could not help goading.

"If you've pored over them all, you'll know there's quite a lot of them, Mr Kennedy. And, like everything else, it all depends on the context. If this comes from where I think it does, on the Web…"

"That's correct."

"If memory serves, I was discussing the use of language. Would that be right, Mr Kennedy?"

"You answer the questions, Mr Crane."

"Your Honour," Trask rose. "Mr Crane is entitled to know where the passage comes from, what the context is; absolutely."

Kennedy shrugged as if he couldn't care less, but knew he had been wrong-footed by Matthew.

"Yes. You were discussing language."

"Does Mr Kennedy have the passage there?" Trask smelled blood.

Silently, Kennedy handed him a copy. Still on his feet, and out of his turn, Trask read aloud triumphantly:

"'We use some of the language of religion: the fundamental union of God and Satan; good and evil. It is useful, because it is familiar, it makes a point without needing to develop it entirely anew; but it can also be misleading, because we do not believe in God and Satan in themselves, we do not believe in them as gods or anti-gods, we do not believe in them as people or images of people.' Thank you, Mr Kennedy." Trask sat down grinning broadly.

Carey too smiled with relief: it's just an idea; it's just words. She has nothing to do with Satan, black magic, absurd rituals, obscene orgies.

"Let's look at some more, Mr Crane. How about this – 'Is it not time to acknowledge that all of your feelings, all of the impulses, all of your reactions and aspirations – all of your demons within – have an equal claim to represent you, an equal validity in themselves?' Demons are valid, Mr Crane?"

"You either acknowledge them and deal with them, or they take you over. Again, it's not an especially original idea. All religions use the imagery of demons; psychology has other names, but it's the same point; you cannot control what you cannot see."

"Control, Mr Crane, that's what we're talking about here, isn't it? You're telling people they're out of control, aren't you? You're offering them control, aren't you?"

"Mr Kennedy, if I call out – right now – that people in this room are hungry, it'll strike a chord with a lot of them."

"Including the bench," the judge said. "Let's resume at one thirty, shall we?"

* * *

"Cassandra," Paimon hissed.

She strokes her brother's face, drawing it towards her, they touch lips, mouths ajar, jerk back before their tongues can connect; they do this once, twice, a third time – lead us into temptation, let us wallow in it. The other members are taut with anticipation: this is ultimate. The siblings kiss again; that is all for now.

Paimon rises. He tucks himself away, buttons up his jeans. He goes and sits with his back to Christopher, between his legs, leaning against him. Christopher kneads Paimon's shoulders. Caleb gestures Leah back into her cell, but her door is left open. It is Anthony's turn. He is terrified, cowering in the cell. He has been here since Caleb locked him in after Matthew left, days and days of stooped isolation, unable to pull himself fully erect or stretch the defeat out of his limbs. The stock-whip was hanging where Caleb had threaded it. Daily, he has been given water and pitta bread, with a slice of vegetable pâté just enough to be able to digest it, and a solitary orange for the vitamins: standard cell-fare. He was given a bucket to urinate and defecate into, nothing to clean himself up with.

Tonight, for the first time, he was taken out by Reuben and Ehud, sprayed with liquid detergent and hosed down in the back of the house, flailing his arms as he desperately tried to clean himself.

He has no clue what is to happen to him. He can barely remember his name, where he is. He knows that he has finally been defeated by a more powerful force than father, teachers, psychologists, prescription drugs combined. During the last days, he has hopped from fear to fury, from hatred of his father for putting him into the hell-hole to screaming pleas to come and get him, from belief in The Programme to plans for total revenge. His mind is at sea, bucked and tossed in a furious storm; he cannot hang onto it; there is nothing with which to lash it down.

Like Leah, he is naked. He will not come out of the safe cave that is the cell. He is no longer shy: he understands that nakedness is a return to innocence. He is physically frightened. He can smell the sex that has taken place in the basement but which he has not seen. He fears buggery: Caleb has buggered him many times; Lemuel, too. It hurts not just at the time but for hours after. He senses – smells – what happened to Leah, is terrified it will happen to him. They are going to hurt him, beat him, bugger him – they are going to kill him. His imagination is raging, disordered, he wants to scream, even merely to cry, but there are no tears left and his throat is rigid with fear.

The two black men enter his cell folded over, drag him from it, fling him into the middle of the room. He falls hard to the rough matted floor, struggles to pull himself into a less vulnerable position, huddles his legs into his chest, buries his head between his knees, sobs silently – what do you want from me?

The Seer intones:

"Anthony, we are going to bring you home."

He succeeds in whispering the magic words:

"I am one, Seer."

Christopher rises for the first time. He has to extricate himself from Paimon, almost trips on his own robe: it is done with good humour, mutual smiles, much laughter. He crosses to the boy, reaches down for Anthony to take his hand and allow himself to be pulled to his feet. The flickering lights distress him, he uses his free hand to cover his eyes. Christopher leads him to The Seer.

She has moved into a sitting position, her legs splayed open either side of the big cushion. She gathers Anthony in her arms, pulls him towards her, tells him not to be scared, rocks him to and fro until, finally, a few residual tears find their way from his eyes. She dries them with her dress, reckless that it causes her to expose herself, pressing herself against the boy's chest, finally she pushes him away, straightens out her dress and leans back against Lee nodding at Christopher that she is done.

Now Christopher leads him to Paimon, seated in Christopher's own place, his back against the wall as Christopher had earlier leaned. Again, he motions Anthony to kneel. Paimon strokes the boy's head, tells him:

"This is the end of the hurting, Anthony. No more pain; just love."

He kisses him warmly on the cheek and gestures to Christopher to move him on.

Now Caleb. Anthony sees the bowl of oil; Caleb has used oil on him before; the fear returns, but he is instructed to kneel facing Caleb. This is not about sex. He sees it in Caleb's eyes. Caleb has been his torturer yet his tutor, even in some ways his mentor. There is affection in Caleb's eyes, the older man leans forward to talk to him privately, their mouths inches away from each other.

"Anthony, it's time to shut the door on the past. What you are being offered – this love – is not to be turned away; you have to allow it into your soul, to take over your soul; it has gone on too long for you; you are my friend, you are my son, I need you to come out, come away, I want you beside me where I don't have to watch my back for your anger, nor push you sullenly forward every day. Do you understand me?"

Anthony whispers hoarsely:

"I think so, Caleb."

"Everyone here loves you, Anthony. Nothing bad is going to happen to you. Go and stand in the middle of the room: you have to learn to accept love, let it in, to let it drown out all the anger you've ever felt, let the good that you and I both know is within you float to the surface."

Anthony cannot speak; he is moved by Caleb's love, and the prospect of love to come. He lets Christopher draw him to his feet, lead him to stand beneath the gong. Paimon is also standing there, at the ready. As Christopher embraces him, Paimon begins to strike the gong, slowly, firmly, ringing loud in Anthony's ears, silencing his thoughts, he returns the embrace, the assurance of love, the familiar exchange:

"I am one."

"We are many."

"Together we shall be whole."

Singly, they come to embrace him, even Reuben, Lemuel and Ehud who have tormented him. Christopher has returned to his place, to his humming. Anthony sees more than hears it over the roar of the gong above his head. He sees others, as they sit down, join in with Christopher. They hold him tightly in turn. Naked Diana goes last. He blushes as he thinks of the times he had studied her from a distance, fantasised about her, he realises he has an erection. She does not pull away, but touches him lightly, kisses him on the lips, whispers in his ear:

"Not me."

Paimon nods towards the cell door:

"Go back inside."

Anthony does as he is told. He has no mind left with which to complain or to resist. He crouches against the far wall. Leah enters, pulls him away from the wall, crouches down beside him, hugs him, strokes his face, his back, his erection returns, she lowers him to the floor, straddles him and takes him into her as Diana did with Christopher, rocking over him as the members gather in the doorway to watch. He is aware that more of them have disrobed, they are holding each other, touching, fondling, he is floating on a salt-lake of sexuality, he is barely aware of it when he comes, not at all aware when she steps off him, strides to the door, someone thrusts the door shut and twists the key in the lock.

All he is left with is the stock-whip, dangling from the air-brick.

Now he knows what it is for.

Outside, the gong starts over: not slowly, but not frenzied; hard and firm; boom, boom, boom, boom, boom – it fills his head.

\* \* \*

"I asked Father Nahum to give it to The Teacher," Amanda said.

Carey let out her breath. As they had entered the court on the first day, Amanda had grabbed her arm. When she had turned to see what was wrong, Amanda was white as a sheet. She had hissed:

"I can't go in; I can't do this," staring beyond Carey at someone inside the courtroom.

"What is it?" Carey had quickly hustled her back out of the door. "Was it your sister?" There had been sharp words as soon as they set eyes on one another. At the time, Amanda had seemed unaffected.

"He's here," Amanda said, shaking.

"Who?"

"At the front; the man in the check jacket."

Carey had been vaguely aware of him: a big man, loud red check jacket, nearly bald.

"Who is he?" she had asked.

"His name is Berlinger; they brought him to the hospital; they let him talk to me. He kept coming to see me. Kept talking about The Programme as if he knew all about it." This was "the man" she had told Matthew about while she was still in the cell; it was the man Phillipe Lamarque had talked about, and to whom he talked in exchange for money.

"Was he a member?"

"It's his job; it's what he does; gets people out of groups, back to their families." Amanda was visibly weakened by the sight of him.

"Don't be scared of him. He's not in charge now. Matthew is."

A day later, in cross-examination:

"This man – Nahum you call him – he was in charge of the – what did you call it? – the mission to America," Kennedy sneered. "That's right, isn't it?"

"No one was in charge of it; he and Jemima were the most senior, that's all. The Programme is The Teacher."

"And is that right – was he your teacher? Is he?"

"Yes," Amanda answered firmly.

The hearing had not begun until after lunch on the first day, evidence not until the next and Matthew had gone first. Their lawyers had taken them to eat at Forlini's, an Italian restaurant on Baxter

Street, at the edge of Chinatown, about a five minute walk from the court. It was a traditional restaurant, with red-clothed tables in booths and a red-sauce menu; it seemed to be jammed with lawyers. Clients eating without their lawyers were more likely to go to Giambone's, a rung down the culinary and cost ladder but likewise on Baxter Street.

Overnight, they stayed quietly at the Chapter, concentrating on keeping Amanda calm, consoling her that neither her sister nor Berlinger could reach her. Emily shared a room with her for comfort.

Carey and Matthew, too, were together, though still warily after that last night in New Orleans. Sitting up naked on the bed covers, she asked him what he knew about Berlinger.

"I've heard of him; I know the type," Matthew replied. "They're parasites. They prey on ignorance and fear. Family ignorance, member fear. They never try to get to the root problems within the family; they spook them with tales combining sex, drugs and the loss of money and property. When they get hold of a member – sometimes quite literally kidnapping them – they do the same to them: they've been known to use drugs, they've been known to use sex, and they cost the families a fortune, often far more than was at risk. They hold themselves out as fighting fire with fire without ever finding out if there was any fire to begin with."

He finished his ablutions, stepped easily into bed beside her: sometimes, it was so normal. He said:

"Quite often, they're ex-members of groups themselves. Huw would have been a prime candidate to become a deprogrammer: unable to have a group of his own, trying to destroy someone else's instead."

Not for the first time, she thought it sounded little different from the dynamics of legal practice. When a lawyer split with his partners, the blood continued to flow through writs, injunctions and motions until, finally, exhausted, they were ready to get on with their lives again.

She lay back with her arms behind her head staring wide-eyed at the ceiling. Matthew also lay down, but on his side, watching her thoughts. At times, he believed she would be the final partner; not meaning that he would never sleep with another member but that he would not elevate anyone else to this position of supreme privilege. At other times, he would step back from the moment and realise she was just one more, not so different from Cassandra or Helen, just new.

Detachment had made them capable of anything; anything, it seemed, except constancy.

* * *

Drained of energy, he crawls across the concrete floor to the wall and uses the whip to pull himself up as fully as the low ceiling allows. There is a short handle, eight feet of leather thong, less only the inches twisted through the holes of the brick. The threaded leather against the brick is firm. Nonetheless, as Caleb had intended him to, he knots it, to make sure that it will hold.

Outside, the gong falls suddenly silent. Except for The Seer, everyone has disrobed – even Christopher. The Seer has turned Lee around to face her, is lying along him, their bodies pressed together. She has her back to the room. She pulls up the front of her dress and raises her leg just enough to slide him into her. It has been a long wait: he comes at once. She hushes his embarrassment with her lips and grips tightly so that he does not slip out of her. Quickly, youthfully, he recovers the erection; she rolls so that she is on top of him but flat; it is their secret; the others may suspect, but they do not know. She faces the room, watching couplings and groupings as they slide into complete abandon, waiting for Anthony to die.

\* \* \*

State Troopers responded to the call. They were still waiting for the ambulance from Binghampton.

Christopher and Paimon met them at the gate.

"D'you want to tell us what we've got here, sir?" the senior trooper asked as he emerged from the car. He was dark – Latin, probably – about five ten, thin, with a hooked nose and a wart on the side of his neck, in the grey uniform of the New York State Police with its incongruous, knitted, purple tie, leaving on the back seat his Mountie-style, flat-brimmed hat.

His partner hung up the radio inside the car and climbed out. He was overweight, wearing sunglasses, with bouffant hair rising in a sea of waves on the top of his head. He was chewing what they thought was gum until he spat a long fat stream of brown juice out onto the ground: tobacco. They could not have looked less like State Troopers were supposed to look.

"Yes. I'm sorry. One of our members has hanged himself."

The two cops exchanged a glance.

"Can you explain that, sir?"

"Hanged himself?" Paimon was unable to suppress the sarcasm.

"You said 'one of our members', sir," the senior cop said, blinking semaphorically to tell Paimon the insult hadn't escaped him. "Members of what would that be, sir?" he asked Christopher.

"We're a religious community, officer." Christopher met the gaze head on. "The Programme. We'll be quite happy to provide you with some of our literature. We have Chapters in New York, Boston and Europe: this is, well, a sort of retreat for members."

They could relate to retreat: that was what priests did.

"You're Catholics?" Chewing-Tobacco asked incredulously.

"No way," murmured Wart-Neck.

Cassandra chose that moment to emerge from the house. Her eyes met those of the Latino officer who repeated, with a hint of awe:

"No way."

"This is Cassandra; she's the most senior member present; she is our Teacher's wife," Christopher introduced.

"How'd'you do, ma'am," Wart-Neck offered a hand. Chewing-Tobacco was likewise openly ogling The Seer. Cassandra took the hand smiling, holding on for a moment longer than necessary.

"Do you have a name, officer?"

He pointed to his badge. "Sergeant Romero, ma'am. Jesus Romero." He pronounced it the Spanish way: Hay-Suss. "This is Officer Allison." He turned away from his partner and lowered his voice: "You'll have to forgive him staring, ma'am; he's a bit of a pig."

"This is very sad, Sergeant," Cassandra drew him aside. "The young man, Anthony, was very special to me. You may have heard of his father: Arthur Rockworth?"

"Nope."

"He's, er, a businessman; that is to say, a rather big businessman, here, in England, everywhere."

"I'm getting the picture, ma'am. Ma'am, I need to see the body now."

He should have seen it sooner, to check the boy was dead; being around these people unsettled him; being around her unsettled him most.

The Programme had lifted Anthony down and left the stock-whip lying on the floor beside him. He was still naked. As he had strangled to death, his bladder had emptied onto the ground. The stench rose from the basement, along with the first strains of decomposition. They covered their noses as Paimon led the way, the two policemen followed, Christopher brought up the rear: Cassandra told them she would meet them on the veranda with tea.

\* \* \*

"She was never a happy girl, I agree," Amanda's sister said, "but she was always careful – especially about money."

"There was plenty of money about, though?" Trask challenged.

"We were well off; not rich."

"Not rich? How wealthy a man was your father at his death?"

"Your Honour," Kennedy complained, "how can this be relevant?"

"Goes to just how big a gift it was, Your Honour; if Ms Kroger didn't think it was that much money, it doesn't call for any loss of free will – more like generosity."

"It's a jurisdiction hearing, Mr Trask," the judge reminded him.

"And a motion on the farm," Trask replied.

"All the same, Mr Trask, I think we're straying a long way from the point. We don't have a jury, Mr Trask." The judge looked steadily at Trask.

Carey leaned towards Trask, whispered to let it go. What Amanda had given Matthew was most of her worldly assets.

"You say she was happy, Mrs Gruenfeld?"

"I said she wasn't happy," Amanda's sister corrected.

"But she was happy in The Programme, wasn't she? You had letters from her, saw her during visits: she was happier than she'd ever been."

"She appeared happy at times," grudgingly conceded. "She ran away in the end."

"Did she run away, Mrs Gruenfeld?"

"She left them; she came home."

"Why do you call it running away?"

The sister flushed.

"It's just words."

"But you had her committed to a home, didn't you?"

"She couldn't settle down afterwards."

"She didn't want you to take this action, did she?"

"She didn't know what she wanted; she wasn't making any sense."

"You mean, it wasn't your idea of sense?"

"Argumentative, Your Honour."

"She wanted to go back, didn't she?" Trask did not await a ruling.

"That's what she said."

"That's what she said?"

"She didn't know what she was doing. I felt, perhaps she only wanted to go back as a way of getting her money away from those people."

Trask raised his eyebrows in mock-amazement.

"She was going back in order to get her money out?"

"I don't know." The sister was flustered. "She wanted to go back; she wanted her money out. That was the way I saw it."

"But she didn't want the money out, Mrs Gruenfeld," Trask

insisted. "That's what she's told us yesterday, in this very courtroom."

"She still doesn't know what she's doing. Look at her, look at the state of her; look into her eyes. That isn't Amanda talking, it's that man."

It could have sounded like hysteria; it sounded, instead, like the truth – concern, barely able to recognise her sister, certain in her heart that The Programme was up to no good. Unable to fix it on anything rational apart from the money, however, she ended up looking greedy.

"Tell me who that gentleman is, Mrs Gruenfeld?" Trask swung suddenly and pointed at Berlinger. "Will you stand up, sir? The gentleman in the check jacket."

Defiantly, Amanda's sister said:

"He's our friend. Mr Berlinger. He's been trying to help us get Amanda back."

"And tell me, Mrs Gruenfeld, just how much money have you paid Mr Berlinger so far to try and get your sister back?"

Matthew too had turned: his eyes met Berlinger's; the big man stared back.

\* \* \*

While the coroner's officers and the police forensic team worked downstairs, guarded by the unpleasant – and, as she had discovered when she stood downwind from him, malodorous – Allison, Cassandra confirmed the account which had already been given Romero by Christopher and Paimon.

"Our members come here for peace; they need peace in order to work something out in themselves, away from whatever's troubling them."

"Okay, so he came here in retreat. Retreat from what?"

"Anthony was," Cassandra hesitated, as if she was still reluctant to expose his secrets, "he was a troubled boy. His father will tell you that Anthony had been a disturbed child more or less since he was first able to talk. There are some, well, some fairly unpleasant stories about him, when he was younger, if you catch my drift."

Romero did not say anything, scribbling busily in his notebook.

"Look, no one wants to speak ill of the dead; and as far as we're concerned, there's no such thing as someone who's evil or lost; that's what we're about here; helping people find themselves, live with themselves. But Anthony was troubled by any standards."

"You're saying the kid was some kind of a monster, right?"

"Right," Cassandra met his eyes with a smile. "Your choice of word though, don't put them down as mine."

"Okay and?"

"And, well, my husband met Mr Rockworth near our country home in England – oh dear, that sounds frightfully grand." She was stomping her usual accent – Welsh with a mild mid-Atlantic twang – into the ground, replacing it with something close enough to English upper to fool Romero. "And Mr Rockworth – Arthur – asked us to help; basically, he asked us to take Anthony in, see if we could do something with him. He was, I suppose, at the end of his tether."

She crossed her legs, watched his eyes follow, leaned down to adjust her shoe. She had always enjoyed her sexuality, but never so much as since the Special Mass; she was walking around in a state of constant heat; she could have slept with this police-clown; she would use it to keep him under her control.

"Okay and?" Romero grudgingly returned to business.

"'Okay and'," she repeated giggling: "'Okay and' we did so, we took him in, we worked with him, we meditated with him, we prayed with him, we tried to keep him occupied and we tried to keep him under control. 'Okay and' it didn't work. There was a problem in London, with a small boy, the son of one of our members."

It all fit together: there was no jigsaw that could not be rearranged.

She recounted how they had brought him over to the States; how he seemed to be settling down; how they believed they were finally winning him over – over to himself, the better side of himself; how he had asked permission to spend some time in isolation, complete retreat.

"That's what those cells are for, right? Isolation; retreat."

"Yes."

"How come they have locks on the doors?"

"It's just the way we bought the doors. I don't have a clue if we even have any keys, but I'll ask."

"I already asked," Romero scowled: and had got the same answer. "What about the stock-whip? Flagellation, penitence?"

Cassandra answered bitterly:

"No, not at all. That's where I blame myself. I don't know how he got it in there. You see, when they go into the cells for complete isolation, they're always naked; I insist on that."

"Why?"

"Just for this, don't you see? Isolation is – how shall I put it? It can be a most healing experience, but it's invariably profound and some people – well, sometimes they can't tell, and even I can't tell, if they're going to be able to handle it. So I insist, completely naked. They're quite alone. It's not cold at this time of the year. In the winter, I let

225

them have a blanket. We bring them food once a day, a bucket of course; if they want, they can come out to wash. All that was what happened with Anthony. I think – I'm guessing now – I think he managed to get the stock-whip while he was outside washing, let's see, that would be Thursday afternoon."

"We're going with some time Thursday night," Romero admitted. "It fits. Where'd the whip come from in the first place?"

"Oh, Sergeant, I really don't know; it's a farm; a lot of people come and go; they may have found it in one of the outbuildings; I hadn't seen it before is the only thing I can tell you; otherwise," she shuddered, "it wouldn't have been here, I can assure you."

\* \* \*

The judge handed down his ruling at the close of argument on the Thursday. Like much of the hearing, it was anti-climactic. Cash had been handed over in England; if there was evidence of oppression, lack of free will, it was likewise based on Amanda's periods with The Programme in England, not during her infrequent returns to the United States. That issue should be tried under English law.

Hammer Reach was a different question: because it related to real estate, it could only be a matter of New York jurisdiction. However, the evidence of manipulation was weak and, above all, insufficient to overcome Amanda's own, assured appearance in court, currently uncontradicted by evidence of imbalance. The judge was not willing outright to dismiss the motion to nullify Matthew's life tenancy of the farm, but neither was he willing to set a trial date until there was more evidence to substantiate the family claim than he had heard in relation to the money.

Carey was – as always after a victory – exuberant. Matthew barely smiled. Outside the Supreme Court building, local television and press journalists surrounded The Programme group, hurling questions which did not bother to conceal their contempt.

"Hey, Matthew, Teacher, whatever your name is, how much does it cost to join?"

"Amanda, was it worth it? What did you get back? What did they do to you?"

One of them fixed on Carey, her excitement quickly supplanted by panic.

"Are you their lawyer or a member? Are you his lover? Is sex better with a god?"

Matthew held up a hand for, and obtained, a moment's silence.

"Your scepticism is deeply appreciated, friends. New ideas, and new faiths, have always been greeted with derision. The court held that Ms Kroger knew what she was doing; it was her property to do what she wanted with. Why don't you compare the sisters: Amanda wants to live in a community in which people give support to one another without reward, and share her money with them; Mrs Gruenfeld wants it for herself."

For a second, it seemed as if he might have convinced them. They were New Yorkers: they saw nothing with a kindly eye.

"Ms Arnott, do you believe in Satan?"

"Hey, maybe The Teacher's got two horns," an unidentified male voice stage-whispered loud enough for the mikes to catch.

Carey was stunned, unable to speak, on the verge of tears. How did they know about her and Matthew? What did it have to do with her position as his lawyer? Would the footage find its way onto English television? Emily flung an arm around her while Matthew protected Amanda. Nahum and Chad pushed their way through. They ran down into the subway and jumped the East Side RIT line before they realised no one was following them: the Gruenfelds had emerged, a new magnet for the media. Sheepishly, the small group huddled together at the train door, to get out at the next stop; by the time they emerged, they were laughing.

They celebrated with ice-cream and sodas at a sidewalk cafe, making plans for the future. Amanda wanted to go back to England with Carey and Emily and, it seemed to have been assumed, Matthew. Carey was cautious, because it could act as an incentive for the family to pursue the action over there where she was by no means as certain of a favourable result. On the other hand, Matthew was not keen to leave Amanda at large, vulnerable to Berlinger. Nahum stepped into the breach – he would look after her.

Chad said:

"I'm going up to Hammer Reach over the weekend; I want to see Tanya – sorry, Leah. Is that all right, Teacher?" His assimilation was complete.

Matthew smiled, stroked the boy's cheek.

"Of course, Chad."

"What about you, Teacher? Are you going back to England?" Chad asked: "Or will you be here when I get back?"

"I'll always be here; one way or another."

They walked back to the Chapter House off Spring Street, still jolly, looking forward to relaying the news and sharing the joy. The Coffee Lounge was shut but not empty. Two New York detectives were waiting with the news that Anthony Rockworth had been found the day before, hanged, in a tiny cell in the basement of their farm in the Catskills. They had a lot of questions. So, they said, did Arthur Rockworth.

\* \* \*

Before he left for Hammer Reach, after he had rejected both her offer to accompany him and her advice that he should take a lawyer with him, Carey told Matthew that she had decided to return to England without him. If he did not need her as a lawyer, especially now when something so redolent with legal implications had occurred, she was not going to stay in any other capacity – lover or Programme member. This was her answer to the questions asked during the strained night in New Orleans after they had visited with Lamarque.

"Of course. I'll take you to the airport," was Matthew's only comment.

Carey had not consulted with Emily, taking for granted that she would return to England with her. It took neither of them long, in their separate rooms, to pack. Carey did not bother ringing ahead for a flight: she would test her resolve by waiting until there was a seat available, however long it took.

Matthew took them to the drop off zone at JFK, not the car park. He pulled in to the sidewalk, got out to remove their bags from the trunk.

On the sidewalk, Carey leaned up to kiss Matthew on the cheek. "I'll see you soon, right?"

"I am one," Matthew said gravely, kissing her back.

"We are many," Carey confirmed.

Neither of them completed the exchange.

Matthew said, instead:

"Go on now, fly away; fly away little bird."

"I'm not sure what that means. It sounds as much like a curse as a blessing."

\* \* \*

They were feet away from the British Airways counter before Emily grabbed Carey's arm to stop her.

"Why are we doing this – going home?"

"I'm a lawyer, remember? I've got work to do."

"I don't want to go," Emily dropped her bag onto the ground for emphasis. "I don't want to go home, Carey," she repeated. "Not yet. I'm not ready. I haven't found what I want yet."

Carey did not ask what it was she was looking for; Emily could not have answered. They were looking for elephants: they could not describe them but they would know them when they saw them. Trying to contain her disappointment, Carey said:

"Where will you go? What will you do? Will you be all right on your own?"

Carey did not understand Emily to be suggesting that she should remain behind with her while Emily had to hide her disappointment that Carey did not offer to stay.

"Are you going to stay with The Programme? In New York? Are you going to stay with Matthew?"

The last question came from nowhere and was all the more frightening for it. Carey could think of nothing she wanted to happen less: it would be a double abandonment.

Emily shrugged: she did not know why she was staying; she had no answers for herself nor therefore for Carey.

"You don't know what you're doing," Carey urged her once last time to change her mind.

"Nor do you, Carey," Emily said gently.

"Stay here, then," Carey replied flatly.

"I'll ring you at home; as soon as you're back."

"Home," Carey repeated, reminding her it was supposed to become Emily's home too.

"I'll miss you," Emily said: the reason she had come to the States.

They both had tears in their eyes. They leaned forward to hug. They kissed briefly on the lips, then – to Carey's surprise – Emily reached for the back of her head to stop her pulling away and kissed her again, on the lips, open-mouthed.

"I thought I was the one wanted you to come home with me," Carey laughed.

Emily was still tearful.

"Don't you think there's a part of me wants to come home with you? Don't you think I wanted, you know, us living – um – in the house together?" The words "in the house" were tossed in at the last moment, to evade the ambiguity.

"Then come back with me now," Carey said fiercely. "Just do it."

"I'm not ready," Emily replied. "That's all. There's things I need to find out about myself – the way you've been doing. When I am, as soon as I am, I'll come home; I promise."

"Do that," Carey picked up her own bag and started towards the airline counter. "Just do what you need to do, Em; come home when you're ready – or I'll come back for you," she warned, only half-joking.

Emily's eyes met hers, locked, nodded in understanding; she turned away, swinging her bag, and within a few moments had been swallowed up by the airport crowd.

# Chapter Ten

"I can't get in, Colin," she sobbed, standing at the top of the stone steps leaning against the solid front door of the office. "You've changed the locks," she accused. "What did you do that for?"

Colin stood at street level, looking up at his sister, waiting for the complaint to pass. Then he cocked his head to one side comically and said:

"Eh, Carey?"

She left her briefcase by the door and ran down the stairs and into his arms, flinging her own around him, repeatedly kissing his cheek, almost urgently.

He could feel the tears on her face.

"Oh, Carey, what have you done to yourself?"

"Nothing," she laughed, cried. "I'm just pleased to see you; it feels like it's been forever."

"Come on, let's go inside before anyone else arrives."

"What's with the key?"

"New lock. Simple, really; they don't make that lock anymore, we couldn't get enough keys for the new people. Don't worry, I've had one made for you."

He stooped to pick up the mail lying in a pile just inside the door.

"When did you get back?"

"This morning." She had come straight from the airport.

In the kitchen, Colin flicked the switch to make coffee: the restaurant-sized filter machine was always left ready for the next morning. Then he led her into his own office, already unwrapping the bundles of mail, automatically sorting it into piles.

"Congratulations on Kroger."

"Yes, well, a bit of the icing's already off that cake."

"What?"

"Anthony Rockworth – Arthur's son – remember? I told you he was in the group? Sort of, a deal to keep him out of trouble?"

Colin shrugged: he had a vague recollection.

"He killed himself at Hammer Reach."

Colin shuddered at the implications, leaping disordered into his mind. He asked, more sharply than he wanted to sound:

"What effect will it have?"

231

"I don't know how Rockworth'll react but, er, I imagine, from what the police said, not particularly well. He's going to blame The Programme."

"There's nothing he can do, is there?"

"About Chesterfield Gardens? No: the lease has got a while to run."

"It's, uh," Colin licked his lips nervously, "it's not exactly the sort of battle we'd most want to be involved in at the moment. I'm sure you know what I mean."

She nodded. She thought he looked tired, worn, and said so.

"I'm all right; it's been a rough time."

"Here? At home?" She asked after Jan, the kids.

"Here," he said shortly, scanning letters as he spoke. "It's been a lot harder than I expected." Compensating for his earlier lapse, he did not tell her about the calls from Richard Fielding.

"In what way?"

"A lot of strutting legal egos taking each other's measure."

"You didn't expect that?" She laughed. "I'll fetch the coffee."

"I'll do it," he surprised her: he liked being waited on.

She followed him back to the kitchen, watched from the door as he busied himself pouring them each a cup. She heard the front door bang: another arrival. He said, facing away from her:

"We haven't sorted all the space out. There's still works going on."

"And?"

"Uh, I had to put someone in with you, for the moment."

She took a deep breath: don't react; it's what he expects.

"Who?"

"I'm sorry, Carey. We didn't know when you'd be back."

"Ah, Colin, you could have waited."

Junior solicitors shared offices, not partners.

He did not reply until they had returned to his own office, shut the door behind them, settled himself behind his desk.

"Could I, Carey? There were times I began to wonder if you'd ever be back, never mind when."

"Who?" she repeated.

"Jessica. Jessica Harvey. You met her."

"Indeed I did," she murmured, remembering the small, dark woman she had wondered if her brother was attracted to.

She felt raw, exposed. Her most immediate thoughts were personal, not professional; she was Colin's sister; they were close; he had put Jessica into her room.

"You'll like her – everyone does, even Charles; I'm sure you'll get along," Colin added lamely. "It's not for long. We've got the decorators on the top floor. They'll work their way down. By the end, it'll be fine."

"Is Charles here?"

"He's at the apartment." Antibes.

"How is he?"

"Worried about you. At least I think so; you know Charles; he doesn't exactly pour his heart out to me."

"I meant – with the merger."

"He's coping."

"You mean he's not?"

"It frightens him: giving up control."

"That's something else you should have expected."

"Who said I didn't?"

"All right then, he should have," she said crossly; she didn't want to come back to family games or wars.

"He said he did, but I think he expected them to fall into line. You know how it is, Carey, all those years of walking on water."

She got up to stretch, uncomfortable in her suit. She came around the desk, leaned against him from behind, massaged his shoulders, kissed the top of his head, rested her cheek against the bald patch in the middle.

"Hi," she whispered. "Long time no see."

He reached around to take her hand, kissed her palm.

"You are back, aren't you, Carey?"

She stood for a moment longer, returned to her seat, lit a cigarette.

"I hope so, Colin; that's the best I can say for the moment."

"Where have you been, Carey? What's going on with you?"

"Could we have lunch, dinner?" To avoid answering now, she promised an answer later.

"I can't, Carey," he apologised. "I'm in conference from midday. How about lunch tomorrow?"

"I'll still be here," she said, barely concealing her disappointment.

"I'm sorry. You know how Jan is about surprises."

She was back in a land where people gave notice.

"Is that it? Or would she be afraid I'd try to convert the children? Or are you?"

"Will you?" he rasped. Then he laughed. "Here we go again, eh?"

He got up to see her out, put an arm around her, hugged her tightly. She hugged him back, shaking, still weepy.

"Do you love him, Carey?" Colin asked quietly, reading her like a book.

"I don't know," she sniffed into his shoulder. "I haven't seen him since yesterday. It's too long ago to remember."

They stood there for a moment longer – siblings – before he sighed loudly and lawyerly.

"Have to get on. I'll speak to you later about tomorrow. We've a lot to talk about." He had Rockworth in mind: father and late son.

"I hope so," she replied, kissing his cheek. "I hope we can talk about it." She meant Matthew and The Programme.

\* \* \*

The publicity hit like a tidal wave.

Within a day, it had been on the local radio stations; by nightfall, it had been picked up by the national news media; by the weekend, on front pages across the country.

"MYSTERY DEATH IN KROGER CULT."

"ROCKWORTH SON IN SECT SUICIDE."

"POLICE INVESTIGATE CULT COUNTRY RETREAT."

The speed would have been surprising if it were not for the Rockworth factor. There were no forensic grounds for suspicion: no signs of struggle or blows, no evidence that the stock-whip had been used for anything other than for the boy to hang himself; there were no fingermarks where he might have been lifted up or other bruising, no drug traces external or internal nor any evidence to suggest anything other than just what it appeared to be – suicide by a boy well-documented as disturbed.

The single issue arising from the forensic examination was how Anthony – supposedly in isolation – came to have traces of different types of sexual activity about his body. That, too, was prayed in aid: shame at breach of both the contact rules and cell discipline might well have been the final straw. Cassandra fought hard to prevent Romero pursuing it – or who it had been. In the end, he let it go – there were no legal grounds on which to insist, let alone on the basis of which to carry out any tests.

\* \* \*

Cassandra had not seen Caleb for a day before the police were called, though she thought nothing of it at the time. She kept Father Christopher at Hammer Reach, sent Paimon – Father Paimon, as she had elevated him – to Boston the same evening, after his initial interview. She had a new toy for him: Helen. The police did not object to people leaving, so long as they could be found if they were needed.

She had told Christopher the day after the Special Mass:
"Stay with Diana."

It was a decision Father Christopher had already reached for himself. He had been uneasy with Helen, she appeared to exist only to serve, but beneath the surface was a mystery. For a short while, it had excited him, to have someone who, he believed, still belonged to Matthew, but it was already turning to resentment. He was pleased to give her up. Something special had passed between himself and Diana during the Mass.

Father Christopher had come into The Programme from computers: he understood the nature and essence of programmes – they were all, always and only about the organisation of information. He did not aspire to lead The Programme. He was happiest as the power behind the throne, whoever for the time being it might be; he liked Cassandra to ask his advice, to watch her make the moves he had designed; everyone else, even his friend Caleb, he kept at a distance. Too many members were merely playing at The Programme; even Cassandra would get up and walk away from it if it no longer suited her; he alone understood that it was a game for life – there was nothing beyond, not even the fire.

It was late by the time Matthew and Nahum arrived. Matthew was outwardly calm but inside he was seething. Christopher greeted him:

"I am one, Matthew." Matthew, not Teacher.

"We are many. What happened?"

"He was never happy."

"Where had he been?"

They were standing in the front hall. Nahum had not come into the house with Matthew, muttering that he could not wait to see his Temple site, if only by the light of the moon and the stars.

Cassandra descended the stairs, trailed by the two Jays. She had kept them around her, to adorn and embellish her presence, the way she was keeping Lee – like a poodle at her feet – for her pleasure. There was no such thing as overkill; small as she was, she planned the whole world for her stage. The two black men would be the granite colonnades of her approach.

"Very good, Matthew; I thought you'd understand."

"What did you think I'd understand, Cassandra?" Matthew kept the snarl out of his voice, not from his eyes.

"Don't worry; we've already told the police he was in retreat, in the cells."

"No," Matthew snapped: that wasn't all.

Cassandra laughed and led the way onto the terrace. Matthew

could only follow. The two Jays stepped aside to let him precede them into the open, but more as if they were guarding him than out of respect. They stood silently, arms folded, behind Cassandra.

"We were trying to heal him; what you might call a healing meditation."

Matthew grunted: he could picture it; Anthony locked in his cell; the remainder of them in the basement meditation area, working on him – at him. It would be enough to shake a less fragile mind than Anthony's.

"What do the police think?"

"They think exactly the way it happened."

"Yes? And how are they writing up healing meditation?"

"Are we ashamed of the ability to heal, Matthew?" Christopher asked sarcastically, feigning the disingenuous tone of a curious student rather than someone who was starting to challenge his teacher.

"We might acquire the humility to be a little ashamed of failure, Christopher. Otherwise, someone might thrust it upon us."

Cassandra reached across Christopher, grasped Matthew's knee.

"I say it was not a failure, Matthew."

"No, that was what I thought."

"What do you think, Matthew?" Christopher asked in the same tone as before.

"Christopher, I've known you for more than ten years. If it wasn't intentional, it will have been the first accident I've known to you to be capable of."

Cassandra clapped her hands with glee, giggled.

"He's right, Christopher, he's right."

"Where is everybody?" Matthew asked, ignoring his wife. If she was pleased by the speed with which he was putting two and two together, there had to be more to the total than four.

"Some people left this afternoon. Paimon started for Boston just before you arrived."

"Caleb?"

"Away," Christopher answered shortly.

Matthew saw a look of surprise flit across Cassandra's face and registered that she had not known. He repeated:

"Where's Caleb, Christopher?" He was The Teacher.

"He's away, Matthew. I sent him away," he added. "I didn't think he'd make a good impression." On the police.

"He has a record," Cassandra snatched the tale from the air and began to work it into her own.

Matthew got up and stepped off the porch, down to the ground.

"I'm going to find Nahum. I'm supposed to see the police in the morning. You come with me," he told Cassandra.

Cassandra nodded, pleased: she did not want him talking to Romero alone.

\* \* \*

The two of them watched as he made his way towards the cluster of outhouses, and the framework of Nahum's Temple project. When he was out of earshot, she crooked her finger for the two Jays to draw near, whispered that they should follow him; they would be her spies in the night, black-faced and unseen. Once they too could no longer hear, she demanded:

"Where has he gone?"

"He went to New Hampshire."

"New Hampshire? What's in New Hampshire?"

"There's a lot of strange people in New Hampshire. Caleb has an old friend there he wanted to see."

She clicked her fingers three times: come on; spit it out.

"Someone he was in jail with is all I know, Cassandra. Honestly," he lied.

She got up and walked around Christopher, leaning against him so his head was pressed to her breasts, she reached inside his shirt, stroked his hairless chest. Something had been unleashed the night of the Mass: either she ran away from it or rode it down the line; the former was not an option.

"What will happen to Matthew?" she asked.

"You're The Seer; you tell me."

Huw had used that line, the night he first left The Programme.

"There aren't that many choices, are there? Not in the long run."

"There are always choices, Cassandra. Some are just easier to make than others."

\* \* \*

From *The Seer's Lesson On Purity*:

*Unification is a symphony of pure harmony. To achieve it, we must perfect all its instruments. The trumpeter must play the trumpet. The violinist, the violin. Let the drummers beat upon their drums. It is not about mixing up all of the talents and all of the instruments until some bland, grey uniformity results, everyone half good at everything, no one excels at anything. When the choral angels sing, let the devils roar. When we can hear them evenly, we will have achieved pure harmony.*

*Pure harmony is ultimate love and ultimate hate. You cannot commit your soul to God and Satan unless you know how to do both. Not love God, hate Satan – love God hate God, hate Satan love Satan. This is The Programme now: realisation of our capacity to do both. Each of these hungry, demanding Gods needs feeding. Admit it, adore it, bring it to life – even if it frightens us, especially when it frightens us, you cannot purify your being by denial, only by exposure.*

*If God and Satan can withstand the tension between them, so can you! If Satan survived the fall from Heaven, you can too! The Programme is just this – a means of bringing to light the darkness within, and for the light to survive the dark! Pure light, pure dark, pure life itself, pure death!*

\* \* \*

Matthew found Nahum at The Temple work-site, shimmery in the moonlight. He was seated cross-legged on the ground. Matthew lowered himself to the ground beside him.

"Doesn't seem like much has been done while you've been in New York."

Nahum nodded. After a while, he added:

"That barn there," he gestured over the top of a cement mixer towards the nearest one to them.

"The Meditation Hall?"

"And a dormitory above. It's strange. They've dug some kind of a hole in the ground. That's what they've been working on."

"I don't understand."

"Nor do I. I didn't get long. I saw a light as I walked over. Part of my building group – there was a section of flooring, in the ground, they were just covering it up, patting it into place, in a hurry like they didn't want to be seen. This time of night," he added.

"You didn't ask?"

Nahum glanced slyly at Matthew.

"You think that would have been a good idea?"

"I don't know. I don't know what that means at the moment; do you?"

Nahum was momentarily confused, then understood, flushed hotly.

"We've been friends a long time, Matthew."

"I know. Forgive me. Others have been with me a long time too."

"I said, we've been friends a long time," Nahum corrected him.

Matthew put an arm around his friend's shoulders, Nahum his around Matthew's waist, rested his head on his shoulder. Matthew stroked his hair, not like a lover, like a father. Shortly after, they went back to the house together. They did not see the two Jays watching them nor, once they had entered the house, return to the barn where they slept, their duty done.

Matthew sat up alone on the porch, smoking a rare cigarette. He wanted the time alone. His children had grown up: that was what the move to America added up to. Even loyal Nahum was making his own decisions. Carey had opted to return to England: he was already missing her.

He barely thought of Anthony. He did not feel sorry for him, more like relief: he was at peace; in Vietnam he had seen deaths of men, bodies torn and guts exposed, and taught himself to care about the state of their souls instead. Because it was such early days in the States, he would have to front for it, take the responsibility. This was why Cassandra had told him as much as she had, close enough to the truth, to implicate him.

The house was silent as he crept up the main stairs to the room he had occupied with Carey just a few nights before. He had been alone on the porch, now he needed company. He climbed another flight to Cassandra's attic suite, opened the door without knocking or pause for hesitation. There were no curtains on the windows: he could see by the moonlight that she was awake, awaiting him. It was not until he had undressed, was about to step into the bed, that he realised she was not alone. He recognised the tousled, sleeping head on the pillow: Lee.

His eyes met hers. She was taunting him, tempting him; he thought about sending the boy away; she glanced down at his erection. He climbed in beside the boy, reached across him for Cassandra's head, eager lips, his penis pressed hard against the stirring youth's backside. He rolled over him and onto his wife, her legs already apart, she did not need to guide him into her, it was second nature. He pulled the youth's body against theirs, the boy's erect penis trapped between them, they fed on his youth, tongues stabbing at one another, first just the two of them then all three mouths in a mangle. Matthew threw one leg outside of Cassandra's, his thigh forced the boy's legs open, he felt his lightly-haired genitalia against his own, against his thigh the boy's rhythm picked up, bucked and jerked and finally came. Matthew too, inside his wife.

He lowered his head between theirs, breathed in the smell of them, crushed his chest against theirs, they both had arms around him, he kissed the boy's mouth: Anthony.

\* \* \*

In the oak-panelled offices of his New York lawyers, Rockworth held a video conference with his lawyers in London.

"I. Want. Them. Out."

Chesterfield Gardens; the London Chapter House; the lease.

Three of his lawyers shook their collective heads.

"There's no way to do it."

The fourth, a young associate, shrugged nonchalantly.

"Not apparently."

Across three thousand miles, Rockworth fixed him with a look of steel that lost nothing in the transmission. He did not bother to ask aloud: his money and their presence implied questions; he wanted answers, not to listen to his own echo.

"I've been through the lease a few times," the associate explained. "I did wonder about the consents clause, but it's difficult."

"Consents clause?"

"They have to comply with local authority regulations, bye-laws, planning requirements. We could use that to harass them, but – as I understand it – they seem to have a temporary permission to use the property for a meeting place, coffee bar."

Rockworth scowled.

"I arranged it."

"I know that." The associate reminded him casually that the problem was of his own making: it was something clients tended to forget. "There are things like health and safety at work, food safety. The difficulty is, they can always just comply, or else there are appeals that can take us, well, literally into the next century."

Into the camera, Rockworth made a beckoning gesture with his hand open facing upwards: gimme, spill it.

"There's also a conventional illegal and immoral user clause. You can forfeit the lease for illegal or immoral use."

"So? They're a religion; at least, that's what they call themselves."

"That's what they say. Some of the time. I've read the New York papers."

One of the partners asked cautiously:

"Sex? In this day and age, I wouldn't have thought."

"No, I agree. The sex on its own isn't enough," the associate replied. "But if we could make out some sort of case on the basis of organised sexual use of members, I would have thought, well, we've got a lot of merits before we begin, haven't we?"

"Merits?" Rockworth's eyes sparkled: this he understood; the hell with the principles – the case would be decided on the merits; all they needed to hand the judge was a peg on which to hang the result. "Yes."

"We don't have any evidence," expostulated the litigation man.

"Get it, then," said the most senior partner.

"Yes," the young associate said: "That was what I was thinking."

* * *

The New Hampshire state motto is "live free or die". Caleb's friend, Al, newly released from jail, had believed in it and moved near to Concord to sell dope to bikers and guns to survivalists.

Father Caleb had not left Hammer Reach because of impending publicity; he would have liked to stay to bare his teeth at the press, watch Matthew wriggle.

He left because he needed to keep moving forward. The Mass had been his fantasies come real. They had proved that there was nothing they could not do to themselves and to each other – no limits. His boys were wired; some of the women too. Left to their own thoughts and devices, there was a risk of counter-purpose, perhaps even shame, trying to put back into the box what they had not known they were capable of; or – worse to his mind than denial – they might rewrite it as nothing more than a sexual adventure. He wanted to keep the spirit of it alive, explore where further it could lead them.

Only Christopher knew where he was going. He took the VW bus in which Nahum and Jemima used to tour. It was an easy journey, just a few hours East along Interstate 88 to Albany, ducking through Massachusetts and North into New Hampshire on 89. There were six of them: Caleb, his three most devoted disciples, and Sisters Mary and Pascale cut loose from Diana, terrified by what they had watched her do, eager for a new role for themselves.

By nightfall, they still had not found Caleb's friend: they slept in the van, fully clothed. In the morning, Caleb took the van and Sister Pascale and left the rest of them to find gas stations and restaurants in which to wash up and eat. If they got bored, they could go donating. He made calls to track Al down. Eventually, he found his way to a biker bar at the north end of the city, where the morning boozers wolf-whistled at Pascale, drank the beers he bought them and – jail-credentials examined and established – sent him on towards Franklin with instructions to cut off the road to Salisbury in the direction of the Merrimack where, with luck and another beer, they would find a mud track that led to Al's deliberately isolated home.

Sister Pascale sat up in the front with him, close enough for their thighs to touch. She was a tall, thin girl, but gawky, with sallow skin, stringy hair: they had found her in London, living in a squat, working in a dry-cleaners. She was scared of being alone with Caleb and excited. When she had watched him enter Diana the other night, ram into her and hold her, her stomach had gone into a free-fall which had not yet ended; she felt as if she was on a permanent trip, better than crack or smack, better than prayer and meditation both. She asked:

"When are we going back for the others?"

"Are you afraid of being alone with me?"

"You seem different," she admitted, but she did not pull away.

"'Individuality comprises several orders of existence'," he quoted Crowley. "Tell me what you see."

"In the Chapter Houses, at Hammer Reach, I don't know, you always seem so in control. I mean, well, to be honest," she laughed, "most of us are pretty scared of you most of the time."

"And now?"

"Now it's different," was all she could manage.

"Where'd you get a name like Pascale?" he asked inconsequentially.

"My mother was French. My father hated it; he wanted me to be English; said I'd get teased and bullied at school if they knew I was French."

"Were you?"

She nodded: unhappy memories.

"Everyone hates outsiders," he muttered.

"You too?"

"I don't do that," he answered.

"What?" she asked, startled and confused.

"Exchange confidences; talk about myself." His eyes were fixed on the road, looking for the junction.

"That's what's different," she said. "This is you, isn't it?"

"What?"

"This; driving; visiting someone you were in jail with; looking for what?"

"You're not as scared of me as you say, are you?"

She shook her head firmly, boldly.

"Do you want me to make love to you?"

Without any hesitation she nods, then says aloud:

"Yes."

"Well, I'm not going to."

She turns bright red, her eyes fill with tears, she has misread the situation, made a fool of herself. She bites her upper lip to stop herself from crying, finally manages to ask:

"Why not?"

"I liked Anthony," Caleb answers.

"I'd heard that. But," she replies, meaning that he also made love to women members – she had seen for herself, "why did you bring me with you, then?"

He turns off the highway, points at the sign to Salisbury, says:

"Watch the mileage," tapping the plastic.

"Why did you bring me?" she repeats. The tears of rejection are gone. She is beginning to see her way through to the answer he will give her. She understands that there is nothing from which she cannot learn, except that which she already knows.

He hears the change in her voice.

"You've got a lot of what I like; you've been a social worker too long." He wants to bring out the pain in her and under his control to turn it on others.

Her eyes flash.

"Then maybe I'll fuck you instead."

He roars aloud:

"Maybe so; maybe so."

It is Al he wants her to fuck; part of the ritual. It establishes good-faith: people working for the government don't sleep with the enemy, not even with a condom. It allows him to take his time, shut by Al into the concealed basement, examining Al's treasures, piling to one side the weapons he can afford to take away with him. It is Christopher's money, the secret fund. He could have bought a single gun anywhere, even two or three; not enough for an army – the army of God and Satan.

\* \* \*

From *Programme and Progression*:

*We do the same with our ideas of God as we do with everything else: purpose and counter-purpose. We approach God with belief, and reserve – by way of counter-purpose – disbelief; we identify God in one way, and an inch below the surface and ten minutes later, we identify God in another. Thus do we seek the best of all worlds and achieve a confused and confusing face of God. This is why we need to give to each of the conflicting directions its own identity – God, Satan, the angels and devils between – to allow counter-purpose its own voice, its own face, its own reality. It must come from within, because otherwise the conflicts are not your own and if you are not composed of your own conflicts and contradictions then there is nothing about you that is unique.*

\* \* \*

Cassandra loved the publicity. By the time they got back from seeing Romero in town, television vans were parked alongside the farm. While Matthew went to meet them, she slipped into the house. She emerged in a flowing robe of black silk, framed by her black body-guards, the silver chain from which hung The Programme symbol around her waist, which she had been wearing constantly since the Special Mass – even in bed – as if to say, it belongs to me now, it – The Programme. The cameras swung from Matthew to The Seer, surrounded her before she could reach him.

"What's your name?"

"Are you the group leader?"

"Were you here?"

"Was he your lover?"

"Why did he kill himself?"

"What's your relationship with Rockworth?"

"One at a time, one at a time." She managed them like a movie-star, face stern, eyes twinkling. "You," she waved gracefully at a man with a CBS microphone.

"What is The Programme, ma'am?"

"You can call me Mother Cassandra." Friendly, no one to be scared of. "The Programme is a group I founded with my husband. He is our Teacher; I am The Seer."

"How come you didn't foresee what Anthony Rockworth was going to do, Cassandra?" a newspaper journalist asked.

"What happened to Anthony is our tragedy; but it was his choice."

"Hey, Cassandra, what was he doing in a cell?"

"It's a small downstairs room which people go to meditate in. Remember meditation? It's how half the world gets by."

"Can we see the room?" asked NBC.

"I'm sorry; we're not going to allow you in the house. This has been distressing enough for us all as it is. The house is our most private place; we've already had the police all over it. But you can visit our Chapters in Boston and New York." She glanced over their heads at Matthew, met his eyes, added: "And in London."

One or two of the press drifted back to Matthew: they had their pictures of the woman, but she was telling them nothing worth printing.

"Matthew, how does this tie in with the Kroger case?"

"It doesn't. We have hundreds of members of The Programme; a lot of things are going on at about the same time – always. That's it."

"Coincidence?"

"There is no coincidence," Matthew answered gravely. "Nor is there chance. Amanda Kroger's sister knew what she was doing; sadly, it looks like Anthony did too."

"Have you spoken to Arthur Rockworth yet?"

"No."

"He doesn't seem to think much of you right now, Matthew."

"He thinks enough of us to let us use a house he owns in London, he made contacts for us in Boston, his son has spent the last few years with us and he seemed happier than he'd been before. I think you should leave Mr Rockworth alone," he added in a measured tone. "He's in grief."

"Hey, he should leave us alone," a woman said. "We don't need to ask; he's telling."

"You're listening," he reminded her.

"We're reporters; it's what we do." She was flustered, finding herself being drawn into debate with him. His eyes swept over her; she felt herself caught up in him, floating; it would never show in a story, but for a moment she understood.

Cassandra finally pushed her way to Matthew's side.

"How long had Anthony been 'meditating'?" The Daily News' stringer sneered.

"Anthony had been properly fed each day, he came out to wash, he was free to leave at any time," Matthew replied.

"A few days," Cassandra declaimed. "It was nothing. Members of The Programme can meditate for weeks at a time."

"What else can they do weeks at a time, Cassandra? How long's a relationship last in The Programme?"

Eyes twinkling, Cassandra said:

"My husband and I have been married for more than ten years."

"Yeah, sure. When d'you last sleep together?"

Cassandra took Matthew's arm and squeezed it.

"Last night. When did you last sleep with your wife?"

\* \* \*

They had rearranged her room to fit in a second desk, placing them at angles in opposite corners, like boxers facing each other in a ring.

For a moment she was confused which was hers, but the mile-high pile of messages gave it away.

She was oddly relieved to see that Patrick's watercolour loaner was still in the room, but it no longer faced her. Defiantly, she took it down and started to swap it around with the William Morris poster. That was what she was doing when Jessica arrived.

"Hi," the woman said from the door, startling Carey as she stood on a chair, the print in one hand, steadying herself against the wall with another. "Here. Let me take that," she added before Carey let it slip.

"Thanks," Carey mumbled.

"This one?" Jessica pointed to the painting on Carey's desk.

"Right."

"It's Patrick's, right?" Jessica said as she handed it up to her.

"Right." Carey wished she could come up with a more original answer: she had been daunted by the woman on the one occasion when they had previously met. "I thought he might have taken it out."

"I think he was planning to." Jessica helped her down from the chair.

"You stopped him?"

The woman carried the Morris print across the room. Carey dragged the chair over. Before she could stop her, Jessica had hopped up lithely, still holding the frame, and hooked it into place.

"There now. Better?"

Jessica was compact, organised, in control and command and not only of herself. She was flaunting it, challenging Carey to match her composure.

Carey asked again:

"Did you stop Patrick taking the picture?"

"Yes."

"Why?"

"I liked it. Why? Did I do something wrong?" She was not disconcerted by Carey's anxiety.

Carey stared at her for a moment, left the room, returned with a fresh mug of coffee for herself. It was the best she could manage.

Jessica sighed.

"We've got off on the wrong foot, haven't we?"

"We?" Carey asked pointedly.

"All right, I have," Jessica corrected herself casually. "This is your office; I apologise. But I'm not newly qualified; it's difficult for me to share a room; perhaps more difficult, in the circumstances." Carey's firm.

"Forget it," Carey said, knowing neither of them would do so.

The long flight and the time difference were catching up with Carey. She gulped her coffee, got up to fetch another, already her third of the day.

"Would you like a cup?" she asked in apology for her earlier childishness.

"I don't drink coffee. I'll come with you, make a cup of tea."

In the kitchen, her back to Jessica, much as Colin had broken the news that she had a room-mate, Carey said:

"I know, er, I know some people think I'm a bit of a screw-up." Patrick sprung to mind. "But I don't screw up at work."

"I know," Jessica replied, squidging her tea bag one last time to prevent it dripping on the counter before she could get it into the bin. "I've been covering some of your files." She hesitated, then added: "If you wanted to talk; I mean…"

"Sure," Carey said, not meaning it.

* * *

Because Carey had given no notice of her return, her appointment book was empty. Her cases were mostly urgent crises which did not wait for an empty slot in any lawyer's diary. New work had been assigned elsewhere. There was enough to do but not too much. Between times, she made calls and visited with others. Alistair acted as if she had merely been abroad on a case, taking a few extra days. Alison was too busy to talk, on the telephone when Carey popped her head around the door, but waved and mouthed "nice to see you". Patrick was at court but came in to see her as soon as he returned. Diplomatically, Jessica withdrew from the room.

Patrick saw at once that his picture had been relocated where Carey could see it, smiled and nodded with pleasure.

"I hear tell you wanted it back," Carey accused.

Patrick reddened.

"I didn't think you'd want it anymore." Not after they had split up.

"Oh, Patrick, I'm sorry."

"Anyway, Jessica said she wanted me to leave it."

"I'm still jet-lagged, everything feels unreal; I'm beginning to wonder if I've stepped into a play called The Watercolour. I'm going to go home soon. Catch a couple of hours sleep."

Patrick rushed in before he could change his mind.

"Would you have dinner with me later? Just to catch up."

"Yes. I'd like that." Carey's voice sounded hollow, ghost-like, someone else's; she wasn't sure what she was doing; maybe she was trying to turn the clock back.

It was hard to tell who was more surprised. He backed out of the room before she backed off her decision.

"Come up to the house after work," she said.

"Seven?"

"Sure."

* * *

After he had finished with his lawyers in London, and handled another session with those in New York, Rockworth met Berlinger. They shook hands; Rockworth offered him a drink.

"I don't," Berlinger said shortly.

"What do you do, Mr Berlinger?"

"I deprogramme, Mr Rockworth."

He had an attitude. Rockworth was used to it: people determinedly undaunted by his wealth and power.

"Yes; that much I knew. It's a bit late for me, though."

"Why did you ask to see me?"

"Have you deprogrammed anyone from The Programme – anyone else, that is?" He reminded Berlinger that he knew of the failed attempt to free Amanda Kroger.

"I've talked to a couple others." He would not tell Rockworth more than he needed to about his operations.

Rockworth studied the man across his desk. He was wearing a dark suit – blue, but dark. He had made the effort. He was younger than he seemed at first: the hair-loss added a decade; for a moment, Rockworth wondered if he might have shaved his head deliberately. He was over six feet. Rockworth's briefing told him Berlinger had been – in turns – a college athlete, a marine, a sports reporter then newsreader on local TV, finally he had made it to network television, only to quit a few months later to engage in his current crusade. He had a daughter who had joined the Moonies, a son who was a missionary in Central Africa, a wife who had died in a car crash no one knew was drink or suicide.

"You don't say much."

"I do when it matters."

"Which is when? When you are persuading someone out of – out of what? A cult? A sect? How do you do that?"

"You said it – you don't have anyone to get out."

His attitude was beginning to annoy Rockworth. He had offered Berlinger five thousand non-refundable dollars to come see him.

"I want to know," he snapped.

"Why did you ask to see me, Mr Rockworth?" Berlinger repeated, sighing as if he was about to give up the interview as a bad job.

Rockworth hesitated. He was not used to refusal. On the other hand, he wanted someone as hard and as unyielding as himself.

"I feel guilty, Mr Berlinger. What I did was wrong, committing my son to their care. I want to make sure it doesn't happen to anyone else; I feel it's the least I can do; I gave them support, that makes me partially responsible. That's why I asked you to come. I want to put them out of business; my lawyers are working on the lease in London; they need information; I want you to work with them; I also want you to work against The Programme in any other way you can – in America, too." No limits.

"You want revenge," Berlinger brushed off the claim to altruism.

"Isn't that what you're doing?" Rockworth answered angrily.

For a moment, he thought he had lost the man. Then, for the first time, Berlinger smiled.

"It's what we're all doing, Mr Rockworth: them too."

"What do you mean?"

"It's the way I see it, Mr Rockworth. The people – these so-called gurus – it's their way of getting revenge."

"For what?"

"Does it matter? Somewhere along the line, they all got passed over – they all wanted something the world wouldn't give them; mostly, I guess, God got there before them. They're all little men, Mr Rockworth, all of them. Even Crane. Little inside. This is their way of saying screw you – I'm going to take it for myself; they especially like taking away your children. Makes them feel powerful; like God telling Abraham to sacrifice Isaac."

"Is that how you feel about your daughter?"

"Mr Rockworth," Berlinger said expressionlessly, "I don't have a daughter. No more than you have a son."

\* \* \*

Carey went home shortly after she had made the date with Patrick.

Before she went to bed, she took a shower and wrapped herself in a towel, sitting in the living room with another cup of coffee, watching CNN and smoking, until she had dried. She drifted off on the sofa, awoke to the sight of Hammer Reach, Matthew and Cassandra outside the farmhouse.

"Last night. When did you last sleep with your wife?"

She did not doubt it: it was pure Matthew, and pure Cassandra to have told the world.

She fought panic, told herself that she did not care. Matthew had made her no promises of fidelity; beneath the surface disappointment, she even managed to be aware that it was mildly exciting. Her hand strayed to her lap; guiltily, she snatched it away.

She switched off the television; she was too tired to think about it. Instead of going directly to her own bedroom, she found herself in what had become Emily's, drawing comfort from the presence of Emily's belongings, wishing she had come back with her, wondering what she was doing, trying not to conjure up the worst images. She stretched out on Emily's bed, still wrapped in her towel, in moments she was asleep.

She dreamed of Matthew, Phillipe, Caleb; they were dancing around something – a sacrifice – a chicken – her heart, raw and red, pumping blood – it was strangely easy, not at all scary – she reached out to touch it for herself, stroke it, it felt sensual, sexual – it was her soul – she was being passed around the men – naked – they were touching her but none of them made any move to possess her – the sacrifice was Emily – now Carey was scared – her heart had been brushed off the altar onto the ground – it started to pump violently – jumping all over the place – she was trying to catch it, grab it, stuff it back inside herself – dead Emily was sobbing – asking her to do it – she mounted her, lay alongside her, cradled her head in the crook of her arm; it's all right, *chérie*, as if they were by the pool at the apartment in Antibes – Charles shook her awake – he was saying something – but it was the doorbell – she fought against its clamour to find out what Charles was saying – the bell won and she came awake without finding out – it had sounded like: fly away little bird.

\* \* \*

She answered the door wearing a silk dressing-gown that belonged to Emily, grabbed from a hook on the back of her door.

Patrick. In a suit.

She was embarrassed; she had forgotten he was coming.

She stepped back to let him in.

He was equally embarrassed, tense, memories of their times together which he had worked to forget were back in a flash. He walked past her in the small hall careful not to touch her, even accidentally.

"Would you like a drink."

Her voice was a mixture of tiredness from the trip abroad and the flight home, her uneasy sleep, and the sudden memory of Cassandra's brash claim coming back to her even as she stood at the door.

It was not cold, but she felt shivery, goose-bumps, tingly, sensuous. She was acutely aware of her nakedness beneath the dressing-gown, Emily's dressing-gown against her skin. She was wet; she pressed her thighs together as if to stop Patrick sensing it. She had been smoking too much; it made her voice sound husky, sexy.

"Sure. Why not?"

He did not know what he wanted. He had loved her, still loved her. They had brought out something special in each other. It had not worked. It had made him unhappy. He had chosen to have nothing rather than not enough. He would be a fool to try again for more than they could make.

He followed her into the kitchen where she struggled with a bottle of wine.

"Here, let me," he held out a hand.

She turned and as she did so, the dressing-gown fell half open. He caught a flash of breast, flushed, looked up to find her eyes meeting his. He took the bottle, the corkscrew already well lodged within, put the cold bottle between his legs; through the material of his suit, he could feel it against an already tumescent penis, he pulled sharply on the corkscrew, she was giggling at him, suddenly the corkscrew popped, he thanked God it was still wine not champagne – the imagery would have been unbearable.

She took the bottle, poured two glasses, handed one to him, held it by the thin stem. His hand seemed larger than she remembered, more lined; it was Phillipe's hand, or Caleb's or Matthew's, from the dream. Instead of taking the glass by the bowl, he wrapped his fingers around hers so they were locked together.

She asked:

"Is this what you wanted?"

"The wine?"

"No."

"No," he said. "It wasn't."

"But it is now?"

She pulled her hand free. She hesitated for a moment longer, then untied the belt of the dressing-gown so it fell open. She stood for a moment then turned to lead the way upstairs to her bedroom still carrying her glass. She took each step slowly, carefully, savouring it. In her bedroom, she lay on the bed, still wearing Emily's dressing-gown, watching him detachedly as he tore at his clothes, using him like a mirror to watch herself.

She had time to ask herself what she was doing, why she was doing it. She flashed on Matthew with Cassandra – with Helen, with the boy Lucius, with Emily. They were all mixed up together. She began to panic. It was not right, it was not what she wanted to be doing: revenge-fucking. She was about to say something, stop him, when he knelt beside her on the bed, pushed one knee between hers, he could not wait, he was already inside her, it was too late, over almost before it had begun.

Afterwards, they showered separately, both of them embarrassed.

"Where do you want to go?" Patrick called from the bathroom.

None of the choices appealed. She suggested they order in: pizza or Chinese. He did not reply for a long time, long enough for her to wonder if he was going to leave, just up and walk out on her, long enough for her to decide she wanted him to stay.

"Okay," he said. "Pizza."

\* \* \*

They ate in the kitchen, either side of the small counter.

"What was it like?" He left her to decide whether he meant America or The Programme.

"Disneyland," she answered promptly.

"What are you saying? That it's unreal?"

"In some ways, yes; not your reality." Her eyes shone: for a moment, she was back at The Programme – the Midnight Meditation when she had joined – Matthew's Introductory Lecture in New York – the evening at Moonlight Inn – before it all got mixed up.

"Yours?"

"I don't know. That's what I meant: it was like a visit."

"Now you're trying to decide if you want to go back or stay here?"

He was astute: she gave him that. She had to be careful what she said. He had too many loyalties to take him for granted. Her position in the firm would already have been somewhere between tenuous and terminal if her name had not been Arnott.

"I know I belong here." She avoided a direct lie though not by much.

"Don't sound so sad about it; it's not the worst place on earth."

"I know. It's just – it's like stepping into a place with a completely different set of rules and objectives; that's what I meant about Disneyland – the objective is to get your turn on the ride; in between, you obey the rules, which are mostly to wait your turn on the ride." She caught the look of confusion on his face, reached across, touched his cheek. "Oh, Patrick, don't try so hard to understand; it won't make any sense to you anyway."

"I know it won't; I was trying to make sense of you."

"What do you think of Jessica?" She changed the subject suddenly.

"I like her, actually." As if it was surprising.

"Everyone seems to. Colin says even Charles likes her."

"He does." Patrick confirmed. "Are you jealous?"

"Of her?"

Patrick nodded.

"Why should I be?"

"Everyone likes you too," he answered elliptically.

"Do you?"

"What? Like you?"

"Yes."

"You know I do."

"No. I know you have feelings for me and I know you're attracted to me. But I've never been quite sure if you liked me, you know, just in myself."

He thought for a moment before answering.

"I'm not sure I know what that means. 'In yourself'. Do people exist like that – separate from what they do, from what you want from them? Is that what The Programme is about?"

"I think that's what it tries to be. Not making demands of each other, to be someone in particular; being ourselves; seeing what we make of ourselves, on our own and collectively. It's about not deciding what we want to happen and going towards it but letting whatever comes out of being ourselves happen, and out of being together while we do it."

"And what does come out of it?"

"Something different every day," she said. "That's the fun part."

"And the serious part?"

"Does it have to have one?" She could not confide in him the inner tensions of the group; he was an outsider.

"We're back where we began, aren't we? What are you going to do?"

"No. That's not the question. It's where I'm going to do it. I believe in the things The Programme stands for. That's what you find hardest, all of you. That I actually believe in it, in anything apart from the law."

"What we find hard is to know what it is."

"It's a group; I suppose you'd call it a religion, but not in a conventional way; articles of faith is the phrase that comes to mind. We all agree on certain principles – propositions – and we agree to live together in recognition of them, out of respect for them, and then we see what happens. In turn, what happens defines the faith. Does that make any better sense?"

"It's far too abstract for me," he grimaced.

"We're fond of one another, right?"

"I hope so."

"But we both know things haven't been working out."

He nodded but said nothing.

"So we decided to do nothing at all instead of struggling to carry on with the bits that did work."

"You've got a short memory, Carey. I thought, just now…"

"That was us again, for a short time, wasn't it? What were you doing?"

He had the answers he needed.

"Having sex," he said flatly.

And:

"That's all," he lied.

"And that's fine with you? That's enough?"

He felt himself growing angry, as if she was playing with him, had been playing with him beforehand. She had changed, she was different, he could not understand her, he did not like what he saw. He repeated the thought to himself, shook his head sorrowfully, said:

"I think you're right."

"What?"

"I don't think I do like you. Anyway, not like this."

She laughed brittlely:

"Well then; don't say nothing good comes out of The Programme – it's what you needed to feel, isn't it?"

\* \* \*

After he had gone, she was lonely. She tried calling the Chapter House. Neither Father Simon nor Mother Naamah – Chapter Mother since the departure of Cassandra – was available. The best she could manage was Sister Rebecca – even Sister Lilith was serving in the

Coffee Lounge, too busy to speak. Rebecca sounded distant, uncomfortable with Carey, they were not connecting.

She opened a second bottle of wine and sat at the window in her study overlooking the street, the way she always used to do, smoking and scanning her computer, waiting for the drink to do its trick. She had gone with Matthew, failed, lost him; Emily had gone over, Carey had come home – lost her too; she had agreed to see Patrick, lost him; Colin did not have the time for her – she and her new room-mate at work were not going to get along; Charles was in Antibes.

She was home, she thought bitterly: this was home. Her head began to spin.

# Chapter Eleven

Three images within as many weeks.

First, The Programme as harmless, almost staid, quasi-New Age – philosophy, psychology, religion, maybe eccentric but well-connected, bordering on the respectable, the acceptable, shrugging off the Kroger case. Secondly, The Programme under siege: death of a member; suspicion; Rockworth's highly publicised anger. They had crossed a line, fair game on either side of the Atlantic. Finally, surviving the media blaze. Even in London, the Coffee Lounge was busy. In Boston and in New York, they slunk nervously around the corner, lined up to slide into the Chapter Houses and cluster outside the Meditation Hall, desperate for acceptance and salvation.

They brought new members to Hammer Reach at the weekends, a handful at a time. Many of them still had jobs; The Programme could not afford to support the sudden influx, needed both the money they could tithe and time to filter them into residence. In the weeks after Anthony's death, they took in nearly a hundred Acolytes, more than half of whom were initiated within a month. To Cassandra's delight, some of the new members brought in children: Matthew had always loved The Programme children, treated them as his own; these would be hers. Now that Anthony was gone, she had asked Hannah – Micah's former wife – to bring Tamar and Thomas over, as soon as their schools broke up for the holidays.

All of the new members who came to Hammer Reach at weekends were already Initiates. Those with children left them in the care of the Boston or New York Chapters. Though they were most of them only weeks into The Programme, it already felt like their whole lives. They were non-resident; if they succeed at the weekend, they will become residents and Junior Messengers.

The hierarchy was wary of spies but hungry for new bodies and blood. A couple of risky prospects were kept on kitchen duty until they failed to turn up again; one more made it into the print shop, but was caught with proofs of The Seer's latest Lesson stuffed into his trousers. The publicity was dying down; Rockworth was quiet. There were negotiations yet to complete with a range of local and federal authorities who had descended on them because of the publicity, but – like Romero – officials found themselves charmed as well as threatened.

The ones who were brought to Hammer Reach were those of whom they were most certain. They had shown the easiest grasp of the ideas and the language of The Programme and had also shown themselves least tied to an outside commitment – job or family. They had turned up to The Programme every minute they were not at work, every day. They had participated in Meditations without restraint. They wanted to move in. They were by no means the loneliest or the most disturbed; to the contrary, they were those who had managed to bring themselves closest to The Programme's conclusions and solutions on their own, wanting someone else with whom to execute them, unafraid and unashamed.

Isaiah 49: 20 – "The children which thou shalt have, after thou has lost the other, shall say again in thine ears, the place is too straight for me; give place to me that I may dwell."

They met The Seer for the first time. They had seen her pictures, read her words, heard her voice on recordings and in videos. They were in awe of her. She was the wife of, and but one step away from, The Teacher himself, about whom they were almost entirely ignorant but who still occupied the group's highest spiritual ground. For years, so many of the existing membership had followed him loyally and unquestioningly – worshipfully – that he could not be pushed aside, let alone pushed under: instead, the process was one of elevation, almost deification, until finally he would float free into the fire beyond.

They were enthralled, entranced by her. They saw this small woman, dark, heavy-breasted, often in the black silk she had worn for the television cameras, framed by her two Jays. Because she was so small, they had to lean in towards her, stooping, almost kneeling, instant obeisance; once within her reach, they belonged to her. They saw those shining eyes and wanted them to shine on them alone. Her energy was unmistakably sexual: they felt it; young men who would have described her derisively on the outside as an older woman shivered in excitement at the idea of her; girls who had never entertained the thought of sex with another woman wondered what it would be like to be cradled naked in her arms. She stroked the Jays as if they were dogs; they were never allowed to touch her in return; they had no sex with her; they were hers, for fucking others with.

In the afternoon of their arrival, new members worked out in the fields. She wanted them fit and lean, and tired and excited. Paimon – up for the weekend from the Boston Chapter of which he was by then in charge – took command of them. They changed into whites: white T-shirts, white shorts, white sneakers. They changed on arrival in the barn-dormitory above the Meditation Hall, boys and girls in a single room without privacy. None of them hesitated: they had spent weeks without sex; they were already disciplined enough to appreciate its more powerful and creative uses.

What started out as exercise became training. Paimon ran them around the fields, laughing and cheering them on. He had them kicking at their outstretched hands in a martial arts movement, learning how to throw each other to the ground and how to fall without hurting themselves. He had them marching and chanting: I am one; we are many; together we shall be whole; left, left, left right left; the army of God and Satan.

Next there were individual training sessions, mental work-outs. Superiors and Senior Messengers took these newcomers into a room, one on one. They were harangued, bullied, shouted at, threatened, broken – to a man and to a woman – to tears, hugged and consoled and kissed and congratulated until the tears subsided and they realised that where they had been – and come safely out of – was the dark place that they would not have dared to visit a couple of weeks before. It was what they had come into The Programme for, they were making it.

"We're here to help you to do things and to become someone you've dreamed about, but never thought possible," they had been told.

They learned to let go, to trust. They were brought back into a group, then paired off. Just as they thought they were over the worst, they were plunged back into the rage. Role-playing, subject – victim – and teacher. Later, they turned to menial activity. They spring-cleaned the house from top to toe, cellar only excepted, changed bed linen, some were put on laundry duty, others to prepare a meal for the weekend household. They were everything that they did; together they were whole.

After they ate, there was a meditation. In the late evening, they were left to their own devices: they took showers and changed back into their own clothes; they could walk – it was the end of the summer but still warm outside; they could sleep; they socialised over hot drinks in the kitchen with people so much more senior than themselves that they had before this weekend not exchanged more than The Programme greeting with them.

In a private room, Paimon, Caleb, Christopher and Cassandra met to discuss the recruits. Shortly before midnight, three of them were selected. One of them was asleep; she was gently woken, a finger placed to her lips – get dressed, come with me. Another, about to go to bed, was told to wait. The third was watching an old movie on TV; gripped by it, he had almost forgotten where he was. Startled, he followed Brother Reuben down the steps, pleased to see faces he knows, first surprised – then proud – when he realised how few of his peer-members were present. Reuben arranged them together, the new people, in the middle of the basement, in a circle, their backs to one another, one of them facing Father Caleb – naked on his throne, one facing Father Paimon in red, one facing a black-robed Father Christopher. As they sat, their eyes took in The Seer, reclining on her bed along the wall, now all in white.

Brother Reuben gestured at them to remove their shoes and socks, put them out of sight beneath the steps, took his own place. The new members could feel each other's pulsing backs. It was dawning on each of them what was about to happen. This was what the abstinence was about, the build up of energy. Each of them had the sudden urge to get up, run away, deny the last weeks, write The Programme off to a bad mistake.

Excitement drew them in, tiredness diminished the will to resist: counter-purpose abated. Each of them was far more scared to go than to stay.

\* \* \*

As soon as she arrived at the office, before Jessica got in, Carey called George Cohen at his own office. She would need his help on the full Kroger trial.

George was guarded, nervous, mumbled a response to her "I am one" greeting:

"I didn't know if you were still over there."

"I got back this morning. How're things here?"

"I, um, well, I haven't been around much," he admitted.

"Working hard?"

"Yes." The truthful answer was none the less misleading. He added: "I moved out, you know." He had been living in the South Kensington flat with Gloria before she went to the States.

"What are you telling me, George?"

A long silence. A loud sigh.

"I needed some time away, Carey. I thought you'd know."

"How would I know?"

"Oh, because of the dispute with Christopher."

"What dispute?" Her hackles were rising; this was news to her.

"I'm not sure, you know, how much I ought to be saying. I mean, well, you're still only an Initiate, aren't you?"

She was not even an Initiate, merely an Acolyte.

"I'm The Programme's lawyer."

"Are you sure? I thought I was their accountant."

"What are you telling me, George?"

"When they first went over, I was still handling all the money from here. It's easy enough by modem. I could even manage the bank account in Boston. Then I found I was being barred, I had to telephone the bank to find out there was nothing wrong with the connection. I spoke to Christopher. He said, well, they were going to run their own accounts, you know, separately, over there."

"So? I mean, George, that's hardly a surprise; it couldn't be very convenient to have to ring you in England every time they want to write a cheque or something."

"No, of course not; nor did they have to. I only managed it. They had access; it's just that I didn't – I didn't have any access anymore."

"Okay," Carey said slowly, absorbing the information. "Is it such a big deal? I mean, the main money's here, right?" Matthew's money, in law.

"Well, that's it. Each of the Chapters has its own local account, for every day expenses. But most of the funds were in the main account; we moved that to Boston, you see."

"You did?" Carey tried to stay calm. "Why? Whose idea was it?"

"Well," George coughed apologetically. "It was mine. With more activity in the States than here, it made sense to place funds there than constantly to pay for transfer – and exchange rates – from here."

"And?"

"And obviously, Christopher had to be a signatory over there; we needed a resident signatory. They both were: Christopher and Cassandra."

"But you are as well?"

"Yes. But two can override one, do you see?"

"What about Matthew? I thought." She knew. "It's all in his name, though. Is he a signatory?"

"He's the account-holder. He can override us all."

"Did you check with him? What did he say?"

"I haven't spoken to him. I thought, well, they've run it all for years; you know Matthew – he's always somewhere else. I assumed he knew."

"George," she said, "is this why you've moved out?"

"What do you mean?"

"Well, do you think you've made a mistake?"

"You mean, fallen on my sword, that sort of thing?"

"That's one possibility." Or fear of punishment.

"I don't think, I'm not sure I can separate things out that easily. I've been with The Programme a long time, Carey: not that long after it began. But I've always maintained a practice of my own and, well, I suppose you could say, I've had the best of both worlds, really, being in it but having my separate position." Much as she had. "I know a lot of people have felt it meant I wasn't as committed as others, and I suppose that's true; it was mutually convenient to let it be. I was already beginning to think, with the move to the States, perhaps I had to make a final choice, one way or the other. Then this happened. Perhaps it was a sign." His voice trailed away.

"A sign of what, though? That's the question," Carey murmured.

"There's so many new members. Where would I have been?"

"I don't know, George. Have you been to the Coffee Lounge?"

"Not for a week," he said miserably. To a resident member, even George, a Programme-week was forever. George was going cold turkey.

"I may need to be in touch," Carey said. "There are some questions around the case."

"I'm not deserting, Carey. I'll still be here. You know where to reach me."

"Take care of yourself, George."

"You too, Carey; you give Matthew my best, too."

"I am one, George."

"We are many," he replied automatically.

He coughed again and hung up.

* * *

Cassandra was bored with Lee. She gave him to Caleb; Lee said no, the way he had when he had refused to leave the Coffee Lounge. Instead, Father Caleb handed Brother Lee off to Sister Pascale in reward for her performance in New Hampshire. Pascale said she was not senior enough to have him under the contact rules so Caleb promoted her Senior Messenger.

One night, he took on the two Jays for the hell of it, fucked them in turns; in the morning, he chased them around the fields with a loaded gun, nearly killing Jeremiah. Cassandra watched from the porch: she knew about the guns, buried in the pit in the Meditation Hall. Father Christopher was cold, Caleb excited, when they had showed her. He named them to her, though it meant nothing:

261

Mitchells and Marlins and Thomsons and Springfields and Rugers. Some were wrapped in, others stacked on, polythene sheeting bought in to damp-proof The Temple, on which were also arrayed cleaning implements and oils. They were stored in a lead-lined trunk which Caleb said had been provided with the guns. While it would not prevent detection by the most sophisticated equipment, it would do so if a run-of-the-mill system was passed over it.

"What are they for?" Cassandra asked.

"To help you make the choice," Christopher answered.

Caleb squatted down in the pit, rifle between his legs.

"We have to protect what's ours."

"Hammer Reach?" Matthew's life-tenancy.

"That too."

Caleb was on a course of his own; Christopher had encouraged him. They were taking steps along a path without a clue where they were headed, for the sake of the adventure.

She drove to Boston. She wanted to talk to Paimon. She could trust him most of all, perhaps only him.

The Programme members in white, selling their magazines, were already a familiar site on the streets of Boston, of Cambridge; also in Manhattan. There were so many alienated people out there; fruit for the plucking.

Behind the scenes, the Chapter Houses were disciplined, but warm: daily routines dominated – teams in the kitchens, preparing new publications, cleaning the houses, washing clothes, conducting public meditations and seminars, talking to prospective members, in the evenings they worked the Coffee Lounge, worshipped in private, looked after the children, sometimes they just hung out, watched TV, like a family.

Jemima was in charge of New York. She was traditional Programme, Nahum's co-missionary. Once, she had been a schoolteacher. The Programme had often attracted teachers. Micah and Hannah – parents of Tamar and Thomas – had been schoolteachers, too. They were good organisers; useful members; lacking in imagination; no threat.

So long as the Kroger case continued – months perhaps years – they needed New York to stay calm, staid even. It was a good place to recruit – better maybe than Boston – but recruits were more volatile. Jemima's calming atmosphere served to weed out the worst of them; Merry's, too.

In Boston, Paimon could not help himself: however hard he tried to impress on recruits the need for self-control, they could scent the danger bubbling beneath the surface; for many, it was what they wanted, worth hanging about for, doing time until it was their turn.

Arriving in Boston in the evening, she left the two Jays to make their own arrangements to stay at one of the satellite houses and visited the Coffee Lounge on her own, dressed in lay clothes. She knew none of the members on duty. She had tied back her thick black hair. No one recognised her. The Coffee Lounge was full: she sat in a booth with a couple of boys, smiled nervously as if it was her first time. She asked:

"Is it okay?" To sit with them.

"Sure," the stronger of the pair welcomed her.

They were maybe twenty, twenty three. She avoided questions about herself, asked them about themselves, it was easy to get them talking. They were from Lowell, where the Massachusetts industrial revolution had begun but that was now better known as the birthplace of Jack Kerouac. They talked of him with pride, like they had known him, but they were not even born when he died in Florida, had not read his books. They were discouraging about the town.

"It's like, dead, you know."

"Did you come in for The Programme?" she asked sceptically.

"We, uh, met this girl, you know. Selling magazines. She said we should come by."

"Would you like to order something?" An Initiate hovered at her side. She had no idea what his name was; he was not seeing her. She suppressed the urge to reprimand him, make him introduce himself the way he was supposed to: be bold; take the initiative; make the visitor want to know you; donate yourself.

"Can I have a cup of tea, English-style?" She remembered the early days; evenings like this – talking to strangers in the Coffee Lounge, getting to know them, to enjoy them, make them want her.

"Milk, right?"

"Right." She felt a brief moment of loyalty to Matthew. He was American; she was Welsh; The Programme had – for all its American members – always been English in style. This lad did not know how to make a cup of tea. "What's your name?" she asked.

"I'm Brother Joshua. What's yours?" He remembered himself.

"I'd like a cup of tea," she said as if she hadn't heard his question.

Peter, the leader of the pair of boys, admitted:

"They're like kind of weird."

"Do you think so? Who was the girl you met?"

"She said her name was Mary," Mike, his friend, answered. "Sister Mary."

"What did she tell you about The Programme?"

"Have you read about them?" Peter reasserted himself.

"I've read a couple of their magazines." The lie was white: she had written most of what they would have read. "How about you?"

"Yeah, we bought one from Mary."

"And?" she prompted.

Peter tossed his head across the table at Mike.

"He thinks it's some kind of a front."

"For what? A front for what?"

"Maybe, like, it's a government thing," Mike answered uneasily.

"He thinks everything's the government," Peter grinned.

Peter thought she was interested in him; she had Mike marked out for recruitment. Peter was a mouth, a distraction. Mike was crying out for an answer he could touch.

Brother Joshua brought her tea.

"That'll be a dollar," he said.

"Here," said Mike, "let me pay for that."

She raised her eyebrows.

"It's all right, Mike; I can manage a dollar."

"I want to," he insisted, tossing a bill onto the table.

"Why?" she asked as Joshua wandered away to another booth.

"I like talking to you." He was embarrassed.

A flurry of activity at the kitchen door. Two more members had come out, were standing there, gawping in her direction. She had been seen. She sighed: she had liked the game of talking to these boys. She broke the news, before they came over to spoil it for her.

"Actually, I belong here."

"You're a member?" Peter asked.

"Uh, yes. Actually," she said sipping her tea, "a bit more than that."

She reached around, slipped her hair out of its grip, shook her head to free it. She was Cassandra again, her face framed by the curly black shock of her hair. Mike picked up the magazine they had bought from Mary from the seat beside him, flashed it at his friend.

"Kind of weird?" He reminded him.

"Government front?" Peter was no less embarrassed.

"Down, boys," Cassandra said, laughing. "You might both be right."

"Cassandra?" Sister Helen had been called. She was Chapter Mother by virtue of her new relationship with Paimon. It was her job to greet the hierarchy when it came to visit. "I am one."

"We are many," Cassandra rose, kissed Helen's cheek like a dutiful sister-in-law which, in a sense, she was – twice over. "Bye, boys," she waved apologetically, asking Helen as they walked away. "Is Mary here? They came in to see her."

Helen nodded, understanding that Cassandra was indulging her young companions, rewarding them for whatever ego-kick they had given her.

"I came to see Father Paimon," Cassandra said.

"I'll find him."

"How are you, Helen?" Cassandra asked.

Helen turned to face her, answered boldly:

"I'm never sure what it is you want from me, Seer?"

Cassandra took her hand, squeezed it reassuringly.

"You've always done what was demanded of you."

"As Matthew asked," Helen corrected her.

"I thought that was your question," Cassandra replied.

Then Paimon, in his new role as Chapter Superior, trying to appear dignified, throwing his arms around his sister, hugging her, Helen watching, thinking what they all thought, that he was in love with his sister but less sure what his sister wanted from him.

In his quarters – the quarters he shared with Helen – he asked her why she had come.

"I wanted to see you, talk to you too."

They were lounging on the couch, his arm dangled over her shoulders, she was leaning against him, he fiddled with her hair, twisting it in his fingers.

"Tell me?"

"Caleb bought some guns. Christopher gave him the money."

Paimon grinned, twisted her hair some more until it almost hurt, turned her face towards him.

"You're scared?"

"Scared of nothing." Her eyes flashed.

He moved in on her, kissed her lips. She broke away, laughing.

"All right; scared of nothing else."

"What, then?"

"Matthew has to go; you know that, don't you?"

Paimon nodded: they all knew but she had never admitted it outright before.

"They're not going to kill him," he reassured her. "They just want to have them, not use them."

"I'm not so sure." She described the scene in the fields with the two Jays. Then: "No, you're right; I don't think they're going to kill him."

"What is it you're scared of? That they might, or that they might not?"

"That I might," she said, surprising herself as much as her brother.

"Or that you might not?" Might not have the courage.

"That too. You seem to be taking it calmly. Did you know?" About the guns.

"No; but I can't say I'm surprised. Caleb's something else. At heart, he's a gangster."

"A gay gangster?"

"Caleb's just not too particular how he has sex. He's no more gay than, well," he looked around for a comparison, "Clint Eastwood."

"I thought you were going to say than you were," Cassandra said.

"Me? I'm queer, not gay; queer for you."

"Is it all about sex?"

"Us? You and me? Or the rest of it?"

"Are they different?"

He slipped off the couch, knelt between her legs. She was wearing a skirt. He pushed it up, lowered his head to rest on her thighs, licked lightly, nibbled. Despite herself, she opened her legs. He licked around her crotch, at the edge of her panties. She pulled her panties to one side; he licked the lips of her vagina until they were wet, slid his tongue over her clitoris, with one hand fumbling at his trousers, trying to extract himself without her noticing. She brought her legs up, crossed them behind his back, stroked his hair: she knew what he was doing.

He straightened himself and placed his palm flat on her stomach to hold her in position. She was open to him; he thrust into her before she could change her mind, she grabbed the back of his neck, pulled his face onto hers, kissed him open-mouthed. Then she pushed him away, lifted herself off him, swiftly tore off her panties, took him back inside, it all seemed like a single, fluid movement.

"God, that feels good," she sighed.

"Why did you leave it so long?" Even a few minutes before, she had been refusing him.

"Why did you?"

As they talked, he was ramming her, deeper and deeper, harder and harder, hurting her.

"I've been ready forever."

"Not ready enough; it was always there; you only had to take it."

She wanted him to rape her. She wanted her baby brother to rape her. It was important that he was her brother; more important that he was younger; most important it was rape.

He looped his hands behind her back, swung her off the couch and onto the floor, flipped her so she was on her stomach, forced her cheeks apart, pulled out and rammed into her behind, as wet as the front of her. She managed to twist enough of her body around to bring their mouths together, bit into his lower lip until he bled, sucked the lip into her mouth, sucked the blood, he gasped but did not cry out, grabbed her by the hair, banged her head onto the ground to make her let go, they struggled and fought and he turned her until she was lying on her side, he knelt with her body gripped between his knees, one leg trapped along the floor, the other hanging limp over his thigh, pulling out of one orifice, into the other, she was strong but he was stronger, at the last moment he pulled all the way out, twisted her head down on it, stuffed his prick into her mouth – covered with vaginal juice and her own shit – and came like that, holding her tight until he was sure she had swallowed it.

They stayed in the same position for several minutes, recovering breath. Then he let go of her, pulled himself up onto the couch, collapsed on it, clothes awry, limp penis on display. She rolled away from him, rose to her knees, shook herself like a dog just in from the rain, shuffled to his side. She bent, kissed his penis lightly, placed her thumb against his lip, asked:

"Does it hurt?"

He nodded proudly. She smiled, put one hand around his head, grabbed his hair to pull his face upwards, mashed her forehead against the raw lip, this time he screamed in agony, almost passed out, she tilted him so he fell onto his side on the couch, she pushed his legs up onto the seat to curl into a foetal position, cradled the whole of his body in her arms.

She loved it like nothing she had ever experienced. She had drawn out his power, dared him to use it on her, taunted him as a coward not to have used it before. While it was out there, exposed, diverted to its immediate task, she grabbed it, slapped it in his face, twirled it around her head. They were not Caleb's guns or Christopher's, but hers.

\* \* \*

During the afternoon, once it was not too early to call the States, Carey tried to call Matthew. She did not care what Jessica overheard or thought: this was legitimate business. At Hammer Reach, she was told he had gone to Boston; at Boston, they said he had never shown up, was in New York; at New York, Jemima told her that Matthew had come down yesterday, but had immediately taken off again.

"Jemima, do you know where Emily is?"

"No, I thought she went home with you."

"We split up at JFK; she wanted to travel."

Jemima thought for a moment, then suggested:

267

"Would she have gone back to New Orleans?"

"No, why should she?" Carey hesitated, then admitted: "Maybe. It's possible." Emily had enjoyed Phillipe a lot more than Carey had, at the least he had piqued her curiosity. "Why do you ask?"

Jemima also hesitated: it seemed like no one trusted anyone anymore. Decision made, she confessed:

"I know Matthew had a call from New Orleans – he has a friend there."

"We met him: Phillipe Lamarque."

"I, er, overheard some of the call." Jemima, too, had been mustering information. "It's just an impression, something he said, I didn't think anything of it at the time. I think maybe Emily may have been there."

Carey shut her eyes, struggling for rationality like air: Emily goes to New Orleans; Phillipe rings Matthew; it made sense, though Phillipe's angle was anyone's guess. Either way, if Jemima was right, it put Matthew and Emily together, exactly where she had feared they might be.

"Do you have Phillipe's number, Jemima?"

"No." Jemima had gone as far as she was willing.

"Jemima – if either of them gets in touch, will you ask them to call me?"

"Sure I will, Carey. I am one," she terminated the conversation.

"We are many," Carey replied.

* * *

Colin and Andrew still played squash regularly: they did so the evening after the day Carey returned.

Andrew had no difficulty beating Colin; he was quite off his game. Afterwards, Andrew had to wait around; Jessica was bringing some papers to sign, the settlement with their former firm. Guiltily, Colin stayed on longer than normal. They talked idly about work, the offices, Andrew's latest female indulgence, nothing that hurt.

They were equally taken aback when – uninvited – they were joined by a big American, in a loud check jacket, who sat down at their table and announced himself:

"Gentlemen."

They exchanged a glance, Andrew said:

"Good evening," with a rising question in his voice.

"My name's Berlinger," he said.

The name meant nothing to either of them.

"I think we know one or two people in common."

Colin said frostily:

"I'm sorry. I wonder if you've mistaken us for someone else."

"Colin Arnott; Andrew Chettle?"

They exchanged a glance.

"How can we help you?" Andrew asked.

"I work for Arthur Rockworth."

Colin leaned forward, picked up his full glass of lager, raised it to his lips, sipped thoughtfully, said quietly:

"A lot of people work for Mr Rockworth."

"You only have one interest in common with Mr Rockworth at the moment," Berlinger said dryly: he was not interested in games-manship.

"Should we be talking to you?" Colin asked, aiming the question at Andrew.

"It's a moot point," Andrew said. "We're not in litigation with Mr Rockworth."

"Yet," Berlinger snapped.

"Are you here to threaten us, Mr – uh – Berlinger, or is that the way you talk to people?"

"Fair point, Mr Arnott. My line of work, I guess I do shoot first, ask questions later."

"What line of work would that be, Mr Berlinger?" Andrew asked.

"I help people," Berlinger said softly. "I help people who've gotten into things over their heads – usually, what I mean is, I help people – and their families – who've gotten involved with cults."

"Like Mr Rockworth," Colin supplied.

"Right. Only Mr Rockworth's already lost his son."

"So what's left for you to do for him?"

"You know the rich; they don't take too well to being on the losing side. I can't see Mr Rockworth being happy to leave The Programme in his London house."

"I read something about that. That's why I asked if we should be talking to you. So far as I'm aware, though, he's done nothing about it. Nor," Colin added quickly, "nor is there anything he can do about it."

"That's for the lawyers, not me."

"What do you do, then?"

"I try to get people out of cults," Berlinger said, with a gentleness in his voice that hinted more care about his job than his demeanour let on.

"Like my colleague said, it's too late for Mr Rockworth's son," Andrew pressed him.

"But not for Mr Arnott's sister."

"My sister's home, Mr Berlinger; she returned home yesterday."

"So I understand."

"So?"

"For good, Mr Arnott?"

Andrew shifted uneasily in his seat.

"Colin, I wonder if I should, well, you know?"

"Stay. I'd like you to." He wanted a witness. "What is it you want to say to me, Mr Berlinger?"

Before he could answer, Jessica Harvey arrived.

"Hi?" She hovered nervously over the table.

Andrew rose to greet her.

"Do you want a drink?"

"I'm driving."

Colin resolved his friend's dilemma.

"Sit down, Jessica. Please."

Berlinger half-rose, held out his hand.

"Mr Berlinger was just leaving," Colin introduced him.

"Yes. Perhaps I was." He started to leave, then hesitated, turned back and addressed himself directly to Colin. "It's a sorry feature of my business, Mr Arnott, how often people don't decide they need me until it's too late." He left without awaiting an answer.

They sat in silence for a moment, then all of them spoke at once.

"What was that about?" Jessica asked, shivering as the man's threatening bulk rolled towards to the exit.

"Have you got those papers?" Andrew asked.

"How about another drink?" Colin suggested.

They laughed at their good timing and his *sang-froid*. Colin felt warmed by their company and by Andrew's loyalty. He repeated:

"Jessica, have a drink anyway?"

"All right. G-and-t."

"Andrew?"

"Same again." Lager.

While Colin was at the bar, Andrew and Jessica exchanged a glance, decided it was better not to start a discussion they would not be able to complete, concentrated on the signing she was there for. Jessica was already stuffing the papers back into her briefcase by the time Colin was back.

"Everything all right?" he asked.

"It went pretty well, all considered. Not so much won't, as sadly feel it's in your best interests if we don't," Andrew said, meaning their former partners had paid them less than they had claimed. "We're free, anyway."

"I hope not," Jessica joked. "Extremely expensive, I'd say. Well, cheers." She clinked glasses with the two of them.

They were the inner core of the new partnership in the way that some would say that Arnotts once had been Charles and Alistair; lawyers automatically formed factions – they found strength in numbers, more people to conduct cross-examination, if the worst came to the worst no one was out on his or her own.

"So? Who was he?"

Andrew said nothing; Colin could explain if he wanted to do so.

"He works for Rockworth. He's what I think they call a deprogrammer: someone who gets people out of cults."

Jessica started to say the same as they had said to Berlinger.

"Bit late, isn't he?" Then she saw – as Andrew had quickly seen – an alternative object of his attentions.

"I told him to piss off. She's not in that sort of trouble."

"Right." Jessica told him what he wanted to hear.

Andrew was embarrassed talking about Carey behind her back, as if she was not quite all there, somehow damaged goods. He said:

"I'm late; I have to be going."

"I should be going too," Jessica said.

"Keep me company while I finish my drink," Colin pleaded.

"Behave yourselves," Andrew said as he left, unable to conceal his amusement.

"What do you really think, Colin?" Jessica asked.

"About Carey?"

"Yes."

"How much time have you spent with her?"

"Not much. We didn't get off to a great start, I'm afraid. Is that why you put me in with her?"

"What do you mean?"

"For me to keep an eye on her – or was it the other way around?"

"I suppose it was an indulgence: two of my favourite people."

"That's nice," she said, conveying more doubt than gratitude.

He blushed: he had not planned to say it.

"I just meant, I thought we'd get along."

She looked down at her hands, studied her fingernails, glanced up to find him watching her.

"I hope we'll be friends." Just friends.

"I didn't mean anything else. Jan and I, we're happily married. It can be difficult, when you're married, to be friends with other women without people getting the wrong idea. It was all right with Carey – she's my sister."

"You don't have to explain. Part of why we wanted to move was to be somewhere there were other people to relate to, not just slices of time for hire. Andrew needs friends: he's only got clients and current lovers."

"And you?"

"Me? I just have clients," she said. "The rest is more trouble than it's worth," she added with ill-concealed bitterness.

He did not say anything for a moment, then commented lightly:

"Probably, you need to know it's what you want beforehand."

Jessica smiled, brushing him off without rancour.

"Andrew said to watch out for your personal insights. He says it's how you relate to people without having to get involved with them."

"He didn't warn me about yours," Colin laughed. "But it sounds like he should have."

They had finished their drinks. Neither wanted to leave. She offered:

"Do you want another drink?"

"I'm driving too. How about a tonic water?"

After she returned, he changed the subject before it got any hotter.

"What did you make of her?" Carey.

"As I said, we got off on the wrong foot. I knew she didn't want me there from the moment I walked in; I didn't handle it very well. Is she having an affair with Patrick?"

"On-off. Mostly off, I'd say. Why?"

"Oh, just curious; checking my instincts are in working order."

"I thought you only had time for clients?"

"I watch soaps on TV like everyone else."

"Yes, that's what I'm afraid of."

"What?"

"That Carey's becoming a bit of a soap opera. Actually, it's not a bad idea. You could do a cult like a cop show or a medical series."

"Why don't I think it would sell? People don't like what frightens them," she answered her own question.

"And it does, doesn't it?" He was talking about himself.

"Sure. Is that what you think?"

"What?"

"That's she's become a signed-up member of The Programme?"

"I think… I think I'm trying to find out what you think."

"I don't know her well enough to judge; hell, I don't know her at all. I just think…" She stopped, shook her head.

"Go on."

"No. It's not my business."

"Please." It was his.

"You won't like it," she warned him.

"Try me."

"All right, then," she said defiantly. "She struck me as immature, almost childish, spoiled too. She's had everything she thought she wanted and it still wasn't enough, so she just shrugs it off and goes off looking for something else without a damn for her responsibilities."

"Professional?"

"No. I'm sure she's a competent lawyer. More than competent, actually. I meant for other people – her father, you – perhaps some of the others," in the firm. "For what you think and what you feel about it. There's a whole myth," she added fiercely, almost passionately. "It's a generational thing; this idea that we have to find ourselves, be our real selves, at any price; it's incredibly selfish because it acts as if the only views that matter are our own; but we're also the reflection of ourselves in other people's eyes – and we should be, and we should give others the credit they are due for the part they play in who we are."

Colin was pained by the diatribe, both because Jessica was so obviously right about Carey and because it was obviously the product of some painful experience of her own. When she looked up at the end of it, she had tears in her eyes.

"What made you so hard?" he asked. "Or should I ask who?"

She shook her head: she did not want his pity.

"You shouldn't ask anything; it's not your concern. She is."

"Perhaps I should have asked Berlinger to talk with her."

"Perhaps you should talk with her yourself," she said firmly.

At the door to the club, their cars parked in opposite directions, he went to kiss her good-night. She turned away quickly so that his lips met only her cheek. He watched her until she was in her car, pulling away. She did not look back. He walked to his own car: time to go home.

\* \* \*

In the evening, Carey went to Chesterfield Gardens.

She needed to see Father Simon or perhaps Mother Naamah, find out what they knew. Aside from disappointment, she had thought nothing of it when she had been unable to reach them the previous evening, but since she had talked to George Cohen she had begun to wonder whose side they were on.

She had to wait to see them. She did not want to go into the Coffee Lounge: her mood was anything but that of The Teacher's triumphant consort paying a royal visit. She sat instead with Sister Lilith at the reception desk, smoking impatiently. Almost immediately, Lilith asked:

"What's going on, Carey?"

"What do you mean?" Role reversal: she had once sat here taking guidance from Lilith.

"I don't know," Lilith admitted. "Anthony – we were all pretty shook up. We hear things – bits and pieces. We get Cassandra's Lessons on the Internet: everything seems different. Some people are even saying The Teacher's not in control anymore."

"Phooey," Carey dismissed. "He's travelling. That's all."

"And stuff about Masses – exclusive Masses for a chosen few? What's that about?"

"I don't know anything about that," Carey insisted: she had heard nothing about any special Masses. "Tell me what you've been doing here?"

"Worrying," Lilith said. "We read that Rockworth is going to evict us from here."

"He was just upset. It's understandable. He'll come around," Carey reassured her. That, at least, she could believe in, as an article of law. "How's membership?" The perennial search for new members.

"One or two new faces; one or two old ones gone. You know about Brother George?"

"I've spoken to him. I know."

Lilith mentioned a couple of other long-standing members who had left. Then she laughed.

"All the publicity's good for the Coffee Lounge. We're run off our feet."

The phone rang. She picked it up, spoke quietly into it, replied:

"We are many," and hung up.

"Father Simon and Mother Naamah are in The Temple, waiting for you," she said.

"Okay." It was a strange place to meet.

She had never been into The Temple before. It was for resident members, where private Masses and other services were held. She was still a non-resident.

Simon was cross-legged on a grand cushion, wearing formal white. Gaunt, ghostlike Naamah was against the wall where The Programme symbol was painted. Simon gestured Carey to sit before him, on the floor. She did so, settling herself with her feet tucked beneath her.

"I am one," he said sombrely.

"We are many," she replied.

"Together we shall be whole," the three of them said.

Simon was Matthew's friend; Simon had sung for them the night she had joined; she had sat with Simon and Matthew in the Coffee Lounge – aware of the sideways glances of awed members – while they made arrangements for their visit to America, leaving Simon in charge in England. She addressed herself to Simon.

"How are you, Father?"

"I'm well, Sister Carey." All junior members were Brothers and Sisters, even non-residents. "How is The Teacher?"

"He's fine. Have you heard from him?"

"Where did you leave him?"

"In New York."

"And now?"

"I heard he might be in New Orleans." It was not what she had come to talk about. "I spoke to Brother George," she probed.

"He is a loss," Simon admitted, watching her closely.

She shuddered: he did not trust her; but then, she did not trust him. She had already decided she would not tell him about the money unless he knew and raised it with her. It was Matthew's business, not hers to disclose.

He caught the mood, nodded.

"It's a difficult time, is it not, Sister Carey? When members cannot talk openly with one another."

"Can I talk openly with you, Father?"

"Only you can decide that, Carey."

"What is going on, Father? Who should I trust?"

"Trust The Teacher. I do."

"I'm frightened: I can't help feeling he's not as much in control of things as he needs to be. Does that make sense? Can I say that?"

"The Teacher sometimes understands things that we cannot. When he decided on the move to America, he knew there would be changes; I think he believed it would be impossible for us to move forward unless it had its own room to breathe; he had to let it do so for itself."

"I know that; I understood that."

"You're still worried. You're thinking perhaps he has let something happen that he can't control? That perhaps it will take over – take over The Programme – and perhaps that it will take him over too?"

Carey nodded: it was exactly what she meant.

"That's why I say that he understands things that we don't. What looks impossible to us may be exactly what he has planned."

She interrupted him.

"But you're worried too?"

"I have known The Teacher for many years; he is The Programme. I think what he would say we should do now is to meditate together, find the inner strength we appear to need to renew our belief in him and our commitment to his way. What do you think, Sister Carey? Shall we meditate together?"

His voice had already begun to drift, he was asking for her confidence to go along with him. Carey glanced at Naamah: neither her posture nor her features had changed: she had simply slipped away.

"Let us close our eyes now; breathe in, deeply now, breathe out again; breathe in deeply, hold it for a moment, think of The Teacher, hold his face in your mind, let him watch you, watch me, watch over us, feel how warm it is, how comfortable, how safe. I am one; we are many; together we shall be whole."

Afterwards, he helped her to her feet.

"Do we need to talk about legal matters?"

"Can I give you a call in the next day or two? Perhaps we can meet to talk."

He nodded sagely, sombre with his responsibilities. She exchanged a glance and a mumbled "I am one-we are many" with Naamah. He guided her to the door, watched her as she walked down the stairs.

He had not asked about Emily. She found it disconcerting that he seemed so uninterested.

"Carey," he called after her.

Carey turned expectantly.

"I am one, Sister," he said.

"We are many," she replied, disappointed on Emily's behalf.

"Together we shall be whole."

They smiled despite themselves as, at the reception desk, they could hear Lilith sing along with them.

\* \* \*

Alone at home, drinking again, Carey made another attempt to reach him – or them. She did not have the number of the hotel in New Orleans nor could remember the name of it; Phillipe Lamarque's phone line was not in his own name. In the end, desperate to connect with and to trust someone, she dialled the Boston Chapter, asked for Sister Helen.

"This is Carey," she said.

"I am one," Helen replied.

"We are many."

"Is everything all right?" Helen asked, picking up the uncertainty in Carey's voice.

"Yes, oh, yes of course. I'm sorry." Helen would think she was still on the road with Matthew. "I'm back in London."

"I see," Helen sounded cautious.

"I think Matthew's in New Orleans and I don't really know how to get hold of him."

"I see," Helen repeated, absorbing the information slowly. "I don't know where he is, Carey. I can try and find out if you like."

"Do you know Phillipe Lamarque?"

"I've heard of him. I don't know him."

"We saw him in New Orleans." Carey knew it was hopeless. She was certain Matthew would have moved on. With Emily.

"Are you all right, Carey?"

She could not tell her that she was a little bit tipsy, a lot lonely, insecure. Doubtfully, she asked:

"Helen, do you know anything about the bank accounts?"

"No, what?" Helen was immediately anxious.

"Oh, it's nothing," Carey regretted asking. "I was talking to George Cohen. He said all the money's been moved to Boston."

"Does Matthew know about it?"

"I'm sure he does," Carey said.

Neither of them believed for a moment that Matthew knew. Helen said slowly:

"I can try, see what I can find out."

They were Matthew's lovers; they were loyalists. Both of them were close enough to the centre to be aware of the schism at the top. Neither of them knew how deeply it was destined to be pursued; both of them feared the worst.

"Perhaps, you know, I shouldn't have said anything. I mean, you should be careful."

"I'm sure there's nothing to worry about. Where can I reach you? Give me your number."

Carey gave her both home and work numbers. She repeated:

"You should be careful, Helen."

"I am one, Carey," Helen replied.

She meant: just one, one who does not matter.

\* \* \*

"Who were you talking to?" Paimon demanded, entering the room as Helen hung up.

"Carey Arnott. In London."

"What did she want?"

"She was trying to find The Teacher." She referred to Matthew as The Teacher when she talked with Paimon; it did not provoke him in the way that reminding him she had been his lover did. He was volatile, frequently violent: since Cassandra had visited him, more so than ever. When he was with her, he was sour, Welsh-broody, on the edge of assault. She stayed as far out of his way as she could, concentrated on running the Chapter: Tamar and Thomas were arriving the next day with Hannah, there were accommodation arrangements to be made for them; there were always small problems; new members needed reassurance – it was enough for her to do.

For Paimon, Cassandra's visit had been the explosion of a time-bomb. He was no longer interested in Helen: it could not be long before she worked out why.

He asked, only half-interested:

"Why?"

"Why what?"

"Why is she looking for Matthew? Has he ditched her too?"

Helen flushed.

"I am one, Paimon."

"Yes, yes. Well?"

"I don't know. She just wanted to know where he was."

"She must have said why."

Helen fidgeted.

"No. Honestly, Paimon."

It was the worst thing to say. He sensed she was holding back. He went around the desk where she was seated, draped an arm around her shoulder, brought his hand up under her chin, gripped it hard.

"I said, why did she want to find him?"

"I don't know," Helen persisted, frightened.

He pulled her head back into his stomach, caressed her face with his free hand, squeezed the bridge of her nose until his thumb and forefinger were almost in her eyes. She squealed:

"Let me go, Paimon, please."

He released her nose but not her chin, squeezed instead at the sides of her mouth until she opened it, rammed his knuckles into the hole, against her teeth, stopping her biting down on them, stronger than her, he pushed harder and harder until she fell backwards off the chair, he stepped out of the way so she fell heavily to the ground, before she could scramble away he was straddling her, holding her shoulders down with his knees.

"Tell me, Helen. I command you; I am your Superior, I am your lover, you have no choice."

Helen stared up at him wide-eyed: what had they become?

* * *

Paimon called Cassandra at Hammer Reach, told her what Helen had been forced to tell him, that Carey was making enquiries about the bank account, was looking to tell Matthew.

Like Paimon, Cassandra recognised that Helen was a problem: they had to decide what to do with her. She had proven a pliant and flexible partner to be handed around the upper echelon, apparently grateful for a role since she had been abandoned by Matthew, but that was the limit of her utility; she had authority amongst the members who had come over from England that derived from her time with Matthew; she was Matthew's eyes, she could communicate with him faster than the Internet.

She told him to come to Hammer Reach.

"Bring her."

"Helen?"

"Yes."

"Now?"

"No, wait until tomorrow. Bring the children too."

"Hannah?"

"Let Hannah take over from Helen in Boston. For now." Until they had fathomed how she would react to the changed order and its new rituals.

After the call, she went downstairs. There was still plenty of activity about the house; it was not yet fully dark outside. She could see Father Nahum and his work crew working a last frantic hour on The Temple. It was a complicated building. He had told no one what he was trying to do, but she had guessed. He was building it in the shape of The Programme symbol. One segment was beginning to rise from its foundations; two more segment foundations were complete; he would not be able to keep it a secret much longer. She doubted he would ever see it complete; he lacked the imagination not to conceive of the project but to finish it.

* * *

Carey was awoken by the phone.

She had fallen into a half-drunk sleep in her chair at her desk. It was dark outside, dark and the streets were empty. She fumbled for the receiver, pushed it at her ear. Her mouth was parched, raw.

"Yes."

"It's me." Emily.

Carey pulled a pack of cigarettes across the desk, shook one out, lit it before she answered her, unable to keep the concern out of her voice:

"Where are you?"

"I'm in Florida," Emily answered. "We are," she corrected. "Somewhere called Jacksonville."

"Why? What's in Florida?"

"I was in New Orleans; Matthew came down." The call from Phillipe that Jemima had overheard. "We're at a motel on the beach outside of town."

"How are you, Em?" Carey asked.

"I'm okay," her friend answered uncertainly. "It's strange. I came here to be with you. Then you went home."

They were silent for a while before Emily offered:

"I miss you."

"You could have come home with me."

"He misses you too."

"Does he?"

"I'm not you, Carey. I'm here, so he's with me, but he's not if you know what I mean."

"I do know – I often feel like that with him."

"It's different. I've seen you together."

"But you're with him," Carey accused.

Emily did not answer.

"Why did you ring?"

"I told you; I miss you. What are you going to do, Carey?"

"I don't know. I've only been back a couple of days."

"It feels like a month since you've been gone."

"What are you going to do?"

"I'm not sure. I suppose I'll go back to New York." Not stay with Matthew in Florida.

"Do what you want; do what you need." Don't do it for me.

"I thought we were going to be together, you and me," Emily said. "I'm frightened; I don't know why; sometimes, I'm even frightened of Matthew. It's like – he's got all the energy of The Programme, but he's separated from all the people to use it."

"Do you want me to come back?"

"No, no; don't." She did not want Carey to walk into the same unknown that frightened her.

"Then come home, come home now," Carey said urgently. If Emily came home, if they were both at home, it would tell her what she ought to do.

Emily sounded listless, almost stoned.

"Perhaps."

"Em, is Matthew there now?"

"No. He's out. Why? Do you want to talk with him?"

"I need to. Something's come up. Can you get him to ring me when he comes back?"

"Sure." A brief silence, background noise. "Hang on, I think that's him now. Wait; I'll go and see."

"Em," Carey called after her: she had not replied to Emily's remark about being together; she wanted to tell her again – come home, come home now.

"Carey?"

She shivered; he could do that to her – with just her name.

"Hi," she said, as she had greeted Emily earlier.

"How are you, Carey?"

"Matthew, I need to talk to you."

"I'm here," he said calmly.

"No," not about us. "About The Programme. Matthew, who's in charge of the money?"

"What money? Programme money?"

"Yes."

"What do you mean? There's no corporation; I thought you knew that. It belongs to me."

"Yes, but who actually has control of the bank accounts?"

"George Cohen," he answered promptly. "He handles it all. Why? Is there a problem?"

\* \* \*

From *The Seer's Lesson on Growth and on Change*:

*With every passing year, there are more hostile forces in the outside world who want to prevent our success. People who have been offended by what we are, people who are jealous, people who fear us – even some former members. At their point of departure from our way, from The Programme itself, their hostility becomes fixed. Because they cease to grow in themselves – because they abandon their hope of change within or around The Programme – they cease to change. All they can cling onto is that one, final point of contact or connection – unchanged, stagnating. With the years, these forces accumulate, more and more of them aiming their disappointment at us with the same glower of fear.*

*When we came to America, change was the objective. Change was recognition of the real, live unification of God and Satan, acting in harmony, in place of the embryonic period in England when we cultivated and nurtured them, fashioned them and committed ourselves to their arrival, burst full-grown from the womb, all-powerful, all-seeing, demanding every ounce of our being, every moment of our attention, every inch of our reach.*

*Since we came here, we have struggled to meet this demand. We have engaged in new activities, new practices, new approaches. With some wonderment, we saw that we were prepared to respond to the demand. With joy, we saw that the demand was for more – like a hungry beast – more growth, more change, growth and change without limit until – like a dervish – we twist and twirl and dance into the fire beyond. This is a whole new phase. New time, new game, new Programme.*

*The Teacher brought us here! The Teacher found the path and led us to it! The Teacher taught us how to find God and Satan within ourselves, and bring them to life! The Teacher was our guardian while we awaited their arrival! Let us never forget what he did for us, indeed for them! It is time to allow The Teacher his freedom again to travel, to travel again beyond and ahead of us, to find the path, the final path, the path to the fire beyond!*

# Chapter Twelve

Father Caleb and his followers formed a team of inquisitors, descending on the Chapters and even Hammer Reach itself with a mission to root out betrayal, corruption, the timid and the meek on whom they could not rely and those who needed a bolster to their resolve. The punishment cells were always full. Punishment was not severe; it was the idea of discipline and control that they wanted to instil. When sinners came out to worship in the basement meditation area where the Special Masses had taken place, they affected a sombre air, but during the days they called out, joked, understood that they were fulfilling a role for the purpose of The Programme: without some who are bad, none can be good.

Cassandra went down into the basement. She frowned: they were chattering, laughing. She said nothing, listened – eavesdropped.

Martha – Mary's Biblical sister – called out:

"Korah?"

"Yup."

"What are you in for?"

"What are you in for, Martha?"

"Enjoying myself too much with a customer in the Coffee Lounge."

"So?"

"I don't think Father Caleb likes people to enjoy themselves."

Standing on the stairs, Cassandra smiled thinly: she had that right.

"What were you doing?" Korah persisted.

She scowled: she knew what Korah was in for; asking too damn many questions. Calvin Wood, his name was, from New York. Carey had been his first contact: small wonder he was problematic.

A long silence, then – sheepishly – Martha admitted:

"I was just holding his hand."

From the other side of the basement, Nadab, the eldest son of Aaron, snorted disbelief loud enough to be heard, dark enough to be seen.

"What?" Martha whined. "It's true," she protested.

"It's not holding his hand that matters, but failure to control your counter-purpose."

"What's the difference?" Martha sulked.

"It's about what you do to yourself, not what you do to others," the fourth voice said: Brother Paul. The other three were only Initiates;

he was already a Junior Messenger.

"Phooey, Martha; hold hands with who you want," Korah said.

Cassandra saw red. He had crossed the line between jocularity and dissidence. She bit her lower lip, knew she should fetch an assistant, wanted this for herself.

She unbolted the door of Korah's cell.

"Come out," she hissed.

He was shocked, perhaps scared. He was crouched down in a grubby white shift, barefoot, he looked like he could use a thorough scrubbing.

He looked down at the ground. She repeated, snarling:

"Come out."

He shuffled from the cell, still hunched over, still looking down. When he emerged, she pointed to the other cell doors, clicking her fingers to tell him to open them. She stood in the middle of the hall, using her finger to beckon them out of their cells one by one, pointing the three of them – likewise in white shifts – to one end, holding a hand up to keep Korah with her.

Ignoring him, she addressed the tiny congregation.

"Why are you here? It is not because you have failed. We do not know failure in The Programme. It is not because of your errors; there are no errors, just choices. You are here because of what you can learn from each other; you are here to shine a light of understanding on one another's choices, to see them from each other's point of view. You," she pointed at Martha. "Brothers Paul and Nadab were trying to help you. But him," she swung on Korah, "all he was doing was mocking you. What good did it do you, Sister Martha, what did you learn from Brother Korah?"

Quaking, Martha shook her head.

"Then you, Brother Korah: what were you trying to teach her?"

He, too, shook his head in silence.

"All of you came into The Programme needing to find yourselves; the first thing you needed to do was to understand yourselves. When Father Caleb ordered you to stay down here, it was because you needed this time to learn more about yourselves."

She paused, breathed deeply, seemed not to let it out, instead she disappeared into herself with her own breath, spoke from somewhere else.

"We believe in the unification of God and Satan; we believe in each of them evenly, and in the many other angels that stand beside them – Lucifer, Beelzebub, Jehovah, the archangel Joel, Zadkiel – the angel of benevolence and of mercy, Sabaoth – one of the seven creators of the universe. I could tell you of powers beyond even these who reach out one to the other, until their hands perfect the circle which protects and contains us. These powers are also within us, within all of us: we have to be taught how to reach down inside of ourselves for them, as if reaching for the bed of the ocean, only there is no bed, no end, we go on and on and we go through, not until we see that there is no bed and decide yet to go on do we begin the journey, not until we become one can be become whole, only then do we earn the right to the fire beyond."

She was hovering like an angel herself. One by one, they dropped to their knees, bowed their heads in shame, even Korah. She reached out a hand to rest it on the top of his head, like a blessing.

"Sister Martha, what did Jesus tell you?"

"'I am the resurrection and the life; he that believeth in me, though he were dead, yet shall he live'."

"'I am the resurrection and the life,'" Cassandra repeated slowly. "This is what Jesus did. He went to the edge – to the bottom of the ocean – and he found there was no end to it all; he did not turn around and come back, but continued through – beyond the fire – and yet he survived. The Teacher wrote this: 'Only when we go beyond the fire and survive do we learn that life and death are stages in a journey without beginning and without end, than which there is nothing more. What is the fire beyond? I will tell you. It is the fire which lights the way beyond the limits we are brought up to believe we are confined by: life ends in death; good ends at the beginning of evil; love and hate are different. When we see the fire beyond, we see across a line we had believed marked the end; the fire beyond calls us across that line, it devours that line, it tells us it is not an end but a beginning'."

She felt no ambivalence quoting The Teacher; nothing they were doing denied or even doubted the vision and wisdom with which he had led The Programme to this point of her departure.

"What you are learning is to take the first steps; if you think you are beyond learning, then walk out of here – go on, if you have nothing more to learn then we have nothing more to teach you. You – Sister Martha? Are you ready to leave? You – Brother Paul, most senior of you four – have you risen already to the point that you can step across to the fire beyond? Brother Nadab – do I need to ask you?" She swung on Korah.

"Brother Korah, then, son of Esau, who led the people against Moses and Aaron, is that what you are here to do, to rebel, to lead them against The Programme, to lead them against me?"

285

"I am one, Seer," he answered, head still lowered.

"Yes," she said, meaning "just one". "Come here, Sister Martha," she beckoned to the girl.

Martha rose and approached her timidly, but no longer in fear.

Cassandra whispered in her ear. The girl unknotted the silver chain belt around Cassandra's waist, ran her fingers along it, held it across both outstretched hands like an offering.

Next, Cassandra beckoned forward Paul and Nadab.

"Hold his arms."

Korah was still kneeling. He did not resist, but held his arms out so that each could take one of them. He looked up and met Cassandra's gaze evenly, calmly.

"I am one," he repeated.

She giggled and – leading Martha by the elbow – walked around behind him. She let go of Martha to grip the neck of Korah's shift tightly in both hands. With her thumbs, she felt for the seam, stared up at the ceiling hook from which Paimon hung his gong, focused her strength in her hands and tore the shift apart. She stroked Korah's smooth, bare back for a moment, then stepped away to leave Martha enough room.

"Just the once," Cassandra said, nodding at her to do it.

Martha let the chain fall from her left hand, so that she was grasping it with her right. The Programme symbol was attached at the bottom of the loop. She twirled the chain to get the weight of it. Then again to pick up speed. With a howl that was instantly drowned out by Korah's scream of pain, she ripped the symbol into and the whole way down into his back.

Cassandra waited for the sound to die away. She said:

"You are free, all of you. Take Brother Korah upstairs; bathe his wound; take him to the dormitory; stay with him."

She held out a hand to help Korah to his feet, as he stood before her she leaned in and kissed him on the forehead.

"I am one," she whispered.

"We are many," he mumbled back, the pain already beginning to subside but the humiliation rising like bile in his throat.

"Together we shall be whole," the others added.

Alone, exultant, Cassandra wandered from empty cell to cell: she could make them do anything she wanted; she could take freedom and she could give it; she could take life – which meant she could give it too; the cells would not stay empty for long.

* * *

Matthew went to the sea. It was the middle of the night, but there was still plenty of light: from the moon, from the city, from the motel behind. He lowered himself into a half-lotus position, on the narrow beach, back straight, hands folded into one another, breathing lightly, unafraid of attackers or muggers, cocooned in a space they would be unable to invade.

Carey's purpose was pivotal. It was about the time that he had gone to Arnotts that he had announced the move to the States; it was at the time that he was getting to know Carey that he had told Helen to go with Cassandra to America; he had been distracted by Carey's interest and admission into The Programme from the direction in which Cassandra was dragging The Programme in the States; even when they were at Hammer Reach, he had spent as much time with Carey as he had with Cassandra's people; at the time he now knew that Anthony was being prepared for his death, he had been in Asheville and New Orleans, with Carey again; it was even in Carey's name that he had gone back to New Orleans for Emily after Phillipe had called him to collect his stray, warning him she was too vulnerable – and too valuable – to leave around for others to prey on.

The Programme was his life. He had wanted Carey; he still did, achingly so. He wanted her in The Programme; he wanted her and The Programme. She reminded him of some of the earliest members: morally or spiritually discontented but not yet given up on finding a way to achieve satisfaction; no loser, not at all – a success in her career, but unfulfilled spirits looking for that elusive something to give it all meaning; he could work with that discontentment, create something of it – like an artist. She was his final painting; he needed her to have another chance at a success of his own.

He was more worried about Helen. He too had rung Boston, New York, even Hammer Reach, and been unable to reach her. Everyone said she was somewhere else. In desperation, he had rung her parents in British Columbia, asking if they knew where she was, ending up reassuring them there was nothing to worry about: a country vet and his wife, members of a fundamentalist Christian sect of Scottish origin, they did not approve of their daughter's departure for The Programme, but they understood it and accepted her absolute faith in Matthew.

He had rung back Boston, insisted on speaking to Paimon, from whom he learned nothing – that she must be between Chapters was the best confection Paimon could be bothered to whip up for him. From early on, he had recognised the unnatural attachment between Cassandra and Huw: he would have been blind not to. He found

Huw physically unattractive, like a toad. The thought of Paimon with Helen made him cringe.

If Cassandra and Paimon were in immediate control, together with Caleb and Christopher, Matthew was confronting evil finally come alive and in action. He had no direct knowledge of any specifically black ritual or act of pagan worship, but he knew Caleb's affiliations and Cassandra had told him of the healing meditation they had conducted for Anthony that had culminated in his death. Things were coming to a head, had been since Anthony's death: Carey's call was confirmation. This was the end game.

He had created the monster; he had to take care of it. If it had happened, then he had to accept responsibility for it: if it had been The Programme's purpose, it must have been his own. It scared him. It was the first time in years he had felt fear, real fear – not since Vietnam. Perhaps not even then; not since he was a child. For a brief moment, he wanted to be Matthew again – not The Teacher but Matthew Crane, an old friend though one whose face he could barely recall.

He heard a noise on the beach, footsteps, turned around, tears still in his eyes.

"How long are you going to sit out here, Matthew?" Emily asked.

The ocean was his meditation-master, that was why Jacksonville.

"Shall I join you?"

She hunched down beside him, studying his face, puzzled.

"You don't know what you're going to do yet, do you?"

"No," he sighed.

His voice betrayed him. Shocked, she stood up.

"You're feeling sorry for yourself," she pronounced. "Why?"

"I never said there wasn't room for a little sadness along the way."

"Sadness is one thing," she replied firmly. "Regret's another. Isn't the past the bottle of rancid water you're always telling us to pour away?"

"I've surrounded myself by too many wise women for my own good," he said wryly.

"I'm not one of them," meaning that she was not one of his women. "What was last night?"

"Something else. Me and Carey. I was her last night."

"Did I make you feel that?"

"No. I did. It's between her and me."

"Are you lovers?"

"Yes." She faced away from him, looked out to the ocean, as if Carey might be watching, listening.

"I didn't think you were. Was that in Antibes?"

"No, it was last night."

"Ah," he understood. "What are you going to do now?"

"I told Carey I was going back to New York. You said you wanted to stay a few days. I'm not so sure now."

"Don't worry about me. I'm fine. You've helped. It's not the past I'm feeling sorry about, it's the future."

She kneeled down again, leaned in to kiss him chastely on the lips.

"I'm going to Boston. Come with me."

"Why?"

"Why not?"

"Are you scared, Matthew?"

What Phillipe had said was:

"If you're facing evil, Matthew, evil is what you'll have to do to defeat it. Remember that, Matthew – Teacher."

* * *

Paimon brought Helen to Hammer Reach with the children. Tamar and Thomas were excited: it was their first visit to the States. They might be children of The Programme, but they were children. America had been brought into their lives through television so early and so much that it felt more like coming home than visiting a foreign country. Almost immediately, they were despatched to New York with Nahum to see their father.

Where Cassandra was going was into an experience that would bind the new hierarchy to an extent that not even Anthony's induced suicide had achieved, the Special Mass that would expunge Matthew from The Programme. Apart from Paimon, only Christopher and Caleb would be tested and proven; the others would come after.

She asked Paimon:

"Do you trust me?"

"Of course; in every way."

"Is there anything you will not do for me?"

He shook his head, took her shoulders.

"You are my life; you always have been; I've been waiting for now."

She let him kiss her, explored his mouth with her tongue: this was Paimon, not Huw; it was no more incest than sleeping with any other member she might call Father or Brother, Sister or Mother. She could feel him hard against her, his hand on her back pressing her against him; he wanted her to feel him. She reached a hand down between them, stroking him through his trousers the way Diana had stroked him the night of the first Special Mass. She had a sudden flash of their parents watching, frowning, wishing they would understand and approve.

Paimon laughed, seized her face in both his hands, kissed her again hungrily.

"What are you up to, Cass?" He asked.

She unzipped him, lowered herself against him, the silk of her blouse, pressed hard against him, pulled at him and burned as she slid down his body. She bathed him in her mouth; he came immediately, repeatedly, she swallowed it hungrily, like an elixir, until it was all gone and he was small again and clean.

He sat down on the bed; she sat beside him, arm around his shoulders; they fell back, twisted their bodies and curled up together, asexually, like children, brother and sister, her cheek resting on his. She whispered:

"I have to know, Paimon."

"What? What is it you want to know?"

"I have to know how far we can go."

His face twitched beneath hers in a smile.

"We've gone pretty far, sister."

"Phooey," she said. "This is nothing; this has always been there; we've had all our lives to get ready for it."

"What, then?"

"Give me Helen."

"That's nothing either."

"Are you sure, Paimon?"

"You're still not sure of me, are you? Even me."

"You more than anyone," she murmured. "I'm only really sure of myself."

\* \* \*

From *Programme and Progression*:

*The good martial arts teacher will tell you that your feet are for running away with; not because you are frightened, but because you are not. People fight because they are not in control of their feelings: rage, self-esteem, fear. When you know that you can fight, you no longer need to do so, not unless someone else forces it on you – not merely challenges, but chases after you demanding that you do so. It is his decision, not yours; you are not fighting in anger – he is. It hardly needs saying that the person who is the better equipped to win that fight is the person who has both the ability and this level of control.*

*So also is it with other kinds of ability, self-knowledge. The fact that we know how to go beyond our limits, that we have found the way to transcend the constraints that have left us unfulfilled, is something we have achieved for ourselves, not for anyone else to explore or to exploit. We are doing it for us, and we must decide what we want to do with it and when. Otherwise, we will have made of ourselves a machine which goes beyond the confines of everyday behaviour, but which someone else can control. If you have looked into the darkest recesses of your mind, seen the demons within, learned to live with them, only you can know how they are to be exercised, they are not there for others to take out and walk around the park, frightening the holiday-makers.*

*How does this relate to the mutual exploration, support, sharing roles, that is the experience of The Programme and that gives The Programme its form, its purpose, its wholeness? The answer is the most difficult lesson – and stage – of The Programme: the temptation to bring it all to the surface, to let it explode – like children unable to wait for Christmas Eve before opening their presents – is considerable and ever-present; resisting it is the most important task of The Programme hierarchy – it is why we have Superiors and Senior Messengers to make sure that every day activity does not accidentally boil over and put out the fire before the meal has been cooked, let alone burn the cook; what we are looking for is the fire beyond to consume us – which is very different from the sort of fire by which we may be burned.*

*The fire beyond is the moment when the collected energies of The Programme – the emergence of the inner voices and impulses we have struggled so long and so hard to identify, listen to, bring into being – our inner gods – have become whole, whole enough that we may step from one side of our beings to the other. This is what is meant by the fire beyond: the fire beyond our beings, which we can step into without harm, because it is not our bodies which we are bringing to it – that is what we have stepped through – but our whole beings – our whole being as The Programme – that mere fire cannot touch.*

*Go back to basics. What we are about is the re-creation of the sense of wholeness from which we emerged; when we have done so is when we have stepped from one side of the mirror in which we look to see how complete is the picture, over to the other: perfect match – not opposite mirror-images but exactness; the mirror does not dissolve, it simply ends its useful life in the final act of completion. So also the fire beyond.*

\* \* \*

Cassandra took Helen down to the basement. Helen had no warning and therefore no fear. She noticed the gong hanging from the hook in the centre of the hall and the lamps for candles between the cell doors, the bale-throne covered with the woven Programme-symbol. She had not been down here before. She had never been put into punishment. It still did not quite occur to her that this was what was to happen as Cassandra pushed her head down and shoved her into a cell, came in after her, kicked the door shut behind her, commanded:

"Take off your clothes, Sister Helen."

"What?" It was still not punishment that came to mind, but the wild sexuality of The Seer. She thought perhaps this was revenge for having loved Matthew, that she was to be made to be with Cassandra instead.

"I said to take off your clothes, Sister Helen. Don't worry; I'm not going to hurt you." Seeing the look in Helen's eyes, she added: "I'm not going to touch you."

"But, why?" Helen protested in gentle Canadian tones, already beginning to do what she had been told. Her instructions were from The Seer herself; the last several years had instilled in her the habit of obeying.

"Put on the shift, Sister Helen," Cassandra pointed at a white shift rolled up and lying in a corner of the cell. "Would you like me to turn around?" She mocked her.

Helen did not answer. She licked her dry lips, swiftly finished undressing and pulled the shift over her head bruising her knuckles against the ceiling as she did so, forcing her to kneel on the ground to finish the job. Cassandra watched her, enjoying her figure, the perfect skin, the moment when her arms were raised above her head and her breasts stretched almost flat. She said:

"Sister Helen, this is necessary. Your relationship with Paimon is at an end. You know that, don't you?"

Helen nodded, with relief at least as much as confusion.

"I have decided. You have spent too long around the hierarchy: first you were with The Teacher, then Christopher, then Paimon. You have been with us, but you have not been one of us. Do you agree?"

Helen lowered her head, nodded again to signify understanding and agreement. This was her punishment for having enjoyed a superior position which she had not earned; she was to be punished to be cleansed to return to the lower orders and take her place in service. If Cassandra believed that this would humiliate or distress her, she was mistaken. It was an escape from the last weeks of Paimon's brutality, from the cold touch of Christopher, from the period of being tossed about after the separation from Matthew. Perhaps it was Cassandra's way of telling her she will never be back together with Matthew.

She had not forgotten the call from Carey: it may even be that Matthew was being excluded from The Programme; it was what she had long feared. If he was out, so also will she be. In her heart of hearts, she cannot pretend that this too would not be a relief.

Cassandra stepped out of the cell, returned. She had a large glass of orange juice for her.

"Drink it. It can feel dry down here."

Obediently, Helen took the glass; she understood that she would not be left with it to drink at her leisure; they all knew what had happened to Anthony in the cells. It was bitter, cloudy, she glanced questioningly at Cassandra as she handed the glass back empty.

Conspiratorially, Cassandra giggled.

"I put a little Valium in it. I don't want you to be upset, I don't want you to suffer. You must understand, Helen: in my own way, I love you as much as Matthew ever did, or Paimon. I am going to take care of you personally – no one else."

* * *

Fortunately, the Disney shop on Regent Street was open late. The children expected something and would not know the difference: Disney was America and America was Disneyland. She could barely concentrate. She was worried about Matthew, Emily too, worried about The Programme. She had lost her easy foot-hold within the firm, her career. This visit was not about the children, or Jan, but for the heart-to-heart with Colin that had been postponed by both of them for too long. She was not looking forward to it: he wanted answers she was not yet ready to give.

Before dinner, she managed to contain her discomfort, prevent it turning into irritation with the children. Jan hovered, telling them to leave their aunt alone: Jan was molly-coddling her, as if she was not capable of protecting herself, treating her like a near-invalid: she wanted to protest, but Jan was right – she was not herself. The nanny was off, so Colin put the children to bed – no staying up for dinner this time, not even Tim. While he did so, Carey followed Jan into the kitchen, leaned against a counter as Colin's efficient wife efficiently completed the meal. She took the initiative.

"How do you think Colin's settling down at work?" With all the changes.

If Jan was surprised by the question, she did not say so.

"At the moment, he's fine; there's more people, which means more work, more things to worry over and fuss about – his idea of heaven, wouldn't you say?" Jan whipped a tray of pastry *hors d'oeuvres* out of the oven, sliding something else inside in effortless order.

"Why do you say 'at the moment'?"

"It's all been too easy. In the long run, some sort of confrontation seems inevitable: you know, two such different sets of people."

"Do you know any of them – other than Andrew, that is?"

"There was a small drinks party at the end of the first week, for people to meet each other really."

"You went?" Jan normally kept herself well away from the firm.

"I wanted to see them," Jan confessed: it was as familiar as they had ever been with one another.

"And?"

"They seemed like a nice group of people. It's more what I've wanted for the firm; you know that. What would you expect?" Jan challenged.

"I was only asking." Carey was taken aback by the sudden attack.

"Well, then," Jan said sensibly, meaning there was no point to Carey's questions.

"Why do you think there's going to have to be a confrontation? If it's what you wanted."

"Nothing's that easy; it's what I wanted, but it's only the beginning. You know Charles."

"Ah." It was not confrontation with the new people that Jan feared, but with the old guard. "Has he been over recently?"

"He visited before he went down to the apartment," Jan admitted cautiously. "But we didn't talk about the firm."

"What about me?" Carey asked suddenly. "Did he talk about me?"

"A little. He's worried about you. We all are," Jan added quietly, a second moment of familiarity. "But of course he doesn't discuss it with me," she added sourly. "He seemed tired. Weary."

"And are you going to tell me what you think?" Carey responded as best she could to Jan's marginal opening.

Jan sighed, then shook her head.

"It's too late for me to get involved, Carey. Just, I don't know, whatever it is you want to do, I hope you make the right decisions for you and I hope, well, that you get on and do it." Stop dithering about.

"Then we feel the same way."

Over dinner, they steered away from the darker side of Carey's adventures in America, although she described the places they had visited and talked a little about the court case and the differences between an English and an American trial. Afterwards, Jan offered:

"I'll clear up; I'd like an early night, so I'll go up to bed after."

"No," Colin said, more sharply than he intended. "We'll go into the study."

He led his sister into his room; it was not the first time they had tackled their problems in there. He carried through one of the dining chairs while she brought in the remains of the wine and both their glasses. Inside, though, he poured himself a whisky from the decanter on the sideboard. He did not sit behind his desk, but rolled his chair around to the other side.

"I gather Jan came in to the office for drinks." Carey put off the discussion they were supposed to be having.

"It seemed a nice idea; make people feel at home."

"Was Charles there?"

"Yes, actually; it was his idea."

"How was he?"

"Did you ask Jan?"

"She said he seemed weary."

"That's Charles in pre-battle posture; designed to make the enemy think he's weaker than he is," Colin said darkly.

"Who's the enemy? You, them – me?"

"All of us, I think. I can't help wondering why he let us go ahead if it makes him so unhappy; then, I think, well – that's Charles, what he likes is to set up battles just so he can win them and prove what a big man he is all over again."

"That's about right," Carey laughed.

"And you?" Colin seized the moment. "What is it you want?"

She finished the wine in her glass, poured herself another.

"As between?"

"You know," Colin said quietly.

"No, I don't think I do know, not at the moment. Spoiled for choice: the firm or The Programme; and there's two different versions of the firm."

295

"Only there aren't anymore," he reminded her that the fight was over.

"That's not what Jan thinks; nor do you."

"What do you mean?"

"This is just the first step: it's what I said before I went to America; a step at a time, that's your style. You said it: what he likes is a battle."

"Yes, battle after battle, time after time, every step by every step. Well, it's not going to happen that way. These are serious people, Carey: you know Andrew, you've met Jessica."

"You told me Charles likes her?"

"So do I," Colin said before he could stop himself, more vigorously than he had intended.

His eyes met Carey's; he had not meant to say more than the words; she was his sister, and knew him better than anyone else in the world.

"Well," Carey drawled.

"Oh, don't be silly, Carey. Just because I like her. That's all. New faces; new ideas. It's what we all want, isn't it? I mean, for the firm."

It meant too much to Colin to tease him; but it was not something that was ready to be discussed seriously.

"What do you want from me, Colin?" she asked suddenly.

"I miss you; I wish I had my sister back, that's all. Running the firm with me. The way it used to be."

"You mean you want me there to help you run your firm."

"Perhaps. It didn't used to be that much of a difference."

"I'm not sure it is now."

"Surely this Programme thing can't mean more to you than the firm? For Christ's sake, Carey – it's us, it's family, it's our life. Whatever it means to you now, it won't last. Can't you see that?"

"Funnily enough, Colin, I can. I don't know if it's true of everyone else who's involved – and I'm sure it's not true of some of those who've been in it for years – but if I'm honest, I don't think I am going to spend the rest of my life in The Programme. I wouldn't say it couldn't happen, but it's not what I expect."

"Well, what then?" He swallowed the rest of his drink to hide his despair. "If it's just, uh, a passing fad, don't let it destroy everything else, you'll need something when it's over."

"It doesn't work like that. Just because it isn't – or may not be – what I'm going to be doing for the rest of my life doesn't make it a passing fad. It's everything now; where I go afterwards starts from then, from when it's over, if it ever is. Otherwise, I'm not really doing it; I'm just playing at it."

Colin walked to the sideboard and refilled his glass.

"Does that make sense to you, Colin?"

"Sense? No. Oh, I can understand what you're saying. I just don't understand what you're doing. Why? What's it all about? Do you really think you can find God through this... this..." He was lost for words: anything he said would alienate her – cult, charlatan, mumbo-jumbo.

"God? I don't know what that means; peace, maybe; contentment; quietude is a much-ignored word that seems to fit my purpose. I can't find it by setting aside a couple of months or years, in order to come back and get on with my career; it doesn't work like that. I have either to do it fully – and take my chances on what's on the other side – or not do it at all. I think that's what I've become most aware of since I came back."

"It's crazy," he mumbled. "People just don't do that sort of thing anymore."

"You mean, since the seventies? Ha, look around you Colin, I can think of more people we've known who've moved on to something else than I can think of people who've stuck the course. People haven't changed, Colin, we just look the other way because we're frightened by the idea that if they can, so could we. What's crazy? Spending some of your life looking for a little bit of peace and contentment – my quietude word – or spending it locked into a job and a life that leaves me lonely, drinking too much, actively unhappy? I feel peace when I'm there; at least, near to peace."

"Where? The Programme – or Crane?"

"No," she laughed. "He doesn't bring me peace – quite the opposite. The Programme does, then he comes along and throws everything up in the air – me too. But," her eyes shone, "he does bring me to life. The combination, well, it's close to irresistible, can't you see?"

"I see you're throwing your life away, Carey."

"It's my life, Colin," she answered flatly.

"It sounds like you've got it all worked out, Carey; like you know what you're going to do."

"No. I don't. I suppose you could say, that's why I'm still drinking – and more than I ought to. And why I'm still thinking about it instead of already doing it."

He remembered what Jessica had said.

"Well, think about us too. We're a part of you. I am. Charles is, for all his sins. The children, too. There are people at the firm who are a part of your life, and of whose lives you're a part: Alistair not least. Perhaps that's why people don't walk in and out of different ways of life: too many other people get left behind. You've got a responsibility to them too."

"I've done my duty, Colin, by you, by Charles, by the firm. Aren't I allowed a little time to decide what's best for me?"

"A little, maybe; but the longer it goes on, the more insecure people begin to feel – about how much they mean to you, about whether you're going to be around anymore – and it doesn't take much to turn that into the notion that if you're not going to be around, they might as well get used to it and start moving on without you."

"I'm sorry if that's what you feel, Colin. You know I love you. I know you love me. I wish you loved me enough to want me to be happy."

"I do. I also love you enough to want to prevent you making a fool of yourself."

\* \* \*

Paimon, last to enter, bolted the door from inside. They had reduced the Hammer Reach population to a bare minimum; those who remained were their most ardent loyalists and even they were locked out of the main house for the night. The door to the basement was supposedly sound-proof but its limits had never been tested. The rest was in the hands of the gods.

Like the others, Paimon wore only a simple shift. At the top of the stairs, he pulled it quickly over his head and dropped it carelessly on the first step where Cassandra's, Caleb's, Christopher's had similarly been tossed. They were all naked.

It was dark in the basement meditation hall: only four candles, one on each wall. The others were in the same positions as on the night of the first Special Mass: Cassandra sprawled on the bed-couch at one end; Caleb opposite her, seated cross-legged on his bale-throne; Christopher with his back to the wall between one pair of cell-doors; Paimon took his place between the other.

There were differences. In the middle of the hall, beneath the gong, was a wooden altar, roughly put together from the lumber with which The Temple was being built, with heavy metal rings screwed deeply into its sides; and, the floor was covered with the same thick, plastic sheet that was used for damp-proofing in the construction of The Temple and that they had also used to protect the weapons in the pit.

Paimon glanced around, smiled, nodded.

"I am one," he said.

"We are many," they replied.

"Together we shall be whole."

"Tonight, we shall see a parting of the ways," Cassandra intoned. "Tonight Matthew Crane is no longer The Teacher. We must liberate him, as all our enemies. We use Helen to help us part from Matthew. We help Helen cross to the fire beyond. When Helen crosses, so also shall he. Are we agreed?"

"We are agreed," they chanted.

Behind her cell door, Helen could hear them but she could not understand. She had been in the cell for nearly forty-eight hours but she was not aware of it: her thoughts were not orderly enough. Anthony could be relied on to sink into his own mental mess left long enough to his own devices. Helen had been helped along by heavy doses of the Valium Cassandra had procured from Leah as she had weaned the younger girl from the habit and retained, if not for this eventuality then for one like it.

Helen knew she had been drugged though not in what quantity. Before they started assembling outside – whoever they were, however many of them there were – she had messed herself. She thought she had called out for help, for Cassandra who had promised to look after her personally, but she could not be sure if she had done so aloud or only in her head.

She was having difficulty focusing on anything: during the first hours, under no more than the first dose of Valium, she had reflected and meditated on Matthew; now, she could not recall his face. Not only as his lover, but as a member of The Programme these last several years, his face was the one to which she had awoken, which watched over her while she worked in the Coffee Lounge or on Reception, which stared up at her from magazines when she was out in the streets donating. Where had he gone?

Caleb called out:

"'God of dead bone, bring forth blood from this corpse!'"

Cassandra reminded them:

"There are only two things we do with one hundred per cent of our beings: being born and dying. We do them with our bodies as a whole, our minds as a whole, and our souls. The rest of the time, we are torn between doing what we most want to do and the rest of us: purpose and counter-purpose. The Programme is about how we free ourselves from that temporal torment, separation – escape to being whole again. We are here to help Helen escape, to be free; if we can help her to be free, then freedom is for us all only one step away."

She swung her feet to the ground and planted them firmly on the sheeted floor, wide apart to display the thick bush between her legs.

Hard nipples jutted from her heavy, swaying breasts. A clear and discernible ring of sexual energy hopped from one of her men to another like lights in a neon-show. Paimon had a proud and fierce erection. When Cassandra let one hand fall from her breast to fondle her clitoris, thrust a finger inside her vagina, Paimon imitated her, grasping his penis, eyes locked onto hers until she turned her attention to Caleb.

He was also in a state of excitement. They were being told that Cassandra and her brother had crossed the line and they were being invited to come across it with them. He and Cassandra had been together on many an occasion, in many a country, when it suited, when it pleased. He had never seen her naked without a savage wonderment, but it was the first time he had thought of what he might do with Paimon, to him, or what it might be like to do it to both of them at once. He kept his hands crossed over his breast: he did not dare touch himself; he would have come at once and that was not what tonight was about.

Only Christopher was not hard. He was the most complex. He knew they were wild; he saw what had happened with Cassandra and Paimon, had guessed it over the last days, smelled it in the air. He was their full partner, but he was the businessman amongst them, their sheet anchor to reality. He had taken part in the Special Masses because he knew that they had to happen and if they had to happen then he had to be a part of them, and he knew too that this ultimate Mass was an essential element in transformation of The Programme. For the others, though, it was part of the end, part of the reward; for Christopher, no more than a means.

He said:

"If you take life, you have to give life; the opposite is also true: if we want to be able to give life, we have to be able to take it. If The Programme is to move beyond, we four must lead it. The Programme needs new capacity, new energy. It is not enough that there are new bodies, new people, greater energetic capacity – we have to be able to use it in a new way, differently. We have to expand our horizons: otherwise, we do no more than dive deeper into the same waters. It is a new time, a new game; it calls for new rules."

Paimon and Christopher rose to fetch Helen from her cell. She put up no resistance as she was pulled into the Meditation Hall, nor as her shift was torn away. Vaguely, in the distance, she had expected something like this. The Programme gossip machine had whispered of Special Masses, she knew Cassandra's nature and, best yet, that of her brother; and they had all long known what sparked Caleb. She crossed her arms in front of her breasts, though only Caleb had never seen her naked, then realised the futility of it and let them drop to her sides. She staggered a little, looked around, registered there were only the four of them. She was still wondering what it meant when Cassandra rose from her couch – as naked as Helen herself – to embrace her.

Beside her head, Paimon sounded the gong, striking it repeatedly.

Cassandra whispered tenderly in her ear:

"Don't be frightened, little girl; we are here to set you free."

Helen was too far out of it to be actively frightened; fear was just one of a number of sensations of which she was aware, watching from the shore as she stepped into the sea.

Christopher, too, was embracing her. She was aware of the gong ever more distant, of Caleb chanting on his throne, of Paimon's and Christopher's penises simultaneously brushing – harder and rougher – against her body, as each had separately touched her in the past, Cassandra kissed her face wetly – her cheeks, her lips, her eyelids. Her lovers were saying farewell.

Caleb chanted:

"'I invoke the source of all power, of all danger, of all pain, of dissolution itself, let the very sinews, the ligaments and joints of Helen be dissolved for all time.'"

Helen felt her knees give way, her body responding to Caleb's curse.

Paimon continued to pound the gong as Cassandra and Christopher lowered her to the altar. The wood was harsh against her skin yet oddly comforting, a normal sensation.

They laid her on her back, stroked her stomach and legs until she parted her legs, Christopher gripped her ankles, Cassandra held her arms out from her sides, they strapped her to the metal rings.

Cassandra knelt down to kiss her face for a last time and stepped back.

"'I swear to the strong angels who stand before Him: turn His dwelling place around to destruction, to hatred, to scattering, to reversal. The people who dwell in it must not be able to look at Him in any way.'"

While he had been chanting, Caleb had risen from his throne and walked around Helen, thrice around and around.

In his hand, he held a knife – a bayonet he had bought in New Hampshire – which he stretched out before him, running the blade lightly along Cassandra's back the second time he passed around Helen, then Christopher's, Paimon's, on the third tour he touched the tip of it to each of their mouths, let them kiss it, brought it to his own lips, kissed it wetly and with his tongue, finally he dropped to his knees on one side of the altar as Paimon dropped to his on the other and without any hesitation made a shallow incision the length of Helen's torso, from her throat to her pelvis.

The bayonet was so sharp, the cut so thin, she so dopey from the Valium, for a moment Helen did not know what had happened. Caleb wet his forefinger, ran it along the cut, drew out blood with his saliva, licked it quickly the way he might lick a cut of his own. Helen struggled to raise her head, her arms tied too tightly to lift herself with her elbows. She saw the cut, fell back exhausted, whimpered aloud for the first time:

"Please."

"I am one," Cassandra reached across Caleb, touched Helen's breast, lifted blood and brought it to Helen's lips. "I am one," she repeated.

"We are many," Helen murmured, believing against reason that this was to be the worst of it – ritual blood.

Caleb reminded them:

"Crowley wrote: 'Any required change may be effected by the application of the proper kind and degree of force in the proper manner through the proper medium to the proper object'."

He glanced around at the others, eyes alight with joy. They nodded and replied:

"Together we shall be whole," as he plunged the bayonet into Helen's stomach with a howl to drown out her screams, so hard it struck through to the wood to which she was tied, and again and again until he yielded to the others in their turn, howling over and over, as if she was a wax doll through whom to inflict his curse:

"Matthew! Matthew! Matthew!"

\* \* \*

At the end, they rose, covered in her blood, stinking of it, laughing, crying, finally free.

\* \* \*

They arrived at the Boston Chapter House shortly after midnight. It was closed. Matthew had no key. He rang at the bell and, when that produced no response, banged heavily on the door. They were not asleep; probably in a Midnight Meditation.

Enoch opened the door. He was dressed in black. That was the first thing that struck Matthew: black; as they used to dress; which they had abandoned years before.

Enoch filled the space. He did not step back to let Matthew in. He stared blankly at Matthew, as if he had never seen him before, as if he had not meant the world to him since he had been found and saved in Devon.

"Brother Enoch," Matthew said, "I am one."

Enoch did not reply; he acted as if Matthew did not exist. His eyes were unfocused, as if he could not bear to look at him.

"Step aside, Enoch," Matthew commanded. He put his hands out to push him out of the way.

Enoch gripped his wrists. Matthew was strong, but none was as strong as Enoch. They stood there, unmoving, until Matthew said:

"Enoch. I am The Teacher, I am your Teacher. I command you to let me pass."

Enoch relented enough to grunt:

"I don't kn...know you," he said. "You don't b...b...belong here. It's o...o...o...over."

He twisted Matthew's wrists sharply inwards and flung him out into the street, slamming the door behind him without looking around to watch Matthew's fall.

*Part Three*

# Chapter Thirteen

They strapped Matthew face down on the makeshift altar on which Helen had been killed. Caleb had not been able to keep from telling him what they had done to her: Matthew could smell the blood that had drained into the wood.

Helen had – Caleb recounted with excitement – been buried in the foundations of Nahum's Temple, in a hole they had dug that would, in due course, lie beneath the focus of future meditations and masses. In Christian terms, they had buried her beneath the cross itself. They had buried her and covered her body in concrete and burned the plastic sheeting. Only the altar itself had not been burned by the time Matthew drove the now weary Lincoln up to the near-deserted complex and demanded:

"Where's Helen?"

\* \* \*

"Everything everybody can think of – that's the only limit there is on the human imagination – which is the same as saying none," Phillipe had said to Emily when she went to see him in New Orleans the second time. "And everything everybody can think of, someday, someone's going to want to see how it feels, try it out for size you could say."

She had drawn a deep breath. She was stoned, drinking beer, in the middle of nowhere – New Orleans.

"Young girl, pretty girl, white girl, middle class. What makes you think it isn't true of you too? What makes you think you're exempt?"

"Exempt from what?" she had asked hoarsely: they had been talking for hours – a demanding, challenging discourse from a man she would in the normal course of her life never have heard of, let alone spent this time with.

"Exempt from," he had paused for thought. "Exempt from the worst excesses, child, from the furthest extremes. From people who start down a path they've got no idea where it's leading, who lose control so bad, the only thing they've got left to believe in is being out of control itself, 'till it become the only thing left to worship." He stopped, dragged on his joint, offered it to her: she shook her head – enough.

"Tell me about Matthew, Phillipe."

"Matthew, hm." He thought a while, then smiled. "Matthew, he wants to be pure."

"And Cassandra?" The unmet Welsh witch.

"Her too. Purity is like a drug, an addiction: they're in competition, to see which one the most pure."

"And you? What are you?"

"Me," he had laughed from his belly. "I thrive on the heat; the heat, yah, that's what turns me on. Now you: what is it you want?"

* * *

They had driven through the night in grim silence. Emily could feel the changes happening to Matthew as tangibly as if he was shifting form from god to man, from man to beast. They stopped for fuel, coffee, toilet, with no more than a half-dozen words between them. Matthew focused on the road, refusing her offer to drive. He was not hurt but already joined in battle.

Emily had stared out the window, smoking heavily, trying to reach outside to hold the night still. She had come to the States to be with Carey. She suspected that she had done so anticipating being with her sexually, even though she had known about Matthew and – before she came – Carey had known about Simon. It was not, she thought, that either of them was gay; it was about completion – it needed to happen to complete the connection that wove through the ending of her marriage, Carey's separation from her firm, their union with The Programme, their union with each other: I am one, together we shall be whole.

She wished she could replay Antibes. Her hand brushed the inside of her bejeaned thighs. She wanted to lie next to Carey, kiss her face, her breasts, to lie between her legs. The images spun like the wheels of a pinball machine, flashing just as brightly and as loud.

She caught a sideways glance from Matthew, blushingly wondered whether he knew what she was thinking; he had a knack of reading other people's minds. His eyes flicked blankly back to the road. He had more important things to think about.

They drove for about six hours before Matthew pulled off the freeway, spun across minor roads through one end of a sleeping town, over a bridge, up into woodlands. It was too early for people to be about. He deposited her outside Moonlight Inn, gesturing to the chairs by the lake.

"You'll be all right here; they'll be up soon."

Emily shivered: it was autumn and the mornings were already noticeably chilly. She lifted her small travel case from the rear seat to make sure he did not drive away with it; there was extra clothing within.

"I want you to check in here, wait for me. You've got a credit card?" Emily nodded. "Get a room, a couple of rooms. I'll be back later."

"And if you're not?"

"Go home, I should think." Emily looked lost. He reassured her: "They're good people," he meant the inn-folk.

Her eyes had met his. She wanted to ask: "Yes; but are we?" Instead, she said simply:

"Be careful, Matthew."

\* \* \*

"Where's Helen?" he demanded of Christopher, seated at the long kitchen table, calmly sipping his morning juice, being waited on by Diana.

"Come," Christopher said, "I'll take you down."

Matthew was not surprised that she was in the cells, bait; they had wanted him to come for her.

The cell doors were open, the cells empty, the stench appalling.

"She was here," Christopher said idly, pointing to the scarred and blood-stained altar, the last evidence yet to be removed. "Helen was here," he repeated.

From behind, Caleb sneered:

"Hello, Matthew. I thought you'd come."

As Matthew – tiredly, resignedly, knowing what was to come – turned to face his enemy within, Caleb struck him with a length of wood across the back of the head. Completing Matthew's turn, their eyes met and held as Matthew tumbled backwards, falling unconscious to the ground.

\* \* \*

When Matthew awoke, he was strapped naked and face down to the altar. He was gagged: the cloth filled his mouth; he could barely breath.

He made out that he was not in the basement cells. The smell was earth, damp and raw and untreated. There were tiny chinks of light: it was still day. He guessed he was in the pit that Nahum had seen them digging. There were other smells: apart from Helen's, something else that was familiar but that he could not place, perhaps machine oil.

309

He could not hear a sound nor sense movement. They would have moved the members out of the barn. He could barely move his head. Even if he had not been gagged, it would have been futile to try to call out. The barn was too big and he lacked the strength. He would need the body of an ox and the strength of a bull to raise a cry that would be heard in the farmhouse itself.

His mouth was dry; the gag had soaked up his saliva. He remembered Christopher gesturing at the altar to which he was now strapped, remembered the stink, remembered the rusty stains sunk into it, the cuts in the wood that – he understood – represented the cuts in Helen.

He was not shocked. He had been frightened for her for several days. Perhaps he had known since Anthony's death that something like it had to happen. Nor could he pretend to feel grief or guilt. It was as it was; regret was purposeless. He hoped they had killed her quickly, that she had not died in pain. He hoped she had managed to keep faith to the end, to embrace the release, to welcome the fire beyond. He hoped he would do so too.

They had not killed him yet. That did not mean they did not intend to do so. He had been their leader, their teacher for years; they would want to claw back to themselves the pieces of their minds and souls that they had yielded up to him, inch by inch, savouring every moment of it. Caleb was pure evil: Matthew had known it for years, could not complain if Caleb wanted to exorcise his power and his influence in the way he knew best and would most enjoy. That was a given: there would be pain to come at his hands; Matthew could take it – Christ on the cross.

Then Christopher: if they had killed Helen, he would know that Matthew too must die. So long as Matthew was alive, he would be a threat. Christopher would know that Matthew could never forgive the way they had used Helen. Matthew wondered about the others. Paimon had long hated Matthew. How great was his current influence over Cassandra, what were he and she up to, what would he be able to make her do? Where were Micah, Jemima, Meredith, Hannah – even Nahum? With whom did they stand? Was Simon in on it – Naamah?

Finally, it was Cassandra who raised the greatest number of questions: far too many to answer; too many even to ask.

He heard movement above his head, could not turn to look but a portion of the pit lit up. The pit was deeper than he had assumed: perhaps five feet. It was supported by a crude timber-frame: uprights holding up the ceiling at breaks along the walls, a couple of cross-struts between each upright, nothing else to contain the packed-earth walls. Out of the corner of an eye, in a still-dark corner, he spotted metal, made out the stock of a gun, the edge of a handful of weapons half-stacked in some sort of a trunk: not machine but gun oil; small wonder it was familiar – some things never changed.

Someone dropped into the pit beside him. A hand – a man's hand – ran its way up the inside of his right leg, gripped his scrotum, squeezed to hurt. He gritted his teeth so as not to cry out but it had already changed the rhythm of his breathing and disclosed that he was awake. Caleb laughed.

"Here I am, Matthew."

Matthew could not speak. He did not even try to do so. There was nothing to say. Phillipe's words rang in his ears: he had to be prepared to do evil. If evil was what it took, he was ready for it.

Caleb ran a finger lightly, lovingly, up Matthew's spine.

"I wonder how it feels, Matthew? I do. Oh," Caleb explained, "I don't mean this, to be strapped down, helpless, completely in some-one else's possession. That's not such a new idea. But to have it happen to you, Matthew, you, that's something else. What's it feel like, Matthew? You used to own us; now look at you." The swift, hard fall from grace.

He was outside Matthew's limited line of vision. He stroked Matthew's hair tenderly then, suddenly, as if to get his attention, gripped it tightly and jerked Matthew's head up so that the strap across the back of his neck cut into him. He leaned down, whispered in his ear:

"I killed her, Matthew, I killed her."

Still Matthew did not make a sound. Caleb resumed his ranting.

"When I was in jail, there was this man, he used to be some kind of a businessman, rich man, powerful; he'd raped and killed a young girl, so he wasn't doing soft time, white collar time; you can only imagine what it had to be like – to fall from those heights, down to this. He had the hardest time of all: sex crime, a crime against a child, he was white and he'd been rich. They used to do everything to him: he'd have the shit beaten out of him just about every day – not just the prisoners, the guards too. They pissed in his coffee, put shit in his food, stood over him 'till he ate it. They fucked him, too: riding him like a horse, everyone in turn – giddyap. I used to wonder how that felt, how he could manage to make the move from a life like he'd had to that. It excited me, you know? I fucked him too, just to see what it felt like. But he'd never tell me. You think, maybe, he couldn't describe?"

Caleb crossed his line of vision, crouched down beneath a section of the cover that had not been removed. He was barefoot, jeans, no shirt. He hunched beside the weapons, busying himself with his back to Matthew. Matthew thought it was going to happen just like that, here and now: Caleb was going to kill him.

Caleb walked around behind him. Again, he ran a finger along the inside of Matthew's leg. His finger was cold, greasy wet. He opened his hand wide and slapped it down on Matthew's backside, forcing the cheeks apart, rubbing his anus with gun oil, he thrust a finger into Matthew, then another.

Caleb remarked conversationally:

"Aleister Crowley said – 'Every man has a right to fulfil his own will without being afraid that it may interfere with that of others; for if he is in his proper place, it is the fault of others if they interfere with him.' We've done that, haven't we? Done it to others, done it in the name of good, in the name of experience, in the name of love, in the name of The Programme. I figure, it's about time to get honest about it. Let's do it for the sheer hell of it, let's do it 'cos we like doing it, let's do it for Satan."

With that, Caleb mounted Matthew, gave himself a final coating of oil and plunged into The Teacher, thrusting himself up to the hilt in a single motion, then withdrawing, waving his glossy wet erection triumphantly at an imagined gathering as if it was a Special Mass before he plunged back into Matthew, falling flat against his body, biting his shoulder with uncontainable glee, humming into his ear, over and over:

"I killed her, I killed her," until Matthew could have no doubt that he was next.

Matthew's eyes fixed on the guns in the corner. There were many guns: they were planning a war – the army of God and Satan. He and Helen were the testing rituals, to bloody the leaders before they sent the troops out to die.

It had been excruciatingly painful when Caleb had entered him. He felt raw and – humiliatingly – as if he badly needed to shit, which made him clench his cheeks which, in turn, made Caleb's thrusting all the more painful. It seemed like Caleb wanted to go on and on forever, without any wish to come. There was no lust in it, only power.

Caleb paused. They could hear voices outside. A couple of members, perhaps three, on their way to some task in the fields or at the other barn, perhaps construction had re-commenced on The Temple. Maybe they were just going for a walk. Matthew could make out no more than the hum of conversation, not a tone that might have told him who they were or what they were saying. They were both silent, motionless: Caleb with his prick inside Matthew, still hard, still not come.

The members passed. During the stillness, the pain had begun to subside, he had relaxed. He sensed that Caleb could feel the difference. Caleb began to move in and out of him again, this time without quite the same intense hammering. He wanted to come. As far as his bonds permitted, Matthew spread his legs, raised himself to meet Caleb. Caleb rested his face against Matthew's back, Matthew could feel his breath on his skin.

Matthew turned his head as far as he was able, until their eyes could meet. Matthew's were gleaming, excited, telling Caleb that he was enjoying it, feeding Caleb lust in place of power. For a moment, Caleb was caught up in it, forgot what he was doing, and to whom.

Matthew saw the change in Caleb's eyes as Caleb discovered Matthew's ploy.

"Fucker," he screamed, grabbing hold of Matthew's head and slamming it back onto the wooden altar, jerking himself out of Matthew.

As he emerged, Caleb came, messily, foolishly, without relief let alone release, shooting globs of semen onto Matthew from which he leapt back as if frightened he might be infected by them. As his feet hit the ground, he raised his hands in a clenched fist above his neck and brought them down with a crash on the back of Matthew's. Matthew blacked out again.

\* \* \*

Squatting in a corner of the barn, one level up, unknown to Matthew and Caleb both, Christopher listened. He would have had to creep a few feet nearer to the pit to see, but he had no particular wish to do so. Matthew's humiliation meant nothing to him; he was finished. He was not interested in what was being done to Matthew; only in what Caleb was doing.

\* \* \*

Http://www.the-programme.org.uk (turn on sound card if available).

*The Programme is back. We have been into the furthest and darkest corners of our plan, our game. We have explored the recesses of our capacity, dragging from hidden cupboards and boxes aspects of ourselves of which we were barely aware. We have broken ourselves down into our smallest parts, and rebuilt ourselves in a different shape. The Programme is back, but you will pause before you recognise us.*

*We need you now, all of you who are out there and who have followed us on this Website, who have come to our Coffee Lounges in London, Boston and New York, or who perhaps once committed yourselves and since withdrew. The Programme is under attack. It has been under attack from within, it is still under attack from outside. Our ranks are depleted at the time that we face the greatest external conflict, when our enemies seek to take advantage of our momentary weakness: some seek to take away our Chapter Houses; others, to rob us of the money we need to perpetuate The Programme; predators seek to steal away our members.*

*We are beginning our last, our final voyage. The lesson we have learned is that the time for which we can expose the raw contradictions of which we are each composed, and of which The Programme itself must therefore be comprised, is not infinite. If we are to complete the reconciliation of our opposing instincts and become whole once more, we must press on with it without any further delay or distraction. Sometimes, we have described The Programme as a way of life; but it is a way of life that exists only to achieve an objective, not a way of life that is an end in itself; we must direct all our energies to its attainment.*

*When we came to America, we became an army – the army of God and Satan. We set out to prove that God and Satan can exist as equal forces, opposites yet in harmony. We have sent God and Satan around opposite wings of the battlefield, and at the hour when the bugle sounded they joined hands – we heard them say: I am one, we are many, together we are whole, are whole mind you, not shall be whole – together we are whole. The millennium approaches; many people believe that it marks the end of the world, the final accounting; others acknowledge its symbolism. The Programme does not know if they are right or wrong nor truly do we care – we shall long beforehand have stepped across to the fire beyond. Come across with us.*

\* \* \*

"What're you doing, Cassandra?" Matthew asked, not for the first time.

"Are you tired, Matthew?"

She had brought him juice.

He mumbled indistinctly:

"Not tired. Take path – become what path made us. Am I tired, now it's here? No. Frightened? No. Enjoying? No." He was silent for a moment then repeated: "What're you doing, Cassandra?"

She was huddled on the ground, within his easiest line of vision, though partly in shadow. When she dropped into the pit, through the same section of floor that Caleb had removed, she had been carrying a paper sack. From it, her first act had been to withdraw a small carton of juice, the sort the children liked, with a straw attached to one side, which she had held for him while he sucked it dry. From the same sack, she had taken a bottle of Johnson's Baby Lotion, shown it to him. For a second, he thought it heralded another assault, bodily invasion. She rubbed it gently into his back, working her way down his body, soothing, massaging, healing. Then she had sat down where he could look at her.

"I think, you know," she finally answered him. "When it all comes down to it, I was sick of words – I was sick of your words. Words, words, words: it felt like you had been filling my head with them for the last God knows how many years; first my head, then others, members, casual visitors to the Coffee Lounges. When our heads were overflowing with words, your words, you used the magazines and the Website and set out to fill the heads of unknown people all over the world, as if you'd never, never stop."

"What do you want instead? This – killing – for the sake of it?"

"Not for the sake of it. Never for that."

"What?"

"You know how it is, Matthew: if you've got power, one of these days you have to use it."

"That's wrong. You know it's wrong. It's one thing to understand what we're capable of; it doesn't mean we have to do it."

"You see what I mean? Words, words, words. Clever, clever, clever. Boring, boring, boring."

Still in a crouch, she came to sit close enough to touch his face. Briefly, she darted her face towards his, touched his lips, backed away before she did more or he could try to do so.

"It's the most interesting resource of all, power: stimulating, challenging. Money's good, too, but if all you can buy with money is inanimate, that's all you can become. It's power over people that matters: you can feed on them, on their energy, engorge yourself."

"Their blood," he reminded her.

"That too. It's happened forever, Matthew: human sacrifice not to appease the gods but to renew yourself – to recreate that most whole of all experiences, birth by passing through death to the other side."

"Where are you taking The Programme, Cassandra?"

"I wish I could tell you. It's complicated at the moment. Caleb wants one thing – well, you know that. Christopher wants something else – but I'm not sure what it is. And me? I want Paimon; I want Paimon to have your place, your position, your authority, your power."

"Authority and power are different," Matthew said wearily.

"For most people it's the same. I don't think Paimon's been ready before, not really. You knew, didn't you? That I wanted to be with him."

He nodded. Knew she'd wanted to; knew now that she was.

"I think, oh, he says he's been waiting for me all this time, waiting for me to be ready; but I'm pretty sure, if I'd let it happen before, it would have burned him up. Maybe both of us. We needed something around us, strong enough to sustain it, feed it: I think you did that for us, Matthew – I think you built up The Programme until it was a group, an organisation, a community strong enough even to absorb the idea of Paimon and I together."

"And Helen – what was that about, Cassandra? Why did that happen? She didn't threaten you. Why did you choose Helen?"

"No," Cassandra admitted, "she wasn't a threat. But she represented you. I thought, you know, at first, when I could see she and Nahum weren't going to happen, I thought perhaps if Christopher took her for a while – then later, Paimon – it might drive you out of her, but it didn't – there was always something about her that was still you – you could see it in her eyes."

"You killed her because of what you could see in her eyes? Christ, Cassandra." With what was in his eyes, what would they do to him?

Cassandra giggled.

"No, silly; not at all. That was why I chose her for death, not why I chose death itself. It could have been anyone. It had to happen. Death is the closest we can come to the essence of it: and, so long as each of us lives, that has to mean someone else's death."

\* \* \*

"I have to go back to the States, Colin," Carey said, standing in the door of his office. "I've booked a flight in the morning."

"What, now?" Colin half-rose from his desk in fury. He stopped, a gleam of hope in his eye. "Is this for the case?"

"No," Carey admitted, "it's for Matthew."

"Carey, Carey," her brother sank back into his chair. "You've only just come back. If you leave now, I don't know what people are going to think. Can't it wait – just a few weeks? Please."

"No, it can't. It can't wait a few days. I can't help what people think. This has to be, Colin. I'm sorry. I'm truly sorry. Matthew's in trouble; he needs me. Emily's over there, waiting for me."

"And the firm? You can just walk away from that? From me, from Dad?"

"Invoking Daddy? You must be desperate."

He shut his eyes as if he could make the conversation go away.

"I am desperate, Carey. Can't you see that?"

She came into the room, closed the door behind her. Went around behind him, placed her hands around his neck, kissed the top of his head. She rocked him and herself from side to side, then kissed him again, went and sat on his desk, the way she liked, like a child.

"What is it, Colin? It's not just the firm, is it?"

"No," he admitted. "Oh, I can tell you that if you walk out now the others won't let you back – and I'd mean it and they'd mean it, and the day you wanted to go back to work, you know I'd do anything – Dad would do anything – I mean, if this is what you wanted to come back to."

Because she had tears in her own eyes, she did not see his own.

"That's the point, Colin. I can walk away from you – and Dad – because I know you'll still be here when I get back. You're my brother: I know you love me; I know you'll always be here for me."

"Is that what this is about? Matthew Crane? Are you frightened you're going to lose him, as a lover?" He did not try to conceal his scorn.

If he had not been in such obvious pain, she would have snapped back any one of a dozen tart replies. Instead, she repeated quietly:

"He's in some kind of trouble. I don't know what's going on. To tell you the truth, I'm a bit scared. There are elements in The Programme who, well, seem to have turned a corner. Perhaps Anthony Rockworth was the beginning. Then a friend of Matthew's disappeared – a girl called Helen, a nice girl. Now Matthew's disappeared too."

"For God's sake, Carey," Colin cried, "what are you talking about? Call the police. Call The Programme's lawyers in New York. If you don't want to use them, we'll find someone else. You're not… You're not…" Because he still was not entirely sure what she was telling him, he could not finish his sentence.

"I've got to go, Colin, I've got to go myself and see he's all right, do what I can to make sure The Programme's all right – that he's all right with The Programme. After that, I'll know what I'm going to do next: that's what I was trying to say the other night – you have to do it before you can see the next step. But if I don't go over and help – afterwards'll be too late, I'm afraid it won't be there anymore. That's what I meant when I said I know you'll still be here when I get back."

"And what I mean is, I don't want you to go because I'm scared you won't be coming back. At all. Ever."

"I know," Carey said, slipping off the desk. "I know that's what you're saying."

He waited for reassurance. He was still waiting when she left the room and shut the door behind her.

* * *

Next time she brought him two cartons of juice as well as an orange which she peeled and broke into segments before she fed them to him. Also, a small plastic bucket of water, a wash-cloth and some soap. As she cleaned him up, she asked artlessly:

"Has he been back?"

"Caleb?"

"Yes."

"Yes."

She did not need to ask if Caleb had assaulted Matthew again. The tone of her question was matched by the tone of his reply. Around his anus, she could see dried blood and traces of semen.

"Not only Caleb."

"How many?" Her questions represented sincere enough concern but did not convey any hint that she might do anything to stop it, as if it was just one of those things and out of her control.

Slowly, he said as if he had been struggling to remember or to work it out:

"Two, three." His guess was that there had been more than one who had tried, but only one other than Caleb who had succeeded.

She shuddered.

"You must be a mess inside."

"We're all a mess inside, Cassandra; rather my sort of mess than yours." His voice muscles were beginning to respond to the juice.

It was news to her, bad news. She knew it would not have been Christopher – who was exclusively heterosexual – nor would it have been Paimon, who might have been tempted by the experience but who would not have failed to tell her. Caleb had brought some of his own, private army to play with Matthew: Reuben, Lemuel, Ehud or perhaps the Jays who had, since Paimon took up residence with her, attached themselves to Caleb, fascinated by someone who had so completely mastered them. None of them was senior enough or should have been trusted enough to have been allowed near the barn.

"Poor Matthew," she murmured as she finished washing him.

"What about when it's your turn, Cassandra? Is that what you'll say then – poor Cassandra?"

She giggled, poured out the dirty water, tidily piled the empty juice carton, orange peel and washcloth into the bucket, and put it beneath the open section of the ceiling of the pit ready to carry away with her, before she settled herself closely down in front of him.

"If it gets that far I'll be gone."

"Dead?"

"Gone," she repeated. "You're the one who feels fine about your own death."

"I don't recall saying," he replied, though she was correct: his death did not bother him; only his life. "It's just other people's deaths you feel fine about?"

"I don't feel fine about it, Matthew. It was necessary."

"Like this?" What they were doing to him.

"If you like. It's only what you've been saying all along; letting it out, letting it happen."

"I never hurt anyone."

"Oh, that's crap, Matthew, and you know it, complete shit. There've been countless members you've hurt: members you've made love to and left them to cope with it; members from whom you've wormed their darkest secrets; members you've humiliated for some transitional purpose; and what about the members you've let give us their money, go back out into the world with nothing, telling them that too was meant to happen?

"How many members have there been, Matthew, who've left us – left you – in tears and shame and confusion and all you've ever said was – they could come back when they were ready?"

She did not wait for an answer; she did not believe he had one. She demanded instead:

"Tell me what you've done with those two girls?"

"Carey? Emily?"

"Yes, them. You couldn't help yourself when you saw her, could you, Matthew? Just decided you had to have her; break up her pathetic little career to make yourself feel better, like a big man. Tell me that's wrong," she challenged him.

"It's your version of events, Cassandra. Did it ever occur to you that I might love her?"

"Did it ever occur to you?"

"Yes," he used the last of his reserves to snarl back.

"Where is she now?"

"She went home."

"Yes," Cassandra admitted. "That's what I heard. And the other one?"

"She went back with her," Matthew replied.

"In a mess, the pair of them?"

"You'll have to ask them, Cassandra."

"We all did the same thing, even me," Cassandra said quietly. "You'd never say the word – the L word – you made us dig it out of ourselves, take exclusive responsibility for it. That was how we were truly hooked, much more than if we could have blamed you for it."

"Oh, Cass," a diminutive unused for years. "Is that what this is? A feminist revolt? Please."

He wanted to laugh but it came out as a croak.

"You're trying to dress this up as something positive, a Programme-happening. But it's turned, hasn't it, The Programme? Apples turned rotten in the barrel, too late to turn into cider."

She giggled.

"Now I'll say it. That's your version of events, not mine."

"Where are we going with this, Cass? Do we have any idea yet?"

"Some," she admitted not all. "We're in for a time of it. Rockworth's getting ready to strike; he's hired Berlinger."

"I assumed, from what Phillipe told me."

"Don't trust Phillipe," Cassandra warned, as if they were still working together. "He'd betray you as soon as spit on you."

"And you." He reminded her that neutrality was Phillipe's article of faith.

"None of them matter, except Rockworth and his man."

"Why do they matter?"

"Rockworth's got the money; Berlinger's got the knowledge; between them, they think they've got the cause."

"So?"

"So they'll come for us. Don't you think?" She was asking him to help her work it out, for her, for The Programme, the way he always had. It did not strike her as odd. What made Matthew special was his capacity for utter detachment. It was the final quality she needed to suck out of him.

"It seems likely. What can they do?"

"Harm enough," she muttered. "If we don't get the better of them first. Chesterfield Gardens. Kroger. There're two other cases which had gone to sleep that we've had new signs of trouble on."

"Is that what the guns are for, Cass?"

"The vultures are gathering," she answered darkly.

"Forgive me if I don't share your concern about Rockworth. I've got other vultures to worry about first."

She leaned in close to him, staring into his eyes, studying them as if she could not believe her ears.

"First? You don't think there's going to be any after, do you?"

He did not reply; despite himself, his eyes fell shut.

"Do you think I'll stop them? Is that what you believe?"

"No, not anymore. I don't believe it anymore."

"Fool you to believe it at all."

He had angered her: more than angered, he had infuriated her. He was not sure how or why; it was difficult to work things out; his mind often wandered. If breaking it down was their first order of business, they were beginning to succeed.

"Does it hurt? When Caleb buggers you, I mean? They say it's much more painful for men than for women."

"That's what he wants to know: how it feels. It's what he keeps asking, over and over, lying on top of me: how does it feel, how does it feel. That, or he tells me how he killed Helen."

"Caleb," she giggled admiringly. "God, he's got no limits, has he?"

"And that makes it all right?"

"It makes sense of it."

* * *

Http://www.the-programme.org.uk (turn on sound card if available).

*This much is certain: the end is approaching. The only questions are about the form it will take, how we will recognise it, who will survive it, who even will thrive.*

*Remember this from Matthew 24. Jesus was sitting on the Mount of Olives when the disciples came to ask what would be the sign of his coming and of the end of the world. He told them: "For many shall come in my name, saying I am Christ; and shall deceive many. Ye shall hear of wars and rumours of wars: see that ye be not troubled: for all these things must come to pass, but the end is not yet. For nation shall rise against nation, and kingdom against kingdom: and there shall be famines, and pestilences, and earthquakes, in divers places. All these are the beginning of sorrows.*

*"Then shall you be delivered up to be afflicted, and shall kill you, and ye shall be hated of all nations for my name's sake. And then shall many be offended, and shall betray one another, and shall hate one another. And many false prophets shall rise and shall deceive many. And because iniquity shall abound, the love of many shall wax cold. But he that shall endure unto the end, the same shall be saved. Then shall be great tribulation, such as was not since the beginning of the world to this time, no, nor ever shall be."*

*No, The Programme has not joined the prophets of imminent doom, final holocaust, Valhalla, Armageddon, though there is plenty of evidence that it is around this corner and that one all of the time. The God and the Satan we unite are within ourselves, not those of others. Their army is marching towards our own, exclusive end. It is for this final adventure that we have endured – the final adventure of the fire beyond. Come into it with us.*

* * *

Carey rented a car at JFK and drove directly to Hedgerow. She arrived late afternoon. She was surprised to feel a mild sense of home-coming. She had only visited the Inn the once, for dinner with Matthew, but from the moment she turned off towards Moonlight the countryside felt warm and familiar.

Emily was waiting for her, seated by the lake in jeans, reading a Programme book, peering at each car as it rolled up the rough track. As Carey climbed out stiffly, Emily let out a yelp of joy and relief and ran to hug her, they stood beside the open door of the car, rocking, crying.

"What are we doing here?" Carey half-laughed, half-cried.

"Husht," Emily stroked her hair, pressed Carey's cheek against hers. "It's going to be all right."

She took Carey's bag and led the way into the Inn. The innkeeper was behind her antique desk, rose to greet Carey like an old friend.

"Hello, my dear. Your friend said you were coming. And, uh, Matthew is it? Is he coming too?"

Carey bit her lower lip.

"I'm not sure. He's over at Hammer Reach."

The woman's eyes were filled with speculation which she did not voice. It was not her business unless and until someone made it so,

322

or asked for help or advice, when it would become as important to her as if it was her very own problem.

"Are you going to want another room?"

"We can manage for the moment, if that's all right?" Emily said quickly. "I mean, until Matthew comes. Is that okay?"

"Sure. It's a double. Do you need any help?" With Carey's bag.

"No," Emily laughed. "We can manage."

"What I'd like most of all is a bath," Carey said.

"Okay. Do you know if you want to eat with us tonight?"

"Yes," Emily said firmly, "I'm sure we will." There was nothing they could do for Matthew until the next day and she wanted them to have at least this night for themselves.

They were in one of the rooms in the annexe. They had to go back outside to reach it. It was at the far end of the building, on the upper floor, approached along a balcony overlooking the tennis court, the car-park and the lake itself. They had barely run Carey's bath when there was a knock at the door and the innkeeper's son was standing there bearing a tray.

"Mum thought you'd like some tea," he explained briefly, disappearing shyly almost before Emily had taken the tray from him.

"Wow," Carey's eyes shone. "It's unreal."

"What is?" Emily sat in a low armchair; Carey was half-sprawled on the bed. "The Inn?"

"Being here; us; in the middle of nowhere, a couple of miles from Hammer Reach. Don't you think, sometimes, it's just a dream, you'll wake up and you're married to Richard, late for work, that sort of thing?"

"When I started, I used to feel that during the Meditation: hey, Em, what are you doing here? I still feel it sometimes."

"So? What are you doing here? For one thing, what were you doing in New Orleans?"

"I think, I felt maybe Phillipe understood more about things – The Programme, people, me, maybe I mean people like us who joined something like The Programme – I thought he could explain what I was doing, what we were doing."

"Could he?"

"I'm still trying to figure it out. I'm sure he was warning me off, though."

"Off what? The Programme or Matthew?"

"Well," Emily laughed, "that's something else I'm still trying to figure out."

"But he called Matthew," Carey reminded her.

"Yes," Emily admitted the contradiction. "I think he didn't want me to be alone, but he didn't want me to stay around either."

"Did he?" Carey asked the underlying question.

"Not a finger. It was quite chastening. I thought he'd try, after some of the things he said." That first night they had visited. "I think, actually, he's really quite a kind person."

She brought Carey up to date since they had last spoken, when she had told her what had happened in Boston.

"Have you tried ringing him?"

"No. I asked him what I should do if he didn't come back; he told me to go home. I suppose I wasn't too surprised when he didn't come back that day; I didn't really expect him. It was when there was still nothing yesterday that I rung you."

"Why didn't you ring there?"

"I think, well, if he's all right, then he wouldn't have wanted me to; if he's not, he'd said to go home – I thought, maybe I shouldn't let anyone know I was here. Does that make sense?"

"I think so. We have to think through all the possibilities – what could have happened to him – before we decide what to do, so I think that was right. Except, unless..." Unless they had already done something to him; Anthony was on their minds; Helen's disappearance.

"Even so," Emily insisted. "What would he have wanted. I couldn't have called the police, could I?"

"No, of course not." It would have been a humiliation more final for Matthew than any that either of them could imagine might have been inflicted on him by Cassandra. "Have you tried New York? I mean, just in case." In case Matthew had gone straight there from Hammer Reach.

"After Boston, I thought, you know, I didn't know whose side they'd be on. Anyway, he wouldn't just leave me here."

"We have to see him, Em." Or find him.

"I've been looking at maps. If you go through the woods on the other side of the lake, you sort of come down onto Hammer Reach – I mean, it's a long way, three or four miles. What if we hiked up there, see what we can see? You've been there; I haven't. Does it make any kind of sense?"

"Yes and no," Carey thought about it. "It's a farm, there are some barns, you could draw pretty close and see what was happening in the fields or maybe even outside the main house, on the porch." Where she had sat, talking with Leah, watching Matthew and Helen walking. "But it's not close enough that we could creep up to the house: there's too much clearing between and, besides…" She did not finish the thought.

"We're not exactly the cavalry? Sure, but it might give us more of an idea what's going on there."

"I'll have that bath," Carey got up and went into the bathroom without answering.

Emily heard her turn off the tap, was aware of her movements as she undressed, the rustle of her clothing falling to the floor. She lay her head against the back of the chair and closed her eyes for just a moment, choosing between two opposing states of mind: concern – rising to outright fear – over Matthew, or sheer relief that Carey had arrived and that they were finally here together.

When she leaned her head back, when Carey stepped into the bath, it was still light outside. She must have drifted off, because dusk was falling when next she looked out of the window. She pushed herself up stiffly from the chair and went into the bathroom: Carey, likewise, had fallen asleep stretched out in the huge tub. Emily knelt down beside the bath smiling, reached out and touched her friend's shoulder.

"Hey, Carey," she woke her gently.

Carey shot bolt upright, sending a wave of bathwater up the walls of the bath. drenching the front of Emily's sweater.

"God, I must have been tired."

"I dozed off too. How about I add some hot water to this?"

"Mm," Carey lowered herself back into the tub. "Lovely."

Emily busied herself with the tap, across from her, in the centre of the bath.

"We'll stay here tonight, decide what to do tomorrow, okay?"

Carey was in no mood to argue. Though the water was still cool, she felt warm inside; the worst of the tiredness had worn off but she did not yet have the energy to get out – she was sensuously comfortable.

"Ugh," Emily pulled the wet sweater over her head. She wore only a thin T-shirt beneath. Carey's naked body was inches from her touch. Her nipples were visibly erect against the cotton of her T-shirt. Her eyes met Carey's, then as she allowed her own gaze to drift she saw that Carey's nipples too were hard. They leaned towards one another until their lips could touch, kissed briefly, pulled back for a moment to see that they were both in the same place, next time their lips met their mouths were wide open, tongues darting. Carey put a hand on the back of Emily's head to hold her. Emily gripped Carey's side, the heel of her hand barely touching her friend's breast, then sliding around until she could cup it. Their mouths still clung to each other. When they broke apart, gasping for air, neither wanted to be the first to let go of the other.

Emily reached out to turn off the hot water, stood up, pulled her T-shirt over her head, slipped out of her jeans and panties and stepped into the bath. She relished the moment their legs connected, made electric currents, the moment that neither of them drew away from. She knelt between Carey's open legs, reached out to touch her face, her breasts, her slender hips, lifted her in the water until she could hold her up with her knees, touched between Carey's thighs, sunk one thumb lightly inside her, brought it to her lips.

Carey slipped off her, came to her own knees, they knelt up straight now, breast to breast, kissing again, stroking. After a while, they stopped kissing, held each other in the same position, heads on shoulders. Carey did not want to be made love to unequally. If they were going to move on from this, every version of the fantasy had to be unleashed. She saw the soap bowl behind the taps, stretched around Emily to reach for it; as she did so, she buried her face in Emily's neck, kissed it, licked it, sucked the flesh into her mouth, ground her mark as Emily groaned aloud, their pelvises hard against each other, a perfect fit.

Carey soaped both her hands until they were frothy and ran them over the fine skin of Emily's lean back that she had looked at in the sun at Antibes where the first inklings had begun. Again they kissed. Carey's hand was soaping Emily's bottom, rolling the cheeks in her hands harder and harder, she plunged a finger into her friend, first in one place then the other then both at once. Emily's mouth broke away, for a moment Carey thought she had misplaced it but the grunts and gasps from Emily told her otherwise. Emily fell back onto the arms with which Carey was encircling and handling her, almost causing Carey to lose her balance. She flung her legs around Carey's waist. Carey could no longer keep her grip from behind. Emily thrust herself hard against Carey, jerking, coming.

For a while they lay there while Emily recovered her breath. Then, awkwardly, Carey extracted herself from her embrace to return to her own end of the tub. Smiling shyly, Emily took Carey's ankles and arranged them across her own thighs, running her hands down the backs of her calves. She lifted Carey's foot until she could kiss it. For the longest time, neither of them said a word, frightened to get it wrong.

Emily took the initiative, stepping from the bath and holding out a hand to help Carey, leading her to the bedroom where they lay on their backs, glistening and wet, on top of the quilt cover, still holding hands. After a few moments, Emily rolled onto her side, leaned down and kissed Carey open-mouthed but gently, and started to work her way down her body until finally she was crouched between her legs, her mouth buried in her, sucking out the very juice of her. She felt Carey grow taut, bring her body up, rubbing against Emily's mouth so hard Emily could barely hold on until, with tiny gasps, Carey reached her own climax and fell back exhausted.

Emily lay between Carey's legs, her head on one shoulder, trapped and trapping. Like that, they fell asleep again until they were awoken by the sounds of cars drawing in and out of the drive – visitors for dinner, a few guests off to try another restaurant: the real world.

Emily knelt on the bed beside her, looked down at her.

"How do you feel, Carey? Are you okay?"

Carey reached out a hand to pull Emily back down on top of her; they kissed again, not as deeply nor for as long as before but with as much affirmation.

# Chapter Fourteen

Simon sat passively while Colin read the letter and its enclosure. Carey's brother was taking longer than he ought to have needed. Simon knew what was going on; he had no intention of making it easy for him.

Colin licked his lips: he did not want this; on the other hand, it was Carey's business, Carey's thing – it made him feel a little closer to her.

"When did this come?"

"Before the weekend."

Colin studied the man opposite. He was a stocky man, dark hair in a ponytail, wearing a neatly pressed, white suit. His skin was slightly pock-marked: enough to take the edge off an otherwise striking face. Matthew, The Teacher, was the only other Programme member Colin had met. Matthew had floated into Colin's office; this man, Simon, landed like a rock-fall.

"This isn't really our sort of thing, you know."

Simon smiled knowingly: Colin was getting to the point.

"Do you realise what it means?" Colin asked.

"More or less. Rockworth wants us out; so he's saying that we've broken the terms of the lease. He's claiming that the way we live is immoral – a course of immoral conduct. I'm not sure I follow that entirely." Simon's manner was measured, careful. This was how he was in The Programme: calm, stable, trustworthy. He used it both to sell the group to the outside world and to help junior members through their troubled times. When on private occasions he undid his ponytail – quite literally – to play his guitar, it served to reassure members that it was all right also to have fun.

"It is an odd approach, I agree. The principal point of note is that they're claiming that the breach is irremediable."

"Which means?"

"If a breach is remediable, like failure to repair, the landlord has to give you an opportunity to remedy it, in which case the lease won't be forfeit. But some kinds of breach are said to be irremediable: typically, use as a brothel – because, uh, it attaches a stigma to the premises themselves, so they say. That's what they're saying here."

"Rockworth knew what we were going to use the property for.

He even helped us get a temporary permission for the Coffee Lounge. How can he say that's a breach of the lease?"

"What they're saying is that, uh, The Programme has exploited members – uh, sexually. That's what they say is the immoral user." Colin was embarrassed: it was an image he did not want to bring to mind.

"How can they say that? On what basis? What evidence?"

"Uh, well, they've been quite clever. You see, if they said the breach was remediable, they'd, uh, have to specify what they wanted you to do to remedy it, which means they would have to be quite specific about the breaches. This way, they're making a general, unparticularised charge, and they don't have to provide any details until they issue the proceedings, not even immediately then. It buys them time and there's the chance that you might just up and leave. The way it works with a forfeiture, it's up to you to apply to court for what's called relief; if you don't apply, or if you give the action up – and of course if you lose – the tenancy has simply gone."

Matthew had warned Simon by telephone that Berlinger might be snooping around, but that was after his visit to New Orleans and before Anthony died; it would have had nothing to do with Rockworth. On the other hand, Rockworth had publicly said that he would get them out of Chesterfield Gardens: Rockworth would have heard of Berlinger – at least as a result of the Kroger business – and it was probable that he would approach the best-known contemporary deprogrammer for information and help.

"I don't know how he's going to get any evidence. I mean, well, The Programme is just not about that."

Colin set his elbows on the desk, locked his fingers, rested his chin.

"It depends how you see things. Look at Amanda Kroger. Some of the, uh, questions at court?" They could have given Rockworth the idea.

"Yes, and she denied it. There's nothing like that; if you don't believe me, you can ask your sister."

Colin winced.

"I'm not the enemy – remember? I'm, uh, well, you're approaching me as your solicitor."

"A careful choice of words?"

Colin had the grace to smile.

"Yes, well, as I said, it's not really our sort of thing."

"Carey is our solicitor," Simon reminded him, not without a hint of cruelty. "Doesn't that make you – the firm – our solicitors, too?"

"Well, strictly, unless you pay a retainer, we're only your solicitor on a case by case basis."

"What are you saying? You can't handle this for us, or you won't?"

Colin steepled his fingers.

"It's not up to me alone. I'll have to talk with my Management Committee."

"If I came in here about being evicted from a flat, would you need to consult your Management Committee before deciding to act for me?"

"Are you being evicted from a flat?" Colin asked dryly.

Simon laughed aloud, a somewhat brutal laugh.

"You and Carey are a lot alike."

"Are we?"

"In some ways. She has a dry, detached side – like you. Don't you think you're alike?"

"I don't know anymore," Colin confessed. "I used to think so. What's going on over there?" he asked suddenly. "In America, I mean."

"I don't know, I honestly don't know. If I did, I'd tell you. I know The Teacher will be all right; I know it will all work out. It's just a muddled time." Colin could hear not only the faith in Simon's voice when he referred to Matthew, The Teacher, but also the love. Irritatedly, he said:

"I'd feel happier if my sister wasn't jumping feet first into a muddle you can't even explain to me."

"But she wasn't happy here."

"No," Colin admitted. "No. Look, I'm sorry, I really am, but I do have another appointment." Simon had come in on short notice.

"And this?" Simon gestured at the letter and notice.

"This. Yes, this. Look, I'll be candid with you: our sort of firm, well, it's not the sort of publicity we're used to or, I think, many people want. They like the clear-cut issues. This, uh, suggestion – sexual abuse: there are a number of our lawyers – women – who aren't going to be happy with that. I'm sorry, but I'm not prepared to take this decision on my own."

In the back of his mind, not sure how it fit, he was also thinking of the calls from Emily's husband, making similar accusations; there had been one more a few nights ago, and a couple of suspicious hang-ups, one that he had taken and another taken by Jan whom he had finally told about Fielding.

"I understand; we're used to people turning us away. I'm surprised, though."

"Why?" Colin rose to end the interview.

"What it says about Arnotts and Carey," Simon also rose.

"That's a matter for me to think about, isn't it?"

"I was wondering what Carey would think."

Colin could not tell whether Simon was trying to blackmail him into taking the case, or whether he was indeed genuinely concerned for what he had rightly assessed Carey would see as a rejection of herself. He had still not decided what to do: to safeguard the firm by refusing to act, or to use the case to keep closer tabs on his sister.

\* \* \*

They met in the kitchen, around the long, pine table, Cassandra at its head like the chairman of the board. She demanded:

"Well, did you?"

"Yes."

Cassandra shivered: the image of Caleb and his men mounting Matthew was instantly horrifying; at the same time, her body tingled at the thought of them banging into him. She bit down hard on her lower lip.

"'Every man and every woman has a course, depending partly on the self, and partly on the environment which is natural and necessary for each.' Crowley," Caleb added unnecessarily. He was quoting Crowley more often than before; it was his principal grip on himself.

"Whose course is it, Caleb? Yours or his?"

"The same passage continues: 'Anyone who is forced from his own course, either through not understanding himself, or through external opposition, comes into conflict with the order of the Universe, and suffers accordingly'. I'd say that fit Matthew, wouldn't you?"

"Cassandra decides our course." Christopher was worried. Caleb's admission that he had taken his closest troops into the pit put them all at risk. "It's dangerous," he added aloud.

"It's all dangerous," Paimon contributed. "Anthony was dangerous – Helen more so. It's dangerous to play with fire; we've walked into the fire, arms outstretched." He was developing as The Seer's companion; soon even Caleb and Christopher would acknowledge his authority. "Without danger, there is nothing; without risk, no new ground. We are not The Programme alone. Every one of those who attended the first Special Mass belongs to us – irrevocably, indivisible, we are many and we are whole."

"Why, Caleb?" Cassandra asked.

"'Until the Great Work has been performed, it is presumptuous for the magician to pretend to understand the universe, and dictate its policy. Only the Master of the Temple can say whether any given act is a crime'. The great work has yet to be done." He was challenging her: until she was willing to perform the great work, he could do what he wanted with Matthew.

"Is it what you want, all of you?"

"Yes," Caleb said flatly. "Nothing less."

"Yes," Paimon said. "I agree."

"Yes," answered Christopher. "There is no option."

"Didn't you say, there are always choices?"

"I also said – some are easier than others."

"So be it," she said, signing her husband's death warrant. "Tonight."

\* \* \*

Emily got up first and went to the bathroom; while she was inside, Carey rose and dressed. They hardly spoke as they made their way to the restaurant for breakfast. They drank juice, coffee, ate toast in silence.

On the way back to the room, Emily asked listlessly:

"What now?"

"I thought we were going to take a look, see what we could see?"

"Yes," It was not what Emily's question meant.

Carey caught her tone.

"I don't know, Emily. There's too much going on; I can't see clearly. But I'm glad it happened. Is that enough for you? For now, I mean."

"I suppose it has to be. But I'm glad you're glad. And, sure, you're right – there's other things to sort out first."

They were on the balcony, unlocking the door to their bedroom.

Emily shut the door behind her, stood with her back to it. Carey turned around and, head askance, studied her friend. It was time for her to take control of – and responsibility for – her life again.

She smiled and crossed the few feet to Emily, cupped her face in her hands, said nothing but kissed her lips, gently, wetly, opening her mouth to insert her tongue, though only briefly. Emily put her arms around her, held her tightly.

"Okay?" Carey asked.

"Okay," Emily replied.

Before they set off across the hill and through the woods, Carey and Emily drove into Hedgerow to buy more suitable footwear and clothing for their hike, and equipment – a small knapsack, water bottle, binoculars, torch; a hunting knife too.

By midday, all their excuses were spent: it was time to go.

\* \* \*

Both Andrew Chettle and Jessica Harvey had taken seats on the Management Committee. Alison Hansen and Alistair Mathison had kept theirs, but Graham Engel and Patrick Preston had stepped down. In Carey's absence, however, Patrick attended as a substitute.

"And that's the turnover," Colin concluded his first financial report on the new partnership.

There was silence while they reviewed the figures – the primary one of interest was billable units, secondarily the breakdown between legal aid work and private.

"It's early days," Alistair said cautiously, "but there doesn't seem to be a downturn in legal aid work." They wanted a new image, but they did not want to lose the business that had been built up over the years before.

The door swung open. Colin jerked his head up: they were not to be interrupted during a Management Committee meeting. It was Charles.

"When did you get back?" Colin asked.

"This morning," Charles answered shortly, looking around. "Where's Carey?"

"She went back to America," Colin replied.

Charles looked much older than when Colin had last seen him, when he had flown to Antibes after the party with which the negotiations with Andrew Chettle and Jessica Harvey had concluded.

Andrew offered Charles his chair, pulled up another. Charles thanked him quietly, sat down before he asked:

"I thought that case was done with for the time being. That's what they said on CNN." The apartment was equipped with cable.

"We're talking about the figures, Charles," Alistair stepped in. "We should talk about Carey later."

Carey's conduct was essentially a private matter. None of them knew that Colin was going to raise The Programme; the visit from Simon had occurred too late to reach the written agenda.

Alistair handed Charles a copy of the financial report. Charles took it, held it in his hands, looked down as if reading it, but found himself staring at it blankly, a blur of figures and typeface that he could no longer relate to.

He had thought almost incessantly, about Carey while he was at the apartment, about her involvement with this so-called cult, community. The more he thought about it, the more he believed he understood it. He had flown home determined to talk it out with her, make her see herself the way he now saw her. At the beginning of the visit, it had all been about Marion – bloody woman with her bloody religion. By the end, it was his fault alone, he had failed Carey, and only he could make it right.

Colin broke the silence.

"Well, there is one thing I have to bring up about, uh, all that."

Alison grimaced: she had clients to see in another half hour.

"Go ahead." Andrew was increasingly performing the role of deputy to Colin's managing partner. Nor did he believe that Carey and The Programme could continue to be swept under the carpet.

Colin explained Simon's visit.

"On the face of it, there's no reason we shouldn't help them. We've plenty of landlord-tenant skills available. If it's going to run the distance, it should produce substantial fees; they always say there's no such thing as bad publicity. They've also been first-rate payers."

With the exception of Charles who was not interested, all of them looked down at the column containing individual billable work done: all of Carey's work would, over that period, have been for The Programme – 200 hours even at a discounted £100 each came to £20,000. Her expenses would be additional, neither profit nor product; presumably, however, a hefty loss if not reimbursed. If they alienated The Programme now, by refusing to represent the group against Rockworth, there was a risk they would have difficulty – at least delay – getting paid any of it.

"Never mind the money," Charles snarled. "The real question is, why shouldn't we act for these people? Rockworth's a bully: he's always been a bully," he added as if he knew him personally. "He's using his power to punish these people – for what? Because he had a half-crazy son no one could control?" The background had not escaped the press. "So he washes his hands of him, hands him over to these people, complains when they don't have any the more success."

"As a matter of fact, they did," Alistair said quietly.

No one had realised that Alistair knew anything about The Programme – or about Rockworth.

"I've been following the stories – asking around, too."

Charles stretched out a hand and gripped his oldest partner's forearm to thank him. Alistair had used his concern constructively.

"What did you mean?" Alison asked in spite of herself.

"The boy was bad; if he'd been anyone else, he would have been sent to a detention centre – or some other kind of institution – probably before puberty. He was a vicious, violent child. Rockworth seems to have done little to try to cure him, mostly just to protect him from the consequences. Putting the boy into The Programme appears to have been quite effective, oddly enough."

"Still, he hanged himself," Charles said grimly. It was the greatest, the unspoken fear: that Carey was so far out of control, she too could end up taking her own life.

"Better himself than someone else."

"I can hardly believe you said that, Alistair," Alison shuddered.

Jessica exchanged a glance first with Andrew, then Patrick: this was not a discussion into which to step carelessly, if at all.

Colin caught the exchange between Jessica and Patrick. He frowned: what was that about?

"What are you saying, Alistair?" he asked. "That we ought to be helping them?"

"There's an argument in favour," Alistair admitted. " How would Carey take it otherwise?"

"That's precisely what this Simon chap said."

"Well, he's not wrong," Charles snapped.

It only needed Charles to take one side for Colin to take the other.

Alistair had seen this too many times before not to be able to read the signs. If they allowed Charles to have his way, this would not be the end of it: The Programme could come to dominate the firm and its meetings – its internal politics – for months to come, if not years. If they went with Colin, it could be contained, but Charles' anger would not be. Cautiously, he tested the force of Charles' resolve.

"On the other hand, we may be too close to this one to handle it objectively. After all," he waved a hand: the lawyer who acts for himself has a fool for a client.

"Poppycock," Charles growled. "If we're not here for one another, for family, who are we here for? You know me, Alistair. I've no time for religion, and I've no time for charlatans, and I've no time for people who don't live up to their best and put it to the greater good; but Carey's allowed herself to get involved with them and – whatever we think of it – we have to stand by her until she's back where she belongs, here at the firm. She's too good a lawyer to lose. We should act for them," he concluded.

Alistair had gone as far as he was willing, nor would Alison take against Charles on such a personal issue. If Colin wanted to argue, that was different: he was family.

"I'm not happy with that," Jessica said. She had no such inhibitions.

"Nor I," Patrick supported her.

Colin glanced at Andrew, who waved a hand airily: whatever views he held, he did not feel the need yet to express them.

"Why not?" Charles demanded. "We've acted for some pretty

strange types before now."

Jessica pursed her lips.

"I daresay, but that was, as you say, before. We've got a broader range of interests now and the same questions we're asking might have to be asked about other cases in the future. I don't mean to seem unfeeling about this, but we're in business here. I don't want my professional and financial well-being jeopardised by a careless decision. You said it, Charles: you haven't taken work on the basis of value alone; well, I've not either. On that basis, we'd take their case and their money. I don't want their case, and I don't want their money, because it's the wrong sort of client for this firm to represent and I believe it'll do long term harm. Alison – how would your union clients like it?"

The older woman nodded: Jessica was right; there was nothing so socially conservative as a trade union leader.

"I can't help wondering," Alistair challenged, "what you'd do with some of my cases?"

Jessica flushed: it was not tactically smart to take on Mathison nor was it what she meant: criminal law was in a class of its own.

"Everyone understands that people need a defence." Patrick came again to her assistance. "However bad the crime, people understand that the criminal has to be represented."

"These people don't need to be represented?" Charles thundered. "They can take on Rockworth's lawyers with what – a prayer and a chant?"

"What I see is that this is the most divisive issue we've yet had to confront," Andrew at last declared himself. "We're not hard up for work. Especially with Carey away, we're even under-resourced. I suggest that's what we tell The Programme: that with Carey away, we don't have the resources to handle it."

Without Colin, they were tied: the three older – more tolerant – members willing to work with The Programme, the three younger ones not. Colin said nonchalantly:

"I'll let them know we can't help them on this occasion."

It was his turn to win.

Angrily, Charles rose and stomped from the room, slamming the door behind him, shouting, as if it made sense:

"This isn't what I came back for."

* * *

Cassandra did not visit Matthew until late afternoon. She did not want a long break between parting and ending.

336

He was in better shape than she had expected. He had found a cache of inner resources, conserving the nourishment she had brought him to spread across the hours between her visits, releasing it in even doses.

As before, she brought him juice, fruit and the facilities with which to wash him down; as before, they did not begin talking until after she had cleaned him up and he had eaten.

She loosened the strap across the back of his neck.

"Here, use this," she said.

She had brought mouthwash too.

He swilled it around his desiccated mouth, spat it onto the ground beside her, gestured for more and repeated the exercise.

"Good," he said when he was finished. "Good."

Settling herself on the ground, she laughed.

"You've still got it, Matthew. Nothing ever touches you. It's what's always made you so special, that unique ability to rise above everything around you, even if it's happening to you. It's what makes people believe in you. They're in awe of it and when you make yourself available to them, you make it available to them: they feel they can rise above their own conditions by latching onto you. Look at you now: you're as Christ-like as ever."

"They killed Christ; they only buggered me," he retorted. "If Christ could rise above his own death, we too have to be able to rise above anything."

She reached out, stroked his cheek.

"But you're not Christ, darling. There's the difference. When you're cut, you bleed."

"When I'm killed, I'm dead?"

"Right," she giggled her high-pitched giggle. "That's right."

She leaned in, licked his dry lips, kissed them, stroked his long hair, normally fine but now matted with dirt, knotted it around her fingers. She knelt upright, shrugged her arms out of her shift and pulled it down until her breasts were free. She placed a breast against his mouth, forced the hard nipple between his lips, pushing it in and out like a tiny penis until he began to respond, sucking on it like a lover, like a child.

She did the same with the other breast, alternated between them, humming, forcing more and more of herself into his mouth, cramming each heavy breast inside until his mouth was as wide open as he could make it and his teeth were biting into her, marking her. One of her hands was between her legs, she rubbed herself, came with tiny controlled shrieks of glee, spiteful and vengeful, she had fucked him one last time.

She rested herself back on the ground, not covering herself up.

"We were always good together, weren't we, Matthew? I don't want you ever to think, ever," she stressed, her voice shrill, "never think you haven't meant a great deal to me, for a time everything. You've been the biggest, best influence, a great love, the most exciting, joyful adventure of all. Just because I've moved on doesn't mean it wasn't real; I can still taste every second of it," she licked her lips for emphasis. "From the day I set eyes on you to now: it doesn't matter what we were doing, if we were doing it together or with someone else, you've been there for me, at the centre of it all, and it's been, oh…" She squeezed her eyes shut as she sought the words. "Oh, magnificent – like being married to God. I love you, Matthew – don't you forget it," she instructed him fiercely.

"And that's why?"

"Why what? This – tonight?" She admitted the end was imminent.

"Yes."

"Sure, yes, of course. It has to be, don't you see? I can't take you with me where I'm going. This is the only way to seal our love, the only way to keep it whole – whole and perfect and complete, the only way to keep it alive really, in a funny sort of way. You do understand, don't you?"

Apart but alive, she would grow a new life that had nothing to do with him. In time, it would erode the old, eating up the emotional energy needed to keep it alive, in due course the old life would fade until it was little more than memory and distant shadow. Killing him now would imprison it, allow her to hold onto it eternally. He had never suffered the same difficulty – he could keep them all and equally alive; she was as jealous of that ability as of his others; it would die with him.

"The others – do they want to keep their memories of me whole?"

"No: you know what that's about." To be finally free of him, to cut him down to size, to kill him and to be certain that he did not arise.

"Well, then," he said.

"Well what?"

"You're not doing it with the same purpose. What is not shared is divided."

"Maybe. The Programme's different now. It shares at a different level than you're used to. We can share the act, while it means something different to each of us. That's what The Programme is about now: action, not words."

Matthew chuckled.

"Why are you laughing?"

"Because it is funny. Don't you think so? We take an idea, a group of people – find a way for us all to live together – form it into a community that yet more people can join – we raise money, acquire property, grow until we are on both sides of the Atlantic – hundreds of people living and breathing as The Programme." He paused: it was still not easy to talk.

"And?" She was eager to hear what was funny.

"And what it all comes down to, in the end, is a cheap little drama – sex games, rituals maybe?" That was a guess, but an educated guess – he knew Caleb. "Murder in a jealous rage."

"Did you realise – when you came here – that it was beyond recall?"

"Pretty much, yes."

"Then why did you come?"

"What were my choices, Cassandra? I built The Programme – not you. Was I supposed to leave it, leave Helen, leave everyone? It was my duty to come back, whatever that meant."

"Good old American duty. I'd almost forgotten you were a soldier."

"I hadn't," Matthew said. "I've been thinking about those times – looking at those guns, I suppose. Some sort of full circle."

"It doesn't have to go round and round: that's what The Programme is about, isn't it? Breaking out; the fire beyond that prevents us coming back to the same old same old cycle."

"That's what The Programme was supposed to be about," he corrected her. "Getting it right, doing it right; just the once but for always."

"Ah, you've lost your faith, " she said, genuinely sad for him.

"No, I've not lost my faith. But one of us has lost the way."

"Us? You or me?"

"I or The Programme." He met her gaze. "You're not The Programme, Cass. You're not; they're not; I am. Kill me, you kill The Programme."

* * *

They managed to get lost a couple of times, but eventually they found their way through the forest overlooking Hammer Reach. It was already approaching dusk; they would not be able to see in another hour. Nervous but determined, Carey led them to the edge of the trees, pausing occasionally to listen for other people. Using the binoculars they had bought in town, she swept the farm, focusing on the deserted porch, beginning to wonder if anyone was there at all until she caught sight – between the barns and the farmhouse – of a small group working out and marching.

As she turned back to the farmhouse, she spotted Cassandra emerging from the larger barn – the one they called the Meditation Hall – alone, slipping a padlock into the hasp of the doors. It was odd for Cassandra to be alone; more so to have been alone in that particular building; most so, for the building to be locked. There was a dormitory on the upper floor: members would need access to it and it should therefore be left unlocked. The lawyer in her computed: more likely, something was locked in – someone.

A short while later, she secured some confirmation when the work-out group dispersed not into the Meditation Hall but into the second of the barns, which – when Carey was last at Hammer Reach – had been used for animals, not members. She swung her binoculars to the third and smallest out-building: a fenced-corral had been put up around it, enclosing its door; hay; dung. The dormitory, she concluded, had been moved into the second barn.

Not long after, Cassandra came out onto the farmhouse deck, accompanied by Paimon and Christopher. Finally, they were joined by Caleb. They sat comfortably, smoking and laughing.

"What do you think?" Emily whispered in her ear.

Carey turned to answer: their mouths were only inches apart but sex could not have been further from her mind. They were soldiers now: not soldiers in the army of God and Satan but soldiers of The Programme, Matthew's troops.

"There's not much happening. That's unusual. No work on The Temple, look there, you can see where it's being built." She handed Emily the binoculars, pointing in the general direction. "Also, there aren't many people here: that's significant. There were a few people doing something – some sort of exercise; but less than ten – that's a very small group. He's here," she concluded. "I'm certain of it; he's here and they're keeping him a prisoner. It's the only thing that makes any sense."

"Where? In the punishment cells?"

"I don't think so. This is The Teacher, remember. If they're holding Matthew prisoner, they won't want to run the risk of ordinary members finding out about it. Look at the larger of the barns: you can see the door; it's got a padlock on it. Cassandra came out of there, on her own, locked it behind her. I'm not sure, I could be wrong, but I think he's in there."

Emily put down the binoculars, her brow furrowed as she tried to remember something Matthew had told her.

"Something about a pit in one of the barns. I don't know what he meant, he didn't know what it meant."

"It doesn't have to mean anything," Carey shuddered, banishing the association between pit and grave.

"What now?"

"Now we wait," Carey decided. "We wait until it's dark." They would have to wait longer than dark – until the members sleeping in the second barn were asleep.

Emily glanced about them, shivered: she did not like the idea of staying out there in the night – she was not a country girl.

Carey laughed, put an arm around her shoulders.

"There aren't any snakes in this part of the world."

"How do you know?"

"I don't. But I'm going to believe it until something tells me different."

"What are we going to do when it's dark?" Emily asked.

"I'm going to go down and take a look," Carey said. "You're going to wait here, in case anything happens. So you can go for help."

Carey was the leader, it was her job to protect Emily.

"Like hell," Emily whispered. "Not as long as you're only guessing about snakes."

Carey smiled and turned back to watch Cassandra and her cohorts on the porch at Hammer Reach: what were they up to?

\* \* \*

Colin worked late: he had lost too much of the day on Simon and on the Management Committee; before he could change his mind or have it changed for him, he had written to Simon returning the top copy of the letter and notice, explaining that they could not act. Though he included the agreed line that, in Carey's absence, they did not have the resources to handle the case, he did not think that Simon would be fooled.

It was after eight when he dictated his last letter of the day. He was working slowly, attention constantly distracted by Carey. He had rung home, told Jan not to hold dinner; his family would not do a better job of putting her out of his mind.

He wandered towards Jessica's room. The light was on and the door was open. As he approached, he heard Patrick saying goodnight to her, something else Colin did not catch, a light laugh. Without knowing why he did so, he held back from the final corner in the corridor to give Patrick time to leave; his heart was beating; he wanted to be alone with her.

"Hi, working late?"

It was what they all said to one another when they popped around towards the end of the day, when the support staff had all left and the last lawyer in the office had to lock up for the night.

"Just finishing up. You're late." Colin – the family man – was not often amongst the last to leave.

"You wouldn't, uh, I suppose, fancy a drink? A bite to eat?"

"No," Jessica replied without thinking about it. "No, thank you," she said, to soften her answer. "Shouldn't you be getting home?" She reminded him where he belonged.

He sighed, lowered himself into a chair across from her.

"Should, shouldn't. They'll have eaten without me. Sometimes," he admitted, "it can be difficult to make the switch."

"Not a problem I have," she said dryly.

He studied her for a moment, then smiled nervously.

"That's ambiguous."

"Is it? How so?"

"It could mean because, there's no one else; or because there is, but he's on the same wavelength." He felt himself redden as he spoke.

"It isn't really any of your business, is it?"

He mumbled an apology.

"But since we're dealing in ambiguities, what is it you want to know?"

"All right – I had a feeling you and Patrick were somewhat lining up in the meeting today. What was that about?"

"Lining up? That's a bit paranoid, isn't it? Couldn't we just happen to agree?"

"It's odd, though; Patrick and Carey, well, you know – I told you when you asked. I suppose I expected him to, uh, stand by her regardless. He always has in the past."

"You decided against," she reminded him.

"I'm not complaining about the outcome."

"Just the means?"

"Something like that."

"And the complaint is?"

"Am I being cross-examined?"

"I think perhaps – yes. You seem to have chosen to go into the witness box."

"I didn't think that was what I was doing," he complained.

"Or just didn't think?"

The words were hard and fast; the atmosphere more relaxed than they suggested; it was as if they were burning up spare fuel before landing.

"I didn't think Patrick would fail to support her."

"I think, perhaps, Patrick and Carey reached some sort of resolution while she was over," Jessica conceded.

"She hardly had time to reach the office, never mind a resolution with Patrick."

"What is it you really want to know, Colin?"

He did not answer.

In the end, fiddling with her pen, suspecting he would not leave until he had what he wanted, she continued:

"I think perhaps that Patrick has come around to the same sort of view as mine."

"Meaning?" Colin asked stiffly.

"I think I used the word spoiled, didn't I? Immature?"

"Is that what that was all about? You wouldn't help The Programme because you think Carey's spoiled?"

"No, of course not. We didn't want to act for them for the same reasons as you and Andrew; at least, I didn't; I can't speak for Patrick. You know how these things go: they always come to a head on the back of something completely different, even irrelevant."

"I suppose, what I really wanted to know," he was tired of pretending. "What I'm more interested in is why Patrick's changed his view of Carey – now, suddenly, after all this time?"

"I'm trying to think what someone in The Programme – or some group like it – would say. How about this? 'Just because people can run five miles doesn't mean they can run ten'. Will that do for a bit of instant philosophy?"

"Not bad."

"It isn't what you meant, is it?"

He shook his head.

"What you're asking is if there's something between me and Patrick, right?"

He nodded glumly.

"Funny – Patrick says Carey asked him the same thing."

"I'm sorry." Colin no longer wanted the answer. She was right: it was not his business; and, it was beginning to look as if it would be the answer he did not want to hear. "Forget I asked."

"Oh, come on," she protested. "That's hardly likely – or fair, is it?"

Colin rose, picked up his briefcase to leave.

"I'm sorry," he repeated. "This whole business with Carey has turned me upside down"

"Patrick's a nice guy; he's easy to talk to. He's just a friend."

"Thank you," he said automatically. "I still like talking to you," he added, referring back to their last personal conversation, at the gym.

"Feel free," she said kindly, meaning it.

It was enough to keep alive an inconsequential fantasy.

* * *

Without the hunting knife, they might not have been able to get into the barn. Their first instinct was to go in through the door. It was on the opposite side of the barn from the farmhouse, which was why they had been able to see Cassandra locking it from the forest. Carey thought they could jab away at the wood to which the hasp was fixed until the screws were loose enough to pull free. She was just about to begin when she said:

"If anyone comes, they'll know we're inside."

"Shit." Emily breathed out.

They walked along the side of the barn, avoiding being seen both from the farmhouse and from the second barn: there were windows to the upper floor, but if they broke the glass it would be heard from the house.

"There," Carey pointed to a stack of thick timber planks, designated for use on The Temple.

They stood – sweating despite the cold – working out how to do it. Then they hefted half a dozen eight foot lengths and laid them in a stepped ramp against the wall. Carey still needed to stand on Emily's shoulders to reach the window-frame, hacking away at it until she could insert the knife to work the handle loose.

There was neither light nor sound within. Carey hauled herself up and crawled inside. Emily handed up the torch they had bought in Hedgerow that morning. Carey checked quickly around before she leaned out to help haul her friend into the building.

For a few moments, they caught the giggles: cops and robbers.

Had it not been for Matthew's reference to a pit, upstairs was where they would have begun the search. There were two long halls, each with open cubicles down both sides – four rows of cubicles in all. The ends of both halls opened into a common washroom; there were timetables on each of the doors with separate hours for Brothers and Sisters.

They found the stairs at the front of the barn and stepped carefully down to the ground floor where they stood with their backs to the wall, breathing deeply, adjusting to the dark. After a few minutes, they realised that the only sound they could hear was the uneven rasp of their own nervous, smokers' breaths.

There were no separate rooms on the ground floor – just the Meditation Hall with painted walls and floor, and a few stalls like Coffee Lounge booths.

"What now?" Emily whispered.

"Where's this pit?"

"I don't know." There was no sign of it.

Carey paced the sides of the Hall, playing the torch into the stalls, finding nothing apart from cushions and cloths. She swept the torch back and forth across the main floor until finally she brought it to rest on the painted symbol of The Programme within a circle in the middle. The circle was what deceived the eye: in its turn, it was within a square. As soon as she could see the square, she could also see that it was made up of four sections, painted elsewhere and not laid in place until it was finished.

"Give me your lighter," Carey told Emily.

She played the flame along the line: there was a flicker where the air passed into the pit.

Now they could see marks where sections of flooring had been removed, where knives or other implements had been inserted to lift them up. Carey stuck the hunting knife into a groove in the section nearest to the barn doors: it took very little effort to lift it far enough to push the knife beneath the section, then her hand.

When Emily, holding the torch, first shone it into the pit, they thought they had been mistaken: there was nothing there to see except a pile of something or other in the middle, and a box or another pile in a far corner beneath another section. Gradually, they made out the form in the centre.

"Oh God," Carey cried. "Oh Matthew, what have they done to you?"

\* \* \*

Caleb came into the barn singing an ancient Hymn to Pan:

"'Thrill with lissom lust of the light,
"'O man! My man!
"'Come careering out of the night
"'Of Pan! Io Pan!
"'Give me the sign of the Open Eye,
"'And the token erect of thorny thigh,

"'And the word of madness and mystery,

"'O Pan! Io Pan!'"

He was wearing a shift, sandals, The Programme symbol around his neck, carrying a large bag – candles, oil, cushions and cloths – and a knife with which he had lifted the section of floor nearest to the barn doors. He shoved the section itself over to one side and stepped out of his sandals, pulling the shift over his head before he dropped the four feet into the pit.

"Oh, Matthew, yo Matthew," he called. "Here am I, Matthew."

He chuckled: Matthew was hardly breathing; his body was still, just enough movement for Caleb to be satisfied he had not cheated him by expiring before the next and ultimate Special Mass.

He had ten or fifteen minutes alone with Matthew before the others arrived. He licked his lips: he told himself he did not need to do this again, at the same time as he knew he would; his penis was rising, the ache began, when he touched himself it felt like metal sheathed in silk.

He put down the bag and ferreted in it for the oil: this was a scented massage oil, not the rough gun oil he had used before. This was his treat. This time it would be with love. Matthew had to be turned over for the Mass, to face them; he would turn him over without awaiting the others – Matthew had no strength left, there was no risk. Then he would tie his arms down, lift his legs, take him from the front, covering his face with his kisses, his mouth. He was so excited, he almost came as he stood there.

He crouched around the altar, knelt in front of Matthew. Matthew's eyes and mouth were both shut. He was unconscious. Caleb reached out to undo the strap across his neck.

Before he could touch the strap, something cold was in his chin, cold and hard: a gun. Matthew – swift as a snake – had a gun beneath his chin, pointing it up into his head. The straps had been undone but left lying in place. Matthew slithered off the altar and forced Caleb backwards until he fell onto the ground.

Caleb giggled in awe.

"God, I love you, Matthew."

"I can see that," Matthew hissed, gesturing with the gun at Caleb's penis locked in erection.

"You're not going to use it, Matthew," Caleb said of the gun. "You can't; it's mine."

"When will the others be here?"

"In time for midnight, when else?"

Matthew dropped his knees to Caleb's scrotum. Caleb screamed.

346

"What did you do that for?" he cried.

"It was beginning to annoy me," Matthew said, removing his knee: Caleb's erection had gone. He straddled Caleb, the gun still at his face.

Carey and Emily emerged from behind the gun-trunk where they had been crouched in hiding. Carey said:

"We should get out of here, Matthew."

"No. I'm not going. You go; if you want to, you go."

"You don't know how many there'll be, Matthew," Emily urged.

"Four – including Caleb, just four." He had sensed Cassandra's anger when she learned that others had been down into the pit to use him.

"What are you going to do?" Carey whispered.

"You'll see," Matthew said grimly. "Are you going to stay?"

There was no question of leaving. He had told them about Helen and what had been done to her; he had told them what Caleb had done to him. Huddled behind the trunk, they had listened to him in horror, in tears, shame too, as if – because it had happened in The Programme – they were also to blame. They could not expect him to walk away and they could not walk away without him.

Matthew ordered them to hide again. While they weren't looking, he struck Caleb once, across the chin, enough to stun him for a few moments but not to knock him out for long. He dragged Caleb quickly up onto the altar, face down, and had the first strap across him before he began to come around: once one was in place, the others were easy. Then he gagged him.

Matthew had not attended a Special Mass, but it was not difficult to imagine how it would be set up. He placed candles at the head, foot and sides of the altar, lit them, cushions at a distance behind each. Then he settled himself in the dark, next to the trunk of guns.

He was ready just in time. He heard the barn door bang as they pulled it shut behind them. The candles in the pit flickered confusedly. He sat on a cushion in the darkest part of the pit, cross-legged, head bowed, watching as Paimon and Christopher dropped naked into the pit.

"I am one, Caleb," Christopher said.

Paimon started to speak.

Cassandra lowered herself at a corner of the open section, one hand on each edge, still fully dressed.

She recognised him instantly.

"Matthew," she screamed, pushing herself back up with a strength bred of pure panic.

Matthew came half to his feet, gun pointed.

It was too late to follow Cassandra: the barn door flew back, banged against the outside wall, she was gone.

Matthew reached forward and jerked the gag out of Caleb's mouth with his free hand but left him strapped down.

Christopher said:

"Teacher, we can work this out."

"You can't kill us all, Matthew," Paimon said.

Caleb said, head raised, grinning crookedly at Matthew:

"He won't shoot anyone. He's The Teacher; he's our father. Father's back in command – father knows best – father's going to punish us – fathers don't kill their children, right, Matthew?"

Matthew could hear Phillipe's prophecy, as if the Voodoo man was standing at his shoulder:

"If you're facing evil, Matthew, evil is what you'll have to do to defeat it. Remember that, Matthew – Teacher."

"You've forgotten something, Caleb. While you were in prison learning how to rape, I was in the army."

With military precision, Matthew shot him once between the eyes. Caleb did not even have time to blink.

# Chapter Fifteen

"This must all stop!" Matthew raged.

They were gathered around the pit in the Meditation Hall barn: The Teacher and Father Nahum, Carey and Emily, Sisters Diana and Pascale, a half-dozen others who had been kept at Hammer Reach to serve. Of those who had stayed during what was intended to have been Matthew's final days, only Brothers Reuben, Lemuel and Ehud were under lock in the cells. In addition, the two children – Tamar and Thomas – were present. Nahum had brought them with him from New York.

Matthew, Nahum, Carey and Emily were washed and had dressed in the cleanest white clothing they could find: likewise, the children were in their Meditation best. The others wore simple shifts, or grubby T-shirts and shorts, working gear – the nearest thing to hand when finally they were let out of their dormitory and brought to this barn.

The altar was burning in the pit: Matthew had sprinkled it with the gas used to fuel the cement-mixer; flames cackled at them, licking at the sides and the supports of the pit. There was no sign of the guns: Matthew had dug into an open side of the pit and buried the trunk deeply within it; he planned to fill in the pit, but if it was opened up, they would dig downwards not out to the sides. Paimon, Christopher, Caleb, Cassandra – likewise gone.

"They planned to tell you that I, I who created The Programme, I who built it idea by idea, member by member, vision by vision, would abandon you," Matthew screamed: "That I – I, The Teacher – would desert you and leave you to wallow in your ignorant experiments; and you were ready to believe them.

"Listen to the Bible! 'Ye have wearied the Lord with your words' – Malachi 2! 'Wherein have we wearied him?' You ask. By saying, 'Everyone that doeth evil is good in the sight of the Lord, and he delighteth in them.' There never was a time for evil in The Programme: we recognised evil but we did not do it! Who are you – who are you all? How dare you defile The Programme, how dare you play such games in my name, mine?

"This must all stop! This must all stop now!" he roared. "I know what has been going on here! I have been forced to bury my head in the dirt and taste it for myself! They kept me in this pit, like an animal, so they could play foul, decadent games with each other, even with me! Even with your Teacher! They did unspeakable things to me – to The Teacher!"

Carey, listening, was surprised: she would have expected him to keep the abuse secret. Matthew was using it, wearing it like a badge, a badge that read: you cannot touch me; not even this can touch me; there is nothing from which I cannot arise; I am one, and only I am whole. "Thou art a teacher come from God: for no man can do these miracles that thou doest, except God be with him": John 3:2.

Yet it had touched him and the wounds would take time to heal. It was her task to help him heal – hers alone.

"You," Matthew thundered, "you and you and you! Look me in the eye and tell me that this was what you came into The Programme for! You, Diana," he bellowed, "tell me what you have done! Be rid of it!"

Diana dropped to her knees, head bowed.

"I was weak," she cried. "Forgive me, Teacher." Forgive me, Father.

"Sex," Matthew ranted. "You had your head turned by sex – you Diana, blessed by beauty, had your head turned by sex! And at the moment they were bored with you, they would have abandoned you!

"I am telling you this, that there will be an end to it now! If sex and The Programme are incompatible, then it is sex that we will abandon, not The Programme! This is the new order! Until we find the way back, let us all pay the price for their deviance! Get up, Diana, get up."

Hurriedly, she scrambled to her feet.

"You, Pascale, what filth did you enact? What was your purpose?"

He knew it all by now, had guessed what Cassandra meant by a Special Mass and ordered the details out of Diana. They all had to know about it, to share in it so that their energy as a whole could be brought to bear on it. They had to place it on the pyre and pledge it to the fire beyond.

Pascale was shaking with fear and shame – and hatred for Caleb who had led her into it and who had now abandoned her. She moaned:

"There were guns, Teacher. I," she stumbled on her words and physically wavered but no one came to her aid, "I had sex with a man – for guns. Caleb's guns," she added.

"The guns are gone," Matthew told her. "Gone with Caleb, gone with your innocence, gone with the love you gave The Programme all the years since you joined and that The Programme gave you – that you traded for guns," his voice rose to a near scream. "You traded my love for guns," he howled in fury, thrusting his hands in the air, clenched into fists.

"Oh, God," she groaned clutching her stomach, sinking to her knees as Diana had done. "Oh, God, forgive me."

"I forgive you? I cannot forgive you: you can only forgive yourselves, redeem yourselves, cleanse yourselves – as I have to forgive myself and redeem and cleanse myself of what you have done in my name."

He looked around the few of them: they were enough to make a start; he would use them to recover those who were still at the Chapters in New York and Boston – and he would bring others over from London who were untainted by it all – and he would grow anew, with fresh people, fresh blood, clean flesh, until this abomination was not even a memory.

"This pit," he raved, "it is to be filled in as if it had never been here. I want it full, tightly packed until there is no trace of it. Put out the fire with earth! Fill it, pack it, cement it over and stamp the floor back into place while the cement is still wet so it can set and no one can ever know what took place here! I want it destroyed: this is my challenge – destroy the hole, fill the vacuum. Father Nahum will lead you. Do it, do it now! All of you!"

The pit was to exist no more, for any of them but himself.

Matthew nodded once at Nahum, raised his arm like a platoon leader and led Carey and Emily from the barn: in turn, as they passed them, they each reached out a hand for one of the children; thus, in procession, Matthew, his women, his children.

Behind them, Nahum began to direct the members, men and women alike, to the edge of the field where the soil that had been dug up from the pit had been taken and spread, to dig it up again and bring it home in wheelbarrows, buckets, cement sacks or even by the shovel-load.

They went to the task with more than enthusiasm, they went to it with joy: it was less punishment than they deserved but it was time for the healing process to begin; if The Teacher was willing to allow it to begin, then one day he would allow it to be complete.

\* \* \*

By the time he got to the farmhouse, she had gone.

They lost time gagging Christopher and Paimon and securing them with the straps that had held first Matthew then Caleb. Carey helped, but Emily was in a daze. Matthew made them wait in the barn while – throwing on a shift – he followed Cassandra. He took

351

with him the gun with which he had surprised then shot Caleb: he did not know how many were at the farmhouse or how involved they were in recent events.

Carey and Emily waited in the barn proper, not in the pit with Christopher, Paimon and Caleb's body. The two men had been tied to the sides of the altar, Caleb's body between them. As she hustled Emily out of the pit, Carey turned to look at Christopher: Paimon was out of her line of vision. He had nothing to do with the cold but distinguished Superior she had met in London months ago. Their eyes met: she saw fear, he saw ice; reversal of roles.

Emily crouched in a corner of the vast barn, hugging herself. She was shaking, sobbing. Carey put her arms around her, rocked her gently, kissed her hair, her face, whispered:

"Husht now, husht; it's going to be all right."

"Oh, God, Carey, what's going to happen?"

She finally calmed down enough for Carey to let go of her. For the first time since they came down from the forest, it was safe to smoke.

"What Matthew did – no court in the world would convict him. I doubt anyone would charge him. He didn't know if they were outside, if there was time to get away. They had guns, Emily. Where would we have run to? They would have followed us, shot us."

Emily licked her dry lips. wanting to believe it; Carey was Matthew's lawyer again, hers too; the ten minutes or so between seizing Caleb and killing him – and the fact that he had been tied up at the time he was shot – were now mere detail.

"Waiting was the only thing Matthew could have done."

"But he shot him, Carey," Emily reminded her, still distressed.

"Yes," Carey had said flatly. "He did."

"I can't help it," she sobbed. "I know you're right; I can't stop seeing Caleb's eyes, just the moment before, as if he knew."

Carey stubbed her cigarette on the ground. She wished Emily would be quiet: she needed the time to sort her own head out. She knew that a life-changing event had taken place – irreversible – something even more significant than she had been looking for, an epiphany she had either to run from or to embrace as her fate; she would have liked a short while to make the choice for herself, though in her heart she knew that the choices had already been made for her.

"Listen to me, Em. We have to help Matthew get everything back together. We're the only ones who he can trust – here and now. He's been through a terrible time – even Matthew has to have been affected."

"Why can't he just, you know, why can't we all just get away from here? Leave it? For God's sake, Carey: The Programme's finished."

"He can't just walk away: there's too much to clear up. There are going to be questions: about Caleb, about Helen – they'll re-open their questions about Anthony. That's three dead, Em; it's going to be all over the news. Whether or not The Programme's finished, Matthew's not, and there's a huge number of members who are not."

"I don't care about them," she pouted.

"No, but he does." For reasons she could not explain, so also did she, as if her responsibility for The Programme extended far beyond her legal work, and many years back. She seemed to have inherited the responsibilities of his former partners – Cassandra who had betrayed him and Helen who had been killed for him alike.

She drew Emily close and pulled her head to rest on her breast.

"We can't run away, Em; he needs us."

"I know," Emily murmured.

"And I need you," Carey admitted.

"I know that too."

* * *

Matthew had reappeared in the doorway of the barn. He was still carrying the gun.

"She's gone," he announced.

"Where?" Carey rose to her feet.

"I don't know. She's taken the car, the Lincoln."

"Who's in the house?"

"Diana. That's all. There's a dormitory in the other barn: she says the rest are there. I don't think they would have heard anything."

It was unlikely that they would have: the barn door had been shut, the shot had been in a covered section of the pit.

"Where's Diana now?"

"I put her in a cell. I rang Nahum – he's on his way up."

"Alone?"

"No. I told him to bring the children."

"The children? Why?" It seemed such a shocking thing to do – to bring children into this place of death and decadent abuse.

"Micah's in New York; Hannah's in Boston."

"So?" Carey stopped, understood: they were perfect hostages.

"I rang Simon too. He'll ring Hannah." Secure her support in Boston. "Simon's flying over."

Simon had hurriedly filled Matthew in on the Rockworth notice – and on Arnotts' refusal to help. It was not something Matthew would tell Carey straight away – there had been enough shock for one night.

"Where will she go?" Carey asked. She: Cassandra.

"Boston or New York, I should think. After that, I'm not sure. Not the police," he added. "Are you all right?" He meant both of them: Emily was still seated, eyes vacant; she had said nothing.

"We're okay," Carey answered, glancing at her friend.

Matthew helped Emily to her feet, put one arm around her, another around Carey.

"I want you to go back to the house. Make sure Diana's all right: don't let her out yet, but see if she needs anything. If anyone comes in from the barn, send them back there."

"What should we tell them?"

"Tell them Cassandra's gone, and that the others have gone, and that The Teacher is back. That's all they need to know. I'll be in soon."

"What are you going to do, Matthew?"

"I don't know. I really don't know." His eyes told a different story.

"What happened down there, Matthew – it was horrible, awful; but I understand and I can cope with it."

"And?"

Carey shivered, a cold sweat.

"I don't know," she admitted.

"You don't have to, do you?" She did not have to know, did not have to cope.

"I suppose not," she replied slowly, dry-mouthed.

Emily looked from one to another. She knew what they were saying but she had no part in it. She had been the link between them after Carey returned to England. She felt shut out, redundant. She did not want to lose either of them.

Carey smiled at her, a strange, detached smile, as if to say – not now, deal with it later. Emily pushed away the fear that later would be too late, jerked her head towards the door: let's go.

Matthew watched them leave. He always had good luck. He knew now that it would never desert him. Carey was a part of it; she would not desert him either.

He stood at the barn door. Nahum would arrive in less than three hours. He loved Nahum and trusted him, but this was something he needed to do for himself. He walked around Nahum's half-built Temple and grabbed the shovel standing against the body of the cement-mixer. He stood at the head of The Temple where Caleb had said Helen was buried.

He set to work digging holes at the tips of the other three segments of The Programme symbol in the shape of which The Temple was being constructed with concrete pillars and double-thickness wooden walls: once concreted over, they would form additional support for the structure, unsuspicious and unlikely to be uncovered by accident.

He dug with the strength of a soldier, not a man possessed but a man with no choice. He wanted neither sleep nor food or drink, merely to fulfil his purpose. Their time was past; the sooner it was buried, the sooner he could begin to rebuild The Programme.

\* \* \*

Http://www.the-programme.org.uk (turn on sound card if available).

*Enemies do not exist in order to attack you, nor even to kill you. Death is freedom – an enemy does not liberate. Enemies exist to keep you in their place, to drink your blood and to eat your flesh until they have swallowed whole your soul.*

*Isaiah 63: "Who is this that cometh from Edom, with dyed garments from Bozrah? This that is glorious in his apparel, travelling in the greatness of his strength? I that speak in righteousness, mighty to save," came the reply. Then the questioner asked: "Wherefore art thou red in thine apparel, and thy garments like him that treadeth in the winefat?" And the answer: "I have trodden the winepress alone; and of the people there was none with me. For I will tread them in mine anger, and trample them in my fury; and their blood shall be sprinkled upon my garments, and I will stain all my raiment. For the day of vengeance is in my heart, and the year of my redeemed is come... And I will tread down the people in mine anger, and make them drunk in my fury, and I will bring down their strength to the earth."*

*I am The Teacher. Those who tried me failed. They are gone – my captors, my tormentors, my enemies. They have fled because they know that as The Programme moves forward to the final freedom, there is no room on the journey for the flawed and the impure. They cannot bear to watch as we depart on the voyage they have forfeit the right to join. The only question that needs to be asked is whether you are with us or whether you are not.*

*The conclusion of the turmoil that has been The Programme these last weeks and months is that, for all but the few, there has been no difficulty answering – we are with The Programme, we are with you. I in my turn shall take you with me.*

\* \* \*

"He buggered me."

"Matthew, we didn't know anything about that," Christopher lied.

"Christopher, I'll decide what you knew."

"It's out of hand," Paimon whined. "I don't know what's happening any more."

"Did you ever?" Matthew tickled Paimon's chin with the gun.

"Oh, man," Paimon moaned. "You know what she's like, for God's sake. None of us ever stood a chance."

"Oh, brother-in-law," Matthew mimicked cruelly, "I gave you nothing but chances."

"Matthew, we're out of here," Christopher reassured him. "You won; you know, you won. Isn't that enough?"

* * *

Cassandra drove like a fiend. She needed to get help, support. Nahum was in New York, so she headed for Boston. Several of the favoured members were there: Gloria, Mary, the two Jays, Lee. She had time to grab only a handful of clothes, her purse, the keys to the Lincoln.

She felt like a fugitive: she was running from wrath and revenge; her head spun with fear for Paimon. She was exhausted; she needed coffee; the car was running low on petrol – gas. A few more miles and she saw the lights of a fuel and food stop: Burger King. She grimaced but it would have to do. She paid for the fuel with a credit card: she needed to get to a cash machine, withdraw as much as she could before Matthew put a stop on the account; she did not have access to Christopher's hidden accounts, only to the main Boston account of The Programme in Matthew's name. She also paid for her food with the card: hold onto the little hard money she still had.

She did not hate Matthew; she envied him. She had recognised him so quickly not only because he was her husband and she would have known him anywhere, but because, as she had joined the others in the pit for the Special Mass that was to end his life, a small part of her still believed that he would survive it, rise up in the way the others wanted the Mass to prove he could not – exactly as he had.

Rescue had simply not occurred to her: it was not Nahum's style, she knew that Simon was in London, she believed Matthew when he told her that the women had gone back to England. The only members of The Programme who would have been capable of it belonged to her. The only other person who might have guessed what was going on was Philippe: he, most of all, would not lift a finger to take a side.

What would be going on now at Hammer Reach? The damned

guns; Caleb had bought the damned guns; if he had died by one of them, it was his purpose. Would Matthew put Paimon and Christopher into the cells, or keep them in the pit until they had suffered as he had done, or would he let them go at once?

A couple of young men at another booth were watching her. They were of an age with the boys in the Boston Coffee Lounge, whose names she had forgotten. They were giving her the eye – a lone woman, an older woman but an attractive woman, she still had what it took, she was still Cassandra.

\* \* \*

Cassandra showed up at Boston by morning, by which time Hannah was already primed to refuse her entry. She hung about outside for a while, but the doors did not open that day or the next. When she telephoned, Hannah herself answered, would not let her talk to Gloria, Mary, either of the Jays or Lee: though she did not know it, all of them except Mary were on their way to Hammer Reach by the end of the first morning, while Mary was held back under Hannah's direct control. Cassandra drove to New York instead, where she encountered much the same from Jemima.

Matthew's tactic was to keep everyone moving. From London, Lilith and Lucius were despatched to New York to help Jemima, while Micah was sent to Hammer Reach to confront The Teacher, who was by then aware that he had participated in Anthony's Special Mass. After the first couple of days, Nahum took Diana and Pascale, ashamed and afraid, to Boston to see Mary, to confer with Hannah, and to keep an eye on the three women for a few more days before giving them back their liberty and returning to his mission to complete The Temple.

The loyalists Meredith and Chad went up to Boston from New York; Korah – the former Calvin Wood – who had joined in New York but subsequently moved to Boston via Hammer Reach, now returned to his home town, bringing Martha with him; Nadab was exchanged for Paul. Matthew could barely keep track of them himself; if he could not do so, nor could anyone else.

At Hammer Reach, Matthew took Lee aside, put his arm around him, reminding him of the night they had been together, telling him that he was Matthew's child as much as Cassandra's, it was a gesture of love and forgiveness that Lee took straight into his heart.

Jeremiah and Jeroboam stood tall in Matthew's presence – giants, like warrior-priests, expressionless.

"I am one," they said, as one.

When they arrived at Hammer Reach from Boston, they had been wearing suits; Nahum had ordered them into shifts as a mark of humility before they were sent to see Matthew.

They were in the Meditation Hall, where the pit had been filled in and the floor cemented in place precisely as Matthew had ordered.

Matthew was alone, unprotected but unafraid; they were servants, not leaders. He sat on a cushion, cross-legged, did not invite them to sit. He had physically recovered from his ordeal, was putting weight back on, he was fit.

He studied them openly, did not reply to their greeting.

"Cassandra is gone," he said. He did not shout at these men as he had bellowed at the gathering after his release. The violent power he wished to impose already resided within them.

Jeremiah, younger but more articulate, said:

"Yes, we know."

"How does that affect you?" This was Matthew's way: let members decide for themselves while he held up the mirror in which they could see their choices until they decided for themselves what he wanted them to.

Jeremiah was unsure what the question meant. He asked frankly:

"Do we have a place in The Programme?"

"That's what I am asking you."

"We did what we were told," Jeremiah replied.

"You were only following orders?" Matthew reproved him.

Jeremiah looked down at the ground, at his own feet not at Matthew, leaving his head hanging while his brother took over.

"We lost our father."

"I know about that."

"This is what we have now." This is all we have.

"If this is what you want, then you have it. But if you want it, you have to give to it. What have you given to it?"

Jeremiah shook his head in admission that what they had given was to Cassandra, not to The Programme.

An idea was beginning to form in Matthew's head. There were too few black people in The Programme; a member here and there in the past – now the two Jays; something about The Programme failed to attract them, whether it was his Southern manner or the English, middle class influence; yet blacks were religious, capable of great commitment, often eager to lose themselves in the body of Christ and the worship of God. He liked the idea of more blacks in The Programme – big men, violent men like the two he saw before him.

He would separate the two Jays, send them respectively to New York and to Boston on a mission of recruitment: it would be a source of growth and of change.

He sent them now to fetch Reuben, Lemuel and Ehud from the cells. It was time to deal with Caleb's three bullies. They were brought to him dirty and sullen, tired but still defiant. Without needing to be told to do so, the two Jays remained in the barn, one on either side of the doors, standing with their arms crossed across their chests like guards or centurions.

Lemuel was their self-appointed spokesman.

"Where is Father Caleb?" He glowered at Matthew.

"Caleb? Caleb has gone, of course. Where do you think Caleb is?"

"Father Caleb would not leave us," Lemuel protested.

"He is no longer Father Caleb," Matthew snapped. "There is no Father Caleb, no Father Christopher nor Father nor Brother Paimon. Come here, Lemuel." He deprived him of his title. "Come here," he commanded.

Reluctantly, hesitantly, Lemuel approached Matthew, seated at the head of the symbol painted on the sections that had covered the pit but that were now cemented into the flooring. Matthew gestured to him to kneel. Lemuel glanced around: any ideas of revolt or attack sank at the sight of the two Jays – Cassandra's blacks, he thought of them.

Lemuel knelt before Matthew, legs apart, still strutting. Matthew leaned forward, sniffed at him: the time Lemuel had spent in the cells without washing almost disguised his personal scent, and Matthew's own stink had all but obscured others' smells when he was strapped to the altar, but there was enough of it for Matthew to be confident – this was the one who had mounted him.

He had planned to forgive them, to return them to constructive uses: he thought of them as boys because that was how he had first known them – youngsters when they entered The Programme, youngsters he had thought so little of that he had been willing to convey them to Caleb. He, Matthew, was as guilty as Caleb himself: he was the only one left to punish.

The boy's sneer was too close. Matthew reached beneath his shift with one hand: he was not wearing any underclothes. Matthew felt for his genitals. Not even Lemuel thought this was sexual, no one else could see what he was doing. Matthew found his target, grasped Lemuel's testicles tightly in his fist. Lemuel squealed but gritted his teeth: he had given pain, he would take it. The Teacher pushed himself upright, still gripping him, it was only when Lemuel tumbled backwards and felt himself being tugged off the ground by his balls that he finally let out a howl of anguish.

"Help me, help me," he flung his arms to the floor to try to take some of his weight.

Neither Reuben nor Ehud moved a muscle. They, too, had been in the pit with Caleb, had mounted Matthew even if neither had gone as far as Lemuel: all they could think of now was how they could avoid Lemuel's fate or one like it.

Matthew started to drag Lemuel around the cushion: it took monstrous strength. He loped around Reuben and Ehud, distantly aware of Lemuel's arms flapping and flailing like a seal in a squall, half-aware of the two Jays' impassive faces, ignoring Lemuel's terrible screams. Before he lost his hold, he flung Lemuel to the ground in front of his two comrades, his shift up around his neck, scrotum torn open, blood smearing his groin, and threw himself back onto his cushion: within seconds, he was not even breathing heavily.

"Go on," he shouted at them. "Kiss him better, get down on your knees, kiss him, lick him clean, that's what you like, isn't it? Animals, pigs," he spat. "Do it, do it."

They dropped to their knees and buried their faces in Lemuel's groin, mouths squeezed tightly shut, wetting him with their tears mingling with his blood.

Matthew looked up again at the two Jays: their expressions were unchanged. He watched them as they watched him. Finally, he nodded.

"Leave him," he ordered Reuben and Ehud. "Come here."

They knelt before him, heads bowed, weeping.

"I know what you did and I forgive you," Matthew said grandly. "Do you understand me?" It was an act of such enormity they might be incapable of grasping it.

They nodded slowly, weakly, defiance spent.

"Go on, now. Go to the barn, go and wash yourselves, go to bed, go to sleep. Do not talk to anyone, not even to each other. Do not speak again until I tell you. Do you understand me?" he repeated.

In silence, each would have to reach inside himself, back to a time when Caleb had not been the master of his soul, back to the plea for help – the prayer for a life – that entry into The Programme represented, each in his different way: reach back and start over.

"Go," Matthew said again.

They rose and slumped from the Meditation Hall, stepping around Lemuel: he was not their business but The Teacher's.

When they were gone, Matthew himself rose. He hovered over

Lemuel, looking down at him as he lay there, curled into a foetal ball, sobbing, humiliated, agonised, clutching himself. Matthew shrugged and strolled from the barn, muttering to the two Jays to throw him back in a cell: Lemuel was no longer a threat, sexual or otherwise.

\* \* \*

Http://www.the-programme.org.uk (turn on sound card if available).

*This is the parable of the Resurrection, according to Matthew, 28: "In the end of the sabbath, as it began to dawn toward the first day of the week, came Mary Magdalene and the other Mary to see the sepulchre. And, behold, there was a great earthquake: for the angel of the Lord descended from heaven, and came and rolled back the stone from the door, and sat on it. His countenance was like lightning, and his raiment white as snow: And for fear of him the keepers did shake, and became as dead men.*

*"And the angel answered and said unto the women, Fear not ye: for I know that ye seek Jesus, which was crucified. He is not here: for he is risen, as he said. Come, see the place where the Lord lay. And go quickly, and tell his disciples that he is risen from the dead; and, behold, he goeth before you into Galilee; there ye shall see him: lo, I have told you. And they departed quickly from the sepulchre with fear and great joy; and did run to bring his disciples word. And as they went to tell his disciples, behold, Jesus met them, saying, All hail. And they came and held him by the feet, and worshipped him. Then said Jesus unto them, Be not afraid; go tell my brethren that they go into Galilee, and there shall they see me."*

*What Jesus Christ stands for – to this Matthew – is the ability to descend into yourself, to find unseen layers, unknown strength, untapped resources, and learn to survive on them alone. That is the key to it. If we put our minds to it, we can any of us grow strong by drawing upon our inner resources, even if they are resources which we conceal from others, or which others do not recognise or are unwilling to acknowledge. We can any of us learn to withstand our enemies, even to survive where others would lie still and die.*

*That is what the tale of resurrection is about – the precedent of survival. Was it told in order to inform us that there is but one child of God, whose spirit we can never equal – as the priests would have it? Or was it told in order to show us what is possible, what we too must learn to achieve?*

*The way that people have been taught to seek to emulate Christ, to secure the right to resurrection, is by a division between God and Mammon, Good and Evil, Belief and Denial, from which you are obliged to choose – it is a programme which has been a dismal failure. If division has failed, it is only wholeness that can succeed. The Programme's instruction is to bring Mammon back to God, Evil back to Good, Denial back to Belief, to reconcile and re-unify them – the reconciliation and re-unification of opposites – welding them back together as a whole – a whole that is loving and which of definition must therefore be a whole that hates.*

*This is the army of God and Satan – one that can walk into the fire beyond, be swallowed up by it, and yet emerge on the other side! This is the journey that I told you we would embark upon! I invite you, and you are welcome to join it!*

\* \* \*

"Who will win?" Berlinger asked.

"It depends what you believe in," the black man teased him, the usual neck of a bottle of cold beer tucked between his fat fingers.

"On what? Good and evil?" Berlinger humoured Phillipe. He had no brief to tackle Voudon and he was glad of it. A cult, he had read somewhere, meant not enough people to make a minority: in New Orleans, Voodoo was bigger than a cult.

"No," Phillipe chuckled. "More like between so rotten to the core you don't think it's possible let alone recognise it, and maybe just a little bit amusingly offbeat."

"Which is which?"

"That depends on your point of view."

"For you?" Berlinger pressed him. "Who is evil, and who is merely – what did you say – offbeat?"

"No, it's not for me to say, to choose. I cannot bless one of them, curse the other. What I'm saying, what we mean about gods is they are pure – pure good or pure evil; that is the ultimate distinction of the gods, to be pure in a way that we mortals can never achieve. Your question is, which one of them thinks he or she is a god, which one of them thinks they are that completely pure?"

Berlinger shook his head, rubbed the back of his neck.

"Bull," he said. "They're just as evil as each other." He paused, then asked: "Tell me this much at least – my man inside, he'll be okay?"

"That depends too, on who wins, and of course if he or she finds out. You want to tell me who it is?" Phillipe was teasing Berlinger: he neither wanted the information, nor would Berlinger give it to him.

"You're giving me nothing in exchange."

"No," Phillipe sighed, suddenly weary. "It's you. You're still not seeing what I'm giving you."

\* \* \*

"Afternoon, sir," said Romero. "Sergeant Romero."

"Good afternoon, Sergeant," Matthew replied, offering his hand. "Thought I'd come out and see how you're all doing."

"We're fine, thank you," he said. Romero's visit was not coincidence.

They were standing outside, at the front. Carey hovered in the doorway listening. Matthew turned to invite her to join them.

"Carey Arnott; our English lawyer."

"Pleased to meet you," Romero shook hands with her too.

"Would you like to come in? A cup of coffee or tea, perhaps?" Carey invited.

"Coffee would be fine, thank you."

Matthew led him to the kitchen, the hub of routine activity around the house. Members went about their business, smiling or nodding at the policeman until, gradually, the kitchen emptied of all but the three of them.

"How's Mother Cassandra?" Romero asked.

"Cassandra's travelling, Sergeant," Matthew met the trooper's eyes. Was he another man on whom she had cast a spell?

"There seem to be a lot of new people here," Romero commented, lifting the mug of coffee to his lips, watching Matthew over the rim of it.

"There are a lot of members of The Programme, officer; we move around a lot."

"Let's see – Father Christopher, I remember, and another man, unusual name?"

"Paimon. They've both left Hammer Reach."

"As well?"

"As well? Oh, as well as Cassandra. Yes, you could say so."

"Together?"

"Is that really any of your business?" Matthew was finally annoyed.

"Just making conversation, sir," Romero held up a hand in the universal gesture of pacification.

"What about your partner – the one I met at your office. What was his name?" Matthew asked, for no good reason but to gain time to bring himself back under control.

"Allison," Romero replied promptly.

"Yes, that's the fellow."

"You could say, he's moved along too. Got caught up in that fingerprint business." The scandal that was sweeping through the New York State Police. "He was helping out a friend, turned a blind eye to the evidence once too often," Romero shrugged to say it was fine by him. "Stupid, I used to think; now I'd have to say deceitful, too. Sometimes I think he did it for the hell of it – you know the type? Preferred to lie even when the truth would serve as well."

"While you prefer the truth?" Carey had been silent until then.

"Right, ma'am."

"Which is why you said you came by just to see how we were doing?" she asked sarcastically.

"Good, that's very good, ma'am. I almost forgot you're a lawyer." Romero chuckled.

Matthew drummed his fingers on the table impatiently. He had much to do. He had personally to deal with many of the members who had, under Cassandra, gone wrong: deal with them, heal them; cure them and punish them. Later, Brother Enoch was due. Just before Romero arrived, Matthew had realised that Brother Micah – as he had become – was overdue by several hours from shopping in Hedgerow. Sister Gloria had not taken well to her own demotion, was asking to return to England.

"Why did you come, Sergeant?" Matthew asked flatly.

"I had a call from the father of one of your members," Romero admitted. "Woman called Helen Atkinson: you know her?"

"Of course I do. The reason her father's worried is because I rang them, looking for her."

Romero stumbled: that was not something he had been told.

"Is she here, sir? Could I see her? Speak to her myself."

"No," Matthew replied too quickly. "I'm sorry, she's not here."

Romero's eyes narrowed.

"Is she travelling too, sir?"

Carey's eyes met Matthew's: the lawyer in her was telling him to be careful what he said.

"I don't know, Sergeant. I just don't know," he was tired of these questions. "She's not here, all right? She hasn't been here since I've been back. She's the main reason I came up here when I did – looking for her. She wasn't here, she's not at any of the other Chapters – here or in London. That's why I rang her parents, all right?"

"Seems like a lot of people aren't here," Romero continued to probe.

"Sure. There's been some changes. It happens."

"I know about that."

Carey cut in:

"What do you know?"

"Fact is, I've had more than one call about you people."

Carey waited.

"Had a call from a man said he was helping out Mr Rockworth: man named, er," he took a notepad from the breast pocket of his shirt: "Berliner, would that be right?"

"Berlinger," Carey corrected. "What did he want?"

"I'm not so sure," Romero laughed wryly. "Seems like, at the time he called me, it all made sense. Afterwards, it didn't seem like he'd said much of anything. That the Berlinger you know, ma'am?"

"I don't know him. I know about him. He's what they call a deprogrammer; he tries to get people out of, er, groups."

"Groups like yours, ma'am?"

"I'm not sure there are any groups like ours, Sergeant. You need to know that he is a witness in a civil action against The Teacher, er, Mr Crane, Matthew."

Romero studied her shrewdly: she was not his type, not the way he had fancied Cassandra, too skinny, but there was no denying she was fine-looking and bright.

"Why would I need to know that, ma'am?"

"I don't know how it is here, Sergeant, but in England we'd probably regard him as someone with something of an axe to grind."

"Doesn't make him wrong, though, does it?"

"Wrong about what, Sergeant? That's what you haven't said."

"I think he was just suggesting maybe I ought to keep an eye out."

"On The Programme?"

Romero nodded.

"He, er, asked you to let him know, perhaps? What was going on here?"

"Something like that. He knew there were changes happening; I guess, the way he put it – who knows what's going to happen."

"I would have thought you don't want to get dragged into any civil litigation," Carey reminded him.

"Sure," Romero agreed. "But once I've been put on warning, I wouldn't want anything to be happening that, well, maybe I could have prevented, right, ma'am?"

"There's nothing going on here. If you want to check back with

Helen's father, he'll tell you I was the one who called him," Matthew said.

"Make that call, Sergeant," Carey concluded. "If they can confirm that Mr Crane was the source of their concern, well," she shrugged, "that would seem to be that, right?"

\* \* \*

Another day, another game of squash.

For the first time since the two practices had merged, Andrew and Colin had arranged to have dinner together afterwards. They used to do so a few times a year. Since Andrew had joined the firm, there was less of a need – they saw each other most days.

They took a cab to the gym so they could drink over dinner.

They played with their usual determination, unrelentingly competitive, two men who knew each other's strengths and weaknesses and played only to the latter, a personal – almost intimate – game, gloating at success, cursing failure, on the very edge of the rules, there was only one, dedicated aim: to win by the largest margin.

In the locker-room, in the shower, they unwound: unembarrassed by their bodies or those of others. They did not loiter in the bar: just a quick juice then a cab to Langan's in Green Park. Andrew lived in Bloomsbury, Colin in Fulham – it was not equi-distant, but near enough to qualify.

Andrew waited until the main course had been served before he dropped his bombshell.

"I had a call from an old pal of mine the other day, Iain Macpherson. He's at…"

"Southwell, Grace."

"I didn't know you knew him."

"I don't. His name's on the letter-heading."

"I'd forgotten about that memory of yours." Colin had seen the name on the letter Simon had showed him. "He's not handling the matter."

"But that's what he was calling about." Colin prompted Andrew.

"Right."

"And?"

"We had a drink last night."

"And a chat about what – The Programme? Carey?" Colin stabbed at the food on his plate: lamb brochette; it had tasted good when he began.

"Both."

"If he's not handling it, what's his interest?"

"Client like Rockworth? What would your interest be?"

"To stay sane, I imagine; and hang on to him," Colin conceded. He gobbled the remains of his meal, washed it down with wine. He was losing his appetite but he did not want to be hungry when he reached home and have to explain why to Jan. "What did he want?"

Andrew put down his knife and fork, pondered the remains of his own meal, met Colin's gaze and admitted:

"Our help. No," he corrected himself. "What he wants is your help."

Colin reached for his glass of wine, realised it was empty; it was not the waiter's fault – he had knocked back a full glass a mere minute or two before. Andrew reached for the bottle, refilled his friend's glass then his own.

"Cheers," he said.

"Is he out of his mind? Has he heard of conflict of interest, professional privilege? Why are you even telling me?"

"That's more or less what I told him – at about the same point in the same conversation."

"So?"

"So I think he has a point." Andrew trod carefully. This was where the ground got soggy. "He knows we're not acting on the eviction thing."

"Forfeiture," Colin corrected automatically, then waved a hand for Andrew to ignore his pedantry. "Did you tell him?"

"He already knew. There's a new firm acting: No one, Nobody and Nonsense." He could not remember the name.

"Go on," Colin invited cautiously.

"Do you know what they're saying?"

"More or less: that they seduced members into The Programme." It began to dawn on him where the conversation was heading.

"More like, seduced them once they were members." Andrew's eyes met Colin's; it was on the table. "That it was a set-up for the senior members to, well, take advantage of the new ones."

"I see." Colin let the waiter refill his glass, noting that Andrew's was still full, but waved away dessert menus: it was not the time for sweets.

He thought about it. They had acted on the Kroger case and, if The Programme still wanted them to do so, could be considered to be under an obligation to continue to act in it when it returned home to England, though Carey's involvement could give them an excuse to withdraw. The Kroger case, however, had nothing to do with

Rockworth's forfeiture proceedings, although – based on the New York transcripts – there would be an evidential overlap.

Rockworth was asking for his evidence: that Carey had become involved with The Programme, had been seduced by Crane, The Teacher or whatever he called himself, that she had lost her mind to him, to the group.

It was true enough, though to recount his sister's fall in open court was a different matter. He had no wish to contribute to her humiliation amongst her peers, or to the embarrassment of the firm by association. On the other hand, he wanted her back. A brief detour, the result of emotional abuse, would soon be forgotten: lawyers attracted attention, and occasional scandal, and they did not need to lose their careers as a result.

His mouth felt dry; he licked his lips. He realised he had drunk too much, was drunk. He pushed the glass of wine away as if to put it out of temptation. Pushed back his chair, too.

"I'm sorry, Andrew; I don't feel well. I'll settle up with you tomorrow, okay?"

Andrew reached out a hand, gripped his wrist to stop him rising.

"I'm sorry too, Colin. I don't want you to think," he fumbled for the words. "It's not because of the firm, you know."

Colin absorbed what he was saying. Andrew, too, was fond of Carey; wanted her out of The Programme; wanted them out of the picture.

"Let me see you home," Andrew urged.

"I'm all right. I want some time. I'll talk to you tomorrow."

\* \* \*

"What I say is the law," The Teacher commanded.

The Meditation Hall at Hammer Reach; Midnight Mass. No wild dancing or trance-like messages from The Seer. Matthew was robed not in the simple shifts they had taken to wearing about the farm, but in a full-dress robe with a hood that fell down his back like a monk and broad tassels over its shoulders that he could throw around his face, a robe that fell in thick sheaths to the ground, that seemed almost to stand of its own weight, stiff and erect – and as austere – as its wearer.

The members were seated cross-legged on the ground, not on cushions: from where they sat, Matthew was ten feet tall. There were over thirty of them, including Carey and Emily, about a third of the remaining residential strength of the group. Enoch sat closest of all:

he had thrown himself at The Teacher's feet to find forgiveness waiting before he needed to ask; his had been the slightest sin, and the stammering with which he had executed his orders testified eloquently to the counter-purpose by which he had been riven. Now he said aloud:

"You are the law, Teacher."

"You are the law, Teacher," others joined in.

"I am the law, one law, I am one," he responded.

"We are many; together we shall be whole." Many of them cried: it was like coming home – the first time he had allowed them to say it since the recovery.

Emily was watching Carey out of the corner of her eye. Carey was heavily involved in restructuring The Programme, much more so than Emily. Emily took upon herself the practical burden of organising the house, arranging members into work teams pending Nahum's return from Boston, and setting up meditation groups, but nothing more spiritual.

A few days ago, Simon had arrived, greeted her warmly but without emotion, asexually, spent almost two whole days with Matthew – attended some of the time by Carey – before he departed for New York, taking Jeremiah with him.

Emily was hurt and lonely, felt abandoned: by Simon, by Matthew, by Carey too. She would not add to the demands on her friend, but the distance from her, as well as from the two men, added up to a distance from The Programme. She had heard a rumour that Gloria might be allowed soon to go back to England: she was wondering about asking to be allowed to accompany her.

She tuned back in to Matthew.

"I am the law, the one law: this is not the time to listen to all the voices in your head, listen only to me. Those voices in your head have had their time, as have those false voices that claimed to speak in the name of The Programme: words and prophecies both, they spoke. That time may be gone, the voices may be receding, but they can still be heard in the distance, muttering as they retreat."

Members nodded their heads in agreement: The Teacher was right; The Teacher was always right.

"Micah has gone," he announced. "Micah has left us. Micah was a part of what happened here and is yet in its grip. I offered him a right to return; he tried, I believe he tried to take the hand that I held out; he was weak and he has run away. Micah was once a Superior. Consider this: if even Micah was not strong enough to hold on, how can you be sure of yourselves?"

Now they shake heads, some more violently than others, still in agreement, willing The Teacher to look down and take notice of them.

"Close your eyes now. Breathe deeply, slowly: breathe in, hold it there, let it out slowly; again, now; keep your eyes closed, start to let go; breathe in, let it out slowly; empty your mind of all but this thought – I am The Teacher, I am the law, I am the way forward – take that thought with you, let it comfort you, let go of everything else, you do not need anything else, see how it feels, see how warm it feels, you do not need anything else but this: I am The Teacher, I am the law, I am the way, I am life itself."

\* \* \*

Colin felt extremely foolish. He had never done anything like it before. He had ordered the cab to Holland Park, where Jessica lived in half a house on a road that ran down the side of the park. He had not called ahead on his mobile phone but was standing at the door, ringing at the entry-phone, leaning against one of the two columns which held up the porch, confused that he was there, confused that there was no reply.

He saw from the position of the buzzers that hers was the upper half of the house; after a few minutes he stepped back onto the path and looked up – no lights, no sign of life. He glanced at his watch: just after ten; surely she would not be asleep already. He gave the buzzer a final jolt but turned to leave almost as soon as he had done so, without giving her a last chance to let him in, feeling oddly relieved.

She was standing at the gate, watching him.

Neither of them spoke for a while, then he shrugged.

"Pretty stupid, huh?"

"Why?" she asked simply.

"Have you just got back from work?"

"No. I went to a film." She added despite herself, "with a friend."

"I had dinner with Andrew. Langan's."

"Hardly your way home." She entered the tiny front garden, automatically shut the gate behind herself, was standing only a foot away from him.

"Could be, if you'd had, uh, as much to drink."

"Yes, I suppose so."

"We were talking about Carey; it upset me."

For a moment longer she hesitated then slowly, almost reluctantly, she said:

"We'd better continue this indoors, before we wake the neighbours."
"I don't want, uh, to keep you up," Colin started to say.
Jessica smiled enigmatically.
"Yes you do."

* * *

Cassandra was only just awake, taking a shower. She answered the door of her hotel room wearing a bathrobe.
"I am one," she said automatically.
"We are many," Micah replied.
"Together we shall be whole," they both said.
Smiling as if the exchange proved that they were still in possession of The Programme, she stepped back, held the door open for him.
The contact barrier was not as solid as Matthew would have liked. The Chapters were active again, Messengers and Initiates were selling on the streets, in Boston as elsewhere there were satellite, non-resident members who hovered around the edges of The Programme, hoping that some of its aura and mystique would rub off on them even if they made no greater commitment. While resident members avoided her, walking away if she approached them in the streets, non-resident members were easy game – to join The Seer in a local cafe or bar was like an invitation to dine with royalty; to gossip with her as an equal more than any of them had dared dream of.
She could learn a great deal from them, although on one subject there was resounding silence: the whereabouts of Paimon, Christopher and Caleb. With each passing day, she was more and more convinced that they were dead – she had seen Matthew with a gun and heard a shot. Paimon, at least, would by now have found her, beloved Paimon, beloved brother.
On other topics, though, resident members talked amongst themselves as they worked in the Coffee Lounges where non-resident members were also allowed to work. It was part of the function of resident members to strike up relationships with non-resident members, help them to cross over. Members, Cassandra learned, had been to-ing and fro-ing at a startling pace. She was told, you never knew if a resident would be in Boston or New York from one day to the next, or even across the Atlantic.
Leah – she learned – had left The Programme, resumed the name Tanya. She was in dispute with her brother, Chad, who was still involved. She wanted The Programme out of their father's house. Their father, however, had still not been tracked down and her mother

would not take sides between her children. Cassandra would seek out Tanya: the girl had access to money; Cassandra's own funds were running low – she was living in a cheap hotel that was little more than a boarding-house; their relationship had been special, close, intimate – she could build on it.

It was from such Acolytes that she also learned – within a few hours – that Micah had turned up at the Boston Chapter. He was not banned from the premises. He had come to visit with Hannah, to talk about the children: so far as Cassandra knew, they were still at Hammer Reach; an idea began to form. She told her confidant:

"I want to see him."

It was another couple of days before Micah received her message, and the address where she was staying. He tried calling, but the phone line was constantly busy and the one time he got through he was left holding until the line cut itself out. He went round to see her.

They stood just inside the door. Cassandra was calculating how to handle him; Micah, unsure why he had come. Cassandra was the enemy; she had turned him against himself; she had provoked the battle for The Programme which she had promptly lost; within the defeat he had been separated from his children, in a way that was not true when they were merely on opposite sides of the ocean and they had all still belonged to The Programme and thence to one another.

Cassandra read his confusion like a script. She asked him if he had any news of the others – Micah knew nothing of their fate or where they might be. In silence, Cassandra gradually drew him nearer to her and put her arms around his waist, leaning her head against his chest.

"Hold me, Micah, hold me."

Whatever had happened, she was The Seer, part of his life forever – actively, dominatingly, sensually so. The night of the Special Mass, as they had entered Leah in turn, when later it seemed as if they all of them had entered one another, they had all been making love to Cassandra.

She pulled his head down towards hers; he had to fold over to reach her; then his lips were on hers, tongues twisting and tangled. One hand let go of his head, before he knew it she had sprung him loose, was fondling him, he was terrified he was going to come in her hand, she let go, slid down his body, he thought he heard her mutter his name, she took him into her mouth, she was thinking of Huw, the day of Helen's sacrifice, not Paimon. For that moment, Huw was alive again.

"Just lie with me; curl up with me; hold me."

He lay beside her: they were not the right sizes for each other. He did not know whether to remove his clothes or to do up his trousers so he did nothing. He lay there, staring over the top of her head, thinking about his children, the argument with Hannah. Hannah was loyal to Matthew; Hannah knew what he had done – the Special Mass. Hannah would not agree to take the children away from Matthew. If Micah wanted them, he would have to fight from outside, leave The Programme altogether, become a non-person to all members. If Micah wanted them out, he would have to fight both his wife and The Teacher. Maternal rights plus weird but sexually fairly normal group versus paternal rights plus perversion: it would be one for the law books as well as for the newspapers.

"We can do it," Cassandra said, reading his mind.

"What?"

"Tamar and Thomas: we can get them back."

Micah rolled onto his back, not trying to conceal his amazement.

"You really can see everything, can't you Seer?"

She had him back now: she giggled.

"How? I've got no place for them to live; I can't afford a lawyer."

"Don't worry, Micah; I think there's a way. You can trust me."

She rose to her knees beside him and slipped the bathrobe off her shoulders, her breasts hanging over him as she unbuttoned his shirt, held him while she pulled the sleeves from his arms. Next she unbuckled his belt, slipped the trousers off him.

Something was holding him back: he was not hard. He was not tired but he was exhausted: over the period since the first Special Mass, his life had been in constant turmoil. First, they had abandoned Matthew's way, then Matthew himself. He had taken part in the Special Mass. He had led the New York Chapter. Just as swiftly, Matthew had regained control and Micah, like a prisoner in chains awaiting court martial, had been ordered to Hammer Reach. For a couple of days, in the contented presence of his children, he had struggled to accept demotion. Even when he fled to Boston, he had still felt like a member; now this.

Cassandra was neither angry nor disappointed. She rested on her heels, legs ajar: he felt the beginnings of a response; he did not want to be hard; he did not want sex with her, not until he understood.

"This," she touched a finger to her lips then pressed her hand against her heart. "I loved The Programme: I love The Programme. I loved Matthew: I love Matthew. I loved all of you – I love all of you. I loved most especially the Superiors: I love you all still. The Programme is a moving feast, a revolving stage, I am at the centre of it. Once, it was

Matthew's time; there have been others – you knew that." She paused, then continued: "I loved Paimon, too."

"I knew that," he said.

She shut her eyes, thought of Paimon, tried to think of him alive, tried to come to terms with the notion that she would not see him again.

"Now it's your time, our time. Don't think less of it because I have loved others; I love you with all of the love for them before and all of the love I will have for you."

During her announcement, wanting it to be true, he became fully erect. She drew him into her, leaned down until her heavy breasts were pressed against him, her mouth only inches away from his:

"You love me too," she commanded.

"I shall; I do," he murmured as her lips closed on his and they made a perfect whole.

Later, he knelt in the shower, his head buried in her breasts, as she shampooed his full head of red hair, massaging away the turmoil, humming as she might soothe a child, he cried gently for a while and when he arose he was strong.

"What now?" he asked as they dressed.

"Now I have to make a phone call," she replied, endowing the banal explanation with mystery. "Sit by me: listen; learn."

## Chapter Sixteen

Rockworth was in New York. Cassandra had read that he was due to attend a Charity Gala in the city the night before: it was a sign.

"Can I speak to Mr Rockworth, please."

"I'll put you through to his office," the receptionist said.

"Mr Rockworth's office," an English woman answered next.

"I'd like to speak to Mr Rockworth, please."

"Can I ask what this is in connection with?"

"Yes, The Programme."

There was a distinct pause before the voice asked:

"Can I ask who's calling, please?"

"Would you tell him that it's Cassandra."

"Cassandra?" The voice repeated: is that all?

"Cassandra; he'll know."

\* \* \*

At first, Carey thought Matthew did not want sex because he was physically wrecked by his ordeal: whatever reserves he had managed to sustain after they released him had been spent re-imposing his authority on The Programme. Then, once he had regained his physical strength, she was unsure whether it was a reaction to the nature of the attack on him, or because when he had said there was to be no more sexual activity in The Programme, he meant it to include everyone, even them. Sometimes, she feared that he might have lost interest in her.

They slept in the same bed. He liked to hold her, stroke her hair, sometimes he touched her breasts, in the night she could feel him brush against her with what she believed was an erection but that she did not have the courage to reach out and check, fearful of his reaction.

One morning, he rose from the bed, naked and erect, and stood at the curtainless window staring out at the barn where he had been held.

He did not know that she was awake until she said:

"Do you still think about it?"

"No," he replied without turning around. "Do you?"

"I try not to. In my dreams, I still see you, the way we found you."

"What did you feel?"

"There were a lot of feelings. We were shocked, scared that some-one would come, not even sure if you were alive to begin with. Shame, too, as if I'd been a part of it."

He turned and leaned with his elbows resting on the window-sill. He still had an erection but seemed to be unaware of it. It seemed bigger than she remembered: that was frustration. He had recovered his physique. He was like a marble statue: she wanted nothing so much as she wanted him to come back to bed, lie atop her, make love to her.

"You know I can't do that," he read her mind.

"No, no I don't know that," she bit her upper lip defiantly.

"It has to be: look at what happened."

"I understand that. But I was no part of it. Is that all I am, Matthew: just another member?"

"You said it," he replied grimly.

"What? What did I say?" She sat up in bed.

"You said – shame, as if you had been a part of it."

"It wasn't what I meant."

"Why did you come back from London, Carey?"

"Emily rang; we were afraid for you; we were right to be."

"You came back. You've stayed. You belong. You are a member."

"Yes." Carey conceded she was more engaged with The Programme than ever before. "But I also came back for you, and I'm here with you."

"I want you to be," he admitted. "I want you to be closer to me than anyone; I want you to share this with me; I want you in The Programme, and to be with me."

"God, you can be so frustrating sometimes, Matthew."

He came and sat on the bed beside her. With a twinkle in his eye she had not seen since before New Orleans, he said:

"That's where this conversation began, didn't it?"

"I don't get it," she said. "You obviously want to make love, you make corny jokes about it, you say you want it to be me, then you don't do anything about it."

"Nor are they: if they can't, we can't. It's not about punishment, Carey; it's about purity. That's what she did: she made up these contact rules which forbade the members to have sex, while she and her puppies were fucking each other and everyone else at will."

"In so-called Masses. I don't want to make a ritual out of it." It was embarrassing: she was asking him to make love to her; she had never wanted someone so urgently.

"The Programme has to be abstinent – not only the members, The Programme as a whole. It has to purge itself of what was done with sex, in the name of love. If we made love, there would be love-making

376

within The Programme, and it would be ours, us, right at the head of it, just like her."

In a small voice, she said:

"If that's what you want."

"What about what you want, Carey?" Matthew did not mean sexually: he was moving on.

"As if I had any choices," Carey muttered bitterly.

She had taken the news of her family's betrayal – the firm's refusal to act – badly, blaming her father for the decision: Colin would not turn away paying work, but Charles would cut off his nose to spite religion.

"There are always choices."

He leaned down to kiss her forehead, her nose, chastely her lips. She asked:

"Where does Emily fit in?"

"You'll have to ask her. You're closer to her than I am."

"She's talked about going home."

"Yes," he was not surprised.

Matthew rose from the bed, started to dress. This was a day of light, he would dress in white: other days, he reverted to his practice of wearing black to reflect his mood; recently, he had worn black much more often than white.

"I don't think she should be allowed to go." Carey said. This was the lawyer speaking. Emily's state of mind was too frail; who knew what she would disclose to whom once she was back in England and on her own – especially when Carey did not come back with her.

"Then don't let her go," Matthew said simply.

"It's not my right to tell her what to do."

"Isn't it?"

Matthew smiled knowingly at Carey but left the room without awaiting her reply.

\* \* \*

After Matthew left, Carey rose from the bed, wrapped the sheet around herself, looked out the window towards the barn as if it might bring her to the same peace of mind as Matthew. It had been strange to hold a simple conversation with him: he shouted more often than he spoke; or he glowered at them in a silence bordering on a hatred from which she was not always exempt.

She smiled at the sight of Nahum hard at work on The Temple. She could make out Chad, Lee, Mary – up from Boston, Nadab from

New York, even Lemuel – let out from the cell for a few hours each day – working his way back to grace.

It would not be long before the project was complete. Nahum had designed and built it to survive an earthquake or a bomb. Instead of windows, it had slits in its solid walls, with concealed ventilation shafts emerging at the peaks of the four segments which were now identifiable and which meant that the roof had three or four times the support it would have had if it had been constructed as a conventional, single space.

She heard the door open behind her and turned, hoping for an improbable second that it was Matthew with a change of mind.

"Hi," Emily said, pushing the door open with her foot. "Coffee," she was carrying two mugs.

"Wonderful."

"Matthew said you wanted to see me."

"Did he?" She laughed. "Did he say I said I wanted to see you, or that he thought I wanted to see you?"

Emily smiled wanly.

"Matthew doesn't go into that sort of detail with me."

Carey tucked the sheet into itself, walked around her friend, pushed the door shut.

"Stay. I do want to see you."

She took one of the mugs from Emily, sipped, put it down on the sideboard. She crossed to the hand-basin, ran water to brush her teeth, wash her face, brushed quickly through her hair, smiled radiantly at Emily.

"There – that's better."

"You looked fine to me." Emily reminded Carey it was not the first time she had seen her when she had only just awaken, not yet washed or brushed her hair.

Instead of getting dressed, Carey sat on the bed, upright against the wall, clutched her coffee mug for warmth.

"How are you doing, Em?"

"Missing you," Emily replied promptly.

"Still want to go home?" Matthew had decided to take the risk with Gloria, let London heal her where in the States she was continuing to fester; in a few days, she would fly back.

"Part of me," Emily admitted. "It's not that easy, though. Too much has happened."

She could have meant what had happened between them or what had happened in the pit.

The fate of Christopher and Paimon was a game of bluff, double bluff and keep on bluffing until the bluff is so far away from where it began it is almost impossible to remember what it was about. There were times when Matthew seemed positively to want the members to believe they were dead and that he had killed them, telling them that The Teacher could give life and he could take it away. It was not intended to intimidate but to inspire – they were in the presence of a god. "I am the law," he had told them. "I am life itself". Yet he was also their father, who could not harm them.

Carey would have preferred not to talk about it at all: she could cope as long as she did not have to confront it, though there were times when it preyed on her mind and she found herself needing almost physically to push away the accusing finger within her head, insistently reminding her that it was death she was dealing in, violent death, and she a lawyer from London. The game, the game, was all she could cry back – it's all in The Programme's game.

Emily asked the same question that Carey had asked Matthew:
"Do you think about it?"

"I don't know any more than before," Carey replied cautiously.

"Don't you, Carey?"

"What are you getting at?"

"He must have killed them." If Carey would not take the initiative, then she would have to do so. "No one who'd been through what Matthew did would have let them go; and if he did, even if they'd fled through the woods in what – next to nothing? Don't you think they'd have come back, been in touch in some way – even just to get their clothes?"

"If he had let them go, they'd be too ashamed and too afraid, to come back – just for clothing."

"I think you don't want to know what happened to them, what the truth is; I think in your heart, you know he did it – I know that's what I believe; but you don't want to admit it."

"That sounds pretty much like what any lawyer would do," Carey said, thinking that her instincts had been right: Emily could not be allowed to stray too far from the fold.

Emily brushed the hair back from her forehead defiantly.

"It doesn't change what I said."

"Why did you come here?" Carey asked her, changing the subject.

"To New York?" Before their travels in the South.

Carey nodded.

"To be with you."

"Why?" Carey repeated, like a child's game.

"I love you. You know that. I thought, I could be with you without being, oh, without being oppressed, abused, a victim." She held up a hand as if to pre-empt any interruption, though Carey had not intended to say anything. "I want to say, I need to say – it wasn't about wanting a woman instead of a man, it's about you, Carey – I love you. I'm trying to say," she was half crying, half laughing. "I think I'm trying to say that it's like chance, a coincidence, that you're a woman. Do you understand that?"

"Then why didn't you come back with me?" From New York to London.

"I don't know," Emily sniffed. "You didn't seem to know what you were doing; nor did I. I wasn't ready to go back."

"Come here," Carey patted the space beside her. After a moment's hesitation, Emily came over and sat beside her, they hugged briefly.

"What do you feel now?" Carey asked.

"I'm not sure. I feel responsible, I suppose; I asked you to come back – for Matthew but also for me; because I'd stayed, you had to come back."

"I want you to stay, Emily."

"I know you do. Why?"

Carey reached out a hand to touch Emily's cheek, letting the sheet fall away. Despite herself, Emily leaned in towards her. Carey pulled herself forward. Their lips met, they kissed. Carey's hand fell to touch Emily's breast, Emily broke away in surprise.

"What are you doing, Carey?"

"I wish I knew," Carey laughed her off. In prospect, on those occasions that she had thought about making love with Emily between Antibes and Moonlight, it had seemed such a momentous thing to do; yet it had been overtaken almost immediately by the events in the pit – to have had sex with another woman was a trivial occurrence in comparison.

"It's not right." Emily pulled away.

"Why? Because of the rules?"

"No; we're neither of us much good at obeying rules."

"What then?" Carey asked.

"I don't know what you want from me."

"I want to do this, Emily." Stay with The Programme, with Matthew. "I need to do it. Putting it all to rights again: it's, oh, I'm not sure what I mean – just, it's the biggest thing I've ever done – me, that is, it's the biggest thing I'll have done for myself."

Carey listened to herself, watched Emily being drawn back in, this time Emily stroked Carey's face, agreeing to stay with her.

Carey watched herself from a distance, thinking that she reminded herself of someone: she wondered if this was how Cassandra had kept people by her side.

\* \* \*

"Matthew, we're out of here," Christopher had reassured him. "You won; you know, you won. Isn't that enough?"

"Absolutely," Matthew had replied, looking at Paimon as he spoke.

Paimon was watching Matthew's eyes. He saw what he saw. He felt something warm between his legs. He had pissed himself. He begged:

"Matthew, Teacher, don't do it, please."

"You stole my wife, Huw – remember?"

"It was something else, Matthew, nothing to do with that."

"Christopher, here, he just stole money – didn't you, Christopher? Nothing much wrong with that – a bit of stealing here and there; it's what people do," he spat, meaning ordinary people, people without significance. Matthew moved around the altar and stared at Christopher. "We used to be friends, Christopher – you used to believe in me. What happened to you?"

"You were just too big, Matthew; too strong. I think I needed to find out just how strong. Until I knew you were always going to be stronger than me, how could I trust you – trust you with everything?"

"That's Cassandra talking," Matthew snapped. "I asked you."

\* \* \*

Http://www.the-programme.org.uk (turn on sound card if available).

*"When thou passeth through the waters, I will be with thee; and through the rivers, they shall not overflow thee: when thou walkest through the fire, thou shall not be burned: neither shall the flame kindle upon thee. Fear not: for I am with thee" – Isaiah 43. The fire is a symbol for every religion in the world: the circle of fire – fire and destruction and rebirth – is an Eastern symbol, fire of redemption in the West. The fire beyond our grasp, the fire beyond the pain and suffering of life, the fire beyond good and evil, love and hate, that appears to consume us but that releases – the fire beyond, that we shall survive, that is our symbol.*

*Compare this from Isaiah 47: "Thou art wearied in the multitude of thy counsel. Let now the astrologers, the stargazers, the monthly prognosticators, stand up, and save thee from these things that shall come upon thee. Behold, they shall be as stubble; the fire shall burn them; they shall not deliver themselves from the power of the flame." He might as well have said, also the seers, as it says in Daniel 7:11 – "I beheld even till the beast was slain, and his body destroyed, and given to the burning flame."*

*Some say that this slow but sure advancement on the fire beyond is a new idea for The Programme; some are resistant – The Programme, they say, is and always has been a way of life, not death; The Programme, they say, is about the unification of opposing forces and feelings, not their mutual elimination. That is correct: The Programme is not a way of death. If the fire beyond were capable of destroying us, we would be insane to engage with it at all, let alone to march so determinedly towards it.*

*We are not insane. We are not on a march to death. We are not bent on self-destruction. The fire beyond is the ultimate proof of life, our very purpose is to emerge from it liberated from the conflict between opposites – alive and free. The purpose of learning to bring love and hate together, or good and evil, each in one harmonious force, is to be capable of surviving the fire beyond. There has to be nothing between them to feed the fire, for the fire to inflame – not a lock of air. This wholeness is our protection from the fire, our immunity. Those who seek to divide us seek therefore to condemn us – false seers who would burn us as stubble. Let them burn instead – save yourself.*

* * *

"Did you know about it?"

"Not directly, no."

"Which means – what?"

Jessica stroked the bowl of her glass with one finger: armagnac.

"You know how it is with partners – you don't need to say half the things you mean. I knew Andrew'd had a call from Iain. I knew his firm acted for Rockworth. I don't believe in coincidences."

"Is he a friend of yours too?"

"Macpherson? Not really; I know him through Andrew. Why?"

"I was wondering what sort of a person he was. I mean – it takes some gall – and some deviousness – to come up with the idea."

Colin had sobered up: the visit to Jessica had been the result as much of distress at the invitation Andrew had passed along as of drink.

"He's just doing his job; using whatever's to hand."

"All the same. I mean, we've been acting for them."

"He knows we're not any longer; he may have read that as an opening."

They were seated at opposite ends of her living room sofa. The decor, her furniture, the bric-à-brac about the maisonette, did not match his expectations: there was something old-fashioned about it, as if it had been designed by a much older woman from a different age – fireplace with grate and brass safety-guard, print-clothed, three-piece suite with round edges and arm-covers and a matching foot-stool, floral-patterned wallpaper, heavy drapes, Limoges figurines in a glass-fronted walnut cabinet, crystal-drop chandelier, gilt-framed paintings – a fruit-bowl still life, Yorkshire moors, a portrait – and in one corner a set of Victorian cameos arranged in three tidy rows. It was womanly but not sexually so.

She watched him studying the room.

"Don't worry, Colin; no one understands me."

"Don't say that – you sound just like Carey."

"We're more alike than you realise: why do you think I can understand her so well – and why I'm so critical?"

"The difference is: you wouldn't throw everything away for some – well – charlatan."

"You don't know that. I don't. Maybe for the charlatan who fit into this room – or the ones I date in my dreams. Why do you think I stay as far away as I can from all of you – them?"

"I don't know: I assumed, because you'd been hurt before."

"Perhaps; perhaps not. I'm not planning on it happening again."

"Do you think maybe, you got it the wrong way round the other night: perhaps I'm the safer bet than Patrick?"

"Why? Because you're married?"

"Sure."

"So that means you can't be a charlatan?"

"Not quite, but close. I'm safe because I'll never leave Jan."

"That's what Andrew says."

"Do you talk about me?"

"Not quite all of the time," she said dryly.

He did not rise to the sarcasm, waited for her to regret it: only then did he reach his hand out along the back of the sofa towards her, open and inviting. At first, she appeared not to see it. Then she looked at it curiously, studied it in the way that he had studied her room. Finally, she laid her own hand in his, allowing him to pull her towards him.

They kissed just the once: at first tentatively, then fully, then passionately. She was lying half across him, her body pressed to his, one hand around the back of his head, one of his supporting her shoulders. For a time, he was careful to keep his other hand politely at her back. As he gathered confidence and tried to bring it around to her breast, she let go of his head, caught the hand and wove her fingers into it, held on for a few more moments before, reluctantly, pulling away from the kiss.

For another minute or so, she sat across from him, faces inches apart, breathing each other's breath, eyes locked. Then she pushed herself away from him and onto her feet, laughing.

"What's that hugely original saying I'm looking for – oh, right, this is it – 'I think you'd better leave now': that's the one, isn't it?"

She did not make him leave at once but poured them both another drink:

"What you're doing – you're doing what she's doing."

"What do you mean?"

"Your private life is Jan and Carey: maybe Jan for main course, Carey for dessert or the other way around. Carey's gone off the rails; you're crashing after her, trying to keep up with her."

"I don't seem to be doing very well," he said ruefully.

"Nor is she, so far as any of us can tell." It was said without malice.

"There's a lot I don't understand."

She laughed, hiccoughed.

"Now there's a really original thought."

"I don't really understand what you're trying to say."

"I'm not trying to say anything."

"All right," he said crossly, "I don't understand what happened just now."

"We kissed. It was nice. In a different time, different circumstances, I'd want you to kiss me again; but I don't. Why do men find that so hard to understand?"

"I've never done that – even that, you know. Not in all the time we've been married."

"Colin, you're confused. It's not surprising. You've been so close to Carey all your life, not just as kids but as adults. You're trying to pretend it's not happening, or it'll all be all right, and you're behaving out of character because in a perverse way that proves it's all right, you know you can pull yourself back in and if you can do so, so can she. That's the way the logic's ticking over, even though it's wrong – syllogistic. What you're not doing," she hesitated but carried on without waiting to be asked, "what you're not doing is the one thing you ought to be doing – putting everything you can into saving her from this, this nonsense."

"I thought you wanted us to have nothing to do with it?"

"Right: as a firm, I don't; definitely. But as her brother you ought to be looking for every way you can get her out of it. Don't confuse the two."

"You're saying – I should help them?" Southwell, Grace; Iain Macpherson.

"I don't know. That's for you to decide: I'm not taking the responsibility – or the blame if it doesn't work out."

"Is it what you'd do?"

She shook her head firmly.

"Asked and answered, counsellor, as they say on the tele. Same question, different wrapper."

"It's such a big thing to do. I can't get my head around doing it – to her, I mean. Holding her up for all the world to see like that. She'd hate it. It's the worst thing I can think of for her. But I also can't get out of my head the idea that it's right. Fighting fire with fire."

He sat for a while longer in silence then rose to leave.

"Do you want me to ring for a cab?" she offered.

"No. The fresh air'll do me good." He held her hand for a moment, squeezed it, let it go. "I remember what I said to you at the gym that day."

"So do I."

"I should have asked what made you so wise."

"I expect I would have given you the same answer." Not his business.

"Thanks, Jessica," he kissed her cheek as she let him out the front door of the house.

She shut it behind him without answering and climbed the stairs to her flat. In her living-room, she began automatically to clear away their glasses, pausing to dribble the last from one of them – she could not remember whose it was – into her mouth. She looked at the glass as if seeing it for the first time. Then she flung it into the fireplace, watching it shatter with a single curse:

"Damn."

* * *

Rockworth met with Cassandra in New York, the day after her call, Berlinger in attendance together with another man to whom she was not introduced.

Micah did not accompany her: she had sent him to see what he could learn at the New York Chapter.

She wore the one decent outfit she had managed to grab from Hammer Reach: beige dress; silk, of course; buttoned down the front; thin, flesh-coloured bra providing inadequate support; as she shifted in her seat she felt her breasts sway; men were never indifferent – not even Matthew, not even after all these years, not even when he had been drained and imprisoned and about to die.

From behind his desk, Rockworth's face was impassive: he was willing to take her help but he was not so foolish as to believe that she did not have a major responsibility for The Programme.

"I'm sorry about Anthony. I was very fond of him."

Berlinger was seated behind Cassandra: Rockworth's eyes met his briefly, vacantly; Berlinger's eyes flickered in response. They were focused on their common task; respect was growing between them.

The third man was seated at the side of Rockworth's desk: in his late twenties, fit but looking tired, he was paying earnest attention, taking occasional notes, his eyes narrowing when he looked at her so she could not see in to read them.

Still Rockworth said nothing. Cassandra had used the same technique on others. If she had not needed to make a deal so badly, she could have out-waited him. She heard herself babbling, on the verge of a giggle she only just managed to contain.

"I mean, of course, I feel very guilty about it – I should have paid him more attention in those last few days, much more attention, I had no idea he was so upset; I thought he was coming to terms with it."

"With what?"

Cassandra looked down at her hands folded demurely in her lap.

"There had been some, well, some – some exchanges between Anthony and my husband."

"Matthew Crane was travelling at the time, he was in New York that day, before that in New Orleans," Berlinger reminded her from behind.

"He'd been at Hammer Reach just before. I think now, it brought it all back for Anthony, but I didn't see it at the time, in time. Matthew was due to come back after the Kroger case. Anthony was upset by the first visit, that was why he asked to be allowed to engage in a private meditation. To be honest, I should have stopped him. I should have known he wasn't ready for that sort of intense confrontation with himself."

She looked up, failed to find a response in Rockworth's eyes, plunged on regardless.

"You have to understand, Mr Rockworth: you know what sort of frame of mind Anthony came to us in. It had been a long time, some progress but slow progress. For Anthony to ask to undertake the exercise was a major step forward in itself – it was hard not to feel that it was some sort of breakthrough."

"Why was my son so upset by seeing Matthew again?" Rockworth signalled to get to the point.

"Things had happened between Matthew and your son. That was the main reason I wanted to bring him to the States with me – to separate them."

"I understood, at the time, it had something to do with Anthony and a younger boy?" Rockworth cross-examined.

"I saw you with Matthew, if you remember. There was a limit to what I could say."

"Are you saying that was a lie, it was made up?" Rockworth was angry: there was a limit to the price he would pay for her assistance in bringing down The Programme; finding out that they had so easily made such a fool of him was beyond it.

"No, it was true. But I think it was something we might have been able to handle in England; it was only part of the reason."

"What are you telling Mr Rockworth?" Berlinger asked.

She turned around to look at him as she answered. She had either to convince him, or to assert herself in spite of him. It was hard to tell which would be more difficult.

"I'm telling Mr Rockworth that Matthew took advantage of Anthony. You know exactly what I am saying – sexually. Matthew took advantage of many younger members – male and female."

"Which you did what to stop?"

"At the time, nothing. I don't mean to offend you, Mr Rockworth, but Anthony's sexual orientation was far from clear. It was not at all obvious that a relationship with Matthew would be harmful – it might even have been what Anthony needed in the longer term, love and stability from an older man."

As she spoke, she had turned back to Rockworth. It was Berlinger who continued to interrogate her, however.

"That's not what you're saying, Cassandra, nothing about love or stability. You said Matthew abused a lot of the young members."

"Mr Berlinger, I'm sure you're well aware, there have been periods when we have not practised monogamy in The Programme. That has not stopped people maintaining strong, permanent relationships."

Berlinger snorted and brushed a palm over his smooth and hairless scalp.

Rockworth held up a hand to tell Berlinger not to pursue the issue: it was going nowhere.

"Let me see if I have this straight, Cassandra. You're saying my son had sexual relations with Matthew Crane, in London?" She nodded but did not interrupt him. "You're saying you knew he was unhappy about it, that was one of the reasons you brought him here?"

"Yes."

"You're saying Matthew came up to Hammer Reach, which upset Anthony because he thought – what? That Matthew had come to resume their relations?"

"I think so."

"Bringing Carey Arnott with him?"

"I don't think you understand, Mr Rockworth. That would only increase Matthew's, well, appetite. When I said he had abused members of both sexes, I didn't mean necessarily at different times."

The young man at Rockworth's side, in his first visible reaction, raised an eyebrow in surprise.

"So Matthew goes off, but is coming back, which is why my son goes into your meditation cells, which is why he kills himself. Is that it?"

"Well, yes, and whatever had happened while Matthew was at Hammer Reach the first time," she took her final shot.

"Ah," said Rockworth. "Which was what?"

"I believe, I've come to believe that Matthew was alone with him. It's what makes sense. I've spoken to several members. Matthew went for a walk with Anthony, in the woods above Hammer Reach."

"They went for a walk together?" Berlinger sneered from behind her.

Again, Rockworth held up a hand to silence the other man.

"Look, I wasn't there. I can't tell you what happened. Other members told me they'd been for a walk, one of them said Anthony looked unhappy on his return – and dishevelled. You can draw your own conclusions or not. It's all I can tell you, but it's what I believe. I know him, remember, I know him better than any of you."

"Who told you that – about the way Anthony looked?"

"Micah," Cassandra answered promptly. "Father Micah – he was Father Micah until Matthew demoted him."

The young man at Rockworth's side passed the tycoon a note. Rockworth looked down and read it, reminded her:

"Anthony was nearly twenty; even if it was true, it wouldn't have been a crime."

"Perhaps not; not here. Before, when we were in London, that was before they lowered the age of homosexual consent."

The young man nodded firmly, enthusiastically: that was correct. He looked at Rockworth for permission to speak, said:

"In view of what you're saying, Mrs Crane," he fumbled over what to call her, "I think I ought to introduce myself. My name is Grant Phillips. I am a solicitor. I work for a firm of solicitors in London: we act for Mr Rockworth in England – including in the matter of Chesterfield Gardens."

The reason he looked tired was because he had flown to New York on no notice the previous night, at Rockworth's insistence, in order to attend this meeting with Cassandra. It was either him or Iain Macpherson. Macpherson was in the middle of a delicate negotiation for evidence from another source.

Cassandra knew of Rockworth's general threat to evict them.

"You should have told me that before, shouldn't you?"

"I didn't think we would be discussing The Programme in England," he offered lamely. Rockworth had insisted he keep quiet, in case it made her clam up too quickly. He had agreed, with the stipulation that if she started to talk about matters they would want to raise in the case, he would be professionally obliged to identify himself. It was a thin line even for an artful lawyer. Clients like Rockworth could make a lawyer walk on air.

"But now we are, because?"

"It's part of the case against The Programme that the way the property had been used is immoral – which would include sexual abuse of a minor, especially if it was illegal at the time."

"Which you have to prove?"

"Indeed. That's why we're meeting, isn't it?"

"Well, I didn't know about the case, but it seems, if you want to get Chesterfield Gardens back…" She did not need to complete the sentence.

Phillips said, protecting his client's position in the negotiation:

"I think Mr Rockworth will be able to get Chesterfield Gardens back without your help."

"Easier with it," she said, eyes glistening.

"Perhaps; it depends exactly what you can testify to first hand. Or, perhaps, arrange for others to tell a court."

"If we got hold of others at Hammer Reach, would they be able to confirm what you say Matthew did to Anthony?" Berlinger followed up, an uncharacteristic note of uncertainty in his voice. He had no brief to defend Matthew but he felt uncomfortable with her whole account of Hammer Reach. It was a gut reaction and – without knowing whether it would help Rockworth or not – Berlinger wanted to know the truth.

"I don't know. I don't think there's anyone left at Hammer Reach who was there at the time."

"What's been happening over the last weeks? You said Matthew had demoted Father Micah, right?" Berlinger had no difficulty talking hierarchy: these groups were all hierarchic. "There's been a split; you tried to take over – he won; you're out of it?"

Cassandra was starting to loathe the balding, burly man. She had been able to handle Rockworth in their past dealings. She had known he and Berlinger were working together – Phillipe had told her so – but she had not anticipated his presence. Whatever hostility Rockworth currently had towards The Programme – and herself – he was an intelligent and sophisticated businessman whom she believed would be unable to keep himself from responding to an intelligent and sophisticated, business-like approach. Berlinger was brutish – he reminded her of Caleb more than anyone else in The Programme.

"How did you know?" she asked.

"I visit the Website, read your newsletters, even the internal ones – what do you call them? Lessons, right. And I talk to people. People who know you."

"A lot of people know me."

"Yes, I got the impression you like a lot of people to know you."

Cassandra turned back to Rockworth.

"I didn't come here for cheap insults."

"What did you come here for, Cassandra? Forgiveness, perhaps?" Rockworth, too, could be sarcastic when he chose.

"Mr Rockworth – I had nothing to do with Anthony's death." She was impassioned. "The Programme had nothing to do with it; just Matthew. I'll bring Micah to you: let him tell you; make up your own mind. There's a lot of good people, people in need, in The Programme: as long as I was there, I could keep some balance; Matthew in charge on his own is out of control, dangerous – I'm frightened about what's going to happen to The Programme, or the people in it. Don't throw the baby out with the bathwater, please, it means too much to too many people, it means too much to me – I've put too much of my life into it."

"How so, dangerous?" Berlinger asked from behind.

Cassandra started to cry. She sobbed:

"I think he may have killed my brother."

"Paimon?" Berlinger rose for the first time, came around, stood against Rockworth's desk. "Matthew may have killed Paimon, you say?" Berlinger was excited: when members of a group began to kill one another, the end-game had begun and he would come into his own, struggling to get more people out than died within – an easy score-card to keep.

"Not just Paimon: perhaps Christopher, Caleb." She took for granted Berlinger knew the names.

"You saw him kill Paimon? The others?"

"No." She did not know for certain that they were dead. If she claimed to have witnessed any killing, and the wrong person turned up alive, her credibility would be shot and with it any chance of using Rockworth to regain control of The Programme.

"How do you know, then?"

"I heard there were guns at Hammer Reach. What for? And where are the others – my brother? Micah says they've disappeared; ask members at the Chapters. It's the only thing that makes any sense."

"Where did they get guns?"

"I don't know; maybe I heard a mention of New Hampshire." She wanted to give it colour without admitting the guns were there at the same time that she was.

"Whose guns, Cassandra?"

"Matthew's, I assume."

Berlinger resumed his seat behind her, thoughtfully stroking his ample chin. The death of Paimon and the others was not the only explanation that made any sense, but enough sense might be made of it to put to use.

Rockworth waited until Berlinger was done before he asked:

"Have you been to the police with any of this?"

"No."

"Why not?"

"I don't think, you know, Mr Rockworth, if I didn't see it for myself, there was anything they could do about it. Not on my say-so."

"But on mine," Rockworth concluded dryly. "Is that what you came for?"

"I thought, perhaps, there might be some advantages for both of us in some mutual cooperation," Cassandra admitted.

"What are you looking for, Cassandra?" Rockworth's eyes were flat.

"Like I said – I want it back." The Programme.

"You want me to give you The Programme back?" Rockworth could not conceal his astonishment at her gall.

Behind her, Berlinger laughed openly.

"Be clear, Cassandra. Tell me exactly what you want," Rockworth said.

"You want The Programme out of Chesterfield Gardens: that's not a problem. I've heard there could be similar pressures in New York. But Boston, that came through you, you could help me get it; and I want to keep Hammer Reach."

Rockworth wanted The Programme out of Boston, out of Hammer Reach, off the face of the earth.

"You don't want much, do you, Cassandra? Let's see: that means I have to ask some people I know to let you stay on in Brookline – I could do that perhaps." The easiest way would be to buy the house from them, without letting her know; evict Matthew Crane's Programme and dangle it in front of her until he was done with her; he might even go as far as letting her back in, evict her again when it had all quieted down. "I've got to make a deal for you with the Gruenfeld family to drop their case to get Hammer Reach back – maybe I could do that too; but then I'm going to have to deal with Matthew's claim to Hammer Reach. Is that about right?"

Cassandra met Rockworth's gaze without embarrassment.

"There's The Programme bank balances too. And Micah's children are still inside; if you want his help, he needs help to get them back. He needs somewhere for them to live."

"What you really want me to do is to destroy Matthew, isn't it?" Matthew, not The Programme.

"Sure. That's what this is about."

"Which I'll do why? Because you say he's responsible for Anthony's death?"

"I would have thought it was cause enough."

"If I believe you."

"Mr Rockworth – it was either caused by Matthew or it was a straightforward suicide. What on earth could I have wanted it to happen for? It's done me – and The Programme – nothing but harm."

The critical moment; either he bought in or he did not.

Rockworth looked past Cassandra to Berlinger, for once expressionless: it was Rockworth's call, not Berlinger's son. He glanced sideways at the English lawyer, scribbling assiduously in his notebook. Rockworth said:

"And for my help, you're offering me what?"

"I would have thought, more or less everything you want." Public accusation; evidence in court.

Rockworth nodded glumly.

"More or less is right." It would not undo Anthony's death. "All right: here it is. I don't want to see you again. You'll deal with Mr Berlinger. He'll deal with the police, and he'll deal with my publicity people. If you co-operate with him, with them – with Mr Phillips here too, I think you can say we've got a deal."

After she was gone, Berlinger said:

"You do know, don't you?"

"What – that she was responsible for Anthony?"

"Yes."

"I expect so," Rockworth said tiredly.

"And the rest of it – do you believe a word of it?"

"No."

"So?"

For the first time since Berlinger had met him, Rockworth smiled, though it was a smile without warmth or humour:

"So what?"

\* \* \*

Paimon pleaded from the other side of the altar:

"This doesn't have to happen, Matthew. You were right; you won; what else do you want?"

"You tried to steal The Programme, Huw. You too, Christopher. You tried to steal The Programme – that was to try to steal me, steal my soul? At least Caleb understood that much: when he fucked me, he was fucking The Programme. What do you think my life's been about?" Matthew cried. "The Programme, that's all; if it wasn't for The Programme, I'd have done nothing, I'd be nothing."

\* \* \*

Colin found the memorandum in his tray first thing in the morning. It was brief to the point of arrogance. Charles wrote as Senior Partner to Colin as Managing Partner, invoking his right to call a full meeting of the partners. He had specified as the sole item for the agenda – "Carey Arnott."

It was still early; there was no one at the office to whom Colin could carry his anger. He picked up the phone, dialled Charles' home number, disconnecting before it rang; he did it twice more before, steeling himself, allowed it to connect only to find that Charles' answering machine was on. He hung up without leaving a message.

It was not until midday that he caught him in the corridor as Charles was on his way into a meeting with Alistair. They spoke in hushed tones:

"What are you doing, Dad?"

Colin thrust the memorandum at his father's face.

"Exercising my rights," Charles replied stiffly.

"Flaunting them, more like."

"You'll make your arguments."

"Like you've been doing, I'm sure," meaning that Charles would have been working his way around the firm, drumming up his support. "Fine campaign slogan she makes, my sister."

"My daughter," Charles hissed back.

"They've probably got other lawyers by now," Colin dissembled.

"Not the same as having Arnotts," Charles said: lawyers can be changed more than once.

"For God's sake," Colin began.

Charles held up a hand.

"Not here. Not now. Lunch." Colin was shocked into silence; he could not remember the last time his father had invited him to lunch on their own. "I'll pick you up in an hour," Charles called as he escaped.

The memorandum killed the morning. Colin poked his head into Jessica's room, but she was out. Alistair was off-limits – locked in session with Charles, probably about Carey. For a moment he toyed with barracking Alison Hansen, finding out where she stood, but Colin was no longer sure what he wanted and until he knew there was no point trying to get anyone else to agree.

They were both meat eaters. Burgundy Ben's on Clerkenwell Road was part of a modern chain but it might as well have been serving since Dickens – panelled booths, framed cartoons on the walls, steaks, pies, ribs of beef, platters of ham, washed down with tankards of ale and vintage ports.

"Tell me what this is about?" Colin had brought the memorandum with him and laid it out on the table like the invitation to a duel.

"It's about Carey," Charles said calmly.

"Carey's private; why are you making it firm business?"

"Since when were Carey and the firm different?"

"Since when were they the same? I'm not the firm; she's not the firm; you're not the firm."

"The firm is my life; you're my life – both of you."

"The world's moved on; the firm's moved on. Everything's too big for one-man operations. Even a man, his daughter and his dog." There was no humour in it; something closer to hatred.

"Did you think I'd let it go at a Management Committee?"

"What do you want, Charles? What do you want the firm to do – stand on its head? Jump up and down because you're telling it to – or because it won't stay still while Carey makes up her mind what she's doing with her life? These are serious people, Dad: serious about law and about money. That's all: law and money and I'm not so sure about the law."

"Don't talk at me as if I were a fool, Colin; I've known more lawyers and I know more about what makes them tick than you've played games of squash with your young friend."

"He's your partner now, Dad, or did you forget?"

"No, I didn't forget. I might regret it, but I didn't forget it."

"Do you?"

"What? Regret it?"

Colin nodded.

"I may be beginning to. I didn't think I would; I've always liked Andrew." He picked up his roll and put it down in one movement.

"But you don't like him any longer because he doesn't agree with you on this?"

Charles eyes lit up as the waiter brought their heaped plates.

"I find I'm enjoying my food more and more these days; I suppose, the less I'm interested in other things." He was looking for a vein of detachment to bring to the discussion. "I spent a lot of time thinking about Carey while I was at the apartment: Carey and her mother, your mother," he corrected himself.

"Here we go. It's all her fault, I suppose?" Marion's.

"No." To Colin's surprise, Charles' eyes began to water. "That's not what I realised. Quite the opposite, as a matter of fact."

"Who, then? I mean, there aren't many others around, are there? If it's not Marion, it won't be Carey, will it?" Not Charles' precious girl. "That leaves me," Colin bit into his meat as if he was snapping at his father's neck. "Let's hear it, shall we? It's all my fault because I gave her the blasted case to begin with, right?" His voice was raised loud enough for people to glance over from other tables, enough to force him to lower his volume. "It's my fault because I shouldn't have let her go to the States?" His tone had turned from what started off as sarcasm to something much more ambiguous, something tainted with fear – truth.

Charles caught the change instantly. He put down his knife and fork, sat as far into the back of his chair as he could manage, almost shrivelled into it, realising for the first time what Colin had done, how he had ushered her off to the States in order to push the merger through. He murmured:

"My God, what have I made you?"

"You didn't make me anything," Colin snarled. "No one makes anyone else – you told me that a thousand times over. That way, we all have to take responsibility for ourselves, and you don't get any of the blame."

"It wasn't what I said," Charles protested. "I said I couldn't tell you what to do with your life, that it was your choice, both of you – your choices. It's not the same thing."

"Well, Carey's made hers." Colin's fury abated temporarily.

For a few minutes, they ate in silence. Neither was hungry: it was something to do to keep them apart.

Charles spoke first, softly, soothingly:

"It wasn't your fault, Colin; it was mine."

"Yours? This is a first."

Charles ignored the cynicism. Nothing would change their relationship; it had gone on for too long; he had let it go on for too long. He was not going to let it prevent him doing what was needed for Carey.

"Yes, mine."

Colin gestured for him to explain.

"I don't think I gave either of you enough direction in your lives. I suppose, it was partly the philosophy of the times, my generation; we'd suffered too much interference from our own parents, too much control, too much, well, direction. We went to the other extreme. I suppose we didn't want anything different from what our parents wanted: we wanted our children to be successful, happy, the usual things; we wanted our children to be like us, too – like most parents do, in one way or another, at any rate the ones who haven't yet seen what failures they've made of their own lives. But we wanted to do it without being seen to tell you what to do: that way, we didn't have to feel guilty about interfering.

"We made a big deal of leaving you to your own devices – but we didn't really, we were still marking out the lines, trying to get you to go in the right direction without letting on that was what we were doing; subtle direction; secret direction."

"What's it got to do with mother?"

"You know how it was with Marion and I – about religion."

"I'm hardly likely to forget," Colin replied dryly.

The waiter hovered: neither of them had touched their food for several minutes. Colin gestured to take their plates away.

"Would you like a dessert?"

"Coffee."

"I'd like another beer," Charles said, surprising his son and challenging him to join him.

"All right," Colin said: "Two." He did not have to drink it.

"And some cheese," Charles pushed.

"Cheese for two," Colin repeated. Nor did he have to eat it.

Charles said:

"We've barely talked since Simpson's."

The annual holidays had been disrupted by the partnership negotiation. For some of his time in Antibes, Charles had no company at all. Colin had taken less time off work. There had been no family visit to the South of France.

"There were easier ways of getting me to lunch." Than the memorandum.

Charles continued:

"I put a solid wall up marked religion – off limits. Too proud to admit there was enough in Marion's beliefs to be worth talking about, that there was even the remotest possibility she might be right. There were other walls too, I think."

"Like?"

"I'm not sure: business, perhaps? At any rate, money as a goal in itself. Politics, too."

"Why politics?"

"Perhaps because I never had the guts to try my own hand at it."

"What are you saying? That it was a mistake? That you should have encouraged us to – what? Make money an object? Go into politics, religion?"

"Don't belittle what I'm saying, Colin. Of course that's not what I mean: I just said, I was trying to push you in a particular direction, both of you, while trying to avoid the responsibility for doing so. That was the mistake – pushing without admitting to it; not the direction itself."

"I'm having a difficult time," Colin stopped mid-sentence as their waiter brought their drinks and the remainder of their meal. He watched his father chomp on a stick of celery: there was nothing wrong with his teeth.

"Go on," Charles said.

"I'm finding it hard to understand what this has all got to do with Carey – and with this," he nodded at the memorandum.

"Because I put up walls around things, I never took the time to work them through with either of you. I left you too much to your own devices. You couldn't express mild, normal interest, curiosity – I didn't leave you that choice. It was selfish, and it was risky. If you didn't ignore religion – which, because of Marion, wasn't possible –

and if you couldn't embrace it – because of me – it either withered away inside – which I think is true of you – or it built up into something too big to contain, and, if you like, too big to handle." Which he believed was true of Carey.

Charles' analysis was typically egocentric: he could not even leave Carey with flaws and mistakes of her own making; they had to be his. It struck too many chords with him, however, for Colin to deny.

"How does it translate into this?" The memorandum again.

"Carey won't come back until she decides she's got it out of her system, decides for herself that she's done with it. You know that. Everything I've taught her, and you, says neither of us can tell her what to do."

"So?" Colin raised his tankard, glanced into it, was disconcerted to realise he had drunk almost half his second beer. He put it back on the table untouched.

"We have to stay as close to her as we can; we have to stay close to her so we can help her to want to come back, until she can come to see things our way, my way. That's why I want us to go on acting for The Programme – to keep open the lines to her, to Carey." This, too, struck a chord in Colin: it had been one of his alternative reactions to Simon.

"I'm not saying that a lot of what you said is wrong, but just because it was your mistake doesn't mean you can undo it. If you like, just because you broke it doesn't mean you can fix it. That sounds like something you'd say, right?"

"No," Charles flinched: it was exactly what he would say in appropriate circumstances. "I'd say if you broke it, you owe it to yourself to try to fix it."

"Owe it to yourself may be right; I'm concerned with what we owe Carey."

"What's your alternative, Colin? Let her fend for herself? Wash our hands of her?"

"No. No, I want to help her too. And I'm going to. As a matter of fact, I've already put something in hand."

"What?"

"I've decided to give a statement to Rockworth's solicitors – about The Programme, and about the effect it's had on Carey – about what that man's led her into, and about what he has been doing to her."

"You can't give evidence for Rockworth, for God's sake."

Before Charles could begin to lecture him on his duties as a solicitor, Colin cut him off to rehearse the arguments that had first been relayed to him by Andrew: though it might be close to the line, there was nothing unethical in what he proposed; and, even if close to the line, it could not stop him helping his sister.

"How will it help her? It just adds to the pressure on her."

It was a good thing the restaurant was by now nearly empty: Charles was bellowing at his son, enraged in defence of his daughter.

"That's rich coming from you," Colin shouted back. "I thought that's exactly what you always did – add to the pressure."

"Professionally, Colin, only professionally."

"This is my professional judgement."

"When it comes to this sort of thing, we're all rank amateurs. All you're doing is helping Rockworth bring The Programme down."

"Yes – right – good. That's precisely the point. I've listened to what you have to say, Dad, but it's bull. It may have been the right approach to the problem if this was something Carey'd done while she was at university, or just after – let her have her head, blow it out of her system, come around when she'd grown up a bit, that sort of thing. But it's too late for that now. She's over there – well out of your reach, even if we snatched the case back and threw all of our resources into it – she's over there, on the other side, in the enemy camp – Marion's camp, Dad. You can't undo it all the moment it doesn't suit you anymore – you'd drown her in confusion with your sudden conversion to fallible man."

If Colin was aware of the effect the attack was having on his father, he showed no sign of it. Charles was slumped back in his chair, breathing rapidly, shallow breaths, mouth hanging open. Colin continued relentlessly.

"The only thing to do is to destroy this blasted cult, this Programme thing, and if that means helping Rockworth, I say why not – what's wrong with Rockworth? He's a decent enough man doing a decent thing – the same thing we should be doing – to protect our own. The way to get her back is to break up The Programme, and God, yes, I'll help do it. Where will she go without it? Back to us – that's where she'll go – she'll come back to us."

Colin too slumped back in his seat, exhausted by his tirade.

For a moment, he thought he'd gotten through to his father. Charles was sitting completely still, white-faced. Charles said flatly:

"Sometimes, I think that you don't understand her at all. Or me. I still want my meeting."

Colin could have cried.

"For God's sake, Dad; you'll rip the firm apart."

"I started this firm, Colin; I'll shut it down if I have to."

"I won't let you."

"You can't stop me."

"Bill, gentlemen?" the waiter asked, before either of them could storm out of the restaurant leaving it unpaid.

* * *

"This is the first time we have conducted a Mass with a loudspeaker, telephone link-up to London. Mother Naamah, can you hear me?"

"I am one, Teacher." Enhanced by the tinny-ness of the loudspeaker system, Naamah's normally reedy voice seemed almost eerie.

"We are many," The Teacher replied.

"Together we shall be whole," the congregations yelled at each other across the Atlantic Ocean. The exchange was followed by some laughter, whooping, one or two members called out to friends – Sister Rebecca to Sister Lilith who had been together in London for so long but who were separated as part of the recovery – they were like schoolchildren on an outing.

"With this Mass, we welcome the spirit of The Programme into its home – the first home that has been designed for it, built for it, that is built in its image."

Matthew – standing at the pulpit – was in his richest white robes, but he had converted them to the high purpose of the occasion by winding around his arms and neck sequinned scarves of silk that had been found in Cassandra's abandoned wardrobe in red and black and turquoise and gold: he was The Teacher and The Seer both.

"I am one," Father Simon led, robed in his own combination of colours, seeming so much smaller than Matthew down on the level floor below him.

The Mass was being held on a Sunday afternoon – allowing all the members from New York and from Boston to drive up, with the exception of a tiny, house-keeping presence at each – Sunday morning in London. Save for that small number, The Programme was – including the London presence – in its fullest session since before the move to America. Even non-resident members had been invited to attend. Many had taken up the invitation.

"We are many," The Teacher replied. "Truly many," he indulged himself.

"Together we shall be whole," the congregation chanted.

The Teacher intoned:

"We raise our voices in harmony in thanks to Father Nahum, in whose heart was conceived this building, under whose direction it was constructed, with whose hands so much of it was built."

"I am one," Simon shouted, turning to Nahum beside him and raising his arm above his head like a champion.

"We are many," Nahum roared with joy.

"Together we shall be whole," the congregation responded, Matthew first amongst them.

The Teacher sang:

"We symbolise our deliverance from destruction, and our coming back together – our re-unification – stronger than we have ever been, more numerous, with greater purpose."

"I am one," the congregation spoke with one voice.

"We are many," Matthew replied.

"Together we shall be whole," cried Naamah from London.

The Teacher pronounced:

"We bring into this very moment the initiation into the inner ranks of The Programme two of our most loved, most loyal, most proven outside members – Sister Carey and Sister Emily."

"I am one," called Mother Hannah, one arm around each of her children.

"We are many," sang Carey and Emily, exchanging a final, quick, private glance.

"Together we shall be whole," the congregation, led by Matthew, roared in delight.

"It is your decision," The Teacher told them as they stepped forward from the congregation and stood, holding hands, at the foot of the pulpit. As befit the solemnity of the occasion, they wore simple robes of white, more than shifts, less than cassocks. Around their necks, they wore their stainless steel symbols of The Programme, now to be replaced with brass. "Do you wish to take new names?"

"I do," said Carey without hesitation: it was long past time to say farewell to Carey Arnott.

Honouring the pledge to stay with her, Emily had come to this point with Carey, had planned even to take a change of name of her own. At this very last moment, she could not do it. It was as if her name was all she had left for herself, even though the realisation did not come upon her with any sense of dignity or pride, more like the Emily of old, the victim the rest of whose belongings had been robbed. She was not changing, Carey was. Accordingly, she did not reply to Matthew's question.

When Carey had discussed her own new name with Matthew, made passing reference to Emily's ideas for herself, Matthew had forewarned her that Emily would not go through with the change. Now she thought: Matthew was right again; it dissolved any last doubt.

"And your new name shall be?"

Her voice strengthened by her faith in Matthew, Carey said, clear and ringing as musical as crystal:

"I shall be Esther."

"Esther," Matthew repeated. "Esther, the cousin of Mordecai and his adopted daughter. Esther, the Jewess who became a Persian queen – Queen Xerces – and who delivered her people from destruction. Esther, who was of outstanding beauty, charm, and courage. Yes, you shall be Esther; you too shall deliver from destruction."

"I am one," Esther said.

"I am one," Emily repeated, back in the loop of the event.

"We are many," The Teacher intoned.

"Together we shall be whole," the congregation sang, voices rising, hearts full.

The Teacher looked around, beaming at his children. He wished he could see London: he missed the old haunt; he had been happiest there. The thought of it made him happy again. He cried out:

"We love you, London."

"We love you, Teacher," came back from the congregation.

"I love you, Teacher," one voice could be heard above the others.

"Sister Gloria, is that you?"

"I am one, Teacher. Here's a friend for you all."

"I am one, Teacher," growled Brother George Cohen.

There was more laughter, more names were called out, Matthew held up his hand for silence.

"I am one," came from the congregation.

"We are many," Matthew sang the words until they rose to a high hum which he held for several moments. "We are many."

"Together we shall be whole," they thundered in reply.

"Where shall we be whole?" Matthew cried.

"In the fire beyond, in the fire beyond!" they sang back.

"How shall we be whole?" He bent the words around a tune.

"In the fire beyond, in the fire beyond!" they repeated in tune.

"We shall be free!" he screamed, beginning to dance.

"In the fire beyond, in the fire beyond!" Several members stomped their feet in time, others started to clap.

"God and Satan!" Matthew waved his hands above his head.

"In the fire beyond, in the fire beyond!" They were abandoning themselves, waving back at him, beating a rhythm for his exhortations, losing themselves in their response.

"Love and hate!" Simon jumped onto the platform on which the pulpit stood, beside his long-time, closest friend.

"In the fire beyond, in the fire beyond!" Matthew joined in the response, one arm around Simon's shoulders so that they were dancing like Greeks in a tavern.

Nahum hopped up beside them: the three elder statesmen of The Programme, robed, kicking up their feet, Matthew in the middle one arm around each of them, the others each with a free arm in the air.

"We shall survive!" Nahum contributed.

"In the fire beyond, in the fire beyond!" The members below and down the wire cheered.

Naamah's clear voice could be heard over the loudspeaker:

"We shall see!"

"In the fire beyond, in the fire beyond!"

Their movements were frenetic, yet seemed to form an image: flickering flames in the fire beyond.

Esther jumped up to the platform, was caught from falling by Nahum, sang:

"We shall be whole!"

"In the fire beyond, in the fire beyond!"

Mother Meredith – as she had recently become – put her hands to her mouth to shout from below, barely capable of containing her laughter:

"We shall eat beans!" Bring back The Programme's humour, she was saying.

"In the fire beyond, in the fire beyond!" They raved and laughed and one or two of them quietly cried for joy.

"We shall sing!"

"In the fire beyond, in the fire beyond!"

"We shall make love!" offered a daring, if anonymous, soul from London.

"In the fire beyond!" Matthew shouted back loud enough for everyone to hear who it was, but eyes twinkling – he could deny them nothing, not even some good-willed cheekiness.

"We shall dance; in the fire beyond, in the fire beyond!"

"We shall be reborn; in the fire beyond, in the fire beyond!"

"We shall see God; in the fire beyond, in the fire beyond!"

"We shall re-unite; in the fire beyond, in the fire beyond!"

"We shall survive; in the fire beyond, in the fire beyond!"

"We shall survive; in the fire beyond, in the fire beyond!"

"We shall survive; in the fire beyond, in the fire beyond!"

Nothing could be more certain; and, nothing more could be certain.

# Chapter Seventeen

Esther's chilling response to the news of the latest, ultimate betrayal was silence. She did not call Colin for an explanation, any more than he had called her before he made his statement for Rockworth. Nor did she tell Emily about it. She saw now that it had not been Charles alone who had been behind the firm's refusal to act for The Programme, but Colin too: they had both deserted her; she had never expected it. She took it hard and it made her harder. It was another defining moment, as important a junction in her path as Caleb's death.

When Matthew told her about it, showed her Colin's statement faxed from London by Mother Naamah, she seemed barely to absorb the information.

"The Programme is your life; it is your family."

"I know." She could not blame him deriving satisfaction from it. She was his partner; until now, she had somewhere else to turn.

"What are you going to do?" He picked up the firmness of her resolve.

"I'll do what it is my purpose to do. Isn't that always the correct answer?"

"I am one, Sister Esther."

"We are many, Teacher."

* * *

It took Berlinger's men not much of Rockworth's money and even less time to track down Tanya's father. He was – ironically, given how spiritually important the country was to The Programme – in Bolivia, living on the shores of Lake Titicaca, high in the Andes but away from the more heavily populated centres of the Altiplano, working with the inhabitants of the floating islands – islands of reeds where lived Indians for whom nothing had changed since Inca times.

Michael Sokolov – Dr Sokolov – had no interest in how his New York townhouse was being used; he seemed to have not much more interest in how his children were doing and none at all in his wife. He was a man who had been locked into a career by his parents. He had not married for love but for solace; solace had turned into a trap. He was not without a sense of duty to the children that had followed: duty was his strongest sense of all; he believed that he had now

404

discharged it.

He was a tall man, carrying to the jetty a battered medical bag in one hand, a sack of supplies in the other, striding like Gulliver amongst the stocky Aymará and Quechua, waving in response to cheerful greetings that matched their colourful dresses and fringed shawls and the good-humoured bowlers and trilbys and knitted backpacks so many of them wore, that belied their forlorn, squat features. He said:

"I read the papers once in a while, a few weeks late; tourists bring magazines, leave them lying about in cafes and hotels; my friends pick them up when they go to the market to sell their produce. They bring them back; makes them feel they're doing something for me. I don't like to tell them I don't want to know what's going on."

"You've heard of The Programme, though?"

"I guess. Your client – his son was a member, hanged himself?"

"Right."

"So I'm supposed to be worried about my own children? I guess there's some kind of logic in it."

"Just Chad; Tanya's out. She wants them out of the house – your house – but so long as Chad's happy for them to be there, it isn't that easy."

"And Marina?"

"I don't know how things stand between you, sir. The house is in your name, I understand."

"Right. Marina's lawyers'll want a slice of it."

"Mr Rockworth would be prepared to make you a very reasonable offer – a very good offer for it."

They had reached the jetty and Sokolov handed down his baggage to a young Indian woman in Western clothing – jeans, chamois shirt – who seemed to be crewing his boat. He said something to her in a language the investigator knew only was neither Spanish nor a local dialect based on it. She replied. The doctor laughed. The investigator could not make out her age: far as he could tell, she might have been anything from thirteen to thirty-five – they were creatures from another planet.

"Is that right?"

"I can assure you, sir."

Sokolov thought for a moment, nodded, exchanged a few more words with the woman in the boat.

"A good offer, you say?"

"Right."

"Tell you what, see what he thinks of this as a good offer. He can have the house for a dollar."

"A dollar?" The investigator's eyes boggled; he was a New Yorker; he would take it himself for a dollar.

"Right, a dollar: and you can send the cheque direct to my wife's lawyers, tell'm I don't want my share. The other thing is, these good people could use a hospital around here, for the island people. Just a small, local hospital and some money for equipment, supplies – you could set the whole thing up for under a million, run it for forty, fifty thousand a year; it'll be tax deductible. That's my offer to Mr Rockworth – see if he thinks it's a good one, why don't you?"

He cast off and hopped down into the boat, chuckling to himself.

\* \* \*

Micah said, looking directly at the camera not at the interviewer:

"I want my children back."

"How old are they?"

"Tamar is thirteen, Thomas is twelve."

"And they're with their mother inside The Programme?"

"Their mother is in Boston; the children are at Hammer Reach."

"And that would be with the man they call The Teacher, right?"

"That's right."

"Would you mind if they were with their mother?"

"Yes, I would, so long as they're in The Programme."

"What do you think is going to happen to them in The Programme? What are you frightened of?"

"I don't want to say. I want them to be with me, I mean, it's natural."

"It's natural for them to be with their mother, too."

"It would be natural for them to be with their mother at home in London, going to school, playing with friends of their own ages, doing the things children do. So long as they're in The Programme, with their mother or not, they're living unnatural lives."

"Unnatural lives? Would you like to say a few more words about that?"

"No, I said, I don't want to." The way the interviewer brought him back to the same subject, and his refusal to be drawn, spoke volumes more than if he painted a graphic picture of the sort of abuse that would be in the minds of most viewers: thirteen year old girl, twelve year old boy; mysterious cult; two and two.

"But you were a member of The Programme yourself, right?"

"It was different then. It's changed. That's why I left. That's why I want them out – whether my wife leaves or not."

"In what way has it changed?"

"I don't want to say."

"Are you going to court to get them back?"

"If I have to. I hope it won't be necessary."

"I'll bet you do," Matthew mocked the TV screen. "I'll just bet you do."

\* \* \*

Colin had snuck in to see Rockworth's lawyers after hours, feeling like a traitor. They had several offices: he had asked to meet with them in one of their annexes to reduce the chances of being seen. As he had entered, he noticed the brass placard identifying the only other occupiers: Everley Ashurst, Richard Fielding's solicitors. He remembered the call from Gatehouse, the calls from Fielding himself – another one last night, more abusive than the ones before; "your cunt sister took my wife away". He rushed through reception feeling exposed, it was too small a legal community.

Even after he had told Charles he was going to do it, Colin had continued to struggle with his conscience. If The Programme was an ugly entity, it was an ugly way of using the law to get back at it: it smacked of persecution, exactly as Matthew had forewarned in their first – and only – interview. If Carey had not been involved, he would have condemned the move to evict them. Yet Jessica was in favour of what he was doing and so was Jan.

Colin had repeated Charles' accusation that he did not understand Carey.

"There's only a thin line between understanding someone and indulging them," Jan said.

"And you think I indulge her?"

"No. I think you understand her; what you should do is act on it in her best interests, not indulge her by doing what she thinks she wants."

It was this ambivalence that had kept him from calling Carey to discuss it first; it would have been contradictory – she would only talk him out of it, he told himself, using the new-found zeal from which it was his purpose to wrest her away.

He ran through the basics with Iain Macpherson. He could confirm that his sister had changed – and dramatically so – since she had met Matthew Crane and become involved with The Programme. He could also confirm that she had lost her interest in the law, in her boyfriend, even in the home she loved. He had received a letter from her containing a notarised power of attorney and asking him to put her house on the market. He was stalling for the time being, he had told Macpherson, but she was doubtless trying to raise funds for The Programme, possibly to cover the legal costs of this very action. Finally, he knew that she had been sleeping with Crane.

"It's not much," he admitted to Macpherson. "But you seem to have plenty else, if I believe what I read in the papers. Crane's wife?"

"She's made a statement implicating Crane in, well, the sort of conduct we'd like to prove. Whether it stands up, we'll have to see."

"You want my evidence to back it up? It's a different thing, isn't it? I mean, uh, for one thing…" Cassandra was accusing Matthew of homosexual abuse.

"How much of their information have you read? Have you looked at their Website?"

"Yes to the first, no to the second. It didn't really occur to me that they'd have one, though now you mention it, I seem to recall a Web address on their literature. Why?"

"Even if you've only read their magazines, it's pretty far out stuff. God and Satan united in harmony, that sort of thing."

Colin began to see where Macpherson was going.

"Did you and your sister ever talk about what The Programme stood for?"

"A little bit," he had replied cautiously.

"Did she seem, well, rational on the subject?"

Colin shook his head, but added:

"People often don't when it comes to religion. My mother was very religious; I, uh, don't think my father would describe it as rational."

"What we're talking about here, there are distinct strains of, well, black magic, Satanism even."

"Yes," Colin had realised that, the cold weather notwithstanding, he was sweating. "I've read the newspapers, I know how the argument goes. And, yes, it worries me. But even so, in law, there are some respects in which it would still be regarded as a religion. What I'm trying to say is, it doesn't really help you much just to call them Satanists, does it?"

"Not on its own. But if, well, we can show it's being used to bring people in, bend their wills, take their money, use them sexually, well," Macpherson held his hands out, palms upwards. "There you have it."

"Is that immoral user in law?" Colin had replied sceptically.

"Maybe; we're going to find out. I think it's fairly immoral, don't you?"

"This is about the merits, isn't it, Iain? Because of who she is, who I am too if you like?" They wanted a lawyer to talk about one of their own.

"Possibly. Does it make any difference?"

Colin had shaken his head tiredly.

"Probably not. All I want is to see her out of it. If I'm going to be of any help, I'm, uh, going to have to emphasise some of the, uh, changes in her, aren't I?"

"Within the parameters of the truth, sure."

"The thing of it is, Iain, if I do that, I could end up doing Carey more harm than good – sort of a baby and the bathwater thing."

"That's the risk, Colin; it's your decision; you know that."

Colin had nodded unhappily.

"Yes, I know."

He had exhaled: it was not a time for faint-heartedness. It was a done deal; it would only be a short time before Carey learned of it. He knew she would be angry, but hoped she would none the less ring him; at least they would talk; perhaps she would finally realise how important it was to him that she give it up and come home.

He had also told Macpherson – the only person he had told apart from Jan – about the calls from Richard Fielding, sketching in the background. He had not been sure why he was doing so: probably just that, because he had told almost no one else and needed to talk about it. He had known though why it made him uncomfortable to do so: Fielding was saying that Carey had done to Emily what The Programme was accused of doing to others.

"Have you rung Gatehouse?"

"No." Colin had looked sheepish. "I know I should have. I was, uh, embarrassed."

Gatehouse had rung him to forward the same complaint from his client; to complain back to Gatehouse could only provoke an enquiry about Carey's current circumstances that Colin did not want to have to answer.

"I think you have to, professionally, you know." However unsolicited, one-sided and unpleasant, it was still contact with the client of another lawyer.

"I know," Colin sighed wearily. "I'm having my home number changed," he added, which was tantamount to admitting that he would not.

\* \* \*

409

The legal costs of actions on both sides of the Atlantic were draining The Programme's funds, already depleted by Cassandra and Christopher.

Somehow, in all the movement around the Chapters, they had let Amanda Kroger slip through the cracks. When she resurfaced, she was spitting fire in the media, supporting her sister's claim that she was a victim of mind-control. When it was put to her, for the appearance of impartiality, that this contradicted her evidence in court, she said, wide-eyed:

"He can make you do anything, I'm telling you, just anything."

Superficially more credible was the claim of her friend, Rosalyn, a former room-mate, that before the preliminary hearing Mother Jemima – of the New York Chapter of The Programme – had discussed getting Amanda out of the clinic where she was being treated, in time enough to get her evidence back on The Programme's track.

Amanda, crying, said:

"My father loved Hammer Reach; I feel like I let him down; all I can think of is getting it back so I can go and live there like he wanted me to."

It was enough to justify an application for a new hearing date for the substantive action: more costs.

\* \* \*

In England, Rockworth orchestrated his action to recover Chesterfield Gardens. What had been at first a gleam in the eye of an ambitious associate became a solid reality. Backed by the news coverage, the idea of using the immoral user covenant in a lease against a modern cult ceased to be laughable.

The Programme's new lawyers tried to strike out the claim for possession – even if all of the allegations were proved, so went the argument, it would still not lead to eviction. A High Court Master denied the motion. Rockworth's lawyers filed and won a counter-motion to have the case set down for trial, offering early disclosure of witness statements as evidence of their preparedness.

Much of the grunt work of instructing their lawyers fell to George Cohen, back in command of the accounts, closest to the financial reality that awaited them if The Programme's fortunes did not take a sudden turn for the better. The South Kensington flat had been sublet for its income: on her return to London, Gloria moved into Chesterfield Gardens; there was plenty of room – so many London loyalists had been moved to the States in the aftermath of the failed revolt.

Since he had moved out of South Kensington, George had been

living in one of the back rooms of his office, effectively camping. Now he too moved into the Chapter, abandoning his independent life. He had thought he was moving in one direction, but counter-purpose had proved stronger. Father George, they called him now, except for the new lawyers who called him Mr Cohen; George, Naamah murmured affectionately as she passed him on the stairs. He understood that he had not been saving himself from The Programme, but for its hour of need.

Naamah rang Matthew.

"How do you prove a negative?"

"That's a lawyer's question. Ask them if they can disprove faith."

"They have witness statements, people who claim that they came into The Programme and were made to have sex, for God's sake. If that's what they think happened to them, who am I to say it's not true?"

"Who?"

That was when Naamah told him.

"Colin Arnott is one of them."

Matthew grunted ambiguously.

"I met him once."

"He can't talk about what you told him."

"More's the pity. I'd like him to. I assume this is about Esther."

"Yes, sure."

"Can you let me have his statement?"

"Sure."

"Who else?"

She gave him those they had disclosed. One or two were relatively recent, but most were people who had hung around The Programme in much earlier days, when lust was free and the lines between residents and non-residents less rigid. They had come out of the wood-work in response to the publicity surrounding Cassandra's allegations.

"They want to know if you'll come back for the trial, Teacher. They say nothing will be so effective."

From his bunker, there was a long silence. Naamah was taken aback: she had assumed he would do anything he could to save the London Chapter, yet he seemed to be in doubt. He was torn between fighting on their ground and making them to come to him.

"They say we may lose if you don't," Naamah prompted.

"If we lose, we lose. Then you could come home to Hammer Reach, Naamah – I miss you."

She heard this and smiled down the phone.

"None of it matters, right, Matthew?"

"It matters to us how we handle ourselves. Not whether we win or lose in their eyes, but whether we have handled ourselves in the way that is right for us."

"Somewhere, back in the mists of time is the way it feels now, I committed my life to The Programme, Matthew; mostly, I guess, because I knew you had committed yours to it – or maybe I mean I believed you had committed it to me – amongst others, but me too. I did it, and I'm glad of it; I don't think I've ever seriously doubted I was right; I know I've never doubted you. I suppose, what I'm saying, it's some sort of final gamble now – we're right or we're wrong." She had invested too much to turn back.

"The other afternoon, during the Mass, I could hear you singing, clearly, as if it was at a pitch no one else could hear: I thought you were singing to me. Sing to me, Naamah, and if the others cannot hear it – so be it; together we shall be whole."

"I am one, Teacher."

\* \* \*

As winter replaced fall, Esther rose rapidly through the ranks. Within a month, she was a Junior Messenger. Then she became a Senior Messenger, entitled to take her place in senior councils of The Programme – and to attend the most private ceremonies – in her own right, neither as The Programme's lawyer nor as Matthew's lover.

Though all three Chapters were operational again, both membership and attendance at Coffee Lounges, courses and public meditations had finally begun to suffer from the sustained public assault on The Programme: the freak factor which had enhanced attendance after the Kroger case and Anthony Rockworth's death had exhausted itself, even in New York. They were not earning enough to call themselves self-sufficient, to replenish the coffers of The Programme itself or to meet their legal costs.

Mother Jemima rang from New York. She had been written to directly by Rockworth's lawyers. Rockworth, they asserted, had bought the house from Leah's and Chad's father and wanted them out. That made a hat-trick: London, New York and Hammer Reach. Boston was the only place they were not being hassled to leave. In view of the way they had secured it, it could only be a matter of time.

Intermittently, Romero or another local authority turned up to ask after missing people – children, siblings, even a lost parent – and though they would finally leave on Matthew's angry assurance that they were not at Hammer Reach or elsewhere within The Programme, there was a persistent threat of recurrence.

Matthew would not step outside Hammer Reach, as if he feared that the slightest absence might lead to the loss of it. He wandered the dormitories at night counting souls, slept late, stayed up until the early hours, between times he meditated alone or lectured to the members who came and went between Hammer Reach and the Chapters, specifically to hear him: sometimes he kept them up for the whole night, haranguing them, meditating for hours on end, chanting, dancing.

In order to demonstrate that they too were observing the rules, Esther had moved into the room next to Matthew's that hitherto had been occupied by Emily. In turn, Emily – still a mere Initiate – had moved out to one of the barn dormitories. She and Esther saw much less of each other; they grew apart by the day.

One evening, though, tempted by the new-fallen snow, they went for a walk in the fields after supper, wrapped in robes and sweaters, a hooded anorak for Esther, full-length coat and scarf for Emily. It was dark; they could barely make out each other's face.

Emily took Esther's arm, walked with her, clutching it.

"I wish I could let go more."

"What do you feel?" Esther asked, the way she might have asked a visitor to the Coffee Lounge: "what does that tell you about yourself?"

"Stuck; at a standstill. Time-warp. This," she waved a hand around to take in the hills beyond, the farmhouse behind, "it's like a quarantine zone, an island, something like that." She blurted: "I heard from Richard."

"What did he want?"

Emily laughed hoarsely.

"Me. Me back."

"Are you tempted?"

"No. I won't go backwards. I'm just stuck going forwards. This was, well, your thing most of all."

She was testing, probing.

"It is my thing," Esther corrected her bluntly. "I'm sorry if it isn't enough for you; it's where I am; I'm happy with it."

"Why?" Emily demanded fiercely.

For a moment, Esther was tempted not to answer: she did not owe Emily an explanation. Briefly she relented, stepped out of rank.

"What was out there for me?" She shot a glance at her friend, failed to make out her expression. "It wouldn't have made a difference."

"You don't know that," Emily said, knowing what Esther meant:

it would have made no difference if they had gone back to Islington to be together.

"Is that why you've stayed on? Hoping I'll change my mind?"

Emily avoided the question.

"During a Mass, I look at you and I see you – you seem – so far away, totally absorbed; I ask myself – who is that? Is there any part of her that is still Carey?"

"No. Absolutely not. Can't you feel the way we're working – like we're weaving ourselves, our bodies, our minds, into – the image that comes to mind is a hanging bridge, rope-bridge, what do you call it? It's like we're giving up all the bits of ourselves we used to hold back, contributing them to the task, to the very elements of the bridge – a bridge none of us could build alone. Can't you feel any of that?"

After a long silence, Emily answered hesitantly.

"Sometimes I can feel as if I'm contributing something of myself to it. But I find myself asking – if I throw so much of myself into – all right, use your image – into the materials for the bridge – who's going to be left to use it? We'll have a bridge without anyone to cross it. Doesn't that worry you?"

"Not at all. The more I give, the more I have to give; it's self-renewing; there's so many layers left, peeling one away – giving it away – is nothing, even when it's one then another and another. It's infinite."

They were almost back at the farmhouse.

"But in the end, there won't be any more, will there? I mean, if you truly do it – ultimately, it'll all be gone."

"So what? If it's all gone – who's left to complain? It's like death – you're not there to moan and groan about how you don't want to be dead; the same thing – if all of me is bound up in the bridge, I have become the bridge, I'm not worried about how to cross the river any more."

"The fire beyond?"

"Right. The fire beyond."

"I don't believe in the fire beyond," Emily admitted. "Do you?"

"I'll be ready when it happens," Esther answered simply.

They passed between The Temple and the barn in which they had found Matthew. Emily glanced at Esther, a knowing look, the secret shared. Esther looked straight ahead. Emily said:

"I look at you and see you happier than I've ever seen you: happier even than Antibes or, well, you know." Moonlight Lake – another forbidden topic. "I don't want to take you away from that. I want it for myself. I want to share it with you."

There were lights on in every room of the house, activity in the living area off which the deck led, figures moving about. They stopped a few feet away. Esther placed her hands on Emily's shoulders like a teacher insisting on the attention of a pupil.

"Stay then, share it with me."

"And if I can't?" Emily asked. "If I can't make it work?" She gripped Esther's shoulders in return, so that their arms formed a circle, seeing Esther's eyes brimming with intensity.

"I am one," Esther said quietly and with a sad smile but without answering her question.

A man was standing on the porch, watching them, laughing.

"Hey – what all this white stuff on the ground?"

Emily recognised him first.

"Phillipe?" she cried, thrilled to see him, an apparition of warmth after the disappointment of the walk.

"Yah. And you? Esther, is it?"

* * *

"What are you doing here, Phillipe?" Emily laid a hand affectionately on Phillipe's.

Though it had only been for a day and a night, Emily had formed a relationship with Phillipe that worried Esther. She did not trust the Voodoo priest nor did she trust his reasons for coming – unannounced – to Hammer Reach.

"Come to see how you doing, see if I can find out something I can sell Berlinger, maybe buy me a new car, what do you think?"

Matthew scowled at the mention of Berlinger.

"Has he been to see you again?"

"Yah, sure. Him, her too."

They had retreated from the living room to the kitchen. In some ways, it was like old times – New Orleans, Matthew, the two women. There was no beer, no dope, but Esther and Phillipe were smoking cigarettes and Emily repeatedly got up to pour more tea for her superiors and their guest.

"They're working together?" Berlinger and Cassandra.

"I'd say."

"Why, for God's sake?" Esther demanded aggressively. "Surely he can see what a phoney she is, that it's just opportunism?"

"Well," Phillipe dragged on his cigarette. "Maybe that why."

"I don't follow."

"He understands phoneys. He sees Matthew here like he the real McCoy and it freaks him. He got to be the devil, got to take him down."

"Hey, Phillipe, there's no one to hear except us. How about lightening up the street talk?" Esther suggested.

"You don't know that," Phillipe replied, complying with the request.

"Don't know what?" Esther asked sharply.

"He means that you don't know there's no one to hear us," Matthew explained, eyes fixed on Phillipe, drilling for more.

Emily watched with amusement. Phillipe had been good to her when she went back to New Orleans on her own, before Matthew came to fetch her. Nor had he taken advantage of her – which was more than could be said of Matthew.

She had meant it when she had told Esther that she wished she could find in The Programme the fulfilment Esther appeared to have found. That did not mean she expected to do so. To the contrary, it was a reflection of her continuing sense of detachment from it. She felt a tingle, watching Phillipe spar with Matthew and Esther: it was nothing to do with her, but he was.

"What are you saying? You're saying there's someone here, at Hammer Reach – someone who can't be trusted, right? A traitor, a spy."

Phillipe turned his substantial bulk to study Esther.

"You've changed more than your name, girl."

"That's not your business, Phillipe."

"Esther." Matthew did not want to alienate one of his only sources of good information from the outside world.

"Why are you telling us, Phillipe?" Esther persisted. "Do you know there's a spy? Do you know who?"

Despite herself, she flashed a glance at Emily, relieved when she did not notice. Those who were not inside ultimately owed their allegiance elsewhere.

Matthew caught the look, smiled to himself.

Phillipe chomped on a home-baked biscuit, his fifth or sixth.

"I don't know who. Berlinger said as much."

"Which means what – that Berlinger wants us to know, or that he trusts you not to tell us?" Matthew demanded.

"I don't understand him any more than you understand me."

"I do," Esther said flatly. "I think that's exactly what you like: for no one to understand you; I think that's as far as it goes – you don't know there's someone here, but you want us to think so, so we can spend our time wondering why you're telling us."

"Just like you're doing," Phillipe grinned broadly.

He was unaffected by her hostility: affection, hostility – it was all the same to him. He had come; he had told them. What they did with it was their own business; no one could ever say that he had taken sides.

"Tell me about Cassandra," Matthew urged hungrily.

"Yah, that woman. Something else."

"What's she doing?"

"Blaming you for every bad thing happen here. What d'you think she's going to do?"

"Did she come to see you with Berlinger?"

"Sure, they travelling together."

Matthew raised his eyebrows; Lamarque shrugged – he did not know.

"She's angry about that brother of hers. Paimon she calls him now; Huw, I knew him. The runt, that's what I call him."

In spite of her antagonism, Esther laughed aloud, barking:

"Right, the runt."

"Seems to think, maybe you killed him?"

"Ah." Phillipe had finally got to his point. Matthew said: "Which she was coming to ask you. How would you know?"

"I think, maybe, what she wanted, she wanted Berlinger to hear, were you up for it."

"What did you tell him?" Matthew asked casually, as if the answer was a matter of indifference to him.

"I told her, she knew you better'n me." He had refused to be drawn.

"What else?"

"Maybe you whacked Caleb, too."

"And?"

"I told him, anybody whacked Caleb did the whole world a favour. Never saw so much twisted evil ugly fucker like that before. No, and I've seen forms some of which ain't exactly picture postcard." Phillipe grinned. He lit another cigarette. "You sure you don't have no beer?"

"How many times has Romero been here, Matthew?" Esther asked.

"Romero – why? Three or four, since we've been back."

"They're looking for an excuse to come in and search – right?" If Phillipe had told them that Matthew was capable of killing either Paimon or Caleb, it was something Berlinger – with the help of a creative lawyer – could translate into an affidavit. Whether or not it was enough depended on the judge, what else they had to use it together with, and what Cassandra herself was telling them above and beyond what she was saying in public.

"Maybe. He should ask. There's nothing to hide."

Phillipe rose, bumping the table as he did so, stretched.

"I've been driving a long ways; I'm going now, maybe come back tomorrow."

"You're welcome to stay here," Matthew said, meaning it.

"I already checked in to an inn."

Matthew shrugged. Esther was pleased, Emily disappointed.

"I'm tired too. I'm going out to the dormitory." Emily stood on tiptoe to kiss Phillipe's cheek.

"I didn't mean to make you feel unwelcome," Esther said politely. "She's still trying to make trouble for us; too many people are."

"I am one." Emily said.

"We are many," Esther and Matthew replied, hardly noticing.

She slipped out of the room quietly, then from the house.

Phillipe yawned.

"I got to use your bathroom."

It was not the first time; he already knew the way.

While he was gone, Esther whispered urgently to Matthew:

"Make sure he comes back tomorrow; he knows more; we need to know what he knows."

"I don't think he does know more; he wants to know more. That's his style. He shows you what he's got, which is always true. It works like a spell to make you want to tell him something in return; that's what he's doing now."

"Do you believe him – that there's a spy? Berlinger's spy?"

"I believe him."

"Why would he tell us?"

"Like I said – he shows you what he's got. Maybe we talk back. He won't force it, but he'll take it. That way, it's our choice; if we give it him, he can use it; otherwise, it's something he took."

"You're not going to tell him anything, are you?"

"I told you, I've got nothing to hide."

"I know what you told me."

They stood outside and waved until Phillipe cleared the bend in the road; for a moment longer they could see the dull, disappearing glare of his tail-lights against the snow, then nothing.

* * *

He kept his eyes peeled for her.

She had run across the fields, skipping like a rabbit, hoping she could keep ahead of him.

He saw her before she got to the road, pulled in, opened the passenger door for her. She fell inside, gasping and laughing.

"You sure you know what you're doing?" he asked her.

"No," she giggled. "But I have to do something."

"You're not a prisoner," he reminded her, shifting into gear. "You can always walk away."

"I wonder," she mused aloud, lowering herself in the seat, settling her feet on the glove compartment.

"Hey, be careful; Mistah Hearse gonna want this back in one piece."

"You're so – oh, I don't know – you're so conservative, Phillipe, deep down, aren't you?"

"I'm what people want me to be. Only things I know for sure – I'm fat, I'm black, you're skinny and white but you're in my car."

"Mr Hertz's car," she corrected him, reaching out to touch his hand on the wheel.

"What do you mean, you wonder if you can walk away? You think they'd stop you?"

"No," Emily said too quickly, "I'm sure they wouldn't. Why would they?"

"So do it then."

"I did that before," Emily said melancholically. "Ran away from my husband; ran away from Carey, too – when I came to see you. I don't want to spend my life running away."

"You're running away now." He pulled up outside the hotel, a substantial wood-fronted, brick-sided construction with balconies along the front and a porch on the ground floor. "How's this gonna work?"

"Put me in a suitcase?" Emily suggested.

It was nothing to do with his having a woman in his room, or one so much younger; everything to do with colour.

He told her to wait while he went inside. It was late and the bar was empty. At the hotel desk, there was a lone clerk. Phillipe asked him what the chances were of getting something to drink, a bottle he could take to his room.

"Bar's shut," the youth replied indifferently.

"You could always open it." Phillipe placed a twenty dollar bill on the counter.

"I thought you wanted a drink, not a soda," the boy sneered.

"Right." He put down another bill, which the boy whisked out of sight.

"Wait here," he told Phillipe, "I'll be right back."

While he was gone, Phillipe signalled Emily to come in and run upstairs, holding up two fingers to tell her the floor. A few moments later, he joined her, grinning as he unlocked his door and ushered her inside, a pint of Southern Comfort tucked between his fingers, his thumb hooked into the spout of a plastic jug of ice.

As he shut the door behind him, she swung around and almost jumped into his arms, flinging hers right around his vast head, resting her body on the mountainous bulge of his stomach, bringing her lips to his, wet and warm.

He waited passively for her to clamber down before he stepped into the bathroom to fetch a pair of tooth-glasses. When he emerged, she was standing with her back to the window, arms crossed, biting her lower lip.

He struggled to open the bottle, pulling at the seal with his fingernails.

"Damn things. Used to be, quick twist and the cap flew off. Remember them gold caps – like cups? Now, they got this plastic, can't hardly get it off."

Despite her embarrassment, she smiled.

"I think you're supposed to cut it off."

"Shit," Phillipe finally succeeded in breaking the seal.

She waited until he had poured her a drink before she sat down on the bed, leaving him the only chair. She threw the liquor into her open mouth, to swallow it back in a gulp, but it was so long since she had drunk anything strong that she gagged, spat of it out again, coughing so hard she almost let the glass drop.

Phillipe sipped his own drink thoughtfully, waited for her to speak.

"I'm feeling a bit of a fool. You thought I wanted to talk, right?"

"Sure. What else you want with a fat old black man like me?"

"You seemed game enough the first time we met."

"I was yanking Matthew's chain – just a bit of fun."

"I thought, when I came back that time, you were being kind, leaving me alone."

"Maybe I was."

"But you're not interested, right?"

"You're a pretty girl; you're not interested in me, that's what."

"You shouldn't be so sure. You know The Programme's celibate now? It's been a few months."

"I didn't say no, if it's what you want. I said, it wasn't what you wanted."

"And you don't want it unless I want you?"

"Listen to yourself: me, I've got to want 'it'; you, you're talking about

420

wanting me. You've got it all confused. What do you think – this Voodoo priest is just another mumbo-jumbo artist, take every piece he can? 'Nother old man using a young girl's joy juice to come himself alive?" He was talking pure street, as Esther had characterised it – self-mocking to keep the criticisms of her light-hearted.

"I don't know what to think – I don't want to think Matthew's a mumbo-jumbo artist – as you put it – either." She crossed her legs beneath herself, sipped again on her drink, much more carefully.

"Tell me what you want to tell me," he suggested. "Maybe we'll know better after."

"That's why you waited for me? To see what you can find out? Why did you come here, Phillipe?"

"I use what people want to give me, sure. But I came because I wanted to see how you all were. Pieces here and there in the papers, on the TV; shit about Matthew and that boy. I thought about you, and your friend – you know about her brother, helping out Rockworth?" he threw out suddenly.

Emily shook her head: but it explained a lot of recent changes in Esther, changes she had not been able to break through.

"Maybe I was worried about Matthew, too," Phillipe continued. "He's my friend. You are. I wanted to see how you were holding up."

"What help can you be, Phillipe? We've made our own beds; we'll lie in them."

"Not with company, you saying." Laughing, he held up the bottle to offer her another. "I tried to help before. I thought, maybe if you both went back to England. I thought, maybe if she went back you'd go with her. Tried to make that happen."

"What do you mean you tried to make it happen?"

Phillipe shrugged, his body quaking from neck to the stomach that had settled on his thighs.

"I wanted it to happen," he replied in a tone that pre-empted a request for further explanation. "She went back; you stayed. That made you my problem. Just like now."

"Like now, what?"

"Like now, you know this is getting to be bad news, you've got to get out of it, instead you keep telling yourself you got to stay."

"I told you," she said crossly. "I don't want to have spent my whole life running away."

"This is what I think," Phillipe said calmly. "You be what you are or maybe you won't be anything; you be a runaway, or maybe you won't have any kind of life instead. You ever think about that?"

Emily's eyes flooded with tears.

"I'm frightened, Phillipe."

"Frightened what – what you've got with The Programme, or what you've got without?"

Emily could not answer him. She could not talk about it any more: it was all mixed up inside and more words would not unlock it. She finished her drink, placed the glass on the floor, untucked her legs and lay back on the bed, hands above her head, spread out on the pillows, gripping their sides. Phillipe watched her small breasts rising and falling, the way one leg was crooked to one side beneath her shift, like a door half-ajar he was being invited to push fully open, her eyes too were open but looking up at the ceiling not at him.

He came and sat on the bed beside her. It sank so far with his weight that she rolled towards him without intending to do so. He leaned down, kissed her on the forehead, chastely on the lips, using his arms to support his body to prevent himself collapsing onto her.

"I drive you back there now, will you get in all right?"

"Everyone trusts me." She sounded bitter about it.

"I think, you're a pretty girl – lovely girl. Clever too; and kind – looking after your friend, looking out for her. I think, I wish I was twenty years younger, hundred pounds less of me. I think, you get it together, leave that place, you want some place to stay, you know where I am." It was as far as he could go. "Come on now, I'll take you back."

The night clerk was asleep as they slipped out. In the car, they spoke only the once, when they had almost arrived.

"Don't you think," she started, then began over. "If you think I should get out of there, why are you driving me back?"

"I'm driving you back because you haven't decided to leave. You need to make that choice, not for me make it for you."

"You sound just like Matthew," she replied before she could help herself.

"Yah," Phillipe said, "I know. That's the thing of it. We do; we are."

"Will you come over tomorrow?"

"No. I think, maybe I don't want to be used the way people want me to be. Some other time, maybe."

"Here," she said tiredly, crossly. "I can cut over the field from here."

* * *

Corroboration of Cassandra's account of guns from New Hampshire took longer to find than Sokolov. They did not have enough to go on and were looking for the wrong way in – it was Matthew whom Cassandra had accused of acquiring weapons. On the journey back from New Orleans, Berlinger pressured her: she was not giving him enough. Finally, she admitted that the guns might – maybe – have been there while she was, maybe they had been acquired by Caleb – from someone he had known while he was in jail. It was all she could say without putting herself at risk.

The Bureau of Alcohol, Tobacco and Firearms arrived early in a convoy of cars and trucks, some fifteen officers in all. Romero was with them, with a new partner, a bored-looking female officer who watched from their car as Romero witnessed service of the warrant.

Matthew studied the warrant for several minutes before handing it on to Esther. He asked the lead officer, a tall, sharp-featured man in his late forties with a crop of thick, grey hair, a deeply-lined face and eyes that squinted from too many years peering down night-glasses:

"What does this mean?"

"It means what it says, that we can search for weapons."

"It says 'visual search only'. What does that mean?"

The Inspector – Faulkener – scowled.

"It means we don't start digging the place up – for the moment."

Matthew caught a flurry of amusement cross Romero's face.

"It means you've got nothing more than suspicion, right? Something you've been told? Cassandra, I suppose."

Berlinger's investigators had found Al in New Hampshire without a problem once they ran the connections. Making a deal with him had not been difficult: Rockworth was money, not the government, not the oppressor; Rockworth could protect him, promising to conceal his identity in exchange for an account of The Programme members who had come looking for guns – one with money, the other with sex. He could only identify Caleb – not even Pascale by name – and Caleb, the purchaser, was not known to be at Hammer Reach, believed not to be. Which was why the most the ATF had managed to obtain was a limited warrant: no digging without obvious cause; no machinery.

"It means what it says; we can do a visual search. Do you have any weapons here, sir?"

"Sure," Matthew replied caustically, "the weapons of freedom of association, freedom of thought, freedom of religion."

"Then you won't object to us taking a look around," Faulkener replied.

"Go right ahead. Let me know if you find anything that interests you."

"Do you have a man here called Keyte – Howard Keyte? Sir?"

"No; not that I'm aware of. Some of our members take new names."

"He was known as Caleb – Father Caleb."

"He's long gone – ask my wife, she may know where he is; he may even be with her."

The ATF men split into teams. About ten of them went directly up into the panoply of snow-capped firs and maples that were the woods, carrying land survey maps on which the farm-limits were marked. A couple of them had hand-held metal detectors, but they would only register if something was close to the surface and in substantial quantity; for anything more, they would have needed to drag their equipment vans up into the woods and that was precluded by the warrant; so, probably, were their hand-held models, but the notion that what was not to be seen did not exist worked both ways.

Though it was not deck weather, that was where Matthew settled himself as the remainder of the search party began their work at the top of the farmhouse, methodically proceeding down to the cells, monitored by Esther. Any questions the officers might have had about use of the cells appeared to have been answered by Romero, because, when they emerged from the cellar, all they asked was to be taken to the outbuildings.

Matthew accompanied them, striding across the snow in a cape that billowed behind him, an incongruous escort for the tightly wrapped officers in their blue dungarees with the acronym of the Bureau stencilled across their backs.

Esther went ahead to waken members in the dormitories. They were lined up outside each of the barns in military rows, a tired-eyed Emily amongst them, shivering in white shorts and T-shirts. As the ATF party approached, they came sarcastically to attention, saluted, then raised their hands in the air by way of surrender – and to make the point that they were not carrying weapons about their persons.

"For Christ's sake," Faulkener snarled, "you think this is some kind of a game?"

"Yes. I think this is my wife's little game and I think you're players in it. Surely you've seen what's been in the media? You're being used to put pressure on us – nothing more."

Faulkener had formed something close to the same opinion for himself: the difference was, after Waco, no one was taking any chances.

"I'm just doing my job, sir."

"Nazis," Esther muttered, loud enough to be heard.

The ATF man was used to the abuse; it washed off him with the sleet that began to fall fat and heavy while the inadequately attired members of The Programme were still standing at attention. He said:

"How about letting your people get some protection before they freeze, huh?"

"They've all the protection they need, Inspector. You look after your people; I'll look after mine."

Faulkener studied Matthew's expression closely, did not like what he saw: fanaticism. Over his shoulder, he noticed for the first time close up The Temple with its medieval slits.

"Now what in God's name is that? Some kind of a silo?"

"That is our Temple, Inspector; and I am about to hold a Mass. You are welcome to join us."

"Can we search it first, sir?"

"No, Inspector, you cannot. You may search it during."

He snapped his fingers, waved in the direction of The Temple, unlocked it with the heavy key of which he alone – not even Nahum – enjoyed possession, and led the members hurriedly within before Faulkener could stop them.

Stubbornly, Faulkener elected to join his own men inside the nearest of the dormitory-barns, that which was also the Meditation Hall. While his men searched the cubicles on the upper storey, using portable ladders to poke into the roof-space, he stood with his back to one of the walls, staring at The Programme symbol that made up the floor's centre-piece. From one angle, in a dim light, it was evocative of an Iron Cross; from another, taking one line from each segment, it could even have suggested a Swastika; moving in towards the middle of the hall, studying it close-up, he understood that it was four segments designed to make up a whole.

"Nothing here, sir," the team-leader reported, pocketing his hand-held detector while he stamped on the floor to indicate that it was solid.

"I didn't think there would be," Faulkener acknowledged.

He was standing directly above the lead-lined trunk.

His hope was that, by leaving The Temple to last, Matthew would have concluded his petulant Mass. Instead, they were still hard at it not only when they finished with the second barn – and the smaller outhouse where the animals were – but even when the woods-party returned to confirm that there were no further buildings or other structures in the rest of the property in which weapons might have been hidden, nor obvious signs of digging or concealment. On a "look-see" warrant, The Temple aside, they were done.

Faulkener took only a handful of his people inside with him. He wanted neither confrontation nor to expose more of them to humiliation than necessary. He led them through the door, opening it no further than necessary before slipping apprehensively inside. The construction was fortress solid, including the door. It took him several minutes to appreciate its shape. Each of the side segments was filled with members; only the head segment, where the pulpit was sited, had its space intact.

The Teacher was hectoring them from the platform.

"'And whoso falleth not down and worshippeth shall the same hour be cast into the midst of a fiery furnace' – Daniel 3:6. This is the distinction: to be cast into the fiery furnace for our failure to worship, and to walk into it with our eyes open as an act of faith in the fire beyond."

The ATF men scrambled around the kneeling members, rapping knuckles along the walls and banging on the floors, acting as if they did not want to disturb the worship yet not merely disrupting but dominating the proceedings. It was precisely the effect that Matthew had wanted.

Faulkener cut through the middle, now as certain that they would find no weapons as he had gradually come to the conviction that these people were a major danger. Part of him did not want to let Matthew draw him into his game; the greater part was incapable of walking away from it.

"Excuse me, sir; I need to examine this platform."

"Of course, Inspector," Matthew stretched his hands out, first to the sides then to the fore, turning them at the last moment into an instruction for the congregation to rise, from where they would the better be able to stare down on the ATF man as he snooped around the base of the pulpit, the construction of the platform, looking for a cupboard- or trap-door or any hint of usable space within.

There was silence as he worked, except for the occasional giggle or snort choked quickly back. As he rose, the membership broke into spontaneous applause. As the search team left, the members filed out after them. As Faulkener looked back, he saw Matthew's face, wracked with malice, watched him bellow:

"'All our enemies have opened their mouths against us.' 'Mine enemies chased me sore, like a bird, without cause' – Lamentations. I told you – I've got nothing to hide, nothing!"

Gradually, clapping slowly and in harmony, the members began to shepherd the ATF contingent off the grounds, towards their vehicles in front of the farmhouse. Romero had accompanied them during the search of the farm-house but had declined to follow them to the other buildings, settling himself in his car with his partner and a thermos of coffee. They both stepped out to watch the throng approach, not sure whether to intervene to save faces or stand back and save themselves from a riot.

From the middle of the crowd, at the back of his men, Faulkener caught Romero's eye, shook his head: this further humiliation he would take; not the one beyond.

Esther began to sing, her voice as clear and as loud as a church bell:

"We shall be whole..." Drawing out the line.

A couple of members responded:

"In the fire beyond."

"We shall survive..."

"In the fire beyond."

Matthew held up a hand to stop them, then shouted at the policemen assembling around their vehicles:

"God and Satan!"

All of the members shouted back in harmony:

"In the fire beyond. In the fire beyond."

\* \* \*

The mission to the ghettos entrusted to Jeremiah and Jeroboam had produced a small handful of new resident members whom Jeroboam had initially been intended to lead to England. Many of David Koresh's Waco followers were black Britons. At the last minute, Matthew cancelled the trip: he decided to bring them to Hammer Reach instead.

The long-anticipated letter from the owners of the house in Brookline arrived: in view of the publicity they could not allow The Programme to stay. Without Chapters, it was impossible to continue to attract new members. Matthew was alternately angry and amused. The ATF visit was the deciding factor: anger in the face of the inevitable was purposeless. There were good reasons to let the Chapters go. Nor did Matthew need them. The Programme had become what it was to be.

Matthew called a Council Meeting in the Meditation Hall, attended by the Superiors of the two American Chapters: Mother Hannah and Mother Meredith from Boston, Mother Jemima and Father Simon from New York, the peripatetic Father Nahum. The local Senior Messengers were also entitled to attend: Sister Esther, Sister Lilith, Brother Enoch, even young Brother Lucius had risen in the ranks. Pregnant Sister Diana – it was rumoured to be Christopher's child – Sisters Mary and Pascale had been allowed to resume their positions

427

of trust, but not so Brothers Reuben, Lemuel and Ehud. Also missing were Mother Naamah and Father George, Sisters Gloria and Rebecca, all in London.

"We are small," Matthew said, "but we are whole. We have said it so many times, we may have begun to forget: together we shall be whole."

Solid, loyal Simon spoke up.

"I see more members than enough. This is a Council Meeting; it has to be kept small; there are many beneath us who need certainty, not debate."

There was a rumble of agreement around the Hall.

Hannah announced:

"Micah is going to try and claim the children," she added.

"I will not let them go." The children were his at least as much as Hannah's and now they were Micah's not at all; to give them up would be to give up the future.

"Teacher – tell us what is happening," Jemima urged.

"What is happening is what is supposed to happen, Mother Jemima. We are being attacked, persecuted – just the way we need."

"Need, Teacher?" asked Nahum.

"Need, yes, Nahum. We can only go so far alone: it is only when we are surrounded by hostility that we can finally be sure that we have built something whole, something perfect, something that is unaffected by the world outside, complete in itself, in ourselves." His eyes were shining. "This is our time, the best time of all; this is when we are finally put to the test, when we finally learn that nothing can destroy us, that we are stronger even than all of them."

"Where, though, Teacher? If they take away our Chapters."

"Oh, they will not take them away," Matthew replied carelessly. "We shall give them up."

They were shocked: most of them had believed until now that to hang on to the Chapters was their primary purpose.

"We came to America thinking we were going to grow; but this is our home, and this is the final size of it. I want to bring everyone back here, while we still can. Those people won't be the end of it," he added, referring to the ATF visit. "If we don't move soon, we may lose the opportunity to be together, to be whole." English members could be refused entry to America; Hammer Reach itself might even be closed off.

Esther reminded him quietly:

"Hammer Reach is also under threat."

"No," Matthew said, much as he had dismissed Micah's claim against him for the children. "I won't give up Hammer Reach."

He gave them a litany of reasons for the decision to let the Chapters go.

"The money is slipping away. We can't afford the Chapters, even if we could manage to hold onto them: and don't forget what will be said about us in order to take them away from us – true or false doesn't matter to the media. The efforts to destroy us are already beginning to intensify. We have to consider what is most important to us. The most important thing is that we should all be together: big or small does not matter; only being whole."

Simon studied his old friend and Teacher and read between the lines: Matthew had said he had no intention of giving up Hammer Reach; he wanted everyone here to defend it. It was the final battle, fight to the end, the fire beyond. He nodded approvingly.

"The more of us there are here, the less they will be willing to force us to leave. The presence alone may be enough. What do they say, Esther? Possession is nine points of the law?"

"It's the tenth they tend to hit you with, though," Esther laughed. "I think, perhaps, I don't know, but it may be possible to make a deal."

"Who with?" Nahum reminded her. "The Chapters are Rockworth; Hammer Reach is Kroger."

"That's one of the attractions," Esther said. Matthew should have been a lawyer, she thought: the strategy was brilliantly simple. "If we give up the Chapters, Rockworth doesn't have a direct interest – or a legal platform. As for Hammer Reach, what the Gruenfelds want is money. Don't forget that it's the more difficult action, too: The Teacher has a life tenancy of Hammer Reach; real property is always more tricky to upset than a gift of money. With money, we can settle with them."

"Where would we get the money to settle with them?" Hannah asked. "Most of it's gone – The Teacher said."

"There'll be money," Esther said with such confidence that they did not ask from where. Only Matthew knew about the sale of her house in London; even he had not thought of her interest in Arnotts.

"The tenancy makes a difference," Nahum observed. "We haven't got a tenancy in New York, and we're no better than visitors in Boston. Giving them up makes us look good. What about London – we've still got a lease. Doesn't that mean Rockworth still has the chance to bring a case?"

"I'm not sure that's right, is it Esther?" Simon recalled something Colin had said. "The lease has gone – it's up to us to get it – I've forgotten now – reinstated?"

"Relief – we have to get relief from forfeiture. Simon's right: if we

429

drop the claim, we have no lease and Rockworth has no case."

Diana rose awkwardly to her feet: she had shown from an early stage, now she was huge. She placed her hands on her unborn child.

"These legal things aren't important. What's important is that The Programme should survive, that it should be here to welcome my child, to nurture her, rear her. I have an image of Tamar heading up a Chapter – it doesn't matter where, maybe in Outer Space by then – and of my daughter serving in its Coffee Lounge." A simple image to which they could all relate. "I need The Programme for her – she needs it too, more than most." The Programme would be her father, not Christopher. "I feel us curling up into a ball, the ball that can fly through the fire beyond and emerge unscathed; this – Hammer Reach, everyone here together – this is that ball. I am one – we are many," she concluded, speaking for herself and her daughter.

Mary helped her to sit down on the extra large cushion they had sewn and stuffed for her. From behind, Pascale supported her back until she had regained her balance. They were still together, these three, the way they had promised each other when the mad times had begun.

"It's agreed," The Teacher concluded. "I am one."

"We are many," they chanted back.

"Together we shall be whole," he said.

"In the fire beyond," they responded.

Before the meeting broke up, The Teacher said:

"There is one other thing that needs to be taken care of. There is someone here at Hammer Reach who is not to be trusted. A traitor, a spy," he used Esther's words deliberately. "If there is a leak, we are not whole."

Matthew's eyes met Esther's with a gaze packed with compassion. "And we know who it is."

For an irrational, insane, panic-stricken moment, Esther thought he meant her; then she realised who it was and glanced to her side to see if Simon, too, already knew. As if he could hear the question, he turned to look at her and nodded: Matthew had told him.

"Then we shall have to take care of her," Esther said softly but not at all gently. "She will need all the care we can give her."

\* \* \*

It was nearly a week later before they acted, a week of hectic activity at Hammer Reach and at the Chapters. Everyone worked until they dropped, even Emily, Emily most of all.

At the farm, they worked to expand available sleeping space. In the second of the barns, downstairs was converted to sleeping stalls. Inside the farm-house itself, they split up some of the larger rooms into cubicles. At one side, they erected a second lean-to to serve as a dining area and built a vast table at which members could eat in relays. No one was sure exactly how many members there would be at Hammer Reach – maybe ninety to a hundred. Aside from Thomas and Tamar, already at Hammer Reach, there would, however, be no children: Matthew had specifically instructed that none of the children, from London, Boston or New York, be brought. They had to be found homes, guardians – family and friends; a couple of parents stayed behind, unable to leave without them.

In New York and in Boston, it took little time to quit. They abandoned larger furniture, taking mattresses but not beds, chairs not tables, as well as all the adaptations that had formed the Coffee Lounges and which with more time would have been worth dismantling: only The Programme symbols had to be removed – mounted symbols from walls and ceilings, embossed curtains, some had to be painted over.

They took bedding, clothing, food, cooking implements, televisions, computers and related equipment – they took all their cash from the banks. They filled every car, VW bus, smaller vans, and they still had to rent U-Hauls and two Ryder trucks. By the third day after the Council Meeting, power supplies disconnected and bills paid in full, it was as if they had never been there – gone as quickly as they had arrived. Keys were left with neighbours. A press announcement would be made once they were all safely at Hammer Reach – The Programme did not need to stay where it was not welcome.

There was even less they could take from London. Some equipment went into store, food was given to non-resident members who were staying behind, technology sold off at a hefty discount. Then there were flights to find – preferably discount, though there was no time for advance booking reductions. There were seventeen of them in all: it would attract too much attention if they all flew together. Nor was it sensible to fly into the same airport. One way and another, it was not until the fifth day that the last of them took off from London Stansted, not until the sixth that they arrived home.

Only then was it Emily's time.

\* \* \*

They were gathered in the punishment block meditation area, one cell door open, the others closed. She had been in her cell for several hours, without food, water or light. Esther had come to fetch her from her work party before lunch, ordered her to come with her without explanation, even as she was led down the stairs she had not understood.

"Take your clothes off, Sister."

"What?" The look in Esther's eyes left her no room for either doubt or hope. "What are you talking about?"

"Take your clothes off, Sister," Esther repeated. She met Emily's gaze full on. She did not see a friend but a member who had betrayed them.

"No," Emily said. "No, I won't. I'm getting out of here, Carey. Let me go."

Calling her by her former name was the wrong thing to do. So fast that she did not see it coming, Esther slapped her across the face, so hard that Emily fell back against the wall, almost to the floor.

"Take your clothes off, Sister," Esther commanded for the third time.

Emily pulled herself to her feet. She cried:

"This is crazy. You're crazy. I want to leave."

Esther reached out a hand. For a split second, Emily thought she was going to lead her out, out and away. Then Esther grabbed at the neck of Emily's white polo-neck sweater, twisted it and began to tear it over her head. Emily lashed out but had left it too late, the top already covered her face. Esther stuck a foot between her legs to trip her over, then was kneeling beside her, pulling so hard Emily felt her arms jerk upwards like a child's to allow the sweater to clear her head.

Esther fought as if possessed. She straddled Emily's shoulders with her knees, pressed them to the ground, wrestled with her slacks pushing and grunting to Emily's ears like a rapist, like Richard. The last time she and Carey had been entangled, she had buried her head between Carey's legs, buried her mouth in her, drinking her, Carey's head had been between her legs, they had come together in love. Now, Esther tore her trousers and panties off in one downward thrust, jumped up, dragged them over Emily's feet, horrified at Emily's nudity, seeing not sex but shame.

Esther flung the clothing out of the cell. Now Emily was wearing only a bra. Esther stood at the door, holding out a hand. Emily was still on the ground. She reached behind herself to unclip it, threw it hard at Esther, started to laugh madly through her tears, lay back, legs apart, fondling her breasts, writhing sexually, raising her pelvis.

"Oh Carey, Carey," she moaned, mocking Esther, mocking herself.

Then, as she watched the door slam and the cell turns dark, as she heard Esther locking the door, she screamed after her:

"I'm not Colin, Carey; I'm not the one who betrayed you."

She was alone. She had seen a blanket in a corner, neatly folded, awaiting her. She groped her way towards it, and wrapped it around herself. For a while, she sobbed gently in a corner, for herself, for what had happened to Carey, for what was to come. She pulled herself together: she had known worse than this; the fact that it has been done to her by someone she loved, who had professed to love her, was nothing new; after the walk the week before, after the display of fanaticism before the ATF search-party the next morning in which Esther had played a leading role, she was not even sure she was surprised. Since Antibes maybe, certainly since she joined The Programme, she had followed Carey into the forest, hoping they would find a path to lead them out, knowing in her heart that each step was a step further away from survival.

Someone had found out about her visit to Phillipe: Matthew probably, always awake, watching from the farmhouse or wandering the sleeping dormitories like a night-guard. Phillipe sold information to Berlinger; it was understandable that they should mistrust him. She needed to explain it to them: Phillipe was a kind man; he had only wanted to help. It was his purpose to remain on the side-lines, but he wished them no harm and had come to tell them so. Yes, she had gone to see him; she would tell them she had gone to see him to find out what he was up to – they had failed, maybe she could do better.

It did not hang together in her own head; it would not sound true to them. Tell them the truth. She was sick of The Programme, sick of what it was doing to Carey, sick of their paranoia and their contempt for the outside world, their passion for the fire beyond.

She felt no hostility towards Carey. It was not Carey who had attacked her but Esther. It was who Matthew had turned Carey into – Matthew and Colin between them. Matthew was crazy – as crazy as Cassandra. They had set up The Programme together; they had made The Programme what it was – it was foolish to think that Cassandra could have been wholly bad, Matthew the angel of pure light.

Then there was Colin. Phillipe had told her Colin was helping Rockworth. He could not be acting for him; he had to be giving evidence. Knowing the general nature of the attack, it was easy to work out what evidence Colin would be giving. It cut too deep; she did not blame Carey for going off the deep end.

Doggedly, Emily told herself there was only one certainty, only one redemption: following Carey into The Programme had served to block Carey's retreat, helped push her further inside as surely as if she had led and pulled her after; she had to get Carey out. It did not matter what followed, not even if they never saw one another again – Emily needed to do it, for herself as much as for Carey.

She must have fallen asleep, lost some time, because she did not hear them coming down – Matthew, Carey – Esther, Simon. The Teacher himself opened the door, bent down to step inside, carefully wrapped the blanket around her.

"I am one, Sister Emily," he reassured her that she was still a member of his flock.

"We are many, Teacher," she mumbled automatically, coming awake to the realisation that she was still a prisoner.

"Come out now, Emily; we are not going to hurt you."

Groggily, she allowed him to pull her to her feet, lead her tamely out into the area between the cells, her eyes searched Esther's, begging for a response, found none. She turned instead to Simon; they were briefly lovers, but he had abandoned her when he came over and they had hardly exchanged a word since. He, too, acted as if she was a complete stranger.

Except for Matthew, they sat cross-legged on the floor. The only furniture was a block of hay, tightly bound and covered with a silk cloth woven with the symbol of The Programme. It had been there when they retrieved Hammer Reach; none of them knew what it was for; Matthew mounted it, sat atop it also cross-legged – The Teacher and his followers.

"I am one," Matthew said.

"We are many," they replied, Emily too.

"Together we shall be whole." All four of them.

"In the fire beyond," Matthew.

"In the fire beyond," Esther and Simon.

"Sister Emily, where did you go with Phillipe?" Matthew asked.

"I went to his hotel." No point in lying.

"Why?"

"I like Phillipe; I liked him when I went back to New Orleans, after Carey – Esther – went home. When he came here last night, it felt as if we were not finished up, there was something more between us."

"Were you going to sleep with him?" Esther demanded.

"I don't know. Maybe."

"Did you sleep with him?" Simon asked.

"No. He's not that kind of man."

"It's what he wants you to think," Matthew snorted.

"I was unhappy." She looked at Esther. "You couldn't help me." When they had walked in the woods.

"Help yourself, Emily," Esther replied. "You can't rely on anyone else."

"Apparently," Emily flashed.

"This serves no purpose." Matthew held up a hand. "What did you tell him?"

"Nothing. Nothing at all. He told me things."

"What?" Simon snapped.

"He told me about Colin, Esther's brother."

Phillipe had said nothing about it when they had talked in the kitchen.

"Berlinger," Esther guessed.

"Sure," Matthew agreed. "How long have you been working for Berlinger?"

"Berlinger? Me? I've never met him, I've got nothing to do with him. You're..." She bit her tongue off from telling The Teacher he was mad.

"You were spying for Phillipe – it's the same thing."

"I wasn't." There were only blindly obedient servants and conniving enemies; she was no longer the former.

"You're lying," Simon announced. "You said you were going to sleep with him?"

"I said I might have."

"You're lying," Simon repeated. "You're under a rule of abstinence; you couldn't have."

"What do you want from me, Teacher?"

"I am The Teacher," Matthew shouted. "I am The Programme. You are a member of The Programme. You cannot question me."

"I quit," Emily shouted back at him. "I quit, right? Keep your Programme – keep Esther, too," she added, regretting it as soon as the words were out of her mouth.

"No one keeps me, Emily," Esther said. "Not The Programme, nor you."

"Is that what this is all about – jealousy?" Matthew asked. "You couldn't have Esther, so you decided to betray us instead? What did you think? Bring down The Programme and she'd come running back to you? Or was it me you wanted to hurt – because Esther wants to be with me?"

Esther slid across the floor to sit directly in front of Emily.

"Oh, Emily," she put her arms around her shoulders. "Is that what you thought? I could have loved you here, Emily; I couldn't love you out there."

Emily whispered back, as if the two men could not hear:

"Esther, Carey – I know you've been hurt. I love you, come away with me; before it's too late."

"Too late?" Esther pushed herself away as if Emily was contagious. "Can't you understand? I want to be here. I told you – stay here and share it with me. But to stay here and betray us – how could you do it?"

"Who's betraying whom, Esther? I never betrayed you."

Simon had risen, stood behind Emily, grabbed her hair with one hand, pulled her head back, held her by the chin with the other.

"You have to tell us, Emily, you have to tell us the truth."

"I am, I am," Emily spoke between her teeth.

Esther closed in on her mouth, hissed directly into it:

"Tell us what you told Phillipe, Emily, tell me."

Matthew watched from his throne: this was proof of his decision to bring the whole of the membership to the farm; they would achieve a level of pure purpose, a unity, an army that no one could displace from Hammer Reach.

"All right," Emily cried, "I'll tell you. I told him – I'm frightened," she said.

"Yes," Esther believed her. "We're all frightened. We need to be."

They would get nothing more from her for the time being. Matthew gestured at Simon, who took hold of Emily's arms and raised her to her feet, guiding her into the cell before she knew what was happening, turning the key to lock the door before she began to scream:

"Let me go, let me out of here."

Esther, too, rose and crossed to the locked door. For a moment it seemed as if she might be about to respond, to unlock it, then she turned around and stood with her back to it, barring the way to prevent either Matthew or Simon releasing her, as if they would.

\* \* \*

The interrogation of Emily took place while members of The Programme were eating supper. There were too many people squashed into the farm-house to deal with her during the night when sounds would carry. Afterwards, almost all of them gathered in the Meditation Hall, leaving only a skeleton staff on guard-duty to look after the buildings and the grounds.

One of those on duty was Korah – Calvin Wood – newly arrived from New York with the mass exodus, waiting until Matthew, Simon and Esther loped across the fields towards the barns.

He knew what he had to do. It was dangerous, but if he left it too long, members would return to the farmhouse, settle in for the night. He had to act now or not at all.

During this and earlier tours at Hammer Reach, he had heard rumours about the night that Cassandra had left it, along with the triumvirate of her closest advisers, tales of people running between the Meditation Hall barn and the farmhouse, one person was alleged to have told another that she had heard either one shot or several shots, another was said to have spied on a midnight digging party, several people had heard the noise of the cement-mixer while it was still dark and well into the morning. Many had attended Matthew's fire-ceremony, when he had filled in the pit.

It was not enough for Berlinger. He needed more than assertion to persuade the authorities to take another look at Hammer Reach – and this time with an open warrant. In their one call, when he had warned his boss that they were quitting New York, Berlinger had insisted on hard evidence while all Calvin had was gossip, rumour, second-hand hearsay, speculation.

What was close to certain was that Esther and Emily had been party to the events of that night. Whether or not Matthew had been present earlier – and allegedly Diana could confirm his arrival – the two women had not been. Berlinger could place Carey in London a day or two before Matthew was back in control; credit card slips put Emily at Moonlight Lake.

The way it fit together was that Matthew had been imprisoned by Cassandra and the others – which was consistent with what he had subsequently written and said – and the two women had rescued him. Imprisoned and – if his own experience was anything to go by – physically assaulted. Calvin was a professional: he had been trained by Berlinger – after Berlinger had helped him make his way out of the Healing Family – to analyse; if this was not close to what had happened, he was at a loss for an alternative explanation.

He had to take the chance that he was right, that Emily had solid information and that – if he could get her out – she would disclose it. He scurried about the farmhouse stuffing his pockets with things she would need. T-shirts could fold up small, so he had plundered three of them. Shorts not trousers. Woollen socks. A pair of trainers beneath his sweater. A card with Berlinger's phone numbers on it. Money – people always needed money – but only enough to get to the nearest town, he did not want her getting away before Berlinger could come for her.

\* \* \*

Later that night when everyone else was asleep, exhausted by the week's activities, building or travelling – intense spiritual activity too, Matthew sat on the deck in the cold night, smoking one of his occasional cigarettes, smiling secretively, admiring his design. His children were here, his family, his worldly achievement. The thought of them kept him warm.

They had come to a crossroads and gone ahead. The Programme was coming to an end; he had foresworn the opportunities to turn it around; it could only drive forward towards its ineluctable end. If he did not rise to greet the end like an old friend, invite it in through the front door, then it would sneak in and destroy The Programme from the back.

He tossed the cigarette end into the dark, onto the damp grass, waited for it to sizzle and fade, then returned to the house and climbed the steps to her bedroom. It was a new time, a new game and he needed her.

Esther awoke as he slipped into the bed beside her, parted her legs to receive him without question or hesitation and abandoned herself to him gratefully. She almost succeeded in banishing Emily from her mind.

Afterwards, when Esther had slid back into sleep, Matthew rose and made his way down to the cells.

Emily had witnessed Caleb's death. She knew there were weapons. It was time for her to tell. On the way, he slipped into his own bedroom and bundled up some of Esther's clothes still there from when she used to occupy it with him. From beside the front door, he picked up a pair of sturdy shoes that seemed about the right size and – indiscriminately – a coat from the stand.

He found the door to her cell open, the cell empty. He frowned, not in anger that she had gone but because he had not expected it. Then he laughed aloud: someone had beaten him to it. It was not Esther; it could not have been. It mattered not who it was: he would find out in due course. The important thing was that she had gone. Everyone served their purpose – everyone served his. His purpose was to ensure that The Programme be preserved – it was more important than anything, more important that The Programme be preserved than that its members should be. Her purpose was to put his to the test.

\* \* \*

"What do you think my life's been about," Matthew had cried. "The Programme, that's all; if it wasn't for The Programme, I'd be nothing,

I'd have done nothing."

"Matthew," Paimon moaned, "Caleb's dead – an eye for an eye."

"Helen was my eyes," he ranted, waving the gun in one face after another: Paimon's, Christopher's, even Caleb's, already dead. "An eye for an eye? She was my eyes," he repeated.

"Where will The Programme be if you kill us, Matthew? What will you have made it into?"

"What did you make it into, Christopher?"

"It was sacred," Christopher whispered. "It was an act of worship."

"So's this," Matthew said, raising the weapon to shoot.

"No, Matthew," Christopher begged him. "This is killing for its own sake." As Matthew had challenged Cassandra.

"That doesn't make it wrong. Couldn't you say, in one sense, The Programme is death for its own sake too?"

Christopher had no arguments left. He squeezed his eyes shut believing, to the end, that Matthew would not do it.

Paimon had a different last thought. Matthew was who Cassandra had loved, more even than she had loved him. She would have shot him. So did Matthew.

# Chapter Eighteen

"It is all about love. Finally, what we are doing here is all about love. It's ironic, isn't it? What they see from outside is our resistance to their interference, which they call hostility. From within, all I can see is the love: we will not let them in, because to do so would mean to give up love: we have nothing else to hide. Look around you now. How many people do you see? Seventy or eighty the last time I counted."

The congregation crowded into The Temple, a more secure building than the larger Meditation Hall, was somewhat less than eighty, closer to sixty, because of the guards on duty at the farmhouse, and in the barns and the outbuilding, keeping watch on the Federal and State police who were, in turn, keeping watch on The Programme.

"This is what we have been trying to achieve since the beginning of The Programme, since the beginning of time. The Programme is the product of everything that went before, just as it will touch everything that follows. The beginning of time was the moment when we left wholeness behind, when we began to think that there was a you and me, an us and them, people and animals, materials and ideas, this country and that, different races and languages – all and any of the divisions you can think of and that cry out for reunification."

He stretched a hand out to touch The Programme symbol carved out of wood and mounted on the wall behind him.

"Even the greatest divisions of all do not exist: fire and water; air and earth – the four so-called elements. There is but one element – one being, one energy.

"Somewhere out there and in here, this one thing – energy – decided it wanted to express itself. That's one of the definitions of energy: a force for expression. And that's the only certainty that there is or ever has been: that there is energy." He had slipped into a concept of which he had often spoken and written; reminding them where the journey had begun. The repetition of old ideas represented the absence of the new – The Programme was at the end of its course, had completed its cycle; if they tried to continue it, they would find themselves going around and around in a circle, the ultimate denial of progress.

"Ever since that one moment of time or feeling or idea, energy has been trying to recapture the way it was when it was whole, the way it was the moment before, the way it was where it had just come from."

He looked around. They were silent, rapt, devoted. He could do them no wrong.

"Conscious life is the mirror in which we work on a giant jig-saw, trying to arrange ourselves – and everyone around us – into a shape or pattern that feels like that wholeness. That's why countries go to war, or why people argue and fight: my way, m*y* way, they cry – it will only make sense if we arrange it all my way.

"It is also why we form alliances – to make a fixed arrangement of some portion of the screen or mirror – and why we seek love with such desperation. It does not work: even in a mirror, if you are looking at it you are not in it; if you are thinking about it, you are not doing it; you cannot see what you are a part of – you have heard this before: the room in which you stand – and therefore, if you can see it, it cannot be you. The only way to achieve that sense of completion, love, wholeness is to be it. That is what we are doing – here, now, today; that is what we are going to do together."

He said, his voice rich and rolling like the hair that flowed down his shoulders, slowing hypnotically with every word:

"I want you to think about the person nearest to you, not about yourself. It doesn't matter who it is, or how well you get along together. Think of him or her as the most loved person in your life, until he or she matters more to you than your life itself. Fix that idea in your head as you begin to meditate, as you begin to float, stop thinking about it, let the idea take you over, let it become you, let it be your very breath, let it be your very last breath – love that person as he or she  is loving you, become one another, do this for each other, until between us we are whole being called love. You will never know this love again; you will know it forever. We are one, we are many, together we are whole, whole love. This is what they cannot destroy or take away: it is the fire beyond that is too hot for them to handle."

\* \* \*

"Why?" Emily asked just as Calvin was about to leave her at the edge of the woods to make his way back to the dormitory. "Why go back?"

"Someone's got to be there. When I was in the Healing Family," he had told her as they walked how he first come into contact with Berlinger, "that was what I used to think. The bit of me that wanted out but couldn't find the way to do it, I used to think – there must be someone else who feels the same way but who does knows how to get himself out, maybe he can help me get out too."

Emily leaned against a tree, cold but glad of the rest before the long and lonely – perhaps dangerous – trek through the woods in the night and down the other side to Moonlight Lake. They had taken the long way round to the woods – along the road – to stay within the sector Calvin was supposed to be watching. As they had slipped out of the house, she spotted Carey's hooded anorak on a hook and had grabbed it to wear: she would have frozen without it. It was almost as if Carey had left it out for her, though she knew it was the last thing Esther would have done.

"Were they, you know, actually stopping you – I mean, like, well, you know?" As she had been.

Calvin – leaning against a tree a couple of feet away – shook his head:

"No. I could have walked at any time. Walked out – walked through a couple of doors, caught a bus to town was all. The thing was – if no one else left, they had to know something I didn't, so I didn't leave either. Being your own guard, man that's the best deal for them: you're under twenty-four hour supervision, better than handcuffed – you can't escape because you're both the prisoner and the guard, they don't even have to feed two of you."

She laughed at his graphic metaphor: his eyes were sparkling; she had never seen him so animated. She remembered first meeting him, at the New York Chapter before their trip to the South: he was older than most of the others. He gave the appearance of a commitment and an interest as great as any other Initiate. Yet he was reserved, never abandoned, acting as if he knew something that the others did not, as if he alone had the sufficient degree of sobriety to appreciate the taste of The Programme. She had sometimes wondered about him, what he was doing there. Now she knew.

"Did someone pay Berlinger to get you out?"

"He was trying to get someone else out. It didn't work. Along the way, he met me and, I guess, he could see I really did want out even if I wasn't able to say it. So he took me out instead, I guess you could say."

"The other person – what happened to him?"

"Her. She killed herself. I think Berlinger felt responsible – like, because he'd put pressure on her too. He's a good man; I think a lot of people don't see that – they see someone who takes money for doing a job that's, well, heavy – dirty maybe, the way it's talked about. I've seen the way people talk to him – parents: it's like they're paying a hit man to kill someone they haven't got the nerve to do themselves."

"How did he get you out?"

"He made a big play of looking around to find the one I was looking for – you know, like I said, the one who could help me get out. Went on looking until I saw him for myself."

"You, right?"

"Right."

"Then you went to work for him."

"Right."

He had begun to clam up; he had given her enough to feel confident in him – that the escape was not the prelude to a trap – but now he was beginning to wonder if she was asking too many questions.

She watched him watching her, laughed.

"Good way to learn trust – The Programme, huh?"

He pushed himself upright and away from the tree, stretched.

"You have to go; I have to get back. After this is over, you know, maybe we could meet up, talk about it."

"I'd like that." He was her saviour; she wanted nothing so much as one day – soon – to be able to see him in the light of day, talk, laugh, wash away the horror of today and the trek that lay ahead.

"You're sure you know where to go?"

She realised that she was crying, wiped the tears away with the sleeve of the anorak before they turned to ice.

"I'm okay. Go, go." She wished he would come with her; so long as he went back, there was more chance it would work out for all of them, Carey too. Purpose and counter-purpose.

\* \* \*

It felt like it took far longer to make her way through the woods and down the hill to Moonlight Lake than it had taken Carey and her to cross to Hammer Reach the day they came to rescue Matthew. That day, though, had still been relatively warm and she had been more suitably clad. She had Carey's company, too, in which she had delighted; no idea how awful what awaited them would be, there had been an air of adventure and excitement – it had still been a game. Tonight, she was freezing, often crying, terrified, confused, betrayed: some of the journey, she was barely conscious, slipping and sliding, bumping into trees, clinging onto a trunk when she mistook night noises for animal.

In fact it was quicker – in a couple of hours, she could see Moonlight Lake, shimmering in the night, the moon dancing on the ice, frozen row-boats seeming to rock as the light caught them in shifting shadows, the jetty seemed longer from a distance than when she had paced it awaiting Carey's arrival.

Her feet were solid blocks of ice themselves, the trainers, though sturdy, were soaked through to her soles. Her shorts chafed her thighs until they, too, were so cold she could not feel them any longer. Her legs were scratched and bruised. By the time she arrived at the Inn, her teeth were chattering so loud and fast she could not hear herself think about whether to ring to be let in or else to find somewhere – maybe an unlocked car – to wait for the morning.

She did not have a choice: she needed warmth and immediately. Nor did she need to ring for long: the innkeeper was quickly at the door; she slept lightly, watching over her guests and her family even as she rested, an ear open for the mythical wanderer needing shelter from the storm; all these years of being ready and it was Emily.

"My God, dear," the woman pulled her inside and wrapped her arms around her. "What happened to you? No, never mind, let me make you a hot drink, I need to fetch you some clothes, here, take off those wet things, put this on," she whipped off her own dressing-gown, "before you freeze."

She physically hustled Emily into the games room at the side of the main house in which she left her, returning a few minutes later in her husband's dressing-gown, with dry clothing rooted from her own and her children's cupboards and a quilt for Emily additionally to wrap around herself. While Emily – in a daze – dressed, she fixed coffee, a sandwich, a generous tot of brandy. Not until she had helped Emily to drink, and forced her to eat, did she ask what had happened.

Still unsure how much she wanted to be known, Emily haltingly recounted that Matthew seemed to have gone completely mad, had lost touch with reality, was behaving like a tyrant; Carey was going along with it. Emily had been locked up. One of the members had helped her to escape.

"That's all there is to it, I suppose," Emily sounded wistful, as if nothing serious could be implied by such a brief and simple explanation. "I'm sorry about waking you," she said for the third or fourth time. "It was the only place I could think of to go."

The woman waved the apology away as unnecessary.

"I need to make some calls, to England. I've got a little bit of money – the guy who helped me out gave me. I don't know if it's enough. I thought – you'd still have my credit card number. I don't have it with me but I haven't cancelled it."

Again, the wave of a hand: detail, didn't matter.

"First thing is, I have to call the police for you."

"Please, let me make my calls first. I'm not hurt – no, really I'm not." It was her turn to wave away the protestation that being locked up and having to escape through the night in summer wear was hurt enough by the innkeeper's book, more than enough to report to the police. "I have to call London – Carey's brother. I have to let him know how much trouble she's in."

The woman snorted: Carey's trouble wasn't her problem right now – Emily was. On the other hand, family registered.

"It's still the middle of the night in England too," she made one last attempt to persuade Emily to call the authorities before anyone else.

"It doesn't matter," Emily said dully.

The hall that was reception was also the office. No one was up and about to overhear. The woman stacked a couple of logs in the fire-place, stoked the glowing embers of the fire to get it up again, went off to make more coffee shaking her head: she'd seen a bunch of things in her time, but these Programme people were headed right to the top of the list.

Emily called International Information to find out Colin's number, which put her through to Directory Inquiries in England. It was strange to be in the middle of nowhere in upstate New York talking to a stranger with an English provincial accent. Strange gave way to frustration when she was told that the number was ex-directory. She heard herself pleading that it was an emergency, life-and-death: if you call the police, love, the voice told her trying to be helpful but making it worse.

She got Charles Arnott's number instead, but there was no answer.

That was when – desperate to make some contact with Carey's family – she dialled the only number she could still remember, her own.

"Hello?" Richard answered sleepily – drunk too, in all probability.

"Richard," she whispered, almost glad to hear his voice.

"Emily?" He awoke at once.

"Ah, Richard," she mumbled.

"Where are you, Em?" Em: Carey sometimes called her Em.

She started to sob.

"It's all gone wrong, I don't know what's happening."

"Em, Emily – where are you? Tell me where you are."

"It doesn't make sense, Richard. I've forgotten why I'm ringing you. I'm sorry I woke you."

"Emily, tell me where you are," he repeated, excitement in his voice. She was in trouble; she had rung him; he would have her back.

"I don't know," she said, realising how absurd it sounded. "I can't tell you." She would have to give him the number for Colin to ring her back; he would be able to work it backwards. It did not matter: there were priorities and Carey was hers.

"Tell me where you are, damnit, Emily: I'm worried about you. Is Carey there?"

"Carey? No. Esther is, though. Sort of," she said, making no sense.

The innkeeper had come back into the hall, stood with her back to a wall, listening grim-faced: she had to get the girl to bed; she was beginning to fear that she was more damaged by her long journey through the hills than she had at first seemed; maybe she should call a doctor as well as the police.

"Richard," Emily said, suddenly clear, "I have to make contact with Colin Arnott. I can't reach him: they say his home number is ex-directory."

"What about it?" Richard challenged defensively for no reason that she could understand. "Why are you asking me?"

"It didn't used to be: they told me that. In the phone book, there'll be an address; it's Fulham or somewhere like that."

"What are you telling me for?" Richard knew where Arnott lived.

"If I give you the number where I am – will you go round and wake him, tell him to call me?"

"What?" he screamed. "Are you crazy. No. Fuck you. What do you think I am? Your servant? Errand boy?"

"Richard, please," she whispered. "Carey's in trouble. I've got to talk to Colin. I can't think of anyone else who'll help."

"The fuck with Carey. I hope she's really in trouble – dead trouble. I'll help you," he said. "Only you. Tell me where you are. I'll come and get you."

If she had seemed to be losing her way earlier in the call – enough to worry the innkeeper – his insistence on coming to get her was enough to snap her back to clarity.

"No," she said. "I can't do that. Will you please, please go round to see Colin? Please, Richard."

"You can fuck off, Emily," he shouted as he realised she was only ringing for Carey's sake, had no interest in him. "Fuck off," he repeated, slamming down the receiver.

"Emily, now," the woman stood over her, Emily's head slumped in her hands, choking back her tears.

"He was a bastard, such a bastard. I was a fool to ring him."

"You need to sleep, Emily. I'll put you in a room upstairs. In the morning we'll call the police." She was dissembling: she would call the police as soon as she got Emily to sleep.

"Please. One more call. Please. I've got one more idea."

"Go ahead, dear; I'm just trying to help," she shrugged off her disappointment.

This time, the International Information she wanted was in France: Antibes, to be precise. If Charles Arnott was not at his London home, he might be at the apartment.

Because France was an hour ahead of England it was already approaching morning. It would not have mattered: Charles had not slept. He snatched at the phone.

"Yes, hello, yes."

"Charles – it's Emily."

"Emily? Emily? Is she all right, Emily? Is she with you? Put her on. Let me speak to her."

"She's not here, Charles," Emily cried.

"Is she all right, Emily?" His voice started to fade.

"She's, she's all right Charles," she tried to say, though her tone told him the truth. "Charles – have you got Colin's new number?"

"New number? Colin? I don't know Colin, I mean, I don't talk to him. Emily, tell me what's wrong."

"It's all gone crazy, Charles: The Programme. Matthew's mad. Carey's – she's – they locked me in a cell, Charles, she took my clothes away, she hit me, Charles." She was half-screaming, half-shouting.

The innkeeper bit her knuckle: she was worried about guests waking; not so much because they would be disturbed – though that would be unfortunate – but because she did not think Emily would be able to cope with seeing anyone else right now, or being seen.

"Carey hit you? What are you talking about?" Charles sounded calmer but distant, unreal, automaton-like. "I don't understand, Emily. Where's my daughter? I want to speak to her."

"Charles, Charles," Emily moaned, "I'm trying to tell you. There's a farmhouse, The Programme's all there – everyone – they've cut themselves off. Some terrible things happened – some things happened to Matthew. Now he's hurting other people – me, he thinks I betrayed him. She does too. They put me in a cell; she took my clothes away; she hit me."

"I don't think I understand," Charles was suddenly lucid, his voice high and clear projecting like an actor on a stage. "I really don't think I can understand."

Emily felt for him but she needed to make him understand.

447

"Charles, people have been killed. We saw someone get killed."

The innkeeper was fully erect: she would not even wait for Emily to fall asleep before she called the police.

"Is Carey all right, Emily?" Charles asked, as if he had not heard.

"I don't know what to do, Charles," Emily sobbed.

There was a long silence, then Charles said again:

"Let me talk to Carey, Emily. Would you let me talk to Carey?"

"I can't, Charles," Emily wept. "I wish I could."

Another silence, longer than the last.

Then a thump, like the phone falling to a stone floor.

The silence continued.

"Charles, Charles, Charles, Charles," Emily was calling. "Please, Charles."

The other woman took the receiver from her hand, listened for a few moments, then pressed the bar to break the connection. Immediately, she pressed a button – redial. After a long wait for the connection to be made, the piercing insistent high-whine like short bursts of a siren told her the receiver was still off the hook at the other end.

She broke the connection again and dialled – 911.

\* \* \*

The innkeeper's call to the police brought them to fetch Emily and, across the Atlantic, their counter-parts to find Charles. He had had a stroke, could not move his limbs, but it was not fatal, nor had it affected his mind. They took him to the hospital in Antibes – the South of France was rich in advanced medical facilities for the elderly: he was rational, insistent – no one was to tell his son. Within a couple of days, he was out of intensive care, well enough to move to a private clinic – one which would allow him to watch the cable TV news to which he was addicted.

\* \* \*

Emily's call to Berlinger was a debt of honour: she had to let him know that Calvin was safe. She telephoned him from the police station to which Romero and his partner drove her on Faulkener's instructions. She slept the whole way. At the station, she was examined by a doctor. They fed her and tried to persuade her not to call anyone, but she insisted. It took Berlinger less than two hours to arrive, calling Rockworth for the use of a plane out of Boston.

Faulkener was neither stupid nor proud. The local FBI had been brought in: Emily's detention was kidnapping, there had been inter-state transportation of minors, arms too once they had Emily's confirmation that there had indeed been weapons at Hammer Reach, whatever had happened to them since. Only Caleb's murder – and the possible deaths of Christopher and Paimon – were purely state affairs. When Berlinger arrived, Faulkener brought him in to advise: none of them had his experience of cults.

Berlinger urged them:

"Go, go in now, before they've got time to react to her escape."

"We have to wait for a warrant," Faulkener insisted.

"Why? Pursuit – imminent danger – aren't they enough?"

"What danger, Mr Berlinger? Your man went back voluntarily."

Berlinger flushed: there was no basis for disputing Emily's account of Calvin's return; besides, he knew Calvin – had trained him – he had no doubt he would have gone back to report on further developments, and – if the chance presented – perhaps also to help others escape.

The local FBI contact agent was a black man called Weitz.

"Jewish grandfather," he had explained before anyone could ask the question he had heard ten thousand times before.

"Bill?" Faulkener asked him.

"I'm sorry, Mr Berlinger – I agree with Bruce." Faulkener. "Unless you can give us something more solid to go on, we'll have to get a warrant. They've already been in, found nothing; that's going to count against us; I think the girl should swear out an affidavit herself – elsewise, we're going to look like we're in some kind of vendetta here."

Berlinger shook his head in frustration.

"When these people go off, they go off fast and they go all the way. It's the way it always happens. For years, they live in a world of their own, then something happens to bring it to a head; there's only a small window of opportunity left, while the final struggle is going on inside."

"I thought you said, this Crane character, he's already won the power struggle?" Romero interrupted.

"No, yes. I'm not talking about the power struggle. That's just the trigger. The real struggle is between the cult's faith, whatever it is, and the real world; the struggle between realities, that's what's coming to a head. The cult and the world are going head to head. What do they do? Stick to their own, weird, cult-view, or face up to the fact that it's a load of baloney and get back to the reality the rest of us believe in? That's the final struggle and that's the last opportunity to get in there and help them."

"Help them?" Faulkener asked in surprise, though Romero nodded slowly, beginning to understand the big man's surprising thoughtfulness.

"Sure, yes, help. You saw them – they're way out of it, him too. That was the big mistake at Waco: you can't treat them as enemy, like gangsters holed up in a bank with a bunch of hostages; it's not about saving some of them from the others; they're all locked into each other – mutually dependent – whether the members on the leader, or the leader on the members – that's how they got there in the first place.

"There's a tendency for us to see the leader as our enemy – which maybe he is – and forget that he's not theirs; we also need to remember that he's only our enemy because that's how the situation has panned out. It isn't what he set out to be – not our enemy, not theirs. It's gone as badly wrong for him as for them; just because, in that situation, he's got maybe ninety per cent control doesn't affect that."

"What about the girl here? She had no control at all." Faulkener.

"Right at the end, sure. But until she got herself locked up, she had some – like you said about Calvin, she went back after she saw Lamarque. Yes, sure, at the end, the balance can shift, you can get a situation where some of them are literally locked up, like Emily was. But that's the result of something that's happened over a period of time, and you can't just ignore the way it got there. It's a part of what I said: the struggle for reality."

"What about the woman, what did you call her – Cassandra?" Faulkener asked.

"We've got her stashed in a house in Boston – her and the other one, Micah, couple others," Berlinger admitted.

"What're you thinking, Bruce?" Weitz asked Faulkener.

"The way Emily tells it, this girl Helen was killed before Crane got back to Hammer Reach – when it was under this Cassandra's control. Do we pick her up? Conspiracy, at least."

Berlinger said tiredly:

"You're still looking at the crimes, gentlemen; we should be looking at the people – the ones who're alive; while they still are."

\* \* \*

Early in the morning, Matthew gathered Nahum and Simon, Lucius too, the two Jays. They assembled in the Meditation Hall.

450

"Emily's gone – escaped," he proclaimed.

"How?" Simon asked. "How could she?" His eyes narrowed accusingly, there was one name on his mind.

"No," Matthew said quickly. "She was with me."

"Then how?" Nahum repeated Simon's question, understanding that it was of seminal significance without yet having worked out exactly why.

"I don't know," Matthew replied. "I went down to see her, she was gone." He did not tell them that he had gone down with the intention of releasing her himself. "It's not the most important thing right now."

Timidly, Brother Lucius, promoted to Senior Messenger when he had come to America after Matthew recovered The Programme, said:

"Tell us what we have to do, Teacher." Matthew's eyes rested on the boy. He remembered the night in The Temple at Chesterfield Gardens that seemed now to have been in another lifetime. He asked:

"What do you feel?"

Lucius' eyes shone.

"Agony."

"Right. Agony. We have always known this moment would come, when we would be tested in the fire – and it will be, as Brother Lucius says, agony, and we shall, as I have told you, survive it. I am one."

"We are many."

"Together we shall be whole; in the fire beyond."

"Here is where they taught me their kind of agony," Matthew stamped on the symbol on the floor. He backed up until he stood outside the four sections that had formed the false-floor that had covered the pit. "And here," he tapped, "is where I buried the weapons with which they intended to inflict their agony on The Programme itself."

The three more junior members drew in their breaths in surprise. Simon nodded – he had not known of the weaponry, but he knew Caleb. Nahum had been told about them as he concreted in the exposed holes of The Temple foundations the next morning.

Matthew paced out an area about four feet by six.

"Jeroboam, Jeremiah, get shovels – and a pick-axe. Hurry; there's not a lot of time."

While the two black men ran to the outhouse where most of their farm and other implements were stored, Lucius going along with them to help, Simon and Nahum huddled around Matthew.

"What's going to happen, Matthew?" Simon asked.

"Emily will tell them about the guns – that's what they were looking for last time; she knows they were here; she saw them; she can give them enough evidence for a full warrant."

"What else will she tell them?" Nahum had not been told what the holes he had filled in with concrete contained, though he had suspected. Matthew's refusal to tell him protected him, and he had been grateful for it at the time; that time was past.

"There was no choice. I couldn't let them go. After what they'd done, they would have had to come back to eradicate it – which meant eradicating me, one way or another. Out there – the three of them together – the war between factions would never have ended, it was all that The Programme would have become."

"Now it's a war between – what? The Programme and the world?" Simon said, licking his lips.

"Something like that. Does it frighten you, Father Simon?" Matthew noticed the mannerism.

"Does it frighten you, Teacher?" Simon licked his lips again. "It's time; I'm looking forward to it." His eyes met Matthew's: do not doubt me again.

"Nahum?" Matthew asked. "I love you, you know that. If this is something you can't do – I won't love you the less for it."

Nahum shook his head firmly.

"No, Teacher. I've had my time; it's been a wonderful time; I never knew there could be so much love or so much fun. I wouldn't have missed it for anything."

Matthew put out his arms to embrace them both.

"It's not over – the fine times, the fun times, the love. It's just beginning. We must be ready for it."

The three other men returned with the tools. Matthew seized the pick, the others took shovels. They began to work.

\* \* \*

The first person Matthew had told was Esther. In turn, she broke the news to Mothers Jemima, Naamah and Hannah. Then she summoned the remainder of the members into The Temple, even Mother Meredith and Father George, mounting the platform to stand behind the pulpit, feeling the nervous tension that she used to feel when she appeared at court as an advocate.

She was dressed not in court gown, but a flowing silk gown that had belonged to Cassandra.

"I was a lawyer; I know the law. They are going to come in the name of the law. They will say that they are coming to search for guns but they will be coming to destroy The Programme. Make no mistake about this. They are working for Rockworth: Rockworth holds The Programme responsible for the death of his son and, it has to be said, he is right – The Programme is responsible."

She had their attention: no one moved, not even to breathe. Matthew had not told her what to say or how much to tell them.

"The Programme is responsible because The Programme allowed him to die. Some of you have heard rumours about what happened. By and large, those rumours are true. I was no more here than most of you but I have talked with others – we have all heard of so-called Special Masses, some members here today attended one of them." She watched heads lower in shame. "Let them speak up now if I am wrong to describe those Masses as the low point in The Programme's history, its pit of shame. The things that happened then led to Anthony's death, as surely as I am standing here." She paused. Diana was nodding firmly, Mary crying, Pascale and Lee could not look her in the eye but their faces told it all.

"I gave up being a lawyer to become a member of The Programme. I will not let them use the law to break up The Programme. I was not there that night, but I was already an Acolyte and even if I were not it would not matter: The Programme is everything that it does, and everything that it has ever done. There is no escaping my responsibility for it, or any of us. We are collectively The Programme. We are what The Programme has become and was at any time. The only way to honour Anthony's death is to place it where it rightfully belongs – in the fire beyond. The only way to ensure that it can survive the fire beyond is to carry it with us as a part of The Programme, as part of the whole that The Programme represents, as part of The Programme of which we are each also a part."

She looked around, encouraged by nodding heads, smiles of recognition and support.

"There is more. There were guns. They were brought here by Caleb with the knowledge of Cassandra and Christopher, Paimon too. They had commenced a war on The Programme itself. Left to themselves, they would have turned it on all of us. Sister Helen, once the close companion of The Teacher, our sister, was killed here at Hammer Reach. That, too, was a Special Mass. Though no one who is now a member of The Programme had any part of it, they will come to see if there are bodies and there will be such a body, Helen's body, buried and hidden not by The Teacher, but by those I have already named, who are gone.

"What do we say to them? That was them, not us – we are the

good version of The Programme, and they were the bad? It may be true but it is not right – there is only one Programme, we are whole, we are all a part of it, good and evil alike; to try to separate us out is to undo the work of decades – it must fail."

Meredith – dear Meredith, New York friend – perceptive Meredith – called out:

"Sister Esther – is there more?"

Esther had not planned to go further – enough at a time. She could not lie to Meredith, she did not like to lie to any of them.

By the time she decided, her hesitation had hinted at the answer.

"Yes," she said flatly. "Yes, there is more. You have also heard rumours of what they did to The Teacher. The Teacher has not concealed it, though he has protected you from the worst of it, knowing how you would react to the pain they inflicted on him, how it would become your pain too. The Teacher was kept prisoner in the pit – the pit beneath the Meditation Hall that some of you helped to fill in the day after he was released." She looked up, eyes shining. "The day after it was my purpose to release him. For several days he had been kept a prisoner, strapped to a block of wood they called an altar, with little food or water, subject to ritual humiliation and physical abuse."

She let her carefully chosen words sink in. While she did so, she looked around for three members in particular: Lemuel, Reuben and Ehud: they alone – of those remaining in The Programme – knew the truth.

Lemuel was terrified, the other two barely less so. His terror was not an obstacle but an attraction. She hissed:

"Tell them Brother Lemuel – tell them what The Teacher forgave you."

Lemuel could not speak; he was shaking, crying, in a fit. He grabbed at Reuben, Ehud: they pulled their arms away, distanced themselves.

Meredith's eyes met Esther's. She was asking her to stop it; she had the authority to command her to do so; Esther was speaking directly for The Teacher – it was an authority she could not use.

Father George was the first to realise what she was telling them had happened in the pit, what Esther was demanding that Lemuel confess. He was at the front of one of the crowded segments; Lemuel only a little way into another. George strode across the short space between them, roughly pulled Lemuel out and flung him angrily to the ground. He did not strike him but spat at his face and turned his back on him, glowering into each of the three segments in which congregation was gathered – all but the fourth, in which the pulpit was set, the segment of fire – silently challenging the others to follow suit.

The men went first, shaking their heads in disbelief; the women followed – what had been done to The Teacher had been done to many of them in one way or another but he was The Teacher. As they passed, they spat on Lemuel before turning their backs, shunning him. Meredith was last. She could not spit. She held a hand out to help Lemuel to his feet, saying:

"Brother Lemuel, even you are a part of The Programme."

Then she, too, turned her back on him.

His face and his T-shirt were covered with globs of spit. He made no effort to wipe them off. He stood there for several minutes before he advanced on the pulpit, praying silently to Esther, before turning and repeating what she had said, in a haunting tone that echoed through The Temple:

"The Teacher forgave me. The Teacher is The Programme. The Programme forgave me. I forgive myself."

Gradually, they began to turn around, responding to his pride that if he was capable of forgiving himself, they too must do so. He had been beyond; The Teacher had welcomed him back; he was a messenger from the fire.

Ashamed of their cowardice, Reuben and Ehud stepped forward and turned to stand with their backs to the pulpit, shoulder to shoulder with Lemuel.

"I am one," Reuben said.

"I am one," Ehud repeated.

"We are many," said George, first to understand and first to forgive.

"Together we shall be whole," Esther led the response, reminding them that this was her gathering. "In the fire beyond."

"What happened, Sister Esther?" Meredith asked.

Esther knew it would come to this. She wanted it to. Whether they stayed or went would be about Matthew – deserting him or standing by him. The quicker she brought them to that choice, the less distracted they would be by the irrelevant details that had so bothered Emily.

"Matthew shot Caleb with one of his own guns. I saw it. I saw everything that happened. Caleb had been going to do it again. I saw that too. I saw Caleb, naked as a baby, naked as a madman. I had released Matthew; Matthew shot him."

"Freed him," Father George corrected her. "Matthew freed him. It was an act of love."

"Love," other members repeated, tasting the word, realising it fit what they felt. To have shot Caleb was to have freed him was to have loved him.

"Love," cried Lemuel, tears coursing down his face in a flood.

"Caleb is free," Esther screamed. "In the fire beyond."

"The fire beyond," they repeated, dancing, grabbing each other, clinging on for the sheer joy of it; those nearest to him dragged Lemuel into their midst – forgiven. "Caleb is free in the fire beyond," they sang.

Neither Esther nor Meredith took any part in their celebration. They were watching each other. Meredith was asking silently: "Do you know what you are doing?" Esther held her gaze, answering: "It is the only way." Meredith asked in return: "Do you know what will happen next?" Esther came down off the platform, walked around the dancing throng, unlocked the door, returned to the pulpit.

"I am one," she called for silence.

"We are many, Sister," they called back.

"Together we shall be whole," she said. "But only if we are together can we be whole. Only if we are whole are we The Programme. The Teacher is The Programme. We are The Programme. If any of you are in doubt, if any of you want to leave The Programme, then now is the time to do it. From this moment on, there is only one way forward – one way, one fire, one fire beyond."

\* \* \*

It was another two days before they came. It should have been one but the Federal Judge they wanted to issue the warrants was lecturing five hundred miles away and her substitute was too unreliable, preferring constitutional niceties to nasty realities. Without a warrant, they could only watch.

From an unmarked car parked where they could just manage to see the nearest junction, they saw a small number of members of The Programme drive out in a VW van and a car, separating at the highway, the car turning North, the van towards the East. As best they could tell, less than ten members. Though they might have been able to justify picking them up on the basis of Emily's account of events, it was a legal long-shot; of more concern, it would give too much forewarning to those still inside.

Meredith had gone to see The Teacher.

"I am one," she had said.

"We are many. Esther tells me you want to leave." Esther was sitting cross-legged on the floor beside him. Occasionally, he reached out a hand to squeeze hers for reassurance. Meredith remembered the girl she had first seen in the London Coffee Lounge – scared of The Programme, angry at just about everything else, a prime candidate with something special to offer, uncertain where to put it.

"Teacher, I do. Can you understand?"

"It's not about understanding any more, Meredith. It's about doing what we've talked about, being what we know."

"I don't find it that simple, Teacher."

"What will you take away with you, then, Meredith?"

"Complexity, I suppose. I told Esther once," she glanced at her, "if I found it too complex – I'd move on." Esther nodded, remembering.

"Leave with love Meredith – my love; when it's over, look up and feel me watching over you, look within yourself and know that I am still there, loving you. Someday, tell them that's what you remember: love."

"Some others want to come with me, Teacher. Sister Gloria."

"Ah, Gloria." Gloria had taken part in Anthony's Special Mass but there was nothing she could tell the police that would equal what Emily knew. He had forgiven Gloria, let her fly away to England to find herself over again. He had forgiven the two Jays, forgiven Lemuel and his brothers, forgiven even Micah. If Gloria left, she could yet go back to Cassandra. "Take Gloria with you," he decided: take a message to Cassandra – I am strong enough to let her go. "And George, is he leaving too?"

"He wants to leave, Teacher. He feels he let you down before; he can't bring himself to do it again."

"Tell him to come and see me. George and Gloria – they belong together. I think they're the only ones who don't realise it. I'd like to think," he smiled. "Perhaps, if it's a boy, they can call him Matthew. Who else?" He felt like a statesman trading prisoners with the representative of a foreign power.

"Will you tell Diana to leave with me?" Pregnant Diana.

"No. Not Diana." Not Christopher's child.

Nadab and Martha, Paul, one of the new black members, a couple from Boston, Karen too, Tanya's friend. Matthew signed their paroles with barely a murmur, counting instead those who had decided to stay.

Before she left, Meredith knelt beside Esther, tried to hug her, looking for the chance to whisper: "Come with us, Carey, you don't belong here." Esther pushed her away stiffly.

"Go now," was all she would say.

\* \* \*

Http://www.the-programme.org.uk (turn on sound card if available).

*They say that I killed Anthony Rockworth. If I did, I killed him with love. I loved him, I drew his pain into me, I encouraged him to see that if he brought to the surface where for so long he had known only hatred and contempt the love he had felt as a baby, he could bring them into a harmony that would liberate him from the need to shout from the roof-top: "I am bad, I am evil, you must hate me as I hate you." Anthony was not bad, nor evil; he simply did not know how to deal with the hatred and evil that were within him, no more than do the best of us. His father told me he could not help him; asked me to help instead. I helped him by loving him and teaching him but in the end he still killed himself. In that way, it is said that I killed Anthony Rockworth.*

*Did I kill Anthony Rockworth? I was a thousand miles away when the boy I loved died. Was Anthony afraid of me, as they hint in the press and on the television – did he kill himself because he was afraid of my return to Hammer Reach? Yes, sure: the way he had seen me every day for years in London, a 'phone call or a taxi ride away from his father, travelling unaccompanied from one to another of The Programme's homes in that most free of all cities, even visiting with his parents for a weekend here, a few days there, but – they seem to be saying – he could not tell them that he was afraid of me. Instead, so they tell it, he killed himself to avoid seeing me again. While I was a thousand miles away.*

*Did I kill Anthony Rockworth? Who says it? Cassandra – The Seer as once we called her – who could see into the future but had never foreseen this. Cassandra – my wife – who helped me to find The Programme but fled shrieking that it was nothing to do with her. Cassandra – at Hammer Reach when he died. Cassandra – who brought to a dark and frightening hole in the ground a boy who was more afraid of his own shadow than he was to lash out at those around him who loved him. Cassandra – who brought to that hole in the ground her naked coven, to chant magic curses, exploit pagan myths, to inflict the whore of Babylon upon nature's lost child, until he understood that just as good had rejected him, so too would evil. It was an irresistible truth and, ultimately, he did not resist it.*

*The evidence of evil is too great to ignore, however hard you try. Why even try? Why not admit it: there are bad people and there are good people and what we want is to be whole. But it's not enough to say it; we have to do it; we have to become whole. One thing that means is that there has to be a part of us capable of doing evil; something else it means, because everything has to exist in contrast, is recognising that some are not and never will become whole. Whole, not whole. We call ourselves The Programme; it is a way of life – a way of being; also, it is a way of dying. Sometimes, only death can make us whole; for some, death is the ultimate achievement – a beginning not an end. It is not brainwashing to share with another what we have learned and experienced about our capacity to make a whole of our lives. It is a gift.*

\* \* \*

They rode in convoy, Faulkener in charge. He had been first on the Hammer Reach scene and ATF was always looking for opportunities to redeem the Waco disaster and that at Ruby Ridge: nor was it a leading brief that the FBI fought to keep. Fourth car in line, Berlinger brought Emily. They were followed by the technician's van with the more powerful detection equipment that could not be brought onto the land the previous ATF visit.

Emily talked openly with Berlinger, even about Richard and how she had met Carey, about everything except what had happened at Moonlight Lake the night Carey had arrived from London. That was the one thing that she preserved for herself, that was not to be written off to The Programme. He was flattered, reassured, he could still pull one more back: one day, maybe his daughter.

She had sworn the affidavit with which they had secured their warrant. She had been willing to help them, not keen. She wanted something back, without which she would not only refuse to swear it, but threatened to retract her account. Her condition was that she went with them to Hammer Reach while they executed the warrant, to give her a further chance of persuading Carey to leave. She was adamant, stubborn, bull-headed: between them, Faulkener and Weitz exchanged a few less palatable epithets but Berlinger told them – sometimes, it only takes a few words to bring someone out. They had relented far enough to take her with them; what happened on the ground would have to be decided at the time.

At first, it seemed like it was going to be cool. Simon came out to greet them, ghostly Mother Naamah with him. They had a warrant, Faulkener explained: they were going to search again for weapons; also, they had information there might be bodies buried in the grounds. Simon was calm but implacable. They had been to Hammer Reach only a few days beforehand. They had found nothing and, he said, there was nothing to find. He insisted on reading the warrant word for word, went back inside saying that he was going to telephone their lawyers in New York.

Once his initial advice to raid the farm without delay or warning had been rejected, Berlinger changed tack. Let the members adjust to the incoming reality; let the presence of police – of the law – strike a chord of recognition. If they responded peacefully and let them draw up to the farmhouse, play on it for as long as possible, establish a relationship. Premature confrontation could set them off.

While Simon was – so he had told them – calling their lawyers, Emily made her move. Romero was distracted, on the radio to his barracks. Berlinger, too, was making a cellphone call to Rockworth. She pushed her way through the other agents until she was face to face with Naamah.

"I am one, Mother Naamah," she said, as if they were passing in the fields.

"We are many," Naamah replied gravely.

"Can I see Esther, Mother?"

"Of course," Naamah replied.

"Hold on," Faulkener grabbed Emily's arm.

"You promised," Emily broke away.

"Wait up," Weitz intervened, taking Faulkener's arm in turn.

The two agents whispered to one another. Faulkener did not want her to go inside. Weitz reminded him that she had talked once, she would talk again. They did not have enough information. Her friend might have more. They could be useful. Faulkener hissed:

"If they ever come out."

"They've gone to phone their lawyers," Weitz replied – they were dealing with reasonable people.

"You don't know these people," Faulkener had been inside.

Emily did not await the outcome but ran into the house before they could object.

"Carey," she called. "Please, Carey – talk to me."

A few minutes later, Naamah said:

"I'll go and see what's happening, okay?"

A few moments after that, Romero joined the two Federal agents.

"You what?" He exploded when told that they had managed to let Emily go inside. He mocked them with laughter when they justified their actions on the grounds that she might be able to get her friend out. "You won't see either of them," he asserted.

They waited for the best part of an hour before they were certain that no one was coming out voluntarily. Faulkener and Weitz crossed the remaining few yards to the house, banged at the door, demanded to be allowed to see Emily.

A window flew open on the second floor. A gun pointed out at them. As their manuals dictated, they retreated.

\* \* \*

They had made preparations during the extra day faith had granted them: they dug shallow trenches between the two barns and The Temple – it was too far from the barns to the main house, or from the barns and the house to the out-house where the animals lived, and the ground was hard beneath the snow; they fortified some windows on the upper storeys of each of the barns, covered up the remainder; they moved all their clothing and other belongings from the farmhouse to the barns, so that no one would have to sleep at the vulnerable front of the property; they moved furniture and nailed wood across the several entrances to the farmhouse, and likewise protected the upper windows so that they could be used to keep watch; and, Matthew and a few others familiar with firearms taught a larger number how to load, aim, fire. It had all arrived home: from Xuan Loc to Hammer Reach.

\* \* \*

Http://www.the-programme.org.uk (turn on sound card if available).

*I know this – that I have lived for more than fifty years, travelled the world, taken part in wars and in marches for peace, studied from philosophy to religion, watched those I have known follow the path that seemed closest to match their aspirations, yet none has ever secured the fulfilment, the joy, the faith, the sense of belonging that The Programme has provided to its many members over its years. Wherever The Programme is now to lead us, whatever is now to happen, they can never take that away from us – from me; there are enough members of The Programme who are not with us at Hammer Reach to make sure that it is never forgotten – who have carried away the very seeds for its survival.*

*It is not about one God but one being – a being who is all men and all women, all good and all evil, all faith and hope and all the feelings of rejection and despair, hatred and contempt, that anyone has ever suffered, all love too. What we have tried to do at The Programme is to create that one being, to stride the world in harmony and at peace – if there is but one, there is no one with whom to fight. You might say: no one, either, with whom to converse – and you would be right. What are words, though? A way of expressing a thought, a thought that is an idea, an idea that is a representation, a representation which seeks to recreate what it is, how much better simply to be it instead.*

*No more words now, just the deed – not several deeds, just the one. The Programme is that one being who is all men and all women, one God who is Satan, and when it acts it will do so as one and in only one way. No more quotes from the Bible; no more lectures from The Teacher; no more arguments and invitations; no more explanations or exhortations. For many months now, we have advertised – openly, publicly, on this World-wide Website – where it is that we are going and now is the time to do it. The fire beyond awaits us; do not be frightened for us – we await the fire beyond. When you read this, we shall be not ashes but at peace.*

* * *

Charles was asleep when the news broke in Europe – mildly tranquillised for the night in the clinic where he was beginning to recover from his stroke. There was nothing wrong with his mind, nothing that the doctors could see, beyond the melancholy of an old man, distant and distanced from his family, unwilling to allow them to be brought to him, confronting death alone.

In the daytime, he could have the television on: the nurses scolded him at first for watching so many news programmes. He needed comforting images and all the programmes brought him was one form of war or another. Eventually, they gave up the effort and, on their breaks or when the clinic was quiet, would join him to watch the news from around the world.

There was no nurse with him when he switched on the television the morning after the raid, channel-surfed until he found the most current news, his arm was still outstretched, finger pressed on the remote control, when the nurses responded to the screech of the heart monitor, the flashing of the light at the central monitoring station, his mouth was open, eyes fixed, his daughter on the screen in a flowing white cloak waving a gun at the camera, grasping the neck of a woman – Emily, he believed – and yelling:

"Get away from here. Get away from us. Get away – she'll die."

* * *

Colin flew over by Concorde. He rented a car at JFK, only got lost a couple of times, the motorway led directly to Hedgerow. The signs to the town were unnecessary: it seemed like most of the traffic on the road was heading in the same direction. He was at Hammer Reach – he remembered the first time he had heard the name, been amused by it, a memorable name – soon after midday, about five thirty at home, a mere eighteen or nineteen hours since he had seen her on the news.

The State Police had set up barriers to keep sightseers away. Most of those turned back stayed to watch even though they could not get close enough to see anything, leaving a long, thin strip between the beginning of the cars and the police barrier barely wide enough for one car, let alone to pass others being turned back.

"What is your business, sir?"

For a moment – tired, confused, inane – Colin almost said that he was a lawyer, before realising in time to catch himself that the Trooper meant business at the farm.

"My name is Colin Arnott. That," he hesitated to say it, to make it real, "that was my sister on the television last night – the one with the gun. I've flown over from England this morning."

If the officer lived up to caricature, there would be a scene, low farce, Colin would either be turned away or end up under arrest. Instead, the Trooper spoke into a radio mounted on the lapel of his lined winter jacket. On an instruction, he asked Colin for some identification – Colin gave him his passport. He told Colin someone would be down to see him, he could take his rental through the barrier, but park immediately on the other side, off the road, please.

Another officer pointed Colin towards a small area where there was already a small number of unmarked cars – from a beat-up old station wagon to a smart maroon Mercedes – around which clustered a group of civilians, pacing, some of them smoking, a couple arguing, another couple was kneeling in the snow praying aloud. Colin sat in his car, reluctant to join them. They would be families of members, those living near enough to arrive before he did; it was quicker to arrive from London by Concorde than to fly in from the West Coast.

"Mr Arnott? Sergeant Romero."

He held the door open for Colin. Another man was standing behind him, of whom Colin had taken no notice.

"Are you all right, sir? Do you have a coat?"

"Mr Arnott," Berlinger stepped into view, proffered a hand.

For a moment, Colin hesitated, reluctant to take it as if doing so would admit that Berlinger had been right all along. Berlinger had been right all along. He took the hand and found that instead of the iron vice he expected, it was soft, almost gentle, comforting.

"I do know what you're feeling, Mr Arnott – may I call you Colin?"

Colin nodded; kindness was the last thing he had expected or could cope with; he could not speak or he would have choked up.

"I've met your sister, Mr Arnott," Romero offered. "She was fine when I saw her at the farm. I want you to know, we're here to help her, help them all. We want to get them all out without a fight. That's our absolute objective. I promise you that."

The long speech helped – as, Colin suspected, it was intended to. It gave him time to recover himself. He was three thousand miles from his home; his sister was on international television waving a gun at the police, holding her friend – and client – hostage; it was freezing cold and all he had worn to the airport was a light mackintosh which in turn he had forgotten at the rental office; he had last seen Berlinger at his gym in London – people didn't decide they needed him until it was too late, he had said.

"If you want to say you told me so," Colin tried for humour, failed, eyes began again to water. It seemed as if all the tears he had suppressed in his life, since he had been a child, since Marion's death, were being released.

Berlinger gripped his shoulder.

"It's not too late, Colin; get that into your head; it's not too late. The police are doing all they can – they're cooperating with each other, they've let me contribute what I know about The Programme, other groups; there's no reason for anything to go wrong; we're not going to let anyone get hurt."

\* \* \*

Matthew and Esther sat cross-legged on their bed. Apart from the guards at the windows, Emily in the basement, they were alone in the house. They were naked, had made love, she stroked his face, leaned forward to receive his kiss, his hand fell to her breast, cupped it, her nipple rose again to his touch, she lowered her head and buried it in his groin, breathing in the smell of their sex, she took him in her mouth, not for response but so that they would be whole.

He started to talk while she had him inside her.

464

"It had to happen – there was no other way to go. I'm not sorry about it because it would mean being sorry for The Programme, for everything I've done. I'm not sorry, because I would end up being sorry for my life – for all our lives – and that would be a denial of life itself."

Esther sat up, put a finger to his lips to silence the apology.

"You've got nothing to be sorry for. I wouldn't want to be anywhere else in the world, just here with you."

He gripped her wrist, sucked on the finger until she opened her hand, he licked her palm, kissed her lips, told her:

"I love you, Esther; I love you, Carey."

Her eyes filled with tears.

"You don't have to say it, Matthew."

"Maybe I should have said it before. Maybe it would have been different."

"Too late for maybes," she said.

"I don't want you to be hurt, Esther; when it all comes down, I don't want you to be hurt."

It was ambiguous: he could have meant that he wanted her to escape; or, that he wanted her to feel no pain when they died.

Because death was not what they were confronting, she could not ask.

There was a sudden noise below. A bang – not a shot, a door slamming open or shut. They froze: was it happening already? It was far too soon.

Matthew scrambled into a pair of jeans; Esther pulled a robe over her head. They heard a voice, two voices.

"I am one," Simon was saying.

"We are many," Lucius replied.

Matthew opened the door, looked out onto the landing.

"It's only me, Teacher."

"How did you get across?"

Simon gestured at his white robe.

"Not easy to see in the snow."

"Why did you come across, Father Simon?" Simon was in charge of one of the barns; Nahum, the other.

"They're asleep," Simon replied. "Comfortable, anyway." Some would probably not sleep at all, but would sit up or huddle for warmth in a bed with those to whom they were closest; others were on duty at the windows, watching the lights of the camps or staring intently towards the woods from where, Matthew had warned, it was most likely that an invasion would be launched. "I think," he hesitated, then shrugged and said what he had come to say: "We have to know, Teacher; we can't afford a traitor amongst us, not now."

"No," Matthew admitted reluctantly. Simon was right, but he would have preferred not to have to tackle Emily; the fight was outside – the fight within was over.

* * *

By the third day, the relatives' camp had grown as large as the press camp, and as the several encampments the police had set up, reflecting both their different jurisdictions and their strategic choices. They had taken the decision that morning to cut off electricity to Hammer Reach; the telephone inside would only connect to Faulkener or Weitz; water would be shut off last of all – there were known to be children inside, and dehydration bred erratic behaviour faster than lack of food.

The hotels and motels within a hundred mile radius were full, doing thriving business not only in lodgings but also in meals. Only one was empty. The Moonlight Inn had been shut. It was not accommodation guests would have been after, but information, gossip, an interview with the innkeeper. They would have wanted her to describe Matthew Crane as a fiend, Carey Arnott and Emily Fielding as his portable harem – or each other's. Viewers were bored with the same old, same old faces: Cassandra and Micah, Tanya Sokolov and Amanda Kroger who appeared regularly together, a few members who admitted they had been nowhere near The Programme for several years; none of those who had left the day before had surfaced – the police did not even know their names.

Some of the relatives found lodgings; others did not want to stray from the farm in case they missed the moment they were hoping for when their loved ones emerged, or the moment they were scared of when it all went down. Local social services put up a marquee-sized tent, provided sleeping bags, benzene burners and lamps, food and hot drinks, warmer clothing than family had managed to bring, some smaller, individual bivouacs.

Berlinger had advised, the more family, the closer they were to the farm, the better the chances that some of them would come out. Rockworth paid for it all, authorising Berlinger to spend whatever he wanted: if it all went horribly wrong, some sections of the media would blame his campaign against The Programme. The longer it went on, the less and less evidence there seemed to be to hold against Matthew or those now inside. They had found New Hampshire Al:

even the guns, it now seemed, had been brought in under Cassandra.

Colin was one of those who never left. He went into town to call home the first full day after he arrived but Jan had been cold, unsympathetic, he belonged in London, helping her to help the children cope with the publicity that had begun to roll over them – at school, cameras outside the house, the firm was under siege as surely as Hammer Reach. She told him that no one had yet managed to reach Charles – Alistair had decided to fly down to Antibes – it was Colin's job, however bad the rift. If Jan was invoking his responsibility for Charles as a way of persuading him to abandon Carey, they were no longer communicating.

He kept a polite distance from the other relatives, even Crane's sister, knowing they all felt the same way about their loved ones, needing to isolate his own, greater pain. Some of them seemed to understand, they talked with him briefly and gently. Sokolov had – almost despite himself – flown up from Bolivia. A black man called Phillipe had been allowed in on Berlinger's authority, claiming a special relationship with Emily Fielding.

The worst encounter of all had been with Richard Fielding, their first time face to face, strutting – he was a star, he had been on English television, they had interviewed him at the press compound; he sneered, threatened, shouted accusations until the police had physically restrained him. He had managed to build up a clique of supporters around him, who shunned Colin and were even beginning to shun those who refused also to shun him – factions were forming, one of these days they would start to elect leaders.

Late at night, when there were the fewest new arrivals, Colin would stand in the dark at the rope the police had put up to mark the line beyond which they could not go – for their own safety as much as for the integrity of the police strategy – straining to make out the shapes of the buildings, wondering which one contained Carey. He would mouth her name. Once, forgetting himself, he had broken the stillness of the night with a howl no one for a hundred miles around could have failed to hear.

"Carey, please Carey."

There had been no response. Of course there had been no response. They had told her, she was Carey no longer: Sister Esther, like a nun, wedded not to Christ but to fire – the fire beyond, they called it, like a game or a competition. Who can first cross the frozen ice to warm themselves at the fire beyond?

"Colin," a voice spoke from behind.

He did not turn around. He recognised it instantly. He was in tears. He did not want her to see him in tears. He had never allowed Jan to do so.

He felt her arms go around his waist, squeeze him from behind, she tucked her ungloved hands into the down jacket he had bought at the store in Hedgerow the day he had gone in to call home, rested her head against his back.

"What are you doing here?" he asked dully.

"I wanted to be with you," Jessica replied. "I, I wanted to come before but I didn't know whether Jan would be here, whether you'd want me here. I didn't know what people at work would think."

"I know what they think. Charles told me clearly enough."

"He wasn't speaking for us, Colin; he was speaking for himself."

"So what do others think?" He had still not turned around.

"A lot of people are worried, Colin. For you, for Carey too – not just the firm. It's funny," she laughed nervously, "almost no one's admitting to being worried about the firm, not aloud anyway. It's like some baptism of fire." She realised what she had said and switched metaphor. "A traumatic event that's awful to go through, but that a lot of people seem to realise will end up bringing us closer together."

"It's the last thing I would have expected," Colin admitted. He took his hands out of his pockets and closed them over hers; she unlocked her fingers, turned her hands around, gripped his until they were all tangled up together like lovers' limbs akimbo and entwined. "Or Charles."

The mention of his father caused her to tense. He felt it, gripped her hands tightly, said:

"Tell me."

"He's all right," she said quickly. "He's had a heart attack; apparently he had a stroke a week or so ago when Emily escaped." The outline story was now general knowledge. "She rang him."

"She had no right," he snarled. "He's an old man."

"She tried to call you – she didn't have your number, couldn't get it. She called him instead."

"Bastard," he said.

"Who? Charles?" Jessica was shocked.

"No – Fielding. He's here, you know. He was calling me – he couldn't get through at the office, so he was calling me at home – making all sorts of allegations, accusations – that's why I changed my number. He's here, doing the same thing: it's all Carey's fault; Carey seduced Emily; Carey dragged her into The Programme; I've even heard, Carey set up orgies, made Emily take part."

"For God's sake," Jessica sympathised.

"How is he, Jess?" The first time had called her that.

"He's going to be all right. But the second one was a lot worse – a full-blown heart attack. He's tough; he'll survive."

Colin was working out the timing. There had been a couple of days between Emily's escape and when he had tried to call his father in Antibes.

"Why didn't anyone phone?"

She squeezed his hands by way of reply until Colin understood that Charles had not wanted them to call him.

Colin heard a movement off towards the camp.

He let go of Jessica's hands, extracted himself from her arms, turned to peer into the gloom.

Fielding was standing with his back to the tents, arms crossed, watching them: Colin could make out the smirk on his face – jealous smirk.

He gently pushed Jessica to one side, muttered grimly:

"Fielding," and marched across towards him.

He was not afraid: he was strong from years of squash; the man was a wife-beating coward.

He would have struck him too if someone had not emerged from between the tents, behind Fielding, seized him by the arms. As Fielding struggled, Lamarque said:

"Come now, Colin; hit the man, make him bleed, maybe that make everything all right, yah?"

* * *

They had been at Emily for hours – well into the morning. Neither Matthew nor Esther had the stomach for violent assault, though both of them suspected that Simon would have gone for it left to his own. He had been betrayed as well as The Programme, Matthew and Esther.

Emily was weak: they had stopped feeding her yesterday, the day before, she could not remember when.

Frequently, Simon grabbed her head from behind, held her head up until she could barely breathe, but none of them struck her with blows, only questions.

"Who was it, Emily? Who's the traitor, Emily? Who let you out, Emily? Why did you betray us? What did you tell them, Emily? Do you know how you will suffer for this, Emily? You have broken the whole, Emily, you and you alone are responsible for what will happen.

You are the murderer, Emily – the one person who has destroyed The Programme – more than Cassandra, more than Caleb. Tell us, Emily, who's the traitor? We won't hurt him, we just need to know – he has to leave – tell us, tell us, together we shall be whole, you can be whole again, make yourself whole."

When it began, Emily tried to reason with them; then she begged, pleaded – once, she screamed at them to kill her, she would never tell; after that, for more than an hour she was silent. In the end, though, exhausted, incapable of thinking straight, desperate for water, she had mumbled Calvin's name and – finally – they had let her fall unconscious to the floor.

* * *

They had Calvin in the kitchen at the farmhouse when Phillipe crossed the police line and started across the field.

Naamah appeared at the door to the kitchen, beckoned at Matthew – come and see. Simon stayed with Calvin, guarded by the two Jays, while Matthew and Esther went upstairs to watch.

Matthew burst out laughing.

"Phillipe Lamarque," he told Naamah.

She had met him once, several years before, in London, but had failed to recognise him.

"God, he's big; I didn't remember him so fat."

"He wasn't," Matthew replied dryly.

"What do we do?" Esther asked.

"Let him in," Matthew shrugged. "He's a visitor."

"Be careful," Esther cautioned. "He might be armed."

"No," Matthew said simply.

"Out for a walk, old friend?" Matthew greeted Phillipe once they had finally removed the bars nailed across the front door.

"Yah – a stroll. Cold, though; damn snow."

"What do you want, Phillipe?" Esther demanded.

"Sister Esther, I say; or is it Mother now?" His eyes met hers, met her hostility head on. "Where is Emily?"

"Come through," Matthew led the way into the kitchen.

Simon rose angrily.

"Lamarque – I didn't think you'd have the guts to come for your spy," he gestured at Calvin, each shoulder held by one of the Jays, locked to an upright chair, face bruised, eyes gaunt.

"This man? I've never seen him. What's your name, boy?"

"Calvin Wood," Calvin shot back before they could stop him

sending his message to the outside world.

"You're the one got Emily out of here." Phillipe settled himself down at the table, looked around. "Don't suppose, no, you don't got no beer. This is not my man," he added carelessly. "Berlinger's."

"Same difference. Berlinger. You. This creep. Her," Simon included Emily without saying her name.

"Yah, we're the enemy all right. Simon, you used to be a good man – what happened? You start believing your own shit?"

Simon came around the table as if he was going to strike Phillipe. Matthew held up a hand to stop him.

"Why did you come, Phillipe? Don't you think you've done enough damage?"

"What damage did I do, Matthew? What damage did I ever do you?"

"The girl came to see you; that was when it began."

"Yah, sure, it all began when one girl run off with me for a few hours to talk and drink like, what have I got to say here, like normal? Like she wanted to touch normal again."

"Normal – from you, Phillipe?" The Voodoo priest.

"Is that why you're here?" Esther asked. "For Emily?"

"Yah, sure. She's my friend. The po-lice," two words, "they've fucked up bad. I told them, I'm going in to ask my friend Matthew here, he let her fly away with me, like a little bird, yah Matthew?" He was not asking for the permission, merely if Matthew understood. "They couldn't rightly say no – 'sides, his friend," he tossed a head at Calvin Wood, "he said you wouldn't hurt me."

Esther was watching him with the growing realisation that she had him all wrong. He did care for Emily and had the courage to come in to ask for her. He had cared for her, too: she had understood that their night in New Orleans – it was what had made her suspicious of him. Why should he? She had heard the words before: fly away, little bird. Matthew had used them at JFK. How did Phillipe know? They were his words, planted on Matthew. She had flown away, but come back. This was when it began to gnaw at her, the wish that she could fly away again – this time, keep going. Was that also why he had come?

"Is that what you think, Phillipe?" Matthew asked.

"I think you, the po-lice, Berlinger him too, no one cares about fat old black Voodoo man – not me either. If it does something for you, you kill me – hey, okay, yah?"

Matthew shook his head, unsuccessfully trying to suppress a smile: Phillipe could make him laugh in the jaws of hell. That was Phillipe's purpose: to remind him how to laugh.

Esther caught the mood, threw off her own, chuckled: it wove its way around the table until they were all laughing, even Simon, and Naamah who never laughed, and the two Jays who had hardly dared smile since Matthew had allowed them to stay on in The Programme. Only Calvin did not laugh: it did not look funny from where he sat.

"How much bad you done, Matthew?" Phillipe asked.

"What did you say last time – anyone killed Caleb did the world a favour?"

"You're telling me, now, you done that?" Phillipe was reminding Matthew that he was liable to repeat what he was told.

"Proud of it. Paimon, Christopher too. What they did – well, I guess you know about that by now." From Emily to the police; the details had not been broadcast but the tenor of the news over the last few days had become distinctly less hostile as more information was allowed to seep out: it was becoming accepted fact that Matthew had been pushed over the edge, had not jumped. "No one else; nothing else. I'm telling you the truth now, Phillipe."

"I hear you. I believe you." Phillipe saw Calvin's hopeful look. "You stop it all here, it ain't so much of a problem, the way I see it."

Matthew's eyes glazed over.

"I don't think it works like that, Phillipe old friend; I'm not sure there is a problem – just an ending."

"Oh, shit, boy, don't you do this now. You don't have to. You've got a lot of people love you Matthew – me, I love you Matthew; it doesn't matter about them boys, they were just squawking chickens and you know what I do with chickens."

"I know you love me, Phillipe; it's mutual. You remember that."

Phillipe looked about him: what they were planning was – in their own terms – perfectly sane and normal, inevitable and not to be resisted.

"You do it, you got to do it, Matthew, but you let these people go – however many of them want to go, you let them go now. You hear me?"

"They went, Phillipe; I let the ones who wanted to go leave."

"What about Emily – let me see her, she tells me she wants to stay, that's one thing."

"Emily's in a special position – she's where it started. I'll tell you what I'll do," he added casually. "You can take Korah with you. Him." He tossed his head at Calvin Wood.

Esther felt warm inside: it was going to be all right; this was the first concession; every lawyer knew that once the concessions began, it would end in a negotiated settlement. Her impression of Phillipe had revolved through a hundred and eighty degrees in considerably fewer minutes; even if Matthew did not let her leave with him, Emily would be all right.

Phillipe had risen, knowing that he had gone as far as he could for the time being, reaching out a hand for Calvin.

"Don't hurt that girl, Matthew; hurt her, hurt me."

Matthew smiled, held out his arms to hug his old friend.

"I wouldn't hurt you, Phillipe."

"I know," Phillipe patted his back, though his eyes were on Esther. He was beginning to wonder how he could get her out too: one thing he saw, she was ready to leave.

At the door, he dug into his pocket and extracted a small, plastic, electrical packet – transmitter. Casually, he threw it to Matthew.

"Here, they told me to leave this here. Told me I should stick it under a table, something. You do that for me, yah?"

Laughing, he stepped through the door, leading Calvin by one hand, holding the other up towards the watching, waiting policemen – angry policemen, too, maybe, if they heard his last exchange. Didn't Berlinger warn them? He always told everyone everything.

Inside the farmhouse, Matthew tossed the transmitter to Simon.

"Break it," he said tersely, making his way upstairs.

Esther started to follow him.

"No," he called without looking around.

Upstairs, he took Lee's rifle from him and lined it up through the foot-square opening that was all they had left to shoot through.

Esther was still at the door, watching Phillipe plodding back across the field, holding onto Calvin's hand as if frightened that he, too, would run back even though they were more than halfway to the police line.

Simon and Naamah had returned to the kitchen to find something with which to open up and deactivate the transmitter.

The single shot from the floor above blew Calvin's head away. As he fell forward, he dragged Phillipe to the ground; Esther slammed the door shut and ran screaming back into the house just before the fire-storm began.

\* \* \*

"Why? What did you do that for?" She cried at Matthew, flailing at his chest with her fists while he gripped her shoulders.

"What? He's all right. I didn't hit him. They didn't either."

"I saw you, I saw his head."

"That was Korah; Phillipe's all right."

"Why?" she sobbed. "Why? You told Phillipe – just the three of them, no one else; it was okay; he told you it would be okay."

"You still don't understand, Sister Esther: my purpose must prevail; I don't want it to be all right in their terms, only in mine. That's what they want out there, that's why they're waiting, hoping our purpose will erode, people will start coming out – me too. It's not going to happen; it mustn't happen."

Her eyes narrowed, she enunciated carefully:

"The morning after, when you told me Emily had gone – when I was getting dressed, I noticed a bundle of my clothes tossed on a chair – trainers, a coat – not mine – that didn't belong there. I didn't think about it until now."

He shrugged.

"Where did they come from, Matthew? Why did you go down to see Emily? You were going to let her go yourself, weren't you? You wanted her to escape – you wanted her to talk. Tell me that's wrong, Matthew; tell me."

His face was expressionless; he would not lie to her nor was there any reason to do so.

"Why, Matthew? Why did this have to happen?"

"What else could have happened, Esther? After what they'd done?"

"To you? To The Programme?"

"Same thing," he replied, picking up the rifle. "Are you coming?"

She shook her head, biting her tongue: there were too many things she wanted to say, none of which he would want to hear, to some of which she could not predict his response. The word largest in her mind was: monster – how could she have failed to see it?

He did not worry about leaving her. There was nowhere she could go. They could hear the front door being nailed shut again. Only the back door was not barred or locked, but there was a permanent – and armed – guard on duty. She would calm down, begin to see it his way, it was his purpose, therefore it was hers.

\* \* \*

From her cell, Carey brought Emily up to date. After describing how Phillipe had come to the farmhouse for her, how he had made Carey start to see sense herself and how she had fought with Matthew, she continued:

"I hid in the attic. He didn't come looking for me – I don't know if he forgot about me or just assumed I'd turn up when I was ready. Once it was dark, he made his way across to The Temple, set up a meditation. I don't know how many people attended, but it was quiet at the farmhouse, maybe half a dozen people on guard duty, looking outwards, not in.

"I had this idea. There was no way to escape, not without being seen. I knew the phone had been cut off but I knew it could still be used to call the police – like a line of last resort. Colin's out there: they said so on the TV. There's a lot of families. Richard, too."

Carey paused to see if the snippet of information might be the one that, finally, persuaded Emily to talk to her. When it did not, she resumed:

"I left it too long. I didn't hear him come in. They'd just picked up, Weitz, the FBI man: that was all he said – 'Weitz'. I was about to tell him who I was, that I wanted to talk to Colin. Matthew came up behind me, reached across, cut the connection. That was it, really."

It was not it: there was more to tell. There was no point talking to Emily – even if she would not reply – if she was still going to lie to her.

"Matthew let Calvin go, Em. He let Phillipe take him. I thought, you know, it was a real sign: maybe it was all going to be okay. I was watching from the door, before they nailed it shut again. He shot him, Matthew shot him, Calvin. Emily, Emily, I'm sorry."

"What happened, Carey?"

"They killed him," Carey sobbed.

Emily froze. She had been exactly halfway between relenting, answering Carey at last, and continued contempt. She said – her last words to the friend she had loved more than she had ever loved anyone:

"Then you're responsible for that too."

* * *

"I wish I could make you understand, Em," Carey said.

By the fourth day of the siege, food was running low at the farm and the first to hurt was Emily: Matthew believed that Esther was in a temporary state of denial that would pass. Emily, however, was unrepentant: no point wasting supplies. The cell-diet of pitta bread, vegetable pâté, an orange for vitamins, which Carey still enjoyed, had days ago been reduced to water; in another couple of days, Emily would not even have anything to drink.

"I know you love me, Emily; anyway, I know you did." Carey

admitted her conduct was beyond forgiveness. "I loved you too. I couldn't see how it could ever be enough. I've loved someone before, in my way. The reason it didn't work was not because they were men. I couldn't feel, the way you did, if it was with another woman it might be different. I wanted something completely different. I wanted a love that I had built for myself, a love that was a way of life, a love that made me feel I had room for everything: to be me in all my moods, me at work and me at rest, creatively me and passively too. I wanted a love I could look around and say it's enough, not just for now but forever. That's about love and hope and faith and much, much more – more than another person could ever be.

"Pretty stupid, huh? It's what I was brought up to believe in though, oddly enough. It's what Charles was telling me – grow up his way, I'd never want for anything else. Colin too: it's what I'm doing; you can do it too. There were whole lives on offer: Arnotts was the word and the world. I wanted to be Marion, Em, but a Marion who stayed, who could handle God with one hand and Charles with the other. I wanted a life in which faith was not the antithesis of reason, where a rational view could sit hand-in-glove with eternal love. I think that's what I've loved about Matthew: he was so reasonable, and so loving, and he had so much faith – so much faith that all these people, many of them good and smart, had bet their whole lives on it, and I wanted to be like them: if I could just learn to let go, I'd learn to fly.

"Giving up the law was easy. It's dry, full of petty rules and the pretension that they are important. In crime, I suppose, and in some family work – like your case – or defending a tenant's right to his home, I could feel I was doing something for people's lives, but what I was doing was still confined by the law and its procedures, the highest achievement was legal victory, a momentary attainment that did not change anyone's life for the better, landing on a ladder knowing that the board is still riddled with snakes. I don't know whose pain I was feeling: my clients' or my own; I suppose I was projecting mine onto them – all they were looking for was that imminent gain; I wanted to give them more because I wanted more.

"I'm sorry I slapped you, Emily; it would have been worse if I hadn't. I'm not sorry for what happened at Moonlight Lake. I'm not sorry for what Matthew did to Caleb and the others. I'm sorry, truly sorry, for what happened to Korah – Calvin. I wanted you to tell because I couldn't stand to see them hurt you any more; I never believed they would hurt him – I thought maybe they'd just put him down here until it was over, maybe even let him go. Did you know

Matthew let those who wanted to leave do so? They went before you came back – even Superiors." It was news to Emily, deliberately withheld from her until they had found out who had released her, to prevent her falsely identifying one of those who had gone.

"Matthew – I've told him this sometimes, he laughs at it – there's so many ways he's like Charles, a bit like Colin at times, very lawyerly. He was mine, though, and what we would do together would be ours – even The Programme, even though it had been around for years, with Cassandra, with Helen, with everyone else, none the less, when we were together, it would be The Programme that was ours, and that I had helped to build.

"Only, by the time I got here, it was too late, it was already unravelling, there were too few choices left. I thought, you know, even in that time, I could make a difference, make the outcome – the next stage – better; even when we knew they would be coming back with a warrant, after you escaped – I still believed it could all be worked out. I still believed he wanted to work it all out: I don't think I stopped believing that until yesterday." She paused, corrected herself. "No, the day before.

"I was blind, Emily; I couldn't admit just how badly wrong I'd got it all, how badly wrong I'd gone too – it's like a drug, all my life, fearing I'd screw up, for myself, for the firm, for my family – and all along, I think that was what I really wanted to do, more than anything, to make it all go wrong, to fail – so I'd never have to try again to get it all right; and, now I've done it, I can't believe just how badly I've done it, how many people I've hurt while I've done it – above all, how much I've hurt you."

Carey stopped talking, pressed her ear to the door as if she might be able to hear Emily's breathing. Not for the first time, nor for the last, she cried out:

"Emily. I'm sorry. Please, Emily. Please talk to me."

There was no answer from the cell across the hall.

\* \* \*

"You were my favourite, Esther. You were always my favourite".

"Then let me go, Matthew," she begged.

He came often to see her, whenever he was at the farmhouse, usually after dark when it was safest to move between the buildings, sometimes two, three times a night. For the hours after he had killed Calvin, it had seemed that an invasion was imminent. Something stopped them – fear of Waco carnage, he supposed. It was exhilarating, waiting for them, knowing that at any moment they could storm the building, bring it all to an end.

"I can't let you go, Esther, surely you can see that? You belong with me; you have to stay. What would they make of it if you were to leave? It would be like pulling the bung from an already leaky boat. It would be the opening of all openings."

"I wouldn't tell them," she pleaded. "I won't tell them who I am."

It was too ridiculous to bother answering: by now, the whole world knew who she was; her face was as familiar as once had been that of David Koresh at Waco or, to an earlier generation, Patty Hearst cradling a gun during a bank raid with the Symbionese Liberation Army.

Those first days, they brought her food, though it had already been running short before Phillipe's visit; Emily, she knew, was on water only. Then there was a day when Matthew did not come at all. There was no food that day, nor the next, just water.

When finally he returned, he seemed weaker. He slumped on the floor opposite her, resting against the cell wall, long legs outstretched until his bare feet were almost touching hers.

He was not eating either. He admitted that there was no food left. The police had offered food in exchange for the children being released – Diana, too, who was pregnant.

"Let them go, Matthew." She was barely able to speak above a whisper. "They don't break the whole."

"Christopher's child?" He snorted – no way.

"Thomas, Tamar, then – you used to say, they were your children, your future. Please, Matthew, let Hannah take them out."

"Hannah won't let them go to Micah. That's what would happen now; she can't let that happen. There are other children." The ones he had ordered not to be brought to Hammer Reach. By then, it was not news to Carey that it had been planned from before the command to abandon the Chapters, regroup at the farm. Matthew did not want all the children to die.

"Matthew – is Emily all right? She won't talk to me; I need to know she's all right."

"She's quiet, but she's okay."

"Matthew – what's to become of us?"

"Who's us, Esther? The Programme – you and me – you and Emily?"

Carey shrugged: she had meant the latter.

"That's what I thought."

"How are the others?"

He tossed his head from side to side.

"Apprehensive," he laughed, she thought, a little nervously.

"Why are you doing it, Matthew?"

"What's the Luther line? *Ich kann nicht anders*: I can do no other."

"That's not good enough, Matthew: you're not Luther."

"Did I ever tell you what I used to say in Vietnam?"

She shook her head: she was not sure what he meant – to himself or to others.

"When the bombs were actually falling, when we were crouching for cover, I used to say, over and over: 'Give me until tomorrow, and then I shall start again'."

"So?"

He laughed again, not nervously this time but derisively.

"I got it wrong; what I meant was – please don't let me see tomorrow, please don't let me see any more of this damned, damned fire." This was his addiction that matched her terror of making a mistake until – exhausted by the effort – all she had wanted was to do it, never to have to try again. Horrified by the fire, the only thing left was to run headlong into it.

"We've made such a fuck-up of it all, haven't we, Matthew?"

"Not you. The thing I've most admired about you, from the very beginning, you were always trying to make it right – everything, whatever you were doing, out there, in here; that's the big difference between you and Cassandra. Don't ever forget it. She wanted the chaos and destruction."

She smiled through tears: Matthew caring for her, the way it had begun.

As if idly, he stretched his toes until they hovered above hers. Before she knew what she was doing, she had lifted her feet to press against the soles of his. Their eyes caught, held: his twinkled; she could not resist him; they laughed together – for a moment, it was once more all and nothing but a grand joke.

He pulled his feet away so that hers fell to the floor, crossed his own and used the pressure of his heels to pull himself forward, away from the wall, until he was sitting upright in the middle of the cell. He held out a hand to help her come forward to him. Not for the first time, he stroked her cheek. Not for the first time, she thought he was going to take her there, on the floor. Not for the first time, part of her wished he would. On previous occasions, it had been clear that physical power over her was not his objective; this time was different.

"I told you we shouldn't have made love," he whispered.

They had made love after the siege had begun but before anyone had been hurt – neither Emily nor Calvin.

"It can't be undone."

For a moment longer he hesitated, then pulled his own shift over his head; she did the same.

For the last time, they made love, neither ritualistically nor eagerly, but slowly, gently, each of them wishing it would never end.

Afterwards, spent, he lay on top of her, not crushing her but protecting her with his body.

They lay like that for the longest time. She sensed the moment when it was over, his body tensed, he pushed himself to his feet.

He was too tired for a long discussion; Matthew, beyond words – the end was at hand.

"I want you with me, Esther; I want you with me – but only if that's what you want too. If you're still a part of The Programme – come with me now, it's not too late, we can still be together, be whole. If you're not, then I'll leave you behind – both of you." He paused and added, not to persuade but caring for her still: "Have you thought about what's out there for you now? What you ran from plus the ridicule – they'll say they admire you, but really they'll pity you, or worse – despise you for being a coward."

"What's in here, Matthew?" She could hardly speak, partly because she was physically weakened, mostly because there was nothing left to say.

"Ah, Esther, just your own people."

He stood at the door, looking at her one last time, willing her to come with him, but weakly, the energy draining from him like blood.

He let himself out the door, shut it behind him, she heard the key turn in the lock.

\* \* \*

They played tricks to confuse the police. Two crossed from barn to house, creeping along the ground, knowing the police could detect the movement, perhaps make out their shapes, but not clearly enough to know who it was, whether it was men or women or even a child, nor to be sure how many. Then four returned, in pairs clinging to one another. Gradually, they emptied the farmhouse of all of the members except for Esther and Emily, locked still in the basement.

It was much easier to get everyone into The Temple itself, only a short distance along the shallow trenches, or around the outhouse which obscured part of the view from the woods above. By four in the morning they had brought everyone inside. There was no turning back. When the light came up and the police realised that there was no life at all in any of the other buildings, they would move in. They could not survive for long in The Temple: there had been next to no food for days; the children – Thomas and Tamar – were fading; the membership as a whole was in the final throes of a terrible rage at the way they were being starved into submission.

The smell of gasoline was overpowering. Their last supplies of fuel had been used to sprinkle the walls of The Temple and the decorations within – symbol, platform and pulpit included. Nahum said:

"They will tear it down; I must do it first."

In the leading segment, the remaining Superiors knelt with each other and with The Teacher, heads bowed, arms around each others' shoulders, a circle of prayer and of life. Simon and Nahum, Naamah and Jemima, Hannah and Matthew. Three men, three women, opposites, a perfect match. In other segments, members imitated them, forming into groups, three or four to each segment, mumbling farewells.

At five, Matthew rose to conduct the last Meditation. They looked up at him, hovering like a father watching his child asleep, his eyes so full of shining love they lit up The Temple and everyone in it within it, not flames but glowing embers. It was the moment before the day, when life would start over again.

"I said to you that you would never know such love again. We are one, we are many, together we are whole – this is the final, the ultimate, the whole love we have been looking for these last ten years or more. They cannot destroy it, nor can they take it away for themselves. It is the fire beyond that is hotter than they can handle.

"Close your eyes now, breathe deeply, take your time. Breathe deeply, take your time, slowly, it's easy now, let it flow, let it go. You are sinking, dissolving, you can feel the flames that devour you and they do not burn you, do not even hurt you: they cannot touch you – you are not there to be touched, you are no longer who you were when you entered the fire beyond, you are your neighbour, the neighbour that you love, and your neighbour is another neighbour, we are all one another and no one of us exists alone. Breathe deeply, take your time, slowly, let it go, let it burn; you are the fire beyond, the fire beyond that is born of love."

When he was quite certain that they were meditating fully, a half hour or so later, Matthew rose quietly. Because Hannah was a Superior, Tamar and Thomas were meditating in his group. He touched each of them gently on the shoulder, urging them to their feet with one hand while a finger of the other was at his mouth, husht. He led them carefully through the meditating members to the main door. As he unlocked it and ushered them out, he turned to see that Hannah was watching him, eyes wide open, tears running down her face, tears of joy. She mouthed:

"I am one," thank you, Teacher.

He mouthed back:

"We are many," he would return.

Outside, he re-locked the door and knelt to tell the children what to do. He hugged them, kissed them. Tamar, nearly fourteen, said:

"I am one, Teacher."

"We are many. Together we shall be whole."

"Why can't we come with you?" Thomas was confused by the separation from his mother and the man who meant more to him than his father.

"You have another purpose, Thomas; kiss me again – both of you."

He stood with his back to one wall of The Temple, between two segments, where he could watch without being seen. There was a rifle already lodged in the gap with which to hold the world at bay. In his pocket, he fingered the book of matches with which to start the fire beyond.

The children – both in white robes – lowered themselves to the freezing, snow-covered earth and, as if not touched by it, began the long crawl towards the farmhouse. They were his messengers – his message was to Esther; he had listened to her – now she should listen to him.

\* \* \*

Carey heard the key turn in the lock. The door open. She expected Matthew. It was Thomas. Across the basement, Tamar was opening Emily's cell door.

"I am one, Sister Esther," Thomas said gravely.

"We are many," she replied. "Can you help me stand, Thomas?"

The boy held out a hand, helped her to her feet, let her put an arm around his shoulder to cross to Emily's cell.

Tamar was kneeling over Emily. Emily was unconscious but alive. Tamar was squeezing her shoulder, rocking her, saying over and over:

"Wake up, Emily, wake up."

Carey took in the situation. She glanced back into the basement area: no one. The door at the top of the stairs was open. There was not a sound from above.

They tried to lift Emily between them. The children were too small, Carey too weak.

"Who's upstairs, Tamar?"

Tamar shook her head, signifying that no one was.

"Who sent you here?" Carey asked, hoping for the answer she got.

"The Teacher."

"Where is everyone? Where's The Teacher?"

They gave different answers.

"In The Temple," Tamar said.

"In the fire beyond," Thomas replied.

Carey shut her eyes. It had come. Matthew had heeded her plea on behalf of the two children – and on her own and Emily's account. He was giving her a last chance to save all of them. There was no time to lose: Emily would be all right here; if there was no one in the farmhouse, it would not be in danger.

As best she could, she hustled the children up the stairs. In the hallway, she hesitated in order to make sure it was as deserted as they had claimed. She told them to wait a moment, rushed up the stairs to the bedroom she had shared with Matthew: she knew it was vain, but she could not face the world in the filthy shift she had soiled during her days in the cell. Lying out on the bed, awaiting her, was the brilliant white, silk robe she had worn the day she had stood beside Matthew to warn to world to leave them alone, and when she had addressed the members on his behalf. She flung her shift onto the floor, slid her arms into the robe.

Downstairs, the front door was not nailed up. It had all been planned, all prepared, it all had a purpose.

She pushed the door back gently, hoping it would not make enough noise to attract attention,

Instantly, a spotlight came on with such force that they were momentarily dazzled. They held their hands up in front of their eyes, fingers splayed, then raised them so that the police could see they were unarmed.

A voice on a bull-horn shouted:

"Keep your hands up; walk towards the fence; don't run."

They had the clearest view of The Temple when they were halfway between the house and the fence. Carey stopped to look at it, lowering her hands. The bull-horn ordered:

"Keep moving; keep your hands up."

Because of her position, she – but not the police – could see him step out to the front of the space between two segments, a rifle shouldered on one arm, in his other hand a book of matches, one of which was bent over, ready to strike. He was standing less than three feet from one of the slits into The Temple, within his long reach.

Carey looked at the police line: a crowd had gathered a hundred feet or so down from the agents – the family compound, woken by the bull-horn. Though dawn was only just beginning to break, she made out her brother's figure at the rope, at the very front.

Colin's arms were outstretched, she could hear him screaming:

"Carey, Carey – I'm here, Carey."

The bull-horn bellowed:

"Get back. Everyone stay back. Miss, Miss – you've got to keep moving, keep coming towards us," waving to show where the agent wanted her to go.

She hissed at Tamar and Thomas:

"Go, go on," shoving them forward hard enough to make them run, not too hard to knock them over.

"Esther," The Teacher's voice rose above a rush of sound. Behind him snippets of white smoke seeped from the slits in the sides of The Temple. He had set the fire while she was sending the children to safety.

"Carey," Colin screamed again. "Carey, please. Carey, I love you."

"Esther, it's time, Esther," Matthew shouted. "Come with me, Esther, I love you."

She was torn three ways. The police agents were still commanding her to run towards them, even as they pulled the children under the rope to safety; she could hear Colin, make out the shape of him; she could see Matthew clearly. She remembered their last conversation: what was out there for her – ridicule – pity? She had asked him what was here – her own people, he had said. She remembered, too, their first conversation.

"You never answered the question," she reminded him.

"What you do if you've filled the canvas up and it still doesn't work? Oh, that's easy. You paint it all over and start over again."

She had loved him and followed him; it could never be undone; the best she could hope for was to start over.

She turned, her robe swirling in the night air, and ran towards him. He stepped back into the shadows, then she saw him unlock The Temple door in readiness for them to step together into the fire beyond.

"Come back, Miss, you have to come back here – for pity's sake."

The police were beginning to cross the rope as they realised that what they could see was smoke, The Temple was on fire, there were flames darting from the slits, a hole had already burned through one of the walls, they were advancing slowly, wary in case it was a trap, weapons held steadily in front of them, firemen unrolling their hoses behind.

Colin jumped the rope, ran at her, howling still her name.

As if it was a race to reach her, as she neared The Temple, Matthew came out to greet her.

She heard someone shout:

"He's got a gun, look out he's got a gun."

She flung herself at him as she heard Colin's voice:

"Carey, I love you Carey."

The police opened fire, a stupendous roar, bullets she could see fly past her head.

Matthew threw an arm around her, they turned together to dive through the blazing door into The Temple.

Colin screamed:

"No," as a second wave of bullets blasted the two of them, his sister and her Teacher, to the snow-covered ground. "No, no, no, no."

They went down, then helped each other struggle to their feet to stumble into The Temple.

They just caught Colin in time, running after her screaming, blinded by tears. It was the FBI man Weitz who tackled him, covering him with his body as The Temple finally erupted, its segments each like a single furnace turned on one another to meet in the centre with a roar of combustion, its roof and its multiple sides blew up and out to the skies and to the fields beyond, there were bodies, some quite literally flying, others shot sideways onto the field beside them, some still alive, burning grotesquely yet singing, Weitz pressed Colin's head into the snow, he must not see this, must not hear it.

"The fire beyond, the fire beyond."

And:

"I am one," in what could only have been Matthew's voice.

Weitz had to let Colin up before he suffocated. He rolled off him, sat up, Colin rolled over. Weitz took him in his arms – the hell with what they said – and rocked him like a baby. Damnit if he wasn't crying too.

At the end, Colin had seen her as an angel. In her flowing – fluorescent – white robe, running back towards the fire. It had seemed to part to welcome her.

# Postscript

As soon as Charles was well enough to travel, Colin flew down to Nice over a weekend to fetch him from the Antibes clinic. There was no one else to do it and he had little else to do with his time outside the office. He used the opportunity to put the apartment on the market, staying in a hotel instead of sleeping there; neither he nor his father would use it again.

Charles was morose more than he was angry at himself or at Colin. They could barely look each other in the eye: shared guilt deprived them of the opportunity to share grief. They had only just managed to save Charles at the time, but his body – though slower – had recovered. It was his mind that had suffered the more serious damage: intermittently, he forgot where he was, sometimes he forgot who; his eyes would glaze over, he would be anywhere else but present or maybe nowhere at all – there was no way to tell.

When he did focus, he had acquired a polite detachment, as if nothing mattered. It enabled him to make his personal arrangements, tolerate visitors, even spend time with his son and grandchildren, without engagement and therefore without concern. The roar for which he had been known had been cut out like a tumour, and the electricity switched off. Even when he spoke about Carey, he was in neutral gear.

"It's the cruellest fate," he would remark in the same tone of voice he might use to express preference for a flavour of ice-cream, "for a parent to bury a child."

Charles was returning to his flat in London for the time being. Colin had arranged for live-in help. It would get them through until he required full-time nursing and the arguments began with the health insurance company over how much they would cover for how long; if he still lived on, next would come residential care, probably a geriatric nursing home.

He visited Charles at his flat; they sat together, sometimes watching the news or in silence, no better able to communicate now than before. Colin would stay for an hour or so, ask his father's helper after his health, make necessary household decisions. When his father slipped out of the present, Colin would study him like a painting in which he had been told was to be found the secret of life. He saw only decay, and thought of something he had read recently in his Bible.

> *"The children which thou shalt have, after thou has lost the other, shall say again in thine ears, the place is too straight for me; give place to me that I may dwell" – Isaiah 49: 20.*

* * *

Fifty-two people died inside The Temple at Hammer Reach on the night of the fire beyond; another fifteen had survived the night but were so badly burned that over the following month all but three of them had brought the total to sixty-four. The surviving three were still critical, though it was expected that they would live, albeit scarred beyond recognition.

A further half dozen had escaped with only minor injuries. They had crawled through the multiple sides of The Temple or had been blasted out of it.

Mother Jemima was the most senior of these. She was being held by the State on charges of murder and attempted murder, which included everyone in The Temple that night, even her alleged co-conspirators. Privately, it was thought doubtful that she would ever be brought to trial: there was negligible evidence against her directly; it was in no one's interests. She was being held because the State was not yet ready to admit that something like The Programme could happen within its frontiers without being able to hold someone to account for it.

Brother Lucius – sole surviving Senior Messenger – was also being held, but as a State's witness. He had given up the names of those who had departed between Emily's escape and her return, though – with the exception of George Cohen – he knew only inside or first names and they were proving surprisingly difficult to trace; George and Gloria themselves had gone entirely to ground. Federal authorities repeatedly issued reassuring messages through the media that there was nothing to fear; there were no criminal charges in the offing nor would they have to give evidence against others unless they had directly witnessed a crime. The main concern was to ensure that the night of the fire beyond was the last of The Programme deaths, not the first: sixty-nine members of the Order of the Solar Temple had taken their lives in four separate incidents, in two continents, over sixteen months.

Helen's body, and the bodies of Caleb, Christopher and Paimon, had been dug out of the ruins of The Temple. Matthew's admission

490

to Phillipe Lamarque meant there would be no charges based on the men's deaths. No one was crying for them: conventional media wisdom held that Matthew's torture was the event which had triggered the disaster. Some would have liked to see Cassandra prosecuted for it but the only witness would have been Emily, who could place her entering then fleeing from the pit, which would not have been sufficient.

It was Berlinger who most commonly pointed the finger at Cassandra, in newspaper interviews and articles and on TV talk-shows, though she had dropped from sight, before the fire beyond, as the mood of the media had begun to turn against her, Micah, Tanya Sokolov and Amanda Kroger with her.

The loss of Calvin Wood had made a profound impact on Berlinger. He publicly announced his retirement from "the deprogramming game," saying:

"If you have to play God, even for a few days, in order to get someone out from under the control of someone else who's playing God – who's to say who's right, and who's to say who's mad?"

He wrote his daughter:

"I'll go anywhere to meet you, anywhere in the world, on any terms and conditions. I won't try to talk you out. I'm sorry for the way I've treated you. I have to see you. I need to see you."

He never received a reply.

* * *

If there were charges, Emily was not going to be a witness against Cassandra or anyone else.

She was initially entrusted to the care of Federal authorities while decisions were being made as to how to dispose of what was left of The Programme. Three weeks after the mass deaths, they left her alone in a locked hotel suite for half an hour. When they returned, they found her in a cupboard, naked, her arms wrapped around herself, chanting insistently:

"I am one, I am one, I am one."

A few days later, heeding the advice of doctors and bearing in mind the paucity of evidence on which to prosecute Cassandra, the Federals reached the pragmatic conclusion that Emily was of no more use to them and, with little forewarning, arrangements were made to transfer her to a psychiatric clinic outside London, chosen by her ex-husband, Richard Fielding, the only person willing to take any responsibility for her. Weitz broke this news to Berlinger, for whom

Rockworth had made a slot in his organisation: in turn, Berlinger spoke to Rockworth and the billionaire agreed, *pro tem*, to advance the cost of her treatment to Fielding, who could not afford it himself.

\* \* \*

These events took place over a number of weeks and seemed likely to drift into an indefinite future. Other events, in London, happened more decisively.

Charles was no longer competent to hold the position of Senior Partner. Colin had no wish to continue as Managing Partner: he had little enough drive to move himself forward, not enough to drive forward the practice. In their places, Alistair Mathison and Andrew Chettle formed a new team, with a re-allocation of responsibilities that effectively gave them joint command.

Jessica brought this news home to her flat, where Colin was staying with her while he found his domestic feet after the break-up of his marriage amidst recriminations that he had preferred his sister to his wife, and his sister's disaster to his children's happiness.

It was Jessica, too, who brought him the news at work one day early in the New Year that they had received a writ claiming damages, issued on behalf of Richard Fielding as Next Friend of his former wife. The claim that Emily had been led into The Programme by Carey, in breach of the duty of care she owed her client, derived as a matter of law – it was averred – from the special relationship between them as solicitor and client; it had resulted in serious mental injury and a near total loss of any sense of reality.

The claim also cited and relied on Colin's statement to Iain Macpherson, Rockworth's lawyer. He asked Jessica:

"Why would Rockworth help Fielding?"

"It appears," Jessica explained, "that Rockworth has been funding Emily's treatment."

"So?"

"So – if our insurers have to cough up, he'll get his money back."

"Talk about a leopard," Colin muttered.

"It has a certain irony, don't you think?"

"I suppose I can't complain. Why should I take her side now she's dead any more than when she was alive?"

Jessica shut her eyes: she could not bear his self-inflicted pain, the continual self-recriminations – Carey, Jan, the kids, the firm, he had let them all down, he cursed nightly like a religious chant.

She had been beside him through Carey's death, through the

arrangements he made for the cremation of what remained of her, through the journey home with the jar of her ashes packed into his flight-bag, holding his hand patiently, understanding what he was going through, guessing correctly that when they got back Jan was not going to understand at all let alone help him through it.

The first time they made love had been – fumbling – in a tent, when his pent up terror for Carey and her gesture of support and affection met head on. They had not made love again in the States, nor on their return during the interregnum between touchdown at Heathrow and his take-off from Fulham, nor even as soon as he had moved into her home.

A few days after he had come to stay with her – they did not call it living together – he told her that he proposed to relinquish his responsibility as Managing Partner. The next morning he told first Alistair, then Andrew: neither sought to dissuade him. That evening, he took her out to dinner. At some point during the main course, he had looked up sheepishly.

"It's funny the way it works, isn't it? I've just realised I haven't thought about Carey since this morning." She knew what he meant: the first thought each day was – she's not coming back.

"It's like that. One day, the grief goes away for a bit; next time, for a bit longer. Eventually, it comes in waves that are further and further apart." She paused, then continued: "A friend once told me: you get used to them – they never go away altogether – knowing they'll be back, you even come to welcome them like an old friend."

"A friend told you that?"

"No."

"Shall you ever tell me?" The missing link in her story – who made her hard, who made her wise.

"I was in love with a man; we were going to be married; he killed himself a month before the wedding." A decade later, simply saying the words could still bring the tears to her eyes.

"God, I'm sorry. Why didn't you tell me?"

"Before – it wasn't your business. After?" After Carey's death. "I thought it would be the wrong thing for both of us. You would have thought I was offering it as a way of saying I understood. You don't want other people telling you how much they understand: they don't; it's yours."

"How would it have been wrong for you?"

"I didn't want my grief to be absorbed into yours; I didn't want you thinking you understood how I felt; that doesn't go away either."

He took her hand across the table and gripped it and when they returned home they made love in front of her fire.

Afterwards, he asked her:

"Did you ever find out why?" Would he ever find out why Carey had done it?

"Not really. I could make a fair working theory out of bits and pieces – the sex was never very good, I think he may have been gay – every time work went badly, he thought his career was over – when it went well, he thought it was only doing so in order to drag out the pain of his final failure – he used, I don't know how to put this, he used to hide from me – I mean, both literally and metaphorically – as if he couldn't stand to see himself in my eyes. But those are my ideas about it; he was dead."

"What did he do?" Please do not tell me he was a lawyer – another bloody screwed up lawyer, like Carey, like me.

"What do you think?"

\* \* \*

Phillipe was initially refused permission to travel to England: the Voodoo connection. He appealed not to the British government, but through Berlinger to Rockworth who knew of him as the man with the courage to walk into the farmhouse when everyone else hid behind the barricades. Berlinger, too, had an affection for him: his enduring image of Calvin was of Phillipe holding his boy's hand as they crossed the field, before they fell. Berlinger did not blame Phillipe for Calvin: it might be true that if Phillipe had not gone in, Calvin would not have been offered the false opportunity to leave, but he would otherwise have been killed before – or in – the fire beyond.

Berlinger did not need to provide him with the address: he already had it. It was in Hertfordshire, not a long drive in his Mistah Hearse; he found a hotel nearby, waited for visiting hours to begin, was first to arrive.

"Can I help you?"

"I'd like to see a patient – Emily Fielding." All the short-cut English was gone; he was back in the form of the college-educated man who had travelled around Europe fifteen or more years before.

"Let's see," the receptionist was not hostile: she was checking whether Emily's visitors were restricted.

"I have to ask you this: are you a lawyer, or in any way connected with a legal firm called Arnotts?"

"Ma'am," Phillipe affected his deepest Southern drawl, "ah am a preacher from Louisiana," pronounced as four not five syllables.

494

"Well, I'm sorry, but we have a strict instruction to ask the question; it's something to do with a legal case. I don't know how we'd be able to tell if the answer was true or not."

Phillipe shrugged, though he could guess that – so long as they had asked the question – anyone who obtained entry by deception would be unable to use the information.

She met him in the lounge. She was always slender, now stick thin. She used to have her hair stylishly cropped: it had grown to shoulder-length but, though clean, had received no professional attention. She was wearing clothing that he supposed was her own but it hung off her looking as if it would rather be on someone else. It was her face which appalled him most: it was dull, sallow, her skin was bleached and in places splotchy.

He wanted to put his arms out to embrace her, tuck her into his pocket and walk her out the front door. He was planning to do just that. Whatever it took, he would find a way.

She sat opposite him on a hard-backed chair, sombre-faced.

"You got my letter," she said.

"I got your letter."

She had written to thank him, to tell him that she knew he had been kind to her, and that she wished she could have known him away from The Programme, without Carey or Matthew. She had written to tell him she was alright in words that told him the opposite. She had written to tell him that she would soon be allowed to go home, that her parents did not want her back, and that she had decided to return to Richard. He loved her, she told him; he had forgiven her; what had happened before was in another time, and she was confident she would not make him angry again; there was no one else to look after her, nowhere else to go. He had been promoted at work, wanted a child. She was writing to tell him goodbye.

He had come at once.

\* \* \*

In the end, Jessica could not take it. She flew with Colin to Antibes to help him pack up the apartment, hand over the keys: she was curious to see it before the new owners took it over. On the last night, they went out to a restaurant overlooking the bay. There was no difficulty finding a table; the season had yet to begin – winter was only just coming to an end.

"I need some space," she said.

Colin took her decision calmly – too calmly.

"I understand."

"I mean, I don't want, you know, to stop seeing you."

"We'll see each other at work." He had his cases. Clients still liked to see an Arnott.

"That wasn't what I meant," she murmured.

"No, I know."

"You don't seem surprised; you don't seem," she hesitated, "disappointed."

"I, uh, I care for you, deeply care for you – I love you," he said with a simplicity that she found hard to bear. "But it's been a shocking year, and to pretend I'm through it would be absurd. I'd like to think, uh, I'll get through this, but I think I know, if I go on staying with you while I try to do so, we won't."

"I worry, though," she said quietly. "Worry if you will get through it."

He was going to reassure her: don't worry; I'm tough; I'm not Carey. He did not want to end it on a lie.

\* \* \*

Colin found himself a ground-floor flat in a new, low-rise block in West Kensington. It had three bedrooms, though two of them were tiny, but enough for all the children to sleep over when they came to visit. After the first weekend, however, there was never another when all three came at once: the children had friends of their own, parties, outings; seeing their father did not take priority.

During the weeks, he worked much later than he used to: he prided himself that, with the exception of a couple of months, his billed hours had maintained their former levels, even increased on them; he remained a valued fee-earner in the firm, on that account at least they would never be able to say he had let them down. He had taken over responsibility for monitoring the firm's Website: it was something he did at home, at night, sitting in the window of the dining room which he had set up as an office at the front of the house, drinking whisky, watching people walk by on their ways home – couples, people rushing to see their families, young men and women back from a date.

He drank much more than he used to; even smoked – occasionally at first, latterly it had built up to ten a day, soon it would be more.

Sometimes in the evening until the early hours, or at the weekend if the children were not staying, he would prowl the streets of the capital – from Hyde Park and Kensington Gardens to the river – looking for something or someone, he did not know what or who but feared in his heart it was still Carey. In one corner of the dining room study, there was a shrine to her: framed photos of them together; a couple of professional portraits – one on her admission as a solicitor, the other taken for the firm's brochure; her ashes were still in the cheap jar in which he brought them back from America – he did not want to keep them, had no way to let them go.

Once or twice, he would receive the eye from a homosexual cruising the streets, presumably thinking that he was doing the same. He never had any inclination that way, had not touched or been touched by another male since early school, he hurried away before by accident he created the wrong impression. Once, afterwards, he found himself wondering what it would have been like, not so much tempted as curious; it scared him that he had given it so much as the thought – what was happening to him?

Sometimes he stopped in a pub, sat in a corner, watched the people until he felt his loneliness become noticeable. Occasionally, he stopped in at a coffee bar where the atmosphere was less frenetic. There were a couple of coffee bars run by local churches which he tried out and which welcomed him. Sunday mornings, he had taken to attending services at different churches, never the same one twice. It was religion he wanted, not a particular religion.

Sunday afternoons, there was always a way to pass the hours: a show at an art gallery or museum; a small theatre group; an educational lecture; meditation groups even, or new age religions. He read about them in the local papers, or on flyers stuck to bus shelters, abandoned buildings, hoardings, and noticeboards in bookstores or community shops.

Some of these groups were well-established, others only recently arrived on the scene. One of these, The Fire Beyond, was making its first appearance in a small hall in Notting Hill on Sunday week, at a talk entitled "Hammer Reach and The End of The Programme".

He told no one about it. He scoured both the local and the national press to see if anyone else seemed to be paying it any attention. He called Jan to cry off the children's visit. He went around to the hall itself, to check that it really had been booked as advertised. He was in a state of high excitement which he only brought under control on Saturday by drinking too much.

On Sunday morning, leaving it to last, he went into the office. He had dressed what he thought was the part: jeans, open-necked shirt, a leather jacket with deep pockets. The office was completely empty.

Because he had been hung-over and had left himself insufficient time, he did not dawdle. He had planned exactly what he was going to do.

He went into Alistair's room – neither he nor Andrew had moved to reflect their new positions. For a moment, he could not find what he was looking for: a fat brief, two feet high and tied up in pink ribbon, had been placed on the mantelpiece obscuring the board on which was mounted the rock-climber's pick with which one of Alistair's clients was said to have murdered his boss. He removed the board to his room where he unmounted the pick without causing it any damage and studied closely the diagram of how it had been used.

He took a taxi to the hall. The talk was already underway. There were no more than thirty people present: the hall would have taken two or three times that number. The Fire Beyond was ambitious.

As he slipped into a seat at the back, a woman spied him and came across to join him. She was American, wearing a red dress, more open at the front than seemed appropriate to an afternoon talk, a purple silk scarf wound around her neck with both its ends hanging forward, as if asking to be pulled on to draw her near. He saw that there were a couple of other women, dressed in a similar manner.

"Hi," she whispered.

"Hello," he replied gravely.

"I'm Leah; who're you?"

She made him uncomfortable. She was seated on the next chair and had twisted herself around towards him, so that she was almost on top of him. She had an odd way of holding her hands against her thighs, evidently pressing down, almost kneading her thighs with her knuckles.

"Colin," he answered gruffly.

"Have you been to see us before?"

The question was forward, as if she wanted to get under his skin as soon as she could, to do who knew what within; despite himself he felt a tingle in his stomach, not sexual but distinctly sensual.

He shook his head, nervous what his tone might disclose if he spoke aloud. She smiled as if she understood him and turned to listen to the speaker, leaning back in her chair at an angle that still inclined her towards him.

The speaker was a tall man with long, wavy hair, wearing a bright red shirt. He recounted:

"The atmosphere was evil, pure evil. Here was this man, whose every movement was like the step of a giant ogre, causing other members to reel back in terror, casting their eyes down in the hope that he would not notice them, all too often someone took his fancy, he would beckon, they would disappear, sometimes for days on end, into the cells in the basement or elsewhere for him to play out his fantasies.

"He was not the sole source of evil. His closest companions bred their own; he had two black men who acted as his personal guard, they went before him to clear the way or stood outside a door as if to remind people that to look upon him was to look upon a God. He said: 'I am one,' meaning that he was God; we had to respond – 'we are many,' we are his servants.

"Yet those words had many other meanings, and to many of us they were the most important and meaningful words we could utter: I am but one; there are many others; together we can be whole. That was the central message of The Programme, a message evolved by many of us, over many years, which Matthew had arrogated to himself and his perverted purposes. Now, Cassandra – The Seer as we called her until he stripped her of her authority – will talk about the meaning of those words, and the value they brought into our lives and could bring into yours."

Colin was so entranced that he had leaned forward in his seat, not resting on the back of the seat in the empty row in front of them, but stretching over it. As Cassandra stepped up to the rostrum, Leah laid a hand on his thigh.

"She is incredible, isn't she?"

If Colin heard her, he did not bother to reply.

Cassandra was a vision. She was dressed similarly to Leah. She was, Colin guessed, three or four years older than he was – he would later learn, closer to eight. Once she began to speak, her Welsh voice high and musical interspersed with an occasional giggle that bridged the gap between herself and her audience, he felt her power roll over him like a warm breeze that lingered and found its welcome way to his every pore.

"Why did Hammer Reach happen? For a long time, I was in a state of shock. I had not foreseen it, though to see where we were going was my very function: later, I realised that it was endemic in where we were going that I should not be able to foresee it; by not foreseeing it, I had done what I was supposed to do. Small comfort when so many were left behind dead, dying or merely doomed: faith is sorely tested when friends are lost.

"I would not be telling the truth if I did not admit that for many months afterwards I did indeed lose my faith in the essential tenets of The Programme – that we come from whole energy and to whole energy shall we return; that our task on earth is to recreate the whole until we have perfected it; that it is a task impossible for man or woman alone to accomplish; that it is only when a framework exists in which men and women can contribute their whole beings to one another that – as Father Micah reminds us – together we shall be whole.

"Reminding myself of that – repeating it over and over like a mantra – was what finally explained Hammer Reach to me. The Programme had mistaken its ultimate objective: the purpose was not its destruction; the fire beyond was a way to move The Programme forward by forging a whole, ridding itself only of its flaws: the evil which had overtaken it and which had obscured its purpose; the fire beyond was – in that light – the most valuable stage into which The Programme had moved, because only by passing through it could we emerge without the baggage that had been accumulated over previous decades. This was The Programme, stripped back to pure energy, stripped bare, pure air."

Colin was riveted. The words alone did nothing for him; but the words as she positively sang them, the mood in the hall as people began to respond, almost swaying along with her, the sensation of belonging to something of infinite capacity, infinite love too, touched a place within that he had not known existed: it was the awe of a child, innocent exploration, the joy of new ideas and images; it was the adventure which will continue forever because it knows no limits; and, so long as they are never reached, it is possible to believe that they do not even exist.

The Fire Beyond, she called the new group.

"The Fire Beyond became The Programme's destination; but we survived it – and so now we move on. The Fire Beyond is our point of departure. We are now The Fire Beyond that The Programme became; we are risen out of the fire beyond and own the fire beyond; those of us who were chosen to survive the fire beyond must rebuild the hearth and home, we alone know that there is no limit to life but life beyond.

> "'Only when we go beyond the fire and survive do we learn that life and death are stages in a journey without beginning and without end, than which there is nothing more. What is the fire beyond? I will tell you. It is the fire which lights the way beyond the limits we are brought up to believe we are confined by: life ends in death; good ends at the beginning of evil; love and hate are different. When we see the fire beyond, we see across a line we had believed marked the end; the fire beyond calls us across that line, it devours that line, it tells us it is not an end but a beginning.'"

After Cassandra's talk, there were questions. Colin took no part. The American women – Leah and the other two – moved towards the door. Leah called to one of them – Karen – to make sure everyone got one of the brochures or pamphlets from the table closest to the entrance. While other members of the audience departed, he remained seated until, as he had known that she would, Cassandra – now wearing an overcoat across her shoulders – came to join him after a quick word with Leah.

She sat in the row in front of him, swivelled around to face him, resting her jaw on arms folded on the back of her chair.

Micah watched from the front of the hall, smiling knowingly. He felt a sense of relief. He was not a leader, a teacher, but a follower; he had followed Cassandra, but she had made him perform the role of leader for others; it was not what he wanted – he wanted a leader of his own; he and Amanda.

"Colin, she said," meaning Leah. "Would that be Colin Arnott?"

"Yes."

"Do you want to tell me why you came, or do you want me to tell you?"

"Tell me," he whispered, sweat breaking on his upper lip.

"I am the only link to Carey, aren't I?"

He nodded miserably, exposed.

"But that isn't what's making you unhappy, is it?" When he said nothing, she continued: "What you don't know is if it's a link you want to break, or a link to cling onto. Would that be right?"

"Yes," he said flatly, resigning himself to her. "What's the answer?"

She laughed, reached out and placed a hand against his cheek.

"It's not really in any doubt, is it?" She slid her hand down his arm, then onto the jacket, licking her lips as she openly searched him. When she found the pick, she extracted it and examined it curiously, turning it over in her hands. "Is this for me?"

Dry-mouthed, he could only reply:

"Yes."

"Thank you," she smiled warmly, placing it in the pocket of her own coat. "I shall treasure it. Now come, I must find a way to thank you."

She took his hand and led him from the hall, leaving Micah and the women to clear up after her. Around the corner from the hall's front door, no one in sight, she swivelled towards him, opened her coat and pressed him against the wall, enveloping him, her body against his, her full and welcoming breasts, her lips.

For a long moment he resisted. Then he began to respond.